MW01200286

The Day America Died!

Trilogy Plus 1

New Beginnings   Book 1

Old Enemies   Book 2

Frozen Apocalypse   Book 3

The Final Ending – Book 4

An EMP Post-Apocalyptic Series

AJ Newman

Table of Contents

*

The Day America Died!

New Beginnings

An EMP Post-Apocalyptic Novel

A J Newman

Acknowledgments

This book is dedicated to Patsy, my beautiful wife of thirty-six years, who assists with everything from Beta reading to censor duties. She enables me to write, golf, and enjoy my life with her and our mob of Shih Tzu's.

Thanks to Patsy, Cheryl, Wes, who are Beta readers for this novel. They gave many suggestions that helped improve the cover and readability of my book.

Thanks to Sabrina Jean at Fasttrackediting for proofreading and editing this novel.

Thanks to WMHCheryl at http://wmhcheryl.com/services-for-authors/ for the great final proofreading and suggestions on improving the accuracy and helping me to tell a better story.

AJ Newman

Copyright © 2020 Anthony J Newman. All rights reserved. ISBN 978-0-9912334-6-5

This book is a work of fiction. All events, names, characters, and places are the product of the author's imagination or are used as a fictitious event. That means I thought up this whole book from my imagination, and nothing in it is true.

All rights reserved. None of this publication may be copied or reproduced without prior written permission from the publisher.

As they say on TV, don't try anything you read in this novel. It's all fiction and stuff I made up to entertain you. Buy some survival books if you want to learn how to survive in the apocalypse.

Published by Newalk LLC.

Henderson, Kentucky

Main Character List

Even I have trouble tracking all of the characters in my books, so here is a list of the important ones.

Zack Johnson – Divorced, electrical engineer, prepper and car mechanic. He has a 15-year-old daughter and ex-wife. The hero of this story.

Callie Johnson - Zack's daughter who lives in Anderson, KY with her mom.

Joan Johnson – Zack's ex-wife, a slim bossy woman who lives in Anderson, KY, where she is a restaurant manager.

Mike Norman – Joan's brother and Zack's best friend. Like Zack, he is a prepper. He is an auto mechanic and outdoorsman.

Geena Denton – Woman who was headed home when Zack saves her from the bad guys.

Sally Green – Geena's best friend and headed home when Zack saves her from the bad guys

Davi Gold – Woman who says she is an ex-Israeli Mossad agent.

Aaron Gold – Davi's father and an ex- Israeli military pilot. Retired and has a large farm south of Presotum, Ill.

Sharon Gold – Davi's mother and a Professor of Chemistry at the University of Illinois.

Lynn Drake - Ex-girlfriend of Mike's. She still loves him.

Todd – Todd is the bad guy. Joan's boyfriend. Goes berserk when TSHTF.

✪

Chapter 1   The End is Near

Somalia

Sometime in the future:

She was soaking wet, and the temperature was still over 105 degrees as the sun went down on the coast of Somalia. The flies were more than annoying as they took turns biting any exposed flesh. One fly bit the back of her neck, which stung fiercely, but she remained frozen, lest she gives away her position.

Her training had been tough and put her through miserable conditions; however, those damn flies were pure torture. She watched as the missile launcher with its missile was loaded into the 53-foot overseas shipping container. The scientists and team fitting the rocket into the container worked for days to get the top to open far enough for the missile to be launched. Davi took many photos and left without being detected. It took her hours to crawl along the sand dunes back to her motorcycle and safety. She opened the saddlebag, retrieved some antibiotic salve, and applied it to the bites.

Davi caught movement in the bike's mirror and saw a shadow creeping up behind her. She used the bike's mirror to view the attacker without alerting him. Just before he lunged at her, she sidestepped, pulled her knife, and slit his throat. He lay there looking up at her trying to say something but only produced bubbles of blood around the slice in his throat and a mumbling sound. She ripped his mask off and was shocked to see a beautiful Chinese woman dying at her feet. She quickly started her bike and fled the area.

"Mori, I am safe and will be uploading the pictures in a few minutes. A Chinese operative just tried to kill me, but it was her unlucky day and my lucky day."

"Davi, I doubt that luck had anything to do with you being alive and her dead."

"It's worse than I thought. There are three separate facilities fitting missile launchers into cargo containers."

"Oh crap. Have you learned anything about their target?"

"Well, it's not Israel in the first round because these missiles could reach us from Syria or several other Islamic countries. I think they're all to be fired on the USA and Western Europe."

"We know Iran and North Korea are funding this effort. Are any other countries involved?"

"Of course. There are the countries allowing the Iranians to use their docks to construct the overseas container missile launchers, Syria, Somalia, and Yemen. We have strong evidence several of the nukes came from North Korea and Iran. There are flocks of Chinese technicians scampering around all three sites."

"Any Russian involvement?"

"None detected. I think they're a target also."

"What makes you think Russia is a target?"

"My team intercepted communication that pinpoints the coordinates for maximum EMP effect on Russia, the USA, and

Europe. Mori, my team also thinks the plot is much larger than we have found so far."

"How big, and what additional targets?"

"We aren't certain, but the Iranians might be double-crossing the Chinese and nuking them also. Zeb saw a map of China, in Yemen, with GPS coordinates that would match a potential EMP attack."

"The attack on Russia is backed up by the gradual shift of China's military to its northern borders. The bastards are going to attack Russia after the EMP blasts."

"Only they don't know they'll have their balls cut off at the same instant."

"How many more containers have already been produced?"

"There's no way to tell at this time. We know of ten containers that can launch one missile each. There could be four or five more, and they could be in a position to launch at any time."

"Thanks and get your teams out of there to safety. When we get permission to destroy them, it will be scorched earth."

"They're ready. Mori, shouldn't you get your family to a safe location? Mine live in the USA."

"Davi, great minds think alike. I can't say more."

"Cover your assets!"

••••

"We have proof that ten containers have been fitted with nuclear-tipped missiles that can travel 350 miles. It would only take five to six such EMP bombs to blast the USA and Western Europe back to the 1850s. There would be no electricity, planes, cars would not move, and people would starve. The question is, what targets are the other bombs for?"

"We must assume we're also targeted."

"One air blast would take out all non-shielded electronics and our grid."

"I must call the US President and warn the USA. Have any of our people tipped off the CIA or NSA about this development?"

"No!"

"Should we warn the Russians?"

"Hell, no!"

••••

"But Mrs. President, if we don't strike now, both of our countries could be destroyed."

"Mr. Prime Minister, do not do anything rash. I have the utmost assurance from the Iranian Supreme Leader, Said El Khamenei, that there is no plot to attack the USA or any other western power. North Korea has also assured us they have destroyed their nuclear weapons. They'll soon be our allies."

"And you believe our mutual enemies and not your friend Israel."

"Mr. Prime Minister, I believe your intelligence is wrong. Do not attack Iran and North Korea or their assets, or you will face the consequences."

"Mrs. President, we have sent the data to the NSA and CIA, and they should concur with our assessment. Please listen to them, even if you don't listen to us."

"So, you went around my back?"

The phone went dead.

••••

"I must report I have failed to convince the US President about the impending attack. I feel we must warn Great Britain and Germany immediately. I don't trust France or the rest of Europe with the intelligence."

"I'll call my contacts in their intelligence groups while you call the Prime Minister of Great Britain and the President of Germany."

"Our intelligence suggests we have five to ten days before the attack. We must prepare our military and evacuate key people to a safe location. I fear our enemies won't settle for eliminating our grid. They'll rain fire down on our country to kill us all. Plan to initiate Dragon Fire if we're attacked."

"Mori, I couldn't convince that bitch. This is a serious threat. She must be sleeping with that Muslim Supreme Leader to ignore this plot against the western world."

"I'll implement Plan B when I receive word that Dragon Fire has been executed."

✪

Chapter 2   Vacation

West Coast, USA

I was taking a well-deserved vacation in the Northwest when the crap hit the fan. Little did I know the world would end in a few days. My world changed from being a pissed off ex-husband to a devoted father who had to get home to save his daughter and friends. I had to get back home to Kentucky before the chaos began.

There was a sound in the room I couldn't identify, and the smell of stale perfume was in the air. I could hear the traffic out on the road and some woman yelling at the top of her voice, but I couldn't understand what she was saying. My head was pounding, my mouth was dry, and I had to piss so bad, it hurt. My head hurt so bad I didn't want to open my eyes. I tried to roll over and go back to sleep, but something heavy was on my arm. I opened one eye and peered at the thing weighing me down. It had red hair, and all I could see was the back of her head. *"What the hell is she doing in my bed? I thought I gave up whoring around,"* was all I could think.

Now that I was awake, my arm was calling to me. It was saying it was dying, and I felt like a thousand pins were attacking it. I gently tried to pull my arm out from under the lady, but it was stuck. I glanced over the back of her head and saw her face in the mirror. Well, at least she wasn't coyote ugly, and my arm could be saved. Now how could I get her off my arm without waking her?

Crap, this is my room. I can't sneak off in the night like a thief. Damn, that face looks familiar. She was the desk clerk on the second shift at the hotel where I was staying. I had promised myself I wouldn't bring strangers to my room ever again after being rolled a month ago. Alcohol must have been involved again. I've been drinking too much since the divorce and waking up with strange women way too often. I had gone from a devoted husband and doting father to a drunken whore-monger.

She woke with a start. I pretended to be asleep as she slowly got out of bed.

I heard her say, "Damn, I promised to never sleep with a customer again. I have to get my ass out of here without waking him. Damn, we must have been drunk because I don't remember having sex."

She slipped her clothes on and said, "Goodbye, Zack Johnson, whoever the hell you're. You can stop pretending to be asleep. I'm gone. What the heck, stop by the desk tonight after I get off, and I'll meet you for drinks."

I continued to pretend I was asleep. She closed the door and was gone. I could breathe again. I rubbed my arm until it came back to life and ran to the bathroom. I peed for about an hour and then searched in my travel bag for some aspirin, took two, and made some of that hotel coffee. My head was still fuzzy, but I remembered I was on vacation and had driven a rented Ford Escape from Smyrna, Tennessee, to Green Land, Oregon. It had taken a week since I'd stopped at all the sights along the way. I was impressed with the geyser and Cody, Wyoming, and saw a bunch of mountains, streams, and redwood trees once I got to northern California.

The hotel was a luxury since I was a backpacker from way back and wanted the best after long hikes. I hiked to the top of Mount Ashland, visited Table Rock, and wandered through the redwoods in California.

I heard my cell phone playing "Brown Eyed Girl" and knew my daughter was calling me. *Where the hell was my phone?* I searched the room and found it had fallen behind the desk. I hit recent calls and dialed her number.

"Dad, why didn't you answer my call, and where are you?"

"Callie, I'm in Oregon on vacation. Remember, I tried to get your Mom to let you go, but she wouldn't?"

"I know, Dad, and I really wanted to go with you. Mom wants to know if I can come down to Smyrna and stay with you for a month this summer. She and Todd want to travel."

So, I get to be the babysitter, while my wife and Todd get married. "You know I want you anytime she'll let you come down. We'll go hiking and backpacking."

"That would be great. Can we shoot your guns? Dad, I need a new bicycle. Mine's a bit small for me. I've grown three inches since last summer."

"Your sixteenth birthday is a month off. Happy Birthday! I'll drive up to Anderson, and perhaps we can drive over to Murphy to that fancy bike shop and find you a bike."

"Thanks, Dad. Have you been to Crater Lake yet? Send more pictures."

"I'm going there after lunch, and I'll send them to you and post a bunch on Facebook."

"Dad, Mom wants to talk with you. Goodbye."

"Goodbye.......... Joan, what do you want?"

"Look, Zack, don't be a butthole. Can't we be civilized? I want to make sure you're alright with Callie spending the summer with you."

"So you and Todd can have a honeymoon?"

"You know that we're getting married. Married people do have honeymoons."

"They do, but you're taking our neighbor on your honeymoon. Has he even divorced Alice yet? You screw our neighbor, divorce me, and expect me to be civilized?"

"Yes, get over it. Our marriage was stale, and you know it."

"So just like day-old bread, you just toss it aside."

"Why do you care? I hear you're screwing every woman you meet. I hope you get an STD."

"I probably got it from you and Todd."

"Oh, and before I forget, your best friend Mike and I'll never speak to each other again after the stunt he pulled."

"What did your brother do to make me proud?"

"He took a dump in Todd's convertible. He's a moron."

"He's your brother."

I cut off the call and pitched the phone on the bed. Time for a shower.

I needed to call Mike and thank him for crapping in that bastard's car. He also needed to check on my farm over east of Owensville, Ky. The farm had belonged to my Great Uncle Arlo and Aunt Betty, and I'd spent many a summer roaming around the farm and surrounding area. That's where I met Mike and Joan Norman. We were best friends, and I married Joan right after high school. My aunt and uncle didn't have any kids, and my dad traveled a lot and took my mom with him when he could, so I got to stay with Uncle Arlo and Aunt Betty. The farm was a hundred and twenty acres of farmland with a five-acre lake and about thirty acres of dense woods with a stream flowing through it year-round. I loved the time I spent there.

Uncle Arlo had been a hunter, fisherman, and a prepper. He'd been in the Army for twenty years and knew just about everything about survival. He'd spent the last fifteen years of his life preparing for an apocalypse that never came. I'm damn glad he did because his work and the training he's given me saved my sorry ass several times over.

The farm had an older ranch style home, a large barn, and a pole barn sits about four hundred feet off Highway 143 east of Owensville. The metal pole barn has a large storm shelter built under the floor. Uncle Arlo always parked his 1954 Ford pickup over it, to make sure it stayed hidden from visitors. He had stocked it with food, water, and weapons, just in case the Commies attacked, or the banking system crashed.   The farm was pretty much self-sufficient. There were fruit trees, blackberry bushes, and a large garden on top of a hen house, a dozen pigs, and twenty head of cattle. There were solar panels on the house and pole barn that supplied electricity along with a windmill that pumped water from the lake to cool the house through a homemade cooling system he had built. The lake was about five acres and averaged fifteen feet deep. He stocked it with catfish, bass, and bluegill. A large dock went twenty feet out into the water with a large covered deck on the side for entertaining.

I'd spent a lot of time with Uncle Arlo, learning everything from marksmanship to trapping and fishing. Those were the best years of my life.

Aunt Betty died first, and then Uncle Arlo died the next year. He'd sold me the farm for a dollar the month before he died. I still have his old Ford truck, and it's my EMP-proof bug out vehicle. I've set the whole farm up as my bug out "go to" place. I go up there every chance I get, but it's only every three months, or so since I took the job below Nashville after the divorce.

✪

Chapter 3   TSHTF

Owensville, Kentucky

"You took a dump in Todd's new Corvette? You're my hero!"

"I did, and it was right in the middle of the driver's seat. It must have been a good one because the flies started swarming as soon as I jumped out of the car."

"Dude, you're the *man*."

"Look, Zack, I did it for me as much as I did for you. That bastard ruined our relationship with Joan, and I hate the jerk."

"Where was the car parked?"

"At his house under the carport. The dumbass left the top down, and I couldn't resist."

We both laughed until tears streamed down our cheeks. This would go down in history along with the time we flushed M-80s down the toilets at Daviess County High. Everyone knew we'd done it, but couldn't prove anything.

"Does he know who did the dastardly deed?"

"No, but with you out of town, I'm sure he knows it was me who fouled his Chevy."

"Hey Mike, have you been by the farm lately?"

"Yeah, a couple of weeks ago. Sorry, but I took a friend over and soiled your sheets, so to speak. I cleaned up and washed the sheets the next day."

"No problem. I might be paranoid, but this crap hitting the fan with Israel and Iran has me scared. Can you check our food and water and perhaps buy some more beans and rice? I'll pay you back."

"I'll bet you have your bug out bag and 1911 with you. Your uncle had you flinching every time the TV had bad news. I'll take care of it, buddy."

"I don't go anywhere without my BOB and my trusty Colt .45. I also have my 12 gauge and Ruger MKI in the trunk. Just because you're paranoid doesn't mean they're not out to get you. I've had a bad feeling about being away on a trip when the crap hits the fan. I'm counting on you to take care of Callie and that bitch sister of yours if TEOTWAWKI happens while I'm gone."

"You rattle that crap off just like you practiced saying TWEPKSTDHIV."

"Not funny, idiot."

"Calling me names won't get you any favors."

"Okay, pretty please, you idiot."

"Now that's better. Hey, are you getting laid out in Oregon?"

"Funny, you should ask. I have a weird coyote ugly story for you."

••••

Mike Norman has been my best friend since grade school. I'd saved Joan's dog from being torn apart by a Pitbull and

15

received a few bites. Joan fell in love with me that day. I was her hero. Mike slowly became my best friend that summer.

Mike's thirty-six with brown hair and green eyes. He's built like a short fullback at 5'8" and 225 pounds of muscle. He's never married and doesn't have any kids. He is an auto mechanic and works at the Ford dealership in Owensville. He drives a new Mustang convertible, but also has a 1973 F100 that's powered by a 460 with a C6 tranny. I helped him build the truck and helped him make it EMP-proof, in case the SHTF. He has six other vehicles sitting around his house, which were future projects. He never stays with a woman for more than a year, and most couldn't put up with his obsession with cars and junk. He spends most of his time and money on his projects, and a lot of time chasing tail between girlfriends. We both are getting too old for that crap.

Mike's problem is he is so adorable, kind of like a long-eared puppy, so women want to mother and take care of him. Mike just wants to get laid and not deal with having a woman around all of the time. He has one woman he can't get rid of, and she really cares for him even knowing he spends a great deal of time chasing tail. I always called her Janie Sweatpants because she always has yoga pants on, and her name is Polish and starts with Swet.......and I can't pronounce it anyway. She would marry Mike, and that scares him to death.

••••

The next morning found Mike driving on Highway 60 from Anderson to the farm. He drove straight through town so he could stop for breakfast at Lee's Restaurant before cutting across to Highway 54 to go to the farm. He always stopped at Lee's for the humongous pancakes, which were much larger than the plate. He always ordered two along with two eggs and ate every last bite.

"Hey, Betty, the usual."

"Mike, you're early this morning. Who was the young lady with you last week? You know a girl could get jealous."

"Now, Betty, don't worry. I can't even remember her name. She was a date that didn't work out."

Mike's order was delivered, and he ate while watching the FOX news anchor talk about tension in the Middle East because Israel had called up all of its reserves and placed its military on the highest alert. The anchor mentioned there had been an unprecedented number of flights out of Israel that started last week and continued this morning. Many of the trips were to the USA.

Suddenly, there was a break in the news, and the report stated there was an intense air battle going on between Iran and Israel. A few minutes later, the reporter broke back into the news to report that Israel had been attacked with nuclear weapons and had responded by bombing Iran's nuclear processing facilities, command and control, and all major military bases with nuclear weapons. The president would address the nation in fifteen minutes.

Mike took his cell phone out of his pocket and called Zack. The phone rang for an eternity and went to voice mail. Mike had called three times before I answered.

"What do you want?"

"Hey buddy, have you heard the news? Iran nuked Israel, and Israel retaliated with nukes."

"I was asleep. Remember it's two hours earlier here. Damn, it's only 3:30 a.m. You'd better have a good reason to wake me up this early."

"Zack, get in your car and head home right now. The crap hit the fan in the Middle East. Iran and Israel have nuked each other. Turn the news on."

I replied, "Oh crap," as I turned the TV on to FOX News.

I watched for a minute and said, "Mike, I'm getting dressed, buying some food and hitting the road. I don't want to be caught out here with this crap happening. I'll start trying to contact you at 10:00 – 10:15 p.m. every night per our plan. Bye."

"Will do. Bye."

Mike gobbled down his pancakes and drove to Wal-Mart. He purchased 400 pounds of rice, 400 pounds of beans, 10 cases of Spam, and 20 cases of bottled water. He also bought three boxes of every type of ammunition the store had in stock.

He climbed into his truck and was ready to drive to Zack's farm when he remembered to call Joan. "Are you listening to the news?"

"Hell no. I was asleep, you idiot. Yeah, I have it on now. I hear they're fighting again in Israel. Todd says it's no big deal and not to worry."

"Joan, Todd is an idiot. Israel just nuked Iran. Go to the store and buy canned food, dried beans, rice, and lots of water. Oh, buy ammo for your guns. The USA will have to respond, and we might get nuked ourselves."

"You sound like Zack. When will y'all grow up?"

"Joan, the crap is hitting the fan, and if I'm wrong, you won't have to buy beans and rice for two years. Please listen to me."

"Look, Mike, we know it was you who took a dump in the Corvette. Pulling this 'buy beans joke' is stupid and don't call back until you're ready to pay the bill for having Todd's car cleaned."

The phone went dead.

Mike stopped at the other Wal-Mart on Highway 54, and several sporting goods stores to purchase as much ammo as they would sell him. He bought as many .45, .223 and .308 rounds as they would sell him. He was only able to purchase a thousand rounds of .22s since they had a three-box limit per customer. Then he drove on out to the farm and unloaded his truck.

Damn, he wished Zack were here. He always knew what to do. He was worried Joan and Callie would not be safe in town if the crap hit the fan in Owensville.

He called Callie, "Hey, girl."

"Uncle Mike, I'm scared. This is what Dad said would happen in the Middle East. Where are you? Can you come and get me?"

"Callie, so you've seen the news?"

"Yes, I'm trying to get Mom to bug out to the farm, and Todd is being a little turd."

"I can't come and kidnap you, but I do want you to make sure you have your bug out bag, extra clothes, and your guns ready to leave your home if needed."

"I've been packing and gathering extra food without alerting Mom."

"Good girl. I'll come and get you if the crap hits us here in the states. Call if you need me."

"Love you, Uncle Mike."

"Love you too, Callie Girl."

★

Chapter 4   The Apocalypse

Midwest, USA

I checked out of the hotel by 4 a.m., stopped at a grocery store, and grabbed a buggy full of beef jerky, Spam, beef stew, bread, crackers, peanut butter, candy bars, sodas and several cases of water. Then I drove to Wal-Mart and bought several boxes of ammo for each of my guns. They would only sell three boxes of any one type, so I bought some I might be able to trade for bullets for my weapons.

The sales clerk looked at my basket and said, "Are you going to war?"

"Yes, ma'am. I think the damn Iranians will nuke us tomorrow, and I want to be able to shoot as many as possible."

That shut her up quickly, but I suddenly thought she might think I was nuts and call the police. I got the hell away from there as fast as possible.

I filled up the car and was on the road home by 5:30 a.m. I wasn't too worried about a ticket, and I drove as fast as I safely could. There are no fast roads out of Oregon headed towards Highway 80. I did the best I could on the windy-assed mountain roads. Then I finally got on Highway 80 and hightailed it east at over a hundred miles per hour. I had my radar detector on and slowed down a bit around major cities. I had to gas up twice, but otherwise, I was averaging over 90mph after I got on Highway 80.

••••

"Hey, Mike, is everything okay? The news sounds like we're at war with Iran and North Korea."

"It's very confusing, but there have been numerous nuclear explosions in Iran, Israel, Somalia, Yemen, and Indonesia. One of our carriers is missing, and they're speculating it was nuked. I'm at the farm and stopped along the way to get more food and ammo."

"Please call Joan and get them to come to the farm. Todd can even bring his sorry ass over if it will help convince Joan to bring Callie over."

"I talked to her earlier today, and she doesn't believe this will amount to much because Todd says so. I was going to call when you called."

"I'll stay in touch with the cell phone and will call every day at 10:00 p.m. If the cell phones get fried, I'll switch to the portable ham radio and try to get other ham operators to pass messages per our plan."

"Stay safe."

"Stay safe."

••••

I was just west of Iowa City when I saw the blue lights coming up from behind. Damn, this will slow me down. I pulled over to the side of the road and waited on the policeman.

21

"Buddy, what's your big hurry? I need your license and registration."

"Officer, I'm trying to get home before the Iranians nuke us."

"Well, that might be the best excuse that I've heard in a long time. Have you been listening to the news? I heard one of our ships was attacked and sank off the coast of Israel."

"Sorry for speeding, but I'm honestly scared that we'll be at war by day's end. I want to be with my family in Kentucky."

The officer wrote the ticket and handed it to me, saying, "You were zipping along at a hundred and five. I reduced it to eighty, so I don't have to take you to jail. Be careful, and get home safely. Are you a prepper?"

"Yes, sir."

"Tear up the ticket and hammer down. I'm getting my ass home ASAP."

••••

I drove off, stayed below the speed limit until the cop was out of sight, and then pushed the car back up to over a hundred. The sky lit up in the distance, and I cursed my bad luck. It must be a thunderstorm. I hope it misses me. At the same time, I saw a sign that said Iowa City twenty-two miles, my engine died, the SUV's lights went out, and the car became hard to steer. WTF was going on? I struggled to get the car to the side of the road as it slowed down. The damn power steering doesn't work with the engine dead. I opened the door in time to hear a booming sound above my head. I looked up and saw something falling from the sky. It crashed and exploded about a mile ahead of where I'd stopped. Burning fuel lit up the night around the crash. I looked across the highway and saw a fiery explosion. A semi had hit a car stopped on the road, and it was apparent there were no survivors. I heard several more explosions in the distance towards Iowa City and assumed more planes had fallen from the sky.

I looked at my phone to see what time it was, but the screen was black. My head was exploding with thoughts and misgivings. *This can't be it, it can't be. Holy crap, we were hit with an EMP blast. Those had to be planes falling out of the sky. Should I go look for survivors?* I tried to crank the engine to no avail and resigned myself to walking home. I felt like a squirrel trying to cross a six-lane highway during rush hour, then I heard, "Pull yourself together, you idiot. People die when they panic. Get your crap together."

I looked around to see who was yelling at me, and I realized I was yelling at myself. I calmed down and gathered all of my gear by the car. What to take and what to leave was the big question. I've read those post-apocalyptic books my whole life and spent ten years prepping. *Why am I panicking? I can't breathe, and my heart is pounding.* I told myself to concentrate on my gear and start thinking about having to walk home. That's when I strapped my 1911 on my hip and tucked my bull barreled Ruger MKI under my shirt in the back. This made me feel secure, and my heart stopped racing.

I placed my bug out bag on the "must go with me" side and opened my duffel bag to see if I could ditch anything. Besides my shotgun and extra ammo, there was a complete change of clothes, hiking boots, parka, hoodie, army poncho, mini cookstove, army mess kit, and a tent. I took off my tennis shoes and replaced them with the hiking boots. It was mid-April, so I pitched the parka in the car, along with the mini cookstove, a shirt, and pants. I put the hoodie on and repacked the gear I was taking with me in the duffle bag. I put the other stuff in the Escape. Someone might need that equipment more than I did.

Then I took a good look at all the food I'd bought. That's when I realized I was starving and decided to eat a can of cold stew and chase it with a soda while I pondered which food would give me the most nourishment per pound. The beef jerky, summer sausage rolls, and Spam were quickly on my shortlist. I packed the food and eight bottles of water in my duffle bag and filled my canteen with water. I drank several sodas and some water to make sure I was hydrated before I left.

I retrieved my weather and emergency radio out of its metal box, cranked the handle for a minute, and turned it on. I searched and finally found a channel with a broadcast.

"The United States has been attacked and is now under martial law. Stay in your homes until the Department of

Homeland Security announces it is safe to be outside. The President will address the nation at 9:00 am," then there was nothing but static.

I heard an explosion, looked up, and saw another fireball in the darkness about two miles from me in the direction of Iowa City. That had to be another plane trying to glide to the Iowa City airport. Damn, can a passenger jet land without its electronics? I don't know, but the people on the plane knew for at least five minutes they were falling to the ground to be maimed and burned to death. That would be a horrible death.

I forced myself to get my thoughts back on how to save my own sorry ass and not worry about how people died. My bug out bag (BOB) was actually a backpack, which weighed about thirty pounds with all of my gear. I pulled the straps over my shoulders, moved it around to where it belonged, and snapped the front belt into place. I bent over to pick up my duffel bag and quickly knew something had to give. I could lift the duffel bag easily, but would not be able to carry it very far. I had two Life Straws to filter water, so I tossed four bottles of water, clothes, and the tent. The bag was still a bit heavy, but I told myself it would get lighter as the days wore on. I kept all of the food so I wouldn't have to hunt or scrounge for food for several days, which freed me to make tracks for Kentucky.

I looked at the sun starting to peek over the horizon and decided it must be about 5:30 a.m. I looked back at the rental car and started walking east on Highway 80. I made sure I kept looking behind me, got my small field glasses out of a side pocket on my BOB, and periodically looked ahead for danger. I walked about half a mile and could see the wreckage of the first plane. It was in a cornfield on my left, and there were no survivors. There were only a few large pieces of the aircraft frame, and one thing looked like an engine remained of the once mighty jet. I had walked past the wreckage before I saw the first stalled car on the other side of the highway.

An older man and woman were standing beside a Volvo with California plates and a peace sign on the back window.

I got closer to them, and the man said, "Our car died, and we have to get back to California. Can you help us?"

"My car is dead also. Your best bet is to walk east into Iowa City and find a ride. I can't help you," I said and kept walking east.

"Thanks, but we'll stay in our car until the police come to help."

"Good luck with that."

"Could you spare some water?"

"Sorry, but I have only enough for me."

I quickly walked away and continued my hike to Iowa City.

I came to the top of a hill and used my field glasses to scout out the road ahead. I saw two vehicles on my side of the road, and I quickly walked to the other side. I needed to get home as soon as possible, and I didn't have time to talk to everyone who was stranded on the side of the highway. The people waved at me as I got closer, and I waved back and kept walking east at a good pace. I looked back and saw a man running across the road from behind me. He yelled for me to stop.

"Hey, what's the hurry? We want to know if you know what happened."

I kept walking and replied, "My car died, and I'm walking home. That's all I know."

"Can you take a look at my car and see if you can get it running?"

"No. I couldn't get mine running, so what makes you think I can fix yours?"

"I don't know, but we need help. Do you think the police will come and rescue us?"

"Look, man. Y'all will starve before the police come. Walk to the nearest town. Sorry, but I'm in a hurry."

I continued walking as he mumbled something under his breath.

The closer I got to Iowa City, the more I saw cars on the side of the road. I knew I couldn't help any of them and kept walking by them without getting into conversations. Most people waved and didn't try to get my attention, which was fine with me. Others were walking east, and only a few were heading west. I only had a one-page map of the USA, so it didn't have all of the country roads and short cuts. My plan was to go through Iowa City on Highway 80, cross the Mississippi River, go east past Davenport, and take Highway 74 down south to Highway 57 to Murphy. I wasn't going to cut across country, climb fences, and get shot at by farmers. I would stick to the main roads and travel by day for a couple of days, then switch to traveling at night when the fun started.

I have been a prepper for ten years. I've read all of the fiction on what happens when the grid goes down, and people panic, riot, and loot. There is only about three days' worth of food in the stores and pipeline to them at any time. That means the looters hit the electronics stores then the food stores. On the second day, most people are trying to get food, and by the third day, good people are getting desperate. After that, almost anyone will kill to get food for their children and family. I planned to get as close to home as possible in the next three days. I have four-hundred and fifty miles to cover, and needed to find an old car or truck produced before 1975, and fight off anyone trying to take it away from me on my way home.

I was deep in thought when I heard a familiar sound coming from behind me. I quickly turned and saw an old Volkswagen bus heading the same direction I was walking. I waved at the driver to no avail. It was a beat-up old Volkswagen camper and appeared to be overloaded with people. I was walking down a gentle grade and saw the bus for several minutes before it disappeared over the horizon. It would take me hours to cover what they traveled in minutes. I thought, *Damn the lucky bastards. Smoking weed, drinking beer, and going 40 miles per hour. I wish I were with them.*

••••

Mike woke up early and decided to drive back to town to have breakfast at Lee's. He arrived at 5:30 a.m. and ordered his usual pancakes, eggs, and sausage. He called Callie, and as she answered, the morning news was all about WWIII and the market collapse.

"Callie, we're at war. I'm coming to get you."

26

The world was falling apart, and the people in the diner could care less. They were eating and discussing their plans for the day. There were only three other people paying attention to the news. Suddenly, the TV started beeping, the screen went blank, and then an emergency broadcast banner scrolled across the screen. The message said, "Seek shelter immediately. The USA is under attack."

"Uncle Mike," was all he had heard before the phone went dead.

The TV went dark, the restaurant's lights went off, and cars started crashing at the same time. The building shook as a truck crashed into the side, and shattered glass sprayed the people inside. Mike only received a few cuts to his forearm and cheek as he ducked below his table. Several older women were screaming, and their husbands lay on the floor.

"Help, my husband passed out. I think he's having a heart attack."

Mike looked over and asked, "Does he have a pacemaker?"

"Why yes, he does."

"Does he have a pulse?"

She checked and bent down and kissed his forehead.

Several people were attending to the women, so Mike ran to the parking lot. He thought he had to go get Callie and Joan, so he threw a twenty on the table and rushed out to Zack's car. Mike had driven the '79 Cutlass Zack had inherited from his aunt to keep the battery charged and the soot blown out. He got in the car, and it wouldn't start. It cranked but didn't fire up.

Mike sat back in the seat, looked around him to see cars and trucks stalled or crashed up and down Highway 60. He thought, *Damn, Zack was right about what an EMP blast would do to cars. Oh crap, everyone with a pacemaker just died.*

Just then, a tremendous explosion rocked the car, and Mike looked up to see debris falling all around him and black smoke pouring into the sky from a block north of him. His stomach flip-flopped. His best friend was somewhere out west, and his sister and Callie were in Anderson about forty miles from the farm. He knew he had to walk the five miles to the farm, get his truck, and rescue Callie and Joan.

He started running and made about a mile before he came upon a woman sitting beside a wreck. Her face was covered in blood, and she held a dead little boy in her arms. He tried to help her, but she screamed and cried. Mike looked beside her and saw blood was flowing from a large wound on the inside of her leg. She died before he could act. He helped several people pull their friends and loved ones out of wrecks on his way to the farm

Mike finally saw the driveway to the farm and sprinted up the road to the house. He stayed calm, got in his old truck, and tried to start it. It cranked but didn't start. Damn, Zack had told him to keep the old ignition parts for the truck in the case of an EMP blast or sunspots. Now, where did he store them? He looked in the glove box, under the seat, and even in his BOB and still couldn't find them. Mike tried starting Zack's '54 Ford, but it wouldn't even crank. He looked in the pole barn and decided he could walk to the auto parts store on Highway 54 and back before he found the points and condenser.

••••

Callie looked at the dead phone and said, "Uncle Mike? Uncle Mike?"

The lights and TV were off, and Callie began to get worried, she yelled, "Mom! Mom, come here. The phone and TV are dead!"

"Callie, I'm sure they'll come back on. Go over to the Smiths and see if their power is out."

Callie walked outside and saw most of the neighbors were milling around and pointing their phones in different directions. Most didn't even notice all of their phones had a blank screen.

The neighbor boy Greg yelled, "Callie, our electricity is off, and everyone's cell phone is dead."

"Tell everyone to go into their houses and fill their tubs with water so they can flush their toilets if the power doesn't come back on soon."

"Why would the power be off so long? There's no storm. Perhaps a car hit a power line."

"Dummy, that wouldn't knock your phone out of service. Look, your phone has no power. I'll bet your car won't start. See all of the cars stalled in the middle of the street?"

Callie ran back into the house, yelling, "Mom, we've been nuked with an EMP as Dad warned us! We need to go to the farm! Now!"

"Callie, I can hear you. The power goes out from time to time. No big deal. Stop the panic."

"Mom, I'm telling you the power is out, the phones are dead, and all of the cars are dead in the street. Try to start your car."

Joan grabbed her keys and went out to her car. She hit the unlock button on the key fob and tried opening the door. It was still locked. She stood there with a blank face until Callie said, "Try the key, Mom."

She used the key to open the door, got in, and tried to start the car. Nothing. No lights, no cranking of the engine, no radio, nothing.

"Callie, there must be a simple explanation. I just don't know what it is."

There were several explosions in the distance as small planes fell to the ground, but Joan was panicking and didn't notice them.

"Mom, I'm riding my bike to the store. Give me some money."

Joan was in a daze and told her to get some money out of her wallet.

Callie put her backpack on, rode her bike down to the grocery, and saw the power was out everywhere as she expected. The store manager was turning people away when Callie parked her bike.

"Hi, Mr. Parker. I need some supplies. I'll pay cash."

"Hi, Callie. I'm closing down since the credit card reader stopped working, but come on in while no one is outside. What do you need?"

Callie purchased all of the packages of beef jerky, rice, beans, and canned meat that would fit in her basket and backpack.

"Callie, that comes to $107, and we'll forget the taxes."

"Thanks for letting me in your store. Are you afraid of looters?"

"Yes, dear. We're taking all we can carry to our house and locking the doors."

He walked over to the meat counter, grabbed several packages, and brought them to Callie, saying, "These steaks will spoil. Take them as a gift."

"Thanks."

She paid Mr. Parker and headed back home. She saw the police were trying to stop looters at the Best Buy store and peddled faster towards home.

••••

Davi felt like a traitor leaving Somalia and flying to the USA without heading to Israel and helping defend her country. Mori had to order her to get the hell out of the Middle East while she could. They both knew the whole area would be a radioactive wasteland in a few days, and there was nothing anyone could do to stop the destruction. Davi and her team flew from Somalia in helicopters to an airstrip in the desert and boarded an Israeli Airforce cargo plane. Thirty-six Israelis were on board, and all of them were headed to the USA to try to survive the holocaust. The aircraft was refueled in the air over the Atlantic Ocean, and both planes went on to the USA. The refueling plane checked in with the military and faked an emergency landing in Pensacola. Davi's plane had a bonafide flight plan for Champaign-Urbana Willard University Airport. They were all booked as scientists visiting the University of Illinois.

Davi would go on to her parent's home while the rest of her team and the others split up and headed to a secret rendezvous location in the southeast USA. Davi and her family were invited to join them, but Davi's father wouldn't leave his new home. Davi's mom was a chemistry professor at UI, and her father was a retired Israeli Air Force pilot who now farmed over a hundred acres south of Champaign. Her mom, Sharon, had set up the fake conference that had allowed the others to visit the area.

The plane landed after dawn, and after tearful goodbyes, Davi found her mother and father waiting in front of the airport. They hugged and told her how grateful they were she was safe in the USA. The news was painting a horrible picture. They stopped at a restaurant on the way to her parent's house for breakfast.

"How bad is it over there? We got up and ran to the airport."

"The Iranians and North Koreans were about to launch a sneak attack on Israel, the USA and several other countries. We have had to try and stop them without help from the USA."

There was a commotion at the front of the restaurant, and someone turned the TV up very loud. They heard, "Our sources are reporting Israel and Iran have exchanged nuclear missiles and are at war. We're guessing that Israel attempted a first strike elimination of Iran's nuclear program and has failed. There have been numerous nuclear blasts in the area. President Wilton will speak to the country in five minutes."

"Mom, Dad, let's go now," Davi said as she jumped up from the table.

"But darling, let's hear what the president has to say."

"Dad, we don't have time. Let's go now."

Aaron Gold paid the bill, and they got in the car and left heading south on Highway 45. Their farm was only a few more miles when the car's engine stalled and died. The radio had a loud buzzing sound and went off at the same time. The Highway 57 overpass was just a hundred yards ahead of them, and Davi yelled for them to follow her.

"We're under attack. Follow me quickly."

Just as they got out of the car, several planes crashed around the airport, and vehicles were stalled with a few crashing into other cars.

She led them up the side of the hill to a spot almost under the underpass.

"We will stay here for a while until the danger passes. An EMP blast just knocked out all electronics.

They spent several hours under the bridge and then walked to her parent's house. Davi had a metal box in her luggage containing several walkie-talkies, an emergency radio, and extra batteries. They listened to the radio most of that night and kept hearing the same message on a loop.

"The USA has experienced a major failure of its power grid. It will take several weeks to get the electrical system back in operation. The large cities will be the first, followed by smaller cities and then the rest of the country. Stay in your homes, conserve food and water, and be patient. Thanks for your support for our great country."

"Dad, how are we fixed for food, weapons, and transportation?"

"Come, my little warrior, into my garage. Your dad thought this might happen, and I have prepared for years."

He led her to a pole barn and opened a side door, which led them into a typical garage that would be found on a farm.

"Davi, what's wrong with this garage? What do you see?"

"Dad, the inside is smaller than the outside."

He replied, "Yes, I taught you well," as he walked over to the east wall and appeared to rub his hand on the wall.

Suddenly, the middle section of the far wall tilted up to reveal a hidden room. Inside the room were two vehicles, an older Jeep, and a newer Jeep.

"These will get us anywhere we need to go and are EMP and solar flare proof. The barn also has an extra layer of metal all around the entire structure, so even the Ford F250 wasn't harmed by the EMP attack. Follow me behind the Jeep."

Again, he rubbed his hand behind a picture on the wall, and she heard a click.

"Help me push the Jeep out of the way."

The Jeep was easy to move, and she saw a section of the floor had raised an inch. Her father bent over and easily lifted the hatch to reveal a set of stairs that descended below the garage. The room was almost as large as the hidden section of the above-ground garage. It was a small apartment with shelves stacked with food, clothing, and other supplies. There were several weapons in a rack on the wall.

"Dad, this is wonderful. We can survive and hide from the bad guys. Do you have any more ammo?"

"Darling, I have another surprise for you," he said as he opened the door to another hidden room.

"This is the Armory, and our friends in Israel helped me stock it in case they needed a safe house in this part of the USA. We have over thirty safe houses across the country."

Davi saw a rack full of M4s, Uzis, several long-range sniper rifles, and a section devoted to pistols of all types.

"I also have LAWs, hand grenades, and thousands of rounds for every weapon. My little Davi can kill all of the bad guys."

"I hope they only cut the USA out of the world stage and choose not to attack further. I hope to be able to contact our intelligence group and get an update tonight. What communication equipment do you have?

"I have walkie talkies, shortwave, and CB radios. I, too, planned to contact our old friends. I don't think North Korea or Iran will try to invade the USA; however, I wouldn't put anything past the Russians, Mexicans or Chinese."

"Dad, why would the Mexican government invade the USA?"

"They want the bottom half of the USA that used to belong to them and still contains a lot of oil and natural resources."

★

Chapter 5 Hightailing it Home

Iowa

I thought I was in pretty good shape for the shape I was in at thirty-five years old; 5'10" and 200 pounds. I had never been a fitness nut, but I ran, worked out on my Bowflex, and took long hikes through the woods. I was into backpacking and camping, which fit right into my prepping interest. I wasn't dead tired, and I have covered at least twenty-five miles since my car died. I planned to walk twenty miles the first day and try for a minimum of thirty miles a day afterward. That's just two miles an hour. I thought I could walk for fifteen hours and rest the remaining nine hours, so I had more than enough time built into my plan. The twenty-five miles wasn't too bad, but people asking for help or needing water had stopped me a couple of times. I politely helped one woman check her husband's pulse, and he was dead. His pacemaker stopped when his car stopped. She cried and asked me to take them to the hospital. I told her she could walk with me to Iowa City, but she wanted to stay with her husband until the police came. I told her they might not come, and she sent me on my way.

I'd just walked under the Highway 1 underpass when I heard several gunshots to the north of me. I ducked behind a

34

support column and saw several men beating the tar out of a guy in a hotel parking lot. It was about a hundred yards away, so I kept walking on down Highway 80, minding my own business. I have to get home, I kept reminding myself, and I can't get involved in other people's misfortune. Had I stepped in back there, I could have been shot myself, and I don't even know who the good or bad guy was. Keep my nose out of other people's problems would be my motto from now on. I walked faster. From time to time, I heard gunshots in the distance and knew in just twenty-four to forty-eight hours, all hell would break loose.

I kept watch ahead and behind every few minutes with my field glasses. From time to time, I looked at what was going on in the homes and villages along the way. I saw stalled cars and people milling around. I saw a house burning and, as the day wore on, saw more and more substantial fires. Once I saw a house burning in the distance. I walked under the Highway 38 underpass, scanned the highway ahead, and saw two young women waving at me. I waved back and peered through the field glasses for any hidden dangers. Seeing none, I walked closer to them until I saw several bodies strewn around a pile of luggage and boxes. I walked closer and saw four men and a woman had been shot and dumped on the side of the road. Both of the young girls had also been shot, but only received flesh wounds. One had a graze to her side and the other a wound to her thigh where the bullet had passed on through without hitting bone or major blood vessels.

They both were crying and blubbering so much I couldn't understand a word they were saying.

"Ladies, please calm down. Neither of you has a serious injury, the bleeding has stopped, and you'll be okay. Who shot y'all, and why?"

"We were driving along, and several men blocked the road with stalled cars and demanded we give them the bus. When Bob told them to get screwed, they started shooting at us. We stopped and surrendered, but they took four of our friends and shot the rest of us. I'm sure they thought we were dead."

"Were you in that VW bus that passed me this morning?"

"Yes."

"The four friends they took with them were young pretty women, weren't they?"

35

"Yes. Oh, my. They took them to..... Oh, crap."

"Yep, that about sums it up. They're now sex slaves to some assholes at the end of the world."

"You're so calm discussing our friends being kidnapped and probably raped by now."

"I can't go to pieces about something I can't control or do anything about. I'm walking home and have four-hundred more miles to go, so ladies, I'm leaving, and you'd better come with me."

"Wait, we need to go to a hospital and need your help. Geena can't even walk. Please help us."

"See that farmhouse over there? I'll help you to it, and perhaps they can get you to a hospital."

"Thanks."

We both helped the girl called Geena to the farmhouse, which was about half a mile away. I had to stop and cut the fence along the highway with my Leatherman since she couldn't climb the fence. We traveled closer to the house when a voice yelled, "Stop! What do you want?"

I replied, "These women have been shot and need help."

"Who shot them?"

"Some bastards shot them and stole their van."

"Damn, the same assholes came through here and killed Tom, who tends the farm for my husband and me. My grandson and I killed two of them, and they ran over to the highway several hours ago. Come on in and let me look at the girls. My name's Paula, and I'm a retired nurse. This is my grandson, Jake."

"This is Geena and Sally, I'm Zack."

"Geena, let's look at your leg first."

Paula examined, cleaned, and bandaged both wounds.

"You two are lucky. Both bullets could have killed you if they weren't such bad shots. Zack, do you know what happened? We were going about our day when everything stopped working, and planes started falling out of the sky."

"Ma'am, I believe the USA has been attacked with nuclear electromagnetic pulse bombs. They fry all electronics and knock out the power grid."

"How long will it take to get the power back up and working? What about cars?"

"Assuming there's no invasion, it could take six months to a year to get the major cities power and two to five years to get the rest of the country back to normal."

"Well, I guess we can make it that long."

"Ma'am, I hate to bring bad news, but you only saw a small example of what will be happening all over the country."

"What do you mean?"

"Stores are running out of food and will be empty by tomorrow. There are no trucks or trains to deliver food, gas, medicine, or other much-needed supplies to the stores. People will riot and start killing each other for scraps of food."

"Damn, that's scary. Well, we have food and will just stay out of the cities until those bastards starve to death. The emergency broadcast said to stay indoors until the DHS says it's safe."

"Ma'am, it's not that easy. When they run out of food in the cities, they'll loot warehouses, and when those are empty, they'll leave the cities and break into houses and farms to find food. Eventually, they'll come here and take your food. The DHS will only try to keep order in the large cities. They can't be everywhere."

"You really think people will kill us for our food?"

"If your grandson hadn't eaten in a week, what would you do to get food for him?"

"Yes, I would kill to feed my kids and grandkids."

"I hate to say it, but the country just went back one-hundred and fifty years in one day. The America that you know has died. The new America is about surviving. It's getting dark outside. Don't light any candles or lights that would attract attention."

"I'll fix a good supper for you tonight, and then we can figure out what to do. I have a freezer that's full of meat that will spoil, so let's eat like kings before it does."

"Thanks. I'll be leaving early in the morning. I have to get back to my family, and they're four hundred miles south of here in Kentucky."

Paula asked, "Sally, where were you two headed when the lights went out?"

"We were headed to a Grateful Dead concert in Cincinnati. Geena has relatives there. I guess that's where we'll go when Geena can walk."

Paula and Sally started cooking while Paula's grandson and I went outside to make sure no one was lurking around.

"Hey, what's in all of these barns?"

"That barn's where Papa stores his farm equipment, and this one's where he stores his antique tractors and farm equipment. He rebuilds them himself."

"Let's take a look."

We entered the barns, and there were over twenty tractors from the turn of the century up to the late forties.

"Do any of them run? Did your Papa drive any of them?"

"Yes, all but those in the very back of the shop run. He let me drive them, and we took them to tractor shows at the county fair."

I looked them over and had a plan hatching in my mind. I was wondering what I'd have to do to get one of those tractors. It would be slower than a car, but even at fifteen miles an hour, I could be home in a week or so.

Sally called us in to eat. The table was piled high with steaks, baked potatoes, freshly baked bread, and tea.

"Paula, where's your husband? Will he be here tonight?"

"He drove over to Davenport early this morning and hasn't made it home yet. I expect he's walking home just as you're. It's about forty-two miles to the other side of Davenport where he went, and I'd guess it will take a couple of days to get back home."

"I'll keep an eye out for him. I have to go to Davenport to cross the Mississippi before heading south."

She pointed to a picture on the mantle and said, "That's his picture."

I took a good look and hoped he was still alive, then said, "Paula, did you know while your trucks and cars won't run, those old tractors will?"

"Are you sure they'll run? We didn't try them. I just assumed all vehicles wouldn't run."

"I'd like to borrow one of them to take me home to Kentucky."

"Frank would have a fit if he knew that I loaned a tractor to someone I just met, but I have a deal for you. You can take one of the tractors and enough fuel to go home if you let my grandson and me tag along on another tractor to find my husband in Davenport. He went to his sister's home on the east side of Davenport, and I want to go get him."

I was speechless. I had been racking my brain trying to think of a way to convince this woman to give me a tractor, and she solved the problem.

"Of course, I'll help you, and we can drop these two women off at the hospital when we get to Davenport."

"Zack, let's head out at dawn. I have a bad feeling after what you told me, and I want Frank home safe."

"You should bring your guns, ammo, food, and water for a week. Stuff happens, and you have to be prepared. Bring your medical gear also."

"I'll start getting it ready now. Frank has several old wagons that'll work nicely to haul us and the gear."

"I think we should have a guard posted through the night. We should break it into two-hour shifts, so everyone gets some sleep."

They all agreed and quickly put a schedule together. Paula said, "I'll get Frank's 12 gauge pump and load it with double-aught buck for the guard."

I added, "I'll show the girls how to use the shotgun and give everyone a few pointers on what to watch for. I'll also put trip wires around the farm with some bells or tin cans to give us an early warning."

"That's a great idea. I'll let the beagles out of the pens to be guard dogs tonight."

I looked at my watch and saw it was a little before 10:00 and got the portable ham radio out of my BOB, climbed to the top of the barn, turned it on, and listened. There was a lot of chatter about the attack, but most of it was confusing and not too helpful. The radio is line of sight, so it only carried ten to fifteen miles unless you're high above the ground.

I keyed the mic and said, "This is Zack 321, pass on to Mike123 that I am okay and headed home."

I received several replies they would pass my message on to Mike123. One man asked for my exact location, and I didn't answer.

"Zack321, this is Pistol Pete, where are you? We need help."

"Sorry, Pistol Pete, but I'm on the road and can't lend assistance. Good luck."

I let the women sleep, and I slept on the front porch with the old double-barrel shotgun, so I could respond quickly if needed. The night was uneventful; however, I woke to hear gunfire in the distance several times. I had the last watch just before daybreak and woke the others as the sun peeked over the horizon.

The tractors started without any issues. Jake hitched the wagons to them, and the women loaded them with the supplies. Both tractors ran on diesel fuel. I found six five-gallon cans and filled them from Frank's one-hundred-gallon tank. Paula gave everyone a small bottle of milk and two ham sandwiches, and we were ready to leave.

Paula gave Jake, Sally, and Geena their choice of a shotgun or 9mm pistol. She showed them how to use them and gave them a couple of boxes of ammunition.

Paula said, "I hope and pray we don't have any problems, but I don't want to have a bunch of criminals kill us all for a damned tractor. Ladies, shoot to kill if you pull that trigger—no warning shots. Jake, you drive the lead tractor, so Zack can keep an eye out for Papa. I gave Geena a pair of binoculars to watch the road, and I'll drive the other tractor."

I never thought two tractors could stir so much interest along our drive to Davenport. We barely made it to the highway before a family wanted us to take them west. I told them we were headed east and couldn't help them. The man got angry and threatened me, but backed down when Paula leveled her shotgun at him and said, "Look, man, get away from us and start walking home before you get hurt."

I kept watch ahead, and while I saw no obvious threats, it became clear to me every living human could become a threat if they were starving or wanted to take our food, guns, or tractors from us. I saw a large group of people milling around a tour bus on the eastbound lane and waved at Paula to let her know we were moving to the other side before the people saw us. The people saw us and started waving to come over to them. We ignored them and stayed in the westbound lane. When they saw we weren't joining them, several ran over to greet us.

"Hey, we need you to give us all a ride into Davenport so we can get a ride to St Louis."

I replied, "I'm sorry, but we don't have room for you, and you could have been there yesterday if you had started walking when your bus stalled."

One large man came over and said, "Look, buddy, you can give us a ride, or we'll take those tractors from you."

He pulled a small pistol from under his shirt and raised it towards me. I pulled faster, drew my 1911, and shot him twice in the chest. He dropped like a sack full of hammers, and the others backed away. One woman ran up and tried to revive him.

"You killed my boyfriend, you bastard!"

"Your boyfriend drew a gun on me, and I shot him in self-defense. We're leaving, and if you try to stop us, more of you will die. Now get back to your bus."

Two men dragged the lady back towards the bus as she screamed at me, "I'll get you! You don't know who you're screwing with. My dad's a senator, and he'll make you pay for this!"

We kept going towards Davenport while ignoring or waving guns at the desperate people trying to force us to give them food, water, or a ride. No one liked ignoring these needy people, but we couldn't help them all and focused on getting further east.

Just before 9:00 a.m., Jake turned towards me, pointed and said, "There's a sign for the hospital."

I turned off Highway 80 and followed the signs to the hospital. A few people came out and asked us if we had seen FEMA or DHS, but no one tried to stop us. I saw the hospital and drove the tractor up to the emergency room entrance, where a nurse was performing triage on a crowd of mad people.

I heard a nurse say, "If you have a cold, allergies or just feel bad, go home. We're only treating broken bones, gunshot wounds, and the very sick. We only have two doctors, and they're leaving tomorrow to go home to their own families."

A woman in the crowd replied, "They can't leave. They have to take care of us. The law says so."

The nurse ignored the woman and, after two hours, finally made it to Sally and Geena. She examined their wounds, gave them each a bottle of antibiotics, and told them to change the bandages frequently and seek medical attention if the injuries got worse. The girls thanked her, and we were on our way again.

"It's only the second day, and the hospitals are shutting down, and people are beginning to get mean and nasty. Imagine what they'll be like in a week," I said as we pulled away.

A man ran up and yelled, "Where are you going? I need a ride!"

Before I could answer, Paula replied, "Sorry, we aren't taking on riders."

"Look bitch, I need a ride!"

"Look asshole, this bitch has a shotgun. Try to get in this wagon, and you'll get a load of buckshot in your belly."

He walked away, cursing us and waving his hands at the crowd of people. Jake put the tractor in high gear and pushed the pedal to the metal. We were quickly out of sight.

I yelled back to the women and asked them where they wanted to be dropped off.

"I don't know what to do. We just need a safe place," said Sally.

"I want to go on to Cincinnati. Can we ride with you until we have to split?"

I looked back at the two rather attractive young ladies and replied, "Yes, as long as you don't get in the way, help find food, and split all chores with me."

Paula looked at me, winked, and said, "Zack, you aren't married, are you? Do you have a girlfriend back home?"

While Paula was right about her dirty thoughts, I lied and said, "I have a girl, and we're getting married when I get back."

I actually thought both Sally and Geena were hot and could warm my bed any night.

Paula laughed, and we drove on.

We were just outside of Le Claire when we saw a man lying on the side of the road waving at us.

"Paula, help me!"

"It's Frank, my husband!"

Jake brought the tractor to a halt, set the brake, jumped off the tractor and ran over to the man. Paula got there first and was hugging him when I arrived.

"Frank, are you okay? What happened?"

Frank looked up and replied, "When the power went off, and my truck wouldn't run, I decided to walk back home yesterday afternoon. My sister helped me put some food and water in a bag, and I was ready to walk home. I always carry my pistol, so I thought I was prepared. I saw several townsfolk who asked where I was going but didn't have any issues until I got on Highway 80. Then a man who was heading east stopped to talk, and the next thing I knew, I was waking up this morning at the bottom of that ditch with a bum foot and robbed of everything but my clothes. I tried to stand up and walk, but my ankle hurt so bad I was forced to crawl back up to the highway. No one would stop and help me until you came along. I recognized my tractors right away and thought maybe someone had stolen them."

"Darling, Jake and I'll get you back to the farm. Don't be mad, but I loaned Zack the John Deere to help get Sally, Geena, and him to their homes."

"It's the right thing to do. I never thought these antiques would be anything more than toys for an old man. Keep the tractor if it will help you. I don't expect the power will come back very soon."

I shook his hand and said, "Thanks for the tractor. You're right about it being a long while before the power comes back on. Old tractors, cars, and trucks may be the only transportation besides horses for a long time."

Paula filled him in on the attack on their farm and our arrival while we loaded him into the wagon.

"Good luck, and thanks for the tractor. We need to be making tracks east. I need to get back to Kentucky and make sure my daughter is safe. Keep your guns handy and don't take any crap from anyone."

It was 2:00 p.m. when we left Le Claire and were making about ten miles per hour. I thanked God for the tractor because I now knew it would have taken me forever to walk home. We ate a late lunch as we crossed the bridge over the Mississippi. The tractor attracted attention, but no one threatened us or tried to approach since we were making sure the shotguns were highly visible. We were just north of Galesburg when I decided to look for fuel and food. We had traveled thirty-six miles in four hours, and the tractor was burning diesel at an alarming rate. I didn't want to go into town, so I stopped beside a deserted semi-truck and trailer and searched for the driver. The driver was long gone, so I cut one of the air hoses off the trailer, made a siphon, and started filling my fuel cans. I filled the tractor's tank and finished topping off my last fuel can.

I opened a side hatch on the truck and found some tools. There were a pry bar and a pair of pliers. Just what I needed! I went to the back of the trailer, twisted the security band off the door, and opened it. The truck was headed to a store, so it was filled with pallets containing a variety of non-perishable foods. I helped Sally up onto the back of the trailer, and we picked the foods we wanted from back pallets. While Sally transferred the packages to the trailer, I climbed on top of the pallets and found some of my favorites. I pitched packages of chocolate chip cookies, Spam, toilet paper, and beef stew back towards Sally.

"Zack, do you see any tampons? Us girls will need them eventually."

"I'll take a look. That reminds me, I need to look for other sanitation items and some first aid supplies."

I had found most of what we needed when I heard, "Hey Zack, you'd better come here quick. We may have trouble."

I scrambled to the end of the truck, pulled my 1911, and saw a small crowd had gathered. One loudmouth yelled, "Are you going to share the food?"

"Sir, if you'll get out of our way, you can get all you want. If I were you, I'd get what I need and then move on before a riot breaks out when the people up and down the road hear about the food."

"Thanks, and thanks for the advice. You don't need the gun."

"You're welcome, but I do need the gun. I killed an asshole yesterday who tried to take our tractor away from us, and I'll do it again if we're attacked."

Geena raised her shotgun and smiled at the crowd of people and said, "Several men shot my friend and me and left us for dead over a VW bus. As long as I have this shotgun, no one will mess with me again."

The man smiled and replied, "Ma'am, I believe you mean business. I'm sorry I came on so strong, but we have been robbed, and some scum took several women along with our food. They left here an hour ago, and you'd better avoid them."

I watched the guy and his group for a few minutes. I saw how hungry the children were and how happy the families were to get the food. I thought there must be widespread hunger sweeping across the USA. I called him over to the tractor.

"Do y'all have any guns or other protection?"

"No, we're from Illinois, and none of the group had a gun in their cars. The damn state has crazy gun control laws."

I thought for a minute, handed him an unloaded shotgun and said, "Here is our extra 12 gauge. I'll drop a box of shells down the road a piece. Not that I don't trust you, but I don't trust anyone now."

"Thanks, mister. I'm Joe Black."

"You're welcome. I'm Zack Johnson. Good luck."

We finished loading then drove on a ways before I laid the shells on the side of the road and waved back at Joe.

We had driven another hour before I started looking for a place to spend the night. We had about an hour before dark, and I wanted to have a secure spot before nightfall. I saw a series of deep gullies up ahead and told the girls we were going to check the area out. We were about ten miles below Galesburg when I got off the tractor, cut the fence, and drove down into one of the gullies and parked.

"Ladies, I'm going to scout the location to make sure it's safe and will be back in about thirty minutes. Watch for intruders and don't make any noise."

I walked through the trees to the other side of the gully and saw a field planted with soybeans and a farmhouse about four hundred yards away. The series of gullies cut through the farm, and while a pain in the ass for the farmer, they made a perfect place for us to hide. The gully where I had parked the tractor was about a quarter-mile long and a hundred feet wide and covered in trees. I walked along a different gully that ran north towards the house, got within a hundred feet of the house, and watched the house for several minutes. There was a man, his wife, and two teenage kids. They were having supper, and the only issue was the kids were gripping about the internet being down. I was satisfied no dangers lurked nearby and headed back to the tractor.

I stopped about twenty-five feet from the tractor and heard the ladies talking.

"Well, then, we'll just have to toss a coin. Just because I can't walk right now doesn't mean I'll let you steal Zack away from me."

"Look, you're my best friend, but a woman without a man is probably a dead woman or a sex slave to some biker dude, now that the world has ended."

"Let's call a truce and flip a coin for him."

"Do you think he'll go for it?"

"He's a man, isn't he? Once his daughter is safe, he'll be chasing both of us."

I backed up another fifty feet and made some noise as I approached the ladies.

"Lucy, I'm home. What's for supper?"

They both laughed and were very nice to me the rest of the night.

I started a small fire against the bank of the gully, and we roasted a couple of cans of Spam, warmed up some canned vegetables and had chocolate chip cookies for dessert. We sat in the wagon eating our supper, and I noticed that Sally practically sat in my lap during supper. Geena glared at her during the entire meal. I tried to help clean up after supper, and the girls said they could handle the dishes.

"Ladies, if you don't need me, I'm taking this roll of TP and hand wipes out to the men's room. The men's room should be about fifty feet in front of the tractor, and the women's about the same behind the trailer. Since I don't have today's newspaper, I'll promptly return."

"That's a good idea. Hurry up, I have to pee and need your help getting out of the trailer and to the bathroom."

As I walked away, I heard, "Geena, that was a dirty trick. You know I can help you go use the restroom. What did you want him to do, hold your hand while you pee?"

"No, but I want him to steady me while I get to the bathroom," laughed Geena.

I returned in about fifteen minutes, and Sally was struggling to get Geena back into the wagon.

"Wait, I'll help."

I picked Geena up and gently placed her over the low side of the wagon, and she gave me a kiss on the cheek.

"My, such a polite man we have here. Thanks so much. You're a big help. I hope I'm back on my feet before we head to Indianapolis without you. Perhaps we'll go on to Kentucky with you. You seem to be a nice guy, and we don't know what to expect in Ohio."

I stammered and replied, "I'm sure your folks will miss you very much, but you're welcome to find a home in Kentucky. My girlfriend might even introduce you to some lucky men down there."

I was not going to start messing around with these women while on the way home. I had enough bad people out there that might try to kill me without them fighting each other and killing me.

I tried the ham radio again, and no one had heard from Mike123. I asked several to try to pass a message on to Mike123 in Kentucky. One man was telling me his son had driven home from Fort Knox and told him all US Armed Forces were being brought home to guard the USA against further attacks. He went on to say half of our military had been wiped out the first day, and we had retaliated, along with the rest of the western nations.

"Who did we retaliate against?"

"My son doesn't know. He thinks we nuked all the countries that support terrorism."

"Has all of the USA been attacked and lost power?"

"My son says he was told that the USA, Canada, and northern Mexico were hit hard by the EMP blasts. All of Europe, China, and Russia were also without power."

"Thanks for the information."

Damn, this guy could be right or a fruitcake. I chatted with several ham operators and then strung my hammock between the tractor and a close tree. I had the first two-hour watch. I heard a noise from the wagon and turned to see Geena taking her bra off. She looked over at me, pulled the cover-up to her neck, and went to sleep. I had heard some giggling and harsh whispers before it got quiet.

Just before my watch ended, Sally woke up, stood up in the wagon while she stretched. The moon was almost full, so she was framed against the sky. She slid a shirt on, climbed down from the wagon, and joined me in the woods in front of the tractor.

"Hello, handsome."

"You say that because I'm the only man around."

She giggled and replied, "No, I think you're a very good looking man. If you didn't already have a girlfriend, I'd be interested in you."

"Thanks for the compliment, but my girl would crap if she knew that I was out on the trail with two beautiful women."

"So you think I'm beautiful? Well, don't tell her when you get back. Damn, you might have to tell her. Geena is trying to talk me into going home with you to Kentucky."

I thought, *"Oh, crap,"* but said, "That would be nice," and shut up.

"What's your girlfriend's name, and what does she look like?"

Damn, I thought for a few seconds, *I have to tell her something that I can remember,* so I gave her Joan's description.

"Her name is Patsy, and she's about 5'4", 110 pounds with dark brown hair. We're supposed to get married this fall at my farm."

"I think you made that up. It took you too long to come up with her name."

She slid her arm around me and rubbed my back. It was feeling way too good, and I had to get away from her, but I was enjoying the massage too much.

"No, I was trying to decide how much to tell a strange woman that I just met yesterday. I'm not telling you the exact place that I live either."

"So, you're afraid of a tiny little girl like me?"

"No, but honestly, I am afraid you might mention to someone else where I live and any details about me. Sally, this is only the tip of the iceberg. Ninety percent of the USA will be dead in three to six months. Think about it. If ten people were sitting here, nine would be dead in six months. Starvation, disease, and lack of medical help will kill millions over the next 30 days. Criminals trying to take your food will kill much more; women will be swapped for whiskey, food, and ammo. Normal good Christian people will slit your throat to take your food and feed their kids."

She snuggled up to me, and I held her for several minutes and then gave her my watch so she would know when to wake Geena up.

"You need to put some pants on before mosquitoes bite that pretty butt. You'd look funny fighting off attackers wearing a thong."

"I was able to fight you off. Do you think I'm pretty?

"Goodnight, and remember, I have a girlfriend."

"I don't believe that crap, and you didn't act like you had a girlfriend when you held me."

"Well, maybe I forgot when I saw you naked in the wagon," I told her and then went to my hammock.

I thought about her all night.

Geena wiped the tears away and tried unsuccessfully to go to sleep. She didn't want a man in her life but knew she would be safer with one.

✪

Chapter 6   Back Home

The United States of America

Mike strapped on his holster with his Glock 9mm and got an extra mag for it and his Ruger .380 he always carried. He filled his canteen, stuffed a couple of water bottles into his BOB, and started to walk into Owensville to find the ignition parts. As an afterthought, he raised the hood on Zack's truck to check the distributor to make sure he bought the right parts. He had the hood open when he saw the red metal box bolted to the side of the firewall. Damn, that's where the spare ignition parts were stored. He felt stupid for forgetting that he and Zack had installed the box and filled it with the parts needed for when TSHTF. He opened the box and saw two complete sets of ignition parts and wires. He took the top off the distributor and removed the electronic components, and then it was just placing the points and condenser on the distributor plate and securing them with screws.

He cranked the engine, and it fired right away but ran a bit rough. He adjusted the timing, and it ran better, but still had a miss. Mike opened the red box, removed the extra spark plug wires, and replaced all of the wires. The engine cranked up and ran perfectly.

Mike said to himself, *"Damn, I'm great. I must thank Zack for us being prepared for this EMP crap. Now to go fetch Callie and my bitch sister. Damn, I need to calm down and start thinking things through, or I'll get my sorry ass in trouble."*

Mike had reluctantly become a prepper because Zack talked about it all of the time. They'd even watched that show on TV about prepping. He read a couple of the apocalyptic novels over the past year about survival and knew that there was trouble ahead. He went back into the garage and retrieved a hand fuel pump, twenty feet of hose, and four gas cans so he could get gas when needed. The truck had a full tank of gas, and he put a case of water and some food in the cab. Now he was ready to travel, but which way should he go? He knew it was early in this disaster and that eventually, people would try to take the truck from him.

He went back into the house and got a Smith & Wesson MP15 and five 30 round mags from the gun safe. He thought, *"better safe than sorry. If an AR and 150 rounds weren't enough firepower, he was probably screwed anyway."*

He decided to take the bypass around Owensville and then take the Baker Parkway to Anderson to avoid as many city streets as possible. No sooner had he turned onto Highway 54 did he see an old Chevy stopping and the driver waving at him.

"Sorry Mike, I thought it was Zack. That's his old '54 Ford, isn't it?"

"Yes, and I'm heading over to Anderson to bring his daughter back over to the farm until this power shortage ends."

"Good idea. Our antique truck club is spreading the word to fire up their old cars and trucks to help out the police and hospitals. Please spread the word when you go through Owensville and Anderson."

"Hey, wouldn't older tractors still run?"

"Damn, no one thought about that yet. I'll start passing that on."

"Chuck, you might have people check to see if anyone has shortwave or walkie-talkie radios that work. Ones that were stored in metal cabinets or metal buildings should work. I think we were attacked with nuclear EMP bombs. The metal shields the radio's electronics from damage."

"Thanks for the ideas and info. We plan to meet at the Post Office in Philpot the day after tomorrow to see how we can help each other."

"Be careful who you invite. People will be starving in a week and will kill for food."

"I'm not worried about that. We're just good Christian people who will help anyone who shows up for help."

Mike waved goodbye and drove on into Owensville without stopping, even when people tried to wave him down. He couldn't drive very fast since cars were parked where they'd stopped in the middle of the road. Mike wove his way around them while cursing the damn drivers for not steering their vehicles to the side of the road. He saw three more old cars on the road and waved at them. He was just about to the exit for the Baker Parkway when he saw a group of people walking on the side of the road. He slowed down and drove across the median to avoid them. Just as he got going, he saw several of them waving rifles and trying to cross over to block his way. Mike floored the old truck, and the 460 Ford roared to life and went past the men before they could get in front of him.

Mike heard them yell, "Stop you, bastard! We need your truck!" then he heard a blast, and something hit the back of the truck.

He looked back in the mirror and saw that the rear window had several small broken spots and fracture lines. The bastards had shot at him with a shotgun! He thought, *"What makes them think they can just steal someone's truck because they need it?"* He pulled his Glock from his holster and placed it on the seat beside him. *"The next asshole who shoots at me will get a bullet in his ass."*

••••

"Mom, I'm back."

"Young lady, don't you ever leave again without checking with me. I was scared you ran off."

"Well, I might if you and Todd don't start taking this seriously. I ran to the store and got some food. Mr. Parker's store was empty, and he was closing it today before looters come to rob him. The Best Buy store was being looted when I rode past it."

"Darling, you've been listening to your dad too much. This is not the end of the world. Todd will be home soon, and he'll know what to do. Surely they shut his office down and sent them home."

"Mom, Todd is an office manager at the welfare office. His office should be closed every day, according to Dad."

"Don't be a smart-ass."

••••

Todd's office was experiencing a total breakdown of order and chaos. EBT cards were not working due to electronics failure, and stores were only taking cash. There were no police to control the crowd of people who demanded food, medicine, and transportation. When they found out the office couldn't help them, they rioted

Todd said to the crowd, "We're sorry the EBT cards aren't working. We only do the paperwork and follow up on your welfare. We can't make the cards work."

"You'd better get us some food, or there's going to be hell to pay. Get your boss out here. We need somebody who can give us cash until the EBT cards work."

"My boss is in Washington today, and with power out, I don't know when he'll be back. We're closing the office down until the federal government gives us the ability to help you."

This angered the crowd, and they went berserk. They knocked Todd out of the way and stormed the office. The office workers fled out the back door when they saw the horde of angry people breaking down the front doors. They broke all of the windows, overturned desks and stole laptops and PCs before they set the building on fire. Todd got up out of the flowerbeds, brushed the dirt off his suit, and watched as these people tore his office to pieces. He felt sorry for these unfortunate people and would have given them his own money if the banks weren't closed. He had been knocked down and trampled on as the mass of people stormed his office, but he had no severe injuries, so he calmly dusted himself off and started walking home.

Todd's office was on Main Street just down from the courthouse, so he had to walk three miles to Joan's home on Bittersweet Road off of Highway 351 on the east side of town. It was a beautiful large house in a nice subdivision, and Todd was tired of living in a small apartment over a store in downtown Anderson. A junior office manager for the state of Kentucky was not very highly paid, and Todd liked the finer things in life.

He walked down Main Street to 2nd Street and headed east. Joan's house was three miles straight ahead. Todd saw a massive fire with black smoke rising from the shopping center where the Walgreens was located. He stopped and looked around to see that there were several large columns of smoke rising into the sky above Anderson. Cars, pickups, and semi-trucks were scattered about the streets as though a child had been playing with them. Many had been wrecked when the engines lost power. He walked several blocks and saw a large crowd gathered behind St. John's Church with what looked like several men fighting. He picked up the pace to get away from the conflict when he saw an older house on the left explode into flames. He stopped for a minute, and three more houses erupted in flames. Todd ran across the street and ran for several blocks until he felt safe again. He walked up the 4th Street overpass, saw that the Best Buy and Tractor Supply were in flames with people still carrying TVs away from the parking lot. He thought, *"Wait until these criminals find out that their EBT cards don't work."*

He avoided making eye contact with everyone he passed and was soon walking down the street Joan lived on. He ran up to the door, opened it, tripped, and stumbled into the house.

"The damn world is falling apart. Those ungrateful bastards would have killed us."

He looked up to see Joan and Callie, staring at him. He was drenched in sweat, his shirt was filthy, and he only had one shoe. He was visibly shaking

"Todd, what happened?"

"My office has been ransacked. They assaulted me, and the city is in chaos. Walgreens, Best Buy, and Tractor Supply are on fire, and every store is being looted. These people have become animals. I hate them."

"Darling, calm down. Everything will be okay. The government will send help, won't they?"

"Joan, I have never been so scared in my life, but that's right. FEMA and DHS will come in, get the power back on, and get law and order re-established. Everything will be okay."

"Go upstairs and get cleaned up."

Todd went upstairs, and Callie said, "I can't believe you left Dad for that spineless worm. He was almost crying."

"Don't be too hard on him. It sounds like he had a rough day. We'll be all right out here away from town. The riff-raff will steal and loot around town, but we'll stay away from town."

"Mom, what happens when we run out of food?"

"The government will come in, give us food, and put those criminals behind bars."

★

Chapter 7   Tractoring Home

Illinois

Geena woke me up with a sharp kick to the side about 4:00 a.m. and gave me a cup of steaming hot coffee. I put my shoes on, buckled my 1911 to my hip and slid my hoodie over my head as I braced myself for the eventual conversation with Geena.

"Thanks for the coffee. You need to catch a nap before we get ready to head out. I'll wake you two at six."

"Thanks, but I'm wide awake and will keep you company if that's all right with you. I know I'm not Sally, but at least we can talk."

I ignored the comment and went on as usual. I noticed Geena was out of the wagon and walking around. I saw she favored her side and limped, trying to protect it from the strain.

"I see you're better this morning."

"I don't know about better, but I decided that I want to be in that ten percent that'll live. What you told Sally last night scared the crap out of me. Did you mean that or were you just trying to scare Sally?"

"It's true, and yes, I wanted to give Sally a dose of reality. You both appear to be a little too carefree and unconcerned about your future. If you aren't careful, you'll end up as a gang member's bitch."

"Zack, we do get it and don't judge us by the fact that you found us in a bus with a bunch of hippies. Our car quit, as did yours, and a million others. We were walking down 80 when these hippies stopped and gave us a ride. Yes, we traded on our good looks to get a ride on the bus and were scared to death that we would have to pay for our ride. Those men were too stoned to worry about sex; thank God."

"I thought y'all were one big happy family."

"No, Sally and I were on vacation and heading to her dad's place outside of Cincinnati when the power went off."

"Where do you work?"

"We both teach at the high school in Castle Rock, Colorado. It's just a few miles south of Denver. We met there and have been best friends for several years. We ski, backpack, and travel together. I know we may appear a bit desperate, but we both recognize you're a good man who knows how to handle himself. Maybe we're coming on a bit strong, but I believe the dating scene is gone forever. We're heading back to the wild west of the 1850's."

"Look, I kind of like the attention, but I have a daughter and a family to get back to and must think about their safety before I think about myself."

"I heard you and Sally talking last night. I thought you were interested in her."

"You're two beautiful and great people to boot, and yes, I am tempted, but I keep remembering my daughter and what is happening to her."

"You're a strong man and will get back to your family."

"My wife left me for my neighbor. I fell to pieces and began screwing his wife to get even. She was a bitch from hell, and I moved on to a dozen other women over the last couple of years. I haven't been a good man, and I haven't been the kind of man that you or I am proud of."

"So you've changed? What about last night with Sally?"

"I didn't sleep with Sally last night and won't with you for that matter. You both are gorgeous, sexy and all I can think about is my Callie trying to find food and fighting off some gang banger. At any other time, I'd be trying to get you both into bed."

She blushed and said, "Isn't she with her mom?"

"Yes, but her mom and her mom's boyfriend don't possess the skills needed to survive this mess. My best friend, Mike, is her mom's brother and he's going to get them and take them to my farm. They should be safe there."

"So you find me attractive, but are thinking about your daughter first?"

"Yes."

"I think you may have turned the corner. I don't think you're a whore-mongering bastard anymore," she said as she kissed me on the cheek and added, "It is yet to be seen if you're only a regular bastard."

"I hope I can exceed your low expectations."

She turned away from me and said, "Sally, you can stop straining to hear our conversation and get your butt out of bed."

I heard Sally say in a muffled voice, "Screw you and the horse you rode in on."

Sally jumped out of her bed in the wagon and stood up to dress for the day. I glanced over to see her sliding her shirt over her bare chest before I quickly glanced away. I backslid and had a few wicked thoughts before I busied myself preparing for our day ahead. It was still dark, and nature was calling, so I headed to the "Men's Room."

"I'll be back in a few minutes after I finish my job at the library."

"Gross."

I was actually reading a map as I did my business. Suddenly, I heard a strange voice on the other side of the tractor. I finished and slowly crawled over to the tractor and peered around the front end to see a man with a pistol aimed at the girls.

"Ladies, I'm not really a bad guy. The only reason I have this gun pointed at you is that you might try to hurt me."

Geena replied, "That's a load of crap. Get out of here before my boyfriend kills your sorry ass."

"Look, bitch, I don't see any men around here. I think I have you two all to myself."

"Now, you, the one with the big mouth, drop to your knees."

"Screw you."

I had watched long enough to see that the man was by himself, so I snuck up behind him as I drew my knife. Geena saw me and dropped to her knees a few inches from him to keep his attention. He lowered the gun as he watched Geena unzip his fly. I grabbed his head as I dragged the knife across his throat. He dropped the gun and tried to talk but couldn't. I dropped him to the ground and saw him pointing at me, his throat bubbling a bloody red froth as he tried to speak. I stepped over him on my way to check on the girls.

"Are you all right?"

They both swarmed me crying and unusually silent.

"That turd was the nice husband and father that I saw in the farmhouse. Let's cover him with some brush and get the hell out of here."

Neither wanted to talk about the attack until later that night. Both were stunned and talked very little the rest of the day.

I topped off the tractor from one of the fuel cans, checked the oil, and made sure the radiator was full before starting the tractor. I examined it from front to back in hopes of preventing any breakdowns. I saw a hole in the left engine cover where a bullet had pierced the lid and glanced off the engine block. The tractor took a bullet meant for one of us. I patted it and hoped our luck would hold out for a few more weeks.

We were on the road by 6:30 that morning, and everyone was quiet. The reality was beginning to set in for the girls. They had been attacked and would have been raped had I not killed the bastard.

I prepared the girls for driving all day to make up for the delays on the previous day. I figured that we could travel over a hundred miles if we kept going until 6:30 p.m. before making camp for the night. That would put us on the other side of Peoria, Illinois. We continued to see people walking along the interstate heading in both directions. Most only waved, but quite a few tried to stop us to get a ride. Several wanted us to change directions and take them west. It was a long day, but as we saw the skyline of Peoria, I saw a large group of people heading west up in front of us. They were different from the other groups, and I was trying to put my finger on it Geena said, "That large group of people doesn't have any children with them. The women are dressed for a ball, and the men are in suits. They just don't fit the picture."

"Good call out. I was trying to figure out what looked odd about them myself. Oh, crap. Some are crossing over towards us."

Several men left the group, veered off from their friends, and started across the median to head towards us. One of them had a briefcase. They would be in the middle of our road before we could get past them.

I pulled my 1911 out and said, "Ladies, keep your guns down, but ready. I don't like what I'm seeing. These guys want our tractor and food."

I sped the tractor up, but they started waving and blocked our path. I stopped fifty feet from them and yelled, "Get out of our way! We don't want to run you down, but we will if we have to!"

One man stepped forward and said, "Hey buddy, we're stranded here and have to get to Omaha for official government business. It's vital to our country's security."

These men did not look like government employees and certainly didn't dress like government employees.

I replied, "Sorry, sir, our tractor is the only way we can get home, and you can't have it."

"Look, buddy, I'll just take it in the name of the government."

"Sorry, but get out of our way so we can get closer to home."

The man reached into his briefcase, pulled out a wad of cash, and said, "I'll buy your tractor and wagon. Here's $50,000. That should get your attention."

"Sorry, but get out of our way."

"Damn, here's $200,000."

"Your money is worthless. Now get out of the road, so you don't get hurt."

"What do you mean worthless? These are US dollars, and I want that tractor."

The five men started walking towards us, and the one offering the money reached under his jacket and came out with a pistol. I raised my gun at the same time the girls raised their shotguns.

I yelled, "Drop your guns and go back across the highway and live! Try to rob us and die!"

The man laughed, raised his pistol, and shot at us, striking the tractor beside me. I aimed, squeezed the trigger, and he was knocked off his feet. Blood flew through the air as he fell. This wasn't slow motion like in the movies, but it wasn't real to me as it unfolded. Shots rang out from both sides, with the shotguns blasting away from behind me. I shot another of the men, and his head exploded as the .45 caliber hollow point tore through his skull. I heard a shotgun blast and saw one of the men knocked backward when the double-aught buck ripped into his stomach. Several more shotgun blasts followed quickly behind the first. The girls killed the other two, and the battle for the tractor was over as suddenly as it had started. I fired the tractor up and took off before their friends could attack us.

I turned around and yelled, "Are y'all okay?"

"Yes, we're okay. Those idiots would have killed us for our tractor. What has this world come to? Who the hell were those guys?"

"We'll probably never know, but I'm sure they didn't work for the US government. They dressed and acted like mafia hoods."

We heard gunfire, and several bullets pinged off the concrete behind us. One hit the tractor just to the left of the steering wheel. I put the pedal to the metal, and we surged ahead, going at least fifteen miles per hour. The shots continued for a few minutes and didn't hit us or the tractor and wagon.

"Zack, turn around."

I turned to see what Sally wanted, and both ladies pointed at my side.

I looked down and saw a bloody shirt, and then it struck me that I'd been hit during the gunfight. I lifted my shirt and saw the end of a small bolt sticking out of my side below my ribs. Blood was flowing down my side.

"Zack, pull over and let us take care of you before you bleed to death."

I pulled the bolt out of my side and had to bite my lip to keep from screaming. I stuck it in my pocket, then wadded up the tail of my shirt and used it to apply pressure to my wound.

"We can't stop until we put a few more miles between those idiots and us behind us."

I put the tractor in gear, slipped the clutch out, and went down the road with me holding my side and the girls yelling at me to stop. I pulled off the road about five miles later and let Sally apply some antibiotic salve and bandages on my wound. I pulled the bolt out of my pocket and saw that it was from the tractor. The bullet that had struck the tractor beside the steering wheel had sent it flying into my side.

"Ladies, the tractor has one less bolt, and I have a hole in my side. I hope the tractor is tougher than I am because that hurts like a bitch."

"Zack, let's find a safe spot and spend the night here. You're in no shape to travel."

"Sorry, but get your pretty asses back in the wagon, and let's roll. We won't get home if we stop for every boo-boo."

"You're one hard-headed bastard."

"Yep."

We drove for several hours until I knew we wouldn't make our distance goal for the day.

"Ladies, we can't get through Peoria and find a safe place to camp before dark. I'm going to go right at the next exit and take Highway 18 to help us get around Peoria."

Sally replied, "Can you find us a hotel with hot showers, a soft bed, and a five-star restaurant?"

"Of course, I'll put that high on my list of places to camp tonight."

I kept looking for a safe place to camp for the night to no avail until I saw an old barn on the west side of Highway 18. The barn was huge but very old. One section had collapsed, and I was sure it was deserted. It was almost dark, so this place was our best hope.

"I'm going over to the barn and see if it's safe for us to spend the night. Keep an eye out for the bad guys."

My side hurt like hell as I dismounted the tractor, but I hid the pain, as men are supposed to do in front of women. I walked around the barn with my pistol drawn and saw there wasn't much light, so I turned my flashlight on and spooked an owl. It scared the crap out of me, and I dropped my gun and the flashlight trying to get away from it as it flew over my head. I picked my gun and flashlight, hoping that no one saw me in this moment of embarrassment. I turned around to see both Sally and Geena behind me, giggling with their hands over their mouths.

"Big brave man told the defenseless women to stay behind while a bird scares the crap out of him."

"That's all right, Sally. You can go into dark barns in the future to scout them out for monsters, bears, and hoods. It won't hurt my male ego one bit."

"Oh no, you're doing a great job, and you keep us laughing."

I opened the large barn doors, drove the tractor into the barn, and closed them for the night.

"I'll gather some wood while you two clear a spot so we can have a fire."

I found plenty of old 2x4s and a stack of firewood at the far end of the barn and carried several loads to the girls. On one trip, I saw an old wheel for the back of a tractor and rolled it to the stack of wood.

"We can start the fire in this wheel, so it doesn't spread and burn our new home down," I said as I stacked some wood in the wheel.

The wood was very dry and caught on fire quickly. Geena soon had a pan of boiling water and a frying pan filled with slices of Spam cooking. We dined on fried Spam, smashed potatoes, and coffee that night. We were exhausted, the girls were still in a daze, and my side was still on fire. We took our turns at guard duty, but no one got much sleep that night.

The night was uneventful even though I thought a lot about Callie and, in a few weak moments, my traveling companions. We ate chocolate chip cookies and breakfast bars and got underway by 6:45 a.m. We continued around Peoria on side roads and did the same to get around Bloomington. We saw a few people in their yards breaking ground for gardens and even saw one man skinning a deer. They watched us pass, but didn't even pick up their rifles as we passed.

Geena got my attention and said, "Almost everyone has a pistol on their hip or a shotgun in their hands."

"I guess they've either had an experience like we did with those men trying to rob us or have a neighbor who's been robbed. It's been three days, and the food is running short. People will start getting mean now."

Ahead, the road made a sharp bend to the left, and just as it began to straighten out, I saw a roadblock ahead. I stopped about 500 feet from it and used my field glasses to check it out before advancing. There were four men and two women manning the roadblock, which was made up of several cars in a line across the road. They'd heard the tractor and were examining us with several pairs of field glasses. They were clean looking, and I didn't think they would cause us any problems, so I drove up to the roadblock, shut off the tractor, and walked up to them with my pistol holstered. Geena and Sally had their shotguns ready but below the top of the wagon.

One of the men asked, "Where are you going, and why should we let you pass through our town?"

I stuck my hand out to shake hands and said, "We were on vacation and are heading home to Kentucky. I'm trying to avoid the big cities, so we're traveling on back roads. Why are you blocking the road?"

"There are several gangs in the area trying to steal our food, water, and women. We have guards all around our little town and will kill anyone who tries to rob us."

"Look, mister, we only want to get on to Kentucky and have had several SOBs try to steal from us. Their bodies are scattered from Iowa City to Peoria. Both of our ladies were wounded during one of the attacks, and I was shot the next day. We're all right now, but we don't trust anyone on the road, thanks to those bastards. So if you'll let us through, we'll be on our way."

One woman came over to the leader, they whispered for a minute and then she said, "Of course we'll let you go through, but we don't have any extra food. You can have all of the water you want."

She walked over to Geena and Sally, saw that their clothes were dirty and asked, "Would you like a hot shower and some new clothes? As I said, we have plenty of water, and we also have extra clothes."

The ladies looked at me and said, "Please, Zack?"

I looked at them and replied, "Since when do you need my permission to take a hot bath?"

While the girls were bathing, Jim, their leader, and I filled each other in on the events since the lights went out.

"How did you get the tractor running? All of our cars and trucks died at one time."

"Only vehicles with computers and electronics were affected by the EMP blast. Vehicles made before the mid 70s should run. Do you have any older vehicles?"

"I know a couple guys have some old trucks, but I don't think anyone has tried them. We assumed that they were all fried."

Jim looked around and yelled at one of the men, "Hey, Carl! Come over here for a minute."

Carl walked over and sat down on a log beside me.

"Carl, have you tried to get that old truck of yours running?"

"Yes, and it's just as dead as the new ones."

I asked, "What model truck do you have and what engine is in it?"

"I have a 1949 Chevy with a 351 Cleveland."

"What carb and ignition do you have?"

"I have a 750 Holley and an MSD Super Pro distributor with computerized timing."

"Do you have the original distributor, coil, and another set of ignition wires?"

"Why, yes, I do."

"Get them, and I'll get your truck running. We just have to take the engine back to having parts that made it run before electronics."

We walked over to Carl's place, and an hour later, Carl drove us around town with a big old smile on his face.

I looked at Jim and said, "Have y'all been out on the highways and searched the semi-trailers for food? There are thousands of them stalled around the country full of food.

"Damn, we never thought of that. We've always been farmers and hunters around here, so we have fresh vegetables, meat, and fish, but are running out of ammunition, toilet paper, canned goods, and spices."

"Follow me to our wagon."

I folded the tarp back, showed him a wagon full of supplies, and said, "This is one-hundredth of what was in that trailer. You also need to check the local sporting goods stores for ammo and guns before looters get everything."

We went on working on trucks and cars until Jim's wife called us for supper. They fed us roast beef, corn on the cob, green beans, and mashed potatoes with sweet tea. My stomach was full for the first time in a week. Jim's wife cleaned my wound, applied more antibiotic salve, and re-bandaged my side. She also gave me a bottle of some pain pills and made me take two. My side still hurt, but I'd be able to sleep.

"Zack, we owe you so much for helping us get these vehicles running. What can we do to repay you?"

I thought for a minute and said, "We have everything we need to make it to Kentucky, so there isn't anything we need. If you want to repay us, then pass on help to deserving people who aren't as fortunate as we all are. Pay it forward."

We sat around a fire in Jim's backyard until everyone was yawning and ready for bed. I noticed they had guards out on the roads into town, but no one guarding around their houses.

"Don't you need guards in town?"

"No, the guards out on the roads will warn us if anyone approaches."

"What if they're watching your roadblocks and decide to sneak into town at night to see what is so valuable in this town?"

"Oh, crap! We hadn't thought about organized raids. We'll be posting guards from now on."

We had a massive breakfast of pancakes, eggs, and ham the next morning and were soon on our way. Jim's wife made us take a smoked ham. We were southeast of Bloomington trying to work our way around the city and back on Highway 74. I wanted to travel a hundred miles today and not stop for anything.

☆

Chapter 8   Hunting

Champaign, Illinois

"Good morning, Davi. Please join your mother and me for breakfast. Did you sleep well?"

"I had a very restful night. Being home agrees with my body. I feel very rested and ready for battle."

"Good morning, sunshine. I have made your favorite breakfast. Blueberry pancakes, sausage, and cinnamon rolls."

Davi didn't realize how hungry she was until the smell of the pancakes, cinnamon, and sausage filtered into her nose. She ate four big pancakes, three cinnamon rolls, and a half dozen sausage links while her mom fussed over her. Her dad watched her while he finished his third cup of coffee.

"I'd like to take the Jeep and scout out the area this morning. I don't want to draw too much attention to us, but I'll bet many of our neighbors need help."

"Dad, I'll be ready in twenty minutes. I agree with not bringing too much attention to ourselves, but we must take our sidearms. Perhaps you take a pump shotgun, and I'll take that Mini 14 .223, and we should fit in with the other farmers. Automatic weapons might scare some of the locals."

"I agree, but I'll put a couple of M4s in the back of the Jeep in case we encounter some hard cases. I want to check out a couple of neighbors and a few of the small towns and still be back before dark."

Davi's mom gave her a bag with their lunch and some bottled water as she hugged them goodbye for the day.

They drove west for about three miles until they came to the Robertson's farm. They were on a back road, so they weren't surprised they hadn't seen anyone on their journey. Aaron honked the Jeep's horn as they turned down the long driveway to the Robertson's house. Davi saw two men run from a barn towards the house and come back out with shotguns. They drove slowly towards the house with Aaron waving as they got close to the house.

"Aaron, you scared us. We thought some of the scum from the city were snooping around again."

"Has there been trouble?"

"No, but we noticed someone watching us from the overpass, and when we went to see who it was, they took off and disappeared. Last night the dogs started barking, and we saw several men lurking around the chicken coop. I fired my shotgun into the air and scared them off. This morning we found they had stolen six chickens."

"Be careful, things will get much worse when the cities run out of food. It's only been two days, and the stores are empty by now. Most people don't have more than a few days of food in their pantry, and when it runs out, they will kill for a can of beans."

"I hadn't given it much thought, but you're right. Bad times are coming. Hey, who is this beautiful young girl, and how did you get the Jeep running?"

"This is my daughter, Davi. She was on her way home when the lights went out. Davi, this is George Robertson, his wife, Emily, and their daughter Bonnie."

They all shook hands, and then Aaron explained about the effects of the EMP blasts and why older vehicles would still run. They went to the barn, and George had his oldest tractor running in short order.

"Thanks, Aaron, I thought all vehicles were dead. I have an old Ford pickup in my garage that should run after I put the points and condenser back in the distributor. I'll pass this info on to my neighbors."

"Y'all watch out for people flooding out here from the city. Shoot first and ask questions later."

"Now Aaron, we're good Christians, and we'll be glad to help anyone who needs help."

"Good luck. People will come, take your food and rape your wife and daughter. I don't want to piss you off, but you're in danger."

"Thanks for the help and the advice, but we will keep helping everyone we can."

They left and drove due north to visit the Millers next. The Millers had several hundred acres and a large cattle farm and dairy that had been in the family for generations. Davi enjoyed listening to her father talking about converting from a warrior to being a simple farmer and how much he loved tilling the soil and watching the crops grow. They had driven about three miles when they heard gunfire in front of them.

"Dad, that's about a mile away. How far is the Miller's farm?"

"Damn, it's a mile ahead of us towards the gunfire. There is a wooded area southeast of the Miller's home that will give us cover if we go off-road in about half a mile. We'll park the Jeep and sneak up on their house. I don't want to drive up and get shot by the Millers or caught in the crossfire."

"I agree, you know the area. I'll follow," said Davi as she thought, "once a soldier, always a soldier."

Aaron pulled the Jeep into a thicket about five-hundred yards from the house, and they took positions behind a fallen tree to observe the house. The house was surrounded and taking gunfire from the front and one side. Several bodies were littering the ground outside the front door, and Davi thought the fight must have started there.

Davi went back to the Jeep and retrieved both M4s and two bags full of magazines for them. One of the M4s had a scope, and she put it to use immediately. She had fired three times with three kills before the men knew that they were under attack. Her dad had fired but had not hit anyone.

There was a ravine running towards the house, and they ducked down and ran as fast as they could towards the house. They covered half the distance when they heard the sound of ATVs speeding away from the farm. Davi steadied her rifle on the side of a tree and shot several times, but couldn't tell if she'd done any damage. She placed a white handkerchief on the end of her barrel and started walking with her dad towards the house.

A man and a woman came running out of the house, along with several teenaged kids. They stopped at one of the bodies and broke into tears. The woman lifted the young boy's body and hugged it as if the boy were still alive. The man, Mr. Miller, walked over and shook Aaron's hand as he thanked him for running the killers off.

"Aaron, you saved our lives. Those bastards were caught butchering a cow yesterday, and Joe ran them off. They came back and killed him as soon as he walked outside. The damn lights have only been out for a couple of days, and the world is going berserk. That city trash came out here to steal our cows and anything not nailed down. They only took the hindquarters and left the rest of the cow to rot."

"We're glad to be able to help and are so sorry for your loss. We heard the gunfire and knew that you were in trouble. We just did what anyone would do to help their neighbor."

They took turns digging until they made the grave deep enough to bury the Miller boy, then said prayers for him and the survivors of this holocaust.

Mrs. Miller brought out some sandwiches and several bottles of cold beer. They sat on the patio looking towards Champaign, wondering when the gang would return.

"Rick, you need to know they'll be back and bring a small army the next time they come. The food is running low in the cities, and these punks will be leaving the cities in a couple of days looking for food. These people will come back for vengeance. You need to pack up and head south. Take a small herd with you and find a safe location to rebuild. Get wherever you're going as quickly as possible so that you have the rest of spring and all summer to grow some crops and get ready for winter. There won't be any gas or electricity to heat your homes."

"I hate to say it, but I think that you're right."

"Stay off the roads and travel as much as possible at night. Take some wire cutters with you to cut fences and stay in the fields and woods. The roads will be hazardous in a couple of days. Here, take this rifle and bag of ammo. Don't trust anyone. Davi and I have to get back home and check on Sharon. Travel safe, and may God be with you."

They hiked back to the Jeep and headed back home without saying anything for a long time.

Then they both tried to talk at the same time.

Davi said, "Dad, don't we need....."

At the same time, her dad said, "Darling, we need to take......"

"You go."

"No, you go first."

"Dad, we need to take your advice and leave this area. Load up and head south."

"Darling, I was thinking the same thing. What will your mother think?"

Chapter 9   Mike to the Rescue

Anderson, Kentucky

Mike saw the exit for Highway 1078 just as he saw the family stranded on the side of the road. He sped up to go around them when he saw the woman and two children sitting beside a dead man.

"Oh crap, I need to keep going. Mike, don't stop! Don't stop. Screw it, I have to live with myself," Mike yelled at himself as he pulled the truck up alongside the family.

"Ma'am, are y'all all right?"

A boy about twelve replied, "Mom hasn't said anything since those men shot my dad and took our truck. I think he's dead. Can you help us?"

Mike took a quick look around to make sure this wasn't a trap and replied, "Son, I'll try my best. Where do y'all live?"

"We have a farm out in Dale. We came here to get my grandma in Murphy and get back home before the crap hit the fan.

Three men stopped us and killed my dad when he wouldn't give them our old truck."

"Son, I'm going on to Anderson to get my sister and niece. I'll pick you up on the way back and take you to Dale."

Mike looked behind the seat, retrieved an entrenching tool, and gave it to the boy as he said, "Son, I know this is a bad thing to ask, but can you bury your dad and be ready to head home in a couple of hours?"

Tears came to the boy's eyes as it finally set in his dad was actually dead.

He wiped the tears away, took the shovel, and replied, "I'll have it done before you get back."

The little girl and Mom just sat there staring into the distance while Mike drove away.

●●●●

Todd came downstairs and fixed himself a large glass of straight whiskey. He was halfway to the bottom of the glass when Joan came out of her bedroom and sat down beside him.

"How bad was it in town? I'm getting worried. Explosions and smoke are rising from the direction of downtown. Are the police and fire department doing anything?"

Todd took a big drink and said, "Leave me alone. I don't want to talk about it. They were monsters."

"Todd, watch your language around Callie."

Callie snickered and said, "I think Todd has been traumatized by this 'peaceful' situation."

"Don't you smart off to me. I was almost killed by that scum at the office."

"You mean those 'down on their luck' poor people who wouldn't hurt a fly? Dad has been telling mom for years, people will kill you for a biscuit when the crap hit the fan."

Todd jumped up and slapped Callie, who fell to the floor. Joan ran over as he tried to kick her while she was on her back.

Joan jumped on Todd's back as he swung his foot to kick Callie. They both tumbled to the ground with Todd on top of Joan with his hands around her neck.

"Todd, stop! You're killing her!" Callie yelled as she got up and tackled Todd.

She knocked him off her mom only to find him on top of her with his hands on her throat. Joan picked up a lamp and hit him on the back of the head just as Mike crashed through the front door.

"What the hell is going on with Todd? Why was he attacking Callie?" Mike yelled as he pointed his gun at Todd.

Joan replied, "He was attacked by a mob at the office and came home in shell shock. He tried to kill me first. Callie knocked him off me, and then he tried to choke her. Shoot him. He tried to kill us."

"Whoa, wait a minute. I don't like the bastard, but he just lost it for a minute. Let's leave him here and head to the farm. Get some clothes and all of the food you can get in the truck."

Todd stirred and started to get up when Mike clubbed him with the butt of his pistol. Todd was down for the count. Callie had already packed, so she and Mike gathered food while her mom got her clothes and a few possessions. Callie brought her 20 gauge shotgun and Henry .22 rifle. They climbed into the truck and pulled out to the street as Todd came out of the house.

"Don't leave me here. They'll get me. Please take me with you."

Joan gave him the finger as Mike drove away.

"Well, Joan, I guess I don't have to apologize for taking a dump in Todd's Corvette, do I?"

She laughed and punched him in the shoulder.

Before they got to Highway 351, Mike asked Joan to open the glove box and get the Ruger 9mm pistol.

"What do you want me to do with this? You know I hate guns."

"I want you to change seats with Callie and give her the gun. Callie after y'all change seats, point the pistol out the window, and jack a round into the chamber. Get ready to use it if needed. I was shot at coming over here, and we need to protect ourselves."

Joan started to protest, but Mike told her to shut up.

They drove down 351 at about 45 mph dodging stalled cars and people wanting rides. No one tried to stop them, so they got to 1078 and then the Baker intersection in about thirty minutes.

Mike pointed to the family and said, "I told them I'd give them a ride back to Dale. The father was killed when some creeps stole their truck."

He pulled over and introduced his family to them, but again the mom and young girl never spoke.

The boy shook their hands and said, "I'm Paul Stone, that's my mom, Ally, and my sister, Sue. We thank you for helping us."

His mom and sister had that distant stare with no emotion. Paul threw a box and a couple of bags in the back of the truck and joined his sister in the back of the truck. Mike doubled back down the ramp to 351 East and sped away headed east towards Owensville.

"Uncle Mike, why are we taking the back roads?"

"Baby girl, some men shot at me a few miles up the road, and I don't want to tangle with them with you and your mom in the truck. I'll cut over to Highway 60 and head over to Owensville."

The drive over to Highway 60 was uneventful, with only a few people waving at them and no one trying to harm them. Just as they crested the last hill before the bridge over the Green River, Mike saw there was a roadblock before the bridge.

"Callie, be ready for anything. These don't look like thugs, so I'm going to drive up and ask to go across the bridge. I'll stay back away just enough that we can get away if they try to pull anything."

Mike pulled up about thirty feet from the roadblock, which was a couple of sawhorses and 2x4s. Three of the men approached him with pistols in their hands. Mike had his ready, and Callie had hers under a handkerchief.

The oldest man walked up and said, "Good afternoon, how y'all doing today?"

"We're fine, and I hope all is well with you."

"Well, it's looking better now that we have us a pickup truck."

Mike replied, "That's odd. I don't see any trucks besides mine, and I know that y'all don't look like scumbag thieves."

The man stopped laughing, pointed his pistol at Mike's face, and said, "We'll see who has this truck and those pretty women tonight."

Mike grabbed the man's hand, yanked as hard as he could while he floored the truck.

Mike yelled, "Callie, shoot the bastards!" as he crashed through the barricade dragging the man beside the truck.

The gun was still in front of Mike's left arm, as he dragged the man across the Blackville bridge at 50 mph. Suddenly, there was a blast in front of him, and part of the window exploded, showering everyone with glass. There were explosions from the other side of the truck as Callie fired on the men at the roadblock. The cowards had ducked and never fired on them as they sped away. Callie didn't hit any, but she scared the crap out of them.

Mike saw they were getting away, so he let go of the old man who still clung to the side of the truck. The old man screamed as he saw the stalled semi-truck on the left side of the bridge growing larger every second. He yelled stop several times before he hit the bumper and grill of the truck knocking him off the pickup. His gun clattered to the floor, and Mike sped on towards Owensville. He looked back into the bed, and Paul gave him a thumbs up. He smiled at the boy and drove on.

••••

78

Todd sat in the middle of the floor in a daze, thanks to the butt of Mike's gun. He took his time, but he finally got up off the floor, made a sandwich for himself, and drank the rest of the whiskey.

"I'll find those bitches and make them *wish* they were dead when I get through with them."

Todd grabbed Callie's softball bat and started walking back into town.

"First, I have a score to settle with those scumbags. I have their files and know where they live," he said as he hit his hand with the bat.

••••

Joan was silent the whole time they were escaping from the roadblock. She glared at Callie as Callie dropped the empty magazine onto the floor and slid a full one into the 9mm. Then she looked over at Mike and started to blast him for allowing that old man to die. She thought back to Todd, trying to kill her and Callie and kept her words to herself.

"Mike, how long before we get to the farm?"

"Sister, it could be an hour or a day depending on stalled cars and roadblocks. I almost pissed my pants when that old fart stuck his gun in my face."

"That was scary, and I did."

"What did you do?"

"Wet my pants."

"Damn, sorry."

"I don't want to ever be that scared again. Can you teach me how to fight and shoot guns?"

"Yes, big sister. It's about time."

"You and that dumbass husband of mine were right all along about this prepping crap."

"It was a matter of when. Not if. Zack made a believer out of me, but you..."

"I had my head up my ass, as you always say. I want Callie and me to be able to defend ourselves."

"Don't be too hard on yourself. Most people never thought that this would happen. Many of them are dying."

"Oh, don't tell Zack that he was right. He has a big enough head right now. Have you heard from him since the lights went out?"

"One ham operator passed on a message that had been passed on nine or ten times. It said that Zack was safe and traveling with two beautiful women who had to get back to Cincinnati."

"I hope his dick rots off."

"Mom, I heard that."

"You left him, he didn't leave you. We'd better finish this conversation without Callie."

"Yes, that would be best."

"Mom, maybe if you groveled, Dad would take you back."

Mike laughed and got a swift punch in the ribs.

✪

Chapter 10   Rear

Champaign, Illinois

We were making good time heading towards Champaign, Illinois on Highway 150, which ran along the side of Highway 74. When we arrived outside of Leroy, I asked Geena to cut across the fields and go around the city on 74 to avoid as many people as we could. Several people saw us and waved from a distance, and we saw that several of the roads into LeRoy had roadblocks. We heard some gunfire coming from the south side of the city, but there were no shots fired at us. We attempted to drive around Farmer City on Highway 74 as we had LeRoy, only this time, we saw a roadblock about a mile ahead. Sally spotted it with the field glasses and told Geena to pull off the road in the brush. I peered through the field glasses and saw that the roadblock was at the overpass where 150 crossed 74. Sally would have never spotted the barrier if there wasn't an American flag waving above the overpass. I could barely make out people standing on the top of the overpass.

"Girls, I think that these are friendly people, but we need to be cautious. The brush and trees on the right side of the road run all the way up to the overpass. I'll work my way up to them and spy on them for a while. I'll wave you in if they're the good guys. If you hear fighting, cut north across the fields and head for home the best that you can. Don't trust anyone."

Geena replied, "Zack, you just had a bolt removed from your side, and you aren't up to full strength. Let me go instead. I won't make contact. I'll sneak up, listen in, and come back here to report to you before we decide what to do."

"Zack, Geena's right. Let her go."

"So, you can have Zack?"

"Geena, you're my best friend. I would never throw you to the wolves for a man."

Geena broke out laughing and said, "I was just pulling your chain."

They hugged, and Geena prepared to go.

"Geena, wait! Tuck my .380 in your pocket and take the small field glasses. Stay in the brush and trees all of the way there. Watch for sentries away from the others. I'd have a sniper on top of that silo and a lookout at that rest stop. Be careful."

I gave her a kiss on the forehead, and she left. Instead of waiting for her to return, I sent Sally out to the south side of the brush and trees along Highway 150, and I took the north side to look for any other people or trouble. I didn't want anyone sneaking upon us. We met back at the tractor in twenty minutes with no sightings of any danger.

"I saw a couple of women cooking on a grill at that farmhouse about a hundred yards towards town and a couple of men walking towards town on Highway 74. They had rifles slung over their shoulders and were packing a small deer hanging from a pole."

"I didn't see anything, but a couple of dogs eating a rabbit. I am worried about large packs of dogs becoming vicious as they search for food. You and Geena need to be alert to that danger and be careful around strays."

Sally and I were talking about what caused the lights to go out when I heard some leaves rustle about twenty feet behind Sally. I saw Geena hiding behind a bush listening to our conversation. Apparently, she didn't trust her friend as much as she made on. I changed the subject to my daughter, and I wondered aloud what she was doing in Kentucky.

"Well, I'm back."

Sally rushed over to her and gave her a big hug saying, "I was worried to death about you getting killed."

I got on my feet, gave her a hug, and said, "I'm glad you're safe. Any issues? What did you hear?"

"They appear to be regular people who are afraid of some biker gang that has been terrorizing the area between them and Champaign. The college in Champaign has had contact with the state and the federal government. The bad news is that most of the world is in the same shape we're. Most of the large cities in the north and west coast are on fire with rioters out of control. What's left of the military and state police are busy trying to bring peace to those areas. The rest of the country is fending for itself."

"Has anyone tried to invade the USA?"

"No, but Mexico wasn't hit hard, and the government is worried they might try to invade the Southwest."

"Our friends to the south want their land back. I'll bet a bunch of Texans might have a problem with that happening. Did you hear anything else?"

"Yes, most everyone wearing a pacemaker died that day, and people on life-sustaining drugs are beginning to die off. Drug addicts went cold turkey all over the country a couple of days ago. These biker and drug gangs are making drugs as fast as they can, but the raw materials are not being produced anymore. Oh, men are being killed off by these gangs, and they're enslaving women."

"The damn world is falling apart, just like Zack told us it would."

"My uncle was a long time prepper, so it came naturally. I'll walk up to their roadblock and introduce myself. If all is fine, I'll wave y'all to come to join me."

I grabbed a shotgun and checked my 9mm before walking away from the girls. I walked in the middle of the highway so they wouldn't think that I was trying to sneak up on them. I got about a hundred yards away before I saw movement. Everyone at the roadblock ducked behind cover and watched me walk up to them.

When I was about fifty feet away, a man rose up and yelled, "What do you want?"

I replied, "Nothing except to pass on through on Highway 74."

"Walk around, idiot."

"I don't want to cut all of your fences to go through. Let's talk."

"Lay down your arms and come over here."

"You lay yours down, and I'll join you."

"And then you'll just kill us all."

"I could have killed all of you two hours ago. We came up and listened to you talk for an hour. Who is Joe, Greg, and Bob?"

"That doesn't mean we can trust you."

"You don't have to. I'll just drive around your town, cutting all of your fences. I see cattle out there. They might get loose."

"What are you driving?"

"An old John Deere tractor with a wagon."

"Can you help us get some tractors running?"

"Y'all don't have any running vehicles?"

"No."

"Let us pass through, and we'll show you how to get them running."

"We thought they were all fried."

"Didn't that college tell you that only electronics were fried? Replace the points, condenser, and maybe the spark plug wires, and all old vehicles should run."

The leader laughed and said, "I guess you heard everything we said. Come on in and help us, and we'll help you on your way."

I raised my arms, and in a few minutes, the tractor came into view.

"Are those two girls your army?"

"Don't sell them short. They've held their own in several shootouts."

"And beautiful, too."

This was becoming our routine. We helped get their trucks and tractors running, and they threw a big lunch for us. They served us brisket, corn on the cob, and a fresh garden salad.

"I'm sorry, but we have to eat and run. We're only a few days from home, and I have a young daughter I need to get home to protect."

"We can't thank you enough for showing us how to get the vehicles running, and those tips about checking semi-trailers and warehouse are going to be a big help."

Geena was driving the tractor with one hand on the wheel and one resting on the 9mm pistol, lying across her lap. Sally was watching our rear while I was watching Geena's rear. I know that sounds bad on my part, but the tractor seat bounced and jiggled just the right amount to keep my attention. After all, I am still technically a reforming whoremonger and not a totally cured one.

My thoughts turned to Callie, how I would have to stop chasing women and get back to being a good father. I was actually proud of myself because I hadn't slept with either of these two gorgeous ladies. I had always asked myself which movie star would I want to be stranded on a desert island with, and none would beat out these two. I was daydreaming when I looked over to Sally and knew that I was busted.

"You do know that I have one of those also, and I might add that mine is better looking than Geena's." said Sally as she teased me.

"I was watching the road ahead, and you have a dirty mind."

"Seriously, Zack, I am interested in you and would like to get closer to you. Dating is out the window, and it sucks to be a woman alone in this world. You're a great guy, and I think we would be great together. I could help you raise your daughter, and I'd make a great wife."

85

"So I'm your choice because I'm one of the last men on earth?"

"No, smart ass. You know what I mean."

Geena stopped the tractor, turned around, and said, "Sally, you do know I could hear most of what you were saying. My assets are definitely better than yours, and I think Zack has already chosen to be with me even if he did ogle yours the other night."

"Girls, I have a wonderful girlfriend who rocks her jeans and has my heart."

They both chimed in at the same time, "Show her picture to us."

"I lost my wallet."

They called me a liar at the same time and started hitting me gently. We tussled around for a few minutes until I realized that I was getting excited, and jumped out of the wagon and stood there looking at them.

Geena spoke up, "Zack, assuming you don't settle down with one of us, could you teach us how to fight and use these guns properly? We both need to learn to hunt and fish also."

"I promise, Mike, and I'll teach you how to do all of those things."

"Tell us about Mike. Does he have a non-existent girlfriend also?"

"No, Mike pretty much sleeps with them until they figure out that he won't commit, then leave him."

"So, your friend is an asshole?"

"No, quite the contrary. He's a real gentleman and the perfect boyfriend. He just hasn't met the right woman yet. Just like me, he thought he'd found her, and she left him about the same time Joan left me, and we both became gun shy with women."

"Tell us more about Mike and any other men in the area. Kentucky is sounding better all the time."

I spent the next hour telling them about Mike, Joan, and myself. I spent half the time cursing Joan and Todd.

"Mike took a dump in your ex's boyfriend's Corvette? How funny. I already like him."

Geena added, "I think you still have a thing for your ex. You talk way too much about her. Is she pretty?"

"The truth is, she's not beautiful like you two. Now she has a fantastic body, but she's the tomboy next door I grew up and fell in love with. We got married right out of high school, had Callie, and made a good living. I worked in the electronics repair field, and she's a restaurant manager."

"Well, I'm jealous of her."

"Y'all don't have to be jealous of her. She's madly in love with that piece of crap, Todd. Look, girls, we need to get back on the road. We're losing a half day's travel today, and I want to get below Champaign before we camp tonight. We need to cover about twenty-five miles, and the last five will be on dirt roads and cornfields to get around Champaign. I don't want to run into that biker gang that is supposed to be operating in the area."

I jumped in the tractor's seat and quickly covered the miles until we were a mile outside of Mahomet, where I veered off the road and headed south until he turned onto a county road.

I turned around and told the girls, "I'm heading southeast, and we're skirting around Champaign. We'll be on a hundred back roads, but we should be able to keep away from that gang."

Geena replied, "We'll keep our eyes peeled for trouble."

We had to stop and cut fences twice, but as I'd told them, we traveled on at least fifteen different roads before County Road 1000 crossed Highway 57 just south of the airport.

"The sun's going down, and we made it past Champaign; we need to find a place to spend the night. We'll stay off 57 and backtrack to County Road 800 and go until we find some woods or an abandoned farmhouse."

It was twilight, but I didn't dare turn the lights on, so I drove slowly.

"Zack, have you noticed the last four farmhouses and barns were burned to the ground."

"Yes, and that worries me. Let's keep going until we get another few miles down the road. The map shows Highways 45 and 57 crosses up ahead. That puts us ten to twelve miles below Champaign. We'll try the first barn without lights."

About two miles later, we saw a house with two barns and half dozen silos on the west side of the road. There were no lights, so I stopped the tractor a quarter-mile away and walked towards it in the dark to scout for danger.

•••

The bikers were at their post on top of the overpass pulling sentry duty. Their leader had been a private in the Army and had tried to instill some military tactics in his men. They were a sorry lot, but they were well-armed and killed anyone who gave them trouble. They also liked to burn people alive in their homes.

"John, did you hear that noise over there?"

John had his woman in his lap, and both were naked and stoned.

"Nah, I didn't hear anything. Go away until we're finished."

"I thought I heard a tractor putting along out west of us. I'm going to tell Bob."

•••

Davi and her parents were sitting on the back deck when they heard the sound from across the field.

"That's coming from the Steven's farm. They disappeared several days ago."

"Dad, should we check it out? It could be that damn gang trying to expand their territory."

"Yes, get prepared. Dear, start loading the truck while we check this out. When we come back, we'll load up and head out in the morning. Come on, Davi, let's do some headhunting."

• • • •

"What do you mean, you heard a noise? You ran back here because you got scared. You left John out there alone to run and hide."

"No, Bob. I heard a tractor and thought you might want to have it."

Bob shoved the woman off his lap, walked over to the biker, and said, "Now you're thinking. The king of bikers needs a damn tractor."

Bob drew back, slugged the man, and then kicked him while yelling, "Get this pussy out of my sight! Bones, take some men and find my tractor and bring it back to me."

• • • •

I took the first and last watch as usual. We had closed the barn doors and had a small fire to cook supper. The girls prepared roasted spam, pork and beans and popcorn for dessert. I climbed the ladder up to the hayloft and took turns looking out at the countryside from both ends of the barn. My two hours passed quickly, and before I could climb down and wake Sally, I heard someone climbing the ladder. Even though I knew it was Sally, I hid behind a bale of hay and waited. Both doors to the hayloft were open, and I could see her in the moonlight. Geena's beauty took my breath away. Her blonde hair glistened in the moonlight, and she swayed her hips as she walked to my end of the barn. I thought, *oh crap, this can't happen* as I watched her walk towards me.

"Hey beautiful, what happened to Sally?"

"She needed a little extra sleep, so I took her place. Do you really think I'm beautiful?"

"Geena, you take my breath away. It's not your beauty but rather all of you. You're funny, intelligent, and have a big heart."

We sat down on the bale of hay, and Geena put her arm around me and laid her head on my shoulder. I put my arm around her and kissed the top of her head. We both felt the electricity. She looked up at me, and our eyes met and locked. I placed my lips on hers and kissed her deeply and often. She slid her hand under my shirt, lifted it over my head, and kissed my chest.

"Zack, I want you."

I raised my hand under her shirt, and then I pulled her shirt over her head and dropped it in the hay. She reached between us, unbuckled my belt, and unzipped my pants. I stood up, and my pants fell to the ground. Geena pulled her shorts off and let them fall. Just as she pulled me to her, there was a scream and gunfire from the barn below.

"Crap, I finally get your clothes off, and we get attacked."

"Sorry, get dressed, girl."

"Raincheck?"

"Raincheck!"

I pulled my pants up, grabbed my shotgun, and ran to the ladder. Geena put her shirt over her head and grabbed her pistol. I stopped and looked down before getting on the ladder and saw a man with his hands on Sally's throat. My pants fell down, tripping me. I fell down through the opening, landed on him, knocking him away from Sally. He raised his gun, and Geena shot him from the loft.

"Sally, are you all right?"

"Yes, I shot one as he walked in, but this one overpowered me before I could turn and shoot him. Are you all right? That was very brave of you to leap from the hayloft to save me."

"Not brave, I tripped."

"Why the hell are your pants down?"

She saw Geena climbing down the ladder, wearing only a shirt and panties.

I saw Geena and said, "Girls, my whole body hurts from the fall."

"Damn you, Geena. You know I wanted him. Can we share?"

"No!"

Just as Sally finished speaking, two men burst through the door in front of us, and three came in the back door.

"Drop those guns, and you live."

We dropped our guns, and I knew Geena's and my fit of passion had allowed these men to get the drop on us.

They threw us to the floor and tied our hands behind our back with baling twine. I kept thinking we could find a way to escape, but there were five of them, and two kept their guns trained on us at all times.

"These two came down from the loft. The blonde has hay trapped under her thong, and he has his pants around his feet. Those two were screwing in the loft. Nasty, nasty. You people left this woman down here all alone. Some bad guys might come along and rape her. Lucky for her, us good guys came to her rescue."

Sally looked over at us and turned red. I could tell she was pissed.

I looked up at him and said, "Please let us go, we have families depending on us. Keep me and let the girls go."

"I have a boss who likes pretty women, and this doomsday event has made him king of this area. You're going to be a slave in our fields, and these two beautiful women get to be Bob's latest lovers. That is until he tires of them, and then we get them. Not to worry, because they get to join you farming when we get tired of them. Of course, they'll be worn out and ugly by then."

"Bones, let's get a taste of these girls before we take them to Bob."

He stooped down over Geena and ran his hand up her leg before she kicked him in the shin and knocked him on the floor.

"Dumbass, you know Bob will cut your nuts off if you touch them before he gets tired of them. You get his leftovers. Get them up, and let's get back to camp. Girl, you kick me in the balls, and I'll cut your foot off. You don't need no stinking foot to please Bob."

91

They made us get off the floor and loaded us into the wagon while one of the thugs started the tractor.

Suddenly, two explosions blinded everyone and gunfire from all directions. I looked over the edge of the wagon, but could barely see anything.

I heard a man yell, "Davi, they're escaping!" Shoot the bastards!"

Then a woman with a rifle came around the tractor shooting the escaping thugs. The leader was stooped down below me and was drawing a bead on her back. I reached over, placed my bound hands around his neck, and pulled him upwards. He dropped the gun and was kicking and trying to scream as I choked the life out of his sorry body. He stopped struggling and hung limply from my hands.

"Zack, you can let him fall. He's dead." Geena said as she put her arms around me.

The woman walked over to the wagon and said, "Thanks for saving my life. He had the drop on me."

"No, but thanks for saving *our lives!* We were about to be their slaves. We can't thank you enough."

"Well, gather your gear, and let's get out of here before they return. Hell, please put some clothes on. These men actually caught you with your pants down."

Davi noticed that Geena and I were down to our underwear, but Sally was fully dressed. She shook her head and went to join the other man while we dressed and got our stuff together. Geena and I went back into the hayloft, and I took Geena by the waist, pulled her to me and kissed her one more time.

"Later?"

"Later!"

I tried to start the tractor, but it was dead. I checked the engine and saw stray rounds had hit the battery and distributor during the battle. It was down for the count. We grabbed our backpacks and loaded them with all of the food we could carry and followed our rescuers for about a hundred yards to a Jeep.

"Pile in, we only have a short drive. You can sit on his lap. It looks like you two are already quite friendly."

Geena sat on my lap, and Sally elbowed me on my wounded side. I groaned but kept my mouth shut. The fall from the hayloft nearly killed me, and I hurt from head to toe.

"I'm Aaron, and this is my daughter Davi. We live just down this road. We heard the gunfire and came to see who was fighting. Who are you, and what happened?"

We introduced ourselves and told him about the bikers capturing us.

"We're heading south to get back to our families and had covered several hundred miles using the tractor. I found the girls up in Iowa, and we have fought and shot several thugs along the way. All of us have been shot and survived. I screwed up and failed at my sentry post. That's why they were able to sneak up on us."

"These days, you screw up, and you die. We're taking you to our house where my wife is loading up our other vehicle, and then we're heading south. We were leaving tomorrow, but this gang will be after us when those men don't return. That's a bad bunch. Drugs, slaves, and debauchery are their calling card. We're getting out of here, and you can come with us if you want."

I replied, "We're heading to western Kentucky. Where are you going?"

"We're heading towards Alabama through Nashville. We hope to link up with friends and head down to Mobile. We want to get away from the north since there is no power to heat our home. I can stand the heat, but freezing in the winter is not my cup of tea."

"Great, you'll want to travel the back roads, and you have a direct shot at Nashville by cutting across Indiana and crossing the Ohio at Murphy, Indiana or Owensville, Kentucky. My home is actually below Nashville, but I have a farm outside of Owensville."

"I had already planned my route through Murphy. We can help each other until we part there. We need to count on each other, so you can't get caught with your pants down again."

His daughter, Davi, snickered while I tried to find words.

"Sir, that won't happen again."

✪ ✪ ✪

✪

Chapter 11   Mike to the Rescue, Again!

St Charles, Kentucky

Paul tapped on the glass until Joan told Mike to pull off the road.

"My sister has to use the bathroom. Can I take her over behind that tree?"

"Of course, I have to pee myself. Paul and Callie, watch the road while the rest of us take care of business, then it's your turn."

Paul's mother never moved and was still dazed with glazed-over eyes.

"Mike, I don't think that woman is going to make it."

"I was wondering myself. We don't need another person to take care of, but I can't put these kids out to fend for themselves."

"Brother, you always had a big heart."

"Come on, we're burning daylight. Let's get to the farm before dark."

Paul replied, "Sir, I thought you were taking us home to Dale."

"We only have about three hours of daylight left. We can let your mom rest and then take you home tomorrow."

"Okay."

Mike started the truck, pulled back onto the road, and saw two men on horseback coming towards them. He picked up speed and prepared to blow by them when they turned sideways and blocked the way.

Mike told Callie, "Hon, hide your gun, but be ready to use it. These might be the bad men."

He pulled up and saw that they had police uniforms on and had their hands on the 9mms strapped to their hips.

"Son, where are you going, and how did you get a truck to run?"

Mike had a bad feeling about these two, so he lied, "Sir, we're from Central City and trying to get home. All older vehicles will run if you just change the points in the distributor. If that's all you need, I need to get the kids home."

"No, that's not all. We need to confiscate your truck and use it to help our community. Now unload and get on your way."

"Look, my sister lives on this side of Owensville. Could we make it there, and I'll help you get several more trucks running? Her husband has several older trucks and cars."

One of the men leaned over, whispered in the other's ear, and laughed. The sheriff had the right uniform but had dirty tennis shoes and biker tattoos all over his arms. His badge had Constable – Dale, Indiana, on it.

"I think we can let you go to your sister's house. I'll ride upfront with you and drop y'all off there."

"So you're the sheriff of Daviess County?"

"No, we're deputies assigned to this end of the county. We need your truck to patrol. Ralph, I'll be at the station in a couple of hours."

"Joan, Callie, please get in the back. Callie, watch out for the bad men. They're everywhere."

"They can stay upfront. One can sit in my lap."

They got out and joined the others in the back of the pickup, which was already crowded.

"Fine, suit yourselves. Let's go, I have to get this truck back to the station before dark."

"Are you at the new station on this end of Parish Avenue?"

"Yeah, that's the one. Now move it."

Mike knew the guy wasn't from this area and there was no station on this end of town. He drove along towards Owensville and knew he had to choose the right place to confront this fake cop. He saw a house on the right up ahead that had several old cars in the driveway and decided it was as good as any.

"That's my sister's place. I'm sure her husband will let you have a couple of his cars to help protect this end of the county."

He pulled in the driveway, hoping no one was home. He had enough worries about his family being caught in the crossfire and endangering innocent people. He got out of the truck along with the deputy and walked up to the door. He knocked on the door, but no one was home.

"Looks like no one's home. Get your stuff out of the truck, and I'll be heading out."

Mike pretended to unload the truck when he suddenly tackled the man and threw him to the ground as they fought for his pistol.

"Joan, take the kids and run. This guy's a thug."

"I'll show them a thug once I kill your sorry ass."

They continued rolling on the ground with neither getting an advantage until the thug was on top, and he managed to pull his gun on Mike.

"Now you'll die, bastard."

There was a gunshot and then silence as Mike waited for the pain and death. The man collapsed on Mike and then rolled off onto the ground. Callie stood with her gun in her hand, ready to help. The thug was dead.

"Callie, are you okay?" Joan called out as she wrapped the child in her arms.

"Yes, that guy was going to kill Uncle Mike. I shot him, and I would do it again."

Mike hugged them both while getting his breath back.

"That bastard was well over three hundred pounds and strong as an ox. I thought I was dead when I heard the gunshot."

Joan said, "Let's get out of here. They might come for him."

"We need to hide the body and then get our butts out of here. Help me drag it behind the garage."

It took Mike, Paul, and Callie to drag the thug behind the garage. They were worn out before they got back to the truck. Mike checked on the woman and then headed back out on Highway 60.

It only took an hour to get to the Highway 54 exit, and they knew they were only nine miles from the farm. Mike had a big smile on his face until they made the turn up the hill and started right on 54.

"Damn, there's another roadblock. Girls get ready. I'm going to run this roadblock and not give them a chance to rob us."

Mike crept towards the men manning the roadblock, and suddenly a big grin came over his face as he exclaimed, "Thank God, a friendly face."

"George Pool, you old goat! How's it hanging?"

"Not too good since the lights went out. What the hell are you doing driving around? Trying to get robbed? Some men will kill for that old truck."

"George, this old truck has saved several lives today, and yes, one man lost his life trying to take it from us. Why are y'all blocking the road?"

"There was a prison break up in Indiana, and a few of the inmates made it across the bridge before we could get roadblocks up."

"Damn, I think we shot one of them a couple of hours ago. They had badges from Indiana."

"Yeah, they tried to pass themselves off as the police, and we had a small battle running them out of town. We killed six of them and lost Elmer Perkins."

"Damn, Elmer was a good old guy."

"Can we head on out to the farm?"

"Of course, but can you come back tomorrow and show us how to get some old trucks and cars running?"

"Do you have a mechanic in this crew? I can tell them in two minutes how to fix them."

"Hey, Frank. Come over here for a minute.

Mike told Frank what to do, and they were on their way again. It only took a half-hour to get to the farm, and everyone was relieved to be safe and off the road.

Mike turned down the driveway and said, "Oh, crap," when he saw the person sitting on the porch swing.

★

Chapter 12   The Grand Master

Anderson, Kentucky

The young girl was out scavenging for food. Her mom and little brother were working hard to put a garden in their backyard, but their pantry was empty, and their last meal was a Ritz cracker soup that was way too thin on crackers. Her home was on Airline Road, and she'd walked from there up to Adams Lane and planned to break into some empty houses to find food. She knew a lot of people had fled town, and others never came back home after the lights went out. She'd never steal, but if they've abandoned their homes, the food was there for the taking. She had broken into several homes on Quail Run but had only found the leftovers from families who had left after they ran out of food. Her backpack and gym bag were empty except for a few crackers and a bottle of water.

She had a kitchen knife for protection and little else to sustain her. She turned the corner to the next house and walked into the middle of several people.

"Who are you, and what're you doing in our neighborhood?"

"Calm down, Jamie boy. It's a nice sweet thing who wants to join our clan."

"I'm not looking for trouble. I just want to find some food and go home. I'll leave your area, and you can go back to what you were doing."

"Grab the bitch."

Before Carrie could run ten feet, two of the boys tackled her and brought her to the ground. They held her tight until the leader slowly walked over to her. He stood over her and looked her over from head to toe.

"My, oh my, I know you. You're that rich bitch cheerleader at County High. I quit school last year. Learned all I needed to know and look at me now, I'm the leader of the East Side Gang. You get to be one of my women. Tie her up and take her back to the club. Todd will want to see her."

"Who's Todd?"

"Todd's the big Kahuna. He's the Grand Master of all the gangs. He'll like you. He likes them young. Todd's an old dude."

Carrie knew she had to escape before they got to the club, or she would never see her family again. She wondered how Callie and her family were doing and thought perhaps she could escape and get to Callie's house. It was only about half a mile away.

They untied her hands but tied a rope around her neck. They pulled her along as they headed towards their club. The main group and the leader had gone on about their business, and these two scumbags had been told to take her to the clubhouse. Carrie had run track in high school and knew that if she got free, she could outrun these two overweight assholes. When she noticed they were taking her right past the street Callie lived on, she waited and then grabbed the rope, wrapped it around her midsection, and took off like a jackrabbit. When the rope played out, it caught the boy looking the other way, and he slammed to the ground and dropped the line. Carrie ran like the wind towards Callie's house, leaving the two fat asses behind.

She ran two blocks and saw Callie's house up ahead. There was Callie's mom's boyfriend, Todd. She lurched to a stop when she saw him leering at her. She thought, *"Oh crap, Todd!"*

101

Anderson quickly degraded into anarchy as food ran out. Most of the people dependent on the government for welfare began to riot when they realized no one was going to continue feeding them. Many hadn't worked in years, and only a few knew how to plant a garden, so they began looting every store in sight. The police and store owners fended them off several times, with a significant loss of life on both sides. Several gangs sprang up overnight to challenge the few remaining police but were also beaten back. The town had been on the verge of taking back its streets and running the scum out of the city when the massacre happened.

The city council was meeting with the sheriff and police chief when Todd had walked into the room.

The mayor looked up and said, "Todd, I'm glad you came in today. With your background in social work, perhaps you can help us make these people realize we can't keep feeding them. They'll have to help grow gardens and work for a living."

Todd laughed as he pulled a Saiga shotgun from a large bag and began shooting the police first, then all of the city officials. Several escaped the room only to be gunned down by Todd's men stationed outside the room. When Todd had finished, only the mayor was left alive.

"Mayor Jackson, you now work for me, and this is *my* town."

Todd quickly took over the remaining food supplies and shot anyone resisting him. This started a war with the town folks fighting back with all they had. Todd promptly allied himself with several other gangs and became the head of all of the local bands. Looting, rape, and slavery were the norm for the area after that day. The locals continued to fight back but were outgunned and outmanned by Todd's coalition of drug addicts, criminals, and thugs.

••••

Carrie ran all the way back to her home, only stopping a couple of times to make sure that Todd or his gang wasn't following her. She briefly hid in a house a few blocks from home when she heard someone yelling a block away. After a while, Carrie searched the house and found that the upstairs had been looted. She lit a match, went down into the basement, and found that it had been searched, but there were a couple cans of Spam and beef stew that had been lost under a couch. She moved the couch and found a large black bag containing a treasure of food and survival supplies. It was too big to carry, so she thought, *"They must have thought they would hide it and come back for it later. Sorry, but my family is starving."*

She found a smaller bag and filled it with the food and some of the survival supplies. She was pleased to find a .38 caliber pistol and a box of ammunition. Food and protection were now solved. She had to get back to her family, talk her mother into leaving home, and find a safer place to live.

She arrived home after a slow and stealthy trip through her neighborhood. Her mother saw her through the window, hugged her, and asked what was in the bag.

"Mom, I found some food. Here, you and Billy eat some of this while I fill you in on what's happening in Anderson."

Her mom patiently listened to the story and Carrie's plea to leave the area, but finally said, "But where will we go? Is it safer anywhere else?"

She thought for a minute and replied, "I know the perfect place. Remember, my friend Callie? Her dad owns a big farm on the other side of Owensville, and she told me they have a large lake full of fish, gardens, and plenty of fruit trees. I want to go there."

"But sweetheart, that's forty or fifty miles away."

"Mom, it's more like thirty or thirty-five miles, and we can walk there in three to five days. We now have food and can get water along the way. There are ponds and lakes all the way. Did you hear me say that they're raping women and making sex slaves out of them?"

"Don't talk like that in front of Billie. Pack your backpack, put on some hiking boots, and give me that .38."

✪✪✪

⭐

Chapter 13   One Big Happy Family

Highway 57 in Illinois

Davi looked over her shoulder at the newcomers and said, "Dad, can we trust these new people? They seem a bit flakey to me."

"Davi, always trust but verify. We will keep an eye on them until we know they can be trusted. Now, finish bringing up the guns and ammo, and let's get out of here before that gang shows up."

Davi, Geena, and I were carrying the guns and ammo out of the secure room when I saw the night vision glasses.

"Wow, I have to try these out."

I grabbed a pair and headed upstairs with them and a load of ammo. I placed the ammo in the back of the Jeep and put the glasses, which were more like goggles, on my head. I looked out into the darkness behind the house and saw a coyote walking along the fence line. Suddenly he took off, and I saw a head bob where he had been. Then I saw several glowing red dots. The idiots were smoking as they tried to infiltrate our position.

"Aaron, we have company coming up from behind the house. They're about five hundred yards out and slowly advancing towards us. There are about a dozen of them, and they're heavily armed. Wow, these night vision glasses are great. Geena, go down and bring up several more so we can see them, but they can't see us."

Aaron added, "Bring up a couple of the green boxes that say "Claymores" in yellow on the sides. Davi, show Zack how to place and arm them."

Aaron shifted into high gear, had us start turning lights off as though we were settling down for the night and directed us to positions around his house.

"We only have a few minutes before they begin their attack. Stay behind cover while we get prepared."

Davi showed me how to set up the Claymores, and we crawled out about twenty yards from the house towards the largest concentration of our enemy. The men made a lot of noise and were probably half-drunk or stoned. I set the Claymore into the ground with the safe side towards the house, armed it, and started back while paying out the wire to the deadly device.

We barely had wired the mines to their firing devices when Sally yelled, "Damn, they have us surrounded! There are twenty or thirty more coming down the road. Duck, they're dropping to fire on us."

I had hit the dirt behind one of the Jeeps when bullets started striking the house blowing out the windows. Sharon fell to the ground with a blood-curdling scream. Damn, she's been hit in the right shoulder. I crawled over to her and pressed hard on the wound to stop the bleeding. Sally slithered over, and we both dragged her into the house. Sally took over caring for her.

I grabbed two M4s from the back of the Jeep and several magazines. I gave one to Geena, took the other one to the side of the barn, and started looking for targets. They stood out like neon signs. The M4 had a red dot sight, and along with the night vision goggles, I couldn't miss. Every shot I took dropped a thug. I had to move every few shots to keep them from firing at my muzzle flash, but I killed eight of the bastards in just a few minutes.

One of the men surprised me by coming up from behind, swinging his rifle butt at my head when Geena shot his sorry ass. I looked over, and Aaron was wiping his knife on another dead thug's shirt.

He looked up, smiled at me, and said, "This is just like the good old days down in the Sinai."

"You have a very perverted sense of fun," I replied as I shot another thug who was trying to rush our position.

Davi and Geena were also killing them at an alarming pace. It was so dark the thugs didn't realize we were decimating them so easily. Finally, they caught on, and the last five started running for their lives. I killed two, and Davi nailed one more. The others were out of range and got away. The entire firefight lasted eight minutes. Those bikers were stupid, and we were lucky I'd seen them, or we'd all be dead.

"Is anyone else wounded?"

Sally replied, "I caught a ricochet in the butt. It's just a scratch, but I need a Band-Aid. Zack, can you take care of it?"

"Come on in the house and drop your pants. I'll take care of it," said Geena as she dragged Sally into the house and winked at me.

"Those two are in love with you, Zack Johnson."

"I don't know about love, but they do think they need a man to protect and take care of them. I'm focused on getting to my daughter and don't have time for love."

"But you had time for lust, judging from the hay in your shorts and Geena's panties. Your focus was off a bit last night, and Sally knows it. You have chosen Geena, and you're going to have a major catfight. Oh, and by the way, both killed several bastards tonight. I think they're learning to take care of themselves."

"I like both, but I don't know if either would be a great mom to my daughter. Yes, I care for Geena, but I just can't focus on a relationship right now. I promised to help train them in fighting and train them on weapons. Could you help train them also?"

"That hay in both of your pants told Sally all she needed to know, and you're going to break Geena's heart if you're just using her.

Davi left me to help her dad tend to her mom. Before she walked into the house, she looked back and smiled at me.

"Aaron, why didn't we use the Claymores?"

"Son, we had them outmanned, outgunned, and besides, there probably won't be any more Claymores manufactured for quite a while. We might need them if we encounter a serious threat. Now, go gather them up and place them back in their boxes."

Sharon was in bad shape and should be in bed resting for several days before being moved, but there we were driving down the highway to escape from any more gang attacks. Sharon was in the back of the Jeep Cherokee with Davi tending to her while Aaron drove. I was driving the other Jeep with Sally in the front seat and Geena sitting in back watching behind us. Aaron was driving at twenty mph to avoid hitting any stalled cars or rough spots on the road. We were both driving with the aid of the night vision goggles and no lights on the Jeeps. We didn't want to make ourselves bigger targets than necessary. We had to take back roads and dirt roads to get around. Aaron supplied walkie talkies for both Jeeps, and Sally and Davi handled communications. We would only drive at night at a low speed so that we would not jostle Sharon, and as important, we wouldn't run up on any ambushes. You could see a lit cigarette over a mile away, and with a clear sky, it was almost like daylight.

I saw numerous raccoons and opossums on the road, but no humans. Animal eyes glowed like a full moon. Once I saw a light come on in a house as we passed, but no one attempted to follow us. I'm sure a lot of people heard us drive by in the dark, and we probably scared the crap out of most of them when they didn't see lights attached to the sound of passing cars.

"Sally, it's almost daylight, and we're only north of Effingham and Highway 70. Dad will pull off at the next

108

abandoned house or barn, so we can rest until tonight. I'll signal when we get ready to pull off the road."

"We'll be ready when you call. I'm tired and ready for some sleep."

"Zack, can we trust these strangers? They seem so perfect."

"I trust everyone until they prove otherwise, but I also keep a watch on their actions more than their words. These people risked their lives and saved our butts. I think they're more than they appear to be. Davi and her dad are highly trained military types. They have military weapons, and I think I saw a case of hand grenades and LAWs packed in the Jeep. They're probably ex-Israeli and settled here to get some peace. Bad luck there."

"It makes sense. What's a LAW?"

"A Light Anti-Tank Weapon."

"They're loaded for bear or terrorists. Maybe they're here under some kind of Israeli witness protection program."

"Sally, we're pulling off to the right. There's a farmhouse and a barn that looks deserted up ahead. Tell Zack to join me in scouting them."

"Will do."

Geena gritted her teeth and said, "I don't trust her. Be careful."

I almost laughed but kept my amusement to myself. What she'd meant was 'keep your pants on and hands off that hussy.'

I went over to their Jeep and joined Davi as we crept up on the barn. She motioned me to drop to the ground and crawl the last thirty feet to the back of the barn as she walked around to the front door. She motioned for me to enter the back door on her signal. I crawled to the edge of the barn and stood just behind the backside, watching around the corner for her signal. She waved and disappeared. I rushed to the door, and we both entered at the same time to find a horrible smell, but no people. There was a dead horse in one of the stalls, and two more in lousy shape.

I told her, "They're dying from dehydration. We will water them after we clear the house."

"Let's clear the house."

"Hey, why did you make me crawl to the barn when you walked right over to it?"

"It was a test to see how you took orders from a woman. Besides, we women like to see men crawl every now and then," she said as she walked away.

I popped her on the butt with my hand, and she quickly turned and said, "Don't start something you have no intention of finishing, mister. I'm focused."

She left the barn and headed to the house with me, tagging along behind her. She looked over her shoulder and smiled as though she just had to know if I was following her or checking her out as she walked away. Guilty on both counts. Damn, it just dawned on me, did she just come on to me or insult me? I thought it was a bit of both. I wondered if she'd make a good mother. Damn, she's right, I need to pick one woman and stick with her.

"Zack, follow behind me as we enter. You watch the left side, and I'll watch the right. Don't shoot me."

She slowly turned the knob on the door, but it was locked. She motioned, and we walked around to the back door, which opened when she tried the knob. The door creaked and made that annoying sound as it opened. The dead must be awake now, along with everyone who wants to kill us. We searched the house room by room until we had cleared every room and closet.

Davi keyed the radio and said, "Come on in. The coast is clear."

We pulled down the shades, lit several candles, and then started searching the house for food and weapons.

"Davi, I'm going out to give those horses some water."

"Only give them a couple quarts or so at a time. They'll drink until they explode. Don't feed them tonight."

"Okay, Miss Vet."

"I'm not a vet, but I do know about people who were starved and well-meaning people gave them too much food and water before their systems could handle them."

I said, "The death camps in Germany."

110

"Bingo, you aren't as stupid as you look."

She turned to reach up in a cabinet, and I looked at her and thought this might be the one. She filled out her jeans in a most remarkable manner. Damn, I have to get women off my mind. Callie! Callie! Callie! But damn, she filled them jeans out.

I watered the horses, brushed them down, and was telling them about our trip when I felt a presence in the barn. I slowly pulled my gun out of my holster as I brushed one of the horses. There was a footstep to my left when I heard, "You're so gentle with the horses. I would not have guessed you to be an animal person."

"I spent a lot of time with my aunt and uncle on their farm. They had horses, pigs, and chickens to care for. They're so strong, but they depend on humans so much on a farm. I hope people are letting them loose to fend for themselves if they can't care for them."

"Sorry, Zack, but most are barbeque about now when people run out of food."

"Thanks for putting *that* in my head."

I turned around to see Davi only a few feet from me. She still had a pistol on her hip, but she had taken her shirt off and just had a sports bra on. Damn, she looked good and filled out that top rather well. I had to get back to the house before something happened.

I dropped the brush and walked towards the house, saying, "I'm hungry. Let's see what's cooking."

Davi responded by mumbling something under her breath. I thought I heard, "Chicken."

I entered the house and saw that Sally was helping Aaron with his wife while Geena placed food on the table.

"Geena, I don't know what's for lunch, but it smells darn good."

"Dog food."

"What do you mean, dog food? Are you serious?"

"No, but it's the best I could put together with what we have. It's beef stew, green beans, and some sauerkraut. I don't have much to work with."

"I wasn't kidding. It really does smell good."

"I'm sorry. I thought that you were being sarcastic."

"Don't worry. I'm hungry, and I appreciate you cooking for us. Are you all right? You seem a little down."

"I'm fine. I think this whole end of the world, as we know it thing just hit me between the eyes, and suddenly I feel very vulnerable and alone. Zack, you were following that Davi like a puppy dog."

"Geena, I care for you a lot and only need time to make sure my daughter is safe, and then you and I'll cash in that rain check and see what comes our way."

"I'm just feeling all alone, and I'm jealous. Sally is getting mad because she thinks I stole you away from her. I don't want to lose her and find out that I never had you."

I walked over to her and gave her a big hug as I said, "You still have Sally and me, and soon you'll meet Mike and Callie. We'll all have your back. Mike will charm the pants off Sally by the second day."

She sobbed and said, "Thank you. I needed that."

I saw Aaron heading towards the kitchen, and I gently broke away from Geena.

"Aaron, how is Sharon doing?"

"Much better. Sharon is in a lot of pain, but there is no infection so far, and she is not running a temperature."

Geena hugged Aaron and then took a bowl of the beef broth to Sharon.

We ate, and since everyone was exhausted, we relaxed the rest of the day and turned in for the night at sundown. I took the first watch, woke Sally up in three hours, and then slept until 5:00 a.m. The night was uneventful, so everyone got some rest and was ready to move on the next morning.

"Aaron, there's a large horse trailer behind the barn. I'd like to take the two horses and some of the other animals with us unless you object."

"Good idea. Shouldn't slow us down much, and they'll come in handy once the gas runs out. Hell, we might have to eat them. Load 'em up."

"Thanks, I'll load the trailer roof with hay bales and bags of feed for the other animals."

Davi helped me load the feed, horses, and other animals while Sally and Geena prepared a cold breakfast for the team and packed everything back into the Jeeps. We made small talk while getting the horse trailer loaded. Davi told me a brief history of her family and how they got to the USA, with no mention of any military experience.

"You didn't mention you and your dad serving in the military."

"Look back to the west. There is a storm heading our way. It's cold this morning."

"You changed the subject."

"Yes, we both served in the IDF and saw action in several conflicts. No big deal. Everyone is a soldier in Israel."

"But most don't bring their toys home with them."

"Well, Dad has some friends in high places with big diplomatic pouches. Remember, we predicted this for years and were prepared."

"I have been preparing for ten years and don't have a single full auto M4 or Claymore. Are y'all part of a special Israeli covert action in the USA?"

"No, we aren't, and if we were, do you think that we would tell you?"

"Well, I guess not."

"Slowly look over to your two jealous women. They haven't taken an eye off us since we started loading the trailer."

I glanced over my shoulder, and sure enough, Geena and Sally were glaring at us while trying to concentrate on their work.

Davi was right. This could develop into a hostile situation, and I had to admit I sort of liked the attention.

"What we need is some more men for them to focus their energy on and give me a break."

"You use the word focus a lot. I agree with the more men comment, and we need some strong, handsome types."

I caught the slur and poked her on the arm.

●●●●

We pulled out just as the sun poked its head out from behind some ominous dark clouds. We were skirting around the east side of Effingham, heading east on Highway 33. The temperature had dropped twenty degrees overnight, and by midday, the wind was growing stronger by the minute. We had gone from sweating to wearing hoodies as the temperature plunged.

"I don't like this change in the weather. We're in tornado alley, and this is not good. We might want to find cover before we get caught out in the open," Sally said over the radio to Davi just as the sound of thunder rolled towards them from the west.

Suddenly the Jeep swerved, and the trailer swung from side to side as a gust of wind shook them and almost ran them off the road. I grabbed the radio and said, "Tell your dad we need to find cover. That blast of wind almost turned us over. This storm is bad, and the worst is yet to come."

"Dad agrees, and we're looking for shelter from a potential tornado and high winds. We're only a few miles outside of Vincennes, and he wants to shelter at the National Guard Armory until this blows over."

"I hope the bridge over the Wabash is still intact and isn't guarded."

"We'll know in a few minutes."

The wind continued rocking the Jeeps and trailers as they headed down 33 to the bridge.

"Hey, that sign says Vincennes is just a mile ahead. That means the bridge is just ahead. Damn, there it is, and there is a roadblock."

"Sally, this is Aaron. Put Zack on. Zack, let's stop about a hundred feet from the roadblock and walk-up with shouldered arms. We'll try to charm them."

"What if that doesn't work?"

"Then, we'll pray for their souls."

We pulled off the road as planned. I walked up to Aaron, and he handed me two hand grenades.

"Okay, now I get the praying part."

"Son, sometimes you have to arrange their meeting with God. Now, pray that they're peaceful."

We walked up to the barricade that was made out of two old cars and some pipes chained to the cars. Two men and a woman popped out and asked what we wanted.

Aaron replied, "We're trying to get to the National Guard Armory to ride this storm out. Some biker gang attacked my wife and us, and another lady is wounded. We won't cause any trouble."

"You can join us at the high school. We tried to get into the Armory, but without power, it's impossible."

"I can open the door and provide shelter for your people. How many are left?"

"Only a little over a hundred. How can you get in?"

"I have a key."

The wind picked up and almost knocked them down as the man replied, "Come on and try your key, but don't get your hopes up."

They moved the cars, locked the steel poles back in place, and we followed them to the Armory.

"Tell your people to get over here ASAP. I'll have the door open in a minute. Oh, by the way, it will be a bit loud."

Aaron waved for me to help him as he walked to a side door carrying a black bag. We arrived at the door, and Aaron

115

handed me a paper-wrapped block and said, "Cut the paper away and stick the detonator in the block. Now, place the C4 on the door and light the fuse. Oh. and run like hell."

He took off at a dead run with me two steps behind him. He looked up and said, "Did you forget something?"

"Damn," I said as I slapped my forehead. I had run before I lit the fuse.

I ran back, lit the fuse, and ran like hell back to Aaron, who was hiding behind an army tank parked in the side yard. Just as I ducked behind the tank, there was a loud explosion, and I saw the door fly open. The door was still on its hinges but was buckled in the middle.

"Come on, let's open the doors and get the vehicles in the basement. Be alert. There could be others."

There weren't any others, and we quickly opened the front doors and the basement's overhead doors.

Sally and Davi pulled the Jeeps in and placed them by the back garage door, so we could make a quick exit if the crap hit the fan. Aaron and I began exploring our new shelter and quickly saw the basement was enormous and contained several large trucks and six Humvees. We searched the upstairs and found a supply room filled with the typical army supplies. There was everything from BDUs to MREs. There was a large safe built into the back of the supply room, and we assumed it contained the weapons and ammo.

"Will you have to use your special key again?"

"Only if we want to get into that room. I don't need any more weapons or explosives, but could always use more .556 and 9mm ammo."

"I never thought that I would need an army to survive, but after what we've been through, I'd like to take some weapons and ammo back to Owensville."

"Well then, let's blow it and get what we want before the others get here."

Aaron reached into his black bag and handed me some more C4. I quickly got it ready, placed it in the middle by the combination lock, and ran like hell after lighting the fuse. Again, there was a tremendous explosion, but this time the door didn't budge. There was a hole in the wall beside the door, and we could see into the safe. It was at least thirty feet deep and fifteen feet wide and full of weapons and shelves of ammo.

"Damn, son, we need a larger key."

Aaron placed two more charges, one above and one below the hole in the wall. He lit the fuse, and we both hid around the corner on the floor with our ears covered. The explosions rocked the building, and a few tiles fell from the ceilings. When the dust settled, we walked around the corner to see the safe door still intact, but a new entry in the wall beside the safe.

"Let's go shopping. Grab two of those SAWs and come back quickly for the ammo."

I picked up the SAWs, a can of ammo, and headed back to the basement. I came down the stairs and saw Davi arguing with a big man with a badge and a gun. I heard, "We appreciate you opening up the Armory, but you can't just steal government property."

I loaded the SAW and walked up to them.

"Sir, I'm Zack. Have you *seen* the government? Have they tried to help you? Why are there only a hundred people left in this town?"

"Look, you're right. The government disappeared with the event, and we lost thousands due to sickness. Most left town to find food, and more were lost to gang attacks. The bastards are better armed and raid us every month or so."

"There is a safe full of M4's, 9mm Berettas and other deadly and dangerous stuff. We can arm and train you so you can fight off these bastards. We just want two of the Humvees and a small part of the weapons and ammo."

While I was talking, a small group of unarmed men walked up and listened to the conversation.

"Roy, the guy's right. Our best men were killed in that first raid. We lost all of the men who had served in Iraq and Afghanistan in that raid. We give in to the gangs and give them what they want. The only fights have been when they come to take our women."

"Can you train us on how to use these weapons?"

"I can't, but Davi and her dad can."

"This little woman is trained in army type weapons?"

"Big man, follow me outside."

Davi grabbed the SAW and walked out the side door along with the group that had joined the conversation.

"See that white Chevy van?"

"Yes."

She raised the weapon and said, "Back tire."

She started shooting, destroyed the tire, and then called out the passenger side door. The door was riddled in a second. Davi handed the weapon to me, drew her sidearm, and yelled mirror. She fired once, and the mirror exploded.

"Need to see anymore?"

With the help of the sheriff and his men, we changed our vehicles and loaded a ton of weapons and ammo into them. By the time we finished, all of the town's surviving people were safely in the building. Geena and I passed out MREs and water while Sally cared for Sharon.

●●●●

I was playing ball with a four-year-old boy when one of the men came in and told us it was raining very hard and looked bad southwest of our location. Then thunder cracked in the distance, and with each minute, the noise grew in intensity until it sounded like we were being bombed. All of the people upstairs came flooding down the stairs as the storm shattered the windows.

We heard and felt the vibrations as the wind gusts tried to blow the building down around us. There was the sound of walls cracking and straining as the intensity of the wind grew. The noise outside shifted to a deeper tone, and just as it peaked, sounded like several freight trains passing us at once.

There was a steady rumble as the building above us fell in on itself. Suddenly there was a crash, and debris fell down the stairs blocking the stairway. Women were screaming, and kids were crying while I hugged Geena and Sally. We were lying under one of the Humvees, and I'll admit to being scared. It sounded like the world was coming to an end. I prayed to God to save us from this disaster and promised to be good forever. I was thinking, *"Damn the bad luck to survive an EMP and TSHTF only to be killed by a tornado."*

I heard, "Tornado!"

"Hell, yes, it's a tornado. This is a bad storm. Keep everyone in the basement until the sheriff says it's clear."

The storm kept on for another fifteen minutes and started tapering off. I joined Aaron and the Sheriff at the side door and was nearly blown off my feet when suddenly there was a total calm outside.

"Is this the eye of the storm?"

"Yes, get ready for more."

I looked outside, and the area looked like a scene from one of those WWII movies where a town had been repeatedly bombed. Just total devastation west and southwest.

The storm raged on for another several hours before it changed to a hard soaking rain. Aaron and the sheriff sent several teams to check out the building for damage. They found the ground floor was in bad shape, and the second floor was gone. I mean gone, as in not a stick or brick remained. The storm had blown it away. We may have all been dead or injured if not for seeking shelter in the basement of the Armory.

While waiting for the storm to blow over, several of the town's men and I helped Davi and Aaron place twin SAWs on our Humvees and three of the remaining ones. Aaron gave them training on the Humvees and the weapon systems. I held small arms training for three other groups before the rain stopped. It got still outside, and everyone wanted to go out and see what was left of the town.

I was in the first group to leave the Armory, and the sight brought tears to my eyes. Everything west and south of the Armory was in ruins. The sheriff surveyed the surroundings and said, "Thank God no one was killed or injured by this disaster, and I personally thank Him for destroying the gang's headquarters and the liquor warehouse."

Aaron was astounded by what he'd heard and asked, "The gang was sharing the town with you?"

"They stayed on the southwest side, and we stayed east of the Armory. They captured the liquor and beer distributor's warehouses just after arriving and never left. They're only a mile due south of here."

"Let's finish them off and free any hostages while they're still reeling from the storm damage."

I choked while thinking that Aaron could get an old Kentucky boy killed.

Chapter 14   Unwanted Guest

The Farm, outside of Owensville, Kentucky

"Lynn, what are you doing here, and how did you get here?"

"Well, Mike, I'm happy to see you too."

"I'm sorry, but we broke up six months ago, and I never expected to see you again. You know my sister, Joan. This is Callie, Joan's daughter. Callie, this is Lynn Drake."

"Pleasure to meet y'all. When the crap hit the fan, I remembered you told me about you and Zack being preppers. My dad's a prepper, but he lives in Georgia, so I started walking here as fast as I could. I knew that you and Zack would know what to do with the world falling apart."

Mike took Lynn over to the porch swing for some privacy.

"I never thought I would see you again."

"I thought we were good together."

"Lynn, you told me that I was a self-absorbed asshole with a tiny penis. No one says penis."

"Dickhead, I was mad at you. We were together for six months. We were in love, and I wanted you forever. I finally said I loved you and asked you to move in with me. You were scared and dumped me over dinner at a cheap restaurant. I need your help. You owe me."

"Lynn, I don't owe you anything, but I'll help you because it's the right thing to do."

"Mike, can you tell me what I did wrong? I thought that we'd be married and live together forever."

"Darling, a nice young lady like you stole my heart and crapped on me. I don't trust any women and still hate her. I'm not ready to fall in love and live with one woman for the rest of my life."

"I feel so sorry for you. So, you hate all women?"

"No, I just don't trust them."

Mike did his best to make everyone comfortable while Joan and Callie fixed supper. The farmhouse had four bedrooms, and the tack room had several bunk beds. He gave Lynn his bedroom and gave Joan and Callie a room to share. He didn't want to drive to Dale until the next morning, so he gave Ally and her daughter, Sue, a room to share and told Paul that he would sleep out in the tack room with him.

"Mike, is my mom going to die?"

"Son, I don't think so, but she has to want to live. You and your sister have to cut her some slack while she grieves for your dad. Be kind and gentle with her for a few weeks, and she'll come around."

"Do we have to go home in the morning? I'd like to stay here with you until Mom feels better."

Mike thought, *"Oh crap,"* but replied, "Of course, you can stay here until your mom gets better."

"We can't pay you, but Sue and I can do some chores to help out and pay for our room and board. Deal?"

"Deal."

Mike took Paul out to the field behind the barn and said, "I'm going to teach you how to plow, so we can plant a large garden. I'll show Sue how to feed the livestock and chickens. Joan will try to keep your mom busy, so she doesn't have time to think about the bad stuff in her life."

"Thanks, Mike."

"No problem, kid. Everyone needs a helping hand every now and then."

Supper was over, and Mike called everyone to the great room to discuss dividing chores and guard duty. He helped Paul coax his mom into the room and had her sit in the rocking chair.

"I called you together to discuss a couple of things before we turn in for the night. First, Ally and her kids will be staying with us for a while until they can travel to their home. Second, we need to divide the chores in the morning after breakfast. We have to start thinking long term and plant a large garden. Last, we have to set up guards to cover us at night. We also have to be vigilant every day and keep an eye out for strangers approaching the farm. There are bad people out there."

Joan spoke up, "I'll head up the kitchen along with Ally, and also take my turn at guard duty."

Lynn added, "I'm into gardening, and will be glad to become a guard. We also need to think about scavenging for more food, guns, toilet paper, and feminine hygiene products. I'm a fan of Post-Apocalyptic novels, and there are warehouses and stalled trucks on the road full of food and supplies. I even learned a lot from watching that zombie series on TV."

"Great idea. I was thinking the same. We need a scavenging team. Lynn, I'll help you find what can be found before others take it all."

They brainstormed for an hour and made several lists of chores, a "to do," list, and a guard schedule. Joan didn't like it, but Mike included Callie as one of the guards.

"Mike, this is your niece and my daughter. She is just a girl, not a guard. This could be dangerous."

"Look, sis, life is dangerous these days. The three of us adults would have to take three hours each and would be dead tired all day. Two hours is bad enough. Besides, the guard is posted just to alert the rest of us to action if something happens, not fight invaders by themselves."

"I don't care. She's my baby girl."

"Your baby is growing up and had better grow up quick."

Zack's uncle had built a crow's nest on top of the barn that was five feet higher than the roof of the barn. This gave the guards a clear view for hundreds of yards around the house and barn. Mike took them up into the crow's nest and prepped each one with the layout of the farm and the most likely spots where intruders would try to gain entrance. Uncle Arlo had thought of everything.

"Team, we will leave two MP 15s and a shotgun up here in the crow's nest at all times. All three will be loaded with three spare magazines each. The Saiga shotgun will kick like a mule, but with these twelve round magazines, it can throw a ton of that #4 buckshot downrange quickly. Only use it if intruders get close to the barn or try to come into the crow's nest. Now the fun part."

Mike reached into a bag, brought out the night vision goggles and said, "Don't drop these. We have two, but we won't find replacements. You'll be able to see the enemy long before he sees you. Don't leave them on all night. We can't waste batteries. Scan the area around the farm every ten to fifteen minutes, and you will catch anyone trying to sneak up on us. Don't be shocked when you see eyes glowing in the dark. Animals' eyes reflect light very well, and their eyes show up like a full moon. Any questions?"

Callie asked, "What do we do if we spot someone?"

"Good question. If you see someone or something that worries you, just key this walkie-talkie, and it'll wake me up. If I don't answer, pull that string, and a bell will ring in the house that'll wake us all up. If you're sure that we're under attack, call on the radio, pull the string, and shoot a couple of rounds above the intruder's heads. That will give me time to haul ass up to see what's going on."

Lynn asked, "What if you're on duty and call for help?"

124

"Grab your weapons and prepare to repel the enemy. Shoot first and ask questions later."

"When do you give us some guns?"

"Now."

Mike took the nine to midnight three-hour slot with Lynn, Callie, and Joan following with two hours each. The time passed slowly as he thought about his best friend out on the trail, trying to get home. The funny thing was, Mike never feared for Zack's life. Mike was deep in thought when he saw the light come on in the kitchen a few minutes before Lynn was due to relieve him. He watched her leave the porch with her shotgun pointing ahead of her. She looked side to side and was quickly in the barn and up the ladder to the crow's nest.

"Hello, Mike. Don't shoot me."

"You looked like you knew what you were doing while you were crossing the yard to the barn."

"I told you my dad's a prepper. He was also in the Army for several years and taught me how to handle myself."

"Damn, you came across as the typical girlie girl. You had me fooled."

"Most men don't like strong-willed women who can take care of themselves. Y'all like to protect us, poor defenseless little girls."

"Don't you think you sell some of us short? I happen to like a woman who can handle a gun as long as it's not pointed at me."

"Now, don't get me wrong. I like a man to open doors for me and treat me like a lady. I don't want him to have a hurt ego when I jump on top in bed and take over. I like men who aren't afraid of me."

Mike was at a loss for words when Lynn kissed him and locked her arms around him. He held her tight and said, "Wow, that kiss stirred up something that has to wait until later. We can't fool around during guard duty. Only fools get caught with their pants down."

"Oh, don't think you were getting more than a kiss after dumping my ass. I plan to make your life miserable, missing what you had and gave up."

"Ouch, I'm going to bed."

✪

Chapter 15   War

Vincennes, Indiana

The gang's headquarters was in a small motel located a mile south of the Armory between 41 South and South Decherd Street. Aaron's plan was to perform surveillance on the thugs and use the information to draw them out into the open and decimate them with the twin SAWs on the Humvees. The part I didn't like was he asked me to go on the scouting mission to the gang's headquarters. Now don't get me wrong, I can handle myself in a fight and am more than fair with a rifle, but I never went looking for a fight either.

"Aaron, shouldn't we pack up and head south? We've armed these people, and they can easily kill all of the gang without much effort. Why should we put our necks on the line?"

"Because if not us, who will help them? They have the weapons but have no leader. I think they'll turn tail and run when first shot at, leaving the Humvees and weapons behind them. Then this gang will be the best-armed group in the area and can expand and take more territory. Let's kill them off now before they grow."

"I guess you're right. I'd want someone helping my family if they were in the same situation. I'm in."

"I knew you'd be in once you thought it through. Now, here's what I need you two to do."

After Aaron had told me that he wanted me to go with Davi to infiltrate the gang's stronghold, I went to tell Geena. She was not happy I was going off to spend a couple of days with that 'Israeli woman.' We talked for several hours, and I told her she was the only woman I was interested in, but that I didn't want to lead her on either. I really didn't want to think about women right now.

Davi and I waited until dark and walked south along the west side of Highway 41 through the broken houses and downed woods between the Armory and the gang's location. The destruction made for slow going as we navigated around piles of limbs and debris. There was more than adequate cover and no sign of the gang or anyone else for that matter. We only saw a couple of dogs along the way, and they ran when they saw us. We were wearing black clothing and had covered our faces with the dark camouflage paint Aaron had found in the National Guard supplies.

Davi looked over at me as we stopped behind a house and said, "You might not be a soldier, but at least you look like one. Just don't get trigger happy and shoot me in the back."

"You could have stopped with how great I look in camo."

"We're almost directly across from the liquor warehouse and need to proceed carefully from here on. Some of the gang might even be living in the houses around us, but I think they're all in the hotel south of the warehouse. Let's stop here for a while and watch and listen."

"Okay, Boss."

We sat on some cinder blocks behind a felled tree and surveyed the area across Highway 41, where the gang was supposed to be for half an hour before we heard the first activity.

"That sounded like a scream coming from the warehouse parking lot. Look closely at that big RV close to the warehouse. It has lights on inside."

Suddenly, the door to the RV slammed open, and someone ran out screaming and running towards the highway. Following right behind her, a man was yelling for her to stop. He fell down twice and was obviously drunk. She cleared the road and ran right at us. The poor girl only had a pair of panties and tennis shoes on and was terrified. She didn't see the log we were hiding behind and did a header right into us. Davi grabbed her and dragged her behind the house just as the drunken biker tripped over the same log and fell on top of me. The bastard was so drunk that he thought that I was the girl.

"Look bitch, when I get through with you, you won't be able to run away. I'm going to cut the tendons to your feet, and you'll be crawling around instead of running away."

I pulled my knife as I grabbed him from behind and slit his throat.

"You won't be hurting any women now, bastard."

I let him drop to the ground and shoved him under the pile of limbs by the log. I heard the girl whimpering behind the house and joined Davi and her between a car and the home.

"Are you all right?" asked Davi.

"Who are you? Let me go."

"Settle down, girl. We're the good guys. Are you from this area?"

"No, I was driving home from IU to Murphy when these men captured me. I've been that SOB's woman since then."

Davi hugged her and asked, "The rest of our people are straight up the road north of here. Can you walk up to them? They'll take care of you. They're at the Armory."

"I guess so. Can't you come with me?"

"Sorry, but we're on a mission."

"Can you save the others?"

"What others?"

"There are fifteen to twenty women and young girls at the hotel. We were all held captive and abused. Two of the girls are my friends and were captured with me."

I quickly replied, "We'll do our best to save the women and kill every last one of these evil thugs. I promise you."

I removed my bulletproof vest and gave her my shirt and said, "Ask for Geena and Sally when you get there. They'll take good care of you."

The girl headed towards the Armory, and we looked at each other, and Davi said, "Disasters bring out the best and the worst in people," as she kissed me on the forehead.

"What did I do right? I want to know, so I can do more of it."

"You were a gentleman to that poor thing, and you promised to avenge her honor. You must be a knight."

"I'm no knight, but I always try to do the right thing. Sometimes my timing is off a bit, but I keep plugging away."

"I was also proud of you for not staring at her tits and giving her something to cover up with."

"Damn, you must have a low opinion of me or maybe all men."

"Right on both counts! Get your ass in gear. We need to get across the street and see what's going on. I also want to find a position to watch them after the sun comes up. We need to know how many there are and what kind of weapons they have."

She led the way across the highway, and we worked our way around the warehouse with ease. There were three guards, with two being drunk and passed out, and the other was stoned and sitting in a lawn chair gazing at the stars. We checked the warehouse out and then snuck over to the hotel. The situation was much different there. The two guards were alert and manning their posts at opposite ends of the hotel parking lot. We quickly slipped by them and surveilled the hotel before finding a place to watch them in the morning. There had been a beautiful stand of trees in front of the hotel with flowers and concrete planters. It was a pile of broken limbs and flowers. We settled in for a long night when the winds picked up, and another storm came through, soaking us before we could cover up with our ponchos. The lightning flashed all around, and the rain poured down on us. We were both shivering when Davi got close to me and then pulled my poncho up and wrapped her arms around me.

"Look, dude, we can share some body heat, but that's all. Don't take this as a come-on and put your hands where they don't belong. I'll break them off if you do."

"Hey, you're the one who crawled under my poncho. I'll be a gentleman as long as you act like a proper lady. Besides, you're not my type."

"I thought your type was warm and breathing."

"Very funny. I have high standards."

"And friends in low places."

We hid in the tangled up mess, taking turns sleeping until the thugs started moving around. Sharing the poncho made the cold of the night bearable, although Davi snored and wiggled all night. Yes, I kept my hands to myself, and none had to be broken.

The first thing we saw at sun up was two men rolling out motorcycles from the lobby of the hotel. We counted 34 motorcycles and two old VW vans at the hotel that appeared to be used by the gang and another five at the warehouse from last night. That amounted to at least fifty gang members plus twenty hostages, and lord knows how many biker bitches they'd brought with them. Two bikers took one of the old vans to the liquor warehouse and came back with a load of alcohol shortly afterward. Three men took the other van and disappeared for several hours. They came back with a load of food and several weapons. Most of the men wore a pistol on their hip, while only a few had automatic rifles with them.

"They don't appear to come out of the hotel for a large gathering. How are we going to trap them in the open if they don't come out to play?"

"We have to think of something that'll draw them all out at the same time. Now, what would entice men to leave their hotel and come outside?"

I got a big grin on my face and heard Davi say, "Shut up, stupid."

"Wait a minute. I was thinking about a barbecue."

"BS. You were thinking about naked ladies."

"Nope, a barbecue. We find a cow. Bring it over here before daybreak tomorrow and wait for them to come out and figure out how to have a big assed barbeque. That's what redneck Americans would do."

"Damn, I'm proud of you. You do think with your big head every now and then."

I was very proud of myself until it dawned on me that she had slammed me again. We watched the gang until dark and quietly slid out of the area and traveled back to the Armory.

••••

"Davi and Zack, tell me all about your visit to the thugs' stronghold. Oh, by the way, we have gained a wealth of information from that poor abused girl you sent back to us."

"Hi, Dad. We have the information we need and even have an idea of how to get them together for our sendoff party for them."

"Great, please fill me in on what you saw and this idea."

He ushered them to a secluded spot to discuss their surveillance results and filled them in on the events at the Armory for the day.

He had conducted several classes on the Humvees and how to use them in battle, but could not shoot the SAWs for fear of alerting the enemy. He'd seized the opportunity to live fire train when the storms blew in last night. Each crew member had shot the weapons on full automatic several times during the lightning storm.

Davi told her father about my idea to entice the gang into gathering in one place, and he liked it.

"Zack, that is a great idea! These guys haven't seen a steak or barbecue in weeks. They'll be all over that cow. Now, we just have to find a cow that hasn't been eaten by the locals. I'll go make arrangements while you two get some sleep. Oh, by the way, were you caught out in the storm last night? It must have been cold, judging from Davi's lipstick on your neck. You damn well better clean it off before Geena sees it."

I wiped at my neck until Davi nodded and said, "Dad, we just shared a poncho. Nothing else."

I quickly turned to leave and ran right into Sally and Geena, who both ran over and gave me a big hug. We walked over to our corner, and I prepared to get in my sleeping bag.

"I'll hold up a sheet while you change out of those damp clothes. It must have been horrible to share a poncho with that bitch from hell. I know how much you hated that."

"Look, Geena, it was raining cats and dogs and was damn cold last night. Sure, I shared a poncho with Davi, and we both stayed warm, but nothing happened."

"Nothing?"

"Nothing."

"Well, I don't like her."

"You don't have to like her. We just have to get along to survive. This isn't high school with kids fighting over who is dating who's. Yes, I like women, but I've told you I'm not settling down with anyone until I know my daughter is safe. Case closed."

Geena walked away, still upset, and since I was never good at calming down pissed off women, I let her go.

Sally saw her leave and quickly said, "You can sleep next to me to stay warm."

I threw my wet socks at her, pulled my sleeping bag over my head, and went to sleep.

••••

Aaron and the sheriff took a brief tour of the east side of Vincennes and found most of the area was intact. There was damage due to the high winds, but the tornado had stayed on the west side of town, which spared most of their homes and supplies.

"Aaron, why don't you guys stay here with us? You can have your pick of a home, and you would fit right in with us. We need your knowledge, and you need stability."

"That sounds very tempting, but we have family in Alabama and must get to them as quickly as possible. They may be in danger, and I'd hate to be comfortable up here if they're in danger. Sorry, but we'll be moving on after we clean out the criminals."

"Well, I had to make the offer."

"And I thank you for it, but no thanks."

The sheriff asked several local farmers to find a cow but did not tell them why. This intrigued Aaron.

"Why didn't you mention why we needed the cow to the farmers?"

"I think we have a leak in our group. Those bikers know more about my business than I know myself. I'll root the SOB out one day, but that's our problem. Now how will you sneak up on the gang with these noisy Humvees?"

"Damn good question. They're a bit heavy to push a mile to the bad guys."

••••

I woke up kind of groggy and felt horrible. Then I heard Sally say, "He must have hated snuggling up to Davi in the rain all night."

"Yeah, that must have been agony for a man who doesn't want to think about women until his daughter is safe."

"I'll bet he doesn't have a daughter or a girlfriend. I can't wait to meet his buddy, Mike. He sounds like a real man."

"Women, I can hear every word you're saying. I'm trying to sleep."

"It's 3:00 p.m., and Aaron said to wake your ass up. He needs you."

"I'm up, I'm up."

Davi had walked up during the conversation and said, "Ladies, Zack was the perfect gentleman. He was warm and kept his hands to himself. All a freezing woman could want on a cold night. Zack, get your ass up. Saying you're awake and being awake are two different things. I'm counting to ten, and at ten, I'm pitching this bucket of cold water on your sorry ass. 1...2...3...4..5"

I jumped up and out of the sleeping bag with just my underwear on, grabbed my pants, and headed out to the latrine.

"Davi, can we help with the assault on the gang?"

"Yes, Dad wants both of you to become snipers and pick off as many as you can while being on the lookout for anyone trying to escape. Can you two shoot a man running away from you?"

"Hell, yes, we can shoot a murdering rapist. We were both shot and almost raped several times. Zack saved us twice. We've both killed scum like this before."

"Hard times make a hard woman."

"Especially when a hard man isn't easy to find."

Davi and Sally broke out laughing when they caught the double meaning of what Geena had said. It took a few seconds for Geena to figure it out, and she turned bright red.

"Well, y'all know what I meant."

They both laughed, and Davi replied, "Yes, we know exactly what you meant, and judging from that hay in your underwear the other night, you found a hard man."

They both laughed as Geena turned a darker shade of red.

"We didn't do anything. Nothing happened."

"Yeah, the Easter Bunny and Santa Claus broke up the party before it got started."

It didn't matter how much Geena protested, they had a biting reply.

"Come on, girls. Let's go get ready to kill some assholes."

They walked up to Aaron and Zack, who had just ended a training session on the Claymores with the sheriff and his deputy.

135

Zack saw the girls and said, "Geena, are you okay? You look like you're coming down with something."

The other two broke out laughing, and Geena hit Sally on the shoulder, but Davi ducked and bobbed, causing Geena to miss.

"Damn, you three are acting like a bunch of school girls. Get serious. NOW," said Aaron.

All three snapped to attention and saluted Aaron, which pissed him off even more if that was possible. He finally began going over the plans for the attack on the gang utilizing the Humvees. He gave detail on how the town's people would push the Humvees the mile to the warehouse before the engines were started.

"Aaron, a barbecue will be out in the open with people coming and going. Won't they see us coming in those big vehicles?"

"Yes, they could, but it's our best plan."

"The only reason you want the Humvees is for the firepower. Why not have several of the SAWs carried to the area and shoot them at the bad guys without the Humvees. Then have the rest of the Humvees come crashing in after you have them pinned down to finish them off."

We all turned towards Geena and stared for a minute before Aaron slapped his forehead and said, "Geena, I could kiss you. That's what we should have planned all along. Thank you."

Geena blushed some more and replied, "Just trying to help. My brothers and I played a lot of war games online, and I always beat them and most of the guys."

We quickly changed our plans and started preparing for implementing the attack tomorrow morning. We spent most of the day cleaning weapons and revisiting the attack plans. The most challenging part of the plan was to get the cow to go to the gang's area and stay long enough to be caught. Again, Geena came up with a brilliant idea.

"Aaron, let's tie a long rope around the neck of the cow and take it over to the hotel in the middle of the night. Then we'll tangle the end of the rope in some debris, so they'll think that the cow escaped and got tangled up in the debris. You two snuck in on them and wandered around for hours without getting caught. Just take the cow with you this time."

Aaron thought for a minute and replied, "Zack, you and Davi have a cow to deliver at approximately 3:00 a.m. Get to bed early tonight. I have to go check on Sharon. She's much better and trying to do too much."

●●●●

The deputy was on watch at 2:00 a.m. and woke Davi. She woke me up and handed me a cup of steaming black coffee with just enough sugar.

"Thanks, how'd you know how I like my coffee?"

"I didn't. That's how I like mine, and I would have drunk it if you didn't."

"You're a hard woman."

"Don't get that started."

"What started?"

"You're a dumb ass and wouldn't understand."

"Thank you. I'll take that as a badge of honor."

"Would you two get a room and shut up, we're trying to sleep," someone yelled from across the room.

"Let's get out of here."

I heard Geena say, "Zack, be careful and come back."

I whispered, "I'll."

I got dressed and met Davi, and the deputy was outside. Thankfully, it was cloudy, and the moon was nowhere to be seen. I heard a moo, turned around, and saw our partner in crime for this mission. Then I remembered the cow was giving its life to help us kill the gang. I blocked that out of my mind and checked my M4 and my 9mm before following Davi away from the Armory.

"How will we keep this cow from mooing and waking up the gang?"

"Use your manly charms to keep her speechless."

"I need a serious answer."

"See that small bale of hay? Grab it and keep her mouth full as we walk over to the hotel. I could have taken the cow myself. I needed someone to keep the cow quiet. That's your job."

"Is this a promotion? I want more pay," I replied as I rubbed the cow's ears.

"Come on, cow. We have a date with a barbecue."

The trip over to the hotel was slow but uneventful, the area was pitch black, and we had to watch for trip hazards everywhere. The cow kept chewing on the hay and was happy to follow us without needing to be prodded. The gang had several fires burning in barrels and a couple of torches burning that actually helped us spot their guards long before they could see us approach. We strung the rope around a light pole with a branch tied to its end.

"Look, they're stoned and drunk again. We could've driven a semi right in the middle of the hotel, dropped the cow off, and driven away without waking up any of these bastards."

"Don't get cocky until we get the heck out of here. You Americans think you're invincible."

We showed the deputy where he should hide and left him to watch and report to Aaron. We decided to sneak away down the side of the hotel when I pointed and whispered for her to be quiet. I saw the door in front of us, open on the side of the building. The door opened to a small platform with stairs coming down to the ground. We ducked up against the concrete platform and hugged its wall praying the thug didn't look down. He stretched and walked over to the side where we were hiding and unzipped his pants. I knew what was coming and pointed my 9mm at him just in case he looked down at us. The thug finished, closed the door, and disappeared.

"Don't you say a word to anyone, or I'll kill you with my bare hands."

"Damn, I would never say anything that would embarrass you. I hope I didn't make you mad, but then I'd rather be pissed off than pissed on."

"Screw you, asshole."

"What's wrong? Did someone rain on your parade?"

She didn't say another word to me the rest of that day.

The trip back to the Armory was uneventful, and Davi stormed off as soon as we entered the gate. I tried to catch her to apologize, but she ignored me and headed to the restroom where we had jury-rigged some showers. I went on to find Aaron and report in on our excursion.

"Zack, where is Davi?"

"She had to run to the restroom to take a shower. Don't worry, she's okay. They were stoned or drunk as before, so there was no one on guard duty. We dropped the cow off and left the deputy in the tree line with the walkie talkie as planned.

●●●●

Aaron and Davi were the brains behind the operation. I watched them coordinate every detail of the attack. As expected, the dirtbags found the cow, butchered it, and quickly built a grill out of some cinder blocks and some fencing. As they prepared to eat brisket, we slowly surrounded them at the hotel and placed some men at the warehouse to take out the thugs staying there to guard their precious liquor. Aaron told the team to be ready to begin the operation when the team at the barbecue started shooting. He wanted as many of the gang outside, in line for beef as possible before the shooting began.

Davi and I had the front of the hotel covered with two SAWs while the Deputy and some of the town's folk had the backside guarded. Aaron and his team would drive the Humvees into the fray when the battle began. Two Humvees would concentrate on the hotel, with one assisting at the warehouse. The sheriff and his men had the warehouse operation. Geena and Sally were about fifty yards behind the hotel on top of a small garage. They had an unobstructed view of the whole area behind the hotel. They both had .308 caliber sniper rifles and shouldn't miss at such a close range.

Three gang members were cooking the meat while two of the biker bitches prepared the side dishes. We counted on the SOB's not feeding their captives until they had their fill. Filthy men and a few more women came running out of the hotel when one of the women beat on the side of a pan.

"Davi, I count forty-five men and six women. Let's roll."

Davi raised her SAW, and I followed suit as she began strafing the crowd. Even the sound of these terrible weapons couldn't drown out the screams of the dying bastards. Five more came out of the hotel shooting and were dead before they hit the ground. We stayed behind our logs until nothing moved. Then we heard shots from behind the hotel and from the direction of the warehouse.

"Damn those things are loud! Get ready for the rats jumping ship!" yelled Sally as they heard the SAWs firing from the front of the hotel.

"Look, there's one coming from the left and another in the middle. I'll take the one in the middle."

Geena placed the crosshairs on the man and slowly squeezed the trigger as she'd been taught by Aaron. The rifle bucked, and the thug fell dead. Another shot and the one in the middle fell dead. Several more broke out windows and tried to escape, but the ladies picked them off one at a time when they ran across the lawn. Then suddenly the game changed. A woman who was dressed as a biker bitch was holding a shotgun to another woman's head as they came out the back door. Sally watched in horror as the biker bitch used the hostage to getaway. They got within fifty feet of the garage when suddenly Geena's rifle barked, and the hostage's head exploded, and both fell to the ground.

"Sally, don't shoot! The one dressed as a biker is the real hostage."

"How the heck do you know that? You killed the hostage!"

The living woman was screaming on the ground with her hands behind her head. It was several minutes before they decided the coast was clear and safe to go to the woman.

"Lady, you can get up now. You're safe," Geena exclaimed.

Sally kept her rifle aimed at the woman and said, "Geena, how do you know this woman is the hostage?"

"Look at her wrists. See the bruises? Look at the biker bitch. Nice clothes, but tattoos all over her arms and neck. Easy decision."

The lady stopped crying long enough to say, "Are they all dead? My kids are in the hotel. I need to make sure they're okay."

"Sorry, but no one goes in until our leader says so. Hold on until they sweep the hotel for gang members."

Every thug was dead or dying, so Davi ordered us to carefully search the hotel room by room. We laid our SAWs down and shouldered our M4s and began searching the hotel. Thank God, the SOBs were all dead, but we did find over thirty women and female children who had suffered the worst kind of abuse at the hands of this scum. I brought several children out the front door as Geena and Sally brought the captive woman around the corner. When she saw her two girls, she ran towards them and collided in the grass, hugging and kissing each other.

"Well, Geena, I guess you were right about who the hostage was."

"I was scared that I'd made the wrong decision. Thank God I shot the right person."

We shuttled the hostages back to the Armory and let the team feed them and treat their wounds from the constant abuse at the hands of the biker scum. The mayor and sheriff thanked us again and asked us to stay and make a home with them. Aaron and I both told them that we'd be moving on in a day or so.

The mayor said, "Please let us throw a dinner in your honor and help resupply you for your journey home. Your training of our people and clearing out that gang ensured our survival. We owe you guys our lives."

"Thanks, but it was the right thing to do, and besides, we're now resupplied and have greatly increased our firepower thanks to your Armory."

"Aaron, we have a couple of men who want to get back to their hometowns south of here in Kentucky. Could they travel with you?"

"As long as you vouch for them, they're welcome."

"They're both good young men. One taught at the community college, and the other is a deputy for our sheriff."

"Great, they can ride along and drop off when they get close to their hometowns. Where are they from?"

"One is from Anderson, and the other is from Buckville, both in Kentucky."

"I saw Anderson on the map, but I have no clue where Buckville is located. I'll check with Zack. He is from Kentucky."

○

Chapter 16   The Flock Grows

Owensville, Kentucky

The days had been uneventful, but Mike knew trouble was always just around the bend as people left the large cities scavenging for food. A couple of rough-looking groups had wandered by begging for food, and he'd turned them away. They were dirty and mean looking. He told them they were barely getting by themselves and had no food to spare. He did give them a couple packets of seeds to plant when they got to where they were heading. Mike was holding an M&P15 and stayed several paces from them. They cursed him as they passed on down the road. Keeping a guard on duty twenty-four/seven was paying off even though they were a mile off the main road. Eventually, these people would kill to find food. Mike knew that they needed several more people who could shoot, fight if needed, and help with the backbreaking farm work. They needed to be selective but needed to expand their little community.

Mike called a meeting to fill the others in on the need to add some members to their group.

Paul quickly spoke up and said, "Does this mean we can stay?"

"Of course you can, if your mom wants to."

For the first time since they had picked this family up off the side of the road, Ally spoke up, "I want to thank all of you for taking care of my kids and me, but we don't want to be a bother to you folks."

Mike replied, "Ally, y'all aren't any trouble, and in fact, Paul has been a big help around the farm. You and your daughter have helped in the kitchen, and once you're trained, I expect you can help with other chores and guard duty. We need you if you want to stay."

"Thanks. I don't know if we would've survived back at our place. We might want to run over there and bring back my husband's beehives and some of his equipment. He also has everything needed to brew beer."

"Do you know how to brew beer?"

"Yes. After years of helping him, I got quite good at it. We can bring back our beer supply also."

Mike looked at the ceiling and said, "Thank you, God, for small things like beer."

Joan kicked him under the table and got the meeting back on track.

"Ally, can you and Paul take me to your place tomorrow so we can gather your supplies and the beehives to bring them back here? Hell, how do you transport beehives?"

"We'd be glad to, and we have done this many times. My husband rented out hives to help farmers pollinate their fruit trees."

"How many do you have?"

"Several hundred. We also sold honey and honeycomb. I know we can't bring them all, but a dozen would really help with stretching our food supply and give the kids something sweet."

"I'm in. Now, back to why we're meeting. Does anybody know anyone close by who would be a good fit for our group? We need more bodies for guard duty and farming. Several farmers in the area are gearing up to help feed the local population, but we need workers and guards to stop the scum from killing us and taking away our food."

Ally spoke up, "There's a family just down the road from us who are good Christian hard-working people. John and Greta have two sons about Paul's age, who are great kids."

"Great, let's look them up when we go tomorrow."

Joan said, "I know several families on the outskirts of Anderson, but they're probably trying to get their farms geared up also."

"Okay, thanks for the input. I'll check with some of the neighboring farms to see if they know some good people who could join us here. Callie, would you like to go with me? I'm going to check out any stalled trucks on the road and drop by several farms to see if they know anyone who might want to join us. Joan, stay on high alert while Paul continues to plow. Keep your guns handy. We'll be back before dark."

Callie cleaned the broken glass from the interior of the pickup while Mike removed the rest of the window that had been shot out on their trip over from Anderson. Mike found two motorcycle helmets with face shields in the barn, gave one to Callie, and put one on himself.

"These will be our windshield until something better comes along.

"We'll look like dorks driving along in a truck with helmets on."

"But we won't lose an eye when a big fat bee hits us in the face."

Callie slipped the helmet over her head, and they checked their weapons.

"Make sure your rifle and pistol are loaded and in the safe position. I have my BOB, and you have yours, so we're ready. Let's make like a turd and hit the dusty trail."

"Uncle Mike, where do you get those corny sayings?"

"I'm a corny guy."

They turned east on Highway 54, heading towards Dale at a decent pace, only having to dodge the occasional stalled car or truck. They had traveled a couple of miles when up ahead they saw several men gathered around the back of a stalled trailer. The men were loading boxes onto a pickup.

"Callie, I know one of those men. He's a friend. Let's see what's going on."

He drove on towards them, waving as he pulled closer. One of the men raised a shotgun and held it waist-high until Mike remembered to remove his helmet.

"Damn, Mike. Can't you get anyone to fix that windshield? I didn't recognize you at first. We've had a couple of hard cases try to rob us over this trailer full of groceries. The last two are rotting in that ditch over there."

"Glad we found you. I was heading to your place and a couple of other farms to see if you knew anyone who could come live with us and help out around the farm. Someone we could trust."

"We're all in the same boat. This farming done like in the 1800s is backbreaking. We need to get more tractors running and get more help. We'll need a lot of help when it comes time to bring in the crops. Plowing is one thing an old tractor can do, but none of the older harvesters survived the scrap yards."

"Have you seen many strangers around?"

"Yes, several groups have wandered through the past few days, and we sent them on their way. Both groups were hard looking people."

"The same ones came by our place. I'm afraid this will get worse before it gets better. Hey, do you know any Stones over past Dale?"

"There are several families named Stone over that way."

"What about Ally and Marty Stone?"

"Great people. They belong to our church. How do you know them?"

"Marty got killed outside of Anderson. I picked Ally and the kids up and brought them back to the farm with me."

"Damn the bad luck. Hey, Marty raised bees. Do you think Ally would trade a few hives or honey?

"I know she'll. In fact, we're heading over there to bring some hives back to Zack's place in the morning. Why don't you follow us over and bring some hives back? We can work out a trade later."

"Sounds great, of course, we'll share this food with you, but could you deliver a couple of loads to my farm and one to Sam's in trade?"

"I'll be glad to help. Come on, Callie, let's help load the truck up. Hey, are you guarding the trailer? There are about thirty more pickup loads in there."

"We haven't been, but I see your point. Anyone could drive or walk by and lay claim to our stuff."

"I'll deliver the three loads and then bring Zack's horse trailer over and help unload as much today as possible."

They delivered the first two loads and went on to deliver the last load to Sam. He was an older man whose son and family lived with him. Mike knew of Sam and his sons Ben and Greg but didn't personally know them. We drove up and were met with shotguns peering out from the barn and house.

"Hello, I'm Mike. Your neighbor Bob said you could use some supplies."

Sam looked in the back of the truck and laid the shotgun down.

"Sorry, but can't be too careful these days. Hey, aren't you Mike Norman? You ran around with Zack and your sister Joan."

"Mister Hager, now I remember you. You ran us out of your watermelon patch."

"Several times. Why didn't you just ask for a melon?"

"We were kids, and there was watermelon."

"We really thank you for the food."

Mike helped them unload the food into the house and couldn't help but notice that they only had a small garden.

"Sam, do y'all need help with planting a larger garden?"

"No, son, I guess we'll have to move on and find a place to farm. I only have a couple of acres, and they're very sandy."

"Would you consider moving over to Zack's farm? We need help with farming and pulling guard duty. We'll need to work on housing, but we figure that the scum in the cities will be heading our way sooner than later, and a few more farmers with guns couldn't hurt. Zack is on his way back from Oregon and should be here any day. That'll take us to nine people, but only three men. We'd love to have you and your family join us."

Sam looked over at his son, and they talked for a minute, and Sam replied, "We'd like that very much. We could use your truck to pull my travel trailer over to live in while we sort out living arrangements."

"Great, just let me know when to come back."

"We'll be ready in three days. How about 8:00 a.m.?"

"We'll be here at eight sharp in three days."

They had a busy day making five more trips with the full horse trailer, delivering supplies to several neighbors, and one large load back to the farm. Joan held supper for them as they all pitched in and unloaded the trailer. There were many different types of canned vegetables, soups, juices, and meat, plus twenty cases of Spam alone. Mike and Callie loved Spam.

They cleaned up for supper, and the group ate while Mike and Callie told them about their busy day.

Mike had finished telling everyone about meeting their neighbors and delivering the food when Callie burst out with, "We have another family moving in with us!"

Before anyone could react, the walkie-talkie squawked.

"Damn, someone's approaching the farm. Man your posts while I go to the crow's nest to see what Lynn is worried about."

Mike stayed in the shadows as he skulked over to the barn and climbed up to the crow's nest. He saw Lynn and signaled her to make sure that she didn't get spooked and shoot him.

Lynn pointed out to the horizon and said, "It looks like three people. Maybe two adults and a kid. They're walking in the open and don't appear to have any long guns. Here, take the night vision goggles and take a look for yourself."

Mike placed the goggles on and came to the same conclusion as Lynn. He knew that he didn't want intruders close to the house, so he left Lynn and went back into the house to get Callie and Joan to back him up while he ran these people away. They grabbed their weapons from the rack by the front door and slid out the back door. Mike's plan was to circle around the fruit trees on the left of the house and come up behind them. The three intruders were halfway down the driveway when Mike called out.

"Who are you, and what's your business here?"

Mike could see that there were two women and a young boy in the driveway. The larger woman had a pistol in her hand.

One of the women replied, "I'm Callie's friend. We're here to see her and Zack."

Callie replied, "Carrie, is that you?"

"Yes, we need help."

"Tell your mom to drop that pistol, and we'll come on up to you."

The woman laid the pistol on the ground and held her hands into the air. Mike turned his flashlight on and aimed it at the intruders. A woman, a teen girl, and a young boy stared back at him. They looked like they had run through a briar patch and were filthy.

Callie and Carrie hugged for a few minutes, and then Callie introduced her friend and family to everyone.

Mike said, "Come on up to the house. Y'all look like you could use a hot bath, some food and a change of clothes."

Carrie's mom spoke up and said, "Mike, we've had a hard time getting here. There are bad people in Anderson and on the way here. They'll be coming this way."

"Ma'am, we know, and we're getting prepared for them. Now let's get you up to the house."

Joan and Callie tended to the family while the others settled back into their regular routine. Mike joined Lynn in the crow's nest and filled her in on their visitors.

"Callie and Joan know the family, and they want us to ask them to join our community."

"But, you're not sold on adding them?"

"Oh, I know they need us, but do we need them?

"I was thinking the same thing. It's three more mouths to feed without much muscle to help with the farming. Besides, have you noticed you now have six women and one man in this community? I personally don't like the odds of finding a husband, and fights will start in months if not weeks."

"I have the same train of thought, but more on the lines of creeps trying to take our women. I say we take these in but need to start being more selective."

"You need to have a meeting and lay down the rules to everyone. Everyone works and pulls their weight, or we don't need them. Yes, women have to plow and work in the fields."

"I agree. We'll let them settle in tomorrow and then have the meeting the day after tomorrow. I'm going on to bed. Goodnight."

"Don't let the bedbugs bite."

★

Chapter 17   So Close Yet So Far

Southern Indiana

We fueled up the Humvees the day before leaving and found an enclosed trailer to haul all our extra gear. This allowed one of the Humvees to quickly maneuver if attacked. The lead Humvee had the twin SAWs, and the second pulled the trailer. Sharon was much better and rode in the lead vehicle with her husband, daughter, and the man from Anderson. His name was Grant Hughes, and he had moved to Vincennes right after grad school to teach biology at the local junior college. Geena, Sally, and the guy from Buckville rode in my Humvee. His name was Roger Dame, and he had just moved away from home a year ago. Both of these men were keen to get home and check on their families. I told both we would give them a ride to their towns. Both brought weapons, ammo, and enough food to last them several weeks after they got home.

Leaving was bittersweet because we had made so many friends, and they now had a safe place to live while we were heading into the unknown. Only knowing that Callie could be in danger spurred me to get on the road again. I had to make sure my baby girl was safe and sound.

I had tried to contact Mike every night for over a week, but I hadn't heard anything back from him since TSHTF. I thought since we were so close to home, I'd try again. I reached a ham radio operator who went by the call sign "VWPACKRAT" and asked him to pass a message on to Mike321 that said we would be home in a few days. I thanked him and prayed for a return answer. None came that day.

We said our goodbyes, loaded up, and headed down Highway 41 towards Murphy. I had talked Aaron into crossing the Ohio River at Owensville to avoid Murphy and Anderson. Crossing there would've meant traveling through the middle of both cities where one could cross east of Owensville and go around the city. We would go to my farm and rest before I took the men home, and Aaron and his family headed on south. I wanted to invite them to all stay at my farm, but I had no idea what to expect when we arrived.

Just before we arrived at the Highway 64 junction, Aaron pulled off into a truck stop to try to refuel. We only saw a handful of old cars and trucks moving around, but there were ATVs of all types darting up and down the road. As had happened several times that morning, people thought we were with the Army and tried to get us to stop and help them.

Aaron waved the people off and said, "We're not with the government, and sorry, we can't help you."

A man walked up who was wearing a sheriff's badge and replied, "Sir, you've got these people wrong. We don't need help. They wanted to see if you needed help. We're doing very well considering the circumstances."

"Sorry for the misunderstanding. My family is heading south of Nashville, and the others are going just east of Owensville."

I spoke up and asked, "What can you tell us about Anderson and Owensville?"

"Son, the north end of Anderson is a lawless place, along with all of the south side of Murphy. Owensville appears to be in good shape. They have kept the gangs out so far. We're working with the north end of Murphy to push the gangs out of the area.

The gangs barricade the bridge, and we have the gangs pinned down below Washington Street."

"Thanks for the information. My daughter was in Anderson, but I'm sure her uncle took her to my farm east of Owensville."

"The gangs are capturing women and girls to use for themselves or sell to the highest bidder. Hell, we strung up a guy yesterday for buying a fourteen-year-old for sex. Good luck."

"Are the roads safe between here and the Owensville bridges?"

"I can't guarantee anything, but it's been calm over that way. The Owensville folks are doing a great job of keeping the scum from the big northern cities out. They've had a few battles but won all of them. Watch out for people wandering in from the north. People are starving in Indianapolis, Louisville, and all the major cities. We're getting prepared to run them off or shoot them."

"Is there any fuel here? And how did you get all of these ATVs running?"

"You can have all of the diesel you can carry. We have a bunch of old gas burners running, but only a few diesel farm tractors so far. Now, you'll have to trade for the fuel. Nothing's free or cheap these days. The ATVs were in overseas shipping containers to be delivered to several local ATV shops. I talked the owner into trading them to us. He also had a ton of spare parts in the trailers, so we were able to get some older ones running."

"Thanks."

The owner of the gas station was listening in and said, "I'll trade you the fuel if you take my nephew over to Owensville. He was up here when the lights went out and wants to get back to Pineville."

"That's a deal. Tell him to get his things, food, water, and his gun. We'll leave as soon as we stretch our legs and fuel up."

The owner showed me how to use the hand pump and then went on to get his nephew ready to travel. It was only twenty minutes before the owner came back with his nephew, all ready to travel. He had a backpack and a 12 gauge pump shotgun and was dressed in a t-shirt and shorts with hiking boots. We introduced ourselves and headed out on the road again. I had Roger sit between the new guy and Sally so she would feel comfortable. It turned out the new guy was friendly and very talkative. Sally and Roger's ears were worn out in only a few miles. Before too long, we went past Rockport and saw the bridge across the Ohio.

●●●●

Mike was skinning a deer he'd killed early that morning when they saw the Humvee and the older truck come down the drive towards the house. He called the others on the radio and warned them of the arrival.

"Keep your guns trained on these guys. I don't recognize them, and this could be trouble. I'm going over to meet them."

Mike walked out to the middle of the driveway with Lynn at his side. Both had M&P15s ready for action. Joan was in the crow's nest, with Callie and Ally hiding behind some hay bales. All were ready for a fight.

"Stop right here. Who are you, and what do you want?"

"Hello, we're lucky we found you. The starving people around here will be glad also."

"Why will they be glad you found me?"

"I'm the Kentucky FEMA representative for this area, and the government has asked me to develop a list of our resources and to assist in distributing them to disaster victims. You can put those guns down now. You're making my guards nervous, and we don't need any problems. Don't worry, we're not here to take all of your crops, only enough from each farmer to help the disaster victims."

Mike looked the man over from head to toe, and the man didn't fit the part of a Kentucky FEMA agent, and the Humvee had seen better days.

"I don't like being nervous either. That's why there are over twenty rifles aimed at you and your nervous men right now. What you need to do is go on into Owensville and get the sheriff of

154

Daviess County to come back here with you and explain why I should give you a damn thing. For all, I know you're a bunch of criminals trying to rip us off."

"Men, stay calm. Sonny, I'll be back, and I'll bring what I need to convince you that you'll be sharing your food with the rest of the state."

"Sir, don't come back without the sheriff, or you won't like the reception you get."

He got back into the Humvee, sped off, and was soon out of sight.

"Lynn, come with me. I'm going to run over to a couple of the other farms and see if this asshole has tried to shake them down. Joan, keep an eye out in case these thugs return."

Several farmers told him that they'd also run the FEMA man off at gunpoint. Sam told Mike that he'd said the FEMA guy to come back next week, and they would have several trucks loaded up to help their unfortunate fellow Kentuckians.

"But, Sam, you don't have any crops, and you're moving to our place tomorrow."

"That's right, and that government bastard can have any crops he can find on that patch of sand and rock. The dumbass saw our small garden in front of the house and thought that we were big-time farmers. Asshole."

"Perhaps you should come over and spend the night with us, in case those men come back."

"No, we're packing up and want to be ready in the morning to move."

"Okay, see you after breakfast."

Mike and Lynn got in the truck and headed back to the farm.

••••

Taking back roads took more time than planned, so we pulled over and made camp for the night before approaching the bridge. I noticed Roger was showing a lot of attention to Sally when Geena came up to me and sat down.

"That Roger has been bird-dogging Sally ever since we parked for the night."

"She doesn't seem to mind the extra attention, and thank God she's backed off chasing me."

"You're already spoken for, buddy."

"Look, Geena, all kidding aside. I like you and would normally want to date you, but you know what's most important to me right now."

"Yes, I know. You tell me every five minutes. Look, Zack, I do like you, but this attraction has a lot to do with survival. A single girl doesn't stand a chance."

I said, "I will help you learn more about surviving regardless of how our relationship works out."

Geena huffed. "Perhaps I need to check out Grant," Geena said as she stormed off.

I slept well that night with Geena only a foot away as though she was still guarding me from Sally. We had a quick breakfast and were on the road again.

"Look, there's a roadblock just before the bridge. I think it'll be safe. They're flying the Kentucky and US flags."

"We still use caution until we know for sure."

Aaron drove up to a safe distance from the roadblock, dismounted, and walked up to greet the several people manning it. He stayed out of the kill zone so Davi could open up on them with the twin SAWs if necessary.

"Hello, we need to pass on through to Owensville."

"Who are you and what business do you have down here? Where did you get those vehicles?"

I recognized one of the men at the checkpoint and yelled at Aaron. I jumped out and walked up to shake hands with one of my old high school buddies.

"Hey, Frank. How are you and your family?"

"Zack, we thought you were dead somewhere between here and Oregon."

"Nope, I'm still alive, and this is my friend Aaron. We were given these Humvees by the Citizens of Vincennes. Aaron and his family have been helping us get back home. I brought a few people with me to live on my farm."

"Boy, it's going to be crowded over there. Mike has got quite the harem over there, I'm told."

"Damn, that sounds just like my buddy Mike. Will we have any problems getting there?"

"No, but stay on the lookout for outsiders wanting to steal food. We have a report of a gang posing as FEMA reps, trying to take over farms east of here."

"We'll check back in with you after we get rested. It's been a long hard trip."

"Hey, you'd better guard those Humvees. Every crook and law enforcement agency around is going to try to take them from you."

Aaron spoke up, "These are only passing through before I take them to the government down in Nashville."

The drive to my farm was usually about twenty minutes from the river before TSHTF; it took us thirty-five minutes that morning. I was so excited, I was nervous. Happy, but cautious since I wasn't sure that Callie was safe. We turned on the last road that ran across the front of my property and were in front of the farm when a bullet struck the front Humvee.

•••

Mike got up early to check out both trucks and air up the tires in the two trailers. He wanted to make one trip today and then go back later for the camper and anything Sam couldn't live without. He was worried the fake FEMA guy would show back up with a larger group.

157

"Lynn, hurry up and wash your face. I'm ready to go. She came running out the kitchen door with a half-eaten ham and cheese burrito and her rifle banging her side as she ran.

"Damn, even I have to eat every now and then."

"Follow closely, but be ready to haul ass if we run into any of those ass bags."

Mike drove off with Lynn on his tail. They didn't see anyone on the way over to Sam's place, and as they drove up to the front of the house, they could see something was wrong. Instead of being greeted, no one was in sight, and the family's belongings were strewn across the porch and front yard. Mike got out and dropped behind his truck, and Lynn joined him.

Mike called out, "Anybody home?"

"Mike, is that you?"

"Yes, we're coming in. What happened?"

As they went through the front door, Mike noticed the broken windows and bullet holes in the door.

"Those FEMA guys caught us napping. They broke through the door and started shooting. I killed one, and my son, Greg, killed those two, but the bastards shot me and killed my grandson. Everyone else is all right."

Mike looked around the room and saw the three dead men and a small body with a sheet over it on the couch.

"How many got away?"

"None. We killed them all. Greg hid the Humvee in the barn."

"Sam, we have to get back to my place. They might be going there next."

"Load up, let's go. We'll come back and bury Jack later today. Grab your guns."

They all jumped in the trucks with Sam and his son in the Humvee and sped back to the farm. Mike radioed Joan and warned her of the attack. She replied all was calm, and no one had shown up yet. Mike didn't see anyone on the road, and there weren't any vehicles in the drive when they drove up to the house. Mike stopped the truck in the front yard and told Lynn to pull in behind him. He wanted some cover in case these bastards attacked.

Joan treated Sam's wound, and when she finished, he got up, grabbed his shotgun, and asked Mike where his guard station was.

"Sam, now, you've just been wounded. Take it easy and let the rest of us handle these men."

"Sorry, but hell, no! They killed my grandson, and I'm going to shoot as many as I can. I have two boxes of buckshot shells, and I figure I'll kill about two dozen of the bastards myself. You kill as many as you want."

Mike put everyone on guard duty and had Callie stay in the crow's nest. An hour passed without any sightings when he heard a shot, and then Callie called down to him from the crow's nest.

"Uncle Mike, we have visitors. There are two army looking vehicles coming in from the east. I shot at them, and they pulled back into the woods."

"I'll be right there."

Mike scrambled to get up the crow's nest and climbed the ladder in record time.

"Darling, show me where they're."

"There. See, they've stopped in the woods."

"Oh crap. They have machine guns mounted on that front, Hummer. We're screwed. Callie, keep your rifle on them and be prepared to shoot."

Mike called Joan and said, "We have to bug out. FEMA's back, and they brought machine guns. They'll cut us to ribbons. Grab what you can and head for the trucks. We have to leave before they get within range."

Mike climbed down from the crow's nest and ran to the kitchen. As he entered, Lynn called, "Mike, a guy on the radio, wants to talk with you. He says that he's here to save your sorry ass."

Mike keyed the walkie-talkie and said, "Callie, what are the intruders doing now?"

"They're waving at us."

159

Mike took the ham radio mike and said, "Who are you, and what do you want?"

"I want a cold beer and a warm woman."

"Zack! You sumbitch. You scared the crap out of us. Get over here ASAP. We're expecting an attack any minute."

"Glad to see you too, Mikey. Thanks for trying to kill me."

"You know what I mean."

✪

Chapter 18   Home Sweet Home

Davies County, Kentucky

Zack, Callie, Joan, and Mike hugged and cried for a few minutes before remembering to introduce their friends.

I introduced Geena to Callie and said, "Callie, this is Geena. She's my girlfriend, and she'll be living with us at the farm."

Callie hugged Geena and welcomed her to the farm. Joan glared at us and walked away in a huff.

Everyone was starting to share stories when Mike yelled for them to stop and listen.

"Look, I know we need to share stories and get to know each other, but we think there are some people about to attack us or some of the surrounding farms."

Aaron replied, "Fill us in after you repost your guards."

"Oh crap! Callie, take the crow's nest. Lynn the front-drive. Joan watch outback, and Ally, take Paul and watch the other side from the orchard."

I started to protest when I saw Callie pick up the AR and head out the door, but kept my mouth shut. Everyone was growing up fast in this new world.

"Everything was going fairly calm when these fake FEMA people showed up and demanded we share our crops with them so they can distribute the food to disaster victims. They didn't look like government people. They looked more like biker scum that'd cleaned themselves up to fool us. This morning, three of them attacked Sam and his family. They were all killed, but killed one of Sam's grandkids."

Sam filled them in on the details of the attack.

Aaron replied, "Let me see this scruffy Humvee."

They walked over to the pole barn, and Aaron inspected the vehicle.

"Just as I thought, this is a surplus vehicle that the government gave to local police departments, and it's been out of use for quite a while. These men are thugs and criminals. It may even be an organized gang trying to take over the whole area as they have in Anderson and Murphy."

Mike stopped Aaron and had him fill them in on the situation in Anderson and Murphy.

"Ally and her family came from Anderson, and their story supports what you just told us. Hey, Zack. They even say Todd is one of the leaders of that gang.

"Todd? That weak-minded lazy bum? No way."

"Yes, it appears he went crazy and came out of it a vicious gang leader. Zack, he went crazy the day I picked Joan and Callie up. He was trying to strangle Joan and Callie when I arrived."

"And he's still alive?"

"Joan stopped me."

"Damn."

I looked over at Aaron and Davi and asked, "Can y'all stay a few days and help us get rid of these fake FEMA thugs?"

Davi came over, gave Zack a hug, and replied, "Of course, we will. Won't we Pop?"

"Yes, we'll help, but we do have to head further south in a few days. It won't take long after we find their base of operations. I can see another barbecue."

My new friends and I all laughed while the others wondered what a barbecue had to do with this serious threat.

Geena glared at Davi, but knew we needed the extra firepower and knew she had to keep her jealousy to herself.

Aaron got everyone's attention and said, "We need to stop worrying about Anderson and introductions and start acting like a fighting force, or those thugs will be throwing us a barbeque. Team, we need the same operation as before. Davi takes Joan, Zack takes Geena, and Mike takes Sally. Scout out the roads and farms for five miles in all directions. The locals know you and won't shoot first and ask questions later. Try not to be seen by the bad guys and bring back information on the gangs. Zack, you know the area; make assignments. Take the other shortwave radios and give them to your friends and farmers. They can be our outposts. I'll stay here and improve our defenses."

I replied, "We'll give our friends the weapons Sam took from the dead men and some of the Illinois gang's weapons if that's okay with you?"

"Of course. Get moving before they catch us sitting around rotating thumbs."

Aaron wasted no time building up their defenses.

"Who knows how to drive the old tractor with the backhoe?"

Greg, Callie, and Paul raised their hands.

"Greg, I need you to help me. Callie, go get me a can of spray paint from your dad's garage. Paul, gas up the tractor and bring it over here and get ready to dig."

Aaron marked the places to dig with the spray paint and showed Paul the places he wanted the dirt piled.

"Roger and Grant, fetch some shovels and make these piles of dirt into fortifications. We'll place about ten of these around the perimeter of the house, barn, pole barn, and tack room. Lynn, see if any bags can be filled with dirt. Hey, does Zack have any extra building materials?"

"I'll check, I think I saw some sandbags in the barn and I know there's a pile of old barn wood in the back of the barn. I'll get the bags and check on the wood."

Aaron spent the rest of the day directing the team at a furious pace. Ally, Carrie, and Sue kept watching for intruders with Ally in the crow's nest, Sue on top of the house, and Carrie out by the road watching both ways. Her instructions were to radio for help if she saw anyone or any vehicles approaching.

"Callie, does your dad have any strong fishing line and something that will make noise if the line is pulled?"

"Yes he does, Dad's a big fisherman and has gobs of tackle. Do you want monofilament, braided, or maybe some super strong line?"

"Bring all of it."

He showed Callie and Greg's kids how to make warning tripwires and showed Callie how to make some more lethal traps. He told her to mark the traps with reflective tape that faced towards the house. He then warned everyone not to enter the dense woods behind the house because he was going to add several Claymore mines to protect them from an attack from the rear.

They started a little before noon, and by 4:00 p.m., they had built six fortifications around the front of the house stretching from the orchard around the house and pole barn over to the garden. Each one was a large pile of dirt shaped like a big "C" with the mouth facing away from the road. The dirt was dug out from around the "C" and piled along its perimeter, making a wall four to five feet high and five feet thick at its base and two feet thick at the top. They were just perfect to use for cover in a gun battle. With these done, Aaron added two more on the front by the road that guarded them against both directions. While they worked on those, Aaron and Greg hauled sandbags and 4x4s up to the crow's nest to fortify it from attack. Roger and Grant helped finish the crow's nest while they completed the front two fortifications.

164

••••

Davi and Joan drove out to Highway 54 and slowly traveled west until they saw a roadblock before the Owensville city limits. Joan waved, and one of the men manning the roadblock told Davi to move closer.

"Hello Joan, I thought you'd be stuck in Anderson with all that crap over there. Good to see you."

"Chuck, this is my friend, Davi. We're out scouting for some thugs that attacked Sam's place this morning and killed his grandkid."

"Damn, did they come this way?"

"No, Sam and Greg killed all that attacked them, but we think they're part of a larger group posing as FEMA agents."

"Now that rings a bell, we've heard several reports of roving gangs posing as government officials. Glad we set up these roadblocks early in the game. I'll let the sheriff know about the attack on Sam's place. He may be able to spare a few men in a couple of days."

Davi looked at Chuck and said, "The bad guys will all be dead in a couple of days, and you will miss the fun."

She turned, walked to the truck, and waited for Joan.

"Joan, who is this hot looking friend of yours? She might get y'all in trouble talking like that. There are some really mean people out there just wanting to capture pretty young women."

"Zack says she's worth five men in a gunfight. She's some kind of Israeli soldier. Besides, you're married and shouldn't be scoping out other women."

"Got divorced a year ago, and I'm free to look at pretty women."

"Goodbye, before you put your foot further in your mouth."

They left and went back down Highway 54 until they saw a roadblock before the Dale School. They pulled off behind a stand

165

of trees before they were spotted. Davi handed Joan a pair of field glasses, and Joan watched the people manning the roadblock, but didn't recognize any of them.

"Joan, stay here, I'm going to get closer and see if these are part of the FEMA bunch. I'll be back in an hour or two. Stay hidden.

"Davi, I can handle myself."

"Joan, sorry, but I don't know you, and I want you to stay safe for Zack's and Callie's sake. I don't need your help and will actually be safer without you. I have been spying on the enemy for over ten years and have only been shot twice."

Joan shut up and let her slink off into the woods. She was gone for over an hour. Joan saw her coming back through the woods and waved.

"Well, what did you see?"

"The fake FEMA thugs have taken over Dale. There's only a handful, but they have the locals terrorized. Let's get back and report it to Dad."

•••

Mike and Sally checked all of the side roads and farms to the east of Zack's farm. They stopped at several farms and gave arms, ammunition, and a radio to the ones at critical positions that guarded key roads. All of the neighbors were armed but now had some real firepower. They were very thankful, several gave them some canned produce from their farms, and one gave them a ham and five pounds of bacon. They drove up to Ralf Green's farm and noticed there wasn't anyone in sight. All of the farms before had lookouts that'd greeted them when they approached.

"Sally, we need to be careful. Something's not right here. Perhaps it's not a problem, but better safe than sorry. I'll knock on the door. You stay off the porch and back me up."

Mike knocked on the door, and Ralf's wife, Greta, opened the door a few inches and said, "Sorry, Mike, but we're all sick and don't want to pass it on. Tell Zack we appreciate him helping out last week."

"Not a problem and Zack was glad to help you. Are you sure there's nothing we can do to help with this disease?"

"No, but thanks."

"We'll drop back by in a couple of days to check on you and your family."

Mike calmly walked off the porch, waved for Sally to join him, got into the truck, and drove away.

"Sally, don't look back. Someone is holding them hostage. I'm driving out of sight, and then we'll sneak back and see if we can help them."

They drove about a quarter-mile down the road, parked in the woods, and started towards the farm from the backside. They took turns covering each other as they leapfrogged to the barn behind the house. The barn smelled like stale cat piss and gagged Sally. Mike peeked through a gap in the wallboards and saw a man with a wrench working on a large tank on wheels. The punk had a pistol on his hip and a shotgun lying against the tank.

"Sally, these punks are stealing ammonia so they can make meth. I'm going in, follow right behind me. I don't want any noise."

Mike picked up a shovel as he entered and walked up behind the thief, raised the shovel, and brought it down on his head. There was a sickening crunch, and the man fell dead. Mike tightened the connection to stop the loss of ammonia and turned to see Sally puking her breakfast out on the floor.

"Are you okay?"

"I'll be in a minute," she said.

"I thought you've been in several gun battles and killed several men."

"I have, but I've never seen a man's head split wide open, and his brains come flying out."

"Damn, I thought our first date was going along just fine."

Sally attempted a smile. "It is, and I'm looking forward to the second one where we cuddle by the fire and tell each other about ourselves."

"Great, I was going to ask if you and Zack are seeing each other."

"No, I'm afraid that Geena has stolen his heart."

"That's quite a feat. Zack just got over Joan this year and has been scared of women for several years. Enough chit chat, are you recovered? We have to save that family from a bunch of Meth heads."

"I'm good. What's the plan, big boy?"

"The plan is we're going to sneak up to the windows, see how many thugs are in there, and kill them before they kill us. When we know where they're, we'll enter the house with me in the lead and you backing me up. My guess is there are only one or two punks in the house."

They used a kid's playhouse to shield their advance to the backside of the house and slowly peered in each window until Sally waved to Mike.

"There are two of them. One in the living room with five hostages and the other, a young girl, is eating in the kitchen."

Mike took a quick look and saw that both could be shot from the closest window to them.

"Damn, we have to take them both down at the same time."

Sally waved at Mike. "Wait, the girl is only about fourteen. We can't kill her."

"Is she armed?"

"Yes, she has a pistol on her hip."

Mike snorted. "She'll kill you if you get in the way of her getting more meth. I need you to shoot her through the window when you hear me shoot the asshole in the living room. Count to ten when I move to the living room window and be ready to shoot. Can you do this?"

"Yes, I'll. I don't like this new world."

"Sorry, beautiful, but a girl has to put on her big girl panties and shoot the bad guys, even if they're young women these days."

"Thanks for the pep talk, that was sweet, but you still have to buy me dinner before you get to see these big girl panties."

"I hope you like a big steak! Let's roll."

Mike crept over to the living room window and found the punk sitting in a recliner chugging a beer. His shotgun was lying across his lap when Mike squeezed the trigger and placed a bullet through his chest. He heard another shot, followed by another shot, ran to the front door and burst through into the living room.

Sally heard Mike's gun bark but took too long to aim and fire. The bullet caught the girl in the chest as she raised her pistol. The gun fired, glass shattered, and Sally hit the ground.

Mike cut the rope from Ralf's hands and left him the knife to cut the ropes from his family. He rushed into the kitchen and saw the girl lying dead on the floor. He turned to the broken window and could only see Sally's feet. She was down. He ran out of the kitchen door and ran around the side to see Sally lying there face down.

For a second, he thought that she was dead until he heard, "That damned bitch shot me. I'm going to kill her, sorry ass again. Let me at the stringy-haired bitch."

Sally pushed herself off the ground and sat upright. She had several cuts and scrapes on her head and forearms. Blood was streaming down her face from a cut on her head. Mike kneeled down and cleaned the glass from her head and shoulders, then applied pressure to the wound where a bullet grazed her upper left arm, He pulled her against him and kissed her forehead.

"Darling, we have to find a safer place to date. The people here are not hospitable."

"I'd prefer a nice restaurant with wine by a fireplace afterward, but it is what it is. Hey, I forgot. Is the girl dead?"

"Yes, she can't hurt anyone else. You're lucky she had an old .32 caliber pistol without much power."

"Can I shoot her again?"

"If it makes you feel better."

"Damn, I froze for a second, and she tried to kill me. That poor sweet young girl became a killer because of that crappy drug."

Mike picked her up into his arms and carried her into the house where Greta could treat her wounds.

••••

Geena and I cut over to Highway 142, heading to the Ford Parkway. There wasn't an on-ramp there, but a Humvee can pretty much make its own road. We stopped and gave out arms, ammo, and a radio to several neighbors I knew along the way. All were friendly and thankful I had made it home safely.

"Honey, can we make it official and move in together? Your daughter is safe, and you promised to give us a chance when you felt that she was safe."

"I'm falling in love with you, and yes, we can move forward. I want to formally introduce you to Callie before she sees us in bed together."

"Darn, it will be nice to sleep in a bed again."

"You can have my room to yourself for a couple of days until Callie gets to know you."

"What if she doesn't like me?"

"She will don't worry. Hey, that's the Ford overpass. Let's go cross country to the highway."

I steered the vehicle across the shallow ditch and stopped before hitting the fence guarding the highway from deer and other animals. I jumped out to see what I needed to do to get through the barrier. I heard Geena close her door and come up behind me as I started cutting the chain link fence. I was going to tease her about my ex-wife living under the same roof but thought better of it before I opened my mouth. Just as I cut the last strand, all hell broke loose with bullets slamming into the Humvee and the dirt all around me. I looked for Geena and heard her scream. I turned and saw her fall to the ground with a red spot on her chest. I grabbed her up and threw her into the vehicle as I felt a kick in my back and burning pain. The Humvee windows were cracking with bullet marks, and the vehicle was being pounded by gunfire. I turned the wheel as hard as I could and took off fast and steered the vehicle for the farm. I held pressure on the wound as we bumped down the road.

"Geena, talk to me."

"Zack, I love you. Take care of Callie and Sally."

"Damn it. Don't talk that way. We'll get you home and put a Band-Aid on that nick, and you'll be good as new."

••••

Mike and Sally drove back to the farm with Sally's head on Mike's shoulder the whole way. She kept the pressure on her wound as Mike drove.

"Mike, will it always be this way in our new world? People killing over drugs and food? I thought people would pull together in times of a crisis."

"Sorry, Sally, but we have a class of people in the country that have been living off welfare for generations and a drug culture with millions of addicts. Most of them will either die off on their own or get shot trying to kill innocent people."

They arrived at the farm ahead of Davi and Joan, and both filled the rest in on their adventures while Joan and Ally tended to Sally's wounds.

Sally told them, "So far, I've had bullets bouncing off my arm and my legs, and I'm lucky to be alive. I don't like being a soldier. I like malls and flirting with men. Damn this post-apocalyptic America."

She had finished talking when they heard a vehicle honking and saw a Humvee blasting up the driveway.

"That's Zack and Geena coming back. This can't be good."

••••

Geena had passed out and didn't respond. I drove as fast as I could and made it to the farm in fifteen minutes. I honked the horn as I got close to the house, ran around to the passenger side, and carried Geena into the living room where I placed her on the couch.

"Geena, hold on, baby."

"Joan, please help her."

Joan pushed me away, checked her pulse, and hung her head down.

"Zack, I'm sorry, but it's too late. She was shot beside the heart, and there was no way to save her. I'm so sorry."

"I'm going to kill every freaking one of those bastards! Grab your guns! Let's go!" I yelled before I passed out.

I woke up the next day with my shoulder bandaged and held Geena's hand for an hour before we buried her in the little plot with my aunt and uncle. Mike and Roger carried me to the gravesite, where I stayed for hours. I cried like a baby all day long and felt ashamed to be such a baby in front of my daughter.

"Dad, go ahead and cry. I didn't know her, but if you loved her, she must have been a great lady."

I already missed Geena and wondered how many more of us would end up in that graveyard.

✪

Chapter 19   Moving Forward

Daviess County, Kentucky

It's been a while since Geena died, and I'm still recuperating from my shoulder wound. The bullet messed up some tendons and muscle in my left shoulder. Joan is already talking about therapy sessions and helping me get full use of my arm. Callie thinks her mom is trying to get back with me before Sally or Ally claims me.

"Dad, I'd love for Mom and you to get back together, but don't do anything until you finish grieving for Geena. I thought Sally was after Uncle Mike."

"Lynn has caught Mike's attention. Don't worry, darling, I'm not the least bit interested in women at this time."

She giggled and said, "You will be. You're a man, and even I can see how those women flirt with you and Mom's the worst. I saw her sneak down the hall last night into your room."

"Yes, and I sent her away when she tried to crawl into bed with me. I'd be lying if I said I don't like the attention, but I'm focused on getting better and killing the ones responsible for

Geena's death. Give me a couple of weeks, and I'll be as good as new."

"What if they attack before then?"

"Aaron and Davi are staying until I'm back up to full strength, and they've been keeping tabs on those punks. If they attack, we'll kill all of them a little earlier."

My little girl is growing up fast and will see her share of grief and sorrow in the future. I asked Davi to train her and make her into another lady warrior. I want her prepared for a future where she has to be able to defend herself and her family. There are many hard days ahead, but if we train and prepare, we can also begin to have some good times along the way.

"Callie, help your old man get dressed. I'm going to the range and practice killing some bad guys."

The End of New Beginnings

and

The start of Old Enemies.

The Day America Died

Old Enemies

Post-Apocalyptic America: After the EMP

Book 2

A J Newman

✪

Acknowledgments

This book is dedicated to my many friends who think I am bat crap crazy for believing the Apocalypse is due any day now. The Apocalypse is coming. Will it be the result of a solar flare, EMP blast, or a failed economy? That's the only question, but it is on the way. This series portrays the lives of regular Americans and how they deal with the issues. I am a prepper and will be prepared. Will you?

Thanks to my wife, who keeps after me to write more books to pay for my prepping, guns, and golf.

Thanks to James Newman and Bob Lovett for beta reading my work.

Thanks to Sabrina Jean at Fasttrackediting for proofreading and editing this novel.

PS - This is not a how-to book, but you might learn a thing or two about surviving if you pay attention.

A J Newman

Copyright © 2020 Anthony J Newman. All rights reserved.

This book is a work of fiction. All events, names, characters, and places are the product of the author's imagination or are used as a fictitious event. That means I thought up this whole book from my imagination, and nothing in it is true.

All rights reserved. None of this publication may be copied or reproduced without prior written permission from the publisher.

As they say on TV, don't try anything you read in this novel. It's all fiction and stuff I made up to entertain you. Buy some survival books if you want to learn how to survive in the apocalypse.

Published by Newalk LLC.

Henderson, Kentucky

Main Character List

-

Davi Gold – Woman who says she is an ex-Israeli Mossad agent. She's a short raven-haired young lady who's as good with her fists as she is with an assault rifle.

Zack Johnson – Zack is a mid-thirties, tall man with a medium build. He is an electrical engineer, prepper, and car mechanic. Zack has a 15-year-old daughter and ex-wife. Zack is in an emotional crisis due to his wife leaving him. He is the hero of this story.

Callie Johnson - Zack's daughter who lives in Anderson, KY, with her mom. A smart and sassy young lady.

Mike Norman – Mike's thirty-six years old with brown hair and green eyes. He's built like a short fullback at 5'8" and 225 pounds of muscle. He is Joan's brother and Zack's best friend. Like Zack, he is a prepper, an auto mechanic, and an outdoorsman.

Ally Stone -Woman rescued by Mike when the SHTF. Has two kids, Paul and Susie.

Joan Johnson – Zack's ex-wife, a slim beauty, but is a bossy woman who lives in Anderson, KY, where she is a restaurant manager.

Sally Green – Geena's best friend and was also headed home when Zack saves her from the bad guys.

Aaron Gold – Davi's father and an ex- Israeli military pilot. Retired and has a large farm south of Presotum, Ill.

Sharon Gold – Davi's mother and a Professor of Chemistry at the University of Illinois.

Lynn Drake - Ex-girlfriend of Mike's. She still loves him.

Chuck Taylor - Sheriff's Deputy. Knows Zack and his team. Becomes Joan's boyfriend.

Todd – The main villain. A social worker who goes berserk to become the leader of a gang that takes over Anderson, Kentucky. Never gets a last name.

Alan Prescott – Owner of a company that hires out mercenaries and high-risk security guards. Ready for TSHTF and uses his men to expand his power.

Geena Denton – Woman who was headed home when Zack saves her from the bad guys. Became Zack's love interest in Book I. She was killed at the end of the book I.

Bert Alford – Daviess County Sheriff. Older man who befriends Zack's group.

✪

Chapter 1 The Farm

Daviess County, Kentucky

I sat on the front porch in my sleeping pants and a t-shirt when Aaron walked by, waved at me, and then walked to the barn without saying anything to me. It was only 9:00 am, and I already had three empty beer bottles lying beside my chair. The mead was some good shit, and Ally was my hero. You have to appreciate a woman who could brew ale when the end of the world as we know it happens. I love beer. Hell, it's 5 o'clock somewhere as the song goes. I dozed off for a minute but quickly woke back up when my mind was flooded with pictures of Geena lying dead on the kitchen table with a bullet in her chest. I shuddered, picked up an empty bottle, and tried to get a drink. I just couldn't shake off these thoughts of her being dead while I was still alive. Damn, I have to go to the barn and get more ale.

The world ended a few months back when the grid shut down, along with all electronics and vehicles that depended on electronics. I was vacationing in Oregon when TSHTF and had to get back to Kentucky to find and protect my daughter. I walked for many miles before I borrowed a tractor and drove it for hundreds of miles until we hooked up with Aaron and his family, who had a couple of EMP-proof jeeps. Did I mention I helped save several people and rescued two beautiful women along the way? They

178

both flirted with me for weeks before I fell in love with Geena but had to focus on getting home to my daughter. Just as things were settling down, she became mine and was killed a couple of days later. I haven't been worth a shit since.

Aaron looked at Davi and his wife Sharon for a few minutes before he spoke up, "I know you like these people, but remember, we're going on down to Alabama. The roads are more dangerous than ever and get worse as people get more desperate. I promised to stay here until Zack recovered, and he has had two months to heal his physical and mental wounds. All he does is sit on the porch drinking ale and thinking about Geena. Well, Geena is dead, and he needs to get off his ass and start being a father to Callie and a leader to these people who look up to him for leadership."

"Dad, I know, but Zack just lost the woman he loves and needs time to heal. He's a strong man and will recover in due time. How many civilians could travel thousands of miles by foot and farm tractor to get home while rescuing people and fighting off killers and rapists?"

"Honey, our girl is right. Zack is fragile and needs time to heal."

"Remember, the whole trip down here, he droned on and on about finding his daughter and protecting her. Well, the world has turned upside down, and if Zack takes much more time, those looters will overrun this farm, kill him and his friends, and take these women as sex slaves. Callie could end up being a biker's bitch. He needs to stop drinking, get off his ass, and man up. These people look up to him, and he's the only one who can pull them together."

"Dad, most of what you say is true, except Joan, Lynn, Ally, Sally, and Callie have done very well in their training. I would put them up against any man in this area and most soldiers. They're definitely not Special Forces level, but they shoot, fight, and can kill as well as most of our soldiers. They're untested, but I believe they have the will to survive."

"I certainly hope so."

I was heading to the barn to get a couple of bottles of Ally's homemade mead ale when I heard Aaron and his family talking around the corner. Damn, I listened to every bit of what was said and got angry with Aaron and the world in general. I respected Aaron, but what right did he have talking that way about me? I loved Geena and barely knew her when those looters shot her dead and wounded me. Then I heard them go on about how I'd to man up and quit drinking my life away. That hurt, but they were right. I looked down at my arm in the sling, removed it, flexed my hand, and walked right in the middle of their conversation.

"Hey, I heard what you were saying, and truthfully, it pissed me off at first."

I waved Aaron off and continued, "I know you're right. I've been a big baby and tried to find comfort at the bottom of the ale bottle. Well, I'm back, and I need your help for a few days to help finish training us before you head south. I want to raid those looters before they raid us."

Their jaws dropped, they were speechless, and then Davi hugged me and said, "Welcome back."

"Davi, would you call everybody together in half an hour? I need to put some clothes on and bathe before I start leading this group."

I caught my best friend, Mike Norman, and thanked him for helping pack my sorry ass for the last month.

"Zack, it's what true friends do. I'm glad you're back to yourself, but there's nothing wrong with the grieving process. It helps you heal."

"Thanks is all I can say."

"I need to fill you in on some changes and additions to our group. We need to decide how big this group is going to get and who makes the decisions."

"Oh shit!"

"*Oh shit* is not here, but it's just around the corner if we don't lay down the law quickly."

"Let's meet after the planning session."

"What planning session?"

"The one we have today."

"Boy, you don't waste time getting back in the saddle."

I quickly shaved for the first time in a week, got dressed in my favorite fire hose pants and a black t-shirt. I strapped on my 1911 Colt .45, stuck my Ruger LCP .380 in my pocket, and checked my belt to ensure I still had four extra mags for the .45 and two for the .380. As I'd requested, everyone but Roger, who was in the crow's nest, was assembled around the front porch. I walked out of the house and smiled at everyone.

"Hello, I'm Zack Johnson, and I'm back among the living. I'm not finished grieving over Geena, but these times suck, and it's time I suck it up and get my ass back in gear."

Mike and Joan started applauding while Callie ran up and hugged me.

I went on addressing the group, "I thank all of you for packing my sorry ass for several months, but I'm back at full strength, and I want payback. Those assholes are going to pay for raiding our farms and killing our people. Aaron, Mike, Lynn, Roger, Joan, and Davi, please come to the kitchen after lunch to bring me up to speed. Now, everybody gets back to work. I've slacked off enough for all of you."

***

The next day the Daviess County Sheriff sent several deputies out to the farms east of Owensville to see if they could band together and help fight the gang of looters working their way to Owensville. The sheriff also told them to check out the farms to see how much food could be counted to help feed their citizens. While I'd been recuperating, Owensville had finally run out of food. Most US cities had run out in the first few days. Still, Owensville was a farming and food processing community, so granaries and large warehouses were stocked with food. Now people were starving, and riots broke out when there was no food to hand out. Many rioters had to be shot to stop the looting and theft from the few who had been prepared for a disaster. The new mayor was counting on the local farms to save her city.

"Frank, take Chuck with you and head out to Zack Johnson's place. We need him to step up and organize the farmers on that end of the county to fight off these looters before they get to town. I'll go over to Hal Burch's place to see if he can get the farmers to share their crops with the city. I don't want to take the food at gunpoint, but we can't let these people die of starvation."

Chuck spoke up, "If we take it this year, they won't plant more than enough to feed themselves next year. This has to be a fair arrangement. What can we do to help them and to make it easy for them to grow more crops?"

"Good questions; I'll work on them. Now go see Zack and the others."

"I don't think he's recovered from the attack that killed his girlfriend and wounded him. I hear he hasn't been worth a shit since the attack."

"What about Mike Norman? I don't know him as well as Zack, but I hear he's a fairly strong guy."

"Yeah, I know Mike and will talk with him as well as Zack."

The deputies drove over to my place in an old, 1950s Chevy truck. Old trucks, cars, tractors, and some ATVs were all anyone could get running since the EMP attack on North America. They stopped at the edge of the farm and got out of the truck. They waved at the guard on top of the barn and then drove down the driveway to the house.

"Zack, you're looking good, and I see your arm is back in service."

"Yep, I've moped around way too long, and I'm ready to kick some ass."

"That's great and exactly why the sheriff sent us over. He wants you to take the lead in eastern Daviess County in our fight against this large group of looters."

"We just put a plan together to wipe them out as soon as we can get a few of the local farmers to join us."

"You said to wipe them out. We don't want a massacre. The sheriff knows some will be killed in the fight but expects you to bring the survivors in to be tried."

Aaron spoke up, "So you want to try them, put them in jail, and have to feed them for ten years?"

"We plan to make them work on local farms to earn their keep. This'll help all of us by allowing us to farm more land."

"And you'll have to have guards to watch over them. Some will escape and kill more people. Tell your sheriff this is not a good idea. Looters must be shot on sight," Aaron said.

I looked Chuck in the eye and said, "We shoot looters on sight and won't bring any captives to you. Oh, there may be some children and prisoners freed, but no looter will be brought back alive."

"Look, Zack, I personally agree with you, but we have a new group running the city, and they don't understand how dangerous it is outside of town. I'll pass this on to the Sheriff. He won't be happy. We can't have vigilantes running around dispensing justice as they see fit."

I replied, "I'm sorry they feel that way. Owensville will be run over by these thugs if you practice what you just preached."

Frank and Chuck continued to update us on the looters. They're based in Ohio County, had raided all of the farms west over to Fordsville and south as far as Hartsville. The Hartsville folks put up a fierce fight and ran the looters away. There were losses on both sides, and the looters didn't know how close they came to taking the city.

They took what they wanted and killed anyone who resisted. They were criminals, thugs, and meth heads who hadn't even thought about growing a garden or what would happen when winter came. They ran out of food, and hardly anyone wanted to take meth in trade for food, ammo, or women.

They had also begun raiding the farms on the west side of Owensville two weeks after they attacked Geena and me by the Natcher Highway just north of Hartsville. They struck a farm two farms east of my farm, killed the owners, and kidnapped their fifteen-year-old daughter. They grew in strength and even set up snipers to harass the team, manning the roadblock on Highway 54 at Thurston Dermont Road.

I shook their hands and said, "Thanks for the update and assure the Sheriff we don't plan to shoot any innocent people, but anyone who's caught looting will be shot immediately."

"We'll pass that on."

***

"Aaron, I know you and your family are in a hurry to get on to Alabama, but could you help me for another two weeks? I need you to train my team some more before you leave."

"We'll stay and help, but they're much further along than you think. While you were looking at the bottom of those ale bottles, Davi and I have been conducting training covering everything from hand-to-hand fighting to constructing IEDs. They aren't ready for the Special Forces yet; however, they can easily defeat any nonmilitary units and hold their own against regular Army soldiers. I hate to say it, but you need to watch your back with the people from Owensville. It looks like some bleeding heart liberals must be taking over. They'll be pissed when you wipe out that gang. They'll try and take your Humvee and those twin SAWs."

The Humvee had two M249 Squad Automatic Weapons mounted in tandem in a turret on top of the vehicle. They could fire several hundred rounds per minute.

"You're right. I wasn't paying attention. Thanks for taking care of us, even though I was absent for the last few months. I agree about the new leaders in Owensville and need to guard against their harming us. They can try to take our weapons, but it would be bad for them."

"I have several gifts and a few surprises for you before we head south. Come into the barn and help me unload the trailer."

I'd forgotten about the trailer we'd towed behind one of the Humvees when we'd left the NG Armory in Indiana. We had loaded it to overflowing with arms and ammunition.

"These KEL-TEC SUB-2000 carbines are from my personal collection. They aren't assault rifles but are very compact when folded and can lay down a large volume of 9mm bullets with good accuracy out to a hundred yards. I have six of them for you and six Glock 17s. They both use the same magazines and 9mm ammunition. I prefer the Glock-17 magazines because they have indicator holes to show how many bullets remain. We liberated over 10,000 rounds of 9mm ammo, and I'm leaving it with you."

"Aaron, I'm speechless. Are you sure you don't need some of it?"

"Don't worry, we just need enough to make it to Alabama and join up with our group there. I have more toys for you, but I'm going to ask you to escort us just north of Nashville in exchange for the toys. This area is fairly safe compared to the unknown between here and Birmingham, and we could use the firepower of the twin SAWs on your Humvee if the shit hits the fan."

"You don't have to bribe us. We would help you just because you and your family are our friends."

"Great, we feel the same way. Now more presents. Here are six - M4s, ten - 9mm Berettas, and two - M4s with grenade launchers. I can spare only five grenades, so use them as a last resort. Grab those cases on the left marked 5.56x45 Ammo 55gr M193 Ball and grab the box behind them. It has five hundred tracers. They'll start a good fire or scare the hell out of some redneck thugs. Now, the last surprise. The metal box on your workbench has six fragmentation grenades. Use them wisely, and don't be near when they explode. These gifts should give you an edge on any known enemy in this area."

"I can't thank you enough. We can defend ourselves and hunt to help get through the first winter until we get a herd of cows and pigs. Thanks."

"We'll try to stay in contact by radio after we see what shape our group is in down there. I'll try to bring you a long-range radio and more supplies if we can spare them. I expect we'll have much more than we need."

After we had stowed the gifts away, we went to the firing range to try out the SUB-2000. I was very impressed with its lightweight and how small it was. I could place it in my bug out bag and keep it with me when I leave the farm. The gun folded in half and fit in my bug out bag along with two - 17 and three - 31 round magazines. I would give a SUB-2000 and a Glock to Joan, Callie, Lynn, Sally, and Mike. The guns were light and didn't have much recoil.

***

I took my small army to the range to give them their weapons and to practice before lunch. Aaron and Davi drove up in my pickup with the KEL-TECs and the Glocks in the bed. They handed one each to the group.

"Each of you'll keep these as your personal weapons. Mike and I'll carry the Glocks and keep the SUB-2000s in our bug out bags. We'll have our bug out bags close by at all times. You'll do the same. I want this group ready to react, fight, and kill anyone who threatens our team. You're our quick reaction squad."

"Dad, are you trying to get months' worth of catching up in one day?"

"Punkin, you're correct. My conversation with the deputies and the attack that killed Geena has me focused on our survival. We need to decide who's on our team, who are friends, and acknowledge anyone, not on our team or a friend as a potential threat."

They all looked at each other and then bobbed their heads in agreement.

"Now, Aaron will give us training on our new weapons."

The training lasted until lunch, and each one left the range proficient in marksmanship and maintenance of their new toys. Everyone liked the idea of the folding rifle that could be stored in their backpacks, and it fired the same 9mm as the Glock. Joan was a little miffed that I'd given our daughter two guns.

"Zack, I know we don't see eye to eye on guns, but don't you think giving a sixteen-year-old two guns to be in her possession every day a bit extreme?"

"No."

186

"Zack, a one-word answer?"

"Joan, the world has changed. Callie is now sixteen and is mature for her age. In the 1800s, she'd be an old married woman with three kids fighting off Indians in the old west. There're killers, perverts, and rapists out there that would love to capture our daughter. I want her to become as good at protecting herself as Davi."

"You just have the hots for the Israeli soldier."

"She's hot, but I don't have the hots for any woman now, and that includes you. You can stop trying to slip into my bed every night."

"Damn, I'd hoped we could get back together for Callie's sake. You know you want me. It's not as if we haven't done it a thousand times. I still love you."

"It's those times you did it with Todd that sticks in my craw. You left me for a whiny assed bastard. That's hard to forget."

"Zack, I made a mistake."

"Yes, you did," I replied and stormed off.

The problem was, I still found Joan attractive and hadn't been with a woman for months. I'd like to keep my mind on my farm and to survive. The new Zack was trying hard.

***

"What do you mean I'm not needed for this meeting? I have a lot to offer and should be included in any planning for our community," said Grant as he glared at me.

"Grant, first, this is not a community. It's my farm, and I say what goes around here. I'll be glad to take advice from those I trust, but this is not a democracy. Besides, you were supposed to head home to Bucksville over a month ago. I'll talk with you later. Now please let us continue our meeting."

"That's not fair. I'm a part of this community."

"Leave now before I lose my temper. Look, this is a meeting with my closest friends to catch me up on anything I've missed. Now leave us alone."

He turned and left the room in a huff.

I got up, closed the door, looked at my friends, and said, "I guess I pissed in his Wheaties. What gives with him?"

Mike spoke up, "That was one of the issues I told you we needed to discuss. Grant has been lobbying for us to begin running the farm as a community. Everyone has a say in all decisions. He has a couple of weak-minded people who are swaying to his side."

"This topic and a few more are why I asked for this meeting. We'll meet about the attack on the gang over in Ohio County tomorrow. The reason I invited y'all to this meeting is I trust you. I haven't known Lynn and Roger long, but Mike and I have learned to trust and respect you. Now, I want to make a few things clear. One, this is my farm, and only Mike and Callie have a right to be here. Two, I make all final decisions. This is not a democracy. Three, I'll take advice, but I still make the final decisions. Four, we must limit who moves to the farm. Outsiders could try to take over if they disagree with the direction I'm taking this group. Five, if you don't like the rules, you're free to leave. There will be more rules, but those are the important ones for now."

Joan hit me on the arm and replied, "So. I don't belong here?"

"Yes, but I don't want you to get too cocky. I'll eventually find a girlfriend and perhaps marry, and I don't want you to harass my new woman."

"I plan to *be* that woman."

"Sorry, but I don't see that happening. Anyone else?"

Aaron replied, "I think you said it well. You have to take charge and do the best you can, but you can't help everyone and give them a place to live. Most people need a helping hand, but you can't support them all."

Roger added, "I'm honored you included me in your circle of trust. I agree with Aaron; we need strong, decisive leadership. I think you'll listen and make the best decisions for your family and the rest of us; however, we can't water down our resources to feed and shelter everyone."

Everyone agreed and asked me to continue.

"I never liked or felt I could trust Grant. I don't know Sam and his group very well, but I trust Mike's judgment. Is there anyone else we need to watch?"

Joan spoke up, "Carrie's mom, Mary, has been close to Grant lately and is asking why the group doesn't have more say in how the farm is managed."

"I think you should ask them to leave. There're plenty of vacant houses around, or they could go to Grant's home in Buckville. I'm heading out to Alabama in a couple of weeks, so I don't have a say in the matter, but that's what I'd do."

I asked about any more malcontents or troublemakers, and no one brought up any others.

I asked, "What about Frank Carpenter and Chuck Taylor? Mike and Joan, you know them better than I do."

Mike answered first, "I like both and trusted them before TSHTF. They're open with me about not liking the direction the new mayor, Alice Bonner, is taking Owensville. They may try to join us."

"I agree with my brother Mike. I trust both, and I've talked quite a bit with Chuck. He would be a good fit for our group."

"The fact that he's been sniffing around you ever since you arrived has nothing to do with his fit, does it?"

"Mike, get your mind out of the gutter."

Lynn spoke up, "Damn, he's been flirting with me a lot also. Not in a bad way."

I broke out laughing and said, "Joan, you need to start flirting back at him. Now seriously, what are you hearing from Owensville? This new mayor's direction is worrying me."

"She's a great person; however, she's a liberal Democrat who thinks the government is the solution to every problem. She doesn't like guns, conservatives, and the police. She's causing big trouble for the police and sheriff. She even proposed that everyone should turn their guns into the police to get crime under control.

About half of the city supports her, but the police and sheriff have rejected this dangerous idea."

I replied, "That would make them an easy target for a gang or a want-to-be dictator to move in and take over. How did she get to be mayor? What happened to Griggs?"

"Heart attack. She was next in line and will be in charge until an election in November next year."

"Joan, please use your feminine charms to get Chuck and Frank out here for a barbeque this weekend. Tell them to bring their girlfriends and kids. I want to see where their heads are at on this new mayor and feel them out on joining us."

Chapter 2 - Lights

The Farm

"Dad, can I have the old exercise bike at the back of the pole barn?"

"What the heck do you want that old thing for? My aunt bought that thing forty years ago, used it a couple of times, and then it went to the barn."

"It's a project Paul and I are doing. We want to be able to exercise during the winter."

"Need anything else?"

"Nope."

"How's your mom doing?"

"You see her every day, don't you know?"

"What I meant is, how is she doing now that she found out what a worm Todd turned out to be?"

"Oops."

"What does oops mean? What do I need to know?"

"Mom's kicking herself in the butt for leaving you for that pervert. He's one sick man."

"What does that mean?"

"Carrie told me Todd has taken over Anderson and has a thing for abusing young girls. His goons tried to capture her, but she outran them."

I thought for a minute before I replied and said, "Anyone can make a mistake. Todd appeared to be a decent sort. He had your mom fooled. I guess I should have been a better husband. I was working out of town a lot back then, and your mom didn't like being home alone."

"She's afraid you think she's a big fool for falling for Todd."

"Callie, I still care for your mom and don't want her hurt, but she hurt me a lot. If Todd had moved in with you, there could have been serious trouble."

"I would've shot him if he tried anything with me."

"I believe that. Now go build your invention."

I saw her go into my shop and take some of my electrical books out to the pole barn, and the light came on in my mind.

I went to the kitchen and found Ally and Joan preparing soup and tuna fish sandwiches for lunch. We have an ample supply of canned goods and can easily make it until the crops were harvested. I was worried about making it until the next harvest the following year if we kept adding people or suffered a crop failure. We had fifteen mouths to feed, and I was planning to add five more if Chuck and Frank's families joined us.

"How are my two favorite chefs this morning? Those sandwiches look awful good."

"Keep your mitts off them until noon. Just because you're our boss doesn't mean you get any favors," replied Joan.

"Ally, I need you to buddy up with Mary to find out if she's on our team. I'm worried she may be up to something bad for us."

"I'll do it, but she's sleeping with Grant, and he's definitely not on our team. He wants to take over and be the big cheese in these parts. If I were you, I'd run both of them out of here today."

"Please go ahead and find out what you can without making her suspicious."

"I'll be glad to."

"Thanks."

I tried to steal a slice of bread, and Joan smacked my hand with a spoon.

Ally winked at me and said, "He's a hardworking man and needs fuel to keep us hired hands in line."

I thought she was flirting with me right in front of Joan. I looked over at Joan, and she was busy spreading tuna on slices of homemade bread. I thought perhaps she's finally moved on. I ignored the wink and stole a piece of bread as I slapped Joan's butt and ran out of the kitchen.

Joan yelled, "Have everyone ready for lunch at 11:15, you pervert!"

As I walked through the fields, I kicked myself for flirting with Joan. I knew I shouldn't send mixed messages. Definitely, I didn't want to fool around with Ally and have another Sally and Geena situation.

Ally spoke up and said, "Joan, I've always been afraid of guns. My father was a staunch anti-gun person and believed the only guns owned by the public should be hunting guns. How are you able to shoot and stand guard duty, knowing you might be shot at or have to shoot someone?"

Joan said, "I grew up with my dad and Mike hunting and target shooting. It just seemed normal. Then I started running around with Zack and Mike in high school, and we were all on the high school marksmanship team. I don't like hunting, but I get a kick out of beating the boys shooting at targets. I can even beat them at clay pigeons with a shotgun."

Ally grimaced. "I'm afraid. You have Mike and Zack to protect you, and I don't have anyone. I don't know what I would've done if y'all hadn't taken me in. I'd probably have hooked up with the first decent man I could find just for protection and survival."

Joan said, "Look, I'll be the first woman to say a good man is great to have around, but a woman who can't protect herself is likely to become a victim these days. I struggled at first when Zack gave Callie her own guns to pack around the farm, especially when Mike had her start pulling guard duty. Now, I'm thinking it's the new normal. I want a man around, but I don't want to be a weakling depending on someone else and afraid of the world. Do you want me to teach you how to shoot and handle a gun?"

Ally cocked her head and slowly turned to Joan. "No, I think I'll get Mike or Zack to teach me if it's ok with you. The way you two were flirting, I thought you two were getting back together."

"Zack still hates me for leaving him and probably won't ever have me with him again. Callie's pushing us to get back together, but I'm trying to move on, and I hope to start seeing Chuck. He and Frank and their families are coming out for a barbecue on Saturday afternoon."

Ally held back a smile. "So, you won't be mad if I get Zack to train me?"

It took a minute for her to answer, but Joan finally replied, "Maybe you should have Mike train you. He and Sally aren't together yet."

Ally laughed and replied, "That's why I asked."

"Thanks."

**

We planted everything from potatoes to wheat. There was a small two-acre garden for tomatoes, cucumbers, radishes, beets, lettuce, cabbage, and a bunch of other vegetables and over ten acres of wheat, corn, and another acre of potatoes. The vegetables and potatoes would ripen about ten days from now, depending on the type. The melons would take another fifteen days. The corn and wheat were a crapshoot because we got bags of unmarked seeds when we liberated them from a looted farm supply store. We also planted five acres of oats to help feed the horses.

We now had two old tractors plowing every day and had Sam and his son scouring the area for more seeds and farm equipment. We had to expand their search since many of the local farms were competing for seeds. We actually had a barter system set up to ensure excess seeds were traded to farms needing them for trade goods or shares on the harvested crops. Heirloom seeds were the most sought after since they made seeds and could be planted from seeds. Many modern hybrid vegetable plants do not produce viable seeds. I'd purchased hundreds of packages of heirloom seeds from My Patriot Supply as part of my prepping, so we were in good shape and shared as much as possible with the other farms. I had ten Survival Seed Vault cans and other heirloom seeds from the local farm supply store. We would save most seeds from our harvests each year, and in a few years, there would be plenty for all of the farms in the area.

Every one of us knew the survivors in the cities would kill for our crops, so we were trying to get ahead of the problem by growing as much as possible. However, Owensville was the big problem. It had been a city of 30,000 before TSHTF and was now down to 3,000 after the deaths due to a lack of medicine, disease, and murders from gang attacks. Along with about another 500 people in the surrounding area, it was still more people than we could feed. Only about half of the Owensville citizens had started growing gardens. At the same time, the other half waited for someone to feed them. There had been riots and loss of life when the stores had run out of food in the first few days after the lights went out.

I asked Roger to put a team together to fence in the crops and set up guards to watch over the animals and crops. This meant we had to visit a farm supply store and talk them out of some fence and posts. To avoid going into Owensville, the best one for us was south of the farm, just inside Ohio County, and too damn close to the gang controlling lower Ohio County.

***

The plan was for Davi and me to drive the Humvee up to Nelson's Farm Supplies and offer to trade food for fencing. Davi would remain hidden and prepared to man the twin SAWs if it got dicey. Mike and Lynn would follow in the pickup with my flatbed trailer and stay a short distance back until we radioed it was safe to join us. The trip over was uneventful, except we saw several horses running wild a few miles from the farm.

I radioed Roger and said, "Roger, there're three horses and a colt grazing on the side of 754 just about two miles south of the farm. Could you take the horse trailer, catch them, and bring them back to the farm? Callie will show you where the feed is that should attract them. She's great with horses. We'll keep them until we find out who they belong to."

"Great, we'll need transportation when we run out of gas. That'll make eight horses."

Davi and I stopped several hundred yards from Nelson's and saw Mr. Nelson standing in front with a shotgun aimed at two men. His wife was just inside the front door with another gun pointed at the men. Several people were standing off to the side, hiding behind some farm equipment.

"Davi, lock, and load. It looks like Mr. Nelson needs some help."

Davi manned the twin SAWs while I drove slowly up to the parking lot. I got out and walked over to Mr. Nelson.

"Hello, Zack. How are you doing today?"

"I'm fine, but you look like you could use some help. Are these guys bothering you?"

"These punks are riffraff from the gang south of here. They thought they could walk in and take what they wanted without paying."

"We offered you some meth for the anhydrous and the kettles."

"I should shoot you for thinking I would take drugs to sell to the folks around here."

I spoke up, "You have disarmed them; now what are you going to do with them? If you're not going to shoot them, you could turn them over to the Daviess County Sheriff."

"I don't think I could shoot unarmed people. Can you get the sheriff out here?"

"I'd recommend shooting them, but yes, I can get the sheriff to take them. He wants to rid the county of this scum. We'll

196

take them with us. Get some large zip ties, and we'll bind them up for the trip."

Davi jumped out of the Humvee. We tied up the gang members and sat them down beside the Humvee. Several of the people standing off to the side came up and asked if we were police.

"No, but the sheriff has asked us to get the local farmers together and help him rid the area of these criminals. He wants to jail them, but we usually shoot looters, criminals, and thugs on sight."

"You don't take them in for a trial?"

"That's what the sheriff wants, but if we catch them in the act, we just shoot them. You're going to have enough trouble feeding yourselves; how are you going to feed hundreds of locked-up criminals?"

The people agreed with what I was saying; however, many were squeamish about shooting anyone, even criminals.

I replied, "If you don't want them shot, then take them to your farms, feed, and take care of them."

One man yelled, "That's what we pay the sheriff to do!"

"How are you going to pay the sheriff now with money worthless, and you can barely feed your family while these creeps are looting and trading meth to your kids?"

That shut them up. Several just wanted someone else to solve their problems, but most were beginning to get it. The big government had disappeared and was not the solution to their issues anymore.

I called Mike to come on in and briefly told him the situation. He and Joan drove up a few minutes later.

"Mr. Nelson, we need some fence and need to know what you'll take in trade. We're fencing in our crops and double fencing around the livestock."

"I'll give you the fence, some posts, and throw in some veterinary supplies if you'll take my cattle over to your place and tend to them. I want just enough meat to feed my family. Counting my wife, son, and his family, we have five. The cows are being poached, and I lose one or two every week. I'm sure it's that drug gang."

"That's a deal. The Carter place has been abandoned and is large enough for you to grow as many crops as you can handle. We're plowing every day with our little tractors and still only have thirty acres tilled. Mr. Nelson, I think the drug gang will retaliate for the action against these two creeps shortly. I don't think you'll be safe here. We're building a small community around my farm of like-minded and armed people to make the area safe for our families."

"I hate moving, but I agree it's not safe here. I'll talk with my wife and give you an answer tomorrow."

He'd no sooner finished speaking when his wife walked up and said, "Will and I heard what you said, and we're ready to move as soon as we can load up. We have two running tractors and a back lot full of antique tractors that Jacob never got rid of. I'll bet you can get several of those running."

I asked, "Jacob, don't you have parts for old tractors?"

"Yes, a whole warehouse of them. What are you thinking?"

I proposed, "Would you help your neighbors by trading them the parts and old tractors for shares on their crops?"

"Hell, yes! I don't know why I didn't think of that."

I then said, "We need a combine if you have an old one."

"There's an older one that's towed behind a tractor that just needs a few bearings to run. I was planning to restore it and show it off at the fairs alongside my two John Deeres."

We approached the others, and they thought it was a great idea. A couple of men were good mechanics and would get as many tractors running as possible.

Jacob looked at me and said, "Zack, you've never been a farmer. I'm surprised you're driving so hard to get all of this antique machinery running and all of these people farming."

I took him off to the side and filled him in on my concerns. "The trucks delivering food to the grocery stores stopped delivering months ago. People are starving and will start killing for food. I'm scared shitless they'll come out to the farms to take what

198

we have. I'm also a Christian and want to help the people who want to help themselves. I want to work up a barter system to feed as many as possible while gaining what we need from them. Engineers, teachers, and mechanics can help us jump from the 1850's rural America up to the early 1900s quickly if we can keep them alive and focused on improving our community. We have to get water treatment and sewage plants back online. Imagine what 30,000 outhouses will do to the water table around here. The disease will be rampant."

"Zack, if you're running for president, I'd vote for you."

"Hell no! I just want a good life for my daughter and friends."

We shook hands and started loading up the fencing onto the trailer. When that was done, we placed the thugs in the back of the pickup.

***

We had arrived an hour before Roger drove up with the horse trailer. Callie had been a big help getting the horses in the trailer. These were someone's pets, and they were starving for attention. Callie fed them sugar cubes, some sweet feed, and they followed her like puppies. All of the kids fell in love with the colt. I kept thinking we needed about ten more horses to be ready for the day when the gas ran out. It would be a while, but we'd better be prepared.

There was alarm about the Nelsons moving near us. I explained they were self-sufficient and brought seeds, fertilizer, farm supplies, plus two more tractors and a combine.

I said, "Mike, you and Roger need to figure out how to get some larger trucks running. There should be a ton of them behind every farm equipment store and some mechanics' garages."

Carrie spoke up, "What about museums? Don't they have old cars and stuff we could get running?"

Roger spoke up, "Way to go, Carrie! That makes me think there're some old steam-powered locomotives around Kentucky. Perhaps we can get them back in operation."

I exclaimed, "Damn! That reminds me, we haven't checked out rail shipping containers for food and vehicles. There must be stalled trains and containers at truck yards around the cities."

"Dad, I know there's a working locomotive with several cars over towards Sailsberg. My class rode on it last year. It operated on a side rail giving rides."

I asked, "Does it connect to the main rail?"

"I don't have a clue."

I said, "Great job, remembering it, girl."

Carrie said, "Mr. Johnson, there's a locomotive just a few miles from here, but it only has a hundred feet of rail. It's in the park over in Parkville. It probably won't help us."

I gave Carrie a pat on the back. "Maybe not, but it could be used to power a large generator or factory. I remember them firing it up on Memorial and Independence Days."

Mike asked, "Jacob, do you know anything about locomotives or steam engines?"

Jacob shrugged. "Not a lot, but remember, I was a machinist during my younger years and can repair or rebuild anything."

I said, "We know where there're two working steam locomotives. I'd like to explore, bring one or both over to this area. Would you go with a team to check them out and recommend how to get them back here? I assume we might have to rip up some rail and lay it back down to drive them over this way."

Jacob grinned, "That's a fantastic idea. I was working on plans to put a machine shop together but needed a power source. We could run a large generator or run some equipment by belts from a pulley on the steam engine. I know we can dismantle one and bring it home in pieces, but wouldn't it be great to have a working train to start up trade with the other communities?"

While we were brainstorming on fixing all of the world's problems, the guys in the back of the truck had been rubbing their zip ties on the edge of the tailgate. They were freeing their feet when Joan sounded the alarm.

"The bastards are escaping!"

She pulled her pistol just as one of them tackled her and drove her to the ground. Lynn grabbed the other escapee just as Davi pulled the other thug off Joan. Ally jumped on the man and punched him with her fists and elbow before he threw her off. Lynn was holding her own while Davi took over for Ally and destroyed the other man. Her hands moved so fast, they made swishing sounds. He was hit, kicked, and then slammed to the ground. Lynn finally kicked the last one in the groin, and he crumpled to the ground.

Davi helped Joan off the ground, and she calmly walked over to the one who'd tackled her and tried to kick him in the head. He blocked her foot with his hand and received several broken fingers for his reward. One was sticking out sideways.

"I need a doctor! Take me to a doctor!"

Joan pulled her 9mm and shot the ground an inch from his ear.

"You're damn lucky I don't shoot your sorry ass."

Ally walked up and kicked the other one in the balls.

Davi caught the women off to the side and gave them some advice, "Ladies, I say 'ladies' because you tried to fight like ladies. You must fight to *win*. You can't overpower most men, but you can outfight them. Use what I taught you about where to hit and how to kill or incapacitate your enemy. Those assholes would have raped all of you had they won the fight. No pulling punches! Take them out with one blow, break their kneecaps, gouge their eyes, and kick them in the balls. Win or die."

***

Mike, Aaron, and I took the captured men into town that afternoon. I sat in the back of the old Ford with my 9mm carbine guarding them. We were stopped at the Highway 54 roadblock until Chuck arrived twenty minutes later to escort us to the jail. He was driving a 1953 Dodge sedan with Daviess County Sheriff stenciled on the doors and red flags waving from the roof.

"Chuck, that's a fearsome sight. You and your paddy wagon."

"Don't laugh. It sure beats walking or riding a horse. Besides, we also have two old Chevy panel trucks being converted to paddy wagons. They'll have a cage between the crooks and the police. Who are these idiots all tied up in the back of your truck?"

"The luckiest two thugs in these parts."

"Okay, I'll bite. Why are they so lucky?"

I laughed, "Because Jacob Nelson had already captured them after they tried to rob him, and we would have shot them on sight for robbery. Then they tried to escape at the farm, and our women beat the crap out of them."

"Well, I guess they're lucky, but you know what the sheriff thinks about murder."

"Protecting yourself is not murder, and when the sheriff clears out all of these criminals, it won't be necessary. Anyway, these guys are yours, and we didn't shoot them."

"Who really roughed them up?"

"It's a bumpy ride from Ohio County to here on the back roads. They didn't complain."

"Well, they probably won't until we pull the duct tape off their mouths and remove those zip ties."

The sheriff greeted us at the front door, and a couple of deputies hauled the men away to their cells.

"Will Mr. Nelson press charges against these two fine citizens?"

I handed him a note from Nelson and said, "He will. They came into his shop and tried to bully him into letting them take what they wanted. When he resisted, they pulled guns on him. His wife and son were ready with shotguns, and these meth heads dropped their pistols."

"I suppose you would have shot them."

I gritted my teeth and firmly said, "Certainly would have. When you pull a gun on a person, that becomes self-defense. I would have shot them for trying to rob me. Stealing a man's food or ability to grow food is the same as attempted murder."

The sheriff said, "Well, our mayor thinks you farmers are almost as bad as the thugs. We've had ten justified shootings in the last week. Attempted murder, rape, and theft at gunpoint were the offenses. The mayor is turning purple and wants it to stop. She thinks we can rehabilitate these scumbags."

I grimaced. "What do you think?"

"I'm trying to please the Mayor without getting my men or the citizens of this great town shot to hell."

I said, "Avoiding the problem by jailing these criminals will just concentrate the problem and shove it forward until it blows up. What happens when you and your men have to leave town to start farming to feed your families?"

"We're hoping you farmers see value in the protection we offer and help us feed our families in trade."

I asked, "Where was Nelson's protection?"

"Zack, in fairness, Nelson lives in Ohio County, and my team serves Daviess County."

I said, "Sheriff, many of us farmers live just across the Ohio County line. Where's this protection we're supposed to pay for? Don't misunderstand. We want to help and are gearing up to trade food for items and services we need, but don't blow smoke at me when you can't protect us anyway soon."

The sheriff said, "We have an almost unlimited supply of gasoline at the depot on the river. There're millions of gallons of diesel and gas. With only a few vehicles, it will last for years. We'll trade fuel for food."

I was happy. "Fantastic. Find some engineers and mechanics to get every emergency generator running to start powering essential services. Hospitals, food production, and light manufacturing are the first targets. Start a major effort to get any vehicle running that can be found or converted. Strip the electronics off the newer diesel trucks and get large trucks moving."

"You need to be mayor. These idiots are waiting on the federal government to come in and save them. Hell, everyone in town is on short rations. We even searched the old Civil Defense bomb shelters and passed out fifty-year-old rations. The crackers aren't bad, but I won't eat any of the canned shit. You're right. I'll start losing my men if I can't feed my deputies and their families. Hell, their wives are doing all they know how to do. They have gardens, and my men are hunting on their off time, but the game is scarce around the city. Can you help us?"

I replied, "Yes, but it's limited this year. Next year we should be growing enough to feed the area. We're getting old tractors running and plowing as much ground as possible. We won't have much food to spare until the crops come in. We'll have vegetables in two weeks and potatoes in about three. We can't feed Owensville, but we can feed any deputies and their families if they come out and help plant and harvest. With their help, we can triple the acreage being farmed. I know that sucks for the rest of the city, but it's the best we can do until fall, and even then, there won't be enough. You can't afford to feed those criminals your do-gooder Mayor wants to salvage."

"Thanks, I'll push for getting the engines running, but don't count on it happening. I'll meet with my guys and make sure they keep this in confidence. I agree with you, but half the town loves the Mayor because she's still able to feed them from the grain silos. That stops this week. There will be riots."

"Bert, some of them will head out of town and try to steal food from the farmers. We can't allow that to happen if we want to ever recover from this disaster."

"Perhaps FEMA will eventually arrive to help."

"My theory is that FEMA got tied up in the big cities, got overwhelmed, and took their supplies home for their families."

"Could be, I've kept a person scanning all radio broadcasts, and we only hear the same canned speech from the president. I think he's holed up under a mountain trying to survive and not worried about his people."

"I've never been political, but we were not prepared for this, and I blame both parties for this disaster. The current party has been in power for thirteen years and gave Iran the bomb. I think we found out what they could do with a few nukes. I'm worried someone will invade us."

"I'm a hearin' a lot of chatter that most of the rest of the world is in the same shape. Only South America, Australia, and some small island countries escaped the EMPs; however, none of this is verifiable."

"Thanks for the update. How about joining us on Saturday for a barbecue at my place? Many of the farmers will be there. Bring your family."

"My sons and grandkids?"

"Yes, if your sons are deputies."

"They're."

"See you Saturday."

Chapter 3 - BBQ

The Farm

Saturday morning was calm until breakfast was over, and then everyone had assignments for the big barbeque in the afternoon. The event was initially scheduled to be a sendoff party for Aaron, Sharon, and Davi the day before leaving for Alabama. Then they invited the surrounding farmers, the sheriff, four of his deputies, and their families. There would be over a hundred people to be fed, entertained, and, more importantly, lobbied to help Zack set up a strong community. Only a strong community could drive out the criminals and drug addicts from the area and survive.

All of the farmers were bringing some type of meat and several side dishes. The women were having a baking contest with prizes for the best cake and pie. Callie and Carrie were in charge of the kid's games while Paul and Susie had the cleanup detail. Mr. Nelson provided half a cow to barbecue and Mike, and I would do the cooking. I already had a large barbecue pit, and we would add chickens, pork, goat, and sheep as the day progressed. Mike and I'd started cooking before dawn.

Ally, Joan, and Lynn had made large tubs of potato salad, baked beans, and fried rice. The whole community had delivered the meat and vegetables the day before. Ally had brought all of her batches of ale from her old home earlier in the week, and we chilled them in the lake. Our guests would be well fed and have a couple of drinks. Life would be somewhat normal for at least one day.

"Zack, we need to find more seasonings. We have plenty of salt but are short on most other spices until the garden can be harvested."

"Callie, go check with Roger. I think they found some spices when they checked out some stalled trucks on Highway 60. Damn, that reminds me. I forgot we have a truckload of canned goods that'll be delivered tomorrow. Sam's boy found an overturned trailer on a sharp turn just about five miles from here. He contacted Jim Mattingly and asked him to deliver a pickup load to every farm. Jim was glad to be of help and to get his share."

***

People started arriving at 11:00 and kept filtering in for the next three hours. I'd freed myself up enough to drink some ale with the ones I wanted to lobby for support. I asked the farmers to choose someone responsible for balancing out our crops and ensuring we weren't all growing the same crops. Another person is to be in charge of a team of scavengers to find more seeds, fertilizer, and farm equipment. Sam and Jacob said they would jointly handle the scavenging tasks. I already had Roger looking for food in trailers, warehouses, and shipping containers, and they would work together. I made sure everyone had a say in the farming and gathering efforts.

"Bert, join Aaron and me for a discussion on our security for our new community. I know Aaron's leaving tomorrow, but I want you two to compare notes and help me deliver the best possible security plan for our group."

"Do you mind if I add Chuck into the conversation? He has military police experience."

"Please, ask him to join. This should be a good fit for him."

"I'd like to start a remote sheriff's station out in this community, and I want Chuck to move out here and oversee the station and its officers. Of course, we'll need some volunteers from your group to help man the station. I'll provide Chuck, Frank, and two other officers."

Aaron replied, "I think that's a great idea."

I spoke up and said, "I like the idea, and of course, they could be back in town in twenty minutes if needed."

"Yes, and support from town could be here in twenty minutes if needed."

We went on to discuss the security needs and a brief outline of how to achieve our goals. I caught Bert off to the side and told him it was a slick move to give us support while we fed Frank, Chuck, Bert's two sons, and all of their families.

"Zack, you're one sharp fellow. I can't get anything past you, can I?"

"Nope, but seriously we need your help, and we'll help you as much as possible."

"Thanks, I'll keep you posted on our wacky mayor's plans, and let's meet to discuss your attack on the criminals over in Ohio County. Perhaps I should say I want to *unofficially* hear about your plans and say I didn't know anything about them. You can trust these four officers, but be careful around my other men. The mayor can't act on guns or anything that affects y'all without my support, so don't worry about Owensville."

"Thanks, I'll focus on the gang south of here. I promise we won't intentionally harm any innocent people. I will still be able to eliminate the drug trade and criminals."

"Thanks for the reassurance, and I'll stay in touch."

***

"Zack, I need a word with you before we leave in the morning."

"I'll catch you on the road."

"We're leaving before the ass crack of dawn, and I want you and my escort sober."

"I was drinking my last drink. Why so early? I thought we were leaving at dawn."

"We want to get as close to Nashville as possible before daylight. I suspect that word of our trip has leaked out, and I don't want an ambush to kill us and take the Humvees. We can drive using the NVG headsets and can see the roadblocks and traps before they see us. We'll make most of the trip at night. I want to give you this military radio. It has a range of about a hundred and twenty miles depending on the weather, hills, buildings, and such. I plan to have Davi contact you once a week. She'll be the main contact with our group. We intend to set up a relay of radios until we can get more powerful radios in operation. She'll send you the channel when that happens. We'll come to your aid if TSHTF and expect the same from you. Goodbye, my friend. I'm going to catch a nap."

"You and your family have saved my life on several occasions. I'll do anything for you."

We hugged, and Aaron went to his room.

***

Joan and I were dancing when Davi broke in and asked me to dance with her. Joan said okay, but had daggers in her eyes.

"Of course, you can have a dance with *my* husband."

"Ex," I replied as Davi grabbed me and moved us out to the middle of the dancers."

"Your ex is a jealous woman."

"That's true, and this won't help."

"Does that mean you're getting back with her?"

"Hell, no! Every time I think about making love to her, I see Todd's fat ass on top of her."

Davi broke out laughing and said, "TMI. Picture, go away."

"Exactly. I can't get that picture out of my mind. I don't hate Joan, and it would be good for Callie, but I can't get over her cheating on me with Todd."

Davi replied, "Good," and kissed me right in front of everyone.

"I guess that was my goodbye kiss. I'll miss you, and I hope to see you again."

"You will."

"I will what?"

"See me in your dreams."

She was right.

***

I saw Mike walking toward me. "Mike, could you have Callie and the girls start lighting the kerosene lanterns? It's going to be too dark to party in a few minutes."

"The lights will come on by themselves in just a minute."

He waved toward the house, and suddenly, all of the Japanese lanterns and fifty hidden light bulbs came on. They weren't as bright as usual outdoor lights, but they lit up the darkness. Callie came out of the barn and took a bow.

Callie addressed the gathering. "That's what can be done with an old exercise bicycle and generator from an old car. We'll have light until Paul runs out of steam, or perhaps some of you would sacrifice a few minutes of peddling to generate some light."

I gave her a big hug and whispered, "I'll get you a bunch of car batteries we can run the lights from, then we only peddle to keep them charged."

"That's why you're the Dad and the electrician in the family."

"Darling, you're the inventor. No one else thought to do this simple thing that'll take us forward a hundred years in lighting technology. We'll eventually get some generators running, but that'll bridge the gap for people who can't obtain a real generator. I need you to go back to the drawing board with Mr. Nelson, improve the prototype, and begin mass production. I'll help you with the electrical work."

Mike and I raised Callie on our shoulders and paraded her around the dance floor while everyone applauded. A simple thing like working light bulbs had given new hope to a hundred people. I knew that we could spread this around to the farms and even to the city.

"I'm proud of you. Keep inventing and repurposing. Go, girl, go."

Callie made sure everyone knew Paul had done a lot of the work with her and deserved half the credit. Everyone thanked her and patted Paul on the back. She was on cloud nine for the next month. Joan and Ally were proud of their children. Paul's legs were sore the next day because while we'd been celebrating the new lights, he was peddling for all he was worth. Callie finally remembered and rounded up a bunch of recruits to share the work. Many of the kids got a kick out of actually making light from their own work.

I seized the moment and gave my planned speech. "Friends and fellow farmers, we have met several difficult challenges and have many threats lurking out in the shadows around us. I have met with many of you. We agree we need to band together to help each other grow our food, secure our farms, and, yes, develop some old technology to make our lives better. I propose we develop a leadership council made up of people we select and serve to focus our efforts. I also propose we meet again in two weeks to vote on who'll be on our board of directors, who'll head up our security and all other important leadership positions."

Most of the group cheered, but a few had questions.

One lady asked, "Zack, is this just a play for you to become our leader?"

I replied, "Hell no. I'll assist any of our elected leaders and any of you who need my opinions, advice, or labor. I'm not running for any office."

A man asked, "Will we have to join this new group?"

I frowned. "I can't speak for the others, but if you don't contribute to the group, why would the members want to assist you if and when you need help?"

The man said, "Because it's the Christian thing to do."

I said, "Yes, helping our fellow man is the right thing to do, but helping someone who won't help themselves is not high on my list."

My last statement brought a round of cheers.

Mr. Nelson spoke up, "I know most of you to be hard-working people who would give the shirt off their back to help a person in need. That's not what we're discussing."

Zack was trying to get the point across that everyone would be expected to pull guard duty, help plow fields, invent new ways to light a dance, and many other ways to contribute. "No one gets a free ride. That's what we meant."

The man said, "Okay, that makes sense. I just don't want anyone telling me what to do and what I can grow."

I replied, "As long as you don't intentionally harm anyone, do your fair share and help others as they help you. Everyone here will be there for you when trouble comes your way."

A woman asked, "Sheriff, the mayor of Owensville wants to take away our guns. Do you support gun confiscation?"

The sheriff replied, "First, the mayor only has control of the city, but she has no say in county politics other than being a private citizen like all of you. I am against gun control and think we'll only survive if good citizens are willing to take up arms against criminals and tyranny, as our forefathers have repeatedly done in our history. The sheriff is elected by the citizens of Daviess County and serves at your pleasure. The sheriff must stay out of politics and perform the duties as prescribed by law. Those are to serve and protect you, the citizens from outlaws, criminals, and crooked politicians."

The sheriff received a round of applause and was about to speak when one of the diehards asked, "If you're supposed to serve us, why are most of your deputies stationed in Owensville?"

"That's a great question. There were rioting and outsiders trying to steal food from the stores and warehouses in town. Had they succeeded, they would have eventually grown in power and been a major threat to you out here in the country. You're self-reliant, and I knew I had time before you needed help. We eliminated over two hundred criminals during the attacks and riots. We lost thousands of citizens and twelve policemen and women during the conflict. I have informed the Mayor, I'm pulling most of my deputies out of town and stationing them in communities like yours all around the county. I'll keep the main office in Owensville, but eighty percent of the officers will be spread out in groups of three to five as needed. Frankly, I have over forty officers that want to help protect you full time, but that means they can't farm or do more than to help farm part-time. I don't want them to desert you to provide for their own families."

A farmer spoke up, "We should all pray for the souls lost in Owensville and make sure we understand, so we help feed the deputies and their families and gain full-time police protection. I like that."

No one disagreed with the concept.

The sheriff said, "I've brought Frank, Chuck, and my two sons, Jeb and Josh, tonight to introduce them as the deputies who would be domiciled in this community. Several of you have already offered to house them until permanent arrangements can be made."

Everyone wanted to meet the new deputies serving our community and gave them a warm welcome.

***

The Deputy Mayor said, "And why should Mayor Bonner want to meet with your leader?"

The stranger said, "Tell her we have common enemies, and there's a plot against her and Owensville. My boss wants to help and form a mutual alliance against all lawless and problem people in the area."

The Deputy Mayor said, "But we hear he has taken over Anderson and is ruling with an iron fist."

"Everyone in Anderson is well fed, there's no crime in the city, and we're spreading out to the county to clean it up of all threats. I hear your people are starving. See those trucks? They have over two tons of food to show our good faith. We can show you how to feed your city and form mutual alliances with all of the farms in your area."

The Deputy Mayor said, "They aren't starving, but the grain will be gone in a week or so. How did you get the farmers to share? They're being stubborn over here."

"That's one of the many things Todd will be discussing with the mayor."

The Deputy Mayor replied, "Thanks for the gesture of goodwill, and I'll pass on your request for a meeting."

"A word of advice. Speak only to the mayor, and don't let the sheriff or his men learn of our meeting."

The Deputy Mayor asked, "What?"

"Trust me."

The deputy mayor reported to the mayor. "I was approached by the new sheriff of Anderson County. He says this Todd character wants to meet with you. They gave us over two tons of canned goods, bags of flour, and rice as a gesture of good faith. He says their citizens are well fed and working together for the betterment of their community."

The mayor asked, "Alan, why did he approach my deputy mayor? That's the man who took over the city of Anderson and killed the previous mayor and city leaders?"

Alan replied, "No, I think those rumors are an exaggeration. I understand he overthrew them in a bloodless coup with the support of the majority of Anderson citizens. He reached out because my brother-in-law is on his staff. We stay in touch."

The mayor said, "Set up a meeting at the gas station on the county line. Make sure the sheriff has plenty of men there, just in case his intentions are less than honorable."

"He warned me to tell you not to let the sheriff know about the meeting. I'll provide security with my people if it's okay with you. After all, I do own the leading security firm in Kentucky. Prescott Security is known worldwide for its excellence."

The mayor said, "I like that. I've always thought the sheriff was a right-wing nut job and knew I had to get him out of office, but he's very popular with the conservatives in the county."

Alan suggested, "Let's meet with the Anderson officials and see where this goes."

"And I guess if Bert goes away, you'll have someone to fill his job? I'll bet you also have as many spies on my staff as you do on his."

Alan said, "And replace all but a few of his deputies. I have several of my men on his force now. Oh, I keep my ears to the ground and gather all types of information."

"What are your spies telling you about the meeting the farmers just had at the Johnson place?"

"The sheriff and four of his deputies were wined and dined, along with their families. I have a friend among that group and hope to have details before too long."

"Alan, we have mutual goals and share the same values. Let's meet again in a week and make long-term plans for Owensville."

"Alice, I agree with what you said, but one thing I must add to the conversation."

"Go on."

"We have more people than can possibly be fed by the local farms, even if we had their cooperation."

The mayor said, "I feel the same way. I assume we'll discuss that in private. If we agree, can you handle the dirty work?"

Alan Prescott replied, "Yes, and I have a plan. My overseas branch has handled several situations that are similar in scope."

"Were you able to protect your client from any backlash or political fallout?"

Alan said, "Not only did we protect them, but we also made the world blame his enemies for the unfortunate disaster."

The mayor smiled. "Let's review your plans next week at my house. How about Tuesday at about 6:00 pm?"

"Good, I'd like to meet your husband."

"He won't be there, but he needs to be included in your disaster plan."

Alan smiled and said, "I'm so sorry, but life goes on."

She pulled him closer and said, "Yes, it does. Alan, we have a chance to remake our little part of the world, and I'm not letting anyone stand in the way."

Alan Prescott got into the backseat of the old Suburban and had his driver take him back to his home on the outskirts of south Owensville. They approached the driveway, the steel gate opened, and the truck drove into the large garage. The door rolled down, and the lights came on. Alan had a T-bone, salad, and wine for supper and then watched an old movie using his blue-ray player. His wife sat in the living room with a bottle of wine for company. She still didn't understand why she couldn't fly to New York for her weekly shopping trip with her friends.

Alan Prescott knew the shit would hit the fan and had moved his world headquarters from New York City to Owensville just after 9/11. He slowly built his home to be a self-sustained fortress, supplied with enough food, water, and weapons for a dozen people to survive for three years. His Olympic swimming pool was actually a way to store more water. There was a much larger sealed tank underneath the pool. All of the electronics, generators, and vehicles were EMP proof. The entire complex was one big Faraday cage and all. Still, his 2020 Corvette had all of the electronics replaced or hardened against an EMP blast. The Corvette was stored in a metal-lined vault in the basement of his garage. He only drove the old Suburban to fool the townspeople into thinking he was in the same boat as they were.

His contacts in the Middle East had given him a few days' warning, which allowed him to pull back his most trusted team members and their families to Owensville. Most were single by design, so there were only twenty-six mouths to feed, and he was milking the city for most of their food.

He had spent years cultivating relationships with both political parties. He had given large sums of money under the table to keep in good standing with the powers in the city. Everyone knew him, and he was envied by some and respected by all. He had the big house, thriving business, trophy wife, and two kids away at college at South Bend, Indiana. That was his one worry. He had sent a small team of his best men to find and bring his daughter and son back to him. It had been over a month, and he hadn't heard a word from them.

His kids had their own problems, and his men never found them.

***

I woke up early and went with Mike, Ally, and Sally to escort the Golds to the Kentucky border. I asked Ally to join us since she had just finished her training. Everyone else was exhausted from guard duty or partying. Ally didn't drink much, so she was rested more than the rest of us. The Golds had loaded up the Humvees and a trailer a couple of days before, and we just had to hit the road after a cold breakfast. It was 2:00 when we pulled out of the farm and worked our way over to the Natcher Highway to head south to Highway 65 and on to Rolling Hills. We would escort them to Franklin, Kentucky, and spend the day hiding until nightfall and then heading back to the farm. As with Aaron's team, night-vision equipment allowed us to drive down the road at forty mph and move while the criminals were sleeping. We could see them, and they couldn't see us until it was too late. The Humvees were noisy, but with no running lights, one didn't know what was coming at them, and it would scare the shit out of most people. We had the twin SAWs and grenade launchers if we were attacked.

The Natcher only had a few stalled cars, and we could reach fifty mph on long stretches where we could see far enough ahead to make sure no roadblocks or ambushes were waiting on us. Rolling Hills was another matter. There was a roadblock a few miles before the Highway 65 exit. Aaron had us stop a safe distance before the barrier, and he tried the radio to see if they were local police.

"You, at the roadblock, are you the police?"

217

"No, but we're guarding our town and don't want anyone going through."

Aaron thought for a minute and replied, "We're heading to Alabama and have to go through to get there."

A man said, "Sorry, go around. We can't take the chance of another gang attacking us."

Aaron said, "We're going to pull up a little closer, and perhaps you can be convinced to let us go through."

The people at the roadblock hadn't seen our three Humvees and probably thought we were a gang trying to attack the town.

Aaron barked, "Fire up the engines and follow me. Man the SAWs and have the grenade launchers ready."

We stopped about fifty yards from the roadblock, and a light was shined onto our vehicles.

"Are you with the Army?"

Aaron said, "No, we're just trying to get home to Alabama."

"Where did you get the military vehicles?"

Aaron sternly warned the man. "We don't have time to play twenty questions. Push the truck off the road so we can pass, or we'll blow it off the road along with y'all. We don't want to hurt you and could even be a big help if you let us pass. We're going through either way. We can be friends or undertakers, your choice."

The truck slowly began rolling out of the way, and Aaron told us to follow him through the gap. "Have grenades ready. We'll be too close to use the SAWs when we go through the barricade. Yell and button up if you drop a grenade."

We kept the SAWs aimed at the people as we passed and noticed they backed quite a distance from us except for one man who laid his rifle down and walked up to Aaron's Humvee.

The man said, "You don't have to open up with those SAWs to show us what could've happened. Who are you?"

Aaron spoke, "Just strangers passing through to Alabama, as I said before. We were stopped at a small community outside of Owensville for the past month and now need to get back home."

"My brother is the sheriff of Daviess County."

Aaron said, "We know Bert very well, or at least my friend in the last Humvee does. That's Zack Johnson back there."

Aaron waved for me to drive up alongside him. "This guy says he's Bert's brother."

I asked him some personal questions about Bert, and he passed with flying colors. "We need to get these folks on down the road, but I'm only escorting them to the Kentucky border. Is it okay if we come back and spend the day here before heading back to the Owensville area? We need to discuss how we can help each other survive this mess."

Bert's brother said, "We'd be glad to have any friend of Bert's visit. Besides, we haven't received much news from the outside. There's a radio station that comes on every night at about 7:00, giving us bits and pieces of news and a lot of survival tips. That's how we got some old trucks running and have a project to have a generator running in a few days."

I said, "We'd like to compare notes. We should be back about dawn. Are you aware of any trouble south of here?"

"Nothing you can't handle with your firepower, but I wouldn't want to be driving a car south of here. There're a few small gangs and some thugs that'll steal anything that isn't nailed down. We shoot as many as possible when we run across them."

We waved goodbye and headed south. The only encounter with anyone trying to stop us was just outside of Franklin when someone took a couple of potshots at us from up on a hill. I had Ally fire a burst at them, and they stopped. We stopped at the truck stop on the border and used the hand pumps to refuel.

Aaron caught me off to the side and said, "I want to leave you with a few words of advice. Find and stock a fallback bug out location. I think your farm is open to attack, and my gut says gangs or even your friends in town will attack you when their food runs out. Trust no one outside of your small circle of close friends. Always be ready to bug out in ten minutes."

"Thanks for the advice. I'd hate to leave my farm, but I've been thinking along the same lines. Y'all be careful, and we'll miss you a bunch."

After fueling up, we said our goodbyes. I got a hug from every one of the Golds and gave Davi a hug and a kiss. "Davi, I need to thank you for the training and guidance over the past months. You've been a big help getting me back on track."

"Zack, you're a very special person and not as bad as you think you're," she said and then kissed me on the lips.

She added, "Remember to think about me every now and then."

I said, "Goodbye."

They were gone.

Mike and Sally started teasing me about Davi, but I ignored them, hoping they would tire and move on. Ally didn't join in and was quiet the rest of the ride back to Rolling Hills.

❂

Chapter 4 - New Friends

Rolling Hills

As promised, we arrived just after dawn, and Bert's brother, Jake, took us to his house to spend the day. His wife fixed us a light breakfast since we had to get some sleep. I chose to leave someone in the Humvee manning the SAWs at all times. Mike took the first watch, and we would rotate every few hours.

I shook Jake's hand. "Thanks for having us to your house. I thought we'd be spending the day holed up in the woods eating MREs."

"We don't have much, but you're welcome to share what we have."

We spent the next two hours discussing any news about why the lights went out and sharing tips on survival. Jake had heard of the takeover of Anderson by a gang, and we filled him in on the details. I later thanked the women for not bringing up Joan's relationship with Todd. When I started yawning, I asked if we could sleep in the barn. I took the next watch and noticed that life in this part of Rolling Hills was much like the rest of the places I'd been since the lights went out. They were nice people who had been sucker-punched and were just trying to get by.

I woke Ally up and took her place in the barn. "Ally, don't let anyone close to the Humvee and keep a grenade handy. Don't hesitate to use it or the SAWS if you're threatened or approached."

Ally smiled. "Thanks. I won't let you down. Hey, are you and Davi going to be seeing each other?"

"No, she's just a dear friend, and besides, she won't be coming back from Alabama."

She said, "Okay, just wondering."

"Goodnight."

I woke up four hours later with Ally sleeping a few inches from me. I looked at her lying there with her head on her bug out bag and a pistol sticking out from under the bag. She was snoring slightly and had a smile on her face. She had long dark hair and American Indian features. She was beautiful, and I couldn't stop watching her. I had my elbow on the ground, and my head propped up on my hand when her eyes popped open and looked into mine. We stared at each other for over a minute, and then I got embarrassed and looked away. I scrambled to my feet, stretching as I stood up.

"Wake up, sleepyheads. It's time to regroup and compare notes with the Rolling Hills folks. Mike and Sally will stay with the Humvee for the first watch, then Ally and I'll stay on watch until we leave. Stay together, stay alert, and see what you can learn. I hate to say this, but only trust what you see and nothing you hear. We want to make friends and help these people if we can, but mostly we want to get out of here alive."

As if on cue, Jake drove up in an old open-top jeep and asked them to go on a tour of Rolling Hills. "I'll take you through the safe areas and show you one of our farms. We're very proud of what we've accomplished since the riots."

I asked, "How bad was the rioting?"

Jake frowned and became somber. "Very bad. On the first day, the SOBs looted the electronics stores, jewelry, and pharmacies. The owners and security put up a fight but were killed quickly. They killed over two hundred drug addicts, criminals, and dumbasses looking to get free stuff before they died. The average person began fighting for food the next day when the grocery shelves were empty. Thousands died the second day and every day until our city shrank from over 60,000 to just over 3,000 for the whole county. The ones who are left shoot first and ask questions later. Our only major issue is the gang that controls the east side of town. They raided several gun shops and have a boatload of ARs and AKs and will use them at the slightest provocation."

I asked, "So, you're coexisting with them?"

"Yes, we trade them food for gas and diesel. They aren't much on farming and control the bulk fuel storage tanks on the river."

"Who controls the granary and the Gen Agra plant?"

Jake said, "We do. Why?"

I wondered if they'd thought about the grain. "Are y'all doling out the grain to your people? There must be thousands of tons of corn, wheat, and oats there. What about the railyards? Have you checked them for food and grain? I saw several of those bulk type tanks along the road back there."

The sheriff turned green and replied, "Hell no. No one thought about the granary or the railcars."

"Man, winter's coming, and you need every scrap of food that you can get. If your crops fail, you're screwed. By the way, what have you planted?"

Jake said, "Yes, most of the farmers and city people have planted crops. We have planted corn, wheat, and potatoes, besides the usual garden vegetables."

We drove on to see a series of roadblocks and cars nosed front to tail, stretching for as far as the eye could see. The open space had been created when all of the houses were burned to the ground during the looting. We drove up to one of the checkpoints and talked with the guards.

"The gang holds up in the houses to the left, and their headquarters is that restaurant where the motorcycles are parked. They have snipers, and we have snipers, so the result is a no man's land and a standoff. They came over under a white flag, and they promised not to attack us if we traded food for fuel. The arrangement has kept the peace for two months."

"How many are in the gang?"

"About forty men, no more than that. There're another hundred women and children. Some of them are captives from the early days. We've lost a dozen women who have either defected to them or been kidnapped."

"Sheriff, you have about a thousand men and five hundred women who can fight. Why haven't you overwhelmed them and killed every last one?"

"We would lose too many trying to cross the no man's land."

Ally added, "Did you think about poisoning their food and then attacking?"

"Our city leaders wouldn't hear of such barbarism."

I replied, "Then be prepared to die a slow death as they get stronger, and you get weaker. It's kill or be killed these days. Take care of the good guys and kill the bad guys."

"I've talked until I'm blue in the face, but the mayor and his lackeys won't hear of these kinds of plans."

"Do you have anyone with any military leadership experience?"

"Only some lower-ranking men and women who served in the Middle East."

"Can you get them together and let me meet with them? I have an idea."

"As long as I'm there, I'll be glad to arrange the meeting."

"Okay. After you give Mike and Sally a tour, let's meet by the Humvee."

An hour before dark, the sheriff walked up, leading a band of over fifty men and women who were armed to the teeth. Mike swung the SAWs around but did not aim at the group.

"Zack, these are our vets. They've fought in Vietnam, Grenada, Iraq, and Afghanistan. They want to hear what you have to say."

"I'm Zack Johnson. I have no military experience, but I have a lot of common sense and have been killing thugs from Oregon to Kentucky since the shit hit the fan. I know you're all going to die if you don't get rid of that biker gang. I have a couple of ideas, but you have the experience. Put a plan together and execute it. Removing the mayor would be my first move. He's being either paid by the bikers or threatened. Meet with Jake. He should be your leader."

One woman stepped forward, "Will you stay and use the Humvee to help us?"

My head shook. "No, it'll take you several days to get ready to attack them. I must leave, and above all, you must prepare in secret. Don't tip off the gang or the mayor of the impending attack. Select three of you to represent the group, and I'll give you a plan that'll work. What you do is up to you."

I took Jake and the three leaders off to the side and had a fifteen-minute discussion, shook their hands, and jumped into the Humvee. "We'll be back in a few weeks to celebrate your victory."

We pulled out and left Rolling Hills. We chatted about what we had seen and discussed our amazement that they were so far behind our progress.

Ally finally asked the question that had been on her lips. "Zack, what's the plan? I'm dying to know what you told them."

"Common sense. Armor plate a bunch of dump trucks, spike the gang's food with ipecac and laxatives, and attack when they're puking or shitting their guts out."

They laughed for an hour.

Finally, Ally said, "That'll be bad for the innocent women and kids, but being gang slaves is much worse. Thanks for helping them solve their problem. That mayor has to be on the take."

"Ally, you just made me think that perhaps Owensville's mayor might be dirty also."

She said, "You need to warn Bert."

The trip back to the farm only took four hours, including the time stopping to relieve ourselves twice since we'd drunk so much sweet tea for supper. We rolled in just before 11:00 pm, and everyone was up waiting for us to return. Callie ran over, hugged me, and told me how she worried so much about me while I was gone. I gave them an update and went on into the house. I fell asleep thinking about mayor Bonner.

I cornered Ally, and she smiled at me. "Ally, what have you learned from Mary about Grant?"

"First, Mary is a good person, but she's fallen for Grant and believes all of his bullshit. He's plotting against us but doesn't have any supporters in our ranks. He has hinted to Mary he's working with or for the most powerful person in this area, and they have a plan to take over everything within a hundred miles."

I was very curious. "Did she speculate who she thinks that person is?"

"No. I guessed it was Todd, the mayor, or both together."

I frowned. "Thanks. What would you do with Grant and Mary?"

"I'd take Grant out into the woods, and he wouldn't return. I'd try to save Mary only because of Carrie and Billy, but I don't think she can be saved."

"Good info, and I agree with your thoughts."

***

Bert shook my hand. "So, Aaron left Sunday morning? I hope he and his family make it to Alabama without any trouble."

"We escorted them to the Kentucky border and spent part of the next day in Rolling Hills."

Bert got excited and said, "Did you see my brother Jake? He's the sheriff of Rolling County."

I said, "Yes, we stayed at his house and had a couple of meals with them. They get by but are in worse shape than we are. They aren't using all of their resources, and the mayor is a problem. A gang has control of a third of their city and most of the fuel. The mayor has set up a deal where they trade food for fuel and a truce. Jake and I think that the mayor is in the gang's pocket."

Bert asked, "Is there anything we can do to help them?"

I passed on the plan I'd left with them and said, "Your brother is a lot like you. He didn't want to go against the mayor even though the signs were there saying the mayor has his own plan, and it isn't in the community's best interest. I think our Mayor Bonner has to go away before she decides to make you and your deputies go away."

Bert grimaced and then said, "I would have argued with you last week, but Bonner brought Alan Prescott to the station yesterday. She told me that she's appointed Alan in charge of developing our long-term security plan, and I should report to him. I explained to both that the sheriff only reported to the county's people and would not report to the mayor or an appointee of the mayor. Alan tried to talk tough, but Bonner asked him to back off, and both left. Since then, one of my deputies told me that the mayor and Prescott had plans to take over the whole county. Their first step would be to make me disappear and then stage attacks against my deputies. They would then replace them with Alan's men. He also told me that Bonner and Prescott are to meet with the leader of Anderson later this week."

My fists clenched, and I took a deep breath. "Damn, Bert! Start by moving your wife and kids out to my place for their safety. If I were you, I'd move out there also. What should we do with this information?"

"I think we should get the leaders from the various communities in Daviess County who we trust and put a plan in place to remove Bonner and neutralize Prescott before they attack. I think we have to get rid of the drug gang in Ohio County first."

I replied, "I agree, but we need to warn the others by tomorrow."

Bert said, "I'm okay with that."

M mind spun with the developments. "We need to add to our army."

"What army?"

I said, "I have fifteen at my place and another thirty fighters in the surrounding farms. You have at least twenty-five loyal deputies. That gives us about seventy people who can hold their own against the drug gang or Bonner's thugs. We can probably double the number after our first meeting."

Bert's head shook a bit. "I agree on the number of people who can fight, but *will they fight* when the bullets fly?"

✪✪✪

Chapter 5 - Todd Reaches Out

Spottsville, Kentucky

Alan's spies told him Todd's men would stake out the meeting early in the morning before the meeting and have men in place to wipe out the mayor's team if the meeting went south. He had his team there two days early. He had set up practically invisible hiding spots with clear fields of fire for likely sniper locations. He also placed IEDs at the meeting site and the roads back to Anderson and Owensville. He definitely didn't trust Todd or his people, and Alan wasn't sure he needed the mayor to take over Owensville. It was a coin toss if he killed both or none. He knew Todd had to go when he outlived his usefulness, but the mayor could come in handy. Both would be the scapegoats in the end. Alan and his team would be the heroes. The citizens would be glad to get rid of Todd and happy Alan's team had killed the evil Todd and delivered Owensville from his clutches.

"Alan, thanks for providing transportation to the meeting and the security coverage. Steve and I had to slip away this morning to prevent anyone from knowing about the meeting. Do you expect this to be a productive meeting or an attempt for Todd to expand his empire?"

Alan looked over at Steve and said, "Is it okay to speak frankly in front of your city manager? I don't want to insult Steve, but how much does he know about this situation?"

"Steve is my most trusted ally, and I trust him with my life."

Alan watched how close they sat together and thought Steve might be why her husband had to be eliminated.

Alan said, "The answer is both. Todd will be quite helpful until he doesn't need us anymore, then he plans to kill us all and take over Daviess County. See, Todd is jealous of the upcoming success of our local farmers. His are beaten down and only doing just enough to keep their lives. He knows that'll mean starvation in the long run. He wants our farms and not our city's people. They'll be expendable."

She asked, "Then why do we want to deal with this devil?"

Alan smirked, "Because you need someone to take the blame for the thinning of the herd, and he's uniquely placed to deal with Zack Johnson and his band of troublemakers."

"How so?"

Alan smiled, "Zack's wife, Joan, left him to live with Todd. Her brother rescued Joan from Todd just after the lights went out. Todd went from a middle management office drone to a raving maniac in a few days. He'll do anything to get Joan and her daughter back while killing Zack and Joan's brother."

She wrung her hands. "Sounds like a fucking soap opera."

Alan leaned toward the mayor. "It is, but it's our best way to kill several birds with one stone. Todd's henchmen will kill Zack's team, be blamed for wiping out half of the people in our town, kill our sheriff Bert and most of his officers. The public will believe what we tell them to believe. We'll be heroes when we drag Todd through the streets and hang him on the courthouse grounds for the mass murder."

"Damn, you're good."

Steve looked from Alice to Alan several times and said, "What happens if the plan goes south?"

Alan beat the mayor to the punch. "That's why I get paid the big bucks. To make sure it goes according to plan."

"What's to prevent you from double-crossing us all and taking the whole area for yourself?"

"Alice, your boyfriend has a vivid imagination. First, I am very rich and don't need anyone or anything to survive. I have a small army to protect me against anything anyone throws at me. I don't need Owensville. Owensville needs my help, and I'm glad to mentor the mayor and be the man behind the power. I guess you might say it's my only hobby, now the world's powers don't need my services."

They'd been waiting for half an hour when Todd's Cadillac came into view. It was a 1959 Eldorado white-on-white convertible with red leather seats. Todd was sitting in the back beside a rather attractive, very young blonde with a driver and a prominent security guard in the passenger seat.

Alan knew by being late, Todd was claiming superiority over the Owensville team. His apology would be bullshit.

"I'm very sorry. We had a flat tire coming over. The roads are not what they used to be."

Todd was dressed in a tailored suit with a flower in his lapel. He actually looked like a gangster from the twenties.

After the pleasantries, Todd took over the conversation. "I want to make sure we all know what each party gets in any deal we make. I........ err .... Anderson wants to rid the area of the rabble that's attacking our farmers and citizens. We want to eliminate the drug trafficking that appears to be located in Ohio County but managed from Daviess County. We also want to cooperate with Daviess County to improve our harvests, share farming equipment, and work together to get our industries back up into operation."

The mayor looked over at Alan and then spoke, "I couldn't agree with you more on the topics you brought up; however, I feel we need to add to the list and clarify one item. We need to add a mutual security effort to protect our citizens and our mutual goals. There're enemies out there who will try to take away our ability to govern and enforce our community's laws. We won't interfere with how each other manages inside their own boundaries. We'll also help you solve a personal problem, the Johnsons, and you'll help me with one of mine."

Todd laughed aloud. "Mayor, I see you've done your homework, and we're on the same wavelength. Let's meet again in two days and introduce our department heads to work out the detail in their areas."

"I agree. Say 10:00 in two days?"

Todd turned to Alan. "Alan, what do you do for the mayor?"

"Security and problem solving."

Todd smiled. "Okay, I have an Alan also. She'll meet with you, and perhaps you two can jointly solve a couple of problems for the mayor and me."

They shook hands and headed back to the office.

***

Alice asked, "Did Todd have his men in place as you suspected?"

Alan looked at the mayor and *thought, she's a bit old for me but damned good looking.* "Yes, and they never knew we had them all covered. He did surprise me with his own IEDs spread around the meeting place. He's a little sharper than I anticipated. He's found a mentor."

***

Todd patted the Latin beauty on the butt. "Imelda, did the mayor have her men in place around the meeting site?"

"Yes, ten more than we had, and they had the escape routes booby-trapped. You were right. This Alan is an expert and will need to go as soon as we finish cooperating with Owensville."

Todd nodded. "That's after I have Callie back, and Mike Norman and Joan Johnson are dead."

232

She said, "I need to give my moles time to dig in and gain the trust of the mayor's and Johnson's people."

Todd pulled Imelda closer. "Get Callie, and I'll give you more time."

"Done. We'll have the bitch in a few weeks. You never asked if I wanted to share you with a teenager."

✪

Chapter 6 - Always Prepared

Southern Daviess County

I kept thinking about the last advice Aaron gave me before heading south. He was right about the farm being hard to defend and not trusting too many people. However, would any place I'd want to live in be easy to defend? I didn't want to think about moving, but having a fallback position fully stocked with supplies was a good idea. I gave it a lot of thought and then decided to bring Mike, Joan, and Sally into my confidence.

I caught Mike before the others, filled him in on the plan, and asked for his opinion.

Mike said, "I like it. We can make this place much more secure, but having a secure place to bug out to makes a lot of sense. We could be overrun, bug out, and snipe the bastards until we retake the farm. I would also bury some food and weapons here at the farm. Any idea where you want to locate it?"

I nodded. "I have a couple, but none are perfect. Down by the river is the old waterworks complex. No one has been there for years and has no reason to go there. It has several concrete buildings that would be easy to defend. You could easily enter or escape the complex by car or boat. The other is the old feed mill on Green River."

Mike thought for a minute and said, "Do you remember your uncle taking us on a hike up Daviess Mountain?"

"Yeah, you mean Daviess Hill? What's up there that would make a good hideout? Damn, are you thinking about the old underground water storage tank?"

"Yes. It has everything that we'd need and would be very secure, and I don't think anyone still alive knows about it."

I agreed. "You're probably right about that. According to my uncle, it was abandoned in the thirties and had been empty ever since. My uncle only knew about it because he stumbled across one end of it that had been exposed due to a landslide after a very wet winter. That was one creepy place."

"Zack, we were eleven the last time we were there. Let's check out all three before we make a decision."

"That works for me. Who should we trust with the location?"

"That's tough. It's not who we trust or don't trust. It's who we trust the most with our lives."

I said, "I'm thinking Joan and Sally."

"What about Ally, Roger, Callie, and Paul?"

I cautioned Mike. "I don't want Callie to slip up and tell her friends. I trust Roger, but we've actually only known them for a couple of months. Why did you bring up, Ally?"

Mike snickered. "And you've known Sally for three to four months, and I've only known her for three, and I trust her. I brought Ally up because you two have been making puppy dog eyes at each other since you got back from Rolling Hills."

"That's bull. She's younger than I am. I made that mistake with Geena. Hell, I'm still grieving over her, and you're trying to hook me up. Anyway, I've been wrestling with who to trust for a week."

Mike snorted, "Damn, you're thirty-five, and Ally is what about thirty-two? That's the same age as Joan. Hell Geena was around twenty-eight?"

"It just seemed more than that. I guess Joan was much more mature than me, so they seem much younger."

"Zack, don't sell Callie short. She's grown up a lot since the lights went out. I think she and Paul will be....."

I choked and then gasped. "If you say having sex, I'll beat the shit out of you."

Mike broke out laughing and replied, "Aren't we a bit overprotective, Daddy? Your little girl is sixteen going on twenty-five. She's proficient with every weapon we have and can knife fight better than most men can. Davi trained her well. I was going to say dating. Zack, your little girl is very responsible, and Paul is cut from the same cloth. I would trust both of them, along with Sally, Joan, and Ally. I'll hold back on Roger, but my gut says we can trust him. It's Grant we have to watch. He needs to go."

Mike and I made excuses the next day and took my truck on a road trip to evaluate the possible locations for our bug out place. We ruled out the old feed mill since people lived in a trailer just a hundred feet away. The old water treatment complex had promise, and we both agreed that it would do, but we wanted something better.

Mike was driving as I watched the countryside roll by.

"Mike, turn right just around the bend. Then we'll stay on the dirt road for a mile or so before turning left and up a big hill."

"Just past the white cow with the black spot?"

I growled, "Shut up and drive."

We started up the hill and came to a flat spot about fifty yards deep and a hundred yards long with a steep hill running the entire length of the backside.

"I remember this is where we camped the day my uncle brought us up here. We pitched our tents over by that big rock and had a fire right here. Let's look for the concrete air vents and the entrance. I know we'd have to climb down a ladder, but the place would be very safe."

Mike led the way and headed through the thick tangle of trees, bushes, and vines until we saw where there had been a landslide. From the side, it looked like the entire hill had collapsed and washed out at a ninety-degree angle heading to our left. There was a fifteen-foot wide flat area leading around towards where the

236

earth had given way. Mike went first, only traveled about thirty feet, and was just around the end of the hill when he yelled.

"Holy crap, there's a big cave! A big ass cave!"

I cleared the side. In front of Mike was a large opening into the side of the hill. The opening was twenty feet wide and at least fifteen feet high. I looked at the edges, and they seemed too regular.

"This is the old underground water storage tank. Part of the wall collapsed and fell down the hill with the surrounding dirt. The floor was on bedrock and is two feet thick. Hell, we could drive a tank into this. Let's go back and get a flashlight and a lantern."

I turned the flashlight on, and Mike lit the lantern as we entered the opening to the underground structure. It had been built sometime around the turn of the twentieth century and was a massive structure for that time. It was as big as a football field and shaped like a giant underground swimming pool, with sides that went up and away at a sharp angle. The concrete sides, bottom, and top appeared to vary from about two feet to three feet, thick judging from the concrete around the opening. There were round columns about every twenty-five feet that held the ceiling up. The columns were three feet in diameter. The roof was thirty feet above the floor.

"No wonder I had nightmares about this place. I think my uncle intentionally brought us here to show us a good place to hide if the shit ever hit the fan. I remember him telling me that this would make a good bomb shelter if the Russians ever got the nerve to tackle the USA."

"I remember the scared part. Let's take a look around."

We tracked our steps as we walked to the far end. One hundred and twenty-five paces should be about four hundred feet. We performed the same maneuver walking from side to side, and arrived at thirty-four paces for about a hundred feet. This would be one big bug out place. We explored the enormous room for over an hour. We found it empty except for the bones of animals and several animal nests. The raccoons had taken over the place.

Mike had a good idea and said, "Let's go back out and look around the area to see if there's anyone nearby."

We walked around the place in ever-widening circles for two hours and saw no evidence of any other people. We found the missing slab of concrete down the side of the hill. It must have fallen over twenty years ago because it had taken down every tree in its path when it slid down the hill. There were already ten-inch thick trees growing back in front of the reservoir.

"Let's take the truck, drive around, and see who the closest neighbor is."

We recognized the old Sim's place, which had been abandoned for what appeared to be a long time. There was no one living within five miles of our new bug out location.

I said, "I say this is what we were looking for. We need to figure out how to move a mountain of supplies in without leaving a trail that can be followed."

Mike replied, "We also have to decide who's going to know about the place and can help get it ready. I say we haul a couple of campers up here to save time building a shack in the cave."

"I think that's a great idea. Let's move as much as possible in a short time and vary our drive in to keep from beating down the weeds and brush. The Humvee has a hitch. Let's load down one of the older campers I stored over at Sam's old place and take as much as we can in one trip."

Mike nodded, "Great idea. We'll find, load down three of the campers over the next week, and only make three trips to get most of our supplies and gear over here to our new hideout."

My eyes turned to Mike. "I say we bring Sally and Joan out here on the first trip and ask their opinions about the others. I'll pull a trailer with the truck, and you take the Humvee and another trailer. They can help us load the supplies. We can take some of the canned goods and dry goods from that last find that we hid away."

"I agree. Let's catch them this afternoon after dinner."

I caught Callie later that day and asked her opinions on several topics, "What do you think about Grant?"

My daughter didn't mince words. "He's a piece of crap and a troublemaker. Carrie tells me about how he's always undercutting what we're trying to do, and he's lazy. Paul and I had a discussion, and he agrees that Grant has to go. I was going to tell you about this after dinner this evening."

"What about Mary?"

"Dad, she thinks the sun shines around Grant. Carrie hates living with them and asked if she could move in with us. I know that Mary is a good person, but she's on Grant's team, not ours."

I said, "Now, the hard question, what do you think about Paul?"

A big smile appeared on Callie's face. "I really like him, and he's my boyfriend. You already knew that, didn't you?"

"I assumed as much. Are y'all....?

Callie interrupted me with, "Dad, we're not having sex. Well, not yet anyway. Paul and I are interested in the same things, and we care for each other a lot."

Holy crap. *Not yet.* I stayed calm. "That's not what I was going to say, but I like your answer."

I changed the topic. "What do you think about his mom? Can she be trusted?"

"Yes, she's a lovely person and becoming a much stronger person. I trust her and Paul."

I thought and then spoke. "You're sixteen years old, and not so long ago, you would have been married, had a bunch of kids, and been plowing fields with your husband. Are you grown up enough to be treated as an adult and keep what I tell you in confidence?"

"I hope you already know the answer to that question. I would do anything to protect you, Mom, and our friends."

I nodded and said, "I knew the answer, but I wanted to hear it from your lips. Is Paul mature enough to be trusted and handle a man's job?"

"Sure, he can handle everything you throw at him. Have you noticed that he's not the skinny beanpole like he was several months ago? He's worked his ass off around the farm and put on twenty pounds of muscles. I like muscles."

I scowled. "Darling, this is touchy, but I think we need to have that sex talk again."

"What do you want to know? Supposing it's not too embarrassing asking your daughter for sex advice. In that case, I'll start with always wear protection until you're in a committed relationship. Then ...."

I broke in and said, "Smartass. I trust your judgment. Just don't do anything that can't be undone."

She snickered, "Is that your way of saying don't get knocked up."

"Damn right, it is. I don't want to have to beat the tar out of Paul."

Callie smirked. "I don't know. Dad, he's getting awful strong."

I gave her a hug and said, "Well, I feel better."

"Me too."

***

We took Joan and Sally for a ride the next morning to check out a small warehouse complex about fifteen miles from the farm out Highway 60 East. Along the way, Joan kept noticing travel trailers sitting in people's yards or for sale in car lots.

"Zack, those trailers could come in handy for visitors to the farm."

"Yes, they could."

What I was really thinking was that they would fit right into our hideout.

The warehouses were tucked in the back corner of an industrial complex with light manufacturing and a few warehouses. The complex was off on a side road and couldn't be seen from Highway 60. We cautiously drove into the complex, keeping vigilant for snipers and trouble in general. We searched each building, starting with the ones at the front of the complex.

We found several items that would come in handy around the farm but no food, weapons, or ammunition. We entered the next to the last building and were disappointed to see that the racks were full of books, CDs, and DVDs.

"Hey gang, we need to search these books for survival manuals. You know the type that has what wild plants you can eat, natural medicines, and army books on how to blow things up. Stuff like that. I'm going to bring Callie and Paul over to search through them."

Sally replied, "Great idea. We may have food now, but next year is a crapshoot."

I waved at everyone to move on to the next building when Joan said that she wanted to go to the back of the building. She's seen some light glancing off something shiny.

"Okay, I'll watch your back while you see what's gleaming back there. Let's don't take too long. Mike and I have a surprise for you two ladies."

We walked on back into the darkness and heard what sounded to be puppies whining and yipping. I turned my flashlight on and saw about twenty eyes looking back at me. There was no growling, but we both drew and raised our handguns.

"Look, Zack, there's a pack of dogs living here. They're friendly and well-nourished. Oh, shit. Look over there."

There was pallet after pallet of dog food, cat food, and all types of pet food. The dogs had torn into several bags and were feasting on the spilled food. I walked on further back and hit the jackpot. There were ten long rows of racks that contained people food. There was cereal, canned goods, candy, flour, salt, sugar, and rice. I called for Mike and Sally to join us.

"Zack, this makes it much easier to stock our new place."

Joan added, "I can't wait until we can tell the others. We need to get a bunch of trucks down here today and take this to the farm."

"No, we're going to take a small part of it to a hidden location before we tell the others. Joan and Sally, this is not what we really took you out to find. This is pure dumb luck that we found what we needed. We were going to take you to our hidden fallback location. We needed you to help us stock it and make it livable, just in case the farm is overrun."

"You don't want to share the food?"

"Yes, but after we have stuck some away for an emergency. You two can't ever tell anyone about our hiding place. We'll bring some others into the plan later, but not now."

Sally replied, "I think it's a great idea. Anyway, we found the food, and most people these days would keep it all to themselves. You say we just take a small part and share the rest. I'm okay with that."

Joan thought for a minute and agreed.

"Mike, I want to use those travel trailers we saw along the way here to haul the food to the hideout and then to live in if we have to. Joan and I'll go back up the highway and bring back the most travel-worthy trailer we can find. You two start selecting the items that we want to fill the trailer."

We stopped and looked at several trailers before finding a big two-year-old camper who looked ready to hit the road. The tires were inflated, and the trailer looked dusty but brand new. I quickly hitched it up while Joan kept guard. We were soon on our way back to the warehouse and arrived a short while later. I backed the trailer down the aisle with Joan guiding me with the aid of my flashlight. There was a big pile of can goods and other food items ready to be loaded. Mike had used a manual pallet jack to move whole pallets to the end of the aisle to be loaded. There was also a pallet made up of toilet paper, soap, feminine hygiene products, and other medical supplies.

Joan said, "Oh, my! Sally, I love you. Where did you find all of this?"

"At the back of the last row. I threw in some perfume also. The girls back at the farm will be happy when we're able to take some back there. Those Sears catalogs were way too rough for me."

I laughed and replied, "Ladies, everyone knows that phone books have much softer paper. Hey, look, the medical supplies have everything you need for first aid. There's even some of the quick clotting powder, WoundSeal."

Sally replied, "There's a whole row of everything from first aid kits, bottles of rubbing alcohol to aspirin."

We stuffed the trailer with as much as it would safely carry, closed the doors, and traveled to the underground water storage tank. Even though I had to weave around some small trees, I could drive the Humvee right into the large opening and took the trailer to the back of the cavern.

I said, "Ladies, let's unhook the trailer and make at least two more runs today before we head back to the farm. I want to move about a hundred pallets of the food here before we start taking food back to the farm. By my quick count, that still leaves approximately 1,300 pallets of food. We can share with Owensville and perhaps keep the mayor off our backs for a while. That warehouse will be over a hundred degrees by summer, so let's make sure we bring anything that will ruin in the heat. This underground tank will stay in the low sixties if we block the opening. I'd bring any medical supplies that will ruin in the heat first. We can share them later as needed."

Sally replied, "Boys, we're going to be traveling on this road a lot to get this food out of here. Someone will notice the traffic and get nosey. Then we'll have to fight for our own food. What if we call Ally on the radio and tell her to get Lynn, Callie, and Paul to bring two trucks and meet us on 60 where the other trailers are? Two of us can take the next load onto the hideout while the others wait for the rest of our team. Let's move as much as we can now."

I agreed. "Damn, you're right. You and Mike take the next load, and Joan and I'll be at that car lot with the blue Northwood camper. You'll have to call them when you cross over to Highway 54 because the radio won't reach them from here. Just tell them we need them and the trucks. Nothing else."

They dropped us off at the car lot on their way, and Joan and I had an awkward forty minutes to fill.

Joan caught my attention and said, "Zack, Callie, and Paul are getting too close to suit me. What do you think?"

"I like Paul, and I think they'll be good for each other. Paul is a great boy and a hard worker. Callie has more organization and drive. They'll make a great team and will deliver some beautiful grandkids."

She poked me in the ribs. "I know you said that just to piss me off. I hate you."

"Then, it'll be easy for you to move on and date Chuck."

She ranted and raved for the rest of the time until they arrived. I ignored her, and that really pissed her off.

The others showed up in a little over an hour, and I greeted them, "We'll explain in a short while. Just help us hook up the trailers."

Ally smiled. "Well, hi to you, too."

I smiled back at her. "Hurry, we don't have much time left."

We hitched the trailers, took them to the warehouse, and backed them into the racks by the food. They were in awe of the row after row of food. Callie immediately wanted a puppy, and I told her she could have her pick after we got the food to a safe location.

Lynn heard me and asked, "Aren't we taking the food to the farm?"

I said, "Most of it will go to the farm, but we're taking about a tenth of it to our fallback location. Mike and I have found a place for us to retreat to if the farm ever gets too dangerous to live there. We went looking for food today to stock it and hit the jackpot. We're afraid that someone will notice us coming and going and try to take it away. That's why we're in a hurry and why we'll leave guards here at the warehouse while we take these loads and three more. The place isn't far, and we can stock our place and get ready to take more to the farm and distribute the rest to our friends."

We loaded the two trailers and had them on their way in just over half an hour. Everyone was exhausted, but I told them to rest on the way to the fallback position. I stayed with Ally and Paul to guard the warehouse. I wanted to see how Paul reacted around me after telling him that I knew about him and Callie.

Paul broke the ice by saying, "Mr. Johnson, I know Callie told you that we're dating. Do you have any concerns?"

"Son, I have a million concerns, but not about you two. Both of you're smart, hardworking, and good people. Just don't tell her anything that you don't mean."

"I won't."

I said, "Paul, I've taken you under my wing, so to speak, and have tried to teach you some skills that should come in handy. I want to continue the mentoring process."

"I'd really like that, Mr. Johnson."

"Let's start with you calling me Zack. You're a man now, and I'll treat you like one as long as you act like one."

"Thanks, Zack. I'm not sure that Joan likes me."

I chuckled, "First, you'd better call her Mrs. Johnson until she says otherwise if you want to stay on her good side. She won't like any boy who's dating Callie until she gets to know him. Take it slow in front of her and be yourself. She'll warm up to you."

Paul went into the warehouse to find the puppies, which left me alone with his mom.

Ally couldn't hold it in any longer and laughed. "I'm sorry, but you're afraid of Joan, aren't you?"

I put my hand on her shoulder. "No, but you know all too well that a pissed-off mother-in-law is not going to be a good start for the boy. He should be afraid of her until I get her used to the idea that Callie's growing up."

We delivered the three loads to the hideout, and Mike stopped the team a couple of times to borrow some cargo trailers. Then we started working on loading some cargo trailers to take to the farm. We used the radios to let our other farmers know about our find, and soon, fourteen trailers were being loaded. We worked on loading and unloading trailers into the wee morning hours. I asked Ally to take a short drive into Owensville with me and radioed ahead for Bert to meet me at the roadblock on Highway 60 East.

I walked up to Bert. "Bert, we found a lot of food and want to share it with you. What you do with it is up to you. We've

245

already taken enough to make sure that your families are cared for and stockpiled enough to take care of all of your deputies and their families until our crops come in. I figure the rest should go to Owensville."

"Thanks, we have plenty of grain thanks to your idea about checking the railcars and trucks. We are running out of other food. Something stinks in Owensville. My men hear rumors that the mayor's getting food from Anderson and keeping it for her friends. If this gets out, there will be riots."

I changed my mind. "Bert, I take back what I said about giving you the food."

"What?"

"Let us farmers hand out the food directly to the citizens."

Bert grinned. "Great. I don't want the mayor to get her grubby hands on the food."

***

"Callie, I want you, Paul, Carrie, and Susie to search through the books to find any survival manuals, medical books, or anything that will be useful for our survival. Then look for how-to-fix stuff books and then finally books to educate our children. Assume that there won't be another book published in the next 25 years."

"Dad, do you really think it will take that long to get the country back on its feet?"

I frowned but was honest. "I don't have an answer, so I'm assuming the worst case. I want to always be positive and hope for the best but prepare for the worst. We'll use the books to develop experts who can train others. Guns are powerful, but knowledge is the most powerful thing a person can have."

"Dad, I'm bringing two of the puppies with us. They're Labs and will make good guard dogs."

I replied, "Well, they might be good hunting dogs, and I guess they'll bark if a stranger comes along. Make sure that you have most of the dog and cat food brought to the farm."

"Okay."

They sorted books for five days. They found a treasure of books on everything from what wild plants to eat to an Army field manual on making deadly improvised weapons and medical books. Callie also brought fifty boxes of CDs and DVDs with movies and how-to films.

"Dad, we found Peterson's - Edible Wild Plants, Alton's - The Ultimate Survival Guide, and Canterbury's - Bush Craft 101. There're many more books on survival, weapons, and food preparation."

"Great start for our library, but what are you going to do with the DVDs?"

Callie said, "There have to be some DVD players and TVs out there sitting in metal cargo containers that are useable. We'll need some kind of entertainment."

***

"Dad, while you were gone, we received a call on that long-range radio that Mr. Gold left us. It was Davi. She said they arrived at their destination, and things were much worse than expected. They were okay but moved on to their second location. She said she might be out of range for several weeks. That was all."

I grimaced. "Darn, I wanted to talk to Davi. Did you tell her what was going on up here?"

"No. I just said things were the same as when she left. I didn't know who else was listening."

"Good girl. Until things get back to normal, never talk longer than a few minutes, and never give away your location."

Callie said, "I guessed as much. Oh, by the way, what did she mean by asking me to ask if you were thinking of her every night?"

"Nothing."

Callie giggled, "Thinking or dreaming?"

✪

Chapter 7 - Free Food

Daviess County, Kentucky

Talking our community of farmers into trading pallets of the newfound food and a small part of our vegetables to the people of Owensville was easy. Convincing them that the town wouldn't try to seize all of our food was the tricky part. We held a meeting the next day after the food was found, and all agreed we should trade the extra food to the local charities and food banks for trade goods. That would set the stage for a *'there's no free lunch'* discussion and still gain goodwill from the people of Owensville. We would also offer free classes on how to grow backyard gardens to help them become more self-sufficient. We asked the sheriff to contact the local church charity groups and the food bank to tell them to be ready to accept our food, with the conditions that they trade for it with items that we needed. He was to inform the mayor after we had started the transfer of food under the watchful eyes of his deputies. The thought was that the farmers would get the goodwill, and the Mayor wouldn't try to seize the food. The mayor was down to less than eleven policemen, and they were rebelling at the long hours and lack of food. Part of our plan was Bert would deliver to them behind the station and let them know we appreciated their service and understand they don't have time to farm. They were told we would keep them fed as long as we could do so. That was Chuck's idea.

We split up and made deliveries to the Catholic and Protestant charities and the Owensville Food Bank at 6:00 am, which was an hour before they opened for the day. I covered the Food Bank since we thought the mayor and her people might show up there over the others. Since there was no major announcement by the plan, the usual crowd of people at each charity was looking for food. The organizers and directors of each group were very pleased with the assistance and our overall plan of trading the food for trade goods. We gave a list with everything from old cars, tractors, farm supplies, and fencing down to gas and diesel. We also offered training on how to grow vegetable gardens for anyone who desired the training.

All but a few people were happy with the arrangement and promised to bring trade goods in over the next week. We told them we would trust them and would keep bringing food as we found it until the crops came in.

The Food Bank director said, "Zack, thanks so much for the help. Only about two-thirds of our people are trying to help themselves, and I'm afraid the others will starve this winter or riot for food. You do know if they start going hungry, they could try to raid your farms."

"We do, and that's part of our reason for helping them with the training. I hate to say it, but we're also ready in case they try to raid us. We have had months to prepare, and it won't turn out good for anyone who tries to attack our farms."

The director said, "I couldn't help but notice that all of your people are heavily armed, and several appear to be on watch."

I replied, "That's right. Every one of our group has had extensive training and is prepared to fight to protect our lives and our farms. Why hasn't the city of Owensville done more to get large-scale farming going in the parks, golf courses, and vacant land around the city? We'll be glad to help even though it's too late for some crops."

"I don't know, but I suspect it's because many of our leaders, including me, thought the government would come and help us through this disaster."

I insisted. "Don't wait for help. Help yourselves, or many of you'll starve. We can help if our crops come in without any issues, but we can't produce enough for ourselves and all of the people in the city this year."

I'd just finished speaking when the mayor's car and a police car drove up. She was red in the face and walking fast at the sheriff and me.

She asked, "What the hell is going on here? You should have obtained permission to deliver this food, and it should have been delivered to the city to dole out."

I spoke out, "Mayor, it's our food, and we'll damn well do with it what we want. The charities we traded the food to have been doing this for many years and are much more capable of handling the distribution than a bunch of politicians."

The chief of police and Bert were talking off to the side when the mayor called them over. "I want this stopped and the food confiscated to be used for the good of *all* of the people of Owensville."

The chief and his deputy looked around, took note of the ten heavily armed farmers, and said, "Mayor, they're trading food for trade items they need. They're doing nothing wrong, and the charities have been handling food distribution to needy people for over a hundred years. I doubt the city could do as good a job as these volunteers. They're not breaking the law, so my hands are tied."

The Food Bank director said, "Now Alice, these fine people are helping feed our people when they could have kept this food for themselves. We should be thanking them, not trying to bully them. Zack, I'm sorry about this, and I'm sure that the mayor means well."

The mayor quickly noticed the people were all standing on Zack's side and pointing at her when one of the crowd said, "Mayor Bonner, are you trying to take this food away from us? What have you done to help us grow our own food?"

That brought shouts from the rest to leave their food alone. The mayor glared at me and said, "I'm sorry. There's been a communication error, and the city just wants to make sure that the food is fairly given away."

I spoke up, "Mayor, we're not *giving* the food away free to anyone. We expect these great people to trade goods to us that we need for food. This is not *welfare*."

She jumped into her car and left.

The police chief came over and said, "Zack, you farmers have made a lot of good friends by getting the barter for food going, but you've made an enemy out of the mayor. Watch your back around her and Prescott's people. He's the real power behind her. Thanks for the food for my men and me. It's hard to work sixteen-hour days and then try to feed your families. The mayor doesn't get that. I have lost over sixty percent of my men and women, thanks to her edicts and demands. We're dropping back to twelve-hour days, and I'm giving every man a day off, thanks to Bert covering for us. Thanks again."

The word quickly spread, and hundreds of people showed up with goods to trade for food. We drove back to the farm after all of the food had been unloaded. We'd received several loads of everything from tools to gas that had been siphoned out of family cars.

Bert said, "Zack, that's another warning about the mayor and Prescott. We need to figure out how to deal with them."

"Well, undercutting their base of support from the citizens was first on my list."

Bert smiled. "Damn, you're way ahead of me."

"No, just a yard or two. Let's get the group together after we deal with the Ohio gang and start planning."

★

Chapter 8 - War

Ohio County, Kentucky

We'd watched the gang members from a distance for several weeks and made notes on their weapons, manpower, and fortification of their compound. I only used a small group of my most trusted friends to plan, surveil the enemy, and conduct the attack. Grant, Mary, and Carrie were kept in the dark. There were only about fifty gang members, along with about seventy women and a handful of children staying at the gang's compound. They were conducting their business from a strip mall at the crossroads formed by Highway 33 and Old Barn View Road. Dense woods were behind the strip mall, and several abandoned farms were across the road from their headquarters. We had our pick of places to watch them.

Sally suggested we throw the gang a barbecue as we did for the biker gang in Vincennes. However, the gang up in Indiana was barely getting by and was ready to throw a party when we helped the cow wander in among them. It turned out to be a slaughter. They also only had a few women and children hostages.

This gang had terrorized the local farmers to bring half their crops into them every Saturday morning. Once we noticed the pattern, it was easy to lace the food with the laxative and ipecac. This had proven very effective down in Rolling Hills. I wanted to avoid as much gunfire as possible around the women and children even though we knew most women were armed.

While the sheriff wouldn't join us in the attack, ten of his men did join us while another nine guarded our farms against attack while we were conducting the raid. He also contributed significantly to our ability to attack in silence by giving me three suppressors that fit ARs. His crew had taken them from one of the gangs that had attacked right after the lights went out.

"Try to bring in some captives. No one will believe you had to kill them all," Bert warned me. "Please, help me out with the mayor."

I said, "I will, but make sure your guys keep Grant and Mary from leaving my farm until we get back. They're bound to notice our absence."

"Frank will handle that and guard against any surprise attacks. I'll personally cruise the roads in your neck of the woods until y'all get back. I don't want any detail, but how long do you think it'll take?"

I answered, "It's a crapshoot, but as little as four hours or as long as two days."

The attack started several hours after the farmers delivered their crops to the gangs. We had four teams of two follow the gang's enforcers out to several farms to ensure the farmers would send a larger load next time. The farmers were not growing enough to feed the thugs and themselves and were holding back enough to prevent starvation. The gangs didn't care. Our snipers shot six of the gang enforcers out at the farms, and the asshats didn't know they were under attack. Lynn and Callie were supposed to get close enough to the remaining two to shoot them with their pistols. Still, a farmer's wife accidentally warned the thugs just as the girls were about to fire.

Lynn suddenly found herself in a hand-to-hand fight with a huge man armed with a tire iron. He was just about to break a farmer's hand when he turned and charged Lynn. Callie started to shoot both men, but the farmer's wife and kids were in the line of fire. The man reached for his pistol when Callie turned, raised her leg, and kicked the gun out of his hand. She came back around and chopped him in the throat, but he turned enough that the blow hit the side of his neck. It gave him a lot of pain, but he was able to charge towards her. She rolled left at the last second, tripped him, and kicked him in the ass as he fell past her.

Lynn ducked as the tire iron whizzed over her head and struck a blow to the thug's ribs as he swung wildly. She then raised a leg, whirled sideways, and kicked the bastard in the groin.

The man attacking Callie pulled his knife and lunged at her, missing his target as she jumped sideways, drawing her own bayonet.

She faced him and said, "You're going to die today. I hope you said your prayers last night."

He faked left, then right, and got a deep slice across his face for his efforts. He lunged wildly again. Callie blocked his knife with her free hand and drove the bayonet through his lower rib cage and up into his heart. He fell to the ground. She turned to see Lynn facing the other asshole as he got up and tried to tackle her. She grabbed his head, fell sideways, and broke his neck on the way to the ground.

Both were battered, and Callie found a cut on her arm that needed attention but was otherwise in good shape, considering the fate of the bastards lying on the ground. The farmer's wife poured the WoundSeal on Callie's wound, and the bleeding stopped immediately. She bandaged the arm, thanked them for taking out the gang members, and asked what they could do to help fight the gang.

Lynn said, "Just watch for any trying to escape down this road and shoot them."

They hopped in the truck and drove on to their next assignment.

Callie asked, "Will they shoot the creeps?"

"I don't think so. Those were good people, but I think they're waiting for someone to do their dirty work for them."

The next task was to take out all four roadblocks without the gang becoming wise to the attack. After that, it was waiting on the ipecac and laxatives to work. It would start within a few minutes for the ipecac and hours for the laxatives after the food was delivered. Even criminals liked fresh garden greens, tomatoes, and fruit.

The four to five thugs manning each of the roadblocks would be attacked at 2:00 pm. Three of the roadblocks could be taken out with the suppressed .223s from over two hundred yards. The fourth had to be taken out the hard way. Per schedule, Joan, Mike, and Ally each fired on their roadblock at 2:00. They were the best sharpshooters and were spread out to three roadblocks with another team protecting them. They started firing, and in under a minute, all thirteen of the gang members were dead or dying. Many had their brains blown all over the road. Roger and I had the job of taking out the last roadblock. The plan was for me to sneak up close enough to shoot any of the assholes that Roger couldn't kill from a hundred yards out. He had an AR15 with a nine power scope, and I had my 9mm carbine.

I figured Roger could kill two and maybe a third, leaving me with two to dispatch to hell. I didn't want to take any prisoners and hoped none would try to surrender. I crawled through the woods, checking the time every ten minutes to make sure I was in position behind a fallen log just twenty feet from the barricade when Roger fired.

I crawled into position with a few minutes to spare when I noticed that I could only see two men and a woman sitting in lawn chairs manning the roadblock. I looked around and didn't see anyone else. This was very odd because our surveillance had always seen four to five people manning every roadblock. Several thoughts went through my mind, and then I saw a man's head explode, heard the crack of Roger's rifle, and another head explode before the next sound of the gun. The third head ducked before I could fire, so I crawled under the log and crawled to the backside of the old car that was half of the roadblock. I saw the thug on the ground peering around the truck's tire, trying to get a bead on the shooter. All I could see was the thug's back and butt from my position, so I fired twice and placed two slugs into his backside. The body rolled over, and I saw it was a middle-aged woman with tattoos all over her face. This distracted me enough that I didn't notice the person sneaking up on me from my right side. I turned to see a gun pointed at me, saw the flash, and heard the explosion when the asshole shot me in the chest twice. I started pulling the trigger as I fell, and everything went black.

***

I heard people laughing and talking about the party that was starting in a few minutes. My head hurt, and my chest felt like it had been run over by a semi. I was dizzy and couldn't open my eyes. I heard the following, "Everything went according to plan until Zack got ambushed by a couple of bikers who decided to go behind some bushes and make love, not war."

Everyone laughed, and then I heard, "The girl didn't have a shirt or bra, and the guy didn't have any pants on when they died. Losing your life over some tail. Go figure."

I tried to get up, and my stirring brought on more talking.

Mike said, "I think he's trying to wake up from his nap."

I felt a cool cloth on my forehead and heard, "Honey, are you okay?""

Then I heard, "Daddy, are you okay?"

Mike snickered. "His damn head is too hard. The bullet bounced off it and killed one of the thugs."

I opened my eyes and saw Joan's eyes looking down on me. My head was in her lap, and everyone was looking at me. "What happened? Where are we? Why aren't we fighting the gang?"

Ally spoke up, "That was yesterday. We defeated them and have already freed their captives and taken the prisoners to the sheriff."

"We won?"

"Yes, we picked off the ones at the roadblocks and the enforcers first, and by then, it was a matter of picking off the rest as they went to or came out of the outhouses. We actually were able to kill another twenty without firing a shot," Lynn said as she drew her bayonet and made a slicing motion.

Mike took over the conversation. "Everyone, even you, accomplished their assignments. Your methods were much more over the top but effective nonetheless. I am very proud of this team. We eliminated the entire gang except for a few mean bitches

256

that threw their guns down when they realized they were being mowed down like hay."

I was confused. "What happened to me? I feel like I was hit by a truck."

Mike held up a bulletproof vest and stuck his fingers in two holes. "Those holes match some pretty black and blue bruises on your chest, and you have a groove in your head. Lucky for you, your hair will probably cover that big ass scar. Old buddy, you're one lucky SOB."

"Did Roger kill the ones who shot me?"

Mike chortled, "Hell no, you did. You were in a gunfight at five feet and survived thanks to the body armor Bert gave to us. Roger killed two from long range. You shot one hiding under the truck right through her ass. Killed her dead. The other two were behind a car screwing in the weeds."

"Mike, there're children present."

"Sorry, the lovemaking couple was startled by the gunfire, dropped what they were doing, ran at you half-naked, and you had the mother of all gun battles. You shot the lady twice in the chest and the man once in the stomach. They both were dead before Roger got down to the roadblock. He thought you were dead at first. A head wound bleeds like a stuck pig. You were covered with blood from head to toe."

Mike, then Roger, Joan, and Paul gave me accounts of 'the battle for Ohio County' as it was known from then on. Then they threw a hell of a barbecue with me lying on a couch that had been brought out into the yard. Callie took Joan's place and helped me sit up, so I could see what was going on. I looked at my little girl and saw the bandage on her arm.

"Callie, did you get wounded during the fight?"

"Yeah, a guy tried to stick a rather large knife into me, but I taught him the error of his ways. Mom doesn't like me saying that I ripped his stomach open on the way to his heart. I must be more lady-like."

I heard a muffled giggle, looked up, and saw Ally covering her mouth.

I said, "Come on over, girl, and sit down beside me and tell me your story of the battle. Everyone knows more than I do. I know you were assigned to take out the four guards at the roadblock. How did that go?"

Ally told me, "I guess it went as planned. I'll never get used to taking a human life, but after we had freed those women and children, I know we did the right thing killing those animals. They were abusing the young girls and raping the women. They set up a brothel and were charging men to abuse the women."

"Wait a minute. Do you mean *local* men?"

Ally said, "The women said that the men were from Anderson and over towards Madison. The gang even sold women for the men to take with them. They said the gang prized young teen girls because they sold for the highest price. The gang took silver, gold, ammunition, drugs, and medical supplies for them."

"My God, how perverted *is* this world?"

Ally snorted, "After helping those women, I can attest to the fact that there're sixty-three fewer perverts in the world. I'm proud to say I sent thirteen to hell myself."

I placed my arm around her and said, "Don't think too much about the deaths of those perverts. We'll probably have to kill a bunch more. They got what they deserved. I won't lie to you and say that that'll get any easier."

Ally cried out, "Zack, what I worry about is that these men were probably doing this *before* the lights went out, and no one did anything about it."

I said, "I've been wondering the same thing myself. Perhaps, Epstein wasn't the only pervert in the world before the lights went out. Maybe, this is a planned cleansing by God. I'm not a religious guy, but I've been wondering about this."

I must have fallen asleep because I woke up with my head in Ally's lap and found myself looking up into her eyes. We talked for over an hour with my head in her lap until the meal was ready. Roger and Mike helped me to the picnic table, and I was surrounded by the people who meant the most to me. All of them were heroes that day, and it was then that I knew that we would survive and make it through these rough times. Tears came to my eyes when I wondered who would be missing from the table this time next year.

✪

Chapter 9 - Trucks and Trains

Central Kentucky

Mike's team looked at every farm, junkyard, and the back of every mechanic's garage to build a list of old trucks that were sound enough to get back into operation. They were able to jumpstart five and bring them back home. The farmers who owned them immediately put three into use. The other two were driven to the farm, serviced, and placed into operation, towing another fifteen that wouldn't start back to the farm to be repaired. Mike asked for and received help from the mechanics in the area and quickly had another seven serviced and up and running. Most had gummed up carburetors and bad batteries; they were easy to get running. The rest had either a blown engine or transmission. They found the best parts and made whole trucks that would run. They made sure the entire community knew what trucks they were looking for and brought the trucks or parts to the farm if possible.

Mike spent several days each week fetching parts and whole vehicles back to the farm. He expanded his acquisitions to farm equipment, cars, camper trailers, cargo trailers, several bulldozers, an old backhoe, and a bi-plane. I told Mike that he needed to get more selective, or he would have to find another storage lot. He had five acres of junk vehicles back behind the lake. Roger took another crew and hit every service station and Wal-Mart to get batteries, tires, and auto parts.

Mike told me, "You gave me orders to get trucks running. I have twenty-eight trucks in operation, a bulldozer, and a large backhoe. The bi-plane has to wait a while. I also found a large VW graveyard, and Roger thinks we can get several of them running. We won't have up-to-date show cars, but we won't suffer from a lack of transportation. You need to find us some gas."

"I'll work on that as soon as I can get in to see Bert. He told me Owensville has millions of gallons of gas and diesel in the tanks down by the river. We can trade them food, trucks, and cars for fuel. I will give Bert the two Ford panel wagons and the city that two-ton green Chevy you got running yesterday. I hope the mayor will want to work with us. Bert floated it past her that we could deliver vehicles for gas and diesel. I'll follow up on that myself if the bitch will talk to me after her rant at the Food Bank. How are Carrie and Sally holding up to the mechanic's training?"

Mike's chest swelled, and he smiled. "Great, Sally's doing very well, and Carrie is a star. We'll be able to turn her loose in a few months. The older vehicles are easy to maintain. Both started out gapping plugs, setting points, and cleaning carburetors. Both of them can now build an engine from parts, replace worn brakes and replace parts that are bad with someone directing them. It will take much longer for them to develop troubleshooting skills.

"Great."

Mike said, "I want you to know Sally, and I are seeing each other, and I think she may be the one I've been looking for."

"Seeing means...........?"

Mike acted offended. "Seeing means dating. I'm taking her on a picnic on Saturday, and on Sunday, we'll be hunting for some redbud trees to replant at the farm."

"So. dating is not dead in this post-apocalyptic world. I'm starting to think I need to find someone to settle down with myself."

Mike said, "I'm glad that you're moving on. Sister Joan?"

I chuffed, "Not unless I can get over her leaving me for Todd."

"Zack, to forgive is to forget. She knows she messed up and would do anything to rewind history and go back to before that happened, but she can't. After all, she's my little sister, and I want the best for her, even if she had her head up her ass on the Todd crap. Try to forgive her for Callie's sake."

I gave my old buddy a pat on the back. "Sorry, old buddy, but I'm just not able to do that at this time. Falling for Geena showed me there was life beyond Joan, and I intend to not look back and get on with my life."

"So, you're going to see Ally?"

"Maybe. I may ask her to go on a ride."

Mike laughed, "Be careful. She's getting very good with that AR and her 9mm. I don't have to remind you that Ally took out four of the creeps over in Ohio County at the roadblock. She also saved my ass when a couple of those scumbags caught me from behind during our little skirmish. She needs some practice with the AR, but she's getting there. She's our second-best sniper."

I exhaled and gave a grunt. "Should I be scared?"

"You were just shot twice, and the vest saved your life. Don't piss her off. By the way, how's your head and chest doing?"

"Okay, until I cough or twist or laugh."

***

Jacob, his son, and Callie spent a week building a mobile repair truck. They took the bed off a service truck from a diesel repair business. They placed it on a two-ton 1975 Ford F350 with a 460 cubic inch V8 with plenty of horsepower to haul the bed and tons of equipment. They added a gas-powered air compressor to run air tools, an oxyacetylene torch to weld and cut, and a host of tools that would help get a locomotive running.

Jacob said, "Callie, the trick to welding is to keep the rod making small circles as you make the weld. Always wear protective clothing and gloves so you won't be afraid of being burned. You *will* get burned."

Callie continued welding the two scrap pieces together and said, "Can you teach me to solder and braze? I'll need to be able to do them for some of my inventions."

Jacob smiled. "I'll be glad to, as soon as we get the engine back home. I plan to head over to Sailsberg in two days. We'll check out the locomotive, determine what it will take to get it running, and if we have a way to drive it back here. I also want to check out the Old Timer's Engine Museum to see if we can get some smaller engines to power equipment. By the way, does Grant always complain all the time and hide when there's work to be done?"

Callie gave a thumbs-up sign. "Yes, that sums up his contribution to our group. Dad needs to make him disappear."

I found Ally and hesitated but built up the courage to ask, "Ally, how would you like to ride shotgun on a trip over to Sailsberg? Mike says you're more comfortable with your shotgun and pistol, and you're ready for guard duty. I'd like you to back me up if we're attacked. The rail crew will be armed, but we'll be their guards while they concentrate on the steam engine."

"I'd be happy to help out any way you need me. It'll be great to get away from the farm and see new territory. Do you think it'll be dangerous? Hey, are you well enough to travel that far?"

I smiled. "My chest still hurts, but I'm okay. Thanks for asking. Everything is dangerous these days, but I haven't heard of any serious threats over that way. Besides, you handled yourself very well over in Ohio County. I know you weren't in the actual firefight, but I know you killed over a dozen of the SOBs and saved Mike's life. I wouldn't take you if I thought we were walking into a battle. Actually, I have a personal reason for bringing you on this trip. I want to get to know you better. I want to ask you out on a date when we get back to the farm."

Ally replied, "Thanks for the compliment. I'd like to get to know you better also, and I can't imagine a date these days. Dinner and a movie?"

"That's funny. I was thinking of a picnic, going swimming in the river, or maybe just picking wildflowers. We have to start thinking as our ancestors did back in the 1850s. Perhaps horseback riding every now and then? Damn, I don't know. I just got up enough courage to ask you out and hadn't thought it completely through."

She took my hand and replied, "I'm flattered you're asking me out. I've been interested in you since I realized I had to move on after my husband's death. You're so good to Paul, and he comes to me every day, mentioning something you've taught him. I just thought you and Joan would get back together. She's trying hard to get back in your good graces. Are you sure you're over her?"

I chuckled, "I'm definitely over Joan. Honestly, I'm still grieving a bit over Geena, but I realize that you can't make it alone in this new world, so yes, I'm ready to date. Yes, Joan still wants me back. Joan and I grew up together and will always be friends, but the day she dumped me for that bastard over in Anderson was the day I wrote her off forever. Frankly, she's tried to get back with me and has even jumped in bed with me while I was asleep several times. I didn't touch her and ran her off. Don't get me wrong, I want female companionship, but not with her. Every time I think of her, I see her and Todd and get sick."

Ally said, "I wouldn't take kindly to her flirting with you if we start seeing each other, and I sure wouldn't want her to be in your bed. It would hurt and be a deal-breaker."

I replied, "I'll make sure she gets the message, and besides, I'm setting her up with Chuck."

"That makes sense. I see Chuck flirting with her every time he gets close."

"So, are we seeing each other, and do I need to give you my high school ring?"

Ally grinned, "We're now going steady, and you can keep the class ring. I'm not a loose woman, so we'll be going very slowly until I'm sure you're ready to go forward. If we go swimming, it won't be skinny dipping."

We laughed at her comments, and her smile was contagious. A smile spread across my face as I thought about the skinny dipping comment.

I replied, "I'm ready to move on, but I guess I'll have to convince you now. I'll go as slow as you want."

She said, "Our kids could be a small problem between us that could go either way. Paul and Callie are getting to be thick as thieves. I expect them to fall in love any day."

I nodded and then said, "Sorry, it's too late. They're in love. I had a great talk with Callie the other day. My problem is, I just don't think of Callie as being a woman, but she would be an old maid if we were back in the 1850s. The heart wants what the heart wants. I tried to give Callie an updated sex talk and let her know that I trust her to make the right decisions. She ended up giving *me* a sex talk."

Ally snickered, "That must have been awkward. I'll do the same with Paul, and I'm confident that he'll be too embarrassed to give me any sex hints. I'd love to have grandkids in about ten years but would rather the world be a bit safer before they're born. I'm glad, and a bit surprised that you didn't freak out. I like seeing you calm and thoughtful."

"Actually, I surprised myself. That's my baby girl."

Ally's eyes bugged out. "What if we get serious, and they get serious? Will that be weird for you?"

I smiled and said, "I *am* serious about you, and I like Paul. You've done well by him. If he chooses Callie to be his mate, it just shows that he has good taste. At the right time, tell him that her father has a gun, and he'd better not break her heart."

"Paul is a good boy. I don't see him just playing with a girl to get sex."

I frowned, "Darn, don't say sex when we're talking about my little girl."

She laughed and said, "Dad, get used to it. Your little girl has grown up."

"I know, but just let me slowly get used to the idea."

Ally pinched my arm and then kissed me on the cheek. "Oh, by the way, I have a big gun, too. Don't break my heart."

"I won't. We'll date, have a good time and see if we even like each other. That should give us time to get over the deaths of our loved ones."

She asked, "Does one ever get over the death of a loved one?"

"No, you just have to move on."

I leaned in, and we kissed.

I left Ally and started thinking about the past few months. I had bounced from the coyote ugly incident in Oregon to the tractor ride across Middle America with Geena and Sally to the recent fight with the drug gang and now, Ally. I'd progressed from drunken whoremonger, to leader of the greatest people on earth during a struggle for survival. Now, I finally fell in love with the woman I was meant to grow old for the rest of my life.

Then I thought I stole that scenario from a movie where the hero was looking over the battlefield, remembering how he got to that point in his life. I was no hero, but I would do the best I could to be the man these people, my daughter, and Ally needed. I need a beer to wash those thoughts down. Damn, my girlfriend actually brews ale. I am the luckiest man in post-apocalyptic America. I wondered if she knew how to distill alcohol? We could trade alcohol and ale.

***

Ally and I gave Jacob's crew an escort over to Sailsberg. Several roadblocks had to be dealt with. Luckily, locals who were just protecting their turf against outsiders manned them all. I talked with their leaders each time and told them about our plan to start a rail service through their communities, and all but one was very pleased with the idea. Jacob and I agreed that there was something fishy about the people manning the roadblock at Beaver Lake. They didn't give us any problems but didn't look like people from a farming community. Don't get me wrong, I have a couple of tattoos, and even Joan has a tramp stamp that I thought was gorgeous until Callie asked for one at twelve years old, but these guys had the full sleeves, wallets on chains, and do-rags. Pretty obvious. A damn biker gang had taken over Beaver Lake.

I warned, "Jacob, we can't do anything now, so don't poke the bear. We'll deal with these guys after we deal with Bonner. If they try to stop the rail from going through, we'll deal with them earlier. Let's make tracks."

Ally and I had several hours to tell each other our life stories and were both open with everything. Her husband had cheated on her several times, but she's stayed with him for the children's sake. He was a good father and actually a good husband, but he just couldn't stop chasing women. I told her about Joan leaving me for Todd and my subsequent fall into woman chasing and excessive drinking. I told her that I'd never cheated on Joan and was devastated when she'd left me. She never judged me or made any comments.

"Is that part of your life over?"

I said, "Well, I slipped a bit on the drinking when Geena was killed, but I won't go overboard ever again. I like beer and will have a drink. I just won't drink to excess, and I won't chase women now that I'm seeing you. Hell, I haven't been with a woman since the lights went out. Geena and I came close, but something always got in the way. God knows Joan tried to get me into bed, but you know how I feel about her."

"And you're okay with going slow?"

I grinned, "No, I'd rather go much faster, but it's what you need, and I care for you a lot."

We chitchatted the rest of the way, and the more I was around Ally, I knew this wasn't a passing fad I was experiencing.

We arrived at Sailsberg, and as expected, there was another roadblock. I asked to speak to their leader, and they brought the police chief out to meet us. I told him that I was from the Owensville area, and Bert had told me to look him up when I got to Sailsberg. The chief knew Bert, and that helped us get our foot in the door. We met with the town council, explained what we wanted to do, and wanted to get the railroad back in operation.

The community was doing reasonably well since the initial rioting and brief lawlessness. The mayor and police chief appeared nervous about our visit but were very accommodating. The area was peaceful and reminded one of a rural town before the turn of the century. They had a large Amish community nearby and had sought out their help in adapting to the new life without electricity. They were using horses and buggies and never even tried to get any vehicles running and had no plans to in the future.

I asked, "Would you trade us some of the old cars and trucks?"

The mayor said, "You can have them. What do you have that we can't provide for ourselves?"

I answered, "What do you need?"

"Some medicine, books, and some more horses."

I said, "We have a ton of books, a small amount of medicine that we can spare, but we also need more horses."

The mayor said, "We'll take the books and any medicine that you can spare."

"Have y'all checked the stalled trailers on the roads, railcars, and warehouses for food and other supplies?"

"No, we hadn't. Wouldn't that be stealing?

I said, "Since it's abandoned and those companies no longer exist, I think that it would be okay to salvage the supplies."

They argued among themselves and concluded they would take a town vote before they seized someone else's belongings.

On a whim, I said, "Would y'all mind if we take what we find out on the roads around here? We won't come into town and look into warehouses."

The chief said, "That's okay for you. We just don't want to before we put it to a vote."

Jacob asked, "Now, is it okay if we see if we can get the locomotive running?"

The mayor beamed, "You don't have to. Billy Gratten is the curator and train engineer for the museum. The train was in operation until the lights went out. He'll fire it up for you and oversee putting the rails back in place to move it to the main tracks. We only removed them after we brought the last locomotive into the museum yard."

Jacob asked, "How many locomotives do you have?"

"Two that are running, two more could be running, but only Billy can tell you how much work has to be done. The other two look great but are only here for the kids to climb around on. By the way, we have a whole wing of the museum filled with industrial and small steam engines that powered America until the

1930s. About half of them are in running condition, and most of the others could be placed back into operation."

I asked, "Don't y'all want to keep most of them for yourselves?"

"No, as you probably see, we have embraced this new, less complicated life. We don't hold it against you that you want cars, electricity, and modern conveniences, but we don't want to go back into the rat race. We would like to keep trading you for things we need, and if you don't mind, you can take what you need on the promise of repaying us with trade goods or help when we need it."

I said, "That's great news. Yes, we agree."

"Thanks, I think that'll be great for both groups."

"I agree."

I said, "Jacob, I think I should go back and bring some men and trucks back to haul some of these steam engines and hit and miss engines back to the farm. I also want to get people started fabricating the ability to power tools."

Jacob said, "I agree. It's safe enough here, and you have the big guns for the trip back. We'll work to move the train to the tracks and learn all about the locomotive while you're gone. I'd only take some of the smaller ones since we should have the train on the main tracks in less than a week."

I said, "Great, I'm just in a hurry to get the lights back on and get a jump start on starting manufacturing again. Besides, I always guard against our plans failing. This way, I'll know that we get at least a few engines."

"I'll pick out some equipment in my spare time and get it moved to the dock. How many trucks will you bring?"

I thought about how large the equipment was. "Probably three or four flatbed trucks."

Ally asked, "Not to question your judgment, but isn't Jacob right? All of the engines could be brought over on the train."

"Yes, he's, and never be afraid to question my judgment. I believe in the brainpower of the many. In this situation, I'm glad you didn't question it in front of Jacob because I'm diverting some of the engines to our hideout. The train doesn't stop there, and even if it did, we don't want everyone to know it even exists."

"Great idea. That's why you get paid the big bucks."

I chortled, "I haven't seen a paycheck in months."

Ally pulled me close, kissed me on the cheek, and said, "That's an advance on your big salary."

I replied, "I need to be paid more than once every four months."

She pulled me close again and whispered in my ear, "Don't get greedy. Where are you going to get coal for the boilers?" and kissed my ear.

"Coal?"

Ally said, "Yes, you'll need to burn something to heat the water to make steam to power the engine."

I'd been short-sighted. "Yes, we need coal and maybe wood before we get back into the 21st century. Believe it or not, there's a humongous pile of coal at the city power plant and at the dock on Green River, and I'll bet in several barges tied up at the dock. We won't have to mine coal for a while."

Ally asked, "Is there any gas or diesel in those barges? There should be thousands of gallons just in the tugs."

"You're one smart lady. I was focused on getting fuel from Owensville and forgot how common it is around the country. I'll have Roger start a crew searching for it."

We enjoyed telling each other stories about our past lives on the trip and returned to the farm in no time. I wished that we'd seen the people watching from cover just a few miles out of Sailsberg.

***

Mike said, "That's a great idea about checking the barges for fuel, but Paul already found a string of barges on the Green

River loaded with gasoline, diesel, and fertilizer. He went fishing this morning with Sam's grandson and came back with a stringer of fish and the good news."

I was proud of Paul. "I'll give Paul a pat on his back for that one. We need some tanker trucks."

Mike added, "Paul came up with something that will work until we can get some real tankers to do the job. His idea is to use empty plastic chemical totes to haul gas. We have a bunch of 250 and a few 500 gallon totes around the farms. Roger has already made two trips over to the barge, and now the problem is storing the gas safely. We don't want 10,000 gallons of gas around the house here, do we?"

"Darn, Paul is our hero."

Ally chimed in, "I'm one proud mom. We need to do something special for him."

I said, "Think of something, and we'll do it."

She said, "I will."

"Hey Mike, we came back early to take some trucks back to Sailsberg and bring some small steam and hit and miss engines back to the farm, which was traded to us for some books and what medicine we can spare. We can stop by that warehouse, get a load of books, and take them back to trade. Three trucks should do with two men per truck."

"Or women," Ally replied.

"That's what I meant," I said.

"Yeah."

***

The men had been watching since the new people arrived but stayed behind cover and reported to their leader. He had already been forcing the city to pay him not to attack and didn't like seeing this new group show up with the Humvee. He knew not to strike while the heavily armed vehicle was guarding the newcomers. His spies came and told him that the armored vehicle had left with two of the people. The others didn't appear to be

271

much of a threat. Three men, an old man, a young girl, and a woman, weren't much of a threat. The spies reported that they didn't see any weapons. That meant the only weapons they were likely to encounter were the deer rifles and .22s that the Sailsberg people had. He wasn't worried about the two cops. He'd have one of his men create a diversion to draw them and perhaps some of the town's people to the other end in the city. He didn't want to hurt the townspeople but would kill the men and capture the two women for his own use. The town's people had to work hard and pay tribute to him if they wanted to live in his kingdom.

Jacob looked up and saw the armed men walking towards them. "Hey, everyone. It looks like we've got company."

He looked at the museum curator and asked, "Should we be worried? These guys are armed and look a little rough."

"Be worried."

The men were still over a hundred feet away when Callie said, "Everyone, slowly get your pistols and be ready to grab your rifles. These are the bad guys, and we're about to be robbed or shot. There're only six of them and six of us. Shoot until they're down if they attack."

The men walked on up, and the leader said, "That's a nice truck you've got there. I know you won't mind if we borrow it for a few years."

Jacob replied, "Sorry, sir. We need our truck, and you can't borrow it today."

The man raised his pistol and started to say something when Callie shot him in the chest and started shooting at the others. Jacob shot one, Callie killed another, and the others killed the rest of the thugs. The thugs were no match for the well-trained group. The fight was over in a few seconds. The attackers were killed, and none of the team had been injured.

"Damn, what have you done? Those bastards will come back with more men and kill us all. "said Billy, the curator.

Callie asked, "Do you know these men?"

"Yes, they've been extorting us to pay them not to attack us. We wanted to kill them and get it over with, but the mayor wanted to pay them to leave us alone. The problem is that they always want more and more."

A few minutes later, the police chief and mayor ran up and were horrified that six men were lying dead on their street. The mayor moaned, "You've started a war. These men will come back and kill us all."

Callie asked, "How many of these assholes are there, and where do they come from?"

"There're about thirty of them, and they just moved in here from Ohio County a month ago. I thought we could pay them, and they'd leave us alone. Now, they'll kill us all."

Callie said, "No, they won't. We can hold them off until my dad returns this evening. Go get more people with guns and let's make a stand here at the museum. Take the elderly and children and hide them until this is over."

"Now, young lady, who put you in charge?"

Lynn answered, "If you want to stay alive, you'd better do what Callie says. Those men had pistols, shotguns, and deer rifles. We have ARs, carbines, and pistols. Moreover, we all have a couple of hundred rounds of ammo each. We can outshoot and outlast them in a fight. Get your asses in gear, and let's fortify this place.

Callie asked, "How many rounds did you fire?"

No one responded with more than six, so they were in great shape on ammo. Callie pulled the magazine out of the SUB-2000 and saw that the indicator holes showed twenty-eight remaining bullets. The extended Glock-17 mags had the numbered indicator holes, which was much better than the magazines that came with the carbine. There was no accurate way to tell how many rounds were left in them.

Callie said, "Only fire if you have someone in your sights. We have to hold them off, but we also need to kill as many as possible. Our goal is one shot, one dead asshole."

The man who led the cops away from the attack ran all the way to the truck hidden on the south side of town. Then, he hauled ass back to the gang.

"It was a massacre! They ambushed us before we could draw our guns!"

One of the thugs said, "Those peaceful, scared people in that town ambushed and killed six of my men? Don't you mean the visitors killed them?"

"No, the two in the Humvee left, and only three people stayed, an old man and two women. We never saw any weapons on them. It had to be the town's people."

The leader thought for a minute and had all of his men rounded up. "We just lost six good men today, and I want to punish that town. We don't want to kill them all because someone has to work in the fields. I want the people at the museum killed or captured, and then we'll gather up the townsfolk and make them wish our men were still alive. We won't kill them. We'll just have a little fun with the women."

The second attack began as an attempt to overrun the museum with sheer numbers. Eighteen thugs rushed the front of the building while another twelve covered them from the woods across the street. They came charging across the street, shooting and yelling. Lynn saw them break out of the woods, shouted to her friends, and started methodically shooting one after another.

Lynn yelled, "Callie, get those two sneaking around the side!"

Her carbine barked twice, and she replied, "Got 'em."

It was a turkey shoot. The dumbasses thought they could run headlong across the street, scare the crap out of the helpless people, and then celebrate. Only five of them made it across the road, and they were pinned down behind a couple of trucks that were there to haul the track and railroad ties to be laid to move the locomotive.

"Try not to damage the trucks. We still need them!" Jacob hollered.

"I'll take care of them," replied Lynn.

She dialed her scope on the AR into the distance and waited for one to reveal a body part. It only took a few seconds, and one lost most of his foot. He fell out from behind the truck, and she shot him in the chest. A few minutes later, another lost the top of his skull as he dared to peer above the bed of the truck. The rest used the trucks for cover and retreated back across the street and blended into the woods.

***

I caught Mike off to the side and told him what the real mission was to make sure he and Sally were one of the teams. We were back on the road in an hour and planned to load up the trucks today and start out early in the morning to bring the engines back home. I drove the Humvee towing a large trailer. We got some come-a-longs, block and tackles, and other gear to make moving the heavy engines a little easier. The ride over was quiet and peaceful until we were about five miles out and heard Lynn on the radio.

"We're under attack! Please help!"

I replied, "Lynn, we're about five miles out. What happened?"

"Some thugs are attacking from the front side of the Museum. We've fought them off four times, but the dumbasses keep attacking."

I asked, "Is everyone okay?"

"Yes. Hurry, they're attacking again."

We arrived in Sailsberg, and all hell broke loose. The fight was going on, and we came up behind the gang attacking our people in the museum.

"Ally, you drive while I man the SAWs. Drive right up behind them. Mike, park the trucks and pick off any that try to escape."

I aimed, squeezed the trigger, and strafed them from behind. The asshats were so busy trying to kill our people that we caught them by surprise. Six were dead before I let up on the trigger, and Mike's crew shot eight more trying to escape. Several escaped and ran into the woods. We didn't follow them, so we could check on our people. I asked Ally to man the SAWs so I could check on Callie. I approached the Museum, and I saw heads popping up from behind rail cars and railroad ties. Callie waved at me, and I ran over and hugged her.

I asked, "Are you okay? Is anyone wounded?"

"They came up trying to steal our truck and then drew their guns. Several of the Sailsberg people were wounded and killed in the first attack. They weren't counting on us to be able to resist them. We had our pistols in our bags and rifles ready but hidden. Six were killed in the first attack, over twelve in the next, and a couple more in each attack after that. They even left, got reinforcements, and came back for this final attack. Ricochets hit Jacob and Grant, but the rest of us are okay. Lynn put some WoundSeal on the wounds, and the bleeding has stopped. The bullets were spent and only grazed them.

The mayor came over and thanked us for helping fight off the thugs but seemed worried that they would return later. The police chief explained the situation, and I asked if he could round up some of his people to help us go over to the gang's hideout and wipe them out. He told me there were only a few fighters in the whole bunch, and that was what had gotten them in trouble in the first place. He left to raise his army while I checked on our team.

I looked them over. "I understand that there're only a dozen men left in the group that attacked y'all, and many of them are wounded. I think we need to hit them hard right now before they regroup. The SAWs will make up for us being shorthanded, and I don't think they'll expect a counter-attack. Who's in?"

Everyone but Grant volunteered, and I had to ask Jacob to stay behind due to his wound. We loaded up and followed the chief's directions to the gang's hideout. It was only a few miles. We arrived and stopped a safe distance away. Mike and Lynn snuck up on them to see if they expected an attack. They left for half an hour and came back with good news.

"Zack, only eight made it back and all, but two were wounded. They're all dead now. The women captives slit the thugs' throats when they returned and tried to get them to load up and move to another town. The women knew the attack weakened the gang, and they killed the thugs when they returned. Chief, they want to join your city. Over twenty of them are from your town."

I rode back with Ally in the Humvee, and we were both thankful that we didn't have to be in another gunfight.

Ally said, "Our people have become very strong. It amazes me that even the meek ones are now helping protect our neighbors."

"Darling, it's a new world. The strong, or at least the ones who can become strong, will survive. Strong doesn't always mean handling a gun. Strong can be plowing fields, canning food, and building a new country without electronics."

"It's the 1850s, and we need to get through the Wild West part as soon as possible," Ally said.

I replied, "You've gone from a reserved person to quite a strong-willed person. When Mike picked you up on the side of the road, he didn't think you'd survive. I'm glad you did, and I like the new Ally."

"Oh, I'm still the old Ally. I just had to suck it up, move on, and protect my kids. Susie is still little, but I'm amazed that Paul has grown so much and so quickly."

***

I made Grant come back with us and asked Joan to stay with the train crew until we could replace Grant. We made up a reason to leave after the others went and dropped three of the small hit-and-miss engines off at our new bug out hideout. Now I just had to hook up a generator to a couple of them, and we'd be in business.

On the way back, Ally had been very quiet. She broke her silence with, "Do we always have to fight and kill people?"

"No, but we can't let the bad guys win either. My guess is that we have a year or two of constant threats, then the lack of food, disease and internal fights will take care of these gangs. Until then, they have unrestricted ability to make meth, grow pot, and kill themselves."

Ally asked, "So, we stay out of the way as much as possible and let them kill each other?"

"Except for the ones who try to take our food or kidnap our people."

Ally asked, "You mean they'll try to kidnap us women."

I said, "Unfortunately, you're right. With no law and order, all types of perversion and crimes will rise until the criminals die off or get killed."

"Can't we find an island and hide until things get better?"

"Darling, it takes people like us to make things get better."

Chapter 10 - Independence Day

Daviess County, Kentucky

Time was passing all too quickly since the lights went out early in the spring. It's now July 1st, and we have made progress towards having all of the advantages of the 1850s plus a bit of technology from the early 1900s. I guess we average out about the 1890s, to be fair. Jacob and his crew found how to hook generators to the hit-and-miss engines with belts and pulleys. They're now tinkering with large generators joined to the steam engines. The important thing is we have electricity at most of the farms in our little community. That means we have lights, and in some cases, we can power a refrigerator or freezer. This may not sound like much, but a candle or kerosene lamp puts out a lot of smoke and fills your lungs with all kinds of chemicals. I love electricity. Of course, Callie reminded me that the power plants gave off pollutants. Right now, I wish we could go back to worrying about contaminants instead of who's going to try to kill us or where our next meal is coming from.

I saw my daughter and Paul heading to her shop and said, "Callie, what do you and Paul have in surprise for us on Independence Day? I know you've been in your workshop with the doors closed, or are you and Paul making out back there? When we get full-time electricity, I might just install a camera to keep an eye on you two."

Paul stuttered and stammered.

Callie said, "Ha! Ha! Dad, you're too funny. Besides, Paul and I go walking in the woods when we want to make out. Paul is a gentleman and is too scared of you and Mom to do much. I have to talk him into everything."

Paul was busy shaking his head to signal no as Callie talked.

"You'd better be kidding. Changing the subject didn't work. I know whatever you're doing involves electricity since there's a drop cord running from the generator to your shop."

They went on into the pole barn, and suddenly I thought, *did Paul's head shaking mean no, they weren't making out in the woods, or she didn't have to talk him into everything.* Damn.

We had a whole cow roasting on a hickory wood fire, along with a goat, pig, and a sheep. We were expecting over a hundred and fifty people plus Bert's deputies and their families. The deputies had kept order in the county since the gang over in Ohio County had been dealt with. The problems were minor compared with a few months ago. There were some drunks, a chicken thief, and several houses of prostitution had popped up. Of course, there was an ongoing drug problem. Still, as we found and eliminated the suppliers, the drug addicts either straightened up or left to find drugs. Selling drugs resulted in banishment from the community, and resisting arrest usually meant an instant death penalty. We had experienced the longest stretch of peace and quiet since before the lights went out.

Most of the vegetables were ripe, and we were preparing for a large harvest of corn, wheat, and oats in the fall. The potato crop was enormous, and we had fried, mashed, boiled, and every other kind of cooked potato that you can imagine. I personally was tired of potatoes but kept my mouth shut since we'd been close to starving several times in the past. Of course, real butter would help the potatoes. I made a mental note to find some butter churns.

Jacob's prototype large generator was taken from a retail store's parking lot. It was a colossal backup generator for a large grocery store that had freezers and refrigerators. It was in an overseas shipping container and hadn't been installed. Naturally, he had it in our barn, and we have to test it to see how much load it would handle, so I'm sitting in front of an air conditioner in an air-conditioned room. It feels so good on a hot day, along with an ice-cold ale. Jacob wanted to air condition one large room of the pole barn to give people a break from the heat and hope that things would return to normal. We'd also made ice cubes and then ice cream yesterday. We planned to make a lot of ice cream for the celebration.

***

We already knew the old L&N Railroad tracks ran between St. Louis and Pittsburgh, with stops in Owensville and Sailsberg. The tracks went through the middle of our new community and were only a quarter-mile from my farm. The tracks had been in use up until the lights had gone out. We didn't have rail service for a few weeks after the Sailsberg people and Jacobs team connected the rail at the museum to the main rail. A train had stopped about twenty miles from the farm and had to be moved onto a siding about ten miles from Sailsberg to clear the rails. There were over a hundred cars hooked to several engines. The steam engine was not up to moving more than a few cars at a time, and moving them was very time-consuming. I had a team sorting through the railcars and dividing them up to share with the Sailsberg people. There was everything from coal to new Ford trucks in the cars. We concentrated on the ones with food, medicine, and any weapons. I had numerous loads of food, weapons, and medical supplies moved to our hideout during the cleanup operation. We had plenty of weapons but didn't want them to fall into the wrong hands.

I caught Sam Hager and asked if he could get some of our friends to help build a small train depot and unloading dock beside the track by my place. They raided the local lumber yards and had built a credible depot for our community within a few weeks. They named it "Bug Tussle Depot" and had a large sign constructed with the name proudly displayed. Their biggest problem had been to build a watering tower for the steam engine. They dragged a large steel oil field tank to the site, raised it up on four telephone poles, and added a spout that filled the engine's water tank. The dock was constructed by placing telephone poles into the ground as legs. Then railroad ties were uses for joists and the decking. You could drive a tank across the dock, and it wouldn't strain a bit. There was a ramp on one end where you could drive a truck right onto a railcar or unload a car with freight stacked on it. Mike had even found an old fork truck that Jacob got running, which the team used to lift the ties. It would be invaluable when we loaded or unloaded freight.

Mike's crew used the old bulldozer to doze a road to the depot from Highway 54. The road was about a thousand yards long and would remain a dirt road until we could cover it in gravel.

Another crew built the depot building by using plans for a fancy pole barn. Again, they placed telephone poles into the ground, wrapped them in 2x4s, and skinned the building with steel siding. The floor had to be made of wood since we weren't up to pouring that large an area with concrete. Sam's daughter-in-law had dug up some old RR signs and antiques to decorate the depot. They even built a large stained-glass window from an old church that had partially burned after a small plane hit it when the lights went out.

We kept this work secret since we wanted to surprise everyone at our Independence Day celebration. Rail service would be one step more towards civilization. With the help of Billy, the Railroad Museum curator from Sailsberg, Jacob and I planned the big surprise for the community on Independence Day.

***

I woke up early on Independence Day and was drinking my first cup of coffee before anyone else was up for the day. It was still dark, and a few mosquitoes were biting. The moon was full, and I could see the guard in the tower. I poured some coffee in my thermos and headed to the building. Ally had been up for several hours and was to be relieved by Joan, who was several minutes late. I climbed the ladder and made my way up to the crow's nest. Ally smiled that big smile of hers, and I walked over to her and hugged her. She felt great in my arms, but I broke off and poured her a cup of coffee.

As she took the cup, she said, "Aren't you, my boyfriend?"

"Is this a trick question? Yes, I am. Am I missing something?"

Ally chuffed. "No, but I didn't even get a kiss from my boyfriend when he saw me for the first time today. Bummer."

I reached over, drew her close, kissed her, and held her for a few minutes.

"I'm confused. You said slowly, and I respect that. Besides, you're on guard duty. We can't get caught with our pants down."

She laughed. "Whoa. A kiss doesn't mean my pants have to come off. I guess you learned your lesson on having your pants down while on guard duty."

"Well, that's embarrassing. Who told you? It has to be Sally. I'm going to kick her butt when I see her."

"I'm not telling on my source. Come here and give me a much better kiss."

Before I moved to her, she placed her finger over her lips and whispered, "Shush, watch the back of the house."

I saw someone sneaking out the back door, still getting dressed. The person stepped out into the moonlight, and I saw Chuck, who was closely followed by Joan.

I said, "Damn, they're sleeping together under my roof. That's bullshit."

Ally laughed and said, "Are you jealous?"

"Not of those two, but they should have their booty calls somewhere else. Callie's sleeping in the room next to Joan's room. Damn, what if she gets pregnant? Callie would have a half brother or sister."

Ally said, "You know we haven't discussed kids. What if I got pregnant?"

"Well, first, that would be an immaculate conception since we've only kissed a few times. Second, I love kids and would be happy. Joan didn't want anymore. I wanted to have a boy. I guess I kind of have Paul now."

Ally grinned at me. "We won't go slowly forever. I think we need to move in together now that Joan has a man. I guess I didn't want to fall for you if she was going to take you away."

I kissed her again as I heard Joan scrambling up the ladder and said, "I love you, and we'll move yours, Paul's, and Susie's things in after the celebration is over tonight."

"Hon, is there room for me and my kids?"

I said, "Yes, with Joan gone and Mike moving in with Sally, there're plenty of bedrooms. Besides, we have my office and the upstairs living room that can be used if needed."

Ally grabbed me, pulled me into her arms, and kissed me for a long time while Joan entered the crow's nest.

Joan stumbled into the crow's nest as we were kissing, saw us, and said, "Well, the two lovebirds are up here in the nest together. I hope Callie doesn't see you."

Ally slowly broke off the kiss and spoke before I could open my mouth, "Hi, Joan. Please tell Chuck to put his pants on after his all-night booty call with you. All of the guards are tired of seeing him run across the lawn each morning with his pants down. I hope you two aren't making too much noise and keeping Callie up all night. Joan, I want to be your friend, but don't pull that holier-than-thou crap on me, and we'll get along just fine."

I opened my mouth. "I'm glad you're seeing Chuck. Callie knows it. I know it, and the entire community knows it. Move in with him tomorrow. You need your privacy, and Ally is moving in with me tomorrow."

Joan was at a loss for words and then recovered with, "I'm sorry, we should've been discrete. I'm happy for you and Ally. Chuck and I already planned to move in together."

"Great, we'll have to help you find a house close by, but not too close. Oh, zip up your pants, and your shirt buttons don't match up. Have a great day."

We left before she could reply.

"Honey, that's the first time I ever saw your ex at a loss for words."

I laughed and said, "Not only that, but she pulled that 'got you crap, ' and you put her in her place. I wish I had that on film for Mike to see."

"Darling, if Joan and I are ever to be friends, we need to keep what happened to ourselves. I want to treat her as I want her to treat me. She's been put on notice that you're mine, and I won't take any shit off her. I think she'll process that, and hopefully, she can be my friend for Callie's sake."

I said, "Even though I want to run to Mike and make his whole year, I promise I'll never repeat a word about it."

"Oh no, we'll talk about it amongst ourselves and laugh our asses off, just never let anyone else know about it. Does Mike hate his sister?"

I aid, "Oh no, he loves her, but he doesn't like her behavior at times. Mike and I have been the jokers in the group, and she's never appreciated our pranks and sense of humor. She's been mad at him since he took a dump in Todd's Corvette."

"Oh my, remind me not to piss Mike off."

"You're too sweet to piss anyone off, except maybe Joan."

Ally winked at me. "If she plays nice, I'll play nice."

"I don't want to be around if you play 'not nice.'"

"Smart man."

We went on down and walked to the house, holding hands. Mike, Sally, and Callie were sitting on one of the picnic tables eating pancakes as we walked up.

Mike looked up and said, "My, my, y'all have big smiles on today."

"Ally is moving in with me tomorrow. We care for each other and are taking the next step."

"Dad, that's great, but can you get Mom and Chuck to move out of her room and get their own place? Their bed is squeaking half the night. I need my sleep."

Ally and I began laughing and couldn't stop, especially after Mike spat a mouthful of pancakes across the lawn and broke into laughter."

"Uncle Mike, Dad, it's not funny."

I spoke, "Callie, it's funny that you mentioned this. Your mom just told Ally that she's moving in with Chuck."

Mike started laughing again and said, "Now, the rest of the story? Go figure the ex and new girlfriend can't live under the same roof."

Ally picked up a biscuit off the table, stuffed it in Mike's mouth, and said, "Sally, could you get Mike under control? We need peace, not war."

Sally replied, "No promises, but I'm working with him every day. I kind of like him as he's. Rough edges and all. Congratulations, Ally. I'm changing the subject. Could you help me with the decorations for our party? I need another set of hands."

"I need to go with Zack for about an hour, freshen up, and will back with you in two hours."

Ally had her bag with her, so we left, going toward the house.

"Thanks."

Mike choked the biscuit down and said, "Looks like Joan and Chuck have found piece."

Sally hit him on the head with a spoon and said, "Watch it, I may have to change my mind about liking your rough edges."

I went into the house, and Ally took me to my bedroom and closed the door behind us. My mind turned to things men think of when they're alone with a beautiful woman in a bedroom with a closed door.

"Zack, the dead animals, half-naked girl poster, and the fishing rods have to go if you want me to sleep in here. Do you mind if we paint the room pale blue and the kitchen yellow? We need to find a furniture store soon. We're sleeping on the floor until you get rid of the bed that you and she slept in together."

My mind took a while to process the information, and I replied. "Yes, to the paint and moving the other stuff out of the room."

"Joan has never slept in that bed, and I like it."

She asked, "What about any other women?"

"Damn, the bed will be gone as soon as we find another. I have one of those blow-up beds we can sleep on until then."

She hugged and kissed me while saying, "Thanks. Those might seem petty to you, but we need a fresh start. I love you. You'll find I'm not demanding and quite low maintenance now that we have those things out of the way. I'm a country girl who likes to take care of her man, as long as he takes good care of me."

She was undressing the whole time she talked, and when she got down to her bra and panties, she disappeared into the bathroom and closed the door.

She poked her head out and said, "Now go help, Mike, so I can get cleaned up and go help Sally. Now close your mouth and get out of here. There's plenty of time for what's on your mind later."

"I was thinking your back needed scrubbing."

"That'll be your job starting tomorrow. I need to talk with Callie before then. Bye."

I walked out of the room, thinking there's never enough time for what was on my mind. I caught up with Mike, and we helped Jacob with his first surprise for our visitors. We had two electric and two hand-cranked ice cream makers and had them manned for several hours, making several kinds of ice cream. Jacob had the generator running, and we had placed several chest-type freezers in the barn to hold the ice for our drinks and ice cream. By the time we finished cranking, our guests were arriving.

I left the barn and waved at Ally as I passed through the yard to the house to get cleaned up. I went to my room and saw several bags and a suitcase. I took off my clothes and entered the bathroom to see a bra and panties drying on the towel holder. She had marked her territory, and the room and I belonged to her. I took my shower, got dressed, and went back out to help set up the extra tables and chairs.

The meal was fantastic, and almost everything on the table had been raised on the farms in our community. You don't think much about fresh vegetables until you have to eat canned ones for months. The barbecue was mouthwatering, and everyone ate way too much. As good as the food was, the ice for the tea was the hit of the meal.

One of the farmers said, "I never thought I'd have ice in my drink until midwinter when I wouldn't want it. If we just had ice cream, I could die a happy man."

I tried not to think about anyone else who might be starving in this world turned upside down, and it was easier than I thought. We deserved the celebration of our successes and hard work. Anyone who had worked hard and fought to protect their families and belongings and helped others when they were able could have accomplished what we did. I did feel sorry for any kids caught up in this mess, but you can't save everyone and have to do the best you can with what you have.

We waited for about an hour after dinner was over and brought out the ice cream.

I saw the farmer who loved ice cream and said, "You can die now. We have ice cream."

The kids ate ice cream until some were sick, and we had to stop serving until we slowed them down. Hell, I ate two bowls full, and I'd been full before I started. Small things mean a lot when you don't have much.

Several men and women had brought their guitars, banjos, and one violin and started playing dance music. Ally took my hand, and I had to waddle out to the dance floor.

"Darling, I'm full of ice cream. I might burst open if I move too fast."

"That's okay. I like slow dancing."

We didn't want to have a fireworks show, even though we'd found a train car full of the stuff since we didn't want to attract attention to our get-together. We danced until dark when suddenly, I heard The Sound of Music playing behind me. I turned and saw Callie and Paul had a video projector and a DVD player projecting the movie on the side of the barn. I'd wondered why this side had a fresh coat of white paint. Now I knew. Everyone stopped what they were doing, sat down, and watched the movie. Several people were crying, and the kids were asking if we had the latest Star Wars movie.

"Ally, it could be fifty to a hundred years before the movie industry makes another movie."

"Well, we'll just have to wear these DVDs out until then."

Ally and I went over to Callie and Paul and thanked them.

I said, "You two make a great team. This means so much to everyone."

That made their day. Only Jacob and I knew that tomorrow, everyone would get a train ride.

Paul switched to a DVD with cartoons for the little kids, then an older Star Wars film. Everything was going much better than even I had expected when one of the deputy's kids got sick. He sweated profusely and was lying on a blanket by his mom when he suddenly started vomiting and having diarrhea. Joan and Ally rushed over to help and sent Callie to our medical stores to get something to help slow the diarrhea.

Ally said, "Here, have your son drink this flattened soda. It'll help with the vomiting. I'll make up something to help with the loss of electrolytes. You need to keep him from getting dehydrated. Oh my, he's burning up. We need a child's thermometer."

Callie came back with the requested medicine and a full medical bag. By that time, one of the deputy's wives came up, said that she was a nurse, and took over.

The nurse said, "This boy is very sick. If I had to guess, he has dysentery. We need to keep him hydrated and try to stop the loss of fluids. We need to get him back to town and get medical help. He needs antibiotics ASAP."

Ally asked, "Is this contagious?"

"Very contagious. It's spread through contaminated drinking water and poor hygiene. People used to die from it by the thousands. I just hope we have enough antibiotics."

The town's people all left after the deputy rushed his son back to town to see the doctor. The party was great but had ended on a sour note.

I caught the rest of the deputies who lived out in the county before they went home and asked them not to go into town until we knew what was going on with the disease. I warned them never to drink the water in the city. We were using well water and felt safe since we had given training on hygiene to all of our community in anticipation of issues like this. We planned to start treating our water with a few drops of bleach per gallon as an added ounce of prevention in the morning.

While I met with the deputies, Ally found Callie and had a talk with her.

"Callie, are you okay with your dad and me moving in together?"

"Yes, it's all right with me. I want my dad to be happy, and you make him happy. The timing is great since Mom has Chuck and won't be pestering Dad."

Ally said, "Thanks, that means a lot to me, and I'm happy for your mom."

Ally then caught Paul, but Susie had fallen asleep long ago.

"Paul, I'm moving in with Zack. Is that a problem for you? You and Susie will move with me. Zack says you'll have your own room."

Paul grinned, "No, I like Zack, and he's taught me a lot and been a good friend. Mom, he's been like my dad since we joined the community."

"Son, that means you and Callie will be living in the same house. No sneaking into her bedroom at night."

"Mom, if it's all right with you, I'll sleep out in the barn. I don't want the temptation for either of us and don't want Zack worrying."

"I think that's a wise move."

It was two in the morning, everyone was gone, and our people had gone to their rooms. Ally and I went to our room and sat on the edge of the blow-up bed. We held each other, and Ally began nibbling on my ear, and well, I guess you can guess the rest. I was exhausted.

Ally said, "Darling, I wouldn't have been such a tease if I'd known what was going to happen. If you're in the mood...."

"Baby, I appreciated the show this afternoon, but I don't want our first time to be when we're bone tired and need sleep. Let's go to bed and hold each other."

We laid in each other's arms and fell asleep before we got undressed.

***

We were the first ones up for the morning. Ally fixed breakfast while I made coffee and set the table. She cooked eggs, ham, toast, and jalapeno blackberry jelly, which was my favorite meal. Mike and Sally joined us and stole some of my coffee and toast.

Mike kidded us, "Well, how are the newly shacked up people doing this morning? I didn't expect y'all to be out and about until noon."

Ally replied, "Mike, we've been up for two hours, and that's all you need to know, Mr. Nosey."

"Zack will fill me in later."

"No, I won't. I want to stay alive."

Ally said, "Sally, please get Mike under control. I have a couple of ideas that'll housebreak him quickly."

"Sorry, Ally. As I told you yesterday, I like the rascal just like he's. Crazy and full of BS, but he treats me like a queen. He only shows off in front of other people. He's like a puppy dog when we're alone."

Ally waved a knife in the air and said, "Even male puppy dogs get neutered to calm them down."

Mike dropped his hands on his lap and said, "Ouch."

Ally gave Mike a kiss on top of his head. "Mike, I actually like you, and I'd never come between you and Zack. Both of you're special people, and many of us would be dead without your help."

We were interrupted by the sound of a train's steam whistle. It was in the distance and got louder as it approached.

I glanced at my watch and said, "The train from Sailsberg is early."

Sally said, "They got the train running. Yeah!"

I said, "It's been running for a couple of weeks. We had to build a depot to fuel and water the train and a dock to load and unload the freight."

The train had two old passenger cars and three flatbed cargo cars loaded to the brim with old steam engines and old industrial shop tools for Jacobs's new machine shop. We unloaded them while everybody waited impatiently for a ride on the train. The train could only travel forwards and backward since there was no place to turn around. There was a large loop in Owensville and Louisville, but we would make do going back and forth forwards and in reverse. The old train cruised at twenty-five miles per hour. The people were thrilled to be riding up and down the rails.

When the joy rides were done, we loaded tons of books, medical supplies, and fresh vegetables for the people in Sailsberg. We planned to run the train every Monday and Thursday until we figured out the schedule. I planned to meet with the mayor of Owensville and the other communities along the rails and get them to start trading with each other. Owensville had an abundance of gas, diesel, and coal, while the smaller communities had crops to sell. Jacob, Mike, and I planned to start trading steam power plants, trucks, cars, and bicycle-powered generators to these towns. We would stockpile what food we needed and trade the excess food that couldn't be stored. Jacob kept reminding everyone that winter was coming. What we harvested was all we could depend on until late spring next year.

***

Bert came to visit me at the farm five days later with terrible news. There was a major outbreak of the disease in the town. Half of his deputies had come down with vomiting and diarrhea.

I said, "Someone needs to check to see where the contamination is coming from. I'd bet on outhouses too close to your wells."

Bert said, "Half the town is getting their water straight out of the river. We told them to boil it or treat it with bleach."

"People are getting complacent."

Bert said, "We need help. Half my staff is either sick or at home caring for sick family members. The mayor is rationing antibiotics and anti-diarrheal medicine. Everyone thinks they're saving it for her supporters and her family. It doesn't matter because there wouldn't be enough anyway. We have had twenty-five kids, and ten adults die so far this week. We just can't keep them hydrated."

I asked, "What can we do to help?"

Bert asked, "Can you provide water for my men in town and take on some more of my team until this is over? The families will stay with some of your people, and the deputies will go on about their jobs by using strict hygiene rules. We won't bring any sick people out here."

I suggested, "I can't speak for the others, but I'm sure they want to help. I'll recommend we put all of your people in some tents and campers here at my farm for a week, and then if they're symptom-free, we'll spread them out into our community."

"My next request is a big one."

I said, "Go ahead."

"Can you send some teams out into the surrounding counties to find some antibiotics?"

"Of course, we will, but you realize we won't find enough for the whole town."

Bert shrugged, "I hate to appear selfish, but I want to take care of my deputies and their families first and then the town. If the deputies can't do their job, the town will fall into chaos."

I asked, "How many sick do you have right now?"

"Only eleven, six kids and five adults. Moving most of them out into the county has been a major help."

I said, "Just a minute, I'll be right back."

I grabbed Joan, Ally, and Mike and said, "The sheriff has six kids and two adults that have come down with the disease. There have been over thirty-five dead in town so far. Are y'all okay with me giving Bert enough antibiotics and anti-diarrheal medicine to treat his people? We have more here and a large supply at the hideout."

Ally said, "Of course, but he can't know about the rest of the medicine."

They all felt terrible about hoarding medicine but knew it could save their loved ones later.

"Bert, we'll help look for medicine, but as soon as you can get all of your people here, Joan's going to give them enough antibiotics to treat the ones who are already sick. We don't have enough to help the town, and giving you medicine to take to town would just start a riot. Let's load your truck up with some clean water and a couple gallons of bleach, so you can treat water in town. Hurry and get the families out here. We'll get their quarters ready and set up a makeshift hospital large enough for the sick. I know you know this, but we can't let it leak out that we have antibiotics, or we'll be overrun by people from the city. We don't have enough for ourselves if there's an outbreak here."

Bert had tears in his eyes when I told him we had medicine for his people, and he could bring the sick ones out here to be treated.

He grabbed my hand, shook it, and said, "Thanks, we'll forever be in your debt."

"You may be paying that debt sooner than you think if this disease gets worse. People will try to leave the city and find a safer place. Our community covers everything southeast of the city, and the river has the northeast blocked. Can your roadblocks send them west or southwest without causing too much suspicion?"

"I'll make it happen, and my deputies will be on board since their families will be in your community."

294

I said, "I thought that would be the case. Thanks for helping protect us. We do appreciate you and the deputies. Joan really appreciates Chuck."

"I know; he has a smile a mile wide since they started dating."

Once upon a time, that would've made me a bit jealous or at least require one of my smart assed comments, but I was just happy for Chuck and my ex.

***

The deputies and their families started rolling in a couple of hours later, and the sick ones were taken to a large tent that we'd set up as a makeshift hospital. One of the deputies brought his sister, a nurse practitioner. With the other deputy's wife, we now had two nurses. They administered the antibiotics and anti-diarrheal medicine and busied themselves with organizing the medical supplies. They both ganged up on me that afternoon to find a permanent building to serve as a hospital.

I asked, "There're numerous medical buildings and a hospital in Owensville. Why do we need a hospital out here in the sticks?"

One of the nurses said, "All but two of the doctors have either died or left town. The hospitals and pharmacies were looted early on when the gangs were looking for drugs. What they didn't steal, they ruined. You have more medical supplies here than all of Owensville."

I gasped. "Why would the bastards take regular medical supplies?"

The nurse shook her head. "To trade and to take care of their own. STDs are running rampant, and the gangs want antibiotics to treat the infected. HIV is out of control, but there're no drugs for that now. Most of those drugs don't have much shelf life. My understanding is most of our supplies ended up in Anderson and Murray. We'd like to set up shop here and take care of our families and your people."

I said, "So, we're looking at several more rounds of people dying off from STDs and other diseases?"

The nurse replied, "Yes, people are dying as we speak in Owensville due to the filthy conditions, contaminated water, and the mayor not helping to educate the people."

I said, "The doomsday prepper crowd has always said that ninety percent of the world would die off the first year. I'm starting to believe those forecasts. The trick is to keep their problems from becoming ours."

I realized that our community had just grown by over forty people because these folks didn't want to go back into town. I had to have a community meeting and determine what to do. We needed them, but this would put a severe strain on our food supply.

I looked at Mike. "We'll have to have a community meeting to decide on the hospital, and if y'all join us permanently."

The nurse said, "We promise we'll help out more than just treating the ill. Most of us have other skills and are willing to learn new ones. I was in the Army and served two tours in Afghanistan. I've been shot at and had to kill to survive. Cops' wives are a hardy bunch. We just have to ditch the city and make a new life. We hope we can join you or other communities."

Her last comment put a thought into my head. I had a solution that would be a win-win for everyone.

***

As I had forecast, the situation got much worse in the city. People were dying by the hundreds, and others were leaving by the droves. Most walked away from the town carrying what they could in shopping carts or wheelbarrows containing their possessions. Bert's team came through for us and directed the people south and west away from us. They told the people fleeing that the area east of the city was worse than Owensville and gave them fresh water for their journey. The ones who arrived in Anderson were not welcome and sent on their way southwest. This situation would get worse over the next few weeks.

✪

Chapter 11 - Win-Win

The Farm

I woke up at dawn, as usual, for the new me. Surprisingly, I felt very rested for having had the midnight to 2:00 am duty in the crow's nest. Ally and I had made it a practice of keeping each other company when we pulled guard duty. I know it didn't make sense, but we hated to be apart. When Mike found out, he gave me a rash of shit and called me whipped. I reminded him that he and Sally walked around hand in hand all of the time. Mike's reply was that perhaps we'd finally achieved happiness. I thought he's right.

I lay in our new bed with Ally's head resting on my left arm and watched her sleep for half an hour before she woke up. Her eyes opened, and she smiled at me.

"Good morning, sunshine."

She looked at me for a minute and said, "I love you, Zack Johnson. How long have you been looking at me? Is my breath bad?"

"For a while, and no."

Ally asked, "Can we just stay in bed all day? I could sleep for another couple of hours."

"We could, but I want to meet with our team and then take some of the team over to Sailsberg."

I gave her the short version of my plan, and she liked my thoughts and made a couple of suggestions.

She said, "Road trip? I'm in. Do I have time for a shower?"

"That depends. Do I still have the job of back scrubber?"

"Of course. Are you any good at your new job?"

I said, "You tell me after I'm done."

I received an A+ for back scrubbing.

Our shower took a little longer than Ally planned. Still, we joined the others for breakfast, and I told them what I planned for the extra deputies and their families who had streamed into our community. I wanted their permission to enact my plan for our newly arrived people from the city.

Joan raised her hand. "So, we build a pole barn hospital here at the farm, and we help spread out the deputies and their families from here to Sailsberg to live? These people will be a big help to those cities. Why do you need us to help with a decision?"

I answered. "Because we would still be adding about ten more mouths to feed right here in our group. Having a hospital could result in every sick person within a hundred miles flocking here for treatment."

Mike exclaimed, "Oh, crap."

I said, "Yes, we have winter coming, and what food we have after harvest is all we'll have until late next spring. I personally think we'll find a way to feed everyone but have to draw the line on anymore. I'm also against building a hospital. Oh, we'll set up a room to treat our sick and injured, but no hospital."

Ally said, "It would be nice to help other people without hurting ourselves."

I said, "We can always help with labor and trading with other communities. We have to always do the right thing for our community when it comes to life-and-death issues."

298

Everyone agreed and took on the task of talking with the deputies about our plan. I asked Chuck to round up the ones here at the farm and to round up the remaining ones for a meeting that evening. I explained the situation, and only a couple of the officers balked at moving further from Owensville.

I said, "Look, I'd love to have all of you stay with us here, but we don't have enough food for everyone to make it through the winter. I know Sailsberg could use a couple of deputies and their families, and I'm sure other communities would be glad to have some of you. We're spreading five of your families around Daviess County and two in Sailsberg. That only leaves three families that will be further away."

One of the deputies replied, "I, for one, don't want to move permanently away from this area. Is there a chance we could move back after the crops are expanded?"

I said, "Yes, we have this year to get through, and then it will get much better at farming and expanding the land farmed. There's enough extra farmland we can eventually grow enough to feed many more people. The wildcard is, can we protect what we have against invaders wanting our food? That's why I feel it is important to keep all of you fighting crime and protecting our community."

After the meeting, Ally, Lynn, Roger, and I headed out to drive along the railroad, looking for communities that would be glad to get their very own policeman and his family. We took the Humvee for added protection and headed east, following the railroad on Highway 52. The first community we came across was a ghost town. On a good day, the unincorporated town of Gillsville only had a caution light, a gas station, and a hundred and twenty people. We moved on to St. Charles and immediately saw people in the fields and around their houses. We drove into the town, and an armed group of men met us.

One stocky looking man gruffly asked, "What do you want?"

I said, "We live over towards Owensville and are looking for communities along the rail to trade with. We have the train that went through here the other day."

The man asked, "How did you get the train running?"

299

I said, "It never stopped running because it didn't have any electronics. Old technology wasn't affected by the EMP blasts. We'd like to share some of our technology with you. We have lights, running water, and several refrigerators back in operation."

We were interrupted when a Catholic priest walked between us and said, "Put the guns down and welcome our guests. Now, you need to get out of that war machine and join us for lunch, I insist."

The people shouldered their rifles, and we dismounted the Humvee and introduced ourselves. We were treated to a lunch consisting of fried catfish, hush puppies, and a salad.

One man said, "No, kidding! You're the Zack Johnson who walked from Oregon to Owensville after the lights went out?"

"I'm Zack Johnson, and I actually drove a tractor most of the way."

"Are you two the beautiful young women he saved along the way?"

Ally replied, "No, we're the beautiful women who joined the community before he arrived from Oregon. If you keep this up, his head will be too big to get back in the Humvee."

"Tell us about the train and your ideas about trading between the communities."

I told them about working with Sailsberg to get the train running and the attack on the city. I filled them in on the situation in Owensville. "Of course, most communities won't be able to trade food for services or goods until next year. We still want to set up the trade routes and stops for the train."

"You said you had refrigerators running?"

I said, "Yes, and we'll have more once we get some of the larger generators in operation."

"If you put some refrigerators or freezers on that train and help us get power to run refrigerators here, we can start trading fish for what you have to trade. We have fish coming out of our ears. We're sick of fish and want something else to eat."

I laughed, "We can make that happen. How do you have that much fish?"

The stocky man said, "As you know, we're on the banks of the Ohio and have always had a strong commercial fishing history. We also have several catfish farms around the town. When the lights went out, we started farming like everyone else, but we have a lot of people who hate to farm but love to catch or raise fish."

I said, "We haven't had much fish since the lights went out. We'll have to start fishing also but need your fish. We'll trade grain and power plants for fish until we figure out what else we can trade."

"Deal."

I asked, "Before we negotiate a fair trade, do y'all have a sheriff or police here?"

"No, but we need several. The county sheriff disappeared when the lights went out."

I said, "You would have to house and feed the cop and his or her family because they wouldn't be able to farm or fish full time. Any problems with a female cop?"

"That would be expected. If they like fish, bring them on. If they can do the job, we'll be fine with anyone."

We spent the next hour negotiating how much fish would be worth a steam-powered generator and how many books per fish. We left a little after 2:00 pm and headed to the following community along the way. We had twenty pounds of smoked fish to take home with us.

Ally said, "I never thought those books would come in handy. Now we can trade them for food. Perhaps we can trade DVDs and CDs also."

I said, "People probably have tons of those around their houses."

Ally said, "Yes, but they'll get tired of watching the same ones over and over. We can be the Movies R US of post-apocalyptic America."

I changed the subject. "So we only have a couple of more deputies to find homes for, and our trip will be a success."

The trip was far more successful than we imagined. While the next two communities wanted to trade, they had no need for more police and little to exchange for our products. They would benefit from our help in survival training and how to get old trucks running. That story changed when we went on past Sailsberg, and the people of Clover Field greeted us. It was another city on the river and was the home to several meatpacking plants. There were four large warehouses packed to the brim with canned chicken, beef, and pork. One was filled with every variety of Spam, and I love Spam. They were tired of a meat diet and were ecstatic about trading for generators, fish, and grain. They were late planting their crops and hadn't had all of the fresh vegetables we'd taken for granted. They also needed several cops. Our first trade mission was a complete success. We spent the night at a house next to the mayor's home. The people had been in Florida on vacation and never returned. We had a good night's sleep and left the following day.

We were riding along in silence when Ally broke the ice. "Lynn, how long have you and Roger been together? He seems like a nice guy."

"We've been seeing each other for a little over two months and plan to get married soon. Are you and Zack getting married?"

"We haven't discussed it yet. We're letting our kids get used to the idea first. We really just started dating a few weeks ago, so we're not in a hurry."

Lynn said, "Well, I'm pregnant, so we'll get married soon."

"Congratulations."

"Thanks, it will be my first."

We headed back to Sailsberg to check in with Billy, the curator/engineer, and start trade discussions. The people were much more outgoing and friendlier than before. Getting that gang taken care of had enabled them to have enough food, and the kidnappings had stopped. The captives from the outlaws had fit into the community and were already contributing. Life was good in Sailsberg.

The mayor said, "We want to thank you and your guys for freeing us from that gang. We didn't show our gratitude last time because we were still fearful of retaliation after being under their thumbs for so long. Once we recruit a few more police, we'll be much stronger and able to resist outside threats."

"I just happen to know where you can find some experienced deputies."

We had a great lunch and trade meeting before heading home.

Ally said, "I think you committed to sending out more deputies than we have available."

I replied, "I know. I'll talk with Bert and work something out. I just couldn't say no when people are in need."

Our little community had several weeks of a plain old dull existence, and I liked it. No one shot, no one robbed, and everyone had a full belly. Life was getting a little boring after the action-packed several months after the lights went out. We all agreed that boring was okay.

✪

Chapter 12 - Disease and Spies

Owensville, Kentucky

It only took a few weeks for Bert, his deputies, and their families to settle into our community. The ones we traded with between Owensville and Clover Field were also doing well. Over twenty homes were still vacant within ten miles of my farm. Our plan was to help relatives and close friends of our community move from the city and occupy them. Bert chose an older two-story farmhouse that had a nice barn and a 60x40 pole barn. We helped him convert the pole barn into the headquarters for his operation. We even installed a jail with two cells made of welded rebar with a concrete floor. We made sure the deputies' spouses or significant others obtained jobs and assignments for guard duty. Bert had fourteen men and eight women deputies left in our community. All but three had served in the military or previous police departments before joining him.

Ally and I rode horseback over to Bert's place to take him a ham and some fresh vegetables. I also wanted to see the jail after Mike had bragged about his welding job.

I saw Bert. "Hello, we rode over to see the new jail and give you a housewarming gift."

"Good to see you."

"Ally, the wife is in the kitchen, trying to get everything organized. Go right in."

Ally went in and visited with Bert's wife and daughter while we went over to the new sheriff's headquarters and jail. I must admit, I was impressed with the quality of the work.

"This looks very professional. How did you get this kind of quality?"

Bert said, "We had professional construction people renovate the pole barn and add the offices and cells. Jacob provided the generator to power the tools, and several local lumberyards provided the materials. The lights went out, but we still have many very talented people just waiting for power to ply their trades."

"I'm very impressed."

Bert said, "I want to bring you up to speed on Owensville. The city continues to fight the illness, but it's been a losing battle. Over half the people fled southeast towards Madison and Perkinsville, with many of them died on the road. The population of Owensville is down to less than 2,000 and shrinking daily. The good news is that they have closed down all of the contaminated wells and forced the people to either boil their water or take boiled water from the city."

I said, "I'm sorry to hear about such devastation and misery. Is there anything that we can realistically do to help them?"

Bert scratched his jaw. "I would like to say yes. However, the mayor took one of the small generators that we gave them to power her house, while the large one powers city hall. Several of the other small ones ended up in Anderson, powering Todd's home and city hall. There appears to be no concern at all for using the generators to assist the city. Zack, I have to add that I think that Bonner and Todd have formed some kind of alliance and maybe a major threat to us."

I asked, "Do you know something new, or just the same Bonner and Prescott wanting to rule our world?"

"She told me she was glad my deputies and I'd moved out of town and told me not to come back. I learned that Prescott's

305

security guards have taken over policing the city and are ruling with an iron fist."

I said, "I hear you, but what has changed that makes you worried?"

"She slipped up and said a couple of things that suggest she has spies in our community. She also said she wants to seize the train to use it for all communities and not just benefit ours."

I said, "The train *is* servicing eight communities and several large farms between here and Sailsberg. We're extending the route to Clover Field this week and keep moving towards Louisville afterward. She knows damn well that we can't go into Owensville until she gets the dysentery outbreak under control. We also don't want food or supplies that might be contaminated. We could increase our trade of food for fuel if she'll take fish in trade."

Bert changed the subject. "What do you want to do to catch the spies?"

I said, "We don't want to catch them. Let's feed them some good juicy information and let them catch themselves. I think Grant and Mary are the spies in my group, and I'd bet the Greens are the spies out in the community."

"So we'll bait the trap?"

I said, "Yes, and we should protect our most valuable assets because when the spies are revealed, they might leave and take things with them. I think I know where you're heading. I'll get Mike and Jacob on board, and we'll handle our end."

Bert said, "I'll double the security on my armory at the back of my headquarters. Tell Mike I need some more welding done."

***

We finished increasing security and then developed a plan to flush out the spies while also springing a trap to catch anyone who took the bait. The bait was an old rail car filled with cattle at our depot, waiting for the train to arrive and take it to Sailsberg for trading. I allowed Mary to overhear me talking with Ally about rounding up twenty head of cattle early the following day and trucking them to the depot to be loaded up on a railcar. Bert had one of his deputies let Mr. Green hear about a truck shipment leaving a warehouse several miles away from the depot. It was to head to Clover Field, with medical supplies and ammunition by truck.

We knew Owensville hadn't had any meat for over a month. The information was that there were 10,000 rounds each of 9mm and .556. This would be impossible to resist for Todd's or Prescott's people. I took command of the operation at the depot, and Bert had the operation at the warehouse. There were only two cows in the truck heading to the depot and no ammunition at the warehouse. We took over a week to set up our positions and only brought our most trusted people into the loop during the planning phase. In addition to Chuck and Frank, Bert loaned me, four deputies to bolster our team for the upcoming conflict. We manned the traps before midnight and watched the enemy slide into their positions to attack their intended targets.

***

I stationed Joan, Ally, and Lynn on top of the water tower, and they had the best field of view. They all had ARs with NVG scopes and were tasked with making sure no one escaped. Besides, I didn't want them to be shot, and the water tank was the safest place to be if you had to be in this battle. The rest of the men and women were placed to have the enemy in a horseshoe that yielded a killing field of overlapping fire. Most were behind stacks of railroad ties that had been delivered earlier in the week. The rest were in fox holes we'd dug after dark each day, and they hid from the view of the depot workers. This should be a turkey shoot, as my uncle used to say.

We had twenty men and six women fighters. I'd spread the NVGs out, so each smaller group had a spotter. We expected ten to twenty in the attacking force. We had the element of surprise, and I'd given Mike and Roger some hand grenades to use in an emergency. If we were about to be overrun, the enemy would get a big surprise.

I placed lookouts with radios about a half-mile down the three roads that could be used to get close to us, and the one on Highway 54 called to report several vehicles heading our way.

I said, "Thanks. Get me a headcount and get on down here and join the fun."

The lookout said, "They aren't expecting any trouble. They haven't turned their headlights off yet. The last group just got out of their car. There're fifteen. I'm on the way."

The men stood out in the moonlight, and we didn't need the NVGs. I waited until the group was in the middle of the field of fire before I squeezed off the first shot. Before I could aim and fire, I heard a volley of shots coming from all around me. I shot two more, but they were knocked down and got back up in a kneeling position and started firing at us, to my horror.

I yelled, "They have flak jackets! Take head or leg shots!"

Bullets were whizzing by my head, and I had splinters from a railroad tie in my face due to a bullet hitting too damn close. I heard bullets hitting the water tank and was scared that Ally would be hurt or killed. I'd die if I lost her.

The fight was intense, but every time they tried to escape our horseshoe, they presented their sides and legs to our withering fire. They started dropping and staying down, and then the fight was over just as quickly as it started.

I shouted, "Check for wounded. We need to interrogate them."

I got out from behind the railroad ties and started checking for wounded. A shot rang out from above me, and blood and brains splattered all over my head and chest. I looked up to see where the shot came from and saw Ally blowing me a kiss. "The bastard was going to shoot you. I had to protect my back scrubber. You owe me, big boy."

"I'll make it up to you tonight."

Another downed thug moved, and I reacted by shooting him twice in the head.

Ally called out. "Damn, Zack, don't you think the lucky bastard is dead enough? You want me to shoot him again?"

308

We only found one more alive, and he was unconscious and only had half a face. Mike shot him before I could.

I waved the women down from the tower, and Ally rushed over to me and hugged me.

Ally sobbed, "I saw that SOB rise up to shoot you and was afraid he would shoot before I could. I couldn't stand losing you."

"I thought the same thing when I heard the bullets ricocheting off the water tank."

Lynn walked over with her hand on her shoulder. "One of those bullets missed the water tank. Boy, this stings."

I ripped her t-shirt to expose her shoulder and said, "It's only a scratch. Rub some dirt on it, and you'll be fine."

I motioned for Lynn to keep the pressure on the wound. It was through and through the flesh on her arm just before the top of her shoulder.

"Lynn, I guess that you'll have to receive the Farmer's Purple Heart for this little nick. Joan will keep the pressure on it until we get you to the nurse at the farm. Seriously, it's just a flesh wound, and it will hurt like hell, but you'll be okay."

Several others received minor wounds from ricochets, but the injuries only needed cleaning, antiseptic, and bandages.

***

Bert and his team watched patiently as they saw the trucks pull into the truck stop about a quarter-mile away and hide behind the restaurant. It was an hour before dawn with a half-moon in the sky. His men hid in the dark under light and sound restrictions while the enemy soldiers were smoking and laughing as they approached the warehouse. Both teams had six NVGs, but the attackers stood out in the moonlight, and the glowing cigarettes stood out like a neon sign. Bert's men were invisible, as were Zack's men. Bert had a mixture of twenty-three deputies and farmers against twelve in the group walking through the field towards the warehouse. They were getting closer, and Bert could hear them talking.

"Men remember there's a bounty from the city on Johnson's and the sheriff's head. Dead or alive. A bounty is on these traitors who were hoarding those medical supplies while your people died by the thousands."

"We'll surprise them and cut them into pieces."

That was the last thing any of them said before a dozen lights came on and highlighted them against the side of the warehouse. Twenty-three rifles started barking and didn't stop spitting lead until every one of the intruders was on the ground and stayed there.

Bert walked up to one of the survivors and asked, "Who do y'all work for? Who is behind this attack on our warehouse?"

The thug said, "You piece of shit. The mayor told us to take the warehouse, hunt you down, and bring you back dead. Go ahead, bastard, arrest me. See how long I stay in jail."

Bert waved at his men, and they started shooting each one of the survivors in the head. "No prisoners. You heard it from their lips. They were going to kill or make slaves of all of us. None can be left alive. Go get the Greens."

His deputies fetched the Greens from the back of a pickup and dragged them to the middle of the battlefield.

Bert asked, "What do you have to say for yourselves? You see what happened to the men who came to kill us. You gave them the information that set this all in motion. If we hadn't suspected you were traitors, we'd be lying dead."

Mr. Green said, "We didn't know they would try to kill anyone. We just thought it was unfair that we didn't share our food and medical supplies with the people in the town."

"Well, you made your bed, now pull your covers up around your ears. Don't worry about your kids. We have them adopted out."

He drew his pistol and shot both of them in the head.

Then he said, "Traitors, looters, and thugs die when and where we find them. I know it's bad to kill a woman, but she was just as guilty as her asshole husband."

I finished thanking the brave men and women who had risked their lives implementing the ambush and then headed over to the warehouse with Mike and Ally. We drove up to see enough lights to light up a football field. I saw Bert patting backs and shaking hands, which was a big relief.

Bert said, "Well, Zack, how did your ambush go? Ours was like shooting blind fish in a barrel. Those NVGs are worthless when you shine a bright light on them. Every one of these fuckers had military-grade NVGs and body armor. We were lucky and could see their vests before we started shooting. Now we have military-grade NVGs, and we'll make sure we observe light discipline when we use them. Those poor bastards marched in as they were going to Sunday school. They were dead before they knew it. Most of their weapons were never fired. Look, we also have eight new AR15s, a bunch of Glock-17s, and seven sets of body armor that survived. We escaped without any serious injuries."

I answered, "Our attackers had NVGs and body armor also. We knocked them down several times before we figured it out. Hell, I thought they were hopped up on cocaine. The bad news is all of the vests were ruined."

"Too bad on the vests, but congratulations on the victory. Was anybody wounded?"

I said, "We caught them by surprise, but they put up a losing fight. We were behind good cover and caught them out in the open. The firefight was intense, but we had cover, and they were caught flatfooted. We only had one lady shot and a couple of minor flesh wounds. What are you going to do with the Greens?"

"They've been rewarded for their treachery with a bullet to the brain."

I said, "Hard men for hard times. I remember you balked when I told you about us shooting looters."

Bert laughed and replied, "That was before the jail was at my house. What are you going to do with Grant and Mary?"

I didn't laugh, but he had a good point. "I don't know. You had hard proof on the Greens. We still just suspect Grant and Mary. I want to put a bullet in both of their brains, but not until I know they're guilty."

Then I said, "Let's have a town meeting after supper at your place and let everyone know about the surprise party we threw for our guests from the city. Do we need to put out extra guards tonight?"

Bert replied, "Yes, and probably until we get a sense of what's going on in Owensville and Anderson. Oh, by the way, one of the intruders told us that the mayor was behind this attack. We also heard the men talking as they walked up. They said that the mayor placed a bounty on yours and my head along with our men and women who resist her."

I cringed, "Damn, we need to quickly throw her a retirement party."

"Amen, brother, amen."

There were no losses on either of our teams, only one serious wound and three minor ones on my team. We planned well, executed well, and had God on our side. We implemented the most sacred rule of any gunfight, which is never get into a fair fight. Always cheat to make sure you have an overwhelming advantage. Overall, it was a great day for the good guys, not so much for the evil people.

***

Alan said, "Alice, you must have spies on your staff."

"Look, Alan, no one on my team even knew why they went with your two teams, other than they were going to confiscate some supplies from an abandoned warehouse."

Alan hit the corner of her desk with his balled-up fist. "These farmers caught us by surprise with two well-planned and executed operations. They cut our men to pieces before they had a chance to steal the cattle and ammo. I lost three at the depot and four at the warehouse, and you lost twenty more. They were waiting for us. We walked right in, and they ambushed us. Not one of our soldiers came back alive. The assholes dumped the bodies at the roadblock on Highway 54."

Alice said, "Did you ever think maybe your spies turned on you or were found out by the sheriff? He could have fed them the information just to set up a trap."

Alan aid, "Two traps and executed to perfection."

"Come over here and love me. We can plan Bert's and that damn Johnson's deaths later."

Alan replied, "Yes, dear," but thought *I'll only have to keep this bitch happy for a few more days.*

Alan had set up the meeting between the mayor and Todd. Still, ever since the meeting, the mayor's town had fallen into disease, famine, and devastation. He had to take over quickly before there was nothing left to take over. He needed hundreds of strong, healthy men and women to take over the entire area, including Anderson. It was his right and his destiny. He would make nice with the sheriff and Johnson until he didn't need them anymore.

She went into the bathroom while he fixed their drinks. He slipped the first dose of poison in the glass and stirred it thoroughly, so she wouldn't notice any undissolved powder. The symptoms of the poison would mimic the symptoms of dysentery, and she would be just another unfortunate casualty of the uncontrolled disease. His head of security was poisoning the drinks of the top five remaining city leaders later that afternoon. The citizens would be looking for the strong leadership that he would provide, and the farmers and sheriff would relish the olive branch. He would open the grain bins for his subjects and share fuel with the farmers.

✪

Chapter 13 - Mayor Prescott

Owensville, Kentucky

Sally, Mike, Ally, and I were playing cards after supper when Callie came running into the kitchen

"Dad, Carrie just came to me and told me that Grant just beat up her mom. Carrie tried to separate them, and he hit Carrie. Please help them."

"Baby girl, why did Grant beat up Mary? I thought they were in love."

"Mary loves Grant, but Carrie thinks Grant was just using her mom. She told me Grant has been stirring up trouble in our community, and at first, her mom tried to be on his side, but he started spreading rumors about you and Uncle Mike that are lies. Her mom called him on it tonight and got a beating. Carrie thinks Grant is some kind of spy for Todd."

I said, "Mike, let's go see what's going on and bring Mary back to our house for her own safety, then we can deal with Grant when Bert gets here. Ally, try to get Bert on the radio. We'll be back in a few minutes."

Ally said, "Darling, be careful. That guy is just waiting to stab you in the back."

314

"I will."

Mike said, "Ally, don't worry. I'll have Zack's back."

We jumped in Mike's truck and sped over to the house where Grant and Mary had set up housekeeping. It was about a mile and a half east of the farm and another quarter mile off the road. We turned down the road to their house just before sunset, and we could see Grant out on the road to the house, waving a pistol. He saw us, took aim, and fired, missing the truck on the first shot. We came to a halt as he fired twice more, hitting the truck both times.

"Mike, you go left, and I'll go right. Try not to shoot the bastard unless you have to."

"Screw that. He's shooting at me. I'm going to kill the SOB."

I said, "Mike, we need him alive to tell us who he's working for."

More shots rang out, and dirt flew around me as Mike cut behind a tree, heading to a yard barn beside the house. Mike was running wide open to tackle Grant when he tripped and fell at his feet. Grant lowered his pistol to shoot Mike when I fired first and shot him twice in the chest. He pulled the trigger as he fell to the ground. The pistol bucked, and the round missed Mike by a few inches. Grant died on his way to the ground.

Mike grimaced. "I thought we weren't going to kill the sack of crap. What happened? He fell for my trick, and I was about to have him hogtied and in the back of the truck in just a minute."

"Mike, you're so full of crap. Your eyes are brown. I just beat him by a half-second. If I'd waited, that bullet would have castrated you."

Mike looked down between his legs and saw the hole in the ground where the bullet had struck and said, "You just saved my private parts, but I still think I could have wrestled him to the ground."

Mary came out from the woods, ran to Grant, and cried over the body.

I said, "Mary, I'm sorry, but he would have killed Mike if I hadn't shot him. Are you okay?"

"I'm okay. I saw the shooting, and he really would have killed Mike. Why did I fall in love with this creep? He could be kind and gentle to me but was mean to Carrie and hated Joan, Mike, and you."

I asked, "What did we do to him? I gave him a ride home from Indiana, and we've fed him for months. The lazy shit."

Mary answered between tears, "I didn't know until this afternoon when I overheard him talking with a couple of the farmers from east of here. He works for his cousin, Todd, from Anderson. Joan and Callie left Todd to come over here, and you beat Todd up for no reason, according to him."

"Well, that answers a lot of questions. We know who he worked for, and good riddance to him and his spying."

Mary said, "Zack, I have to confess. I bought what he was saying and passed on to him everything I heard from Carrie or picked up around your house. I guess I was blinded by love."

"Don't worry about that. Are you okay? Let's get you over to my house and get the nurse to take a look at you."

Before we could head to my farm, Bert and two deputies drove up with guns drawn. Neither Mike nor I recognized one of them. He was a guy who could pass for a Navy Seal, was dressed in black BDUs, and had body armor.

"Zack, what happened? We got the message and headed over here as fast as we could. Is that him over there?"

I said, "Bert, he started shooting at us as soon as we drove up. I had to shoot him when he pulled his gun on Mike. Mike would've been dead if I hadn't shot him."

Bert asked, "Why did you call us if you were going to handle this yourself?"

"Bert, we came over to prevent him from killing Mary. He beat the hell out of her. Take a look."

Bert said, "I'm sorry, Mary, but can I take a look at your injuries?"

"Yes, go ahead. If I'd had a gun, I'd have shot him. He wouldn't let me have my gun except when I pulled guard duty."

Bert looked at Mary and winced when he saw the bruises on her face and arms. "I guess it was a justifiable shooting. I'll do a formal interview with Mary in the morning, and I'm sure everything will be okay. I'll drive her to your farm."

Bert and the deputies helped Mary into their car and drove off.

"Zack, what was that all about? Bert got all official on us. I thought he would ask for our guns, and who was that new deputy? I thought I knew all of his people."

I said, "He could ask and try to take them. I smell a rat, and I don't think Grant was the only one around. We always knew that Bert was a political animal; however, I thought he was truly on our side. He just didn't seem to be himself. Now I wonder who we can trust."

Mike said, "Let's call our normal meeting that we usually have after a big event and see how people react."

"I think we need to underline what Aaron told me when he said to be prepared for anything."

Mike said, "Maybe we're just being paranoid."

We both replied the same exact words, "Just because you're paranoid doesn't mean they're not out to get you."

I added, "And I'll add, keep your friends close and your enemies closer."

"I'm now very glad that you talked us into finding and equipping a hideout, fallback, whatever we need to call it."

I said, "Let's just make it easy and call it the hideout."

We drove into my driveway and saw Carrie and Callie running to meet us.

Carrie moaned, "Where's Mom? Is she okay?"

"Yes, she's riding back here with the sheriff. She'll be fine after some rest."

Mary had been severely beaten, but there was no permanent damage. She had the mother of all black eyes and would limp for a while where the worthless excuse of a man had kicked her. She would survive this, but now we had to decide what to do with her. The big question was-can we trust her ever again?

***

Everyone had left, and Mary and Carrie spent the night with us out in one of the extra trailers. I was sitting at the kitchen table with the others enjoying a glass of sweet tea, and the girls were eager to know what had happened. They listened patiently until I got to the part about Mike almost being neutered, and Sally hugged him.

"Mike, this scares me. I could have lost you."

Mike made light of the situation, and Sally slapped him on the back of the head just hard enough to get his attention.

Then I told them about Bert and his deputies showing up. I was surprised by the reaction.

Callie said, "Dad, there's a new deputy, and the sheriff didn't bring him by the house to meet us when he started? That sucks, and it's not something a friend would do."

Ally said, "Wait a minute. Bert said he needed to investigate before you're cleared, and it looked like the shooting was justified. Has he lost his damn mind? Grant beat Mary. He tried to kill Mike and you shot Grant. What the hell does he want, a videotape of the shooting? Mary backed up your story, and since when does Bert doubt your word?"

Sally interrupted, "Since he got the new deputy, I'll bet. We need to know more about this guy and where he came from."

Ally said, "Darling, this smells like crap and looks like crap. Therefore, it must be crap, as my dad used to say. We have a big piece of the puzzle missing. You've gone from hero to a suspect in just a few days."

Callie raised her hand, and everyone turned to look at her when she said, "Dad, list the facts on a piece of paper. One, Grant was spying for Todd. Two, Mary says Grant was starting rumors

318

that you're doing bad things. Three, Bert has changed and gone all official. Four, there's a new cyborg deputy who probably wouldn't look you in the eye. Darn right, it stinks, and I'll bet it's all tied together. We just don't know who tied the knot and when it changes into a hangman's noose."

I said, "You're wise beyond your years. Let's keep this to ourselves until I can feel out, Roger. I don't trust anyone else until we get a handle on these developments. We need to hope for the best and prepare for the worst, without anyone knowing we're preparing."

"Dad, you don't trust Mom?"

"I trust your mom, but remember her new boyfriend is tight with Bert, and I don't trust him right now. What your mom doesn't know, she can't let slip during pillow talk."

***

Alan asked, "Well, Slim, how was your first couple of days on the job? Did Bert behave?"

"Very productive. We responded to a shooting out at Grant's house. Grant beat up his old lady, and Johnson and Norman killed him."

Alan asked, "What did you do? Are they in jail?"

"No. Bert wouldn't arrest them because the victim said Grant was beating her, and Grant tried to shoot Norman. It was justified. Don't worry, we'll take care of those clowns, and I'll make it look good. Half the farmers bought Grant's rumors about Johnson hoarding food and medical supplies while the city people were dying."

Alan said, "So if you found this stash and turned it over to our guys on the inside, it might tip the table in our favor?"

"Definitely, but we need a bunch of food and medicine to show that Johnson was hoarding."

Alan said, "Let me take care of that. Pick out a hiding spot to tie to Johnson, and I'll have the supplies delivered to the location. They'll turn against him, and then we just need to keep the wound festering until he's a pariah among his friends."

"Boss, I'll make it happen."

Alan said, "Good, I'm traveling over to Sailsberg on a goodwill mission. I'll be gone a couple of days."

"What about the mayor?"

"Ignore her and keep on track."

***

I'd called the meeting for after supper at the new sheriff's office. I started the discussion by covering the events with Mary and Grant.

A woman asked, "So you killed him because he was beating up on Mary or because he was opposing what you're trying to accomplish?"

Mike spoke up, "What the hell are you saying? Grant beat the hell out of Mary. We went to save her. Grant shot at me, and Zack shot him to save my life. That should settle the question."

Several of the men agreed with Mike, but a few others continued to ask questions.

One asked, "Bert, did Mary back up their story?

Bert said, "She gave the same story and said that she would have shot Grant, but he hid her gun. The shooting appears to be justified."

I looked around the room and saw it was divided down the middle. The folks who have always known Mike and me were on our side, and the others were hostile and trying to find a way to make us look guilty.

I looked around and said, "I see that several of you don't believe that Mike and I were justified in killing Grant even though Mary backs up our report. I want to know why. I've done nothing but help each one of you. Why are you acting this way?"

No one spoke up, and no one would look me in the eye.

Finally, Jacob spoke up. "Zack, these people have bought into the bullshit Grant was spreading around about you and your family getting rich off of them and have stockpiles of food and medicine that you're holding out from them."

"The only supplies that I haven't shared are the ones that Mike and I stocked away over the past few years. Some of you know that my uncle was one of those doomsday preppers. He spent the last ten years of his life preparing for exactly the type of disaster that hit us months ago. Even at that, I have shared my medical supplies with the nurse to treat all of you at my farm. Where did you think those supplies came from? Mike and I have shared *every* time we've found supplies the community needs. We even shared with the city."

Jacob replied, "I know you're speaking the truth, but Grant convinced half of the people in the room that you're power-hungry and just waiting to take over and make slaves out of them. He got them scared that you'll turn that Humvee loose on them if they make you mad."

I looked them in the eye and said, "So, you believe Grant over me? What did that lazy asshole contribute to improving this community? Name one thing."

No one answered. The room was silent.

I said, "I brought Jacob and his family into our community and set up a machine shop at my place, so he can fix your machinery and build generators to deliver electricity. Mike scoured the countryside to find old cars, trucks, and machinery to make your lives better. Jacob, Mike, and I had the idea to travel to the museum in Sailsberg to see if we could get a steam locomotive running. Now you have a way to travel and trade goods with other communities. Those are just a *few* things that Mike and I have contributed. I'm leaving now before I say something I'll regret. Goodbye."

The drive back to the farm was silent until Ally spoke up, "Honey, I'm very proud of you and what you've accomplished. Screw the ones who have been turned against you. We need to cut them out of our plans and move on."

Sally spoke up, "Sorry, but I think we have a major revolt going on, and it's not just Grant stirring the pot. Chuck started to speak up for you, and Bert elbowed him. I can't believe Bert didn't speak up on your behalf. This was a major rebuke to our side of the community, and I expect a confrontation shortly."

I replied, "I agree, and I'm going to catch Chuck in the morning."

We were pulling into my driveway when we heard gunfire and flashes from the crow's nest. We got up to the barn, and Roger yelled down, "Go to the shed with the Humvee! Someone was snooping around!"

We had our guns ready, and I carefully moved towards the shed and found it empty when gunfire erupted to my right.

Roger yelled, "Got one. Damn, he's back up and running. I lost him."

I shouted, "How many were there?"

"I saw two and shot one," replied Sam, "but the SOB got back up and took off."

We cautiously walked in the direction the thugs headed and lost them in the woods.

I said, "Let's head on back. We don't need to be walking into an ambush in the dark."

Roger yelled, "Hey, I nailed one! Look over by the dog house."

I headed over to the doghouse while the others covered me. There was a dead man behind the doghouse. He had a big hole in the front of his head and a much larger in the back. He was wearing black BDUs and body armor.

"Ally, please go up and take Roger's place, so I can talk with him. Thanks, hon."

Roger came down and started talking as soon as he approached us, "I heard one of the dogs barking but didn't see anything. Then I heard the door on the shed squeak and fired a round in the dirt by the shed. All hell broke loose, and I saw flashes from three different shooters. I stayed low and tried to keep them pinned down until help arrived. I know I hit another. Are you sure there isn't another body?"

I said, "Roger, the dead guy has body armor. You nailed him in the head. Ally hit another, and he got up and ran off."

Roger said, "What the hell is going on? Someone just tried to steal our Humvee."

"Roger, what do you know about the new deputy who resembles a Navy Seal, and his looks could cut you in half?"

"Which one?"

I said, "How many new deputies does Bert have?"

"I've seen three who match the description, but Frank told me that there's at least five more. Bert sent our men over to Sailsberg to live and replaced them with these guys. I'm sorry I didn't mention it sooner, has something happened?"

I said, "Roger, look at this man. Is he one of the deputies?"

Roger rolled the guy's head over and replied, "He's not one of the three, but he's dressed exactly like them. Could these be Prescott's men?"

I said, "That would be my first guess. My second guess would be that they're Todd's or Alan's men."

***

The mayor died the next day. Her husband took his own life, according to the policeman who performed the investigation. Several other of the town's leaders died over the next two days from the same symptoms as thousands of others had. It didn't matter, they were dead, and no one was clamoring for an autopsy. Prescott was out of town and beyond reproach. He offered his condolences and sent food to the victim's families.

Prescott's men and supporters set the ball in motion for the town to elect a new mayor. Prescott's cronies handed out cigarettes, whiskey, and food to gain enough votes without threatening anyone. The people loved him.

323

Chuck drove up with Joan in his old squad car and asked where I was when he saw Callie. She brought them out to the back porch, where Ally was giving me a haircut.

Ally said, "Stay still and quit acting like a kid."

I sat perfectly upright and said, "Yes, dear."

"I'll shove these clippers up your 'yes dear' ass if you keep taunting me, asshole."

I said, "But you still love me, don't you?"

Ally said, "My love won't make the clippers hurt any less. Hey, there's Joan and Chuck. Hello, Callie, please be a dear and get them some tea."

We exchanged hellos with Chuck and Joan, and then he jumped right in with, "Zack, Mayor Bonner died two days ago, and Alan Prescott is the new mayor. I'm convinced he had his goons kill her and five of the city leaders while away to Sailsberg."

"Slow down. What did the mayor and the others die from?"

Chuck said, "The police told me they died from dysentery, but no one's died for a week, and suddenly the whole power structure of Owensville dies in two days? That's BS."

I asked, "How the hell did they have a vote so quickly?"

"No one knows. A crowd clamored for a vote to elect a new mayor just hours after the mayor died. There're rumors of vote-buying and dirty tricks all over the town. Prescott won by a landslide. He was opposed by one of the deputies and a local lawyer, but their homes were burned down the day before the election."

I looked over at Ally and said, "I guess we know who tried to steal the Humvee."

Cuck said, "Zack, I almost forgot. One of the deputies passed on to me that he overheard two of the new deputies discussing how the sheriff needed to confiscate the Humvee before you attacked innocent civilians. What should we do? It looks like the city, Bert, and some of the farmers are ganging up against us."

"Chuck, can I have a minute alone with my ex? Stay here, Joan, and I'll go outside."

"No problem."

I led Joan out to my workshop and sat down outside on a hay bale. "How much do you trust Chuck?"

"What do you mean? Of course, I trust Chuck. I'm going to marry him."

"Joan, you trusted Todd, and it almost got you and Callie killed. Now, is this your hormones talking or your head?"

"I was stupid to fall for Todd. I know I made a mistake. Chuck is not Todd, and he's a good man. Remember, we've both known him for over twenty-five years. Yes, I trust him. Now what gives?"

"We're under attack both physically and through someone stirring the outlying farmers against us. Hell, even Bert has turned his back on me and maybe part of this overall plot. The mayor and others were killed to allow Prescott to take over. Someone tried to steal the Humvee the other night. I think we may have to stand and fight or bug out. Will Chuck be with us?"

"Yes, there's no doubt in my mind; Chuck is with us."

***

Several days had passed, and everything had been calm. We'd doubled our guards, and I met with all farmers and locals who I thought would be on our side. We all agreed that something terrible was going on behind our backs. Bert and his new deputies were making trouble for those not on Mayor Prescott's team. On several occasions, the men dressed in black BDUs demanded large quantities of food from several farmers. They were given the food, and they left. After hearing this, we buried a large part of our supplies and took the rest to the hideout, only leaving enough for a week's worth of meals.

Sam told me, "One deputy told me that the mayor was taxing us for the protection provided by the sheriff and his team. They had Ben, and I outnumbered, so we gave them the food."

Before I could reply, Paul drove up in my truck with Billy, the engineer from Sailsberg and Jacob.

Sam, Ben, and I were on the front porch and greeted them. I said, "Billy, I haven't seen you in a couple of weeks, and I've never seen you this far from the locomotive."

"Zack, the mayor of Sailsberg asked me to pass on a message to you on this trip. Can we go somewhere private?"

"Billy, you can trust these men. Let's hear what the mayor has to say."

Billy said, "Well, if you're okay, I'll go ahead. Several days ago, Alan Prescott came over to Sailsberg with four men dressed in black who were heavily armed. He said that he was there to set up trade between Owensville and Sailsberg and would be speaking for every community between the two."

"Go on."

"He indicated he would provide protection for the train because it could easily be attacked by criminals in this area, and until they wiped them out. It would be too dangerous to operate the train without their protection."

I asked, "Did he directly threaten the mayor?"

"No, but he implied that we had to take the help. The mayor declined his protection and said we'd be glad to trade with Owensville. Still, we've already set up trading with all of the communities between the two cities. This made him furious, and he said that all of Daviess County would soon be under his leadership, and all business would be conducted through his team."

I replied, "Thanks, Billy. We've seen Prescott's men flexing their muscles around this area. We believe he's going to try to either kill us or run us out. Thanks for the warning. Tell the mayor we're seeing the same actions by Prescott's men over here. Our group will meet tonight and decide on a course of action. I'll send a message with you on the next trip."

I pulled my immediate team together and asked them to meet me for lunch at the farm. I asked Ally to make sure Paul joined us, and I caught Callie and asked her to join us for lunch.

I started the meeting. "I guess y'all want to know why I invited you to lunch. Look around the table, and I hope you see the same thing I see. I trust every one of you with my life and worldly possessions. I know I can count on you when the shit hits the fan, and I hope you feel the same about me. This group is the leadership of our community. I know there're others who we trust and love to be around, but I don't feel as strongly about their loyalty."

"Dad, why are Paul and I here? We're not adults."

Mike spoke up, "You were kids several months ago before the lights went out, but I've seen both of you become adults in a short period. I totally agree with you two being in this group."

Everyone at the table pitched in their comments, backing up Mike's words.

I said, "Now, down to business. I just heard from the mayor of Sailsberg that Prescott paid them a visit and threatened them if they don't pay taxes and join his team. He told them he would be in charge of all of Daviess County as soon as he wiped out come criminals. Folks, I think he means to wipe us out of the county. The question is, what do we do to stop him? The kicker is that I feel Bert has joined with Prescott."

Roger replied, "Bert changed about three weeks ago. Lynn, you know his wife and daughter fairly well. Have you seen any change in them?"

Ally said, "Funny, but I haven't seen them for a month or so. I went over to their house, and Bert said they were in town visiting her sister."

Chuck replied, "She only has one, and she died a few days after the lights went out. Why would Bert lie?"

Callie said, "Dad, Paul and I used to see Gemma every Thursday when the train came in. She loves trains. I haven't seen her in two to three weeks."

Zack put two and two together and said, "Do y'all think Prescott is holding them hostage to get Bert's support?"

I said, "Makes the most sense and fits Bert's sudden loss of loyalty."

Paul asked, "Mr. Johnson, why is Prescott waiting to attack us? We aren't a threat to him. He has about thirty of his own men and the ones who've joined him since Mayor Bonner died."

"Call me Zack. We're all equals at this table. I like the respect, but Zack will do. Prescott is just another power-hungry man who's trying to take advantage of the chaos. The more I think about it, the more I'm convinced the attack is going to happen after we get all of the crops in from the fields. He wants us to do all of the work, so he can get all of the benefits when he gets rid of us."

"What if Prescott and Todd have formed an alliance? Anderson has to steal food because no one pushed the farmers to get back in the fields, and then most of them fled when they found out that Todd was taking most of their harvest. If Todd and Prescott unite, we're screwed," Mike commented.

I said, "Until we develop a plan to fight them, I want to start improving our situation. We need to move as much food, ammo, weapons, medical supplies, and fuel to the hideout as quickly as possible."

Mike replied, "Most of the extra food has already been moved. I'll handle the weapons if someone else handles the transfer of the rest."

Chuck and Roger looked up with puzzled faces, so I filled them in on our hideout.

My face was hot and red. "Sorry we didn't tell you earlier, but with the sudden change in Bert and Prescott's men popping up everywhere, I didn't know who to trust."

Chuck asked, "How far away is the location?"

I replied, "About twelve miles southeast. Do you remember Daviess Mountain?"

Chuck frowned. "Yes, but it's more like a tall hill."

I replied, "It's there in the old underground water storage tank. It was abandoned back in the '30s and is a perfect hideout for our team."

Roger asked, "Will it hold all of us?"

I thought about all of the new people. "Yes, we moved six medium-sized campers in and a mountain of supplies, and it's still empty. It's larger than a football field and completely underground, except for a large opening where a wall collapsed many years ago. I want us all to be ready at a minute's notice to bug out and go there without being followed."

Roger asked, "What else do we need to do?"

I asked, "Paul, have you been reading the US Army Improvised Munitions Handbook as I requested?"

"Yes, and I can make some deadly booby traps."

I said, "Start making them, but make sure they're safe until needed. Keep everything top secret."

Then I turned to Chuck. "Chuck, you're the head of our disinformation department. Make Bert and the others think that we're fat, dumb, and happy. Our Humvee, with its machine guns, will protect our friends and us. Throw in that we plan to work on the town's folk over the winter to have a coup and throw Prescott out on his ear. You know where I'm going. Stall for time without being too obvious."

Chuck said, "I know just how to play Bert and the others. I also have a couple of my own ideas. I'll catch you after the meeting."

I said, "Great. Paul, I need you and Callie to start taking joy rides as often as possible. Hell, what young couple doesn't want to get away for some privacy? Now, what you'll really be doing is sneaking our weapons, explosives, and any booby traps that we don't need here to the hideout."

Callie replied, "You can count on us."

I smiled at Mike. "Mike, strip the SAW's from the Humvee and replace them with broomsticks or something that will fool someone sneaking up in the dark to steal the Humvee. Take the SAWs to the hideout and work with Paul to booby trap the Humvee. I love the thing, but it draws too much attention."

Ally looked at me and said, "I love this place. Do you really think we'll have to leave?"

I nodded, "Darling, I think that we can start a war, attack them first and win in the long run. My best guess is that we'd lose half of the people around this table. I think we set a shit load of booby traps, make one hit and run attack, and disappear. Then we can start a guerilla war in the spring."

Mike said, "Why wait until spring? We can hit them all winter unless it snows. We don't want anyone following our tracks in the snow back to the hideout."

Ally asked, "Don't we need to let our friends know we're leaving?"

I replied quickly and firmly, "No. If our plans go perfectly, everyone, including our enemy, will think we're all dead. We can't have them searching the whole county for us. The bastards could trip over our hideout, and then we might have to bug out all over again. I know I sound like a dictator, but I can't bear the thought of losing any of you."

We continued working out our plans for several hours. We broke away for the day, with each team member having several assignments to accomplish before the next meeting. It was only a week before the harvest started, and a week or two afterward, all of the crops would be in the barns and root cellars. Most of the fruits and vegetables had already been canned.

Joan caught me when Chuck finished and hit me up about encouraging Callie and Paul to sneak away from us. "Damn, Zack. There're trailers with beds in that hideout. What the hell do you think is going to happen?"

I replied, "I think that they'll hold hands, kiss a lot, deliver the goods and come back here without doing anything else. I just told them that we consider them adults, and we trust them with our lives. I think they'll live up to that trust."

"And what the hell were we doing at their age when we got off alone?"

"I think Callie has higher morals than you did."

She said, "You dirty SOB. I should shoot you for that comment."

Ally caught me later and said, "I heard what you told Joan. I agree. Our kids have grown up and have to be trusted. I know they love each other, and regardless of what they do, they'll have a great life together."

★

Chapter 14 - Harvest Moon

The Farm

Todd mulled over the news. "So Johnson doesn't expect a thing, and we just have to wait until the harvest is done to raid his farm and wipe those bastards out. I want Joan and Callie brought to me in Anderson. They're mine. Don't harm them."

Allan said, "I'm sure he thinks that I've taken over Owensville through immoral and illegal methods. But he appears to have tucked his tail between his legs and stopped pestering the other farmers to join him against us. Kidnapping the kids or wives of the outlying farmers and Bert has made this a cakewalk. We'll kill all of them before they can mount their spring offensive."

Todd asked, "Are there any young girls in the bunch?"

"Look, Todd, I believe we can work together and rule this area together, but I'm not going to help you rape kids. What you do over in your town is your business, but don't try to screw around with the kids over here."

Todd pleaded, "But, you'll give me Joan and Callie?"

"Yes, but it will be the last time. I don't want kids molested, and I don't buy or sell women. If a woman wants to work in our brothels, that's her business, but I'm not forcing any to do that."

Todd scoffed, "So, you're a gentleman criminal."

"Todd, I'm not a criminal. I have just taken power to help these people survive this disaster. You're a crook and a pervert."

Todd said, "Keep tabs on Johnson and Norman, and don't underestimate them."

"I have been and will continue."

***

Without drawing any attention, we doubled up our efforts to get the hideout ready in case of TSHTF for the second time. We spotted the men shadowing Mike and me right away and made sure we never headed to the hideout without them thinking we were in my house or barn. We tested them several times, and they only followed Mike and me, which freed up the others to complete our bug out preparations and finish taking supplies to the hideout. Paul had manufactured several dozen IEDs for our booby traps and for roadside bombs.

Since there were only three old combines for all of the farms, the harvest took much longer than we'd forecast. We didn't have a wheat thresher, so we placed the wheat on big tarps and had the kids stomp on the wheat to knock the grain off the stalk. Then we took shovels and tossed the grain into the air to let the wind blow the chaff away. This was fun at first but became hard work after the second day. Thank God, the combine had a built-in corn shelling device, or we would've never gotten the crops in before winter. We were lucky the weather stayed reasonably warm, and there was no rain at all during the harvest. We used an old 1949 Ford to haul grain to our hideout, right under the eyes of the spies. We placed the grain in bags and stuffed them in the trunk and backseat, and then Paul would take Callie out in the woods for some privacy. They would drop the grain off at the hideout and head back home.

***

Callie asked Paul to pull over beside the road a few miles from the farm to relieve herself. "Sorry, I can't make it back to the farm. It'll be just a minute."

Paul sat patiently in the car when Callie returned, got in the car, moved over, and pulled herself onto Paul's lap.

"Paul, slide the seat back. The steering wheel is killing my butt."

He adjusted the seat, and Callie began kissing him. They held each other, trading kisses and telling each other how much they were in love for about fifteen minutes when she saw someone walking towards the car. Callie slid off Paul's lap and saw Frank and another man walking towards them, laughing. She quickly unfastened Paul's belt, unbuttoned his jeans, and pulled his zipper down as she whispered in his ear.

The man in black spoke, "Get out of the car on this side and keep your hands where I can see them."

Paul opened the door and stepped out while attempting to keep his pants from falling down. Callie got out behind Paul as he zipped his pants and buttoned them. His face was red as a fire truck and looked like he'd been caught red-handed.

Frank said, "Boy, get your clothes on. Well, I guess this is one thing that hasn't changed since the lights went out. Young lovers still sneak away in daddy's car to make out."

The deputy in the black uniform asked, "What do we do with them? Should we run them in or let them get back to what they were doing?"

Frank looked Callie in the eye and said, "Let them enjoy themselves. Carrie, I have to tell Mary about this, so you might want to tell her before I do. I'll wait until tomorrow morning. Now, go on home."

Paul fired up the Ford and headed on to the farm.

Paul was confused. "Frank knows both of us. Why did he mistake you for Carrie?"

Callie slapped Paul's leg. "He didn't. He was protecting us from the other man. My gut says that he would've kidnapped us if he knew who we really are. Frank may have saved our lives."

Paul's face was still cherry red. "You could have warned me before you unzipped my pants. I didn't hear them walking up, and my mind was racing."

Callie demanded, "Stop the car."

Paul pulled to the side of the road and looked over to Callie.

Callie said, "I whispered in your ear that men were behind you and to play along with me."

"Callie, I just felt your lips on my ear and felt you unzipping my pants. What did you think I was thinking?"

Callie laughed, "Oh, darn, Paul. You never make the first move. I guess you thought I was attacking you. Half the time, you act as if you're afraid of me. I have to kiss you first before you even kiss me back. Don't you love me?"

He said, "I do love you, and I want to make out with you, but I like you too much to hurt you, and besides, your dad said that he and your mom would kill me if I hurt you."

"Dad's a big teddy bear, and I can handle Mom. You need to start acting like my boyfriend."

Paul pulled her to him, kissed her, and said, "How old do you have to be to get married in post-apocalyptic America?"

She said, "I don't know, but you can kiss me again. Don't get too greedy. I was just kidding about being able to handle Mom."

Paul kissed her deeply and didn't ask for permission for what happened next.

***

Callie walked up behind Ally. "Ally, can we talk for a few minutes while Dad and Uncle Mike are out in the barn with Paul?"

"Yes, darling, what's on your mind?"

Callie began telling her the whole story about the deputies, the unzipped pants, and Frank mistaking her for Carrie.

Ally gulped, "Well, first, I guess Paul about killed himself getting out of the car."

"Yes, his pants fell down, but he recovered."

Ally rubbed her chin. "Callie, that was quick thinking. You kept them from wondering what y'all were doing out in the car and possibly finding the hideout."

"How old were you when you got married?"

Ally stumbled but recovered. "I ... uh... got pregnant, quit school, and was married before I turned sixteen. Life was hard, but we made it okay. What's on your mind? You're not pregnant, are you?"

Callie choked. "No! I mean, I don't think so. We love each other, and I want to be his forever and have his children one of these days."

"Well, I'm glad that you don't think you're pregnant. Are you asking me if you're too young to get married? That's something you need to ask your mom and dad. I'll say that you and Paul are much more mature than I was when I had Paul. I'll support you two getting married."

Callie hugged her. "Thanks, but what I'm trying to get to is, I know Dad and you love each other and will get married. I just want to be married to Paul before you two get married."

"Why rush just to beat us getting married?"

"Ally, if you marry Dad, Paul will be my stepbrother, and marrying your stepbrother sounds like a creepy country song. I can't make love to my stepbrother."

Ally stifled her laugh and replied, "I understand and will have to think about this. Can I get back to you tomorrow? Tell your dad about Frank mistaking you for Carrie."

Callie said, "Yes, that's okay. Ally, I wanted Dad to get back with Mom until I got to know you. Dad loves you, and you two are good for each other. If you have children, I want a baby sister."

Ally kissed her on the forehead, and they talked until supper.

"Hon, Frank was sending a signal to your daughter while protecting her from one of Prescott's men."

I looked at Ally and smiled. "I agree and thank God that was the last trip that they had to make to the hideout. Did she tell you anything else?"

She said, "We talked a lot, but I gave her my word that I would keep it in confidence. On another different topic, Paul and Callie are madly in love, and it's just a matter of time before things begin moving very fast. What do you think about them getting married? I think the sooner, the better."

I fidgeted and then spoke. "Damn, I thought we'd be married for years before that came up. My little girl is a woman, and oh crap, is this you asking, or did Callie bring it up?"

She grinned. "You know I can't answer that. Wait a darn minute. You never asked me to marry you. We just moved in together a few weeks ago, and I don't know you that well."

I pulled her to me. She felt very warm in my arms. "Well, I'll tell you all about myself in bed tonight."

Ally pushed me away. "Whoa. Let's just say that if we get married tomorrow, what does that make our kids?"

I grinned and then choked up. "Stepchildren? Oh, crap, stepbrother and stepsister. Damn, that's creepy."

"Just like a creepy country song."

I laughed, and she punched me in the belly.

I said, "Give me a day or two to figure out how high Joan will jump when I tell her that our kids are getting married. They do want to get married, don't they? Isn't this what you and Callie have been talking around? Is she pregnant?"

Ally continued being coy. "I can't say what Callie told me, but boy, do I have a funny story to tell you after they're married. Oh, and I don't think she's pregnant."

I took a deep breath. "Think?"

***

Alan raged with clenched fists. "What do you mean you think you almost had the Johnson girl? She's the number one target, along with her mother. Did you see her or not?"

His soldier replied, "Boss, Frank and I were patrolling southeast of the Johnson place when we saw an old Ford car parked on the road with two teenagers in it. They were making out, so it was easy to sneak up on them. Frank said that he recognized one of them to be Carrie Linton. He didn't say who the boy was."

Alan asked, "What makes you think that the girl was Callie Johnson?"

"Later in the day, I saw Bart coming back from surveilling the Johnson place, and he mentioned seeing this cherry red 1949 Ford pull into their barn. He said that he'd seen the Johnson girl and a boy leave in it and return a couple hours later. I'm putting two and two together, and I'm wondering why Frank lied about the girl."

Alan exclaimed, "So it was the Johnson girl!"

"The timing fits perfectly."

Alan said, "Bring Frank in to see me now. Tell Bart to come in first and to be prepared to arrest Frank."

Frank stood by his patrol car and saw the guy he'd been on patrol with go up to the black-uniformed men and point in his direction. The guy called Bart went into the office, and the other came towards him, checking his pistol as he walked. Frank knew he was in trouble and had to get the hell out of Dodge. He beat the other man to the draw, shot him twice to knock him down, and once in the head to keep him down. Frank jumped into his car, started the motor, and quickly sped away from the sheriff's station when the bullets began to pepper the back of his car. He felt intense pain as the slug passed through his lung and out the front of his chest. Blood was spurting out of his chest as he tried to plug the hole with his finger. He was dying and knew he couldn't warn the others. He turned the car around and drove it straight back to the station, gaining speed until he went over ninety miles per hour. Bullets began spraying the car again, but they were too late.

The car hit the corner of the pole barn with the office and tore through the wall, killing four men outside and the three inside when the gas tank erupted into flames and exploded. He died with a smile on his face.

Allan asked, "Why the hell would Frank Carpenter make a suicide attack on the sheriff's station? We knew he was not totally on our side, but he appeared to be doing a good job."

Bert said, "Alan, he's close to Chuck and may be closer to Joan Norman than we thought, but I never figured him for something like that."

"Bert, if you ever want to see your daughter again, you'd better flush out any deputies who are not loyal to me. Do you hear me? I'll give your daughter to Todd if this happens again and then kill the rest of your family. That bastard killed five of my best men and two of yours."

"I'll take care of it right now."

Allan said, "You'd better."

"Alan, Alan, your army is shrinking by the minute. I thought your guys were Special Forces hot shit. How did they let a hick town deputy kill five of them without firing a shot?"

"Okay, Todd, you've had your laugh, now let's get down to business. We're taking the two women and their Humvee tonight, and when they're licking their wounds, we'll hit them with our full force and kill every one of those bastards. After that, we'll go farm to farm and let them know who's boss. I'll keep them alive and able to work, but after this visit, they'll tow the mark and crap their pants when my men appear at their doors."

Todd said, "Don't hurt my women. Kill the rest for all I care."

***

All the crops were harvested, and the only thing left was to thresh the wheat, barley, and oats. The wheat was almost threshed and stored away, and we estimated it would take two more days to finish the remaining grain. The entire community was worn out but ready to throw a Harvest Dance two days after the last of the grain was stored. We went through the motions of planning and prepping for the dance, just to keep the bastards from knowing our real intentions.

I prepared my team to bug out tomorrow night, which was the last day of the harvest, before Prescott's men could attack. Mike and I would sneak out and shoot the men surveilling the house, then we would all get in our vehicles and bug out to the hideout. We were loading up the cars and trucks today in the barn and workshop and could hit the road with five minute's notice.

"Dad, we have to remember to set the horses free before we leave. I don't want cooked horses."

I said, "Don't worry. Sally is moving them to the back pasture after lunch. You can help her. How many dogs are you bringing? That's a lot of dog food stacked in the bed of that old Ford truck. You know we stored a ton of the stuff from the warehouse at the hideout, don't you?"

Callie winked, "Yes, but I don't want my pups starving."

I asked, "I guess Paul hated to leave the '49 Ford behind. Where is it?"

"We gave it to Carrie, so she and her mom would have transportation."

I gave her a pat on the back. "Good thinking."

"Paul is very kind."

I said, "Remember to bring all of your winter clothes. It's shorts weather now, but icy weather is just a month or two away. Hey, tell Ally that I'm driving over to Sam's, so I can draw my escorts away from the farm, and you can change vehicles to be loaded. Don't move any until Uncle Mike says the coast is clear."

"Okay, Dad. Be careful."

I got in my old Ford FI and drove down the driveway, turned right, and headed over to Sam's place. "Mike, are they following me?"

"Yes, but there're two trucks. I don't like this. Watch out. We're on the way."

Mike hollered at the rest, drove his truck around, and waited for the rest to join him. Roger, Chuck, and Lynn grabbed their ARs, got in Mike's truck, and took off to help stop the attack. The men were in the bed with their rifles on the roof of the truck and aimed ahead. They went around a bend and saw the three vehicles ahead, and a fierce firefight was going on.

I'd tried to act as if nothing was happening when several bullets struck the back of my truck and blew the back glass over my back and neck. I saw the stalled truck on the right side and slid to a stop behind it while firing at them as I moved into position behind the truck's back wheels. Bullets were peppering the ground beside me and ricocheting off the truck. There were four of them, and I knew I was done for if help didn't arrive soon. I took a deep breath, took the time to aim, and shot one of the attackers in the leg. He fell out from behind the pickup, and I put a slug into his head. That slowed them down for a minute, and then I heard more gunfire behind them. Mike and the others had arrived and were coming up from their backside. They couldn't cover themselves from both sides, and one more fell dead. The other two tried to run out in the brush to their left to escape. Mike never stopped and ran right over them. Roger and Chuck shot both of them as soon as the truck got past them. They aimed and made headshots to make sure they were dead.

I yelled, "Grab their weapons and body armor, and let's get back to the farm! My truck is dead! I'll ride with you!"

We drove back and found everything was normal, except their worry about us. I quickly filled them in and told them we need to bug out now before those men were missed. "Sorry, but we have to chance it now. Those men will be missed in two hours at their shift change. You have ten minutes, and then we need to hit the road."

341

Ally said, "Hon, we anticipated that, and we're ready now. Let's go."

I said, "Paul, set your traps, Mike, set the Humvee booby trap, and I added a small surprise for the thugs in my shop. I hate to blow the house up, but they need to think that we died while under attack. The tripwires will make the rifles fire until empty, and those homemade smoke bombs will confuse them when they attack. The tripwire between the pole barn and the barn will set the timer in motion to set off the rockets in all directions. Finally, the fireworks stash in the basement beside the two fifty-gallon drums of gasoline will make a Hell of a blaze."

I had Ally and her daughter Susie in my truck, along with Susie's puppy. It was the brother to Callie's dog and would be great companionship for Susie once we holed up in the hideout. There wouldn't be any other kids to play with for quite some time. I was glad that Susie was low maintenance like her mom since we were moving into what amounted to be a cave for who knew how long. I had a bad feeling that evil lurked around every corner, and I had to protect my family every minute of the day.

Susie said, "Mom, look! Joan and Chuck are turning around. I wonder why?"

Just then, Joan's voice came over the radio. "Chuck and I have to go back. I forgot something in the house. Don't worry. Chuck knows where the tripwires are located. We'll be on the road in twenty minutes."

I replied, "Hurry up! We'll see you there."

Thankfully, the drive over to the hideout was uneventful, and there was no one on the road. We pulled directly into the hole in the wall and parked the trucks.

I called out, "I want everyone to grab some brush and help me erase our tire tracks. Mike, come with me down to the road. We'll start down there and work our way back to y'all."

Ally said, "Zack, we can't start until Joan and Chuck gets here."

"Damn, you're right."

I yelled at Mike. "Let's brush out the tracks by the road, just in case someone drives by before they get here."

Mike said, "Okay, the rest of you go ahead and get everything unloaded."

Ten minutes passed, and they hadn't arrived.

Mike said, "Something's wrong. Joan said they'd be right behind us."

I replied, "We'll wait five more minutes, and then Mike and I'll go looking for them."

The time passed, so Mike and I got in my truck and headed back toward the farm. We were a mile away when we saw the black smoke and heard explosions coming from the direction of the farm. We turned off the road and drove up behind my place through the woods, stopping a quarter-mile away. I saw my shop, but the house and barn were leveled but still smoking. I got my field glasses and could see men searching the workshop and the '49 Ford car that Paul had given to Carrie. Then I saw the bodies by the shop covered with blankets. I got a lump in my throat, and tears came to my eyes.

I could barely speak but said, "Mike, there're two bodies, and I can't tell who they're."

Mike said, "Let's go down and kill those bastards and get Joan."

"Mike, calm down. There are two dozen heavily armed men down there. We could kill some, but we'd also be killed. We don't know if that's Joan and Chuck on the ground. It appears that Carrie drove up to the house before they could leave. They may be criminals and thugs, but I don't think they would kill women just for fun. Let's go to the hideout until we can find out what happened. Getting ourselves killed won't help Joan."

Mike growled, "I know you're right, but I want to kill all of them."

I said, "Me too, let's go."

I couldn't help feel we should've stayed at the farm while we waited on Joan and Chuck, but reality kept slapping me in the face. Had we stayed, all of us could be dead now. I knew this was right, but it didn't make me feel better.

Chapter 15 --Kidnapped

The Farm

Joan and Chuck were walking onto the porch when the old Ford car drove into the driveway. Chuck had just disabled the trip wires or would all be in the middle of an inferno with explosions all around them.

Mary said, "Hello, Joan. Carrie brought me over to see if we could borrow some flour and sugar."

Joan replied, "Stay there, and I'll get it for you. We're in a hurry to leave and have to be on the road in a minute."

Mary pointed at the driveway. "Does it have anything to do with the men pulling up over there just out of sight? Are they trouble?"

Joan gasped, "Yes, they're Prescott's men, and they attacked us earlier this morning. Find cover and get your guns."

Carrie and her mom ran to the car, retrieved their rifles, and took cover behind the porch.

Mary asked, "Chuck, are you sure they mean to hurt us? I don't want to hurt them if they're just investigating the shootout this morning."

The men continued to walk towards the house and began shooting at Chuck as they advanced. Bullets also struck the end of the porch where Carrie and her mom hid behind for protection.

"I guess that answers your question about them, not meaning to hurt you."

Carrie and her mom began shooting and killed several before the men fell to the ground, trying to find cover. Joan and Chuck had the other side of the front yard covered and hit several men before a dozen more men came running out of the trees in a frontal assault. Just then, Chuck was shot in the shoulder and dropped to the ground.

"I'm hit, Joan. We can't escape. They have us surrounded. Drive the truck into the barn and set the charge as you leave. I'll set the charges for the house. We'll blow the place as we surrender. They have to believe the rest were caught in the fire."

Chuck set the tripwires, and immediately the rifles rigged to fire started shooting. Several charges exploded in front of the house. Chuck returned fire and slowed the attackers down until Joan closed the barn door and ran back to him.

Joan yelled, "We have to get over behind the workshop in less than a minute, or we're all dead! Run!"

All four of them jumped off the porch and ran towards the workshop. Mary fell after being shot in the leg and the chest, but Joan helped her up and on towards the workshop. Bullets were hitting all around them when one struck Joan, and she fell. Chuck looked over and saw her holding her bloody head. That was the last thing he saw. A bullet tore through his chest and destroyed his heart. He fell beside Joan, thinking they were both dead. Carrie tried to drag her mom to cover, but the whole world exploded around her, knocking her to the ground. She blacked out.

***

The explosions flattened the house and barn, killing twelve of the men attacking the farm. The house and barn were blazing, and small explosions were still coming from them.

The leader yelled, "Stop shooting, you dumb SOBs! I told you not to shoot the women!"

A man yelled back. "They were shooting at us! What the fuck did you expect us to do?"

The leader said, "Check them out. The boss is going to be furious if you killed them."

The men turned the women over and checked the damage.

"This one's dead, but the girl is alive and may have a concussion. Her face looks like hamburger. Oh crap, she has a large chunk of metal stuck in her side. I don't think she'll make it."

The leader gasped, "Oh! Shit! Damn, this is Joan Johnson. She has a graze to her head but is alive and might recover. The girl is her daughter Callie. We have both of the women the boss wanted. We just have to keep them alive."

"Load them up, and let's get them into town to the doctor."

They placed Joan and Carrie in the back of the pickup along with two guards and sped towards town.

***

Joan woke up in the bed of a pickup bouncing down a highway. Her head was pounding, and someone was holding pressure on her wound. She kept still because she wanted to know what was going on before her captors knew she was awake. It was daylight, and the sun was still high in the sky, so she hadn't been unconscious for very long. Another person was lying against her, and she couldn't tell who it was, but it was a woman. That made her remember Chuck falling after being shot. Tears came to her eyes as she realized that Chuck was dead, and Mary was probably dead.

She heard one of the men in the bed of the pickup say, "The older one is Joan Johnson, and the young girl is her daughter Callie. Alan's trading them to Todd."

"The woman will be okay, but the girl probably won't make it to the doctor alive."

347

She thought, *Callie was with Paul and went on to the hideout. This can't be her. Damn, it must be Carrie. I'll let them think it's Callie, so at least they won't be looking for her.*

Chapter 16 - The Hideout

Daviess County, Kentucky

Mike and I returned and told the team to use the brush to cover our tracks before we had time to bring them up to speed. Callie grabbed me and asked about her mom. "Dad, where's mom? Are she and Chuck going to join us later?"

"Darling, I don't know. We didn't find them, and I'm sorry to say, but I think they were captured by Prescott's men."

Callie asked, "You think they were captured?"

I told her the truth. "The house and barn were smoking ruins. The old Ford Paul gave Carrie was there, and there were two dead bodies. I think they were Carrie and her mom Mary, but the truth is we just don't know. There were dozens of Prescott's men there, and we had to come back here."

Callie began crying in my arms while Paul and Mike looked on. There was nothing that could be said that would make her feel better, so I just comforted her while she cried.

After an hour, Callie looked at me and said, "I know Mom's alive, and I want you to kill the bastards that captured her and killed Carrie."

"I will."

"Paul, hold me."

She went over to Paul, and they went into one of the campers and sat on the couch for the rest of the afternoon. Paul came out after a couple of hours and said that Callie was asleep on the couch.

I walked over to Mike and Sally's camper and knocked on the door. Mike came to the door and invited me in.

"Mike, are you okay? Is there anything we can do for you?"

Mike had tears on his cheeks. "No, not now. I've been racking my brains on how we can find out where Joan is and what their plans are for her. Surely, they'll release her. She hasn't done anything to Prescott. I guess the only thing that we can do right now is to pray for Joan and Chuck."

I nodded, "That makes sense to me."

I kept racking my brains on how to find out where Joan was and how to rescue her. I was sitting at the table in our camper with Susie while Ally prepared supper.

I said, "Ally, Mike and I need to sneak into town to find out where they're keeping Joan and the others, but I can't think of a way that doesn't end well. We can get about halfway there by truck, but we'd have to walk five miles into town to avoid being seen."

Susie said, "Why don't you ride our bicycles on the Greenway into town? Several of us kids have snuck back into town several times. The paths are open, but the weeds and brush are tall around them. You could drive to Green River Road, park the truck, and ride bikes into town. After dark, of course."

I reach over, kissed Susie on the forehead, and said, "From the mouths of babes comes the solution to my problem. We'll ride bikes into Owensville and slip in right under their noses."

Ally looked at me. "Darling, you do know you won't be invisible and could get shot. Look, I'm all for saving Joan, but I don't want to lose you because you and Mike have to do

350

something, even if it's wrong. Please think this out before you do anything that gets you two killed."

"I promise Mike, and I'll be very careful. We won't try to do anything but find out where they're keeping her."

I looked over to see that Susie was playing with her puppy and whispered, "I just hope for Callie's sake, Joan is still alive."

Ally whispered. "Hon, what happens if you run into someone out on the road? Are you going to shoot them just to keep our hideout secret? What if you get in a gun battle with Prescott's men and get killed or captured?"

"Darling, I'm not going to BS you into thinking it won't be dangerous, but we'll leave the hideout after midnight and return way before dawn. There's no one on the road and only guards at the major roads. We should be able to sneak in and out without being detected."

She asked, "How will you find out where she is if everyone's asleep?"

I rubbed my head and then spoke. "Okay, I need to work on the plan. I promise we won't do anything stupid and get hurt. Is it okay if I share my ideas with Mike?"

She huffed, "You're a grown man, and we're not married, so you can do what you want."

"Wait a minute. We may not be officially married, but you belong to me and me to you. I won't do this without your approval."

Ally replied, "Thanks. I feel the same way. Let's work on the plan with Mike and see if you can safely get the information you need."

I walked over to Ally, kneeled down on one knee, and said, "Ally, will you marry me and be my wife forever?"

"Yes, I was wondering when you would get around to asking. Now stand up and kiss me, but don't think for a minute I'll let you get killed doing something crazy."

We had Jalapeno Spam, macaroni and cheese, and spinach for supper. Susie cleared the table, and I washed the dishes while

Ally had a glass of wine and rested. We finished the dishes, and I sat down beside my beautiful woman and thanked God that I'd met her. I needed someone with a calming influence on me during these trying times. Ally read a book titled Bush Craft 101, and Susie played with her dog while I had a book in front of me, planning how to get the information we needed. I can thank Sally for figuring out how to accomplish that task.

***

Joan continued to keep her eyes closed and didn't react when the men picked her up and carried her into the hospital. They placed her gently on a bed and went back to get Carrie. Joan heard them talking, and then they took Carrie to another room.

One of the men said, "Too bad about that one. She bled out on the way here. Alan will be pissed, but it wasn't our fault those idiots booby-trapped their farm. Only one left alive out of eight to ten. Alan wanted to put Johnson and Norman in jail and try them for stealing food from the people."

The other man replied, "Well, tough shit. They wounded me, and a dozen of our buddies were killed. I'm glad they're dead, and I'd kill this bitch too if I could get away with it."

"I don't know about that. I can think of other things to do with her."

"Keep your paws off her. If Alan found out she'd been messed with, he'd cut our balls off."

Joan could hear another voice in the hall coming towards her. It was Doc Brown.

The doctor said, "I know this young lady. It's Joan Johnson. Her head is covered in blood. What happened to her?"

"She almost got lead poisoning. Stop asking questions and fix her head."

He took a small flashlight out of his pocket, pulled her eyelid down, and shined the light on her eye to check her pupils.

She blinked and startled the doctor. He realized what she was doing and winked at her. She winked back.

The doctor cleaned the wound, shaved her head around it before injecting antibiotics and painkillers into her scalp, and then stitched her injury.

"Let her sleep for the rest of the night, and I'll check her in the morning."

He held her hand and squeezed it. She squeezed his hand and held it for a minute.

The doctor said, "Tell your boss it'll be several days before she'll be able to be moved. I'll have my nurse come over and watch her until the morning. She'll be unconscious for a day or so."

Joan knew she had to escape before they tied her up or handcuffed her. That meant in the next two days. She looked around the room and saw that she was alone. She tried to pull herself up, her head pounded, and she was too weak to move. She would try again tomorrow. The nurse watched over her all night, so she slept through until dawn.

***

I woke up with the strange feeling that someone was spying on us. Ally was in my arms, and I could hear her cute little snore, but the hair on the back of my neck was standing on end. I heard breathing behind my head and quickly rolled over to see Susie's dog staring me in the face. My sudden movement scared him, and he jumped off the bed, yelping to get out of the room. I strained my foot, walking towards the sliding door, and opened it enough to allow Duke to run down to Susie's bed.

Susie had the bottom bunk of a bunk bed on the opposite end of the trailer. Callie had the top bunk, and we had a master bedroom with a sliding door on either side of the queen bed. You actually had to leave the room to walk around the bed. Not much privacy. My movement woke Ally up, and she drew me near and hugged me. Her eyes never opened.

I asked, "Are you hoping yesterday never happened, and we're on a camping trip down at Barkley Lake?"

"Nope, we're in Orlando camped just outside of Disney World, the kids are outside playing with the neighbor kids, and we have time to fool around before you take us to breakfast. If I keep my eyes closed, it might come true."

I joked. "So if the campers rocking, don't bother knocking?"

Ally laughed. "Yeah, something like that. Now, I'm going to open my eyes and go back to our problem-filled world."

I said, "Wait, keep your eyes closed for another few minutes while I tell you how much you mean to me, and I want to live with you forever."

"Well, I'm waiting."

"For what?"

Ally said, "For you to tell me how much you love me, and you want me forever."

I squeezed her hand. "I just did. That was me saying all that stuff you just repeated."

She said, "Oh, I thought you'd add some detail and sweep me off my feet."

"You're off your feet and naked in bed with me. I must have already swept you off your feet."

She laughed, "Too much wine."

"What do you mean? Too much wine?"

"I mean, if that's all you had to say to get me in bed, I must have had too much wine."

I said, "I'll show you too much wine," as I tickled her.

"Stop before you regret it. I get even."

I stopped tickling her, kissed her, and kicked the door closed so we could get dressed.

Ally said, "You gave up too soon."

I said, "No, I looked down the hall and saw Susie peering out of her bunk to see what was going on."

"She's twelve. She probably knows what was going on."

I said, "Darn, now I'll have to slip her a sleeping pill before we can...."

"Shush! The walls have ears, and so do Susie and Callie."

I laughed. "I was going to say, have fun. Now get up sleepy head.

"Bummer. Back to the trouble-filled world."

My belly growled. "Yep, what's for breakfast?"

"Now that's my silver-tongued devil that used the magic words that are the key to her heart."

My belly was still growling. "I try hard to impress."

"Go tell the others that we're having pancakes on the picnic table at our house."

I got up, went to the bathroom, and walked out to the living room when I realized I didn't see Callie. "Susie, where is Callie?"

Susie replied, "Her and Paul fell asleep by the campfire. I'll bet they're still there."

"Shouldn't that be she and Paul?"

"Grammar Nazi!"

I charged out of the trailer and over to the front of our new abode to see Callie lying in Paul's arms under a blanket by the long-dead campfire. They had their clothes on, so my daughter's virtue was still intact. I watched for a minute and wondered what to do about young love and our screwed-up world.

I took my foot, nudged Paul's back, and said, "Wake up, sleepyhead. Wake your woman up. We're having pancakes at our house in an hour."

"Hello, Zack. This isn't what you think."

I tried to sound stern. "Yes, it is. You two fell asleep with your clothes on and slept in each other's arms. You love my daughter, and she loves you. Nothing happened. Did I miss anything?"

"No, sir."

"See you at breakfast."

As I walked towards the other campers, I thought that those two needed to get married before one of them was kidnapped, killed, or pregnant.

I went around the campers and beat on the doors. I told them to wake up and come on over for pancakes. I caught Mike off to the side and wanted to fill him in on my thoughts for rescuing Joan. "How are you doing, buddy? Don't worry. We'll get Joan back."

Mike sighed, "I'm okay. I know. She's too mean to die and has probably kicked their asses and escaped by now."

"I hope so," I said and then filled him in on my plans.

Mike pointed to his girlfriend. "I spent all night thinking the same things. Sally came up with a way to find out what we need. Look at this."

He had a small electronic device in his hand and said, "It's a small sound-activated voice recorder. It uses a memory card instead of tape, so it'll record as long as the battery lasts."

"It's electronic and probably fried."

Mike insisted, "No, it works just fine. It was in that metal-skinned warehouse where we found the food. The packaging had one of those anti-static bags and aluminum foil, so it was EMP proof. All we have to do is to sneak into city hall and bug Prescott's office."

"Oh, I thought you'd come up with something difficult to do. Can I assume we have to go back and retrieve it also?"

Mike scowled. "Yes, but we can do it. It'll be 2:00 in the morning, and there will only be one guard making rounds."

"And you know this how?"

He said, "Well, that's what I'd do."

"I would just put my valuables in my safe, lock up the office, and go home."

Mike said, "That's even better."

356

I changed the subject. "I found Callie and Paul sleeping together this morning."

"Have you given her the sex talk and some contraceptives?"

"Yes and no. Hell, no! I don't want to think about that."

Mike nudged my arm and grinned. "Look, we were sixteen, and that's all we thought about."

"Whoa, they had all of their clothes on and were asleep by our campfire."

Mike laughed. "That doesn't change anything. You're going to be a grampa before you know it."

Sally was coming out the door, heard the conversation, and said, "Mike's right. Even girls have those thoughts, daddy. Of course, I was twenty-five before I had sex."

I said, "Sally, you just turned twenty-five this year."

She chuckled, "I was a late bloomer."

Mike said, "So, I was the first?"

"Oh, yes, dear," she said and gave him a peck on the cheek.

I replied, "My ass."

Mike said, "Let's get back to Callie and Paul. Paul already lives in the extra trailer. Let them set up housekeeping in it. Roger can marry them. He was a policeman once upon a time. Then your grandkids won't be born out of wedlock."

Roger and Lynn walked up behind Sally and me. Lynn said, "Don't worry. Paul was a perfect gentleman all night long. Well, I couldn't see what his hand was doing under the cover every now and then, but I'm sure it was innocent."

I gave her the finger.

"Seriously, Zack, they behaved well. I watched for the first four hours, and Roger had the last four."

I said, "Oh shit, we forgot to post guards."

Roger raised his hands. "No, Lynn and I were the guards last night. That boy has more character and restraint than I ever had at sixteen. That's all I'm going to say about that. Hell, let them move in together. You can marry them. You're our leader."

I gave them all the finger, walked out, and sat down on the picnic table. I knew something had to be done because it was just a matter of time when sleeping would turn into a different meaning than what I'd found this morning. I knew that the world had slid back in time, but I still wasn't ready for Callie to grow up.

Callie and Paul joined me at the table before the others arrived. Callie sat down next to me and said, "Daddy, nothing happened last night. Paul is always a gentleman. I want to marry Paul. He wants me also. We might starve to death or be killed by Prescott's men before we turn eighteen. We're both very mature and have done about all of the growing up we're going to do. Please?"

Before I could speak, I saw the others heading towards us. I waved them off and said, "I think Paul's mom should be a part of this discussion."

"What discussion should I be a part of?"

Callie repeated what she had told me and said, "I promise to be a good wife to Paul, and I know he'll take care of me."

I nodded at Ally. She nodded back and then said, "Paul is this, what you want?"

"Mom, Zack, I want this more than anything. I know I have a lot to learn, but I have you two to help me, and I know that no one could love or take better care of Callie. We don't want to be slipping around behind your backs. We want to be married."

Ally and I looked at each other, and Ally said, "So Callie, you two will be married before your father and me. You two tomorrow morning, and us right afterward. We'll get your uncle Mike to perform the ceremony."

Ally went into the trailer, came back, walked up to Callie, and said, "I like for you two to use my wedding band until you can get one of your own."

I gave Paul my class ring and said, "Use this for your wedding band until you can get one of your own."

Paul choked up. "Yes, I'd like that very much. Thanks, Zack and Mom."

Yes, it got mushy after all of that. I was still in shock, but I loved Paul like a son, and now he would be my son-in-law. The others came over, and we announced the future Mr. and Mrs. Stone. They applauded, hugged Callie, and shook Paul's hand. I was still in a daze. *Joan will kill me.*

"Ally, the pancakes are delicious. Thanks for our first official meal in our new home. "While the ladies are cleaning up, we'll plan the infiltration of Owensville."

Ally put her hands on her hips. "Whoa, wait for a minute, big boy. Y'all do the cleanup while we take Callie inside and give her some motherly advice on how to handle men who try to get themselves killed. Then after we're done, we'll all help make the plans."

"Yes, dear."

Ally frowned. "So, Mike and Zack bike into the city while Paul and Roger set IEDs on their escape route. Mike bugs the office while Zack pulls lookout duty. The rest of us wait at the truck as a backup in case shit happens. All four of you ride the bikes back the four miles to the truck, and we all drive back to the hideout."

I answered, "That sums it up, except we'll hide the bikes in the bushes when we head back here. If you hear gunfire, get ready for a battle."

Paul said, "If the worst happens and they chase us, there won't be many of them left alive if the IEDs work. The worst case is we kill a bunch of them, hideout in the woods, and go back to the hideout later when they're not following."

Ally said, "Looks like we're on for tonight and have weddings tomorrow."

I said, "Okay, everyone, get some rest, Ally and I'll pull the first four hours of guard duty, Callie and Paul, the next four, and then the rest of you can divide up the rest of the day. I want everyone ready to travel at midnight."

I watched Paul and Callie go into their new home together and wondered. As if she'd read my mind, Ally said, "Don't worry, they'll wait until tomorrow."

The time passed quickly as we discussed what we needed to do for the newlyweds. Ally and I got about six hours of sleep and got ready for a long night.

The drive over to Owensville was tricky since we traveled without headlights. We had to go about twenty miles per hour and were nervous we would be heard or seen before we could enact our plan. I drove and had to stop once for a cow and then for a tree branch that had fallen. We replaced it, in case someone had put it there to see if anyone was using this old road. We arrived a mile from the roadblock and hid the truck in the brush. We unloaded our bikes, kissed our girls, and headed on into Owensville on the Greenway. The path ran away from the city to the river and then along the river to the downtown area where the mayor's office was located.

**

"Don't worry, she's progressing well. She woke up and talked with me today. I'm going home, and you get some rest."

The doctor was talking to his nurse. Joan listened to make sure her escape plans were still good.

"Shouldn't she be handcuffed?"

"No, she's too weak to go anywhere. I'm responsible for her, and besides, I gave her a shot that'll keep her knocked out all night. They're moving her to Anderson in the morning, and she would try to escape if she knew that."

"I should've known you had everything covered. I'm going to make up my cot and get a good night's sleep. That'll be an easy night."

The clock on the wall ticked off every second for the three hours Joan waited until 1:00 am to make her move. She slowly slid off the bed, put the nurse's tennis shoes on, grabbed a bottle of water, and slipped out the back door. Joan knew she couldn't walk straight through town, so she decided to make it to the waterfront, take the Greenway around the city to the southeast side of town, and walk to the hideout. She thought she could cover the distance before daybreak or the nurse waking up. Joan didn't know the doctor had slipped the nurse a sleeping pill, so she walked as fast as she could while staying in the shadows. She made it to the Greenway and found three bicycles beside the entrance. She chose one and took off on it. She used to ride ten miles a day, and she enjoyed the breeze.

Everything was going according to her plan when she rounded a bend and saw something coming at her. She swerved but still hit something head-on. She went head over heels and hit something soft. Her leg was under her, and it hurt like hell. She heard voices and felt someone moving on top of her. Someone had her pinned down. She started punching the person and knew that she would kill to get back to her daughter and family.

***

I rode with Mike in the middle, Roger on the right side, and Paul on the left. The air was crisp and had smoke in it from the fireplaces. The temperature getting down in the '40s at night, and a fire felt good this time of year. We had just set an IED and rounded a bend when something flew in, knocked me off my, bike and careened into Paul.

I could hear Paul saying, "Stop hitting me, and I'll get up. It's a woman, and if the bitch doesn't stop hitting me, I'm going to kill her."

Then, Paul yelled in pain, "Oh shit. Get her off me; she's kicked me in the balls."

The woman yelled, "Get your hands off my tits, asshole!"

Mike whispered, "Joan, is that you?"

Joan's voice cracked. "Mike, is that you?"

I spoke up and said, "Paul, get your hands off your mother-in-law's tits. She's small but vicious."

Paul moved away from Joan, and I helped her up and gave her a big hug. She was trembling in my arms, and I could tell that the collision had shaken her up and made her mad at the same time. Her nose bled but quickly stopped.

I said, "Keep your voices down. Joan, we were coming into town to find out where you were, so we could rescue you."

She replied, "The doctor helped me escape. I just walked out."

Paul stuttered, "Mrs. Mrs. ....Johnson,... I'm sorry we collided with each other. I hope you're okay."

Mike hugged his sister, thanked God she was okay, and said, "We need to get the heck out of here and head back to the truck before someone misses her. We can swap stories later."

Joan lifted her bike and said, "The wheel's bent. I'll have to ride with someone."

I said, "Paul, give your mom-in-law a ride."

Joan chuffed, "Mike, I'm riding with you. He tried to play with my.... What's this crap about mom-in-law?"

I replied, "Callie and Paul are getting married tomorrow."

She snarled, "The hell they will."

I barked back at her. "Joan, shut up and ride."

Joan didn't shut up, but she kept her voice low while she cursed and grumbled something about over her dead body. We stopped and retrieved the IEDs, so no one would think Joan had help. I made her take her bloody blouse off and hung it on a limb at the river's edge, so maybe they would think she'd fallen in the river or tried to swim to the Indiana side.

We were back at the truck in a little over an hour and rode up to four amazed women.

"Joan, you're safe!"

Callie hugged her mom and cried. "Mama, I thought I'd never see you again. Let's take you home. Paul, help me get Mom in the truck."

Paul stood there with his mouth open and moved slowly towards Joan.

Joan said, "What's wrong, boy? You shouldn't have any trouble holding my hand after running yours all over my body. Baby girl, you haven't even married this bum yet, and he's already making passes at his mother-in-law."

Callie's head jerked toward Paul. "What?"

Paul replied, "Momma Joan, that was an accident, and you'll scare Callie talking like that. I know you're just kidding about killing me."

Joan screeched, "Don't call me momma. There isn't going to be a wedding, and that's final."

Callie replied, "Mom, we're getting married, or I'm shacking up with him like you did with Todd and Chuck."

She didn't reply, and we drove slowly in the dark back to the hideout.

Joan heard about the details of the wedding and said, "Oh, hell no! If my daughter's getting married, she'll use my wedding ring."

Joan caught Ally and me off to the side and asked, "Did we bring those boxes of birth control pills and condoms from the farm?"

Ally answered, "Yes, are you worried about Callie and Paul?"

Joan said, "Yes, and the rest of you. We don't have a doctor to deliver a bunch of babies."

Joan and Paul told that story about the collision for years, with it growing like a fisherman's story that got bigger and bigger year after year. We had the weddings the next evening after we got some rest. Later, we swapped stories about what happened at the farm and the events around that day. Joan still mourns for Chuck but has learned to love Paul and dotes on him and Callie. This part of our story ends as well as can be expected, and we just need to survive this winter and take one day at a time.

Other than the ring issue, the weddings went off without a hitch. It was challenging to honeymoon in a trailer in a cavern with other people all around, but it can be done.

Chapter 17 - Early Winter

The Hideout

Three weeks had passed since we holed up at the hideout. We were reasonably certain that no one was looking for us, and our lookouts hadn't seen a car on the two closest roads during that time. It was now mid-October and colder in the mornings, then I remembered past fall weather to be. The good news was it was about fifty-five degrees in the hideout winter or summer if we kept the outside air out. It didn't matter how cold it was this winter. We would be able to heat our campers without using too much of our store of propane.

The air was sparkling clear. The sky was electric blue and smelled like burning wood. Most people had to revert to burning wood or coal in their fireplaces. Eventually, this would take a toll on air quality. The only real excitement was a week ago when we'd seen a jet streaking across the sky.

Callie had been watching the road in front of the hideout when she came running in the entrance, yelling, "There's a jet in the sky! Dad, there's a jet! Come on!"

We all came running to the entrance and immediately saw the contrail against the clear blue sky.

"The jet is over there," Callie said as she pointed.

I was coming on guard duty, so I had my field glasses and looked at the jet. "It's actually three jets. One is a B52, and the others are much smaller, probably fighters. I wonder if we're at war, or are they taking our president to a golf outing?"

That brought some laughs and a couple of jeers. We had forgotten politics a long time ago when we had to concentrate on surviving. Funny how staying alive and caring for your loved ones jumps ahead of jobs, possessions, and politics. We started seeing more jets and a few turboprop planes as time passed. The country must have some government or military still functioning, but why they hadn't shown up to help us, we wondered.

It had taken Joan two weeks before she accepted Callie was married and another week before she would talk with Paul without threatening him. Paul handled it very well since Mike had coached him on how to handle his new mother-in-law. It was a mixture of standing up to Joan and kissing her ass. The critical part was when to do the correct one. Paul was a master at handling Joan, and it didn't take long until she was doting on him as much as she doted on Callie.

Paul and Callie had brought several of their bicycle generators with them from the farm, I hooked a bank of car batteries to them, and we had lights inside of our cavern. We also had two larger makeshift generators, but they were noisy and gave off smoke or fumes. We had built a wall out of two by fours and covered it with a large tarp over the opening to have light at night. This wall also kept the cold winter air out. We scheduled group game sessions, showed movies, and started a book club to help pass the time when we weren't on guard duty or doing our chores. We tried to make life as normal as possible, considering being holed up in a big cave most of our day.

We had everything we needed to survive until spring, and then we planned to take back my farm. We would also get rid of Alan and kill Todd. My secret backup plan was to haul ass down to Alabama and join the Golds. I was afraid that too many of us would die fighting the occupying force. I often wondered why I hadn't heard from Davi as she'd promised.

***

Everything was going along very well, boring, but well until two things happened. The first event was a person who stumbled into our camp half dead and dropped several bombshells of news on us.

Roger was watching the road behind the hideout. It was over a half-mile away and never had any traffic. He had set his traps and had a compound bow ready in case a deer wandered by. He would only use his AR15 if he felt the hideout would be overrun if he didn't stop the attackers. Both approaches to the refuge were lined with IEDs, trip wires, and pongee traps. No one could get in without being maimed, blown to pieces, or find themselves hanging from a tree upside down. We had actually caught two deer in the snares. The IEDs were triggered by remote controls if there was an attack on the hideout.

Roger thought he saw movement down the road at the bend and brought his field glasses up to his eyes. Nothing at first, but then he saw something crawling on the ground. He watched for a minute and then decided to get help. He carefully walked back to the end of the hideout, found the line that went down the airshaft, and pulled it to ring the bell on the other end. I heard the bell ring, grabbed my gear, and proceeded cautiously to Roger's location.

"Zack, I saw a man crawling along the road down by the bend."

"Is he trying to sneak up on us?"

Roger replied, "I don't think so. He might be wounded."

I knew we had to check this threat out, but I also knew we couldn't bring anyone into our hideout. "Let's go down and get close enough to see if he's a threat, and more importantly, are there any more people out there trying to find us?"

We took off down the hill, traveling towards the bend but staying a hundred yards away from the direct line to it. We arrived at a point far enough from the hideout to start working over toward where the man was last seen. We stayed low, crawled to within a hundred feet of the bend, and saw a body lying face down on the road. We watched for half an hour and felt safe approaching the body. I walked over to the body while Roger kept guard and nudged it with my foot. A hand whipped out and tried to drag me down while another came up with a knife aimed at my gut. The person was too slow, I knocked the knife out of his hand and rolled him over, pointing my SUB-2000 in his face.

I inhaled. "Davi, what the heck are you doing here? You almost killed me."

She smiled, took my hand, and passed out.

"Roger, take my rifle. I'll carry her to the hideout."

I picked her up and carried her as carefully as possible. She was lighter than I remembered, and her face was gaunt and filthy. I noticed dried blood and a bullet hole in her jacket at the top of her shoulder and another on her thigh. I picked up my pace because I was afraid she was dying.

I entered the cavern and yelled for help, "Ally, Joan, I need help! Davi's been shot!"

I took her into our camper and placed her on our bed. Ally and Joan took over.

Ally shouted, "Get out of here! We have to take her clothes off to find her wounds."

Lynn brought our medical bag, several wound kits, and the blood clotting powder to the camper. They worked on her for several hours and only gave us brief updates. There were two bullet wounds, several broken ribs, and she'd been severely beaten and had small burned spots on her legs. She may have even been tortured. The wounds weren't life-threatening, nor were the rest of her injuries. Still, she was suffering from a loss of blood, severe malnutrition, and dehydration. She was exhausted and would probably sleep for days. Joan started an IV to get some liquids and glucose into her until we could get her to eat. Ally was placing small chips of ice in her mouth to speed up the rehydration.

Ally asked, "Where did y'all find her?"

I said, "She was lying in the road, dying from her wounds. She tried to knife me when I turned her over. Lucky for me, she was exhausted, or I'd be dead."

Ally looked at me. "I wonder what she's doing back up north."

I thought for a minute and said, "Bring me her clothes. Let's look for clues."

Ally came back and said, "There're several strange issues with her clothes. They're men's clothes, and even the underwear is too big for her. She had to tie them to keep them from falling off."

I asked, "She wasn't wearing a sports bra and Under Armor underwear?"

Ally answered, "No, and how would you know?"

I said, "Long story, but I know, and no, we didn't."

She replied, "No, just these ratty worn-out jeans, t-shirt, and a flannel shirt. Oh, she had boots and no socks. I can't wait to hear the long story."

I looked at the clothes, went over the description of her injuries, and said, "She escaped from captivity and didn't tell her captors what they wanted to know. I forgot. She also killed her captors as she left. Probably slit their throats or broke their necks by hand."

Mike replied, "I get the captured, but where did you get the rest?"

I smiled, "The rest was the easy part. I was stalled by the fact that no man on earth could've ever captured her and lived to tell about it. That's one badass woman. Remember, I went on several missions with her, and I've never seen someone so efficient at killing."

Joan took the first watch at Davi's bedside, and I took the first watch outside the entrance. I'd just settled down and was gazing at the stars when Ally sat down beside me.

I grabbed her arm. "Darling, you don't have to worry about Davi. Nothing happened between us."

"I know. I believe you. I am curious as to how you know what underwear Davi wears, so maybe I am a bit jealous."

I told her about Davi's and my missions, including the barbecue for the biker gang, the thug relieving himself on her head, and her dad and her finding Geena and me with our pants down. She was laughing at the end of the story.

I went on. "Davi saved my life on several occasions, and I owe her and her father a debt I can't ever repay, but I'll always be there for them if they need me. Davi will never come between us, I promise."

Ally wasn't a very jealous woman, and she was a big help to Davi during her recovery.

***

The second event was when Joan was manning the radio and heard a transmission from the federal government. She alerted us, but the message was over.

Joan told us, "The announcer said President Hardy would speak to the nation at 7:00 pm every Thursday evening to update the citizens on the progress the country was making. The announcer went on to say she was in a safe but undisclosed location until further notice."

I replied, "Who the hell is President Hardy? There couldn't have been an election, or the chain of succession would've been the VP, Speaker of the House, and then God knows who. Callie, do we have any books on the government?"

"Yes, I think I can find one that not only has the succession laws but should have the current officeholder as of the shit hit the fan."

Her mom spoke up, "*When the lights went out,* sounds better."

"Okay."

Time stood still until 7:00 that evening. While we were waiting, Callie found the books with everything we needed. She shocked all of us because there was only one female named Hardy, and she was a senator from Texas. She was a conservative war veteran who'd been awarded several medals for bravery and had two Purple Hearts.

I exclaimed, "Damn, the whole government must have been nuked. The succession list goes all the way through the cabinet members. I don't see Senators on the list. They must all be dead."

Joan said, "I remember her campaigning and thought that she was a good woman and leader, but she's a first-term senator. This is scary."

We were sitting by the radio when the announcer introduced the President.

"I want to introduce the President of the USA, Laura Hardy, our President and Commander and Chief of our Armed Forces. Madam President."

"My fellow Americans, I know many of you have literally been in the dark for many months and wonder why your government hasn't been helping you recover from this dastardly attack on our homeland. The answer is that the nuclear attack and EMP blasts knocked out all of our communications, destroyed twenty-one major US cities, and destroyed Washington, DC. Yes, our capital is gone, and our complete governing body was killed in a few seconds.

The truth is our past government leaders dropped their guard and failed to protect us from our known enemies. It took months to form a government. During that time, our military and Israel retaliated and neutralized those responsible for the cowardly attack that brought us to our knees. We're guarding our country and fighting a land war on the southwest border with Mexico to wipe out the drug cartels trying to take over our surviving cities in that area.

I'll be addressing you every week with updates on our progress. I have asked the Department of Homeland Security director to set up broadcasts every evening to pass on survival information and give warnings on locations within our borders that are not safe. I'm sorry to say, but we're also fighting drug gangs, criminals, and local despots who have enslaved people and set up their local kingdoms on our own soil. The bad news is that seventy percent of our people perished during the first ninety days. We have few resources to assist you in rural or small towns across the country. We have no supplies, men, or medicine to help you, but we can pass on survival tips and training. I'll speak again next week at 7:00 pm. God bless America."

We were all in shock. Our country was so devastated that our government couldn't help us. They were barely able to help the large population centers. We went to bed that night fighting hopelessness. The following day over breakfast, we decided we weren't hopeless.

Ally started the meal with the Lord's Prayer and then asked me to give grace.

"I struggled last night with how hopeless our situation is. This morning I realized I'm thankful for the friends around this table, for my wife, daughter, and her husband, and my new daughter Susie. I'm thankful we have food to eat, shelter, and I believe that things will get better. Thank you, Lord, for this food and the daily miracles that you perform that go unnoticed. Amen."

Davi woke up at the end of my prayer and said, "I was coming to tell you about the massacre in Alabama, and Prescott captured me," and then she passed out.

I should have asked God for a mild winter.

The End

And start of Frozen Apocalypse

★

The Day America Died!

Frozen Apocalypse

Book 3

A J Newman

✪

This book is dedicated to my many friends who think I'm bat crap crazy for believing the Apocalypse is due any day now. The Apocalypse is coming. Will it be the result of a solar flare, EMP blast, or a failed economy? That's the only question, but it's on the way. This series portrays the lives of regular Americans and how they deal with the issues. I'm a prepper and will be prepared. Will you?

Thanks to my wife, who keeps after me to write more books to pay for my prepping, guns, and golf.

Thanks to James Newman and Bob Lovett for beta reading my work.

Thanks to Sabrina Jean at Fasttrackediting for proofreading and editing this novel.

Thanks to Dee at Dauntless Cover Design for the fantastic cover.

PS - This is not a how-to book, but you might learn a thing or two about surviving if you pay attention.

A J Newman

Copyright © 2020 Anthony J Newman. All rights reserved.

This book is a work of fiction. All events, names, characters, and places are the product of the author's imagination or are used as a fictitious events. That means I thought up this whole book from my imagination, and nothing in it's true.

All rights reserved. None of this publication may be copied or reproduced without prior written permission from the publisher.

As they say on TV, don't try anything you read in this novel. It's all fiction and stuff I made up to entertain you. Buy some survival books if you want to learn how to survive in the apocalypse.

Published by Newalk LLC.

Henderson, Kentucky

Key Character List

Zack Johnson – Divorced, electrical engineer, prepper, and car mechanic. He has a 16-year-old daughter and ex-wife. Had a farm close to Owensville, Ky. He is the hero in this series. Married Ally Stone.

Callie Johnson - Zack's daughter, who lived in Anderson, KY, with her mom. Married Paul Stone.

Ally Stone –A woman rescued by Mike when the SHTF. She has two kids, Paul and Susie. Becomes Zack's wife.

Joan Johnson – Zack's ex-wife. A bossy woman who lived in Anderson, Kentucky, where she's a restaurant manager.

Mike Norman – Joan's brother and Zack's best friend. Like Zack, he is a prepper. He is an auto mechanic and outdoorsman.

Sally Green – She was headed home when Zack saved her. A Strong-willed woman who does what it takes to survive.

Davi Gold – Aaron's daughter. She is an ex-Israeli Mossad agent. Falls for Zack, but has to move on to complete her mission in the USA.

Aaron Gold – Davi's father, 55, and an ex- Israeli military pilot. Retired and had a large farm in southern Illinois. He became Zack's mentor.

Sharon Gold – Davi's mother and a Professor of Chemistry at the University of Illinois.

Paul Stone – Ally's son and becomes very helpful on the farm. Becomes Callie's boyfriend and then her husband at the end of book II.

Mort - Aaron's friend and another ex-patriot Jew from Israel.

Aimee Bassot - A young woman Zack saved from a drug cartel and the daughter of Captain Bassot.

Captain Henry Bassot - Military commander of Martenvous and a dictator.

Lieutenant Devereau - Bassot's right arm man.

Todd – Social worker, who goes berserk, becomes the gang leader that takes over Anderson, Kentucky. Never gets a last name.

Alan Prescott – Owner of a worldwide company that hires out mercenaries and high-risk security guards. Ready for TSHTF and uses his men to expand his power.

●

Chapter 1 - The United States of America

Office of the President

The United States of America

Undisclosed location

The Secretary of State said, "Madam President, we can't tell the people the truth about how bad the situation has become. The truth will cause widespread panic and chaos."

"George, what we have now, is panic and chaos. Our surviving citizens have seen 21 of their cities destroyed, and over two hundred million of their friends and relatives died. They're starving around a campfire as we speak. I think they already know we aren't coming to rescue them. We have to give them the facts and keep up the survival tips program over the radio. I *will* not lie to our people as the past two administrations have."

"Jill, give us an update on the talking points."

"Madam President, they are:

1. Our military forces have retaliated against the North Koreans. We have decimated their military and, we believe, eliminated their entire military manufacturing infrastructure. We have also removed their nuclear capability, their entire government, to include command and control infrastructure.

2. The U.S. and Israel retaliated against the Iranians by again destroying their military, government, and all known military manufacturing facilities. Israel has destroyed the entire country with approximately fifteen nuclear devices.

3. Israel used nuclear bombs against Pakistan, Moscow, Beijing, Lebanon, Syria, Libya...Madam President, the list contains seventeen more targets. Ultimately, they attacked every one of their enemies before incoming nuclear weapons ended their struggle.

4. Israel was hit with ten nuclear devices and no longer exists as a nation. We have evacuated nearly 250,000 Israeli citizens two days before the attack.

"Sorry, but I disagree. We could have saved twice that amount if the president had authorized the mission. He placed his trust in the Iranians. Now, go ahead."

Madam President, I do not think we need to tell our citizens this was done by our military against the orders of the president."

"Jill, while I understand your position and appreciate your desire to shield the American population, I must disagree. Our people have had enough lies from their government. The two former administrations, I believe, put the United States on a collision course to this disaster. They have sown the seeds of near-total worldwide destruction, and now, we have reaped the whirlwind.

The lies end here and now. Please proceed, Jill."

"Yes, Ma'am, of course.

"5. Twenty-one major US cities were destroyed during the attack, and ninety-five% of our electrical grid is down."

6. Approximately 50% of our military survived the initial attacks. Unfortunately, the predominance of our foreign-based forces was caught up in the maelstrom. At this time, we have only been able to retrieve the Air and Naval Forces. There have been no communications with any of our deployed Army personnel since the attacks.

We are currently engaged in combat operations on two fronts.

- Along the border with Mexico from Texas to Arizona, we are actively combating several Drug Cartels.

- We are also engaged in Alaska, Washington, and Oregon. It appears a sizable Russian Force, consisting of an estimated three Divisions, from the 33rd Siberian Army is attempting to start their own country at our expense. This cannot end well for them as their supply trains have dried up, and we can simply attrite them. Time, for once, is on our side.

7. We are pushing the Cartels back into Mexico on the southern front.

- The action along our southern border will be over by spring.

- As we are currently at war with the Russian Confederation, the incursion onto sovereign United States lands places us in a political problem.

- The Russian Confederation no longer exists, and those former Russian Divisions are technically nothing more than rogue elements."

"Jill, enough with the political correctness, already! If it looks like a pile of shit and smells like a pile of shit, you should be able to recognize it as a pile of shit.

I want everyone in this room to realize that political correctness is one of the major contributing factors that have led us to this point in time.

I'm a country girl. PC is dead. I will no longer tolerate it. I warn each and every one of you not to piss on my leg and tell me it's rainin'. Do I make myself clear?"

A chorus of predominantly enthusiastic, "Yes, ma'am's," flew around the table, as those present realized they had a real President of the United States, and not just another politician.

The President stood and said, "Good. We no longer have time, patience, or consideration for hurt feelings. People, we are at war with two factions on U.S. soil and a country to rebuild. So, in the words of one of my favorite comedians, The Cable Guy, let's 'Git 'er dun'!

Jill, again, please proceed."

"Yes, ma'am, returning to the conflict areas, our forces are gathering for a final push to eliminate, once and for all, the drug cartels of southern Mexico. With your permission, we will chase them across the border and into Mexico to put an end to their reign of terror.

Ma'am, at the chance of sounding overly harsh, I would add that, with your permission, it would be the mission of our forces to kill every single one of them. They'll be given no quarter, meaning no prisoners."

Showing a sinister smile, the President said, "I want to make it clear to everyone that no other option will be entertained from this office. Kill them all, then kill their pet goat. Any precious metals or valuables found in their possession will be brought back to the U.S. as the spoils of war.

NO! I do not want to hear about that being property of Mexico. That craphole is not now, nor has ever been a friend of the U.S. Am I clear on this?"

Now, everyone at the table displayed the same sinister grin. It wasn't going to end well for the drug cartels.

"Thank you, Madam President. To secure our borders, we would add that we build a wall similar to the one built by the Italians in Ethiopia during the 1930s. Should this be a plan you may be interested in, I can have the Corps of Engineers present a detailed plan in 72 hours."

"Excellent, Jill, you may proceed."

"And now, Madam President, for the bitter pill, Agenda Item number 8: All of our resources are engaged in the two wars and helping the remaining Port Cities in the Northeast and

California. We must reopen trade routes with the world and better deals than we have had in the past.

Sadly, the rest of the country may have to fend for themselves for several years."

The President thought for a moment before replying, "We will tell the truth and not hide anything from the people. John, I know we don't have much food to spare, but can we supply weapons and training to responsible citizen groups to help them defend themselves and eliminate the criminal elements roaming around the country killing and looting."

John replied, "The short answer is we have ammunition, weapons, and extra vehicles to supply over roughly a million soldiers. We have to find a way to ensure the groups to be armed are both capable and willing to defend themselves.

I'm sure way too many will expect the government to carry their water. If we arm them, we will only end up arming criminals when they take those weapons away from the sheeple of this nation, and that we must not do. Any criminal organization capturing those weapons and vehicles will become nearly unbeatable in their area of operations."

Concerned, the President asked, "Am I correct in understanding you oppose arming the populace to combat criminals?"

John said, "Oh, no, ma'am, not at all. My point is that we must only arm those communities that have already demonstrated a history of defending their homes and families. Let's make the strong stronger. This will enable those communities to not only prevent the incursion of bandits but may enable them to take the fight to the bad guys."

Her brows raised. "General, should we be concerned that local self-defense forces may become the very element we wish to eliminate? I mean, how do we prevent them from subjugating weaker settlements through aggression?"

The General stood and replied, "Madam President, should we embark upon this operation, we accept that we may open yet another Pandora's Box. I wish I had the perfect answer for you, but there it is."

"General, I would like you to take charge of this mission. Develop your team, and get back to me with a proposal one week from today. I would also like an update on the viability of each state's remaining government, to include the State National Guard."

"Yes, Madam President."

"Thank you all for your input. I must now go practice my speech to be ready by 1900. May God bless the USA!"

***

The Water Reservoir

I yelled, "Hurry up with the popcorn. I don't want to miss the president's speech tonight."

Zack, "I'm popping as fast as I can with a pan and a propane camping stove. Darn, I miss my microwave."

"Darling, why aren't you using the microwave in the trailer?"

Ally said, "I'm trying to save the gas for the generator for something more important."

Paul snorted, "Mom, stop talking, and pop faster. Callie and I are the only ones without popcorn, and the President starts in ten minutes," shouted Paul.

The popcorn was finished in time, and they all sat at the picnic tables around the radio. This was a weekly ritual since the first broadcast several weeks ago.

The President started on time, and after the Pledge of Allegiance began covering her talking points.

There was cheering and a round of applause when she mentioned the retaliation against Iran and North Korea.

There were tears when she stated that Israel was a lethal radiation zone and shock when she said there was no help coming for the country's Midwest for the foreseeable future. As always, she ended her presentation asking the country to pull together for survival and then the Lord's Prayer.

381

Presidential Compound

Undisclosed Location

The President watched as the camera crew, radio crew, and her staff left the production room. She saw General John Keene walk across the room and said," John, would you please come to my office for a minute?"

"Yes, of course, Madam President. I'll follow you there."

She asked, "How is your family doing? I know you had to travel up to Virginia to rescue them."

"They're fine now. The kids and I are still grieving over the loss of my wife's parents, but otherwise, they're okay. As you know, I lost my wife to cancer ten years ago. How are you, Madam President? I know you have also suffered a personal loss."

"I'm holding up under the circumstances. My fiancée died in DC, and my parents in New York. I was eaten up with anger and wanted retaliation. We nuked a lot of innocent people to get the traitors to humanity, and that will be with me forever."

"Madam, President..."

"John, please call me Laura in private. It will keep me from getting a big head. I need your help and advice."

"Of course, Laura, what can I do to help?"

She said, "Let's discuss that when we can make sure we have privacy."

John replied, "All right, Laura, I'll arrange for your office to be swept for electronic bugs immediately. Shall we reconvene here in, say, one hour?"

The President stood, offered her hand, and said, "General, why don't we have lunch while your people conduct their sweep."

The current home of the US Government was the Pennsylvania Capitol building in Harrisburg, Pennsylvania. They entered the President's office and sat on the couch across from her desk.

John said, "Madam President, I believe this room is clean. Before we begin with your agenda, may I ask if you have decided on a permanent location for our new capital? You know I'm pushing for it to be located near a large military installation for security reasons."

She said, "That's one of the topics that I want to cover with you. I agree with your concern and assessment. Please formally present your proposal for a temporary site at the next Primary Staff-Briefing. That's where it will be until we have this nation in the firm grip of recovery and have ended hostilities."

"Laura, I strongly suggest Fort Bragg, Fort Benning, or Fort Gordon, with Fort Gordon being my personal preference. We need to close down many of our now excess installations to consolidate our forces. Due to the training infrastructures, those three must never be closed."

The President said, "John, I agree and will approve your recommendation for Augusta, Georgia, to be the temporary home of our government. However, please keep the site confidential at the next staff meeting.

The entire Congress of the U.S. should be involved in making the final decision on a permanent location."

John, I inherited most of my cabinet from the former president, and let's say that many of them do not see things the way I do. I'm demanding a strong military, and they want to draw back from the fight and give up land for peace with the Russian terrorists and Mexican drug lords.

John, with your support, I intend to initiate Martial Law and give near-dictatorial powers to the Executive Branch.

At this time in history, we cannot afford to be weak, especially in the eyes of the world. I'll be replacing all members of my Cabinet and Legislative Branch officeholders that don't support my agenda. I believe the War Powers Act and Martial Law grant the President the authority to execute this action. I need to know if the military is behind me."

John nodded, "Madam President, all of the branches of the military expected you to do this, and it's our intention to support you. Please know that when these extreme powers are no longer required, the military will no longer support such actions and will take action as necessary to return to a Constitutional Republic. Are we agreed on this?"

The president shook John's hand. "General, I absolutely agree with your stance."

John said, "It would be a significant mistake to give up our land to terrorists, who will only come back for more. And, the Joint Chiefs will be happy to recommend replacements for your cabinet positions."

"Thanks for the support and the recommendations. Do you think retired General Joe Phillips would like to become Secretary of Defense and Lt. Col. Roger McNabb Director of Homeland Security?"

John said, "Yes, and they'll do a great job. I'll set up a meeting with them for you."

"John, I want a strong military presence when I ask for the resignations and especially when I kick Feinstein out. I fear he'll orchestrate a coup attempt. Some of his top men are very loyal to him."

"Laura, we already have your back, and you're right. The CIA approached me yesterday with the same concerns. The CIA and NSA are solidly behind you.

However, we feel the head of the FBI must also be replaced. He's loyal but frail and incompetent.

The CIA thinks the Secretary of State and Director of Homeland Security are trying to stir up support for a coup against you. The Director believes he should be the president because you have no experience. Madam President, I assure you the military will *not* let this happen."

The president said, "Damn, I felt something like this might happen. Do you have enough proof to arrest them?"

"Not yet. You should consider firing the entire cabinet and reappoint the ones you trust. I'll have troops stationed to enforce the firings and stop any potential coup."

"Thanks, John. I knew I could depend on you."

"Thank you, Laura, for the confidence."

The president said, "We must get this political crap over quickly, or we will never get started helping our people recover."

"Laura, we are receiving more good reports than bad ones concerning the state of our recovery. Sure, criminals are killing and looting, but there are many more communities taking charge of their own recovery."

***

The Water Reservoir

Ally jumped into our bed, snuggled up close to me, and placed her cold feet against my legs to get warm."

I exclaimed, "Holy shit! Did you just take your feet off a block of ice? I had plans tonight, but you just froze everything."

"I'll bet I can warm you back up."

I cringed, "Not until those feet warm up *a bunch*."

Ally changed the subject. "Zack, did the President's comment about us being on our own scare you?"

"Baby, changing the topic didn't make those feet any warmer. Yes, it worries me a bit; however, we will keep chugging along to survive one day at a time and work hard to make each new day just a bit better than the one before."

Then, I said, "Yes, I was worried. I don't want my wife and kids to worry about being alone as we struggle to survive.

Ally said, "I'm not worried for myself, but I'm terrified Callie, Paul, and Suzie may face horrendous trials over the next thirty years. They'll be living as people who lived in the 1850s. There will be no modern medicine, no rabies vaccine for dogs, no life-flight helicopters. A bad cavity could become infected and kill a person. Women will die in childbirth. Hell, even a tiny skin cancer could kill an otherwise healthy person."

I could take Ally or myself becoming sick or wounded, but I'm afraid my little girl, Callie, may become sick or have an accident. I'll do my best to protect our kids at all costs.

I lay there trying to sleep as I tossed and turned until Ally whispered in my ear, "Darling, we will be okay. We will teach our kids how to survive and give them the best chance of making a good life for themselves and our grandkids. Now, go to sleep."

I said, "I love you and need to hear that, sweetie. Goodnight."

Life is tough enough without losing hope. Having Ally comfort me and tell me everything will work out for the best is what I need.

I always try to keep a positive outlook and make sure my friends and family know we will survive. Deep inside, I still have doubts.

This will be one mother of a winter even though we are warm in our underground water reservoir and have plenty of food.

I fear our friends in Owensville and the surrounding farms are either starving or freezing or perhaps both.

I resolved to focus on daily tasks to make life just a bit better, conduct ongoing training for our kids and friends to prepare them for all possibilities. We will look the unknown in the face and give it the middle finger.

***

The Water Reservoir

Sally grabbed her bag, stuffed her personal hygiene items into it, grabbed her guns, and laid them in the pickup's cab. She helped Mike lower the pallet with the supplies, food, water, and ammo down from the roof to the truck's bed. Mike fired up the old Ford 4X4 up and drove to the front of the hideout. Ally and I arrived just before the remainder of our party.

I said, "Damn, we're good. That was twelve minutes. In five minutes, we would be a mile down the road."

"Dad, how often do we have to practice Bugging Out?"

"Darling, we are going to do it once a week until the threat is over. If Prescott finds out where we are, he'll try to wipe us out. Our lookouts can only give us a few minutes of warning. Stay prepared."

I knew once a month was probably enough drills, but I felt the drill kept us mentally sharp and drove the point home that we weren't safe as long as Prescott existed.

Before we had to retreat to the hideout, we had spent many hours preparing for several scenarios ranging from Bugging Out to guerrilla war.

We knew the hideout could be overrun, so Mike came up with the idea to bury food, weapons, and other supplies in 55-gallon drums in several locations away from the hideout. It took over a month, but we hid 63 drums of supplies. Mike made maps of their locations and gave a copy to everyone to keep in their Bug Out Bags.

We met each week to review our survival plans and made adjustments as needed. I don't think we ever thought we'd have to leave my farm, but we were prepared and made the move as planned.

Joan, being kidnapped, screwed up the process, but even that worked out in the end. I'm very proud of my little tribe.

Paul walked up to me after the Bug Out drill and said, "Zack, I know we have three locations already chosen to Bug Out, but I've been thinking about adding another."

"Paul, I'd be glad to consider another suitable location, but you know we have to be able to scout it before we decide."

Paul replied, "I know and just want us to have fallback locations in an emergency. I'm thinking about Graham, Kentucky, and it is a campground where my uncle had a trailer. We camped there in the summer when I was young. It's the O'Bryan Campground, and it has a fifty-acre lake and some caves we used to explore."

I asked, "Where the heck is Graham?"

"About 15 miles west of Greenville on Highway 121."

I wasn't really interested, but maybe it was worth the effort. "Yeah, it sounds like a place we should consider. I'll add it to our list to check out. Our two primary locations are just north of Rolling Hills. Perhaps you and I can go scout it out if the weather holds. This warm winter won't last much longer."

Chapter 2 – Davi

The Water Reservoir

A month ago, Roger and I found Davi half-dead, lying on the ground outside of the bunker. I walked up to her and tried to check to see if she was alive, and she nearly stabbed me before I could subdue her. She had been almost fatally injured, shot twice, beaten, and tortured. She arrived at the hideout, barely alive.

Ally and Joan dug out the bullets, patched her up the best they could, and we had to leave her in God's hands. Ally and Callie changed Davi's bandages daily, and the wounds appeared to be healing, but she didn't wake up for over a week.

For the first several days, she just laid there and did not move. The last two days before she woke up were painful to watch. She tossed and turned while mumbling words we couldn't understand. At least once a day she would sit straight up and scream. Then she would fall back into whatever unconscious hell tortured her broken body.

Nine days after we found her, she woke up just before breakfast and said, "Those are breakfast smells. I'm hungry. Prescott's men captured me, and they plan to kill all of you. Damn,

I'm hungry. Who found me? What day is it? How long have I been out? Has Prescott attacked? Damn, I'm hungry and thirsty."

Ally fetched a glass of water and handed it to Davi, who drank the glass empty in one deep gulp.

Ally said, "Davi, you've been unconscious for nine days and were shot twice. Be careful about getting up. You were beaten, and I think you have some broken ribs."

Davi moaned, "You should see the other guys."

I spoke up, "I believe I know this story. They all have had their throats slashed and balls cut off."

"No, I shot six, cut three throats, and strangled one with my bare hands. I didn't have time to cut their balls off. That damn Prescott had me tortured for several days, and when they couldn't make me talk, he let me hear his plans for me that night. When he was through with me, he planned to let his men have the leftovers.

The idiot sent in two women to wipe the blood off and clean me up for their fun and games. The bath felt great, and they took my chains off to finish cleaning and dry me while a man held a gun on me. I waited until one of the women walked between us and shoved her fat ass into him. I broke her neck as I sent her crashing into him and quickly kicked the other in the neck, killing her. Then I whirled around and took his gun away. It was easy to beat him to death with his own pistol."

I asked, "Sounds like you had everything in control. Why didn't you steal one of the women's clothes?"

Davi said, "Yes, I was standing there bare assed naked when five men ran into the room after hearing the commotion. Seeing me naked must have frozen them because I shot the first three before they reacted. I got hit a couple of times before I killed the others."

I was still curious. "Still, why didn't you grab the women's clothes?"

"Damn it. They were dressed in see-through tops and panties."

I started laughing and couldn't stop. Ally and Davi gave me a look that could kill, and still, I could not stop laughing. After I had regained my composure, I asked, "Okay, now, how did you get away from their headquarters?"

Davi huffed, "I got dressed, grabbed all of the guns and ammo I could carry, stole one of their old trucks, and blasted off in this direction.

Since I killed everyone at that location, there was no one to follow me. I made it to the roadblock on Highway 54 and blasted my way through the guards killing all but one. Then about five miles from here, I ran out of gas and started walking. It was pure dumb luck that I got lost and passed out close to here."

Ally helped Davi up while saying, "Zack, this is one very scary woman."

I said, "You got that right."

Ally chuckled, "Davi, Zack guessed your story would be about the same as you just told. I never thought a woman could be such a badass."

Davi winked at me. "I can teach you how to be just as bad as I am."

I quickly replied, "Hell, no! She might use it on me."

Ally poked me in the side. "Don't you want me to be able to take care of myself when the big strong man isn't around?"

"Well, when you put it that way. Yeah, I guess I do."

Davi ate 5 eggs and a large steak along with 6 pieces of toast and 3 cups of coffee before declaring herself full. We watched in awe of this small woman's appetite.

Ally finally broke the ice by saying, "Davi, if you're still hungry, we can butcher a hog or a cow and BBQ it for you."

Davi looked up with her mouth still full, gave her the finger, and smiled. She swallowed and said, "If I'm a bother, I can leave now, but I wanted to tell you what I learned about Prescott's little kingdom before they caught me."

I poked her on her arm and said, "You have to stay and work to pay us back for all of that excellent medical attention and breakfast. What's going on out there around us? We only hear a few bits and pieces on the walkie-talkies as we listen in on other's conversations."

Davi said, "Prescott has taken over all of Daviess County and several cities along the rail lines. He crushed all opposition by either killing or running any leaders out of the area. He took charge of the grain silos, all food production, and fuel storage. Half of the town's people are starving and will freeze this winter. People are dying every day in Owensville for no reason other than Prescott wants fewer mouths to feed."

I asked, "Davi, what about the people out in the county. We had just brought the crops in, and they should have plenty of food to make it through the winter. They also have plenty of coal from those barges plus the diesel fuel Paul found."

She said, "Prescott's men went from farm to farm seizing all but a few weeks supply of all food and fuel from every farm. The ones loyal to you knew this could happen, so most of them have hidden supplies, but not enough to last all winter. The rest are in bad shape and beginning to die off."

I replied, "Damn, we have to do something. We have enough food for fifty more people with plenty in reserve. We have to help save as many of our friends as possible. We need a plan."

Davi replied, "It's not my place to tell you what to do, but be careful, adding anyone you don't know really well. How will you get to them and get them back here without leaving tracks that can easily be followed? Saving people is a great Judeo/Christian thing to do, but don't get your group killed trying to save a few lives."

I looked at Davi" "Good points, but we have to do something, or we won't be able to live with ourselves later."

Davi looked around the table and said, "But you will still be alive to have regrets. Do something if you have to, but don't do anything half-baked or irresponsible. Make sure you gather intelligence about what's actually happening out there before going off half-cocked."

I caught Davi a little later and asked, "You didn't tell us about how your mom and dad are doing or anything about the Israeli settlers. Is everything okay?"

"No, our compound below Nashville on the Tennessee River was attacked, and my mom was injured fighting off the invaders."

I said, "I thought your compound was well-armed and prepared for any and all attacks. What could a bunch of local thugs do against the Israeli Army?"

Davi's head shook side to side. "The attackers were well-armed ex-military mercenaries. We fought off the attackers, killing most of them, with only a handful of them escaping. They had three civilian helicopters outfitted with machine guns, rockets, and one had a mini Gatling gun. They caught us by surprise and almost overran the compound before we took out the choppers with Stingers and antiaircraft guns."

I asked, "How many were there?"

"There were approximately ninety, not including the pilots and gunners in the helicopters. They knew exactly where to hit us and the time of day for maximum impact. This wasn't a bunch of punks. These men were part of the Prescott Corporation Security Group."

"No, shit? Prescott's Group is big and controls that much territory."

Davi nodded. "Yes. We interrogated the five survivors and learned they have three large groups trying to control the Kentucky to Lower Alabama region. We kept the Wheeler Dam in operation, and they wanted it."

"Why doesn't the Army deal with them? Hey, how many compounds do the Israeli's have, and where are they?"

"Zack, what's left of your Army is fighting two wars, one with the Cartels on the Mexican border and one with the Russians on the northwest coast. We have 15 compounds in the USA and 15 more spread from Mexico down to Brazil. We also have compounds in Hawaii and other islands.

Our largest is below Wichita, a few miles south of McConnell AFB. I can't tell you the locations of the others for security reasons.

Prescott's group has attacked several of our compounds. We have won every battle, but they're getting stronger as he

392

recruits more ex-military men and women to join him. He offers food, security, and housing for their families."

I exhaled sharply. "Son of a Bitch! How can our little group fight such a large, well-armed group?"

Davi smiled that devilish smile of hers. "Cut the head off the snake, and it will break into many smaller dictatorships that can be more easily dealt with.

✪

Chapter 3 - Rescue

The transition from fall to winter was slow this year until the end of November, then winter fell upon us like a blanket. We had spent the nice fall days gathering nuts, berries, and plenty of firewood in preparation for winter. Callie, Susie, and Sally harvested the vegetables from our small garden while Joan and Ally canned and made preserves. Joan and Ally might never be friends, but they could work together without pulling hair and fighting. Joan was still grieving the loss of Chuck, and Ally did everything possible to help her through the healing process.

We had a little over thirty days of beautiful fall weather and spent most of the time outside but staying in the woods around the hideout. Only Mike and I ventured out to spy on Prescott's men and the surrounding area.

Mike and I traveled through the woods towards Owensville and were careful not to leave any tracks out of the dense brush and woods. It was 5:00, and the sun hadn't peeked above the skyline yet. There was a bite of cold in the air, promising winter was just around the corner. There was a light frost on the grass that could barely be seen by the light from the half-moon. We scurried along tree lines and ditches most of the way. The last two hundred yards were through a subdivision along Miller's Mill Road. We arrived on the south side of Highway 54 at the Thurston Dermont crossing without being seen. There was one narrow escape where a woman surprised us and threw the contents of a slop bucket just behind us. Thankfully, she never saw us, and we moved on.

I said, "Damn, Mike, that was a close call."

Mike held his nose. "Too damn close. Did you catch a whiff of that shit? If it had landed on us, we'd have to call off this trip."

"Yep, it would gag a maggot, and the guards would get tears in their eyes."

Mike and I hid under an abandoned delivery truck and listened to the guards. There were two men and a woman on guard duty, and they were too busy talking to notice anything around them.

***

One of the guards asked, "Why don't Prescott's boys have to pull guard duty?"

Another said, "I was told they're elite soldiers whose job is to fight our enemies and run off all of the drug pushers."

The first man said, "The bastards killed Chuck and probably killed Mike Norman and Zack. I'll never believe they were the masterminds behind a drug gang. I don't like this half rations shit, and I hear the farmers are starving. Those are the ones that don't freeze to death this winter. Damn, it's cold. Ralph, it's your turn to put another log in the barrel. Get the fire roaring."

Ralph replied, "Get off my ass. I'm going now. I'll even put two logs on."

"Hey Sharon, now that he's gone, how about coming over to my place for a little wine and some cheese I scrounged up just for you?"

"So you can get me drunk and get me in bed? Hell no! Not now, or ever. I know you turned the Hager family in for holding back a little food for themselves. I grew up with Sam's son. They're good people, and now they'll starve. You're scum."

"You'd better show me some respect, or I'll tell Prescott you're part of the resistance."

Ralph came up behind the asshole and struck him in the head with the butt of his hunting rifle. The woman checked his pulse and said, "The bastard is dead. What do we do now?"

"Grab the shovels out of the bed of my pickup. I'll drag the body behind the Burger Shack and bury him in the burn pile. No one will find him. I'll tell Jock the bastard got pissed about the short rations and headed over to Anderson."

***

Mike and I listened from the safety of the shadows. "Mike, it appears not all of Prescott's people are loyal to him, to say the least. We should be able to get many of them to join us in the spring. Their story backs up what Davi told us about Prescott starving the people that aren't loyal to him."

"I'm worried that most of them might be dead by spring. You heard what he said about Sam's family. Let's get them to join us at the hideout along with any others we can trust."

"Mike, we need to talk to our group first."

"Zack, you're our leader. Lead, damn it. Let's go get them now."

"I guess you're right. I couldn't live with myself if Sam or Jacob's family starved to death. We're seven miles from Sam's place and another ½ mile to Jacob's home. We need to go back to the hideout and put a plan together and leave the hideout at sundown."

Mike replied, "Sounds good to me. Let's shag ass home."

The trip home was uneventful, and everyone had a million questions for us when we arrived back at the hideout. We filled them in on what we heard and saw while we gorged on Joan's deer stew and Ally's cornbread.

396

Ally said, "They actually killed that asshole and buried him."

I nodded, "Yes, I think he planned to rape the woman, and they knew his plan."

Callie spoke up, "Dad, we have to help Sam and Jacob's families."

I was a bit reluctant. "Darling, I agree. I want to put a plan together to bring both families here as soon as we can safely do it. Who else do we need to bring over here that we can trust?"

We all thought about who could be trusted and couldn't come up with any more names the team thought we could trust our lives with. We came up with several families we wanted to save but not bring back to the hideout.

Ally asked, "If we don't trust some people with our lives but may need them to fight against Prescott, could we help feed a few of these families?"

I replied, "You mean leave anonymous care packages?"

"Yes, something like that. Perhaps we leave a bundle of food with a note from the resistance saying to keep their chins up while the resistance deals with Prescott."

Paul asked, "What's the name of the resistance, and can we have a symbol?"

Mike replied, "How about "The Green River Rangers?""

Sally countered with "The Patriots" for her suggestion."

I looked around the picnic table and said, "All for the Patriots, raise your hand."

Everyone except Mike raised their hand.

"It's official. We are the Patriots. Now, what's our symbol?"

Ally spoke up and said, "Our symbol has to be a Christian Cross."

She drew one on a slip of paper that looked like this - ♱ ."That's what we place on walls, houses, and care packages. If we shoot an evil person, we mark them with a cross."

The group approved the cross as the symbol of our resistance movement then planned the rescue of Sam and Jacob's family.

Davi wanted to join us as we went to rescue Sam's family, but my threat to chain her to her bed backed her off. "Davi, it's just been two weeks since you crawled in here half dead. I know you're better at this type of work than we are, but you're wounded and recovering. You could get us killed if you have a relapse, and we have to carry you back," I implored.

Davi frowned. "I know you're right. I just hate sitting here on my ass while y'all are having all the fun."

I quipped. "Damn, did I hear the Israeli girl say y'all?"

Davi kissed me on the cheek and said, "Your bad influence. Come back safe."

"I will."

Ally caught me as I left Davi, gave me a kiss, and hugged me for a minute before saying, "Be careful. You aren't 10 foot tall and bulletproof."

The plan was for Paul, Mike, and me to drive over to Sam's place, load the family up in the pickup, and high tail it back to the hideout without being seen.

I saw Paul walking towards the pickup with his bow slung on his back and said, "We don't have time for hunting this trip."

"Zack, we might want to take out a thug or two without making any noise."

We slipped away from the hideout after midnight and drove one of the old trucks the eight miles to my old farm, where Sam's family was still residing in camping trailers. We took the side road to the back of the farm and slipped up to the back of the workshop. I blew my house and barn up to make Prescott think we were dead. The trailers were between the workshop and the remains of the house.

We expected to find Sam, his sons, Greg and Ben, and Ben's wife, Millie. The ride back would be crowded, but it was only a thirty-minute drive to where we would stash the truck in the old barn about a half-mile from the hideout.

Mike saw the man guarding the campers and waved to the rest of us. "It's Greg, and he's armed. Let's don't get shot doing a good deed. Let me get his attention."

Mike snuck up closer to Greg's position and kept a large oak tree between Greg and him. "Greg, this is Mike Norman," Mike loudly whispered.

Greg came to attention, raised his shotgun, and said, "Mike, is that you?"

"Yes, Greg, it's me. I'm stepping out from behind the oak tree with my hands raised."

Mike leaned his AR against the tree and walked out with his hands up in the air.

"Mike, I see you. You can put your hands down. What are you doing here? We thought you were dead."

Mike said, "Greg, Zack, and Paul are with me. Can they join us?"

"Of course. What can I do for you?"

I shook Greg's hand and said, "We want you to join us and get away from here."

Greg was hesitant. "I'd like that, but we are running out of food and don't want to burden you."

I replied, "We have enough food for your family and us. Wake them up, and we need to leave now before someone spots us."

Greg went into two of the campers, woke his family up, and soon they were standing in front of us. I saw a young girl I didn't recognize.

I asked, "Sam, who's the girl?"

"Her name is Betty, and she's an orphan. Prescott's men killed her parents while she hid in a brush pile. She's 16 years old, and we took her in with us. Ben and Millie have adopted her."

I stopped at the front door and drew our symbol on the door so Prescott's men would see our ✚ on the door. I wrote 'PATRIOTS!' below the cross.

I said, "Grab a few personal items, your weapons, and ammo and load up in the truck. Millie and Betty get to ride up front with Mike. The rest will ride in the back and watch for Prescott's men. Hold on tight. We will be running without lights, so Mike tends to run off the road every now and then."

Everything was going as planned when I saw lights up ahead around a curve. Mike saw them at the same time, slowed up, and drove off into the brush alongside the road. He stopped a short distance away and cut the motor off. An old truck came around the curve, slowed up, and stopped a few yards past where we'd left the road. A couple of men got out of the back of the truck and walked to the side of the road. It was soon obvious they were Prescott's men, and they were drunk. Two were relieving themselves while attempting to sing 99 bottles of beer on the wall. They finished, got back in the truck, and sped off down the road.

Mike said, "Damn, I'm glad those short dicked fuckers didn't try to write their names on the ground. If they turned just a bit, they would have seen us."

I replied, "Mike, there's a girl present."

"Sorry, ma'am."

Betty replied, "Don't worry, Mike. I was thinking the same thing."

We arrived at the abandoned barn, parked the truck inside, took some branches from a brush pile, and wiped out the tracks leading off the road.

I said, "I'll take the lead. Mike, bring up the rear. Greg help me look forward. Paul, take the left side and Ben the right. Be alert for any danger. Sam, please guard the girls."

We were only a few yards into our trek when there was a howl from our left.

Greg said, "Damn, that sounds like a wolf. Don't worry. They're afraid of people."

We kept on walking but heard something walking in the bushes behind us and on our left side. I looked back and saw Paul draw his bowstring back and fire an arrow just as something flashed into my view. Paul grabbed another arrow and let it fly to the rear of our column. There was a loud yelp and then silence.

We bunched up with everyone looking into the woods around us when Mike leaped away and tackled a dark object flying through the air. There was a struggle, and we heard growling and Mike cursing. I ran over to help but only saw a mass of dark shapes wallowing on the ground. I wanted to help Mike but knew any action could hurt him or his attacker. There was a loud yelp, and the struggle was over. We couldn't see anything, and then Mike came walking towards us covered in blood.

Mike wiped his bayonet on his sleeve and said, "I killed whatever the bastard was, but he scratched and bit me."

Paul stepped out to the left with another arrow ready and came back into view with an arrow in his hand.

Paul said, "Wolves. I killed one and may have killed the one attacking from the rear. We need to move on because this is a large pack, and they definitely aren't afraid of us."

We arrived back at the hideout an hour later, and our team welcomed Sam and his family to our new home. The women had prepared two of the trailers for the Hager family and another for Jacob's family. Ally and Joan showed them to their new homes and promised a tour of the hideout in the morning. Our new team members settled in for the night, as did the rest of us who weren't on guard duty.

Sally and Ally tended to Mike's wounds, and then everyone, at last, turned in for the night.

Ally lay beside me and asked, "Darling are wolves and lions going to be a problem?"

"Baby, I never gave that much thought before tonight. I always worried about stray dogs forming packs and killing people but never thought about lions and wolves in Kentucky. I guess the short answer is yes. We will have to stay on guard for wild animals from now on. They're multiplying while mankind is still dying off."

Ally replied, "Can you get me a bear rug?" Then she paused and said, "Just kidding, maybe a small one."

We had a group breakfast at 9:00 the following day, brought Sam's family up to speed on our recent history, and filled them in on what Davi had told us. They told us about what happened after we bugged out and how ruthless Prescott's black-uniformed men were to the local farmers. They also told us the regular guards and local police tried to treat everyone as well as possible but disappeared if they crossed the line on enforcing Prescott's laws.

We planned the mission to rescue Jacob's family and added more support for the trek to the truck and back. Greg and Ben were both bow hunters, so we added them to the party if we ran into the wolf pack again. I also filled some spray bottles with a ten percent ammonia solution to spray around us if we heard the pack in hopes that would drive them off without a fight.

Sally walked up to Mike and me, handed each of us a large container of MACE, and said, "I'll bet this will discourage wild animals."

I replied, "Damn good idea. They even make "Bear Spray" for hikers to ward off bears. I never thought we'd need this stuff in Kentucky."

We never saw or heard any humans close by but did hear a vehicle in the distance towards Highway 54 a couple of times. We heard wolves, coyotes, and perhaps a cougar. I guess it makes sense animals would take back their natural habitats with sixty percent of mankind dead and gone. Mike even made the point that the animals had an enormous human feast for months after the shit hit the fan. Dead people were everywhere for over a year. The vultures and predators got fat and multiplied.

After the encounter with the wolves, Paul set up an archery range, and we were all trying to learn how to shoot a bow and

402

arrow. We had a dozen compound bows and several hundred arrows that we might have to depend on for protection and hunting if this catastrophe continued for several years. I urged everyone to practice because I knew a gunshot could give our hideout away while an arrow was silent death. We would all pack a bow and quiver when outside the hideout in the future unless the plan called for maximum firepower, and then only a few would pack bows.

We left the hideout a little after midnight and quickly walked the mile to the trucks. We heard some large animals following us in the brush, but a couple of squirts of the ammonia ran them off.

The plan was for Mike, Paul, and me to travel by truck over to Jacob's place while Greg, Lynn, Ally, and Ben waited at the barn to assist us when we arrived back at the hideout.

I left Lynn in charge and gave her orders to watch for both human and animal threats. I told her to use the mace and ammonia to scare off predators and only shoot to save their lives.

***

I saw the red glowing dot of a cigarette in the dark as soon as we cleared the tree line about a hundred yards away from the men. Lowering my Night Vision Goggles (NVG), I could see the men hiding behind a clump of tall bushes another hundred yards from the rear of Jacob's place. We heard the men talking as we crept up on them.

One said, "Hey, dumbass, put the cigarette out! That glow can be seen for miles."

"Stick it up your ass, man. I'm out here playing soldier watching an old man's house because our dip shit leader thinks that old man is the mastermind of the resistance. That's a load of horse shit."

"Look, as long as we keep following orders, we keep our families fed. Where else could we get food?"

"Well, for one, we could grow it, except Prescott keeps taking the crops away from the farmers. When will the idiot learn happy farmers are productive farmers?"

"Put that damned cigarette out and stop changing the subject numbnuts."

"I'm cold, hungry, and I need a smoke. Go fuck yourself."

We stayed low, made it close to their location, and heard their voices, but we could hear everything they said.

"Mike, sneak up on them and see what you can learn."

"Okay, General."

Mike crawled towards them while keeping concealed by staying low and walking in a shallow ravine that ran across the back of Jacob's property. Mike wasn't far from the men when he stopped to watch and listen.

Three men were arguing about being out in the cold, having to watch Jacob's place. Mike listened for ten minutes and then headed back to the others. "Zack, they're just three Owensville locals drafted into Prescott's army to keep the county people in line. They hate the work and hate Prescott even more for forcing them to watch an innocent man."

I asked, "Then why are they out in the cold camped out behind Jacob's house?"

"Because Prescott thinks Jacob might be one of the leaders of the resistance, and if they don't camp out behind Jacob's house, their families won't receive food. We can sneak Jacob and his family out from the house, and the way they're bitching at each other, they won't stop bickering long enough to notice."

I said, "I'll go down to the road and get closer to the house using the barn to conceal me from the men, then crawl across the front yard up to the front door."

"Sounds like a plan, but I don't think these guys would notice if you drove up in a fire truck with the lights on and sirens blasting."

I said, "Key the walkie-talkie twice if something changes. Like maybe, they actually start watching the house. Only talk if you think the mission is in danger. As we've seen here, voices travel a long way."

I went back about fifty yards towards the tree line and positioned the barn between the men and me for as long as possible. When I had to leave the security of hiding behind the barn, I noticed if I stayed low, I couldn't see the men's position, so they couldn't see me.

I was only a few feet from the front door when I saw the movement in the front room. Now, my problem was how I get the person's attention without being shot in the process.

The man opened the door, walked out on the porch to the side, and relieved himself.

I whispered, "Jacob, this is Zack."

"Zack, who?"

"Your friend Zack."

"Oh, I'm Ira, Jacob's son. Slowly come out of the shadows with your hands up."

I complied with his instructions, and he instantly recognized me and lowered his rifle.

"Zack, the whole county thinks you and your family died in the fire."

I said, "That's what we wanted them to believe. Wake up, your dad. We need to get your family out of here and safely to our hideout."

We went into the house, Ira walked into his dad's room, and they came back quickly.

Jacob saw me, shook his head, and gave me a hug while saying, "We thought you were dead."

I said, "We made it look like we were dead, so Prescott wouldn't search for us. He tried to kill my family and me earlier that day and had guards watching us for weeks before."

"How did you get in here? Prescott has men watching us right now."

I said, "I know. They're back behind the house about a hundred yards."

"I don't know about them, but there are two across the road in the trees. They don't know we made them the other day."

I asked, "Are they locals or the men in the black uniforms?"

"They have black uniforms."

I cursed. "Damn, then they probably know I'm in here. I need to warn the others. We have a secure hideout with plenty of food and warm housing not far from here."

I keyed my walkie-talkie and said, "There are two more across the street from the house. They're the real deal. Hold while I check them out with my NVGs."

Mike replied with two clicks.

I peered out the front window and saw a man in the woods facing the house. I watched for a few minutes and saw another man switch positions with him. My only guess was they didn't have NVG equipment, or they would be attacking us right now.

I keyed my walkie-talkie again and said, "Meet me on the west side of the barn in ten minutes. We have to take them out."

I turned to Jacob and said, "Have your family ready to travel in twenty minutes. We have a truck stashed about a half-mile back in the woods, then we'll have to walk another mile when we get closer to our hideout. Travel light."

I stopped twice to watch the men as I moved back to the barn and could see they had not spotted us. What the hell? Maybe we *could* pull this off.

I carefully slipped behind the barn to wait for Mike and Paul to arrive. I could still faintly hear the guards behind the house bickering. Then I heard, "Zack."

I whispered, "Here, behind the tractor."

They joined me, and I laid my plan on them. Then we moved closer to surveil their position.

Mike said, "It should work, but we need some way to distract them when we have to cross that open spot."

Paul said, "I could shoot a couple of arrows over them to fall behind their position. That should make enough noise to distract the guards."

I gave him a pat on the back. "Good thinkin', Paul. How close do you have to be to kill these assholes?"

Paul replied, "I'd like to be within a hundred feet to make sure, but if they have body armor, I'll have to go for headshots and would need to be close to have the best chance to hit them."

I cringed, "Shit, that's too close. Mike and I'll get close enough to charge in and slit their throats when you fire the arrows over them. Close in and help us if you can."

"Zack, you don't have to shelter me from these assholes. I want them dead as much as you do."

I said, "I know, son, but Mike and I have done a lot of this lately. You're new at this, and if you freeze, we could all die."

Paul said, "Okay, I get it. I don't like it, but I get it."

I smiled and said, "Good man, Paul."

I patted him on the back and said, "Let's go."

Mike and I were stationed on opposite sides of their position only a few feet from them when we heard the arrows arch over their heads. They turned to see what was sneaking up on them when Paul launched another arrow. That was our cue to charge the men and put them down.

I heard the sound of something traveling very fast going past my ear and then heard a thunk sound causing one of the men to fall. There was another swishing sound accompanied by another thunk as the second man fell to the ground.

Mike and I ran and saw them lying on the ground with arrows sticking in the backs of their skull. Both bodies were still twitching on the ground. Their bodies did not yet know they were dead.

I bragged on Paul. "Good shootin', ya' done good. You scared the shit out of me, but ya' done good."

Mike barked, "All right, let's strip their weapons, ammo, and body armor, then get the hell out of here."

I spray painted PATRIOTS and our symbol on the door as we left.

Jacob's family marched the half-mile to the truck, and we made tracks for home.

We were a few hundred yards from the barn when we saw several flashes and gunfire. Our team was under attack.

✪

Chapter 4 - Lions and Tigers and Wolves – Oh My

The pack had 38 members and would add twenty to twenty-five pups in the spring. All of the females were still hunting with the pack since none was pregnant yet.

As winter progressed, the breeding season would start, and later, the pregnant females would go to their dens to deliver their pups. The females avoided territorial fights with other packs to deliver in safety.

These wolves had entered Kentucky from Indiana, heading south to find a game. The readily available human carcasses had dried up by the end of summer, so they had to go back to hunting deer and other game. The predator population had grown dramatically as their human predators declined. The availability of human bodies that either weren't buried improperly or just left to rot in the sun was now becoming rare.

The pack was hungry, and winter was approaching. This made them extremely dangerous since they no longer feared man, and man had become an easily taken food source.

The pack stalked a small group of humans. They hoped to dine well tonight.

I'd left Lynn in charge of the group and cautioned her to ensure they kept on guard for Prescott's men and any dangerous animals. I warned her to use the mace, ammonia, and bows if needed to ward off any predators. The barn had a large sliding door on each end plus a couple of standard man doors. The sliding door on the north end of the barn had fallen away from the barn, leaving it vulnerable.

She posted a guard at each end of the barn and planned to rotate that duty through the night until the rescue team rejoined them. Lynn was firm as she posted the guards, "Remember, no smoking or talking, above a whisper. Listen for vehicles and any unusual sounds coming from the woods. We don't need anyone sneaking up on us.

Greg, you and Ally take the first turn at guard duty. Ben and I'll relieve you in half an hour. We'll rotate every half hour until our team gets back."

"Yes, mom, we chillun will keep a sharp eye out for the lions and tigers and bears."

Lynn said, "Look, Greg, I know you're just joking, but if you do what I tell you to do, every time I tell you to do something, you might just stay alive and maybe help keep the rest of us alive."

Ben replied, "He's just having trouble taking orders from a woman. Greg, shut the fuck up and do what she tells you. She has proven her combat skills, and that's something you have yet to do. Now, get your head out of your ass and do as you're told. I'm warning you, she can, and will, kick your ass."

Realizing that he had just been told the truth, Greg almost whispered, "I apologize, ma'am. I'll do what I'm told. I know that was stupid. It will never happen again."

Trying to hide her smile, Lynn said, "Okay, stud, see that it doesn't, 'cause he's right, I can, and will, kick your ass in front of God and everybody if this happens again."

Greg replied, "Yes, ma'am, I gotcha. Can we move on now?"

Lynn asked, "What you think, Ben? You want to add anything else?"

"Oh, hell, no."

Lynn and Ben passed the time by telling their life's story while eating a couple of sandwiches and guzzling tea. Ben had served in the Army with two tours in the Middle East. He told Lynn his brother Greg had never served but *thought* he was a tough guy who could handle himself.

Lynn said, "Ben, Greg may be tough, but until a gun is stuck in your face, or you see friends dying around you, you don't know how you will react."

Ben nodded, "Been there, done that. I was in several firefights with the Taliban and wounded twice. I lost several friends during my last tour. I'll work with Greg to tone him down and get him to fit in with our team."

"Thanks, I don't want him challenging Zack's authority. It would not end well."

Be replied, "Me neither. Zack and the rest of you have saved our asses several times, and my family is grateful for the help. We owe all y'all."

They continued to take turns on guard duty for several hours. Greg and Ally were on duty when they first heard the soft rustle of grass that signaled they were being stalked. Ally was the first to catch a glimpse of a shadow crossing between bushes. Before she said a word, Greg saw something lurking in the shadow of the barn in the faint moonlight. "Lynn, I just saw something out there. It might be a big dog or a deer."

"Hey, I just saw a shadow about 15 yards away. I don't like this," Greg added.

Lynn ordered, "Spray the ammonia as far as it will stream in all directions."

Lynn joined Ally and Ben went to his brother's side. "Use the mace if you need it, but don't shoot your guns unless we're attacked."

"Lynn, look! I can see several eyes in the bushes. The ammonia isn't working."

Lynn said, "Spray some more out there. Animals hate the smell."

They sprayed most of the ammonia to no avail. Several shadows ran very near to the open doors.

Lynn said, "Close and lock your door and join us down here. We don't need to split our forces."

She no sooner got the words out of her mouth than three giant wolves crashed into them. Ally pulled her bayonet and stabbed the one on top of her, then rolled over and stabbed one that had Lynn's ankle in its mouth while Lynn wrestled with the third. She had the wolf by his neck, doing her best to keep it from biting her face when it went limp and fell off her with an arrow in its back.

Lynn said, "Thanks for killing that big bastard. Get the mace ready. Shit, shoot some out in the air to run these wolves off."

Before Ally could spray the mace, a dozen wolves charged the door. Ally drew her 9mm and started shooting. The others joined in and killed all but two that had tackled Greg and Ally. They stabbed the last two wolves and grabbed their ARs to finish off any that continued the attack.

***

We saw the flashes and gunfire just as we were about to pull off the road. "Mike and Paul, follow me. They're under attack," I yelled.

We ran to the end of the barn and saw the Wolves' running back into the woods.

Mike called out, "It's Mike. Are y'all okay? We're coming around the barn."

Ally replied, "Come on in."

We came to the other end of the barn to see dead and dying wolves' lying around the entrance to the barn. Ally ran up, hugged me, and held me tightly as she trembled. "Zack, I know we weren't supposed to shoot, but the ammonia and mace just pissed them

412

off. They charged the first time, and we killed three with our knives and an arrow. There was a dozen in the next charge, and they would have overwhelmed us. I shot five of the monsters myself."

I asked, "Is anyone injured?"

"One of the fuckers bit my ankle," replied Lynn.

Ally replied, "I've got some scratches."

"I'm okay," replied Ben.

Greg didn't respond."

"Greg, hey, Greg."

They turned and started to search the barn when Ben yelled, "They killed Greg."

Greg was lying in the middle of a half dozen wolves and had his throat ripped out. He died quickly, but not before he stuck his knife deep into the wolf that killed him.

I looked at Ben and said, "I'm sorry for your loss, but we need to get you and the Jacobs to the hideout before Prescott's men come to investigate. We'll bury Greg in the back of the barn and cover the grave with that pile of timbers. Sorry Ben, but we can't carry him back home.

Mike and Paul, you stay with me while the rest of you head to the hideout. We have to figure out how to throw these assholes off our trail. We have to assume Prescott's men heard the shots. Go now. If you're attacked again, don't hesitate to shoot the nasty monsters.

Ally, we'll key the walkie-talkie twice, wait ten seconds and key it again four times when we settle down for the night. We'll do the same when we get back to the barn tomorrow."

"Watch out for the four-legged and two-legged monsters," she replied.

We watched them leave, and I wondered how, the hell, we could keep the hideout from being discovered.

Mike said, "Zack, they had to hear the gunshots, but I don't think they could know exactly where they came from. Let's confuse them. Let's take the truck five miles north, shoot a bunch of rounds, go another three miles east, shoot some more. Then we find a place to hide for the night."

I replied, "They won't know what to think. No one attacked them, so they might think a gang is attacking the farmers."

Mike said, "That's what I thought."

***

Ally, where's Paul? I don't see dad or Uncle Mike either. Are they okay? We heard gunfire," asked Callie.

Ally said, "Darling, they're okay. We were attacked by a pack of wolves. We had to shoot them to survive. Your husband, dad, and Uncle are trying to make sure Prescott's men don't come towards the hideout and discover us."

"That sounds dangerous. How will they do that?"

"Darling, I don't know, but you know your dad and Uncle are really good Boy Scouts."

It was only then that Callie saw the blood on Ally's arm.

Callie said, "You're hurt. Let me help you. Mom, come over here and help."

Joan replied, "Boil some water and get some bandages. Wash the bite with cold water and soap. I'm busy with Lynn's injuries."

None of the wounds had severe bleeding. Ally's injuries were just scrapes and not deep puncture wounds, so they were easy to treat with antibiotic cream.

Lynn had several puncture wounds that had to be cleaned and treated with antibiotic cream. Joan also gave Lynn some Ibuprofen for the pain. Joan gave all three a bottle of strong antibiotics and told them to get some rest.

"Ally, I'm scared. I won't be able to sleep until Paul gets safely back home," said Callie.

"Honey, that's what women do when their men are off fighting thugs and wild animals."

414

Callie insisted, "But I want to fight alongside him. I don't want to be stuck in a cave waiting for him to return or die out there without me. If he's going to die, I want to die fighting beside him."

Ally gave her a hug. "Don't wish too hard. Women fight just as much as men do now that the SHTF. Besides, what will you do when you have two or three of my grandkids hanging on to your apron?

Callie smiled and replied, "I'll leave them with my mom or their other beautiful granny."

"The beautiful comment takes the sting off being a granny at my age. I'm just kidding. I'd love to have a bunch of grandkids."

Ally watched Joan treating the bite wounds and scratches and knew they would run out of antibiotics sometime in the next year. Even the pills would have a shelf life and would be worthless in a short time. A bite, infected tooth, or bullet wound could be fatal. Then suddenly, she wondered if the others had received a Tetanus shot lately.

***

Mike drove the five miles and never slowed down as Paul and I let off a barrage of shots. We repeated this several times around the county before seeing several trucks and a Humvee tearing up the back roads looking for us.

Mike drove us into a barn on the side of the road to avoid the first truck full of Prescott's men. Then we finally went off-road into a thicket to spend the night about twelve miles east of the hideout. I keyed the mike on the walkie-talkie and took the first turn at guard duty.

We heard vehicles tearing down the road several times during the night, but none stopped close to us. Our ruse apparently worked. Chalk up one for the good guys.

✪

Chapter 5 - Mayor Prescott

Prescott's helicopter skimmed along the tops of the trees at night with no lights to avoid detection by the military or DHS. The pilots flew with the aid of NVGs and had no problems steering around power lines, radio, and TV antennas.

Prescott was furious about the ongoing failure to take the Wheeler hydroelectric dam on the Tennessee River. He was sure this was due to faulty intelligence. His team had failed to infiltrate the group protecting the dam and only had information gained from surveillance.

His mission was to visit with his Alabama commander and decide if he was the right man for the job. He was hesitant since he only had a few men as competent as the one in Alabama and hoped this was a setback and not a trend.

The helicopter landed in the parking lot of a warehouse complex in Courtland, Alabama. This was a northern outpost of the main compound in Birmingham.

He had complete control of Birmingham and had teams fanning out to control the other major cities. He was promoting his group's ability to provide food and protection to the town's people.

His men killed or ran off the gangs that harassed most towns. They also killed drug dealers on sight. The town's people liked that.

They just didn't know they were trading one evil for a different devil. The Federal Government was too busy fighting Russians and the Cartel to be of any help.

Prescott climbed down out of the helicopter, and Mark Henson, the commander of his forces in Alabama, greeted him. "Hello Mark, let's head to your office."

"Sorry, I thought you would want to go to your room for the night before we meet."

Prescott replied, "No, I want to meet for an hour and then fly to Texas tonight. Let's roll."

"Yes, sir."

Prescott had several compounds across the USA and wanted desperately to consolidate them into a new country that took land from Texas to Arkansas over to Kentucky and then down to the Gulf.

He knew he only had a year to make it happen, and the key was taking over the power generation and the military bases in his new country.

He thought most of the soldiers would join him since there was no hope of help coming from the USA. The government was forcing soldiers to leave their families and fight on the Mexican border and Oregon.

They walked into the warehouse, entered Mark's office, and started their meeting.

Mark said, "Sir, I believe we found the reason our attacks have failed so far."

Prescott frowned. "Enlighten me."

Mark said, "We captured one of the guards at the dam this morning and attempted to question her to learn more about this

417

invincible force that guards the dam. We couldn't break her. No technique or type of torture worked. She passed out this evening after being nearly beaten to death and losing five fingers. She was groggy as she woke up and began speaking in Hebrew. One of our men speaks Hebrew and actually trained Israeli pilots on our equipment years ago. He swears she's an Israeli Army or even a Mossad agent."

Prescott asked, "Can I speak to her?"

"Sorry, but she died a few hours ago. She killed three of my men and maimed two more before she was shot several times."

"Your men were careless."

Mark cringed, "Sir, she was strapped to a chair with her hands and feet bound. She broke the chair and used it to club my men to death."

"So, you think you have the Israeli Army guarding the dam."

Mark answered, "Sir, they're much better armed, have better intelligence, and frankly, their guards are better soldiers than I have. My solution is to bring in some heavy guns and mortars to eliminate them so we can liberate the dam."

Prescott offered a solution. "Have you thought about sending in an underwater team to infiltrate them?"

"Yes, twice, and they were all killed before they could get out of the water."

Prescott slammed his fist on a table. "You might be right about the Israelis, but why are they here, and why guard this dam?"

"Sir, I don't mean to insult you, but what if they're doing the same thing we are doing. Their country was destroyed. Where did a quarter-million Jews go? We heard that many escaped."

Prescott rubbed his jaw. "Damn, I think you're right. Those bastards have set up strongholds in the USA and other countries."

***

Owensville Police Department

Prescott's captain said, "Sheriff, shouldn't you be out on patrol or something? Go find that drug dealer Johnson or his buddy Norman."

Bert cast a dirty glance at the Captain of Prescott's Owensville Police Force and replied, "Did you forget? They're dead. Your boss says so."

"Well then, get out of here, asshole. If you get on my nerves, we might just find out we don't need you to keep the natives in line."

Bert said, "I'll leave after I finish this report for Mr. Prescott. He'll be pissed if it's not on his desk when he gets back."

"Okay, but get it done and get out of my sight, or I may have to visit your wife in the cell tonight."

Bert didn't react because that's what this animal wanted. He would use any excuse to shoot Bert.

The Captain went into his office, closed the door, and made a call on a satellite phone. There was no one in the room, so Bert moved closer to the door to eavesdrop.

He heard, "Yes, I'm sure. We checked all of the...and found a bunch of wolves buried in the brush behind a.............apparently, there's a big assed underground water tank nearby. Okay. I want to raid..........Johnson and Norman are holed up in the ....Yes, sir, I'll wait until you get back."

Bert scrambled to get back to his desk before the door closed and only beat the Captain by a few seconds. He knew he had to warn Zack and Mike, but if Prescott found out, he would kill Bert's family.

Bert watched as the Captain walked past his desk to check on the guard in the back of the station where the cells were located. It was 10:00 pm, and the station was deserted except for the Captain and one jailer.

Bert knew he had to act now, or his friends and perhaps his family would die. He drew his knife, walked up behind the Captain, grabbed him from behind, and cut his neck from ear to ear. The captain dropped to the floor, silently struggling for air that would not enter his lungs. He died within seconds.

Bert walked past him, saying, "That's what happens when you think you're superior to another and don't think they're a threat. Asshole."

Bert took the keys from the dead Captain's belt along with his gun belt and sidearm. He opened the door leading to the cells and called the guard's name, "Fred, the captain needs you."

"Why the fuck would he send a worm like you to relieve me?"

Bert shot the guard twice in the chest and ran to the cell where his wife and daughter were.

"Bert, is that you?"

"Yes dear, let's go. I'm getting you out of here."

His wife and daughter hurried past Bert as he opened the other four cells to release the prisoners.

They all thanked Bert and ran out the door. Bert followed his family and walked from the cell area into the office when there was a gunshot, and he felt a burning stab in his lower side.

He quickly turned and shot the man who had just fired. Bert shot him again and took his pistol. He failed to see if the man was dead and paid a high price for the mistake. Bert fell once as he used the furniture and cabinets to steady himself as he walked across the room. His wife ran back in and helped Bert into the driver's side of the patrol car against her protest.

Bert said, "Darling, I have to drive until we get past the roadblock, then you can take us on to meet up with the Resistance. I'll explain later. You two hide under that blanket on the floor in the back until we get past the roadblock. I'll make it that far."

She said, "Okay, but let me place this wad of cloth behind you to stop the blood. Keep your back pressed against it."

They sped off down Main Street, turned left on Highway 54, and arrived at the roadblock in a few minutes. Bert knew he only had an hour before the night shift guards arrived at the jail and had to get to us ASAP.

Bert cursed, "Damn, it's beginning to snow. Shit, we'll leave tracks that can be followed. Well, at least this old wagon has four-wheel drive, and it's full of gas."

He pulled up to the roadblock, stopped, and waved at the guards.

"Hey Bert, what are you doing out tonight in this snow? Does Captain Asshole know?"

"Captain Asshole wants me to arrest Jacob Nelson. He thinks I can get him to come in without a fight. I'll be back in an hour."

"Jacob will shoot your ass if you mess with him."

Bert replied, "Thanks for the warning."

They moved the sawhorse gate and let Bert drive away. He turned at the next right and headed south towards the underground storage tank and his friends.

Bert, "Darling, take the wheel and take us out Miller's Mill Road and make the third right.

I'll tell you when to turn left off the road. We'll probably have to drive a couple of hundred yards across some grass and brush. Be careful. It's not slick yet, but soon will be."

***

Prescott's Alabama Headquarters

Prescott placed the phone back onto the receiver. "Mark, sorry, but I had to take that call. I have to cancel my trip to Texas and head back to Kentucky. We've located my major pain in the ass up there, and I want to be onsite when we string those bastards up high in a tree on the courthouse lawn. You have my approval on your plan. The mortars and recoilless rifles will arrive next Thursday. Thanks for figuring this out down here. Good luck, and don't fail me."

Chapter 6 - Winter Bug Out

The Hideout

Dad, it's starting to snow, and it's big fluffy wet snow. The ground will be covered in a few minutes. Can we make snowmen?" asked Callie.

I said, "Callie, we have to be extra careful when it snows and can't leave any footprints, much fewer snowmen for all to see. Just watch the beautiful snow and remember how pretty it was when you're cussing it after we are snowbound."

Callie said, "Darn, that spoiled my good mood, but staying alive beats making snowmen any day.

"Ally? Do you know how to make snow cream? We can have something almost as good as ice cream?" I asked.

"Sure, I do. What a good idea. I'll gather the items I need, and I'll have some ready when you get off guard duty at 11:00."

Callie said, "Oh, I better get back out there with Paul."

Ally watched Callie leave. "Zack, do you think it's safe to let those love birds pull guard duty together? They might get distracted."

422

"Honey, they actually behave better than you, and I do when we're on guard duty."

Ally turned to me. "Have you been spying on them?"

"Mike and I make regular checks on everyone to make sure our security stays tight. Other than a quick kiss or a hand that wanders every now and then, everyone stays alert."

Ally asked. "Should I talk with Paul about that?"

"No, Mike told me we were the worst of the bunch."

Ally huffed, "Darn, I like our time together under the stars. I guess I'll keep my hands to myself."

I sounded whiney when I answered, "Yeah, I know, me too."

It was a little after 11:00 when Paul came running to me, saying, "Zack, a station wagon pulled off the road and is heading straight for us."

I yelled to the team," Cut the lights, grab your guns, and follow me. Ally and Joan, stay with the kids."

I arrived in time to see the panel wagon slide sideways in the snow as it came to a stop. Two women got out of the back and helped a man walk towards us. I recognized one of the women and ran down to help her.

I yelled, "Guys, it's Bert and his family. He's wounded. Let's get him inside."

Bert said, "Zack, stop! Prescott knows you're hiding here. I had to shoot two of his men to come warn you. We've gotta' leave now!"

A million things went through my mind, and I'm sorry to say that the one that rattled around the most was, *Shit, we have warmth, shelter, and food here. It's fucking cold out there. I wonder how much we can take with us and still getaway.*

The good news was that we were prepared to Bug Out at all times. We each had a Bug Out Bag, and our vehicles were stocked with food, supplies, and fuel. We couldn't take everything, but we wouldn't starve for a while. We also had the barrels full of supplies stashed around Davies's country that we could dig up in a pinch.

I pointed at Joan. "Joan, you and Ally quickly treat Bert and get him ready to hit the road in 15 minutes. The rest of you know the drill. We are bugging out in 15 minutes."

Ally groaned, "Dear, we can't get Bert ready in 15 minutes."

I said, "Prescott's men know where we are, and Bert just killed two and drove here, leaving tracks in the snow. We could all be dead in an hour if we don't go now. Do the best you can.

Mike, help me put a bunk bed mattress in the back of Bert's station wagon to help cushion him from the bumps.

All right, everyone, we are heading to the church campground above Rolling Hills. We'll stay there until Bert can move or we find a better place. "

Everyone knew their jobs and scurried about loading their vehicles and hooking up the cargo trailers preloaded with supplies. I finished packing my truck behind Paul and Ally. I ran over to help Roger and Lynn drop the pallet of supplies into the bed of Roger's truck and then ran back to mine. Ally and Suzie were waiting for me. Joan was in the back of Bert's truck with Sally driving while Bert's wife and Joan tended to Bert.

Roger and Lynn would bring up the rear with the other vehicles traveling in the middle. We had five trucks, three old Bronco 4x4s, and Bert's station wagon. All were four-wheel-drive vehicles, so the snow wouldn't be much of a problem.

We pulled out of the hideout 17 minutes after I said Bug Out, and we'll never know how close we came to being caught, but we had miles to go before we slept and couldn't think about that now.

Davi rode with me to man the SAW while I led the caravan on back roads over to Highway 231 before heading south as fast as I could, dodging stalled cars and slick spots. We were making 45 MPH and traveling without lights, so we couldn't go wide open. The snow was pouring down, and we had over four inches on the road. I slowed down to 35 MPH and kept trucking.

I turned off 231, got on the Natcher Parkway at Beaver Dam. We then got back on 231 at the Morgantown interchange.

The snow almost reached the whiteout level by this time, and I knew only diehards would keep following us. We drove on south until we were about three miles north of Rolling Hills and made a right on Old Church Road. The snow was eight inches deep, and our tracks were disappearing behind us.

We drove about a mile and turned left into the abandoned campground.

The camp was originally a small resort back in the '50s that catered to the fishing crowd before the Southern Baptist Church in Rolling Hills bought it for a church retreat and campground for church families.

There were 12 cabins, a barn that held the lawn and garden equipment, and a large building with a central kitchen and dining room attached. The large building had been a bed and breakfast long ago. There were several large lakes on the property, and it was only half a mile from the Barren River. We parked the vehicles by the large building, and I gathered the team.

I called out to my crew. "We need to clear all of the buildings before we occupy them. They were empty when we scouted the area, but who knows what has happened since then.

Mike, you and Roger take the six cabins on the right. Greg and Ben search the main building, and Paul and I'll take the other six cabins.

Move Bert into the large building after we clear it so Joan and Ally can continue patching him up.

We'll all move into the large building until we sort things out. Let's move, people."

We cleared the large building that had been bed and breakfast first and got fires started in the fireplaces.

Paul and I then cleared the first four cabins quickly, as did Mike and Roger. Three of the cabins Roger and Mike cleared were full of can goods, guns, ammo, and prescription drugs.

The fourth one we cleared reeked of ammonia as we got closer to it. I slowly opened the door and saw tables covered with chemicals and lab equipment. "Paul, this is a meth lab."

Paul said, "Zack, oh, crap, we got bad guys. Be ready for anything 'cause they ain't leavin' here alive."

I saw Mike. "Mike, we found a working meth lab. These guys will be dangerous."

The last cabins on both sides were a hundred yards down the hill and by the largest lake. The fifth cabin was storage for the thug's marijuana processing.

Paul and I came out of the fifth cabin when he pointed at our next house and whispered, "Look, smoke."

Several trees blocked our view, so we ran across the road to join the others. The cabin came insight, and even through the driving snow, I could see smoke billowing from the chimney. There was also a faint glow coming from one of the windows.

I said, "Paul and I'll knock on the door, and you two cover us."

We carefully walked in the woods to the back of the cabin and circled to the front. I stood to the side and knocked on the door. The door opened a crack, and a man said, "Go away."

I replied, "We're friendly and just want to know who our neighbors are. We're moving into the other cabins up the...."

I didn't get a chance to finish when there was a boom, a hole exploded in the door, and we were covered in splinters. I would have been dead if I had been in front of the door.

I heard Roger shout, "Are y'all okay?"

I yelled, "Yes. Mike, take Roger and break down the back door when I yell. They'll turn to see who's breaking in, and we'll come through the front door. Shoot anyone who resists. A prisoner would be nice to question before we send him to whatever hell meth makers go to."

I waited a minute and yelled, "Go!"

We heard the crash of the door being breached, waited a few seconds, and I crashed into the already damaged door. I saw a scruffy man with a shotgun turning to shoot Mike. I fired, dropping the man where he stood. A younger man dropped his pistol and cried, "You done kilt, my daddy. Wait, don't shoot me, mister, please. Don't shoot me, mister. We hain't done nothing agin y'all. You hain't got no call to barge in here and start a killin' people."

I looked from one man to the other and saw both looked like they had been on Meth for years. Both had a mouth full of rotten teeth, were filthy and hungry to the point where they looked like walking death.

I replied, "Trying to kill me for knocking on the door seems to be wrong in my book. Why would he shoot someone for knocking on the door unless he was hiding from the law or done something bad? What's your name, boy?"

"I'm Billy Owens, and that's my daddy, Alf. We hain't bad people. We jess tryin' to make it from one day to the next, like everbody else."

I tied the man's hands behind his back and shoved him down on the couch. "Paul, shoot him if he tries to get off the couch. Let's search the other rooms and then check the other cabin.

I asked, Scumbag, what's in the other rooms?"

"Just my mom and sisters."

I said, "Roger, cover me while I enter this room."

I moved out from in front of the door and knocked as I said, "I'm coming in. We won't harm you. Put down any guns, and you'll be okay."

No one replied, so I slowly turned the knob and then pushed the door open while staying out of the line of fire. I could see several girls standing in the right corner. None of them was armed, so I walked into the room and saw an older woman behind them. The woman said, "I heard shots. Who got shot?"

I replied, "Come out from behind the girls with your hands up, and you won't get shot."

The older lady said, "We ain't done nothin' wrong. These are my kids. My old man and me's just doing the best we can."

I looked at the girls and saw all three had bruises on their faces and arms. Looking down to the floor, I was astounded to see they all had chains around their ankles.

Looking up at the woman, I saw she also had terrible teeth, and her face was old beyond its years. She stayed behind the girls, and I knew she must have a gun or a knife hidden behind them.

I insisted, "Ma'am, I need you to come into the living room, so y'all can see to your family. Your husband tried to kill us, and we want to know why."

Suddenly, she raised her arms, grabbed the girl in front of her and held a knife to the girl's throat, and said, "Get the fuck out of my house, or I'll kill this bitch."

I raised my 9mm and pointed it at the woman's head. The girl started crying and trembled.

I took a deep breath, "Look, no one has to die today."

"You won't shoot with this girl..."

She didn't finish the sentence because I squeezed the trigger and blew the top of her head off. The knife fell to the floor, and the girls swarmed me, begging for their freedom.

I said, "Calm down. We'll set you free as soon as we can find the keys to the locks."

One of the girls said, "The old woman has the keys in her jeans pocket. Please unlock us so we can go find our families. There are more girls in the cabin across the road."

I found the keys and freed the girls while Roger and Mike checked out the last cabin.

They found three more girls who were also chained to their beds. Girls and young women had been kidnapped from the surrounding communities. They were being traded to gangs for food, drugs, and alcohol.

I asked Paul and Sally to get beds ready for them in the large building and moved them up the hill. I also placed a guard on them until we could make sure they could be trusted. I told the girls the guard was for their protection.

"How do we know you ain't gonna' be just like them and sell us like slaves?"

Ally spoke up, "Ladies, you're free to leave now. We'll give you clothes, food, and that shit heel's truck. Leave now if you want to go. However, you did just walk up here thru 12 inches of snow, and it would be crazy to leave, but you're not our prisoners. We don't know you, and yes, the guards are for the safety of us all."

The older girl stepped forward and said, "It's not that we ain't grateful for you freeing us. It's just that it's hard to trust anybody after being kidnapped, beaten, and raped for weeks."

Ally responded, "Darling, I can't say I know how you feel, but try to put that behind you and move on. As soon as the snow stops, we'll try to help you get back home. Until then, it's our rules because we know how to survive."

Later, I gathered those of my team not pulling guard duty and asked, "I'm going to put that piece of shit down. He's guilty of rape, kidnapping, and drug dealing."

Davi answered, "Of course, we *have* to execute him. We don't have a jail and are not able to babysit a prisoner. Besides, what would be the purpose?"

"I agree, and we need to quickly carry out the execution."

Mike spoke up, "Roger, come with me, and we'll take the bastard out into the woods, and he won't come back. I'll put a .22 in his head."

"Thank you, Mike. Do it."

They came back twenty minutes later, and neither was worth a damn the rest of the day. Even killing an asshole wears on you. I knew this wouldn't be that last up close and personal criminal that we would bring to justice, but nothing could make it feel good.

✪

Chapter 7 - Snowmageddon

The Campground

The snow continued into the next day, and we couldn't see across the court to the cabins. The big fluffy flakes blew around in swirls before ending up in drifts against fences, buildings, and trees. Some cabins had piles higher than the tops of their windows and would soon be just big lumps in the deep snow. There were 18 inches of snow covering the ground between the cabins, making it hard to fetch wood and coal.

It appeared as if the campground had been in operation one day and closed the next. There was firewood stacked beside each cabin, and the coal bin for the large building was packed.

The large cistern below the front porch of the large building was full of water. All of the buildings had gas heat and air conditioners along with the fireplaces. Each building had its own large propane tank. We decided to use the propane for heating as a last resort when the firewood and coal were depleted. We did use it for cooking and hot water.

I could only guess the coal-fired heater was leftover from the forties or fifties. We didn't trust it enough to use it, but we would burn some of the coal to help extend the firewood. Besides, a pile of burning coal lasted longer over the night than wood. The smell was a bit like sulfur, but the heat felt great.

We spent the second day at the campground, moving the canned goods from the cabins to the large heated building to keep them from freezing. I handled that detail while Joan had a team performing an inventory of the other new supplies.

Mike's group unloaded the water and canned goods from our vehicles and moved them to the heated building. We left all other supplies in the vehicles in case we had to Bug Out again.

I said, "Paul, get your old lady and let's bring buckets full of snow in to melt for drinking water. Callie always wants to play in the snow."

"Uh, Zack, I'd rather massage a lion with a hand full of briers than call her my old lady."

I chuckled, "Who's the man of your family?"

Paul begged, "Zack, I know you're kidding, but I want to live longer, so I'll pass.

Callie, would you please come over here, and please help fetch some snow."

My little girl said, "Dad, I'll bet you didn't know that even with this damned snow falling, I could hear every word you said. We share everything, and I know he would never call me names like that if he wants to get in my bed at night. And dad, he really, really *likes* being in bed with me. I take good care of my man."

I flinched, "Shit girl, that's way TMI. Sorry I started this crap. You're still my little girl, and I don't want to know what y'all do in bed. Come on, let's collect that snow now."

Callie snickered, "Dad, don't poke the bear unless you're ready for a fight."

I said, "I'll remember that."

"I'm going to ask Ally if you call her old lady."

I made a slashing motion across my throat. "You trying to get me killed? I was just trying to stir Paul up a bit."

Callie chuckled, "Dad, I might get her so stirred up that you'll be sleeping by yourself tonight. Hee hee hee. Old people don't do much in bed anyway, right?"

I knew I was beaten. "Look, young lady. We are not old, and we do a lot in bed. However, none of it's your business. Drop it. I'm sorry I brought it up."

"Paul, I beat Dad at his own shit-stirring game. Mom will be so proud of me."

I said, "Oh, shit. Don't tell your mom or Ally."

The little witch told everybody in camp. They were all poking fun at me for a week. Alas, I *am* the master and will get even. Shit stirring is what Mike and I do best. Of course, Mike took that to new heights when he took that dump in Todd's Corvette. Damn, that seemed like a million years ago. I wondered if someone had put a bullet in Todd yet.

The going was slow due to the heavy snow, but we got the work done by noon and took a break for lunch. I walked into the dining room and was amazed at how large our group had grown. We had doubled in size, counting the six rescued girls. We now had thirty-one people in our group.

Bert sat sideways in a recliner to ease the pain in his back but was alert and doing as well as could be expected.

I thumped a spoon on a table and got everyone's attention. "I want to formally welcome everyone to our little tribe. I know the young ladies won't stay with us, but I want them treated as though they're part of this extended family. Except for Ben and Lynn on guard duty, this is the first time in days that we have all shared a meal. I'll ask Callie to say grace, and then I want everyone to introduce themselves."

Callie bowed her head and said, "Thank God for delivering us safely to this campground. Thanks for the food we are about to eat, and please help dad learn not to poke the bear. Amen."

That brought laughter from Joan and Ally.

I replied, "I may have to learn to spank the bear. Let's eat."

432

***

Suzie was in bed and Ally, and I were getting our cold-weather gear on when Ally came over to me and nuzzled her lips against my neck and said, "Do I take good care of my man in bed?"

I was slow and started to respond when she broke out laughing. "Darling, I'm sorry, but it just strikes me funny that my son's 16-year-old wife is telling her father that she takes good care of her man in bed."

I replied, "I hope he takes good care of her in bed for the rest of her life. Happy wife, happy life."

She came over and gave me a full kiss on the mouth, ran her hand under my shirt, and rubbed my chest. "Zack, I hope that I take good care of you because you make me the happiest woman on earth."

I started to take her clothes off when she backed away and said, "We have to relieve Sally and Mike. I'll take good care of you after guard duty."

"I love you, Ally. You make me want to conquer the world and make it safe again."

Damn, it was cold outside. The temperature dropped to the low thirties every night and seemed to be colder every new day. The wind blew all night, whipping the snow around and building on top of the already high drifts. We had some of the best winter gear made and still had to keep walking to stay warm. We sweated and became chilled as the sweat evaporated. It was miserable.

I said, "Darling, we have to figure this guard duty out. I don't want anyone to get frostbite or lost in these whiteouts."

Ally replied, "Do you really think anyone will be out in this trying to attack us?"

I thought for a few seconds. "No, but if I wanted to take someone by surprise, I'd attack in the worst conditions. I guess we can switch to one-hour shifts at night. Bert and Davi won't be much help for another month."

Ally said, "That would be a big help. My butt and feet are freezing."

I shivered, "Damn, girl. Your feet are cold on a warm day. Hey, there's Roger and Lynn. Let's get back to the discussion we were having before we came out here."

The snow was now over 25 inches deep, and more was falling every minute. We had teams shoveling walkways around the main building and most of the way down to the lake but had to give up on the path. Roger took his Bronco, drove it up and down the path down to the lake, making a rough path. He tried to figure out how to mount a makeshift plow but couldn't find anything to make the blade.

Paul said, "Callie put your gear on and come with me. I'm going down to the barn to see if I can find something to make a snowplow for Roger's Bronco. This snow will be too deep to plow by tomorrow night."

Callie gave the time-out sign. "Okay, just give me a minute. Hey, while we're there, let's look for some games to help our stay. We need some bean bag toss games or anything that can be played indoors. Every camp I've ever been to had that stuff."

The wind was blowing so hard it made them unsteady as they walked towards the barn. Each step had to be deliberate and vertical because one couldn't swing a foot forward in the deep snow. Paul turned his flashlight on, opened the sliding barn door, and entered with his pistol ready.

The pole barn was 60x40 feet and contained two older tractors and one new one, several mowing machines, along with the expected weed eaters and other lawn mowing gear.

Callie saw some lawn furniture on the left side while Paul turned right towards the tractors. One had a bucket on the front and a box blade on the back. These would work, but he really wanted a grader blade for the tractor.

Paul checked the tractor out and then tried to start it, but the battery was dead. Callie yelled for him to join her as he climbed off the tractor.

434

"Paul, I found some games and a big hunk of metal that would make a great grader blade."

Paul walked over to Callie, saw the hunk of metal, and gave her a big hug. "Darling, that's a grader blade. Let's go get Roger and get his Bronco down here to jump-start the tractor and install the grader blade."

Paul started to walk away when it dawned on him that the wall was covered in animal traps. There were small ones for squirrels and martins all the way up to large ones for bears and lions. "I need to tell Zack about these. We could catch some game."

Callie added, "Or some two-legged varmints."

Roger, Mike, and I came down to work on the tractors. We quickly checked them all and decided to put the blade on the other old tractor and use both to clear the driveway because the new one had electronics.

Both old ones were diesel and hard to start in this cold weather. I found a 5 gallon can with the anti-gel additive and added the correct amount to the fuel while Roger got the first tractor ready to jump. It had taken several attempts before we got the first one running, but the second fired right up.

Before we finished, Paul showed me the animal traps, my first thought was a game, and the second was humans. I guess the Callie apple didn't fall far from the tree.

I got off the tractor and said, "Paul, you found the tractors and blade, so you get to plow first."

"Actually, Callie found the blade, but I'll do the honors."

He drove out of the barn, lowered the blade, and started to plow. It had taken about a half-hour before we got the angle on the blade set right to give the best results, and even then, it took three runs to clear part of the driveway. We took turns the rest of the day and had the driveway cleared all the way down to the lake. We stopped when Lynn called us in for supper.

We came in from plowing snow to the hallway and removed our cold-weather gear and boots before entering the crowded dining room.

435

I was pleased to see that Bert was sitting at the table with his wife and daughter. I was also pleased that the six new girls were mixing in with our people. I hadn't even tried to remember their names because I believed they would disappear when the snow cleared.

I saw Ally walking towards Callie and with three open seats. I started to sit down in the middle seat when Ally nudged me over to the one next to Callie. I wondered why she was so assertive when I saw the cute redhead sit down in the last open seat. Mama Bear was protecting Papa Bear from predators.

"Jackie, how are you doing today," Ally asked.

"Why, thank you for asking. I'm wonderful. I love the snow. I like cuddling up in front of the fire with a good book on a snow day," Jackie said.

I noticed that she was wearing a tight blouse with no bra and skin-tight jeans. She was husband shopping.

Ally replied, "Honey, you'd better put some clothes on. You must be freezing in that skimpy blouse."

Thank God Ally didn't see me looking at Jackie. I felt a poke in the ribs, and Callie placed her head close to mine and said, "Dad, put your eyes back in your head. Ally will cut something off if she sees you looking at that her like that."

Oh shit, as usual, I didn't notice that we had six new good looking women that ranged from 16 to 25 in our group, and every male was spoken for. That's a formula for disaster. I bent over to Ally and whispered, "Hon, you women need to take these girls off to the side and give them some rules on surviving if they want to live with us for a while. The first thing is how to wear proper clothes."

Ally gave me a peck on the cheek and squeezed my thigh. I had actually gotten some brownie points. I caught Callie later and told her that I appreciated the heads up.

"Well, dad, you were staring at her breasts. No woman wants her man checking out another woman."

I replied, "Darling, it was hard not to notice as cold as it was in the room. I asked Ally to tell our women to have a talk with the girls and set some rules. We don't need us fighting among ourselves, and we sure don't need any catfights."

Callie slapped her fist into the palm of her other hand. "I already had to run that little blonde away from Paul twice, and the next time I'm going to punch her ticket."

"Whoa, girl. You don't have to worry about Paul. He only has eyes for his sweet wife. Back off until tomorrow. Give Ally and your mom a chance to explain things to these girls. Remember, the world ended, and a person alone in this world can quickly become a victim."

Callie said, "I know, and you can bet that I'll do whatever it takes to keep those bitches away from my Paul."

My sweet daughter could be a bit wicked when necessary, and I didn't know if I should be happy or sad. I look back at my story, and it saddens me to see a 16-year-old girl acting like a worldly 35-year-old with combat experience. I guess it would be worse if she were a girly-girl in a post-apocalyptic world. At least she could take care of her family when the time comes, and she's put to the test.

The days of mall shopping, texting all day, playing computer games are gone, and survival is a full-time job. An apple now means food and not a telephone. I'll never miss all of the electronic toys, people ignoring each other at the supper table, and watching zombies walking the streets looking down at a damn smartphone.

I waited until supper was nearly over when I called Ally and Joan over to meet with me. "Ladies, we have a problem. We are overstaffed with women and understaffed with men. I can see some hair pulling and general mayhem if we don't nip this in the bud."

Joan replied, "Are you referring to that redhead that was poking her tits in your face until Ally stepped in between you two."

I frowned, and my eyes squinted a bit. "To put it bluntly, yes. Get our women together, have a peaceful discussion with these girls, and lay down the law. I don't want any skimpy-dressed women running around the camp. We rescued these girls and can't throw them out in the cold, but we can't have that kind of fighting in our little tribe."

Joan replied, "We'll get the women together and get a plan laid out before meeting with them. It could get dicey."

Ally added, "I feel sorry for them, but no other woman is going to flirt with you."

As always, Joan was right up front and added, "Zack, could you work harder at rescuing some good-looking men. Remember, I'm the only woman from our team here without a man. It's only been a couple of months since Chuck was killed, but my survival instincts tell me to pair up before the women in our group see *me* as a threat."

I snickered and said, "I understand. The problem is that the men are being killed off in much higher numbers than women are. Our society has always cherished and protected our women. The new world will equalize out as more women become fighters, as our women have.

Good or bad, that's how it's in this screwed-up post-apocalyptic world. Joan, we will scour the planet to find you a man just as soon as the snow clears. Hell, perhaps our friend, the sheriff of Rolling Hills, might have a lonely son."

As her head dropped, Joan said, "Thanks, now I'm the desperate old hag."

Oh, man, was I ever glad that I didn't reply to that...whoa.

The talk with the six girls didn't go as planned. Four of them immediately complied with our request and became part of the group. The redhead and petite blonde told Joan that they would dress as they wanted and flirt with anyone they wanted. Joan and Ally came to me and filled me in on the results.

I said, "I already knew the redhead disagreed with the new rules because she dropped by and invited me to visit her later. I told her to get her happy ass to her room before I locked her in."

Ally got red in the face and said, "I'll kill the bitch if she comes after you again."

Callie walked up in the middle of the conversation and yelled, "That little blonde-haired whore left the meeting and tried to corner Paul in the supply room. I walked by when he threw her out the door. I'm with Ally. I'll kill that whore if she touches Paul again."

I said, "Ladies, calm down. We'll lock them in their rooms until we figure out what to do with them. I'll lay down the law to them and let them know they can't stay here."

"And I'll be by your side," Ally exclaimed.

"Yes, Dear, and I'll ask Mike to go with us."

Mike and I entered the room where the two wayward women were held. Ally stood in the doorway.

Mike said, "What part of our rules didn't you understand? You were told to stop trying to steal another woman's man, and yet you went ahead and made another play for Zack. You're lucky you weren't shot. This won't be tolerated, and as soon as possible, we will take the two of you to Rolling Hills, and you can stay there or go where you want, but you can't stay here."

The redhead got up off the bed, walked up to me, and stared at Ally as she said, "Can't me and your bitch share you. Two women in bed is every man's dream."

Before I could react, Ally tackled the girl and beat her senseless before Mike and I could pull her off. Ally was a raving madwoman, screaming, hitting, and kicking the girl. Hell, she hit me twice before she realized she was hitting me.

I urged, "Ally, calm down."

"You calm down. I'm going to kill that slut."

I held her arms against her sides. "Whoa. You can't kill an unarmed woman."

"Watch me. I'd kill her just like the cockroach that she is," Ally replied through clenched teeth.

"Mike, lock these women in their room and don't let them out. Only let them out to use the bathroom."

I said, "Ally, come with me. We need to talk."

Ally was still seething and mumbling under her breath as we went to our room. I closed the door behind us, took her in my arms, and kissed her passionately. Then I took her to bed and lay with her in my arms as she calmed down. I was looked into her eyes when she spoke for the first time since we entered our room, "Zack, I love you and won't live without you. No woman is going to take you away from me."

I kissed her and said, "I love you, and you're right. No woman can take me away from you. You can run me off, but no one will ever take me from you. Joan ran me off. I would have never left her otherwise."

"Darling, I believe you, but seeing that...that....hussy trying to seduce you drove me crazy. Keep them locked up."

I grinned. "They'll stay locked up until we dump them on Rolling Hills."

Ally started kissing me, and one thing led to another. We were getting dressed when I heard, "I wonder if Callie and Paul are using protection?"

"Damn, Ally, that was a buzz kill, but, yeah, I hope so. Please have a talk with them."

Ally said, "No, you talk with Paul, and I'll talk with Callie."

I shrugged. "So I just walk up to Paul and say. Paul, practice safe sex with my daughter?"

She kissed me on the cheek. "Yeah, well, something like that. You'll find the right words. I'd really like some grandchildren, but not until things get stable."

I had spoken before, I thought, "Or, we have a baby in nine months."

She smiled, looked up to me, and said, "A baby is welcome any time, but yes, we need to be more careful.

Well, that killed any further romance. I got dressed and went out to check on the guards.

✪

Chapter 8 - Intruders

The snow was now three feet deep, with snowdrifts as high as ten feet. We plowed with the tractors three times a day to keep up with the falling and drifting snow. We were now two weeks into this seemingly unending snowfall. There had been only a few scattered days without snow falling, and even then, snow was blown around, making ever-deepening drifts.

Most of the clan was balking at pulling guard duty during the heavy snowstorm. Mike and I held firm and reminded them that a surprise attack could wipe us out. Besides, what else did they have to do?

Damn, it was boring, to say the least. Callie and Joan organized a bean bag toss league, canasta tournaments, and several ongoing board games. My favorite was Risk. I was the master of strategy, warfare, and widespread cheating to win. The games helped pass the time between our chores and guard duty.

I even continued the Bug Out Drills, which were even more unpopular than guard duty. I really liked this place but knew we were open to attack from all sides and was eager to find a more secure location when the snow subsided.

The blonde quietly loaded food and water bottles into two backpacks while the redhead took Lynn's pistol and stole cold-weather gear. They dressed, slung the backpacks on their backs, and left just after midnight.

The blonde asked, "Jackie, how will we find our way in the snow?"

Jackie answered, "Easy, see the tops of the fence posts on both sides of the road. We turn right at the end of the driveway and stay between the posts until we hit Highway 231 and make a right. That takes us into Rolling Hills. They'll take us in, and we will find some men to take care of us."

"How do you know this?"

Jackie replied, "I was raised in Idaho, and we had snowdrifts every year. We had snowmobiles and played in worse storms than we'll ever have here. Let's go."

They made it to 231 in short order and started trudging towards Rolling Hills.

"Jackie, I hate those people, and if we get a chance, I want to get even with those bitches."

"Yes, I'll kill that whore Ally. Zack liked me, and I know it."

They kept walking for the next several hours until the sun came up.

"Jackie, let's take another break. My ass is dragging."

"Yeah, I'm tired, too."

They talked when Jackie pointed to smoke rising from the woods on the left side of the road about half a mile away. "Come on. Let's find out who has a warm fire. This time, we need to be careful, trying to take a man away from his wife. Maybe she needs to have an unfortunate accident. A few weeks without female companionship, and our problems go away."

***

The Campground

I heard Mike say, "Zack, they're gone."

"Who's gone?"

Mike replied, "The two girls that were locked up. They overpowered Lynn last night, tied and gagged her, and then ran away. They stole food, guns, and cold weather gear."

I asked, "Is Lynn okay?"

"Yes, her pride's hurt, but she wasn't injured."

I thought for a minute and said, "Good riddance. We probably couldn't track them, and unfortunately, they'll die walking in circles in the woods. Call everyone together, and let's let them know about the escape."

Everyone except the guards was assembled in the dining room when I walked in. I opened by saying, "Ladies, your men are safe now. The two captives escaped last night and are now wandering around in this foul weather. We are not going to put lives at risk searching for them."

I looked over to the four friends of the two wayward women and said, "I'm sorry, but your friends will probably die out in this snow."

One quickly replied, "Those two were a pain in the ass, and none of us liked them. They were both scum before the lights went out and are still scum. Good riddance."

I said, "Well then, they won't be missed."

There were two days of calm with no snow and hardly any wind before another blizzard came roaring in. The snow fell, the temperature dropped, and the wind blew the snow sideways for three days. We kept plowing through the storm but now had to use the bucket on the tractor to move snow down the hill since there was no place to push it to the side. This was now a full-time job. We had to rotate the work through our group along with guard duty. Everyone hated the task after the first day, but actually, it did break the boredom.

Just as suddenly, as the fierce storm arrived, it left on the fourth day. The sun was out, and the temperature hovered just below freezing. The sun was welcome, and several of the ladies sat by windows and let the sun stream in on them. I joined Ally in the sunlight. The warmth and bright light made me feel great.

I was napping the second afternoon as the sun went down when I heard a shot, then several more. I put my cold-weather gear on, grabbed my rifle, and charged out the door with Mike, and Paul, behind me. We trudged up the hill towards the direction of the shots and saw Roger shooting at something. I looked in front of Roger and saw a dead deer and two wolves.

Roger said, "Zack, keep an eye out. There's a wolf pack out there trying to get this deer. I saw the deer and shot it for the meat when the pack ran out of the woods and charged us. Lynn and I shot several, and they ran back into the woods."

I saw three dead wolves, and another was trying to get up when Lynn shot it. "Paul, would you go get the tractor with the bucket and take the deer down to the barn so we can dress it out?"

"Yes, sir."

Ally, Joan, and Sally had joined us, and I asked them to guard Paul as he took the deer to the barn. These wolves were starving and would attack us for their supper. Suddenly, over a dozen of the pack charged our position, and we began shooting them as they closed the distance. We missed as many as we hit with the ARs, but Mike and Joan had shotguns with double aught buck and nailed any we missed. It was a massacre, and soon there were six more dead, and wolves were lying all around us.

Ally asked, "Hon, what are we going to do with the carcasses? They'll attract more predators if we don't dispose of them."

I replied, "Damn, the ground is frozen, so we can't bury them. What the heck can we do with the carcasses?"

One of the girls replied, "Put them in the metal garden shed, let them freeze, and douse them with diesel fuel to cover their scent until we can burn or bury them."

"Great idea. Let's load the bodies into the bucket and move them to the shed."

I doubled the guard for the next several days in case the wolves came back, and I was glad I did. They tried to pick off one of our guards, but we killed them for their efforts. We had killed another four before the attacks stopped.

There were several other narrow escapes, but I was the only one who was actually injured by a wolf, and that was because I fell down as one leaped at me. I shot it, but the bastard fell on me causing me to sprain my ankle.

We went from boredom to sheer terror back to boredom in a week. Boredom wasn't so bad, after all.

***

The house was a two-story Colonial that would make any millionaire proud to own. It was on 125 acres, had an oversized stable, enormous garage, tennis courts, and an indoor riding arena. The owner had sold his logistics company and retired at 55 to raise Paint horses and collect classic trucks and cars.

The two women watched the house for several hours before approaching. They saw four men and a woman come outside in the sunshine and thought they saw another woman through a window. The men carried firewood into the house while the woman watched.

Jackie looked over at her friend and said, "We need to have a good story to tell these people. I don't think they'll like the truth about us being kidnapped, raped, and then thrown out of our rescuer's camp for trying to steal their men."

"The blonde replied, "We were up in Indiana visiting a dear friend when the lights went out. It's taken months to walk home. We've fought off attacks by criminals and wild animals. We finally got home, and our families are dead. What can a girl do to survive? Boohoo."

"I like that. Let's add some detail and then walk in like we own the place. I'll tuck the pistol into my pants in case these people become a problem."

The women walked up to the front of the house and yelled to catch the owner's attention. Jackie didn't want to be shot because of any misunderstanding. They saw the door open, and two men with rifles walked out on the large porch.

***

"Hey George, I hear someone yelling out front. Grab your rifle."

"It looks like two women. Be careful."

George walked out onto the porch with Wes right behind him. They saw two women dressed in expensive snow gear waving at them.

Wes looked and George and said, "This looks interesting."

"What do you want?"

The women walked closer, and the redhead said, "Sorry to disturb you, but we're from about fifteen miles south of here and are trying to get home. We've been on the road since the lights went out."

"We still want to know what you want."

"Just some water and a place out of the snow so we can rest up. Your barn would be ok."

A voice came from inside the house, "George, bring those girls in right now before you all die from pneumonia."

"Follow us."

They followed the men into the house, and the woman introduced herself, "I'm May Owens, and this one is my husband, George. The other is my son Wes. Y'all must be frozen. Come on over to the fireplace and warm your bones. We ain't had any company since fall. No one travels much, and a lot of them are thieves and scoundrels. Let's get those heavy clothes off you and get you warm."

May was a plain woman dressed in a long skirt and a fancy white blouse. She wore no makeup and looked like she could kill you as soon as look at you.

They took off their heavy gear and sat down by the fire. May brought them a bowl of soup and a glass of tea.

"Ma'am, thank you so much. We camped about five miles north of here in an old barn but couldn't get much sleep because bad men were roaming around. We've been eating jerky and cold soup for days. This is like heaven having a warm fire and a bowl of hot soup."

"Don't worry, you'll sleep good tonight. We ain't fancy people, but we are hospitable."

Jackie knew something was wrong as the drug dulled her senses. She slid her hand under her blouse and tried to pull the pistol free when she passed out.

"The last thing Jackie thought as the drug took effect was that these people don't match the house. Hillbillies don't own mansions."

"Mom, why did you knock them out? They weren't hurtin' nobody. I want the skinny blonde for me. You can sell the redhead."

"Wes, stop thinking with your dick and use your head every now and then. Don't these girls look familiar?"

"Mom, the redhead looks just like the one Uncle Alf has. I'll bet they're sisters."

"Dumbass, it's the same girl. Look at the bandages on her ankle. The last time I saw her and the blonde, they were chained to a bed. Your dad and Alf were taking turns with 'em."

"Mom, why would my uncle let them go?"

May rolled Jackie over, and she saw the pistol on the floor.

"This bitch must have shot Alf and escaped. We'll have to go visit my brother and see if'n he's okay. Meanwhile, chain the redhead to your bed and the blonde to my bed. We might as well have some fun with them until we see what happened to Alf."

Wes replied, "Maw, that's why I love you so much. You let me have pretty toys."

Her husband replied, "I like toys."

"Yes, and it keeps you from rooting around on me all the dadburn time. Enjoy her until we have to give her back to Alf."

Jackie woke up with the younger man on top of her and knew she'd jumped from the frying pan into the fire. Those other people weren't so bad, and now she wished she'd stayed with them and behaved. She heard her friend scream from the room next door and began thinking of ways to kill these people.

**

The Campground

The worst of the snowstorms were over with only occasional flurries for the past week. The sun was shining, and it had been warm enough the past few days to begin melting and packing the snow.

The problem was that at night the water froze and left a sheet of ice covering the driveway. I busted my ass several times, walking out to fetch firewood. I was much more careful now. Even though I wasn't the only one, I was still the one that everyone saw. My friends are a cruel lot.

I said, "Paul, please make some channels in the snow on the driveway so the water can runoff."

Paul laughed, "Good idea, maybe then you won't bust your clumsy ass in the morning."

"Paul, you were my favorite son-in-law, but now you're in last place, asshole."

I turned to walk away, slipped on the wet ice, and nearly fell again. My best friend Mike yelled out, "You look like a chimpanzee trying to roller skate for the first time."

"Screw you."

448

Mike gave me his middle finger. "It'd be the best you ever had."

A snowball hit Mike in the back and another...*splat*...hit him in the back of the head.

"You'd better correct that statement. I have another snowball in my hand," Ally replied.

I looked up, and Davi was throwing snowballs at everyone. She winced every now and then, but she was up and moving around.

Suddenly, snowballs were filling the air hitting anything that moved. I started making snowballs and tossing them to Ally so she could throw them faster. She nailed Mike several more times before switching to Paul then Callie. We frolicked in the snow for over an hour until Joan called us in for lunch. Play, such a novel idea in this new world.

***

May had George bring the two girls to the kitchen table and chain them to the table leg.

"Good morning, ladies. I hope my men weren't too rough on you last night. Blondie, I'll tell George not to hit you in the face. Hell, you look like shit, and we won't get much for you when the slavers come through in the spring if you're all bruised up.

You two need to do what we say and exactly what we say, and you will survive this. If you want to avoid daily beatings, you'd better make my men happy.

Now eat your bacon and eggs and tell me about the people at the church campground."

Jackie looked up and said, "What campground."

May slapped Jackie and knocked her to the floor as she said, "Lie again, and I'll have George come in here with his toys and show you what real pain is. now, tell us about the people in the campground."

Jackie started crying and replied, "What do you want to know?"

449

"Is my brother still alive?"

"No, they killed him and his son."

May went into a rage and knocked the breakfast dishes off the table.

"Tell me what happened and who killed my brother."

Jackie was so scared she was trembling as she replied, "They knocked on the door, and Alf tried to kill them, then they broke down both doors and shot him dead."

She went on to tell everything she knew about the people who had risked their lives to free her.

***

Mike came in from early morning guard duty, caught up with me, and said, "I think someone is watching us from the woods. I caught a flash of reflected light a couple of times on the west side of the property. I waited, made my rounds over that way, and saw some tracks that I'm pretty sure aren't ours. I also found some cigarette butts. I think they came in at night and watched until the sun was up before returning home."

I said, "Let's warn the others and get ready to defend ourselves. I'm thinking some tripwires, bear traps, and ambushes. The guys we killed were selling women and drugs to someone. Those people are probably wondering what happened to their source of goods."

Mike said, "I agree. I think they'll case the place for a day or so and then hit us at night while we're sleeping. We need to get more sleep in the day and have more of our team ready for a night attack. Zack, old buddy, why don't we follow the tracks back to their place and attack them first."

I said, "Oh, uh, yeah, I guess that'd work, too. Let's get the team together and discuss a plan to attack them before dawn tomorrow."

Mike said, "Whoa, Einstein, we haven't tracked them back to their homes yet, and can't track them in the dark. Let's just follow them back to their homes in the morning and watch them a bit before we attack. Whew, man, you're getting quick on the trigger in your old age."

I replied, "Ok, ok, we'll follow them home and make sure they're unfriendly before we start shooting. Let's make that happen. Good plan."

I asked everyone but the guards to attend a planning session after breakfast. I intentionally included the four girls we had rescued since the ones watching are probably friends of their captors. I asked the girls if they remembered anything that would help us against this new threat.

The oldest, Cindy, replied, "I remember hearing the men who captured us say they had a family this side of Rolling Hills."

Another girl said, "They always chained us in our rooms when they were dealing and trading unless someone wanted a woman. Another seven girls came through, but they got traded off to Alf's friends and customers. They'd show us to the men like we were at a cattle auction.

Some men didn't like that they were trading women, but they still traded for drugs. I was shown to more than ten men, but none of them was in the gang. I was loaned to four men for a day or two, and they all lived four to five miles from here. People came from as far as Anderson to buy drugs and women."

I spoke to the team," We could be facing three to as many as ten of these piss ants. Let's set some large traps to take out as many as possible today before they come back. Roger, I'd like you and Paul to work on the traps while Mike and I get at the trip wires and booby traps.

We will follow them back to their camp and be prepared to render them harmless when they get there. I would think they would gather around their returning people to find out what we are doing, and that's when we attack.

They won't expect an attack. We'll take out their guards with the compound bows.

Paul, do you have two of your archers that can handle the bows at one-hundred-fifty feet?"

451

Paul got thoroughly excited and said, "Absolutely Zack, they'll never know what hit them. Come on, it's only half a football field. I guarantee it's much quieter than suppressed ARs. Zack, consider it done."

I smiled and said, "Thanks, Paul, we're all counting on you. I know you'll do us proud.

So, after the guards are laid to rest, we'll throw a couple of grenades through a window and have snipers prepared to take out anyone trying to escape. It should be quick, deadly, and we'll be home before dark. Any questions?"

Mike made everyone smile when he said, "...render them harmless? They ain't big words, but they sure ere fancy."

When the tide of laughter died down, I raised my hand and replied, "Well, yeah, it's a bit fancy, but I'm tired of words like 'killin'. I thought it might in...ter...ject a bit of class into our planning session."

That, of course, got everyone laughing again.

Davi raised her hand and asked, "What can I do?"

"Get well and protect the clan if we don't come back."

Chapter 9 - Operation Hillbilly

The Campground

Callie came along to help set the trip wires and was a big help in making sure they were all well hidden. All but a few were simply noisemakers to warn us of any impending threats. We placed all of the trip wires, booby traps, and animal traps close to the cabins to scare off their scouts. They stayed about a hundred yards out and probably watched us with the aid of binoculars.

Callie asked, "Why are we taking so much time to install trip wires and booby traps when we'll *render them harmless* tomorrow?"

Smiling, I replied, "Girl, what if these aren't the only threats in the area? The same traps will also warn of an attack by wolves and might even trap a few."

She said, "Okay, that makes sense. We really need to make sure our guys don't walk into one of those bear traps."

I said, "I've told everyone to not go past the signs we put up that say "Camp Bear Paw." I can't help them much if they don't pay attention."

Placing the trip wires was easy, but the traps were a bitch in the deep snow. We looked for places where the terrain and trees made natural paths down towards the main building.

Roger said, "Damn, that spring is strong."

"It has to be to hold a bear after it's triggered. Now, you see why the mechanism has to be set with your feet outside of the jaws," replied Paul.

Roger said, "I know we have safe paths for our travel but are you sure we'll be able to find all of the traps when the danger is over? The fresh snow covers them well, but we'll eventually want to take them with us."

Paul showed Roger the black Paracord attached to the trap and said, "I'm tying a cord to every trap with the cord covered with snow and tying the other end to a nearby marked tree that's in our safe zone. We just walk to the tree and follow the cord to the trap. The wind will cover the traps."

We finished installing the traps and tripwires by early afternoon. We watched as the beautiful sunny skies slowly turned cloudy and dark. The dark clouds were scudding across the sky, bringing flurries.

The wind picked up and began blowing the trees and rattling the window an hour later. Then the snow came in from the northwest. This wasn't a heavy snowfall but rather a light dusting with blowing and drifting.

I was pleased to see the front move out quickly and leave enough snow to cover our work, but not bad enough to make the intruders stay home.

We spent the afternoon checking and cleaning our weapons. I had to dig through my supplies to find the grenades and our military-grade body armor.

Our guards regularly wore military-grade body armor, but I wanted everyone on the raid to be more fully protected.

We only had eight military models, so I planned to give them to the six men and then have the women draw straws to see who stayed clear of the fight and sniped at anyone trying to escape. Ally and Sally lost and were to join the men in the raid while Callie, Joan, and Lynn became snipers. Lynn was over four months pregnant, and we did our best to keep her away from danger, but she kept jumping into every fight. Bert hadn't fully recovered, and his wife was useless with a gun.

We covered our plans several times then started playing bean bag toss in the dining room to help settle our nerves down a bit.

Ally and I had the 10:00 pm guard shift, so we turned in at 7:00 pm and tried to get some sleep. The alarm woke me to see Ally watching me wake up. She had her head propped up on a pillow. She was softly rubbing my chest as the alarm sounded.

I rolled over on top of her and tried to get amorous, but she pushed me away and said, "We don't have time. I don't want to be late. We have plenty of time for that after the raid."

I begged, "Yes, we have time, but I'll be cold, sleepy, and probably grumpy."

She replied, "Maybe, but it won't matter because I won't be tired, sleepy, or grumpy."

Guard duty passed quickly with no threats or issues, and we were soon back inside by the fire taking off our cold-weather gear. Ally wasn't too cold, and she was very talkative. "Darling, what if these are good people that feel threatened by us intruding in their area?"

"I think they'd do what we'd do and introduce themselves and try to see what we want. I think these are scumbags and somehow friends or relatives of the ones we sent to whatever hell, slavers go to."

Ally said, I know you're right, but it seems that we have to fight all of the time just to survive. Will we always have to fight? Why can't we move on to another area?"

"Darling, moving on would be easy after the snow clears, but where to? Anderson, Owensville, many other cities, and the countryside have gangs, crooked politicians, and meth dealers. We

455

could end up running every month or so, and every time we leave, we lose what we have built and most of our food and supplies."

Ally sighed, "I know, I know, it's just that I'm so tired of the fighting and afraid I'll lose you in one of these fights."

I said, "Damn, it's 1:30, and we have to get up in thirty minutes."

Before the alarm, we got out of bed, joined Callie and Paul by the fireside, and dressed in our cold-weather gear and body armor. Roger and Joan were on guard duty. Sally and Mike were heading out ahead of us to relieve them.

I heard Joan say, "Mike, you're ten minutes late. You need to crawl off Sally a few minutes earlier and get your ass out on time."

"Look, sister, just because you aren't getting laid, don't jump my ass."

Joan said, "Sally, slap him and get him moving."

"For being late?"

"No, for reminding me that I'm not getting laid."

Callie said, "Mom, I can hear you."

Joan snickered, "Little girl. You wanted to get married and become a woman, so you have to listen to me complaining about my lack of male companionship."

Callie laughed and said, "TMI, Paul, let's go outside, so I don't have to hear this kind of talk from my mom."

Joan took Callie by the hand. "Wait, Callie, I want to be serious here for a minute. In this new reality, there does seem to be a subconscious need for companionship, and love, which, of course, includes sex. I just realized that we all feel that same need. It has to be in our gene pool to repopulate the Earth after such a major die-off. I mean, I don't mean to sound so crass, ok, horny, but it's there, and we all feel it. We simply need someone to hold us, protect us, and love us. Callie, I'm sorry for my language. Do you understand?"

Callie hugged her mother and said, "Yeah, mom, I do feel it. I love you."

They were still in their embrace when we heard a clatter from one of the tripwires and a tortured scream in the woods.

A man screamed. "Oh shit, my leg's been cut off. Help!"

We saw flashes and gunfire from that direction. Everyone poured out of the building, and the attackers greeted them with a hail of bullets. One caught Callie in the chest, knocked her flat on her butt, and scared her out of her wits. "I'm hit. The vest stopped the bullet, but this hurts like a son of a bitch."

Paul checked her out while the others returned fire. Roger yelled to them and then ran over to their position.

I yelled to the others. "Those assholes decided to attack tonight. It sounds like we caught some in the traps, and there are several more advancing from the woods, plus several others sniping from the woods. Use your NVGs and kill any of those bastards that stick their heads up."

I gave Ally my NVGs and said, "Mike, you and Roger follow me, and we'll go around the first cabin and come up behind them. Give your NVGs to the women. The rest of you keep the gang pinned down in the woods. Come on."

Ally and Sally could see the intruders hiding behind trees and logs. A couple of them were hiding behind bushes. Ally carefully placed the cross-hair of the NVG scope on the first man and slowly squeezed the trigger using the pad of her finger. The rifle bucked, and the man died. She taught them the difference between concealment and cover when she placed .556 bullets in their chests.

Sally killed another and wounded two more. The sniping from the woods ended.

We turned the corner of the cabin and crept down the side, using the shadows to conceal our movement. We were in the open about halfway to the back of the dining room when we started taking gunfire from an automatic weapon.

The only cover was the shallow ditch that drained the parking lot. The bullets passed over us but pinned us down, and we could not effectively return fire. We burrowed deep into the snow and kept our heads down.

457

Two men with AK47s were advancing, and all we could do is poke our ARs up and shoot without looking.

I felt a thud on my left hand and intense pain. I had been hit. The shot knocked my AR out of my hands, and I couldn't reach it. I grabbed my pistol and tried to fire it in the attacker's direction, but they kept firing and coming at us.

Mike yelled, "I'm hit. Oh, God, my foot hurts."

The bastards were getting close enough that the ditch wasn't protecting us anymore.

I heard, "I can see them. Kill the bastards."

I heard the AKs firing at us, and other gunfire join in the noise, and then suddenly, they stopped, and I heard someone yelling, "Are you okay?"

It was Davi. She had two ARs in her hands. She walked up to the three men and riddled them with gunfire. "They had M249 SAWS. The turds must also be gunrunners."

"Yeah, Gunrunners with plenty of ammo. Davi, we owe you our lives," I said.

Davi helped me up while Roger helped Mike stop the bleeding and took him into the main building.

Davi said, "Roger, come with me."

Davi and Roger left the room and headed outside to make sure the attackers had been neutralized. Joan and Sally worked on Mike while Ally tended to my hand. The bullet went through my middle fingers, missing the bone and out the back of my hand. She cleaned, placed antibiotic cream on the wound, and bandaged it before she gave me a couple of pain pills.

Mike's left heel had been grazed, resulting in a shallow furrow in his heel. It hurt like hell, but he could hobble around and bitch about the pain. Well, he's just a delicate flower.

Ally told us, "We killed several in the woods. From the blood trails, we must have wounded a couple more. Davi killed the three attacking you, and we took out several more trying to join them."

I said, "Thanks, Ally, you and Joan come with me to help Davi and Roger check the campout and make sure we killed or ran those dirtbags away."

We checked all of the cabins and the area around the camp until we ran into Davi and Roger.

Davi waved at us. "We found eight dead, two wounded and three alive in the bear traps. I killed the ones in the traps, and the other two are heading home."

I clenched my fists. "Why didn't you *kill* them?"

Davi said, "Our mission was to follow them back to their base. One has a shoulder wound and the other a wound in his calf. They can't walk very fast, and I marked where their trail starts. They're boogying back home as we speak. Now, we have two leaving a trail straight back to their base. Let's go."

I started to get up. Ally pushed me back down, saying, "You're wounded. You can't go."

I got up and said, "Ally, I have to go. We have to end this threat now. Mike, you stay here with Lynn, Bert, Sam Jacob, and Callie while the rest of us end this tonight. If, for some reason, we don't stop them, they might attack the camp again."

I took Ally off to the side, convinced her that I'd be okay, and showed her that I had added two thirty-round mags for my AR and extra mags for my 45.

I said, "Ally, I can fire ninety shots. That's just three awkward mag changes, and I still have my .45 for any close-up shit. I can get by with one hand. In a pinch, I can ignore the pain and get it done. I'll join Mike in whining about it later. Besides, I have four hand grenades. I can really cause some severe damage."

She popped two Ibuprofens in my mouth and said, "I love you, and I'll help protect my big fearsome man bear."

I kissed her. We gathered the others and headed towards the woods to pick up the trail of the wounded intruders. Davi was, of course, right. The wounded duo was unable to walk very fast. I hoped that at least one didn't bleed out and leave us searching for their base of operations.

***

The boy said, "Dad, my leg is killing me. We have to stop and rest. They won't follow us tonight. We'll have time to warn Mom and the others."

George responded, "Look pussy, I got shot in the chest, and I'm twenty years older than you. You don't see me wanting to stop every ten minutes. We've stopped twice. Suck it up, Buttercup, and make it past the Miller's shack before we stop again."

"Dad, Joe got his leg in a bear trap. I saw it, and the trap pulled half the meat off his calf and took it down to his ankle. Two others got their damn legs in bear traps. Them sum bitches don't fight fair."

"Don't worry about them. We'll round up every one of the bastards and fuck 'em up. I promise that on your dead sister's grave."

"But Dad, you killed my sister. You ain't got no right swearing on her grave."

"If you tell your Mom, I'll kill your sorry ass, too, and throw you in the hog pen."

"I won't tell mom, but you'd best not swear on her grave no more."

George raised his pistol, turned, and blew his boy's brains out.

George looked down at his son and said, "Pussy.

***

We followed the trail for two hours when we saw where the two had stopped and rested. One was still leaving a blood trail. The tracks showed that the man limping was leaving the blood trail. We kept trudging on, and an hour later, we saw where they had rested again.

I said, "Guys, stop talking. They can't be very far ahead of us due to stopping all the time."

460

We walked another mile or so, and Paul said, "I see them up ahead. See, they're going around the bend in the road. Hey, they stopped. Duck!"

A flash and a gunshot came from the direction of the men we were following.

Ally said, "Zack, did you see that. The asshole shot his own man."

I replied, "Yeah, that was cold. He doesn't appear to be worried about being followed. Damn, he just walked off and left the other guy. That's one less we'll have to kill later."

We stayed about a hundred yards behind the man for another mile when we saw a light up ahead. I noticed he had quickened his pace and guessed this must be his destination. He was almost running when he tripped on something and fell down. We stopped and hid in the shadows while waiting for him to get up and head home.

He must have rested for a few minutes before getting up because he lay still in the snow but then pulled himself up and walked the last fifty yards to the house.

"Paul, follow me and let's make sure these are the outlaws and not just strangers that opened the door. Go to the backside and listen in while I check out the front."

Paul said, "Roger that," before heading over to the tree line behind the house and work his way behind it."

I told the others to hide in the ditch in front of the house while we checked them out. I used a yard shed and a truck to conceal my movement towards the house and made it within a few yards of the front porch when three men came outside to smoke.

I could hear them talking. One said, "I knew those dumb bastards should have waited for us to get here and help them. Hell, theys all dead, but George."

Hal, George is just plain old stupid. That asshole cain't find his own ass with both hands. What the fuck was he doing leading an attack."

"You got that shit right. It sounds like they did some damage, and them folks won't be out tonight. Let's get some sleep today, then go over to the church campground, kill the men, and take their women."

"I need a new one myself. May wants a ton of drugs for that redhead. I think I'll just go get one for myself."

I'd heard enough and worked my way back to the group. Paul arrived a minute later, and we filled everyone on what I had learned. I spoke first and told them, "These are the assholes that attacked us. The attack was premature, and these guys weren't here in time to join in. Thank God, or we might all be dead."

Paul added, "I heard pretty much the same, and I was able to look in several windows.

The blonde and redhead that left us are chained to beds in the back right side bedroom. There wasn't anyone in the other bedrooms. There are a few women and no children. The women are hard cases who need to be eliminated along with the men."

I gave them instructions, "As we planned, Lynn, you take the back, Joan take the front and kill anyone outside when I give the signal. Then kill any who try to escape after we begin the attack.

Roger, take these two grenades and pitch one in the back kitchen window when I whistle. That's the signal for Lynn and Joan to begin sniping.

I'll throw one in the front living room at the same time. Roger, wait ten seconds, and we'll throw the other grenades into the house. Paul and Ally, be ready to follow Roger and me into the house to finish off any survivors.

We won't take any prisoners. The two girls are in the back bedroom and should be okay.

I'll head to the left bedroom. Ally, take the middle one after we clear the living room and kitchen. Be prepared and have your heads on swivels. These rats could pop out anywhere. Oh, and by the way, thank Davi for getting us the grenades. Good luck, and may God go with us this morning. Move into position."

Everyone was in position, there were the same three men on the front porch, and two men and a woman were smoking on

462

the back porch when I whistled. Lynn and Joan took three shots each, and six dirtbags lay dying as Roger and I ran up to our positions.

I started to whistle, and several of the thugs flew out the front door shooting in all directions. Lynn and Joan cut them down, and I whistled as I pulled the pin on the grenade. I threw the grenade into the room and ducked.

Roger's grenade landed under the kitchen table, with six of the criminals drinking whiskey and smoking pot. Mine rolled up against the couch, which had two people all snuggled up on it and four others lying drunk on the floor. Roger's grenade exploded first, mangled their legs, and killed four outright. Two, including May, lay on the floor, screaming in pain.

My grenade exploded, killed the three on the floor, and blew the head off the woman. It only scared the hell out of the man who was shielded by the woman's body.

"Let's roll," I yelled as I entered the living room.

I entered the room, saw the blast, and felt a searing pain in my chest. The man had recovered enough to shoot me in the chest with a .357 Magnum knocking me to the floor.

Ally was behind me, and she shot the man three times. She then shot every one of the thugs in the head. She looked over at me, saw me clutching my chest, gasping for air, and ran to my side. Joan entered the room and watched for any threats.

Ally yelled, "Zack, speak to me! Damn it, are you okay?"

I was still gasping for air and finally caught my breath as I said, "Thank God for these flak jackets."

Roger kicked the back door down and began shooting the survivors.

May looked at her mangled legs and said to Roger, "Why kill us? We didn't hurt you."

"You attacked the church camp. Poke the bear and die bitch."

Roger shot the pervert between the eyes.

463

Ally, Roger, and Joan checked the other rooms, and the first two were empty, as Paul had told us. They entered the last room and didn't see anyone.

Roger yelled, "Jackie, are you in here?"

A reply came out from under the bed, "We're under the bed. Is it you, Roger?"

"Yes, the gang is dead. You're safe."

Both women came out from under the bed and hugged Roger. Joan and Ally kept their distance.

Jackie said, "Can we come home to the camp? These people raped and abused us."

Ally pointed her gun at the two and said, "Hell no. We tried to help you, and you knocked out Lynn, stole our gear, and disappeared. We should shoot you right now. No, we're going to turn you over to the Rolling Hills police."

The blonde said, "Well, we'll just wait and see what Zack has to say."

I overheard them talking, struggled to my feet, and said, "Ally, shoot them if you want. If not, we'll take the ungrateful bitches to Bert's brother in Rolling Hills."

I asked Joan and Ally to keep watch while I checked on the others. Roger had some glass blowback in his face and needed some small pieces removed. Paul tripped and cut his hand when he slipped in a pool of blood. My chest hurt like a son of a bitch, but there were no severe injuries. Well, except for my bruise the size of a basketball. I guess I'm a delicate flower, too."

I doused the fire in the two fireplaces, shut the doors on the houses, and walked out. Frozen bodies don't stink. Someone else can worry about them later. We took several of their trucks, all of their guns and ammo, and then drove back to the camp. We would come back in the morning to retrieve any food or other supplies we needed.

We arrived back at the camp and sat in front of the massive fireplace, swapping tales about our victory and filling in the folks that stayed home to guard the camp.

Joan and Ally played doctor cleaning and bandaging everyone's wounds. Joan checked me for broken ribs while Ally worked on Roger's face.

Joan said, "You're damn lucky you had that flak jacket, else you'd be laying here dead. That bullet hit just below your heart."

I replied, "I know, I'm lucky. We need to get better at this shit before someone kills us. Davi, can you give us some more training on entering and clearing rooms. You know SWAT stuff."

"Zack, I still recommend you all should hide out for the next year until the gangs and thugs kill each other off. This is serious business, and people are going to die if you keep confronting every asshole that comes along."

I was getting hot, and my ears must have been three shades of red when I replied, "So what would Miss Princess Warrior do? Hide for a year."

Davi snorted, "No, I would go out and kill every one of those assholes. Zack, I've been training all of my life to survive and kill to protect my home and family. You're trying to train as you go, and there just isn't any shortcut to becoming proficient at survival, killing, and military tactics."

Davi batted her eyelashes at me and said, "Do you really think I'm a Princess."

Ally responded, "Princess, go find your own knight in rusty armor. This one's spoken for."

I slept straight through the night, thanks to the Ibuprofen Joan gave me for the pain in my chest. I rolled over on my back, and the pills must have worn off because my chest was throbbing. I opened my eyes, and Ally stared at me as she ran her fingers through my hair.

"Good morning, lover," she said as she ran her hands down my chest."

I said, "What are you doing?"

"We've been married for months now, and if you don't know what I'm doing, I feel sorry for you."

I said, "You know what I mean. I'm injured, and my chest hurts like a son of a bitch. I can't...help, help...."

She rolled over and out of bed, saying, "I was just messing with you. I'll get a couple more pain pills for you, but after those wear off, you'll have to tough it out, you wussy."

"So you think that acting horny and making fun of me is the way to show me that you love me?"

Ally stepped close to the bed, took her t-shirt off, dropped her panties to the floor, and said, "Yes, I like flirting with my husband," as she ran into the bathroom to take a shower.

"You forgot my pills, ouch."

★

Chapter 10 - Break in Winter

The Campground

A week had passed since we wiped out the drug and slave gang. The Clan was healing nicely, and my ribs didn't hurt nearly as much as they did the first time my body armor saved my ass. Callie's ribs were still very sore, and she remained on light duty for the next week.

Davi conducted military and SWAT tactics training for every adult, and we gave age-appropriate training to the kids. All of them were taught to respect weapons and proper handling. They learned to reload magazines, put out fires, and hide from the enemy if needed. Even with these events, we still had a lot of time on our hands.

We were all suffering from cabin fever. The classes and the organized games helped a bit with the boredom. Still, as time dragged by, we became overly anxious to do something, anything. Tempers were beginning to take on a ragged edge.

Ally and I caught up on all of the lovemaking we'd missed during my recovery from the shot to the chest. I fell more in love with her every day and thought less and less about Geena until one day, I just didn't think about Geena at all.

Ally had been in an oppressive relationship and bloomed in front of my eyes. She was smart, clever, and very funny. She was always flirting with me and teasing Mike. She played several jokes on Mike, and only I knew the perpetrator's identity.

Mike came to breakfast, cursing and muttering as he sat down with the rest of us. He said, "I was just sitting down for my morning dump when...."

Callie cried out. "Uncle Mike, too much information is bad for my digestion."

"As I said, my ass just hit the seat when a big assed hairy spider fell in my lap. It was a fake spider, but I about killed myself getting out of the bathroom."

Lynn spoke up, "Yes, and he fell into me with his pants and underwear down around his ankles. My friends, I saw more of Mike than I ever wanted to see."

Roger laughed and said, "Did it scare the...," he looked around, saw the kids, and added, "the poop out of you?"

Mike exclaimed, "I think I had a heart attack. Three days ago, it was the clear wrap across the top of the door and the week before the clear wrap on the toilet. That sucked. Who hates me so much?"

Ally replied, "Maybe you have a secret admirer, and they just want your attention, or maybe it's a ghost."

Everyone laughed and picked on Mike throughout the meal.

I caught Ally alone after breakfast and asked, "Ally, how do you manage to set these traps without being caught? I couldn't keep a straight face, and it would only take a minute for everyone to see the guilt in my face."

"Dear, that's because you're an amateur. I'm a professional. I'm akin to the ninja, dressed in black that can walk among mere mortals without being seen. If you tell anyone it's me, I'll make you my next target."

I said, "Whoa girl, I'm on your side. Of course, I'd be insane not to be. Just promise me there will be no blood or violence."

"Deal."

I asked, "What if Mike retaliates and innocent bystanders are pranked."

"Collateral damage is a distinct possibility during pranks."

The pranks stopped, and Mike never knew who'd targeted him. However, about once a week after that, everyone, including me, was pranked.

One night just after we went to bed, I asked Ally if she was the one pranking everyone.

Ally insisted, "Darling, I did not pull a prank on Sally or you. I'm innocent. My bet is that Mike is pranking everyone to make sure he gets the original perpetrator."

I said, "I'm not convinced."

"Babe, the pranks have kept us from killing each other, and they make for great conversation at mealtime. I'll cease-fire for ninety days if it makes you feel better."

"So, it's you and not Mike."

Ally said, "No, I have not pranked anyone but Joan, Roger, and Callie for several weeks."

I brought everyone together and read them the riot act about how the pranks had to stop when, during my speech, a giant black spider fell in my lap. I swatted at it while dancing in my chair. I crushed the damn thing while everyone was laughing their asses off at my expense.

I asked, "Who's the asshole who dropped the spider on me?"

Mike couldn't stop laughing while he answered, "Zack, uh...ha, uh...that spider committed suicide. I guess we won't be seeing him again."

"Yeah, well, I guess that's true. Now, if I can just get my heart rate back to normal. Oh, and please, everyone, stay out of the Halloween boxes."

Ally tried to keep a straight face while she said, "Hon, I think it was a coincidence. No one could get a spider trained to jump on my big Ninja spider killing husband on cue."

I shouted, "Look, this shit's not funny. I could have been hurt."

Everyone just laughed harder and piled on the comments after my statement.

Mike said, "Big man, afraid of a tiny spider."

Roger said, "Zack, you looked like a man in a phone booth trying to kill a snake with a 9 iron."

"Daddy, I'll protect you from those mean ole critters."

I finally calmed down even though my face and ears were fire engine red and said, "Now back to the matter at hand, "No more pranks."

Mike laughed while he said, "Zack, we can't stop the insects or animals from attacking you.

I gave him the finger and left the room. The dirty bastards made fun of my killer spider dance for weeks.

Then, in mid-January, the snow stopped, the weather warmed, and it felt like spring. The snow took several days to melt off the roads. Still, it didn't totally disappear from the shady sides of hills and woods. Still, it was finally nice enough to enjoy being outside. The temperature was in the mid-'60s in the afternoon, and we spent much more time enjoying the sun and warm air.

I knew the good weather might not last and proposed to the team that we send a small group over to scout out Rolling Hills and contact Bert's brother Jake, the sheriff of Warren County. We had promised to come back and check on their progress in eliminating their gang problem but hadn't been able to make it back.

"Ally, I'm going to go over and check things out in Rolling Hills. It would be nice to move back into a house until we can go back home. I'll take several of the guys and Davi just in case we need some firepower."

Ally said, "Take Paul. He needs the experience. How long will you be gone?"

"Probably over and back in the same day; however, we'll pack for a three-day excursion."

Ally said, "Wear your body armor."

"As the commercial said, 'I never leave home without it.'"

"Be careful, and watch out, in case Prescott has spies in Rolling Hills."

I stopped in mid-step. "Damn, I hadn't thought about that happening. I guess that bastard plans to eventually annex all of Western Kentucky. It makes sense that he wants to know what's going on in the towns around Daviess County. I'll have to think of a way to get to Jake without everyone in town knowing about our visit."

***

I walked up to Davi. "Davi, we're going over to Rolling Hills this week. Prescott could have spies there. I want to meet with Jake without letting everyone in town know who we are and our business. Any ideas?"

"You're right. We could be under attack in just a few hours if the news got back to that ruthless bastard. Let me give it some thought."

"Okay, but think fast. We need a plan before we enter Rolling Hills."

Davi said, "Don't."

"Don't what?"

Davi's voice rose. "Don't enter Rolling Hills."

I asked, "So, how do we meet with Jake?"

"We get a message to him."

"How?"

She said, "Ask Bert. He knows Jake the best and should have some way to craft a message that only Jake would understand, saying to meet us at a certain place."

"Great idea."

Bert thought for a minute, laughed, and wrote a few words on a sheet of paper.

I read the note and asked, "Who are Abby and Betty Dill?"

"You don't need to know, but Jake will. You only need to know the location of the barn.

***

I asked Mike to stay back and watch over the camp while Davi, Roger, Paul, and I drove over to the meeting location. Bert was still recovering from his wounds, and it was too soon for him to travel, or he would have gone to see his brother.

"Paul, would you please fuel up my pickup. Everyone check your weapons, bring body armor, and prepare for a three-day journey.

Roger replied, "Zack, it's only a half-hour drive."

"I know, but just in case the shit hits the fan, let's always be prepared."

Then I said, "Ben, please mount the SAW on top of the cab. I know it's overkill, but I never want to be on the short end of a gunfight."

Davi added, "If we get into a firefight, that SAW could make the difference in us coming back alive. Zack, there are some metal plates in the barn that I'd like to bolt onto your truck to give us some armor. Can I have Paul to help me install the armor?"

"Of course, Paul, please help Davi ruin the sublimely beautiful lines of my classic 1949 F1 Ford by installing a machine gun on top of my cab and armor on its body."

It only took Ben a few minutes to mount the SAW. Davi and Paul worked most of the day bolting metal slabs onto the tailgate, bumper, both doors, and behind the cab. The truck looked like a cross between a demolition derby car and a ten-year-old's idea of a tank.

We loaded up the next morning before sunrise and checked each other out before heading over to Rolling Hills. I wanted to travel while most people were still asleep or having breakfast.

We didn't think there would be any issues, but we were always alert for danger. We left the camp and drove for twenty minutes on side roads before getting on Highway 231 South.

Davi rode in the cab with me while Paul and Roger were in the bed. Roger manned the SAW, and Paul watched our rear.

We drove slowly to avoid running into an ambush. There weren't any other vehicles on the road, and we frequently stopped to scout ahead using my binoculars.

As the sun rose, I only saw a few people stirring around in their houses, and no one paid any attention to us. I spotted the roadblock just where we thought it would be before the exit to the Natcher Parkway.

I quickly pulled off the road behind some bushes and stopped a few hundred yards away from the roadblock. Roger stayed with the truck while Paul and I worked our way down the ditch on the south side of the road until we were only a hundred feet from the roadblock.

Davi gave us time to get ready to back her up and then walked up to the roadblock to pass the note for Jake to one of the people manning the roadblock.

She had her rifle slung over her shoulder and pistol on her hip as she approached the roadblock waving a white handkerchief.

One of the men stepped out and said, "Well, what can we do for you, young lady?"

Davi asked, "Do you know Jake Alford?"

"Well, of course, we know him, he's the sheriff, and we work for him."

She handed him the envelope and said, "Take this message to him, and please don't open it."

The man took the envelope and said, "You can stay a while and visit."

Davi smiled, "Thanks, but no thanks, maybe next time."

She turned and walked back to the truck. We watched as one of the guards hopped on an ATV and headed into town with the note. Then we worked our way back to the truck and headed to the meeting place.

We turned around and took two back roads to the barn on the corner of County Road 2665 and Dedmond Road. I hid the truck in the barn and waited on Jake.

Davi snickered, "Zack, I seem to remember another barn a while back, and you getting caught with your pants down."

"That's why we're posting guards front and back. Davi, take the front entrance, and Roger, you take the first hour at the back. Paul and I'll relieve you in an hour."

Davi and Roger took their weapons and gear and then went out for guard duty.

Paul walked up to me and said, "What was that pants down comment?"

I scowled, "Paul, I was supposed to be on guard duty and got distracted. While I wasn't paying attention, some bad men came in the barn and captured us."

Paul asked, "Was that when Sally, Geena, and you were coming here from Oregon?"

"Yes."

I said, "Hey, Paul, I don't want you to answer this unless you...."

"The question is, am I keeping an eye on you?"

I frowned. "Well, sort of. So my wife doesn't trust me?"

"Oh no, she trusts you. She just doesn't trust any woman around you, and she really doesn't trust Davi."

I said, "Paul, I haven't done anything to lose your mom's trust."

"She knows that, but what you don't know is my dad was screwing every woman he could get his hands on. Mom tried to believe him, but she caught him just the week before TSHTF. She'd had enough and filed for divorce. Listen, she doesn't know that I know all of this, so please don't tell her."

I said, "Don't worry, Paul, I won't, and I would never break your trust."

I thought for a minute, then asked, "Paul, did you ever figure out who was pulling all of the pranks on everyone?"

"Yes, it was a mom."

I laughed and said, "How did you figure it out?"

"Well, mom once told me that she and one of her girlfriends had been the pranksters at their high school. Then I saw dad become a primary target every time he came home late or the next day.

She fed him everything from Cayenne pepper to Exlax, and sometimes both together. She found out who some of the married women he saw were and sent them flowers signed with his full name to their husband's work address. That, of course, was just to get their attention...and it did."

I winced, "Oh shit."

Paul broke out laughing and said, "Yes, literally, he also came home black and blue a couple of times."

A few minutes later, Davi yelled, "Truck approaching with two men."

I told Roger to keep a watch on the backside while Paul and I joined Davi to confront the truck's occupants.

I called out, "Davi and Paul will meet the truck while I stay out of sight. No one will know you two."

The men parked the truck in front of the barn and walked up to Davi and Paul. I could hear Jake ask where his brother was. I stepped out from beside the barn and said, "Hello, Jake."

"Hi Zack, where's my brother? I heard rumors that Prescott had killed him."

I said, "Your brother is safe back at our home location. He was shot escaping from Prescott's men, but he and his family made it to our place. He warned that Prescott was coming to kill Mike and me. We escaped and headed this way."

Jake asked, "Can I see Bert?"

I said, "Of course you can. I was hoping you'd come alone. How well do you know this guy?"

"Steve is my brother-in-law and best friend. You can trust him."

I replied, "Move your truck into the barn, and we'll bring each other up to date."

I introduced my team to Jake and Steve and then filled him in on our story since we last saw him.

Jake said, "That damn Prescott is trying to take over the entire country. He came to Rolling Hills a couple of months ago and met with our town council. He tried to talk them into joining his Community Protection Cooperative. We had heard about his dealings with the gang in Anderson, and Bert had already told me not to trust him."

"How did he take that answer?"

Jake said, "He was pissed, but he smiled and said, "There are dangerous people out there, and they'll be coming to your town to take your food, weapons, and women. If you don't join us, I'm absolutely sure that you will regret it."

I said, "A not so veiled threat."

Jake replied, "I told him that he should keep his men in Daviess County, so we don't accidentally kill them when we shoot the thugs trying to rob us. He got mad and left. We hadn't had any problems since we eliminated that gang last summer. Right after he left, the trouble began. We had cattle killed or missing, and several young girls disappeared.

I set some traps and killed a dozen of 'em, and they all pretty much looked like Prescott's security team."

I asked, "Before I forget, tell me about how you got rid of the gang."

"The ipecac made the difference. We spiked the food we took them as you suggested, and the gang never knew what hit them. Those guys were so busy vomiting they hardly knew they were under attack. We shot them like fish in a barrel. It was a slaughter. I lost one man and had three others wounded.

The mayor and city council were pissed at first until we presented evidence that the mayor and two of the Council were on the take. We ran them out of town, along with most of the gang's women. We killed all of the gang except for a few that were able to escape on their bikes. All of the leaders died that day."

I said, "I'm glad we were able to help. Do you want to go to our camp and say hi to Bert?"

"Damn straight, I would. I'd like to see him today."

"By the way, who are Abby and Betty?"

Jake's brother-in-law quickly said, "They're my sisters!"

"Okay, I won't ask."

Jake replied, "No, it's okay. Bert and I were dating his sisters, and we married them. The funny part is we didn't marry the one we dated the longest. At the last minute, we switched."

I laughed, "Oh, boy."

"No, we all get along great."

***

Jake followed us over to our camp and was thrilled to see his brother and his family. We introduced Jake and his brother-in-law to everyone and then left them alone to catch up on events. They talked for hours and started again after lunch.

Before Jake left, Mike and I filled them in on Daviess County and what we had accomplished, getting farming more productive and our successes at generating electricity.

Jake was astounded. "Boy, y'all were way ahead of the farmers back home. We only have a few tractors and large trucks running. We were so busy trying to survive the first year that we didn't look at longer range planning."

Mike looked at me and replied, "Zack, it appears we are stuck here for a while. Shouldn't we reach out to the local farmers and help them like we did around Owensville.

I replied, "I know Callie and Paul can build more of the bicycle and small gas engine generators. I'd also like to help get more tractors and trucks running. Jacob and Sam can fix any old truck or tractor. Let's jump-start this area as we did at home."

Jake grinned and said, "We could really use your help, and you do need a home."

I remembered Prescott and replied, "I'm afraid that it would leak out that Mike and I are in Rolling Hills, and Prescott would attack the city to get to us."

Davi chimed in, "Prescott is going to try to take all of Western Kentucky regardless of where you and Mike live. We have to take him out before he builds his kingdom."

Jake replied, "I think she hit the nail on the head."

I answered, "I know she's right, but we have been fighting thugs and criminals for almost a year now. When does it end?"

Davi quickly answered, "Zack, it will go on until the country is rebuilt, or at least this part of the country gets back to a law and order society. Remember, I'm from Israel. We have been fighting every day since 1949. I think the quicker you kill the Prescott's of the world, the quicker the country moves forward."

I thought for a minute and replied, "So, we put a plan together to take out Prescott with the least risk and loss of our lives."

"Yes, we must remove him, his top leaders, and as many of his men as possible. These are all nasty guys who could take his place and become a true dictator.

We must think this through and execute a plan that has multiple attacks on Prescott's empire. The assaults must simultaneously take out him, his command and control, and most of his soldiers," Davi pleaded.

We all agreed with Davi as the room fell silent. I knew our people just wanted to settle down somewhere and start a new life. Still, I also realized that running away just meant that we would probably run into another Prescott. Yeah, I guess it's time to make a stand.

We agreed to move over to Rolling Hills during the next two weeks. Jacob and Sam's families would go first, and then the rest of us would come over a week later. Jake told us that they had a couple of subdivisions that were ghost towns. Most people had moved closer to town and upgraded their housing during the moves. He thought Mike and I could hide in plain sight on the outskirts of town while Jacob and Sam were actively working with the farmers to get ready for spring planting.

When Jake left, we sent the girls that we freed from the drug gang back with him. Several were from Rolling Hills and knew the Sheriff. They were glad to be going home.

✪

Chapter 11 - Winter is a Cruel Mistress

We relocated to Rolling Hills. We moved all of our gear, firewood, and vehicles and then enjoyed the balmy spring-like weather during mid-winter. Several of us went out hunting or fishing each day to augment our food supply. Mike and I took either Susie or Callie out every day to pass on our hunting and trapping skills to them. I took very seriously the need to pass on skills to the younger generation.

The girls took to hunting as eagerly as any man and became proficient quickly. They knew we only shot animals we intended to eat, and nothing was wasted. The dogs or our neighbor's pigs ate everything we didn't save for ourselves. We taught them how to field dress, clean, and dry meat. We made sausage, sun-dried jerky, and smoked meat. We all loved deer jerky and sausage. I loved the deer sausage with cheese and jalapeno mixed into the sausage.

Paul didn't like trapping animals, but all knew we had to use every method possible to feed ourselves. There were no food processing and packaging plants in operation in the USA, and the existing dry and canned goods would be gone before the end of this year. He never liked taking an animal from a trap, but he did it because it was necessary for survival.

Susie and I were a mile or so south of the subdivision hunting deer. I could see she was growing up in maturity as well as strength, thanks to necessity. She handled her Winchester lever-action .30-.30 as well as any man and had already killed several deer with it.

Suzie asked, "Zack, will we ever get back to the way things used to be?"

"Darling, not for a long time, and even then, it may not be the same. There won't be money spent on cell phones and computer games in my lifetime. Civilization has to rebuild our medical, food processing, and transportation technology before non-essential items can be brought back."

"Zack, can I call you, Dad?"

"Of course. I would like that, daughter."

"Dad, why did this happen?"

I said, "I don't think anyone knows. My guess is some enemies of the USA attacked us to eliminate our influence in the world."

"Will they invade our part of the country?"

"Darling, I hope not, but I won't lie to you. They could. Uncle Mike and I'll do everything possible to protect you and the rest of our family."

"What will we do if they come here?"

I didn't have a good answer. Yes, I finessed the question but didn't have a good answer. This young girl had asked the question that I kept pushing to the back of my mind. I tried not to think about this and was successful until the issue slapped me in the face.

Susie killed a large doe shortly after our conversation, and I forgot about her question. Mike later taught Callie and her how to skin the hide without ruining it to use the deer leather to make gloves and a coat. Mike would later teach us how to tan leather.

We were all becoming more proficient at the daily chores our great grandfathers and mothers tackled every day.

I drug the field-dressed deer back to the house where we butchered it and began processing it to preserve the meat. Ally cut off steaks for supper that night. She sent Suzie out to invite Callie and Paul, Mike and Sally, and Davi to supper. The weather was great, I had some dried hickory wood for the barbecue, and I loved to grill. Ally and Suzie prepared the sides as our guests arrived. I gave everyone a homebrew, and we shot the shit as I grilled the steaks. It was only 4:00 as the sun went down, and the air was noticeably colder than it had been since the snow melted.

My guests moved inside when the wind picked up, and the temperature plummeted. Thank God Callie brought me a coat because my teeth were chattering, even standing close to the fire. The sun was setting, but there was enough light to see the black clouds racing towards us from the northwest. I had hoped we would escape any further snow and cold weather, but the clouds and drop in temperature did not support my hopes. I was glad when the steaks were done and took them into the warm house and shivered as my body took in the warmth.

Mike saw me shivering and said, "I knew the warm weather was just a teaser. Mother Nature was just screwing with us, and now she'll bring all of her fury down on us."

I said, "I hope this is just a brief change in weather and not one of those polar vortex thingies. I remembered back about ten years ago, we had snowstorms and a deep freeze for a week."

"We only have about six to ten more weeks of winter, and I hope it's closer to four."

Callie spoke up, "Dad, remember I told you that the wooly worms have real thick black coats as winter started. They know this is going to be a bad winter. I'm okay with winter as long as Paul and I have a warm fire to snuggle up in front of."

Ally replied, "I second that thought, but I worry about the animals during a blizzard. There are a lot of house dogs and cats that have been turned loose when their human parents died or couldn't feed them."

Sally added, "That reminds me, we need to be very careful and watch for wild and domestic animals that are starving.

Remember the wolf attack back home. We could have lost some friends."

I hadn't worried about that because, with most humans dead, the wild game had flourished. People were hunting, but there was a hell of a lot less of them hunting or ruining the animal's habitat. Hell, you can sit on your back porch and see hundreds of rabbits, squirrels, skunks, and even a porcupine or two any day of the week. Dogs and cats were plentiful. You can hear Coyotes yelping all night. Nature was in a rebalancing period, the strong would survive, and the weak would be eaten.

Susie came running into the family room and yelled, "It's snowing! It's snowing real hard, and the wind is blowing."

A gust of wind rattled the storm windows as if to punctuate Susie's words. The wind picked up in velocity. We could hear it howling, and one of the side doors had a whistle. We all ran to the windows and saw nothing but a white mass of snow hitting the window. I shined my flashlight out the front window, and the beam stopped a few feet into the whiteout.

I looked at my guests and said, "Y'all should spend the night here. I think it may be too dangerous to walk home in this whiteout.

"Dad, we only live next door, and I hate to leave my dog home alone. This storm is probably scaring him to death."

Mike said, "Zack, we live on the other side of Callie, so I'm sure we can make it home."

"Okay, but I offered. Key your mike twice when you're home safely, and Mike, key yours three times."

"Yes, dad," both Mike and Callie replied."

I woke up in the middle of the night and heard the wind fiercely blowing. I got out of bed without waking Ally and went to the living room to look out the window. It was 3:21 am, and the snow was still coming down so fast I couldn't see but a few inches beyond the window. I was wide awake, so I made myself a biscuit and deer steak sandwich. I sat at the front window, watching the snow rain down. I don't know why it fascinated me because it was like watching a TV without a signal. Nothing on the screen to see, but I couldn't stop watching.

Before I knew it, it was 6:00. I started a pot of coffee and fetched some eggs and deer sausage for breakfast. I wasn't much of a cook, but scrambled eggs and sausage were not much of a challenge. The smell of the coffee floated throughout the house, and Susie joined me after making herself a cup of coffee.

"Dad, what are you cooking? It smells great and is making me hungry."

"Scrambled eggs and some sausage from your deer."

"That sounds great, and boy, I'm hungry."

I looked down beside her and saw her Winchester leaning against the counter beside my AR. I had mixed emotions seeing that this little teen girl had been trained to keep her rifle handy at all times. I was proud but saddened that our world had come to this. It was no different from the early settlers who always prepared for an Indian attack.

Ally came down the hall wearing only one of my long sleeve t-shirts, looking beautiful, taking my mind off my cooking.

Before she saw Susie, she said, "Zack, come on back to bed, and we can ... Oh, hi, Susie. You're up early this morning."

"Yes, mom, the coffee smelled so good that I had to have a cup with dad."

Ally said, "Well, since you're up, please let the dog out to do his business."

"Okay, mom."

Susie looked down at her black Lab and called for him to follow her. She opened the kitchen door, the wind blew it out of her hand, and it slammed against the counter. Snow swirled into the kitchen until I ran over and forced the door closed.

Susie said, "Holy shit. The wind almost knocked me down."

"Susie, don't say that word."

"Mom, you say the "S" word all the time."

Ally scowled, "I'm an adult. You're not. Do what I say."

"Yes, mam."

I interjected, "Ally, please finish breakfast while I clear a path for the dog."

While they discussed the finer points of children not cussing, I got dressed and put on a heavy coat, gloves, and ski mask. I struggled to open the door just enough to see what was happening outside. The snow was three feet deep against the house and door. I went out into the garage and found a snow shovel to clear a path for the poor dog. I had Ally and Susie close the door behind me. The snow was only a foot and a half deep but had drifted against the house. The sun was up, but it was twilight outside, and I could only see a few feet in front of me

I cleared a small 10 x 10-foot area for the dog to do his business and came back in for breakfast. I was just in time to sit down and eat. The meal hit the spot after shoveling the wet, heavy snow.

I said, "Darling, we'll have to keep an area clear for the dog, and I think I'll clear a path over to Callie's home before I sit my ass in front of the fire and read a good book."

Ally said, "That sounds like a great idea. How many shovels do we have?"

"Just the one. We'll have to take turns. I hope each house has a shovel. If this crap continues, we'll need to all work to keep our paths open."

Susie exclaimed, "Mom, dad said crap."

"He's also an adult. Cut out the backtalk, or you will be sitting in a corner."

I said, "Before I was interrupted, I was going to say that I'll go check some of the abandoned houses for more shovels while you and Susie shovel."

Ally said, "Sounds like a plan. Please check on Callie and Paul while you're out."

"I planned to drop in on them."

I put my winter duds back on and braved the blizzard once more to walk next door to Callie's home. I knew the house was straight ahead but couldn't see it until I was about five feet away. I knocked on the kitchen door, and no one answered. I waited and knocked louder. I saw Paul through the window, hopping along, putting his pants on.

The door opened, letting a bunch of snow and me in on their kitchen floor.

"What are y'all doing sleeping in this late? Morning is half over. We're burning daylight."

I heard Callie behind me, "Dad, some people like to stay in bed and do adult stuff in the morning when it's too crappy outside."

I said, "Girl, we're spending the morning cleaning a place so Susie's dog can take a crap while Ally tries to teach Susie not to say the word crap while discussing this crappy weather. That's what adults do in our house on a crappy weather day. I'm now officially done talking about crap."

Laughing, Callie replied, "Poor daddy. Is it okay if we invite Susie to a slumber party at my house so Ally and you can behave like adults once in a while?"

"Yes, if you take her dog too."

Callie chuckled, "Poor Dad."

I pointed to the window and said, "Hey, now seriously, there's 18 inches of snow on the ground and three-foot drifts. You need to clear an area for your dog to do his business, and we are making a path from our house to yours. I would like you to make a path over to Mike's house and so on until we are all linked up. This storm is not going away for another day or so, and I don't want to be digging three feet of snow. Let's stay caught up with it as it falls."

Paul answered, "That sounds like a great idea. We have a snow shovel, and I'll bet some of the abandoned homes also have some."

"I'm going to look in a few, and I'll bring you an extra one back here shortly. I'm dropping by the rest of our big family to spread our plan and check on them."

Callie said, "Okay, we'll have breakfast and get to shoveling snow right after breakfast."

"I'll be back in an hour or so."

Damn, I arrived at Mike's place, and they were still in bed. My friends were getting lazy and blaming the snowstorm. Sally finally answered the door and let a ton of snow and me into their house.

Sally fussed, "Damn Zack, you're messing up my clean kitchen floor."

"Well, it's about to get worse. It's snowed all night and is still snowing."

I filled them in on our plan and divided the rest of our group with Mike to visit. We would both search a few houses for snow shovels. I visited Jacob and Sam's homes while Mike took care of the rest.

I found three more snow shovels and a lawn tractor with a plow blade attachment and then drove it back home, plowing a path as I went. The tractor's blade was just a bit shorter than the snow was deep and didn't do a great job with just one pass. I drove it past Mike and Callie's homes to help them with their paths. It worked much better, clearing the already cleared paths. I was happy until I realized that four inches of snow had fallen in the last ninety minutes.

The tractor made short work of clearing a much larger area for the dog, and I ran it up and down the path between Callie's and our house. I was plowing away when I heard a noise behind me. I turned and saw Mike riding a big Cub Cadet with a snowblower attachment on the front. It was throwing the snow ten feet into the air. This was much better than trying to shove snow out of the way.

Mike yelled, "Hey Zack, look what I found in the pole barn behind Roger's place. The metal barn must have shielded it from the EMP blast. I'm going to start plowing the paths between all of the houses and then try to clear the streets if you and Paul will help. The others have already volunteered. We'll all take turns and make the job easier. Paul is firing up the tractor with the bucket and blade to help with the streets."

Okay, I'll admit that we were bored and playing with the tractor and snowblower. They were just what the doctor ordered to get us out in the snow. The first day was fun. The next day wasn't too bad, but the third day was work. Everyone was taking turns, including the women, but we barely stayed caught up.

Mother Nature unloaded this blizzard on us two weeks after we moved to Rolling Hills. This was made much crueler because we were walking outside in shirt sleeves one day, and the next had two feet of snow and 29-degree weather. It snowed for a week piling the snow up higher than most of our houses. We had no warning as we had in the days before the lights went out. There were no three days of warning that a bad storm was on its way, and no one told us to go to the store and buy all of the milk and bread we can get. This was a total surprise.

Thank God Ally had selected a two-story house for us to live in that had two fireplaces and a nice basement. We couldn't see out of any of the downstairs windows by the fourth day of the storm. The snow was about five feet deep and climbing, but drifts were as high as 12 feet against buildings and fences. We had to go upstairs to look outside, not that we could see anything with the blizzard still pounding us with more snow every minute. Hell, even I was praying for global warming each night.

***

On the morning of the fourth day of the storm, Mike woke up at what was supposed to be daylight, checked the time, and rolled out of bed.

Sally cried out, "Mike, it's not even daylight yet. Come back to bed."

"Hon, it's 7:30, and there ain't a bit of sun out there. I'm going to get dressed and get some plowing done before breakfast. I'll be back in an hour and a half."

Mike fueled up the snowblower, but before he took it out of the garage, he heard the tractor fire up and moved out onto the street. Mike pulled the door open with the pull cord and wished the automatic garage door opener worked. This was a sixteen-foot door, and the bitch was heavy. He drove the Cub Cadet out onto the driveway and was shocked to see another foot of snow covering everything he had worked so hard to plow the day before. He started the snowblower up and cleared the driveway. He waved at Paul, who was scraping the road in front of their houses. He saw Paul stop and use the bucket to collect and dump the mound of snow up over the snow wall and onto the top of the now six feet of snow.

Mike then headed to the backyard to clear the dog's area and the path between the houses. He ran on down to Callie's house, then my place, where he stopped and banged on the door. "Zack, roll off your hussy and get your ass out here."

Ally poked her head out the door and replied, "Mike, shut up. Zack rolled off his beautiful wife two hours ago and is helping Sam clear snow away from his garage door. And be careful with that hussy crap."

"See you later, beautiful."

Ally gave him the finger. "That's better. Now, go play in the street."

Mike finished at my house and went back to his to get a tape measure. He measured the wall of snow that surrounded our paths and found the average height of the barriers to be six feet three inches.

I saw Mike making the measurements and said, "You checking to see if it's a record snowfall?"

"No. The snowblower can only blow the snow about ten feet in the air, and at that height, a quarter of the snowfalls back on the path being cleared. This snow has to stop before we can't clear it anymore."

I said, "I know, I was talking with Paul, and he reminded me that the bucket on the tractor can only dump snow about nine to ten feet out of our cleared paths. Then the bucket is so high that the snow just falls back on the path. I'm worried."

Mike looked at his watch and said, "Breakfast time. You can have the snowblower for the next forty minutes."

That was the worst winter North America had experienced since the last Ice Age. We were bored one day and terrified the next. Cabin fever abounded, and we just had to suck it up and work hard to survive. There probably was too much snuggling by the fire that winter because we had several new additions to our clan nine months later.

✪

Chapter 12 - Terror in the Ice

On the morning of the fifth day of the winter blizzard, I woke up with a bright light in my eyes, and Susie was yelling, "Mom, Dad, the sun is shining. The snow has stopped."

I raced to the window and looked down at the top of the snow and then at the sun. The snow reflected the light like a mirror and nearly blinded me, but it was great to see across the snow to the buried houses. I could see the bucket of the tractor scooping snow and piling it on top of the frozen white walls, which defined the path in front of Paul's house.

Ally was stretching and yawning as Susie said, "It looks warm outside. I'll bet the snow melts and is gone in a couple of days."

I performed a mental calculation that I remembered from listening to the local Channel 44 weather lady. Ten inches of snow equals one inch of water, so our seven feet of snow equals 8.4 inches of water with no place to go except through our manmade paths. The water will be channeled directly into our homes.

"Oh shit! Son of a Bitch!"

Susie called me out. "Dad is cussing."

"Damn, Skippy, I'm cussing. Ally, where's the water going to go if we have a quick melt-off?"

There was a moment of silence. Ally said, "Oh crap!"

Susie was getting to be annoying. "You said crap."

I said, "We need to get the clan together, now!"

Ally said, "Susie, get your coat on and run down to Roger's house and ask him to bring everyone past his house here, *right now*! I'll get the rest."

I quickly dressed and ran down to the other houses to get everyone to the meeting. I noticed that it was actually colder this morning than it had been during the last week, so maybe, just maybe, we had some time to develop a course of action to resolve our water problem.

I finished knocking on doors, ran back to the house, and only busting my ass twice on the ice. I walked into the kitchen, saw Callie and Paul, and said, "Ally start a big pot of coffee, and please fry up some sausage. Most of our guests haven't had breakfast."

I guess our Bug Out drills had helped instill a major sense of urgency in our little clan because everyone was in our family room within fifteen minutes of notification.

I started the discussion. "I know you want to know what's so urgent this sunny cold morning, so I'll get right to the point. The sun is out. The weather has to warm up. The snow is going to melt."

I stopped and let the words sink in for a moment before the realization sank in on my friends.

Mike cursed. "Oh shit."

Roger said, "Boy, are we screwed."

Mike joked. "Water wings."

Roger tried to top Mike. "Noah's ark?"

I said, "Yes, my friends, we have made a mile-long swimming pool that will funnel all of that melting snow into our streets and paths that will have nowhere to go except into our houses. We need to brainstorm a solution before the temperature rises."

Paul asked, "Where's the low end of our neighborhood."

"It's the southeast end of the subdivision. The entire neighborhood slants downhill in that direction."

I thought for a second, realized that our home was the furthest southeast, and said, "Oh shit! This is more serious than I thought. Your water is heading down to our house."

Callie asked, "Dad, aren't there storm drains and underground pipes to take rainwater away?"

I answered, "Normally, yes, but not in a country subdivision like this. We have several dry stormwater ponds that fill up during a storm. They hold the excess water and then slowly release it into creeks and the lake about half a mile south of here. Our problem is that the stormwater ponds have seven feet of snow in them and won't take much water."

Paul suggested, "What if we take the snowblower and tractor and make several paths down to the creeks where the stormwater normally flows?"

I replied, "The snow blower won't work because the snow is seven feet deep and heavily compacted. We will have to use the bucket on the tractor, and that will be a lot of work."

Paul added, "We could also build some snow dams to divert the water around the houses at this end of the subdivision."

I patted Paul on the back and said, "That's my boy. You get a gold star for that one. I believe we have a few days before the snow begins a rapid melting. Still, once it does, it will refreeze overnight and become impossible to remove."

"You're right," said Jacob. We need to get these new channels started this morning before we run out of time. We can't move our vehicles or gear and would lose most of it if the paths flood.

We will set up a schedule to work around the clock and pray the tractor doesn't break down."

Roger drew a rough map of the subdivision, and we penciled in some suggested routes for the channels.

I told the team, "Roger, I want you to take Paul and Jacob to the southeast end of the development and choose the routes for the channels. The rest of us will start figuring out where to place the dams."

***

The heavy snow had kept the wolf pack penned up in their den, a small cave that ran into a much larger cavern system. Southern Kentucky had many caves and was famous for being the home of Mammoth Cave. The cave ran back under a large hill and opened up to yield a large chamber that comfortably held the thirty members of the pack. The temperature was a cool 55 degrees in the large room that was forty feet from the opening.

A small stream ran all year long at the rear of the cave, so the water was plentiful though it did have a coppery taste. Shelter and water were not problems for the pack. The problem was the blizzard, dumping seven feet of snow over the past four days, which made hunting impossible. Deer, rabbit, and opossum were numerous now that the human population had been significantly reduced.

The pack had eaten well since moving south until the snowstorm literally locked them inside the cave. The inside of their huge den was utterly dark as the snow had covered the entrance, yet something in their makeup told them that the snow had stopped. They began to dig.

Now that the sun had come out, the pack found that it was difficult to walk on the snow and that there was no game to stalk. They found a few mice but little else. It had been six days since they had killed a deer and a small beaver. The pack was starving.

Becoming desperate, the Alpha male knew they had to have a successful hunt soon. He could smell the human scent from the north mixed in with the smell of dogs and a faint smell of cats. Before TSHTF, wolves would not usually attack or eat humans. Still, dogs and cats would fill their bellies nicely until they could find their regular game. Hunger would drive them to make a raid on the human town tonight.

***

Roger returned with his crew from the scouting trip and pointed out the best route for our drainage path. Sam and Jacob got on top of the garage with a rifle's scope and showed Paul where to start digging and piling snow.

Jacob handed the scope to Sam and said, "See that large oak tree to the left of the red barn."

Sam replied, "Yes, it's by its self, so it makes a good target."

"Just keep the tractor operator aimed at that tree, and we'll be on target. When we get closer to the tree, we have another tree beside the creek to guide us to finish the project. We figure it's about half a mile to the creek. We couldn't pace it off due to having to make our way through the snow and drifts."

Sam added, "Yes, and we wouldn't have made it if Callie hadn't come up with the idea to make snowshoes. Joan and Lynn did a great job making them for us.

The plan was to have someone check the path against the preferred route every half hour to keep it on track. Paul took the first two-hour shift and only dug out eight feet wide by fifty feet long. The path was wider than needed because the tractor had to turn to the side to dump the snow.

I got Mike and Jacob to watch the effort to see if we could develop a better method. "Guys, Paul has only dug up fifty feet of the path, and at that rate, it will take about forty-five hours straight to finish our drainage ditch. We need ideas to speed up the work!"

Mike said, "Let's watch for a minute."

After observing for a few minutes, Jacob spoke up, "Paul is spending too much time pushing the snow from the ground, causing most of the snow to fall behind the blade. Let's have him move the top five to six feet and use the snow blower to clean up the ground as he goes."

I said, "Sounds good, Mike, please get the blower, and we'll give it a try."

I got on the tractor and changed to the new procedure while Mike came in behind me to move the remaining foot of snow. This reduced the time for the next fifty feet by a third.

I said, "Well, that was successful. Let's pass the process on to everyone before they take their turn."

Mike said, "Using the brainpower of the group is always better."

"Mike, please check on the dam building. If this works, the dams won't have to be more than a foot or so high."

Mike pointed at one of our dams. "Hey, big boy, we might have to re-think the dams to keep the water away from the houses."

"Why?"

Mike snorted, "Dams keep water in for the most part. Snow will melt on both sides of the dams.

"Another oh crap situation," moaned Callie.

I said, "No, I say we build the dams, but keep an eye on the water flow. If our project works, we won't need the dams. If there's a backup, the dams could be handy."

I suppose dams might not be the best term. Channels would be more accurate. While they'll perform as dams to keep water out of our homes, their primary purpose was to channel the water away.

I thought to myself, semantics, *good grief!* "Okay, let's educate everyone."

Paul added, "We remind everyone that at night the channels will leave a sheet of ice on our paths. We don't need any busted asses or broken legs."

Smugly, Mike added, "Another great observation."

I smiled and said, "Dude, no one likes a smartass. I know because the only friends I have are smartasses."

***

496

The Alpha male and nine of the pack struggled through the deep but hardening snow to the human's houses that night to bring home a kill for the pack. There was a strong smell of humans, dogs, cats, and raccoons, but only three humans were outside digging in the snow.

The two raccoons raided a garbage can and moved back to the woods when the pack attacked. The raccoons put up a fight but were vastly outnumbered.

The Alpha male ate first, and there was a fight for the rest. Wolves don't typically attack humans, but this pack was starving.

The humans were stuck below the level of the top of the snow. They would be alarmed at the number of wolf and coyote paw prints in the snow above them. The Alfa male knew the pack could jump down and kill a dog but could not get back up the sheer wall of snow and ice.

***

We worked on digging the drainage path for the next two days and could see that we were only yards from the tree line at the creek. By working in two-hour shifts, we dug the drainage path without wearing anyone out, and thankfully, our equipment kept running without breaking down.

We broke through the last few feet and found the creek to be flowing free. The water level was high, and the ordinarily small stream was twenty feet across and opened to the sky. I thanked God that the creek level was five feet below ground level, or we would have just flooded the neighborhood. The ground level on the other side of the creek was three feet lower than our side, so I wasn't worried about the stream flooding the neighborhood.

Paul ran the snowblower to the end of the path and finished the job. "Let's celebrate. Mike, cut up some deer steaks, and let's have a BBQ."

Mike agreed, "Great idea, let's see, it's 3:00, and the sun will be down shortly. Let's go get the pit fired up."

Later, after we had finished eating, we sat around my family room, swapping stories and singing our favorite songs.

"This is as close to before the lights went out normal as it gets these days. People are enjoying their friend's company and having a great time." Ally said.

Joan replied, "And no one is staring down at their smartphones and ignoring their friends. This might be a better world if we weren't running out of medicine and hygiene supplies."

That brought a cautious laugh from everyone.

Callie said, "I need to take Duke out to do his business. I'll be back in a minute. Let's stay up late playing cards."

I said, "Darn, I need to let our dogs out."

Mike said, "Me, too."

I suggested, "Let's take a break and then start a gin rummy marathon."

The ones with dogs went home to let them out and came back after their dogs had finished. Callie and I had Labs from the same litter that we found in a warehouse. Sally and Lynn had German Shepherds, and the others had a variety of dogs. Sadly, most small dogs seem to have disappeared over the last year. Then again, large dogs were a distinctly coveted addition to the family.

We had a ball playing cards, and the time passed quickly when Ally said," The poor dogs must be ready to go out again. Susie, would you and Kate please go let the dogs out."

Susie was playing checkers with Ben's daughter Kate when she heard the request. "What do I get for going out in the cold to take care of the dogs?"

I replied, "My dad would have said something like, you won't get your ass busted, but I'm sure your mom has a better answer."

Ally went over to Susie and whispered in Susie and Kate's ears. They jumped up, put their coats and gloves on, and went to tend to the dogs.

"What did you tell them," asked Lynn?

"I told them the mean old man would make snow cream for them tomorrow."

I said, "When you find a mean old man, you'd better order him to make snow cream."

***

The wolves came up our new drainage channel from the creek. The icy footing was very slick, but their claws made the trek passable. We had unknowingly solved their transportation problem. The wolves searched the areas around the houses when two humans and a large dog came out of one of the houses.

Several wolves followed the dog while the two humans opened the door to another house and let another large dog out. The two humans traveled house to house, letting more dogs and a few cats out. The pack would kill and eat tonight because the humans had cleared a path to the creek, and the wolves could drag their prey back to a safe place to eat.

Several of the dogs sniffed the air and caught the scent of dangerous animals. The fur along their back stood on end, and they began to bark aggressively. Ten wolves were watching the dogs and humans from above the snow walls down to the paths. Another 15 waited down by the houses.

Suddenly, several wolves jumped down from the top of the snow walls and attacked the dogs. The fight was fierce but shortened by the number of wolves. The struggle was quickly over. The smaller dogs didn't stand a chance. They were killed in short order, and the wolves dragged them back to their den.

Susie saw the wolves, screamed, and then yelled for Duke and Gus to come to her. She wanted to protect the two Labs.

Susie and Kate were backed into a corner in Callie's back yard just ten feet from the kitchen door. Several wolves were between them, and the door with Duke and Gus was between them and the wolves. They snarled and gnashed their teeth at the wolves. The wolves were moving in for the kill when the two German Shepherds attacked them from behind.

Susie and Kate were crying and screaming as loud as they could, but the snow walls muffled the sound.

***

We were playing cards when Ally said, "Susie and Kate should have been back by now. Zack, come with me to make sure everything is okay."

"Yes, dear."

Ally opened the door, and there was Jacob's smaller dog trying to fight off a wolf. Ally reached for her pistol and sadly found that she had failed to strap on her gun belt before leaving the house. I drew mine and shot the wolf. The others ran to the door as I yelled for them to get their guns.

"Come on, we must get to the girls. Ally, go back in and get your gun."

Mike, Ben, Paul, Callie, and I charged out the door and only got a short way from the house when wolves jumped down on us from above. They were actually after three of the dogs who had run to us for safety. We were in the middle of dogs and wolves fighting and couldn't shoot for fear of hitting one another.

I yelled, "Shoot when you have a clear shot!"

I drew my bayonet with my left hand and stabbed the nearest wolf. His head came around, and he bit my forearm as he died. Mike stabbed another, got him against the snow wall, and shot him. Ben shot another that was on top of Callie, and Paul wrestled with one on the ground until he stabbed it in the side.

I shot the nasty beast, turned, and stabbed another that had jumped down from the top of the wall. Callie shot two more, and suddenly, dead wolves were piled around us. The others headed to Callie's house. I waved towards Callie's house and yelled, "The girls, let's go!"

Several more of our clan had joined us to save the girls from the wolves. We ran towards Callie's house when we heard snarling and screaming up ahead. Mike and I were in the lead when we rounded a corner and came face to face with a large group of wolves that had the girls, and our dogs surrounded.

One German Shepherd was down but still trying to fight even with his terrible wounds. A wolf was on top of Kate. She was bravely hitting the wolf with her tiny fists. The other German Shepherd had a wolf by the throat, but two more wolves were ripping him apart from behind. Duke and Gus were blocking the wolves from getting to Susie.

The wolves saw us. They turned to attack as we approached. I started shooting when I had a clear shot and killed two. We had to kill more of these vicious beasts to get out into the open. The wolves charged, and we fought them hand to muzzle. I was ripping and stabbing while the wolves were biting all of us.

Mike emptied his magazine, and a wolf grabbed his free hand before he could reload. Paul stabbed the bastard and started shooting his 9mm into the beasts.

I looked up, saw a wolf ripping Kate's throat open, and shot him. I kept shooting until the three remaining wolves ran on out towards Mike's house. I checked Kate, found her dead, picked Suzie up, and headed back towards my house. Ben held his dead daughter and wept.

I yelled at Mike, "Kill every wolf you find."

I headed back while the rest went wolf hunting. The trail was easy to follow.

I ran into Ally on the way and handed Suzie to her as I said, "Kate didn't make it. I have to tell Ben's wife."

I walked into the kitchen, and Ben's wife saw the sorrow in my eyes and fell to her knees.

"Oh, God, no, my baby is dead."

I said, "I'm sorry. We couldn't save her."

Ally walked in, carrying Suzie, set her down at the table, and then tended to her wounds.

I thought, *Susie, is alive. Why did Kate die, and God spare Susie?*

Susie yelled to me, "Go save Gus and Duke. They saved me."

I went back and found Duke guarding Gus, who had died from his wounds. I picked Duke up and carried him back to the house. He had suffered numerous bites, but nothing life-threatening.

I tried to help Ally with Susie, but Susie just clung to her mom, and all I could do is to fetch water and keep Ally company. Joan helped me patch Duke up, and then I went back out to gather the bodies of our dead dogs. I placed them in my garage so the wolves couldn't come back and carry them off. We held a burial service for them the same day we buried Kate.

***

Paul cautioned, "Mike, slow down. The wolves are trapped by the slick ice walls. They know they're trapped and will fight to the death. They have to go through us to get out of this maze to the creek."

"Damn. Paul, you're right. Let's slow down and pick them off as we herd them toward Sam's place."

The wolves tried several times to break through and escape, but they had people shooting every time. My guys kept thinning them down until they were finally cornered at Sam's place. There were only four left, and they had drug several dead dogs with them in hopes of getting back to their pack.

Mike and Paul shot the last four wolves before they could attack. The nightmare was over for everyone except Susie. She would take months to get back to normal and was afraid of the dark for years.

***

We were very thankful that we still had antibiotic creams and capsules. Our wounds slowly healed without anyone developing a serious infection.

The weather got better, and the temperatures slowly rose until we were in the mid-forties in the daytime and barely above freezing at night.

The snow began to melt, and we had a steady stream of water all day long running from Sam's on down past my house. We had to keep an eye out for wall collapses as the snow melted. One night a wall between Callie and Mike's house fell and dammed up the drainage. We ended up with a foot of water before our guard could fire up the tractor and bust the dam open.

It got up into the fifties the following week and began raining. The water was six inches deep, flowing down the path all week long. By the end of that week, winter was over. We killed several more wolves, but none ever tried to attack us again.

Chapter 13 - State of the Union

Rolling Hills

Everyone was trying to put the wolf attack behind them as winter turned into spring. The weather was beautiful, and we were able to stay outdoors again hunting and fishing. I was fortunate to have my dog Duke help us hunt. Only a few dogs and no cats survived the attack.

We licked our wounds and were pleasantly surprised that no one got rabies from the bites. Life got back to some semblance of normal. Well, as normal as it could be in this post-apocalyptic world.

***

The President of the United States was to give the State of the Union Address to the country by radio in two hours. The problem was she didn't know if she should give the feel-good canned political speech or the one from her heart that laid out the bad with the good.

POTUS sat down with her four most trusted advisors, Jill Rayburn, her Chief of Staff, Gen John Keene, the Chairman of the Joint Chiefs, LT Colonel Roger McNabb, the Director of Homeland Security and Gen. Joe Phillips, the Secretary of State.

The president asked, "Jill, what are you hearing from your contacts about canning my cabinet and replacing most of them?"

"Our friends love the move, and our opposition hates it. There are rumblings about a power grab. As I told you yesterday, the ex-Director of Homeland Security wants your job."

Gen. Keene spoke up, "Madam President, the threat has been neutralized. The NSA had a plant in his meeting with the other traitors, and we caught them with their hands in the cookie jar. The asshole even tried to get one of the Joint Chiefs to use his command to forcibly throw you out of office and install him as interim president. The CIA took care of all of those treasonous bastards."

"Damn, a trial at this time would have been a major distraction."

Ge, Keene said, "Ma'am, thanks to the CIA, there will be no trial. A most tragic accident happened as their plane went down on the way to St. Louis. I'm deeply saddened to inform you that there were no survivors. The press will hear about their engine trouble. It's tragic, simply tragic."

The president said, "John, really, you're just so transparent you're almost giddy. Oh, well, I guess it's for the best.

Jill, please bring the new Cabinet on board, not too quickly. Take a week to get them all installed."

"Yes, ma'am. I'll have a press conference, announce the tragedy, and have you say a short prayer for the deceased and their families. Consider it done," replied a seemingly somber Chief of Staff.

Smiling, the President said, "Oh, Jill, well done."

"Yes, ma'am, I have to be convincing for the 5th estate."

POTUS said, "God help me, I'm in the hands of madmen."

Gen. Keene, please update me on the situation in Florida and California."

"I hate to keep bearing bad news, but the Cubans have landed a large contingent of soldiers outside of Miami, and the Chinese have landed over five thousand men, tanks, and artillery north of San Francisco. Both intend to carve their piece of our pie before the Russians and Mexicans take the whole country.

The Chinese are taking prisoners and starting work camps. They currently have almost no opposition. The good news from Florida is that our Naval and Marine forces have the Cubans pinned down in one area. Mop up to begin in the next 48 hours.

I'm somewhat amazed that the Chinese have such poor intelligence sources. They apparently feel the Russians are winning. We'll have them erased in a matter of weeks. Even without a significant military push, the Ruskies have no resupply train. They're toast.

However, unfortunately, as the Chinese have landed, we need to eliminate the Russians to take on their comrades. I simply cannot understand how anyone would begin such an enterprise without a plan to resupply."

POTUS said, "So, they perceive me as weak and the USA as unable to defend itself?"

"Yes, they think we are on our heels, and a couple of blows could knock us out? Our plan is to take out the Cuban command and control in Havana and most of their military with two nuclear devices. We are still developing a plan for the Chinese. I DO NOT encourage you to use Nukes on American soil. Besides, it would invite in-kind retaliation."

POTUS replied, "You have the authority to take out the Cubans as per your plan. Can you wipe out their men on our soil?"

"Yes, Ma'am. Without resupply, air, or naval support, they're doomed."

POTUS said, "Do it. I want before and after pictures to show anyone else who decides to fuck with us. Would nuclear bombs work against the Mexican Cartels inside Mexico?"

Gen. Keene replied, "No ma'am, the Cartels are spread out over too much territory."

POTUS replied, "But, you're sure about the Mexican government backing them with men, supplies, and weapons?"

Keene said, "Yes, we have definitive proof."

POTUS said, "We can't fight four or five wars. I say we get their president on the line and nuke their largest two military installations while I talk with him. I *will* nuke his sorry ass if he doesn't fall into line after the second detonation."

The Chief of Staff spoke up, "That would mean that five to six million civilians would perish."

The Director of DHS replied, "The bastards have killed thousands of Americans in Texas and Arizona. I don't feel we should back off from eliminating any and all threats. The entire Mexican power structure is in Mexico City. With their military neutralized and the command vaporized, we only have drug lords to contend with, and we will begin to take out their boss men with drone strikes. If that doesn't resolve the issue, we'll eventually have to move into Mexico to take them out."

Shocked, the Chief of Staff said, "Laura, we can't kill millions of innocent people. We're the good guys."

POTUS patted her friend on the back. "Jill, the good guys, will be overrun, and we won't have a country if we don't eliminate these threats. Gen. Keene, doesn't the military have a code word for when a base will be overrun. Isn't it something like Broken Arrow?"

Keene said, "No ma'am, a Broken Arrow is a lost nuclear weapon. We're usually a little more definitive about being overrun. It's, button-up, the fuckers are comin' through the wire, or words to that effect. If used, all available military assets must come to the base's defense."

POTUS said, "Jill, we are months, if not days from that scenario, and damned few assets to come to our rescue. John, I want a *Button-up* scenario used now for all of these known attacks on our country. Can this be done without using nukes?"

General Keene straightened in his chair and said, "Madam President, we have the mechanical resources to end the current incursions into our country, but we are beginning to run short of human assets. Basically, we need grunts."

POTUS said, "I'll prep the country to let our people know that we are under attack, and we need volunteers to fight."

Keene said, "Ma'am, don't scare them too much. I'd mention the cartels and the rogue Russian Forces, but not the Chinese."

"General, I have promised to tell our people the truth. I have pledged not to sugarcoat the national situation. If, as you say, we need grunts, we need to let them know why. I have faith in our American will, and they need to know why we need grunts. Clear."

Every attendee felt pride in their POTUS and knew she was right—no more bull shit. Tell the truth, and get the job done!

Smiling, General Keene said, "Madam President, in retrospect, I must agree. I guess we are just not yet, used to an honest politician. No, that's not exactly what I meant. I think I meant a true and honest leader of this once great nation. One that will, because of you, become great again."

"Thank you, General, but let's not put the cart before the horse. You know as well as I do that we as a nation may still dissolve."

There was no response from anyone.

***

Jacob and Sam had worked on several City dump trucks fitted with snow blades. They got them up and running in record time, but too late for the snow. Jacob and Sam also built several small generators from tiller engines and generators to light up the police station, city hall, and the hospital.

They were scrounging to find parts to get more powerful AC generators in operation. They also gave lessons on how to make bicycle generators for a single household. Callie and Paul joined in on that effort.

We changed our last names to help keep the town folk from figuring out who we were. Naturally, Callie was now Mrs. Paul Stone, and I became Mr. Zack Stone. Mike and Joan changed to Newman for their last names.

Only Jacob, Sam, Callie, and Paul mixed with the citizens. At the same time, we kept hidden away from anyone except Jake and a couple of his deputies, the mayor, and town council

508

members. There was little chance of us being outed unless a member of our inner circle ratted us out.

Every night we monitored the Short Wave Bands and other radio channels to glean any news from the rest of the world.

Some of the reports were unnerving, to say the least. We heard that we were gaining ground against the Mexicans and Russians but had new attacks by the Chinese in California and Cuba in Florida. The operators only had rumors from California and Florida. Still, it appeared our enemies were trying to carve out their own little piece of America when we were the most vulnerable.

The rumors were that these were not the old official governments but rather rogue military commanders who wanted to form their own countries at our expense.

I turned the radio off and said, "Mike, I hope the military can quickly defeat these outside attacks while we citizens handle the homegrown enemy like Prescott."

"I agree. We can't pull the military into these local fights and leave the country open to attacks."

I looked at my friends, gathered around the radio, and said, "Let's join in prayer for our country. Jacob, could you lead us?"

We all still got together to hear the President's weekly address to the country and eat popcorn while watching a recorded movie after the President's program. This was one of the few highlights of our week.

***

President's Office

The President of the United States was nervous as she drank a cup of lemon-infused tea and prepared herself to address the nation from her desk. Taking a deep breath to stabilize her pulse and heart rate, she was able to avoid the nearly overwhelming urge to run screaming back to her quarters.

She thought if General George Washington bending the knee to God in the snow of the blood-stained trail to Valley Forge had appeared calm in their hour of terror, then so would she. Like President Truman often said, "The buck stops here."

These thoughts danced through her mind as she willed herself to attain the calm needed to deliver this desperate State of the Union Address to the people of the United States of America. Contemplating her speech brought her to near tears, but tears were not what the American people would hear from their President this night. Her tears would fall later, in her quarters,...alone.

"3 - 2 - 1 – go...."

POTUS began speaking. "My fellow Americans, our country, has survived many seemingly impossible obstacles. They each threatened the fabric and existence of our Constitutional Republic, yet, we prevailed through the dogged tenacity of our people and the Grace of Almighty God. My friends, we face another such crisis that we must not fail to overcome.

The attacks of a year ago did, without question, bring this great nation to its knees. Like our nation's father, General George Washington kneeled in the blood-soaked snow of Valley Forge. We must, as did he, arise with faith in God and the American spirit, continue forward to save and preserve our new nation. This, my fellow Americans, we will do, for we are the world's bastion of freedom. We are the United States of America.

Though not as great as that of the Founding Fathers who pledged their "lives, fortunes, and sacred honor" to build this nation, our task is great. Like the phoenix of legend, we shall arise from the ashes and begin anew to rebuild this nation. As you all must, by now know, this task will be long and arduous. We have a three-front battle on our soil, which we will, in time, win. This is not idle political promise. This is a fact.

Following the final defeat of our enemies, we face many years of struggle to recover from the unprovoked and cowardly attacks on our great nation. I intentionally did not say, "Back to

510

the way it was before the attacks on our homeland." That will not happen in our lifetime.

A goal to return electricity to all in our nation, with rebuilding our grid infrastructure, is an achievable goal. The return of electric power will pave the way for a national resurgence in all areas of human endeavor. It can be done, and it shall be done.

Today, we face several significant threats to our country. Rogue military forces from the former Russian Confederation, the former Chinese military, Cuba, and drug cartels, backed by the Mexican government, have attacked us. They desire to carve out land from our country for their own needs. Cuban soldiers have landed in Miami. Our military is currently engaged in battles with these invaders, as we speak.

We cannot be tied down in large land battles and lose thousands of our brave soldiers. With Congressional approval, I instructed our military to use thermonuclear devices to neutralize the Mexican and Cuban military on their own soil.

Our military has contained both the Russian and Chinese invaders. As they no longer have a means of resupply, they'll be driven back to the coast and into the Pacific Ocean. There will be no quarter and no survivors. Our attack submarines and unimpaired surface components have decimated their fleets.

In mere hours following the assault upon our Republic, our attack submarine service proved to be more than capable of eliminating the governments of Russia, China, North Korea, and Pakistan. To the brave Americans of our Submarine Service, we owe a debt, which can never be repaid.

I wish I could tell you that our remaining resources are being utilized to rebuild the infrastructure necessary to return America to what we were before the heinous attack on our country. I can't. The world is still a dangerous place filled with those who wish us harm for whatever foolish ideas. We have put them on notice that we will use every resource in our arsenal to protect our country.

As President John F. Kennedy once said, *Ask not what your country can do for you, but what you can do for your country.* These sacred words mean more now than at any other time in our brief history as a nation.

We have the hardware to defeat those enemy forces now on American shores. Still, we desperately need volunteers to join our military, so we may more swiftly drive our enemies from our shores. I know that many of you're barely able to feed your families and have no medical care. I promise that the families of every volunteer will be housed, fed, and receive medical attention. They'll be housed at our current military bases and be protected by our military. The adults will be offered jobs in factories and farms that support our war and rebuilding efforts.

Without question, we will prevail, but without overwhelming force, the process will be slow. Therefore, my fellow citizens, in your hands will rest the final success, or failure, of our nation.

Since this country's founding, each generation of Americans has been summoned to give the ultimate sacrifice to preserve our great and exceptional nation. The graves of young Americans who answered the call to service yet surround the globe. Their ultimate sacrifice was given to secure the continuation of the United States of America.

Your Government realizes, full well, that many of you will be unable to join our military. Therefore, we ask you to assist your local law enforcement agencies to eliminate the gangs, drug pushers, and other criminals in your area.

America is down, but we still have a lot of willpower and fight left in our people.

Goodnight, and May God Bless the United States of America."

An unidentified voice added, "We will broadcast details and locations where you can meet with our recruiters.

***

Rolling Hills

512

I looked around the room and saw everyone was looking to see if anyone would say something. They were speechless.

Callie broke the ice with, "Dad, did the President just say we nuked Mexico and Cuba?"

I replied, "That's what I heard, but I'm more scared by what I didn't hear?"

Ally said, "I don't understand."

"The question is why the most powerful country in the world had to resort to nuclear weapons to deal with third-rate military powers unless there are bigger fish to fry," said Davi.

I replied, "I would guess that would be the rogue Russians and Chinese. Still, without military resupply, it's unlikely that they could be successful in the long haul. From what I heard her say, we have fought and apparently won a nuclear war. Dear God, we must have caught them with their pants down while they were dancing in the streets over the report of our demise."

Paul asked, "If the attack in Oregon is by rogue Russian military formations, why don't we just nuke them?"

I said, "We certainly don't want to nuke our own country. Killing untold numbers of civilians and poisoning the land for thousands of years, and the prevailing winds would bring radiation clouds all across the continent. God only knows how much radiation is already in the air from our earlier attacks."

Joan asked, "What about fallout? Do we need to get some Geiger Counters?"

I replied, "I don't know, but let's ask Jake to see if there are any available."

We watched our movie, ate our popcorn, but our minds were on the President's address.

I caught Mike alone after the meeting, "Mike, do we need to think about heading down to South America or Australia? I'm worried."

"I'm with you, buddy. Things must be much worse than what the president told the nation. How the hell would we get there? By boat?"

I said, "I don't know, but keep it between us for now. I don't want everyone to panic."

I left Mike's house and was walking back to my house when Davi stopped me, "Zack, the situation has to be much worse than the President is telling us.

Let's get in touch with my dad or our group in Alabama to hear what they think is happening. I believe the Chinese and Russians attacking the USA are a more significant threat than the President is letting on."

I said, "Good thinking. How do we contact your dad?"

"We must travel south and get within radio range or go to our base."

I asked, "How big a group?"

Davi said, "Two or three. Just you and I should go."

I said, "You know damn well, Ally won't let me go out alone with you."

Davi frowned, "Our lives may depend on this trip."

I said, "Let me think this through, but I agree the trip must happen quickly."

"Let's discuss tomorrow."

I replied, "Okay, but I plan to head south, with or without you in two days."

That night, as I was preparing for bed, Ally said, "Hon, the President scared us more than boosting our morale, and I can't help wondering what she held back. Are we in more danger than she indicated?"

"Ally, I hoped to avoid that question until tomorrow, but Davi, Mike, and I think there's more to the story, and we are afraid that the situation is worse than we've been told. Davi thinks her dad or the Israeli military will know the real story."

Ally asked, "How do we contact them?"

"We will send a team down to Alabama to make contact."

Ally pondered the problem. "Darling, do what you have to do? Will we have to leave the USA and seek sanctuary in another country?"

I said, "That's the question we have to ask. I invited Mike, Sally, Paul, and Davi over for breakfast in the morning. We'll eat and then send Susie out to play while we form a plan. I want to keep this close to the vest until we know what to do. Are you nervous about me traveling with Davi?"

She said, "I trust you, but I'd be lying if I said I wasn't jealous. It's my problem from that lying, cheating, rat bastard ex-husband of mine. He had affairs with most of the women I know and even hit on my mother."

I held her hand. "I won't betray you. Not ever."

"I believe you."

We finished our eggs, bacon, and biscuits then sent Susie out to visit with the Sheriff's daughter.

I started the discussion by saying, "I know the President's speech unnerved a lot of people, and I think we need to discuss it and determine what action we need to take."

Paul replied, "Well, I'm going to concentrate on killing local scumbags and not join the Army even though I'm concerned that there are much bigger security problems. The President may not be lying, but she didn't tell us all she knows."

Mike said, "I wonder if we will be safe anywhere in this country. The east coast, west coast, and southern border are all under attack. The USA used nuclear bombs for the first time in over ninety some odd years. "

I said, "Davi thinks her dad may have more detail about what's actually happening in this country than we are hearing. I think we need to visit him before we make any long-term Bug Out plans."

Everyone agreed, and then the discussion began on who would travel with Davi down to Alabama.

Mike said, "I would recommend three of us go. I also think that Zack or I stay back to lead the team. We need three good fighters to go to improve their chance of a safe return. Davi, you may have to stay with your father, which is another good reason for at least three to make the trip."

Everyone agreed that at least three would go, and then we discussed who to bring into our confidence.

Sally said, "Frankly, I'm surprised that Joan, Lynn, and Roger aren't in the conversation right now."

I interrupted and said, "I wanted to keep the meeting small to make sure nothing leaked back to Prescott. We'll bring them into the loop ASAP. The question is, who can we trust. I also was worried about Lynn being pregnant, Roger leaving, and not coming back. Perhaps I'm overthinking. Yeah, we'll get them into the next meeting."

Davi stated, "I would not go beyond those mentioned because of your experience with Bert. Everyone is trustworthy until someone threatens their family."

We all reluctantly agreed and decided to meet again that afternoon.

We added Lynn, Roger, and Joan to the meeting. While we were waiting on Mike and Sally to arrive, Lynn said, "Roger and I are worried that the USA might be a war zone for several years from what the President said. We are wondering if we should head to South America or Australia. We could be trapped between the Russians, Cubans, and Mexicans. Not to mention Prescott and the other thugs roaming the streets."

"Y'all aren't the only ones thinking like that," Ally chimed in.

Lynn replied, "My dad and uncle have large sailboats close to Mobile."

Mike and Sally joined us, and I called the meeting to order, "We will continue that discussion at the end of our meeting. I think both are related. We all heard the President's speech last night. I feel that we need to contact Davi's father and the Israeli group to get more info on the situation with the attacks on America. I'm afraid we are not hearing the entire story and don't have enough information to make a good decision."

516

Roger replied, "I would normally say we need to join the Army and fight for our country, but I think our country might be doomed, and we'd just die in vain. I'm for getting accurate facts and making a good decision, even if that means bugging out of our country."

Everyone agreed, so I moved on, "My proposal is that Paul, Davi, and I head down to Alabama to visit with Aaron. We will travel at night to avoid trouble, and it should only take three to four days to get there and the same back. Mike will be in charge during my absence."

Davi added, "Zack, please add another to our group. I may have to stay with my mom and dad."

"I'll add Ben to our team, and I think we should leave tomorrow night."

***

The explosions were racking the buildings with deadly accuracy raining fire and debris down on the men trying to protect the hydroelectric dam. The artillery fire was coming from the north while the mortar fire was raining down from the southeast.

A soldier called out. "Sir, they have several hundred men ready to flood in when they have softened us up along with several light tanks and APCs. We can't resist much longer."

Major North replied, "Thanks. Tell the men to get ready to evacuate and head to our rally point in Cherokee. We'll regroup there with the Israelis and then head on to Pickwick Dam."

Major North was in command of the US Army's program to get the TVA dams back in operation. He had a mixture of Army Corps of Engineering, infantry, and volunteer Israeli engineers and Army personnel under his command.

Major North said, "Aaron, we have to bug out. No one is coming to help us, and the best we can do is get the hell out of here and live to fight another day."

Aaron said, "Major, this is the same group that took over Owensville up in Kentucky. We need to crush them before they grow and take over the entire southeast."

517

North said, "I know, but my orders are to retreat and hold the Pickwick Dam. We don't have enough soldiers to fight 4-5 wars at one time. The Chinese nuked five of our Army bases and three naval stations this morning. Hell, they nuked the new US Capitol in Pennsylvania two hours ago. We think the President and some of our government escaped but haven't heard for sure. We retaliated by nuking all of their major military bases. The only way to stop them and the Russians are with nuclear bombs, which renders our country and their nuclear slag heaps. I'm sorry, you Israelis came here. You need to head to South America or Australia."

Aaron paused then said, "I think you're right. I'll contact my superior and make that recommendation. Come with us. You need a new home."

"Before you go, let me know your destination. I have to fetch my wife and kids. I'll try to bring my family and my men's families to join you."

"I also have to find my daughter and her new friends."

Chapter 14 - Heading South

We spent the next day cleaning and checking our weapons after loading the Bronco with enough supplies for two weeks. I loaded two plastic barrels with food, extra ammo, and winter tents and then secured them to the Bronco's roof rack. We were ready to go by noon, and I asked the team to try to get some sleep or at least some rest.

I could never sleep worth a damn during the day, but I forced myself to lie down and close my eyes around 2:00 p.m. and didn't wake up until after the sun was down. Ally woke me up by snuggling up against me. She even had socks on, so her cold feet wouldn't be a shock.

I rolled over, placed an arm around her, and kissed her. She started undressing when we heard Callie yelling.

"Dad, Ally, come here quick. The President's dead."

I threw on some clothes and joined the rest of our group huddled around the radio.

"My fellow Americans, I'm Brigadier General John Keene, Chairman of the Military Joint Chiefs. With deep sadness, I must report that our new Capitol in Pennsylvania was attacked an hour ago with a nuclear device launched by the Chinese forces in California.

Most of our government and high-ranking military officers were killed. I was on the way to the Capitol at the time of the attack and was only spared by luck.

I'm assuming authority for the USA until we can determine if any civilian leaders survived the blast. This is not a coup, and we will place the government back in civilian hands as soon as the situation allows.

I'll keep the country posted on any significant events.

May God watch over us and help us in our struggle to defeat our enemies."

Everyone started talking at once, and this was the first time that I had seen my friends panic.

I yelled to get their attention, "Hello! Hello! ... Shut the hell up!"

There was silence.

"Listen. We need to bug out for the Gulf of Mexico and figure out where we are going along the way. This place is going to be radioactive in a few days. We need to pack and leave now!"

"Zack is right. BUG OUT!" Mike yelled.

We drilled for this very situation nearly every day. Everyone was packed and ready to roll in thirty minutes except for Bert and his family. They told us that they had decided to stay with his brother and ride things out.

"Goodbye, Bert. We will miss you. I don't think we will ever be back here. We wish you well."

After some handshakes and hugs, our convoy pulled out just after the sun went down. There were nine vehicles in our convoy. The lead pickup had one of the 5.56 mm. SAWs mounted to the roof. The trailing vehicle, the Bronco, had the other SAW mounted beside a newly cut hole in its roof. The food and supply barrels had to go on a trailer.

Ally and Joan made a canvas boot for the gunner to poke his body through to keep the cold and, hopefully, rain out while keeping the warm air in. The other seven vehicles all pulled cargo trailers filled with our supplies.

We decided to take Highway 80 over to Russellville and 79 on down to Clarksville, where we planned to stop for the day. We would then work our way south to Florence the following night.

We intended to travel at night because we hoped that most of the assholes, gangs, and criminals would be asleep with only their B Teams guarding the roadblocks.

It was only about sixty miles to Clarksville, but we knew that most roads were still blocked with stalled cars and trucks. There were also roadblocks that towns and some gangs had put up.

The towns just wanted to protect themselves, while the gangs wanted to be paid a toll for traveling through their area. Of course, once in their clutches, if you had anything of value...well, no one really knew what happened because no one ever came out to relate the experience.

Rolling Hills to Florence was only a three and a half to four-hour drive before TSHTF. Now, it could be eight hours or eight days.

As expected, we spent most of our time navigating around stalled vehicles.

We made it to the east side of Russellville before we had any serious trouble. Davi, Roger, and I had the lead pickup while Mike, Paul, and Ben provided rear security as a tail gunner.

We traveled at thirty MPH with our Night Vision Glasses (NVGs) aid when Ben spotted something up ahead in the middle of the road.

I signaled for the convoy to stop and halted at the bottom of a hill. We saw it was a roadblock with at least two people manning it from the bouncing glow of their cigarettes.

Davi went ahead to scout the road ahead and was gone for thirty minutes. As planned, with her red-lensed flashlight Davi signaled for us to come down to the roadblock. We cautiously drove up to the roadblock and saw Davi sitting in a lawn chair, drinking a beer and shooting the shit with a man and woman.

"Come on over, Zack. These are great people. I traded them fifty rounds of 5.56mm for a six-pack of beer. They told me the road is clear to the south side of Clarksville. There we'll run into a crooked mayor and sheriff who work for a guy named Prescott."

I replied, "Yeah, it seems we've heard of him. Davi, we need to hit the road."

"Okay, boss."

We drove around the roadblock heading through Russellville, where we turned onto Highway 79 to Clarksville.

There were fewer cars in the middle of the road, and we could make 35 MPH. We passed through Clarksville an hour later and were making very good time towards Dickson when Davi spotted another roadblock. We were over a half-mile from the lights that she had seen.

These guys had a bonfire and huddled around it. No one appeared to be watching the road, or for that matter, getting more than a few feet from the fire.

Davi and I advanced towards the fire by staying in the bushes on the overgrown side of the road. It had been over a year since any road crews had mowed or cut down the brush on the sides of America's highways. It was relatively easy to sneak up on people sitting around a fire, not paying attention to their surroundings.

We approached within a few feet and saw eight people sitting around the fire, drinking beer, and passing a bottle of whiskey.

Davi put her finger over her mouth and indicated for me to keep quiet and listen. We crawled up close to the group and found them talking so loud we could have driven a semi up to them without being noticed.

One man was arguing, "That damn Prescott and his men are takin' all our food and extra ammo."

"But he protects us from gangs and criminals."

A woman spoke up, "We were doing fine without him. I heard he teamed up with that scum in Anderson. Hell's bells, he ain't nuthin' but a danged dictator his danged self."

"Yeah, I can't wipe my ass lessen one of his men is a telling me to just use 4 sheets.

The police chief done disappeared a week after the county sheriff done went missing'. Hell, the mayor and town council will be the nextuns to go."

"I went hunting the other day, and just as I had me a small doe sighted in, one of them damnable black Humvees came roaring up behind me.

They done scared my deer away.

Then them squirrely bastards started playing' twenty questions about why I was out hunting and did I know that I was hunting on restricted property. I was on the old Newman farm. How did it get restricted?"

"We either got to run these shitheels off or leave ourselves and all y'all know we don't have enough ammo to put up a fight."

Davi waved for me to back away and move back to our convoy with her.

We got far enough away to talk, and Davi said, "Can I take them some of our civilian ammo. They had a couple of .30/.30s and several.30 .06 rifles. I'll take them five hundred rounds, and perhaps they can wipe Prescott out or kill off a bunch of his men."

"Do it. We have a hundred thousand .556 and 9mm rounds. I doubt we'll miss those bullets."

Davi retrieved the ammo, we snuck back up to the group, and waited for the leader to break away from the others. Davi slipped up behind him and disarmed him. I thought he would have to change his shorts until I told him why we were there.

He began to smile like a pig in a manure pile when I showed him the weapons and ammo.

I said, "We are friends and have some ammunition for you.

We overheard your comments about fighting Prescott's men and brought this little treasure to you. My friend will give you some brief training on killing as many as possible without losing any of your men. Your team can take their guns and kill more of them."

Davi spoke to the man for ten minutes and then asked him the best way to get around Clarksville without running into Prescott's men. He told us, and we left.

The bad news was that we couldn't get around Clarksville without going out of our way. The least problematic route was to take Highway 12 east of Clarksville down to Ashland City and then over to Dickson before we could get back on the shortest route to Florence.

This slight detour resulted in us losing two days but probably saved our lives.

***

Undisclosed Location,

Near Owensville, Alabama

Aaron knew that his daughter, Davi, would be listening to the radio every evening for a message from him. He wanted to get close enough to Owensville for Davi to hear his message. This would save several days' travel for Davi and her friends to join Aaron's group before going to Mobile to start their own journey south.

He was driving an old truck up Highway 13 north of Savana, TN. His wife Sharon was trying the radio for the third time that evening when they heard a reply.

"Hercules, this is Athena. I can barely hear you."

"Athena, are you heading our way?"

"Yes, to your location."

"Stop, do not go there. It's not safe. I'll give you coordinates for our meet-up."

"Copy that, standing by for instructions."

'Do you have company?"

"Yes, all good guys." This was code, for had she said anything else, Aaron would know that she was being held against her will, which meant an ambush to free her.

Aaron replied, "Roger Athena, understand all good guys."

"Thank God."

Aaron pulled off the road into a stand of trees and checked his map.

"Sharon, I think we should skip the dam and head straight to Mobile."

"I agree."

"I'll call the Colonel when we get in range and let him know that we have altered the plan, crossed our line of departure, and are moving south."

Aaron unfolded his map and copied the coordinates. He then added a hundred minutes of latitude. He subtracted two hundred minutes of longitude as he and Davi had done so many times before when they wanted to keep their destination secret.

"Athena, this is Hercules, over."

"Copy Hercules, over."

"Proceed to the following coordinates."

He gave her the adjusted coordinates for their meeting place, and Davi confirmed the numbers.

"Hercules, meet you there ASAP. We have a few miles to go, but we are prepared."

"Athena, we are standing by. See you soon. Travel safely and quickly. Oh, check out the SFGC when you get to these coordinates, out."

He gave Davi a different set of coordinates and told her to stay safe.

I looked at Davi and said, "I saw you looking at the map at the Gulf."

"Yes, dad wants to meet us at Saraland, Alabama. He must have the same idea about heading to South America. They must be within fifty miles, but not in Florence. The other coordinates are for a spot southeast of the Pickwick Dam. What's SFGC?"

I looked at the map over her shoulder, saw the Shiloh Falls Golf Course, and said, "It has to be the golf course. What could be there that we need to see?"

"Maybe it's not what we need to see, but it has something we need."

Let's bring everyone up to speed before we move out tonight."

"I agree. I want to study the maps and pick the best route before we spring this on the clan."

The clan, *Davi, had said clan*. She must rightfully feel that she has indeed become a part of our extended family...*our clan*. This is a good thing.

"Let's see if anyone in the group knows the area around Mobile. Damn, I wish I could pull up Google Earth and check the area out."

"Sorry, but it may be generations before the internet is back up and running again."

"If ever."

"Yeah, if ever."

We had supper before I called everyone together to brief them and to ask their thoughts on the trip to Mobile.

I started with the update about the brief conversation with Aaron, "We heard from Aaron earlier today. He has waved us off going to Florence and told us to head to a town north of Mobile after stopping in the Pickwick Dam area. He and Davi's mom Sharon will meet us there."

Then I asked, "Has anyone traveled to Mobile from the Kentucky area?"

Lynn replied, "We always got on Highway 65 in Rolling Hills and headed down to Mobile. We got off above Mobile and headed over to Gulf Shores."

We heard the same thing from several members of our team.

Mike replied, "I'd like to avoid the big cities and Highway 65. Is there a back way from here?"

Jacob cleared his throat and said, "There's always a backroad way to get anywhere since they were here before the interstate highway system.

My family once headed to Gulf Shores but had to pick up my sister and her kid in Jackson, TN. We left Jackson, crossed the river on the bridge at Pickwick Dam, worked our way over to State Road 45, and cruised down to Mobile. There are no big towns and plenty of side roads if we have to detour."

Davi looked at her map and said, "That looks like a winner. We could have trouble on any road, but this looks like we can avoid large towns. I like it."

Lynn asked, "Davi, does your dad have a boat in Mobile or just hopes to find one?"

Davi answered, "I'm not aware of a boat, but my dad is a master sailor and could sail a dingy around the world. I trust him to get us a ship and to lead us to safety south of the border. We have several compounds set up in five different countries. I hope he wants to head to Belize.

There will be hundreds of sail and powerboats abandoned along the coast. We just need to find one large enough to could take us safely around the world."

"We need to keep an eye out for supplies on the way there. We will need food for a three-month journey, "added Davi.

Ally said, "Will it take three months to get to South America?"

I replied, "Just a minute. Belize is 1,100 miles. At six miles per hour, that's 183 hours or 8 days. Columbia is 1600 miles. At six miles per hour, that's 266 hours or 11 days. Now, that's moving 24 hours per day. That also means we didn't stop to hunt for food or water, and everything goes perfectly."

"I added plenty of safety margin to assure no one starves or dies of thirst," said Davi.

Mike said, "We have plenty of guns and bullets. We need food, water, and medical supplies. We'll check along the way to see if we can find or trade for supplies."

I added, "We also have a large quantity of gold, silver, and jewels that perhaps someone still wants."

Ally and Joan both replied at the same time, "I want jewels."

Everyone broke out laughing.

Callie came over to Ally and me and said, "Dad, I thought the South was warmer than the north. It's colder down here at night than it was in Kentucky when we left."

"Darling, we are only at the bottom of Tennessee. It will warm up when we get further south."

We settled in as the sun came up, and everyone but the two guards got some good r.e.m. sleep...exhaustion will do that for you.

***

Aaron looked at the map and said, "Dear, I think we should take a side trip over to Columbus AFB. It's only 15 miles out of the way and might have some supplies we need."

"We already have the pickup and trailer full. We will need to get another vehicle if we find anything useable."

"We need food for thirty people for two to three months. We have no idea what to expect when we arrive in South America. I plan to head to Belize first, but if it's hostile or unsuitable, we may have to travel on to our compound in Brazil or Uruguay."

"Aaron, I was actually getting used to calling Illinois home, and now once again, we have to play *'pin the tail on the donkey'* to find a new home.

Oh, well, it must be in our blood to constantly be searching for a home. It seems Jews have been on the move since we escaped the Egyptians, even before. Will we ever find our promised land and be able to hold onto it?"

Aaron's voice became sad and a bit deeper, "I wish I had the answer to that, the most ancient of questions for our people.

Remember, Sharon, life is full of tests, storms, and tests. I choose to believe that God has a plan for us that will lead us to a new reality where Jews are not considered the pariahs of the Earth.

It saddens and wounds us all that the Jewish people's accomplishments have done more, in all the sciences and arts, than any other ethnic group that has ever existed. No, I just do not know why, but there's a reason, and together we shall build a new world, free of the unwarranted hatred of our people. A new world where everyone can live in peace."

Now Sharon's voice deepened as she said, "Peace, Aaron, peace is not the human way. Conflict is the norm for our species.

We are, I believe, flawed. A flaw perhaps caused by our God's grant to us of *free will*. Peace, has there been peace since Cain and Able?"

"Sharon, we can but try. Now, please, let's return to the present and our current source of tests and storms. I love you, my dear, and *that's* the true constant in the universe."

"Aaron, you're a silly old fool. I love you, too."

Aaron, what if our compounds have been overrun or don't have enough food for additional people? Can we find an unpopulated island and live out our days in peace?"

"Dear, that's my backup plan. I have selected several islands that have little or no inhabitants as a fallback home for us.

Ah, here is the turn-off to the Air Force Base."

Sharon made the turn and headed east on Hazelwood for five miles before dropping down to Highway 50. This enabled them to get around the city of West Point and avoid the potential dangers presented by traveling through a city in broad daylight.

"Take the first left after we cross the river, and I'll give you directions for the side roads to the base. I want to get close enough to watch the place to make sure it's safe before we enter."

Thirty minutes later, they were in front of the deserted main administrative building. Columbus AFB was a flight training center and didn't have any fighters or bombers. They could see numerous A 6 Texan propeller planes and small passenger jets parked by the runways, but no human activity. Still, the houses around the base did seem to have a few families living in them.

"Let's wait for dark and walk in from here to search for any supplies. We will concentrate on the two warehouses, maintenance buildings, and those semi-trailers. I'll bring bolt cutters. You bring our tool bag just in case we have to force some doors open."

Three hours later, it was dark, and they walked onto the base. The warehouses had been ransacked and had nothing of value in them. The maintenance buildings had also been searched and burned.

They moved on to a building housing a dining facility and found the cupboards bare. They found a few pickups and Humvees that would run along with semi-trailers but no food, ammo, or weapons.

"Let's check out the trailers and then head on south."

As they moved closer to the trailers, they noticed several had been forced open. Aaron opened the door to the first one and found crates of airplane engine parts. The next one contained hazmat suits, chemical and biological contamination cleanup gear, and signs stating, "Hazardous Material."

"Dear, let's open every other one that hasn't been opened. Maybe the others gave up too soon."

"Yes, it's worth a try. Keep an eye out for intruders. I caught a flash of light from one of the houses as you were speaking. I think someone is watching us. If we find something we need, don't react. Slam the door in disgust to mislead them."

The third and fifth trailers had MREs and supplies for the mess hall. There was enough food to feed their people for months. The rest of the trailers had office supplies, maintenance parts, and uniforms.

Sharon asked, "Aaron, how do we load these boxes without anyone noticing? Even the good guys will want a share of the food. They may claim squatter's rights and try to take all of our treasure."

"Dear, I have a brilliant idea. Let's check out the three semi-trucks by the maintenance building."

Sharon's head suddenly turned toward Aaron, "What, you're going to hitch up to one of them and drive out like you own the place."

"Yes. I'll drop you off at our truck, and we'll drive until we can find another pickup and trailer so we can head on to Mobile."

Sharon said, "Why not just drive the semi on down to Mobile?"

"It would attract attention, but maybe we can use that to our advantage. I have a weird but excellent idea. Open the next trailer, search it and slam the door and we'll leave here and go check out the semis."

***

A guard said, "Sam, a man, and a woman are over at the base, searching the buildings and trailers."

Aman replied, "There's nothing there. Did they take anything?"

"No, they were pissed when they found the same crap we found when we opened three of the trailers. They left a few minutes ago."

The man said, "If they come back, shoot the man and see if the woman is a keeper."

The guard replied, "They looked like old farts. The woman is old but still attractive."

"Okay, shoot both of them."

***

The Clan

Near Pickwick Dam

We broke camp at dusk and headed over to the Pickwick Dam, which was over 125 miles by the twisting turning back roads. Even though the trip was uneventful, it took over six hours to get to the dam and cross over to the south side.

We noted numerous temporary Army buildings, tents, and broken-down vehicles as we headed south towards the golf course. We also saw a small city of large tents surrounding an old US Post Office. We pulled off the road into the tent area and found they had just been abandoned.

531

The mess hall tent still had plates on the table with food that had not rotted. We found bags of oranges, potatoes, onions, and flour, which we piled into our trailers. There were cots, office equipment, clothes, blankets, and tons of general, albeit useless items that couldn't be shot or eaten.

"The Army bugged out and didn't take the time to pack. We better make like a keeper of sheep and get the flock out of here before we find out what scared them so much."

We hauled ass on down the road about a mile and saw the entrance to the golf course. This area, too, had been abandoned.

I started to question Aaron's sanity when I saw tracks on the side of the road from a tracked vehicle like a tank. I followed the tracks until we were almost to Pickwick Lake. We stopped suddenly when I drove around a bend and saw a parking lot full of military vehicles.

***

Army Bivouac

Golf Course

Forrest Hogg begged the soldiers to take his children and him with them when the orders for bugging out were given. The Captain told the man that he was sorry, but they couldn't take any civilians. He did tell Forrest that they were leaving plenty of food, water, and several vehicles that Forrest could have. Forrest had three kids, two girls and a boy, who ranged in age from three to ten that he had to protect and feed.

Forrest's wife had been killed during a home invasion a few months after the lights went out. He was away looking for food and antibiotics for his youngest child when the bastards attacked. His wife saw them in the street and hid the kids in a yard barn in the backyard. She made the mistake of leaving the yard barn to pick up a doll that the youngest girl had dropped. One of the gang members saw her and dragged her back into the house. The three men took turns with her. They killed her when she told them there were no drugs or alcohol in the place.

He came home that afternoon to find his dead wife covered with a blanket and his three children crying on the couch.

Forrest Hogg taught Biology and was the assistant football coach at Corinth High School before the lights went out.

He had begun prepping a couple of years before and felt the urge to do more, but his wife didn't want any guns in the house. She also thought prepping scared the kids.

His plan had been to bug out to the north end of Pickwick Lake if TSHTF and things got rough in the town.

He was angry with himself because he waited too late to bug out. His most profound guilt ate at him because he couldn't kill the men who had done this to his wife.

He tried to keep his kids in their home, but a gang had recently arrived and had taken over the area. There was gunfire every day. The last straw was when one of his neighbors was killed because he wouldn't give the gang his old truck. That's when Forrest decided to move to a more secure and secluded location.

He made a two-wheeled cart from a bicycle and lumber he scavenged from Lowes. The cart was sturdy enough to haul their food, a tent, and extra clothing.

He could also haul one of the smaller kids if he had to give them a rest along the way. It was only 18 miles to Counce, Ms., and another three miles to the lake. A railroad track ran between Corinth and Counce that avoided the populated areas. It was only a few hundred feet from his house, and they could take it to just south of Counce and then travel cross-country to the lake.

The trip was much rougher than he thought it would be. The kids needed to rest or pee every thirty minutes. The trip was only 21 miles but took four days.

The big surprise was the significant military presence. They had a small hospital tent, took good care of the kids, and gave them plenty to eat. Forrest thought their worries were over until the night he heard the orders for the Army to bug out. Forrest tried to go with them, but they told him not to follow the convoy.

He picked through the massive amount of gear and supplies that were abandoned to find something to help his family survive.

Forrest loaded one of the military pickups with food, two tents, cots, blankets, and anything else he thought they might need. Early the following day, he drove through the golf course to head to the marina in the inlet that he and his father had fished when he was a boy. He knew there were cottages and boats there, and they would live in one of the abandoned cottages.

He drove to the marina, and as he turned right into the parking lot, the truck's lights shone on numerous military vehicles parked everywhere. There were tanks, trucks, Humvees, pickups, and heavy-duty semis and trailers. He had stumbled into an abandoned supply depot.

He drove up to the marina's office and told the kids to stay in the truck.

"Son, keep the girls in the truck while I go in and make sure that no one is here. Honk the horn if anyone approaches."

"Daddy, don't leave us."

"Son, I have to see if we can make this our home. Be brave."

Chapter 15 - Christmas Presents

The Marina

I backed the truck up and signaled to the others to hide their vehicles. "There's a pickup in front of the main building, and I see movement in the cab."

It was almost daylight, and I pulled out my field glasses to see what was going on in the truck.

"Damn, it looks like a truckload of small children. Scan the area for any people or movement, and then we'll sneak in and see what's going on here.

Davi, I see why your dad sent us here. There's a shit load of military equipment, and I'll bet the buildings are full of supplies."

There was no movement except the kids in the truck, so I sent Joan, Ally, and Roger to check out the kids while Davi, Sam, and Ben went to check out the vehicles in the parking lot. Paul, Callie, and I headed to the main office while Mike and the others guarded our vehicles.

Joan followed Ally and Roger into the woods to get closer to the pickup without being seen. They stopped before exiting the woods and saw three children playing in the parking lot beside the truck. They kept the end of the truck between them and the kids as they closed the fifty feet to the truck.

Joan handed her rifle to Roger, walked around the truck, and said, "Hello, I'm Joan. Is your mommy or daddy here?

The oldest boy tried to open the door of the truck, but Joan blocked his way.

"My dad told me to honk the horn if I saw any strangers."

Ally said, "We're not going to hurt you. We want to be your friends."

The boy looked up at her and said, "I'll bet all of the bad people say that before they kill you."

Joan replied, "We're both mommies and would never hurt little children. I have a girl, and Ally has a boy and a girl."

"Can we play with them?"

Joan replied, "Yes, let's find your daddy and mommy, and then you can play."

"Our daddy is in that boat building. Some bad men killed our mommy."

Joan fought through the tears and said, "I'm sorry. I know she's in heaven, watching over y'all."

We peered through several windows but couldn't see anyone in the main building. I sent Paul and Callie around to the back entrance while I entered through the front door.

I heard some noise coming from the right side of the building and slowly traveled that way. I listened to a sound that I hadn't heard in a while. My mouth started watering as I heard another "pop" and then a "fizz."

I was almost to the end of the building when I heard, "My God, that was good. Even hot beer beats no beer."

I poked my head around the corner, saw a man about my age, and build sitting on a table surrounded by beer cans and bags of potato chips. He had an ax on his lap but no gun.

I started to speak when he said to himself, "Crap, I forgot the kids."

He got up, turned, and saw me with a rifle pointed at him.

"I'm sorry. I was hungry and saw the beer. I would never steal and thought this was abandoned."

I replied, "Put the ax down and let's talk. I don't want to hurt you and won't as long as you behave. What are you doing in this army depot?"

"When the Army bugged out, I came this way to find a cabin and live there until the lights come back on. I just stumbled on this massive cache of supplies. Mister, my kids are outside and probably got scared. Can we go to them?"

I said, "Of course. My wife and another woman are out there, and they're very good with children."

We escorted him outside, and all three kids ran to him as soon as he came around the front of the pickup. He hugged them and apologized for being gone so long.

I said, "Roger, have the team pull down here, and we'll camp here for the night.

I'll bet you and the kids haven't had a home-cooked meal in a long time. We'll have dinner and get to know each other. I'm Zack Johnson."

We introduced ourselves, and while we exchanged stories, Davi, Mike, and Jacob inspected the vehicles. At the same time, Roger, Paul, and Lynn searched through the building to see what supplies had been abandoned.

We slept in shifts, splitting our awake time on guard duty or loading the trailers with supplies. Jacob and Sam hitched cargo trailers to two of the Humvees, and everyone helped load them with supplies, food, and ammo. Roger got a Humvee and hooked one of the fuel trailers to it.

Late in the day, I asked, "Forrest, did the Army say why they left in a hurry?"

"No, the captain just said that they were leaving and that I should take one of their vehicles, load it up with food and get out of here quickly."

That worried me, and I said, "When did the captain say this?"

"Yesterday, about noon, as they were leaving. He was very concerned. Actually, he seemed almost scared."

I thought, *Oh shit*, and yelled for the team to join us. "Gather around. Forrest tells me that the Army bugged out yesterday, and the captain warned him to get away from here quickly."

Davi said, "Oh shit, and he waited to tell us that little tidbit of info until now? We have to gather supplies and bug out also."

"I agree. We could be under attack at any moment. Load your vehicles up to the brim with food, water, and ammo. We are leaving here in one hour."

I caught Forrest and said, "Y'all are welcome to come with us. We are heading away from here and looking for a safe place to live away from all this turmoil."

"I think we'll just move on down to the bottom of the lake away from whatever is heading this way. I want to set up a home as quickly as possible for my kids."

I replied, "Okay, but get out of here quickly."

"I'll leave with you and follow you for a while before I split off back to the lake. I'll head south on 25 and take a back road over to the bottom of the lake."

I said, "We'll split off on Highway 365 and head southwest.

I thought about the man's ax. "Oh, by the way, we have some extra guns, and I'd like to leave a pistol and rifle with you."

"I'd like that."

I said, "Come on over to my truck."

We walked over to my pickup, and I handed him a Springfield M&P15 and a Ruger 9mm plus seven magazines for each weapon plus a hundred rounds for each. I showed him how to operate the M&P15. He was familiar with the Ruger.

"Thanks for the home cooking and the guns. I never was a gun nut, but these days a gun can come in very handy. I guess I need to go steal my kids away from Joan."

Laughing, I said, "Yes, she likes little kids."

"They like her a lot. Is she married?"

I chuckled, "No, she's my ex-wife, and her boyfriend was killed a few months back. She loves kids. You need to get to know her. Kids need a mom."

He said, "Well, it doesn't matter. I won't see her again."

He shook my hand and said, "I'll fall in line behind your vehicles and peel off at my turn. Good luck."

"Good luck to you and your kids."

He headed over to the far left end of the main building, where Joan played with the children.

I heard footsteps behind me, and then Ally said, "He seems like a great guy. He and Joan would be a nice couple. She loves his kids."

"I suggested that he stay and get to...." I had said before I was cut off by gunfire from the direction Forrest had just gone.

I yelled, "Grab your guns! We're under attack!"

Several of us ran towards the gunfire while scanning ahead for intruders. There were two more shots, then silence. We got to the end of the building and saw the kids crying. Joan was holding Forrest's head in her lap. He was covered in blood from a wound on his head and another on his left arm. There were three dead strangers dressed in black BDUs lying on the ground twenty yards away.

I asked, "Joan, what happened?"

She replied, "I was saying goodbye to the kids when we were attacked. One just missed me when Forrest started shooting. He killed the first one, and I shot the second as he jumped between the third asshole and me. Forrest killed him as he fell to the ground."

Joan said, "Callie, please take the kids while we tend to their father."

I said, "Thank God he was here, and I just gave him the guns and a quick lesson on how to use them."

Joan held his head in her lap. "You know he was one of those gun control people before the lights went out."

I snickered, "I think he just joined the NRA."

The head wound was just a graze that bled profusely and knocked him out. The arm wound was a through-and-through. Joan and Lynn bandaged the wounds and kept the pressure on them while we loaded him into the bed of one of the pickups.

Joan then applied WoundSeal to control the bleeding. She got in to tend to him while we bugged out. We grabbed the attacker's guns, ammo, ID papers and hit the road at high speed. We got on Highway 25, headed down to our turn, and kept moving as fast we could around the stalled cars.

We traveled the forty miles to Highway 45 in a little less than two hours and kept heading south. The ride was getting monotonous as we weaved around the stalled cars and watched for ambushes.

'Boredom with a chance of sheer terror' is the phrase we coined for driving along the highways of the USA. It was still daylight, and I felt very uncomfortable driving while everyone along the road was up and moving around. Thank God there were fewer stalled cars out on the open road.

We stopped at 1:00 am for lunch and bathroom breaks. As usual, it was a cold meal of meat, crackers, and canned fruit.

Joan opened the conversation by asking, "What do we do with Forrest? He wanted to stay by the lake, and here we are a hundred miles from there."

Mike replied, "We can't stop and wait for him to recover enough to take care of his kids, and we can't just dump them on the side of the road.

Joan is taking good care of him and certainly seems to becoming attached to the children. I say we just have to deal with him when he gets better."

The moon was bright as I looked around at the faces and said, "Look, if we hadn't been there, he would have had to deal with those men by himself. They could have killed him and left the kids to die. Joan, how is he doing?"

She replied, "He'll have one hell of a headache when he wakes up, and he won't be using his arm for a while, but all in all, he's doing okay. I'll be worried if he doesn't wake up by tomorrow afternoon. I agree on taking them with us."

We stopped before sunrise at an abandoned farm supply store on Highway 8 just off 45 for the night. There were no lights on in any of the houses, and we always had guards, so it should be another calm night.

Davi told me that her dad had contacted her, and both exchanged statements that all was going well, and so far, everyone was safe.

Aaron asked if we had found any groceries along the way, and Davi replied that we had seen some, but a bear ran us off before we could get our fill.

I shook my head. "Davi, I guess it gets kinda weird talking to your dad in code words."

"Well, it used to be, but not so much now. Of course, we do have to change call signs regularly to help make sure no one is trying to pinpoint our position. Dad and mom change up talking, and I use Ben to rotate up with me. I know how vital the secrecy is, so I don't mind."

I said, "Well, I want to thank you for all your help. Most of us would be dead or slaves by now if we hadn't met you."

She smiled. "Thanks. That's what friends are for."

Ally and I settled on top of our sleeping bags with mosquito netting above us. The further south we traveled, the more the annoying little bastards tried to make blood withdrawals. The nets worked while we slept, but I wondered what we would do in South America when the insect repellent wore off.

"Darling, I was just wondering about our trip south and the diseases that we could encounter."

I rolled over towards her and said, "Yes, we won't have drugs for malaria, typhus, or a dozen other diseases. Scares the crap out of me."

"Zack, even if we stayed in the USA, all drugs will eventually run past their usable lives. I wonder how far back this will set mankind."

"I'm not sure how the rest of the world was affected. South America could be untouched."

"I think that would be great, but will they want a flood of Americans, Canadians, and Mexicans flooding into their countries?"

"I guess we'll find out in a few months."

I was thinking about a most uncomfortable life in a Brazilian jungle when I fell asleep."

***

I awoke to a gunshot and heard, "Dad, wake up," being yelled at me.

My eyes opened, and I saw Callie standing over me.

"Dad, someone tried to steal some of our food and supplies."

I bolted upright, wiped the sleep from my eyes, and said, "What happened," as I buckled my holster and grabbed my AR, Ally jumped out of bed and joined us.

"Some kids distracted us while someone tried to steal from the trailers. The kids were working too hard to get my attention, so I turned away and caught a glimpse of someone by one of our trailers. I asked Jacob to watch the kids while I checked on the trailers. The man saw me coming and pointed a pistol at me. I shot him."

Ally asked, "What happened to the kids?"

"Jacob caught the smallest two, but the larger two ran into the woods."

"Ben, Joan, and Callie, check the trailers to see what's missing."

I walked over to where Jacob had the two small kids corralled and found a small boy and girl. They couldn't be more than five years old. "Jacob, it looks like you caught some master thieves."

The boy replied, "We ain't no thieves. Joe said we wuz just collecting taxes from people traveling on our road."

I snorted, "The road belongs to you."

"No, Joe said it belongs to him."

I asked, "Is he your dad?"

The boy said, "No. He found us when some bad people killed our mom and papa. We work for him collecting taxes."

I asked, "What happened to the bad people?"

"We never saw them. Joe said he run 'em off. We were sleepin' when they killed our folks."

"Are the other two kids, your brother and sister?"

"No. They were with Joe when he saved us. The girl is Joe's wife, and the boy is her brother."

Ben returned and said, "They only took a few packages of food. They dropped most of what they were stealing when Jacob and Callie surprised them."

I said, "At least we can be thankful that they weren't very talented thieves."

I caught Callie off to the side and asked, "How old were the other kids?"

"Dad, the boy, was maybe 15, and the girl was 12 or 13. I heard what the little boy said. That asshole is a pedophile. We need to shoot him again, maybe 'bout ten more times. He has probably scarred that poor girl for the rest of her life."

I walked back to the kids and asked, "Can you find your house where you stayed with the man, Joe?"

"Yes, sir, it's the next house on the left down that way."

I hoped that we could catch the two teenagers and help them recover their lives, so I picked up my rifle and waved at Davi, Roger, Ben, and Paul to follow me to the house. We got closer to the house, but we were too late. There were taillights a half-mile down the road, and we could hear the engine roar as they drove away.

"They're gone, but let's check the house for other kids and maybe find what they stole from us."

We carefully entered the house and cleared each room and the garage. There was nothing of value, but we saw signs that they had been living there for some time.

"Zack, the bastards are living like pigs. This guy was a filthy sumbitch."

"Okay, there's nothing we can do here. Let's go back to the camp."

We walked into the camp and saw Ally and Callie watching the two kids sleep. Ally told us they were brother and sister, and their names were Johnny and Karen Swope. They're from Citronelle, Alabama. Their family was heading north to live with their uncle in Meridian when the bad guys killed their mom and papa.

The little girl's head was in Ally's lap, and she was stroking the girl's hair.

Ally said, "These two will be okay. They never knew they were breaking the law and harming people. We can help them through this, and they'll become good adults."

I bit my lip and said, "We'll check with a few people in Meridian as we pass through to see if anyone knows their uncle, but it will be lucky if we find him. Perhaps we can find a good home for the kids along the way to Mobile."

Ally replied, "What if we can't find good homes for the kids?"

I replied, "We have picked up one wounded man and five children this week. We simply can't keep saving everyone in this screwed-up world. We have to save ourselves before we can save anyone else."

"You're not proposing that we drop these kids off with the first people we see. Are you?"

I saw the look in Ally's eyes and replied, "Of course not, but we can't keep adding children, or adults, to a boat that we don't even know the size of."

"We can take two boats."

Damn, she had me there, so I replied, "We need to find more food on the way, or these kids will starve on the trip to South America."

Ally kidded me, "We need to find some ocean fishing gear. I heard the Gulf of Mexico has some fish."

I could only choke down my usual smart assed reply and said, "Yes, dear, great idea."

***

Air Force Base

Aaron and his wife checked out the military semis, and none would start. The batteries were dead, and there was no way to recharge them. He walked back to their truck and drove it over to where the semis were parked. He tried to jump-start one from the truck's battery, but the truck's starter only clicked. He disconnected the trailer. Sharon checked each semi and discovered that every single one was an automatic shift...no push start.

"Sharon, let's hook the jumper cables up to the semi and charge the batteries with our truck. It will take a while, but I'm sure it will work."

While the batteries were being charged, they filled up the fuel tanks, five gallons at a time, from the fuel depot.

After several hours, Aaron tried to start the semi, and it cranked over a couple of times and then started.

He drove the semi, and Sharon followed in their truck. As much as they hated the MREs, it still made sense to take them since they had years left on their shelf life and were much lighter than the can goods.

Aaron said, "I'll back up to the trailer, and you be prepared to jack up the dolly wheels after the truck and trailer are hooked up. Keep your rifle handy in case someone gets nosy. We'll both get the gear we need from the Hazmat trailer, load it up and drive away. The whole operation should only take ten minutes."

Sharon nodded, "I'll follow you until we find a place to load our supplies and gear into the trailer."

"Let's do it."

Aaron drove straight over to the trailer parking lot and right up to the trailers, with Sharon following. He started backing up to the trailer they wanted. He backed under the trailer, climbed out of the cab, locked the trailer to the semi, and hooked up the air brake hoses.

Aaron called out, "Lights came on in a couple of houses. We have someone's interest. Let's hurry."

They opened the Hazmat trailer and quickly grabbed the hazmat suits, decontamination equipment, and signs. They loaded them onto the back of their trailer and promptly drove off.

Sharon followed him down Highway 373 over to Highway 50. They pulled off the road and into a deserted barn they had found earlier that day. This allowed them to hide while they transferred their goods and prepared the semi for the remainder of their trip.

"Sharon, pull guard duty for an hour or so to make sure no one followed us."

"Sure, I was heading outside in a minute anyway."

Sharon left the barn, walked up to the road, and immediately saw lights heading their way. The vehicle turned off the road about a half-mile away and then, a few minutes later, headed her way again only to pull off the road again.

She ran into the barn and said, "There's a vehicle about a quarter-mile east of here, and they appear to be searching for us."

"Well, we'll just have to make them sorry they made that decision."

He grabbed his M4 and several extra magazines, then followed his wife out to the road. "If they turn into the barn, kill them all."

She replied, "It's a shame they followed us. They could be sleeping instead of dying."

The truck slowed and turned into the driveway to the barn and house. It moved very slow, then stopped in front of the barn, and two men got out. They were armed with shotguns and pistols. There was no cover, so Aaron knew he had to shoot them. He aimed the M4, squeezed the trigger, and the closest man fell to the ground. He heard Sharon's gun bark, and the other man died as he fell. They dragged the bodies into the barn, and Aaron parked their truck in the barn.

Aaron chuckled, "I have an idea for these bodies. We will take them with us."

Sharon's face puckered. "Damn, are you thinking what I'm thinking?"

He said, "Yes, I'm going to make small burns on their faces, and they'll be our quarantined sick patients."

Sharon winced, "Great idea. A bit macabre, but it should be effective. Let's transfer our gear and supplies quickly. The locals heard those gunshots, and we don't need more company. You move the supplies while I prepare the semi and trailer."

It took over two hours for Aaron to transfer their supplies to the trailer. He even had to secure a large part of it to the top of the trailer because he ran out of space.

Sharon finished her work, attaching signs on the trailer before Aaron finished moving the supplies. Hence, she helped him finish his task. They left their pickup in the barn and drove the semi south on back roads until they cleared the city of West Point and headed south on Highway 45.

Sharon grinned, "Darling, do you think I might have overdone it with the biological hazard signs on the semi and trailer?"

He replied, "You sure are scaring the hell out of everyone manning the roadblocks. The last man nearly crapped his pants when you stepped down from the truck in the full hazmat suit and offered to show him the patients in the back of the truck."

★

Chapter 16 - The Boat

Safe House

Bayou La Batre, Louisiana

They drove night and day straight to Mobile, only stopping for restroom breaks and to get diesel fuel at an abandoned truck stop.

There was only one narrow escape at Meridian when an over-eager policeman ordered them to open the back of the semi to see the patients. Sharon told him that Ebola was tough to treat, and he ran off like a little girl when he saw the two bodies.

Upon arriving at Bayou La Batre, they immediately scared the few locals out of eight of their nine lives.

Aaron led the way to their safe house and drove the semi into a warehouse on a nearby property. Initially, the place appeared to be deserted, but a man walked out of a house down the street and waved at them. "Mort, oh, my God, it's good to see you. Where's everyone?"

Aaron's old friend, Mort, replied, "I'm glad to see you too, Aaron. They all flew out of here two days ago, headed for Uruguay.

The fact is that we didn't have enough planes for everyone. People kept adding people who were friends of friends. We're leaving as soon as possible. The U.S. is being invaded, and it sure looks like Mobile is offloading troops and supplies."

Aaron asked, "Why did you stay behind?"

He said, "Someone had to. I sure as hell hope you're still a champion sailor?"

Aaron said, "I'm sure I can still hold my own on a sailboat."

"Good. See that mast sticking up above the houses?"

Aaron nodded, "Yes."

"Well, you're sailing it to South America while I follow you in a motor yacht."

Aaron asked, "How big is the sailboat?"

Mort said, "It's a Beneteau 62 that we have added extra fuel tanks for the iron sail and extra water tanks."

"How much horsepower is the auxiliary engine?" Aaron asked.

He answered, "165 HP, you can cruise a long way on 365 gallons of diesel when the wind is calm."

Aaron asked, "How many people do you have here that need to go with us?"

"There are ten of us poor Jews left here that are searchin' for a new home."

Smiling now, Aaron looked at Sharon and said, "We'll join you in that search."

Mort laughed and asked, "When will your group arrive?"

"They should arrive tomorrow night."

"Aaron, that's cutting it very close. Boats are already landing in Mobile. If one warship strays over here, we could all be captured or killed."

Aaron snorted, "I can't leave my friends."

"Ok, ok, I get it, but we'll have to sneak out of here at night. Don't be such a mensch. I see you drove up in a semi with Hazardous Biological markings on it. I'm guessing that's how you managed to deliver a 53-foot trailer filled with food to Bayou La Batre without being robbed."

Sharon laughed, "Yes, it scared the crap out of the gangs and police."

Most smiled, "Perhaps we may have to tow a barge to take all of the food."

Aaron replied, "Sorry, my friend, but most of it's MREs that we liberated from an American air force base. So calling it food is a bit of a stretch. One of my friends arriving tomorrow told me that the letters M. R. E. really stand for Meals Rejected by Ethiopia. Oh well, what the hell? They do fill the void."

Mort winced, "A hungry belly will grow to appreciate MREs."

Aaron sighed knowingly, "Let's see the boats and start loading so we can leave as soon as our friends arrive."

Mort introduced them to the rest of the group before they started loading. There were eight adults and five children. All but two of the adults and one child were Israelis. The three had lived next to Mort, and he couldn't leave them here.

Aaron made a mental note that there were sixteen people here now and thirty arriving soon. He would ask Davi how large her flock was. They might need another boat.

***

Aaron called for Davi, "Angel, what's your ETA, and how large is your flock?"

"Soonest, sixteen hours with twenty-four sheep."

Aaron said, "I have new coordinates."

Davi checked her map and replied, "Add twenty minutes to that ETA."

"Angel, speed it up. You may be arriving in a hot LZ. The wolves are close. Come in prepared, but as fast as possible. Be ready to depart this location as soon as you transfer your gear."

Davi said, "We're always ready."

The motor yacht was an older eighty-footer with twin diesels stripped of anything unnecessary to get them a thousand miles to their new home. Beds, couches, and game tables were tossed for cots and sleeping bags. Food, other supplies, and drums of fuel were stored on the open deck. The boat was ready to head out at a moment's notice.

The Beneteau was the most beautiful sailboat that Aaron had ever seen, even with the cabins and lounge area stripped out to make room for cots and supplies. The once beautiful sailing ship now looked more like cargo ships on the inside. Aaron was reminded of the Queen Elizabeth after being converted from a luxury liner to a troop transport in 1942.

They spent the day loading the boats with supplies from the trailer and mounting two SAWs and two caliber .50 MGs on each boat. The .556 SAWs were stored on the deck but had mounts on the rails so that they could be brought to bear quickly. The .50 caliber MGs had mounts on the front decks, and they covered them with tarps. Mort and Aaron stored two Stinger missiles and five LAWs on each boat in case they needed heavier firepower. Mort placed several Russian RPG 9's below deck in reserve.

The boats had no armor but could unleash hell on anyone trying to screw with them. They weren't worried about military, naval ships attacking them once they got out of port, but pirates may be a huge concern.

Aaron asked, "Mort, has there been any pirate activity around Mobile?"

"Yes, they began rearing their ugly heads shortly after the Navy and Coast Guard pulled out and headed to Florida to help fight the Cuban invasion. The first radio report of piracy came only a few days later. We heard distress calls from a boat under attack. It was off the coast by Pascagoula when the calls went silent. There have been several boats and a few large ships attacked since then."

Aaron said, "That's my most significant fear once we head out to the sea. I know we can make the trip without any major

552

issues, barring a hurricane, of course, but we must be prepared for Peg Leg Pete trying to take our boat."

Mort said, "It's worse than that. Some of the pirates want slaves and women to sell in Mexico. It's getting to be a large business."

***

On the road to

Bayou La Batre, Louisiana

We made good time, except for deciding to skirt around Tupelo and Meridian. I didn't want to take a chance on facing a gang in a gunfight trapped between buildings and barricades.

We were still traveling at night, so we didn't meet many people except at roadblocks, and most of them were just like us, trying to survive.

A few asked us for food and other supplies. We had to turn them down. All but a few just waved as we left, but a couple of groups demanded that we share our food with them.

I had to shoot one group leader between the eyes, and Davi fired a burst from the SAW over the heads. This tended to calm them down. People were starving and didn't care that it was our food. They just needed it, but so did we.

Most of these were filthy and didn't try to feed themselves. They were used to feeding off the government teat. They simply could not fathom the concept that Uncle Sam died in the last nuclear attack in Pennsylvania, or perhaps he passed away a year ago.

It was dark when we finally arrived in the area around Mobile.

Davi and I looked at the map during our last restroom break, decided to get off Highway 45, work our way to the west of Mobile Regional Airport, and then down to Bayou La Batre. We turned south on Highway 25 and cruised along when we saw lights up ahead at the Highway 70 crossing.

I signaled the column to stop, and Davi and I walked up the side of the road towards what appeared to be a roadblock. Our luck had run out on good old boys manning roadblocks.

This was a professional crew dressed in black Battle Dress Uniforms, BDUs with body armor, and Humvees with turret-mounted SAWs. We scurried back to our convoy and backtracked to the next turn west. We had to cut through subdivisions and a few dirt roads before finding a road heading south again.

Unfortunately, there we found another roadblock manned by the same type of troops.

Davi said, "Those men are guarding all access to the airport. We either have to go out of our way or run their roadblock."

"I don't want to risk a fight with the kids in the trucks. Let's try to go further west."

We turned around, drove down a road heading west, and came to a dead end.

"We either have to cut across country or head back north to get around Big Creek Lake."

"Let's cut across to the next street heading south."

We drove through a thinly wooded area, crossed a small creek, and found an opening between two houses to get to the next street heading south. Just as we pulled onto the street, I saw a Humvee parked at the house across the street. The lights came on in the place, and a man ran out with a rifle. He walked toward us, and I saw that he had the black BDUs and an M4 pointing at us.

Davi slipped out the passenger side, drew a bead on the bastard, and shot him in the head. Before he fell to the ground, lights came on in all of the houses around us, and armed men came running out, shooting at us as we sped south.

I looked in the mirror and said, "I think we just crashed the neighborhood of the local militia."

"Those assholes were dressed like Prescott's men. I wonder..........."

Davi had to start shooting since we were taking fire from both sides and behind us. Everyone was firing back, and both SAWs were effectively slowing the enemy fire. We had stepped into a hornet's nest.

"Get the fuck out of here. Hit the gas."

We hit the end of the block, and the firing stopped from the sides. Only a few shots were coming in from behind. I floored my truck and got the hell out of Dodge when Ben radioed that we were being followed.

Davi yelled, "We can't let these assholes follow us to the Gulf. We have to stop them now. Keep driving while I grab some LAWS. I'll have Mike and Roger do the same.

I want you to pull behind a barn or house after I tell them the plan. We are going to put an end to this shit, then hurry the hell up to our awaiting Ark. Now, I'm pissed, and I've had enough of people shooting at me!"

"Call them now."

Davi gave them the plan while I searched ahead for something to hide behind when we ambushed these bastards. I saw several semi-trailers parked beside a couple of small buildings. I drove between them, stopping behind the closest building. "Joan, Ally, take Sam and Jacob's wives and the children behind the other building and hide there until this thing is over."

Joan asked, "What about Forrest?"

"Sorry. Leave him where he is. We don't have time to move him."

We positioned the two vehicles with the SAWs so they had a good field of fire. I sent Jacob and Sam to our flanks with the other two SAWS. The rest of us took LAWs rockets for the Humvees charging at us.

We could hear the enemy vehicles approaching. They came around a curve and Davi, and Roger fired simultaneously, and an instant later, two Humvees exploded. Ben, Mike, and I fired ours, and two more exploded. Mike missed his target, and it backed up behind a truck.

Mike was pinned down behind a truck in a crossfire by several of the enemy, now in infantry mode, and couldn't rise high enough to get into position for accurate return fire. One figured out he couldn't hit Mike directly and started firing at a brick retaining wall behind him. Bits of brick peppered Mike from behind, along with the risk of ricochets.

He dropped down below the truck and shot one of the bastards in the head and another through the neck. The last one obviously decided that discretion was the better part of valor and ran away from the fight.

Mike had a handful of minor wounds on his neck and back from the metal and brick striking him but had a more severe injury on the back of his right shoulder.

"Mike yelled, "Damn, I've been hit in my neck and back."

I yelled back, "Rub some dirt on it, then walk it off, you pussy."

We had a brief firefight with four men from the Humvee and killed two before they backed away and sped off away from us. Living to fight another day again is not cowardice. It's called the preservation of forces. I fired a Law at them but hit a damn tree branch hanging over the road.

"Davi yelled, "Let's go before they come back."

"Anybody wounded?"

"Me," Mike yelled.

I chuckled and said, "Oh, good grief, Mike, go see the school nurse and get a Band-Aid. You're such a wussy."

Smiling himself, now, Mike retorted, "Ok, ok, but just remember, what goes around comes around."

Ricochets had nicked both Mike and Ben. There were both crabby and bitchy, but the poor babies were okay.

Sally kept the pressure on Mike's wound, and the bleeding stopped before we made it two blocks down the road. Ben only needed a bandage.

As always, we took the weapons and ammo from the fallen, loaded up, and hit the road. I kept the peddle to the metal for over half an hour, slowing to a more normal pace as we approached the north end of Bayou La Batre.

The only good news was that Forrest woke up. The bad news was he had to be told he was a couple hundred miles from the lake. Joan filled him in on what happened while he was unconscious, and he surprised us by saying we did the right thing by taking him and his kids with us.

Personally, I think that having his head on Joan's lap for the rest of the trip may have sealed the deal. They were bonding, and his kids were already fond of Joan. It seemed strange to me, but there could be no question that relationships developed at hyper-speed here after the lights went out.

***

Sharon called out. "Aaron, vehicles are approaching. I hope it's our girl and her friends."

He replied, "Better safe than sorry. Man the SAWs and call for Mort while I run up to see who it is."

Mort brought six armed people with him, and they quickly set up a crossfire to ambush any undesirables. They lay behind walls, boats in dry dock, and in culverts. They were prepared and professional.

Aaron saw the lead vehicle turn down their street and immediately recognized the woman manning the SAW on the roof of the old pickup. It was his beautiful daughter. He stepped out into the street and waved at the convoy approaching them.

"My Davi, I have missed you so much. I know many of your friends, but when we get them all aboard ship and safely out to sea, you will have to introduce everyone to your Uncle Mort and his people."

"Davi, are you okay?" her mom yelled.

Davi hugged her mother and father, then turned to see her Dad's best friend and cried out, "Uncle Mort, you rascal, you haven't changed a bit."

"And you, my dear, are as beautiful as ever."

They were fed sandwiches and fruit while Mort filled them all in on the progress of getting the boats loaded and ready for the trip.

"My friends, I'm sorry, but we have to immediately load up and get out of here. There are some horrible people a few miles north of here."

I replied, "There are twenty fewer of those bastards. We had to blast our way through them to get here."

Mort looked terrified and replied, "Then we have to leave right away. You see the boats. Start loading them now and prepare to sail in two hours. All hands on deck, and we leave in two hours even if we leave supplies on the dock."

The following two hours were all assholes and elbows as we frantically moved all of our supplies and people onto the boats before the sun came up. Mort was glad to see the four extra SAWs, LAWs, and many weapons and ammo we brought to the party.

Aaron said, "Keep the SAWs handy, but we'll mount them after we get away from this place. Who has sailing experience?"

Roger, Forrest, and Mike were the only ones that had sailed small boats and were immediately drafted to help move the yacht, renamed the Exodus II, away from the dock.

We stacked our supplies all over the deck and in the cabin space. We didn't try to stow it away in its proper place as we wasted no time and quickly had everything piled high on the two boats. "Joan. Please take charge of the children while the rest of us prepare to sail and stow the supplies."

Mike and Roger removed the mooring lines while Aaron started the auxiliary diesel engine. Aaron skillfully pulled away from the dock and headed three-quarters of a mile downstream to the Gulf of Mexico. Navigating only by moonlight to avoid being seen was dangerous close to shore. Still, it wouldn't be an issue in open water.

Aaron said, "Men, we need to get a half mile out before we can be sure we can tack port or starboard. Maintain light discipline. We are living on borrowed time, and I want to get out of sight as soon as possible. Mort, please take the lead and use your depth finder to tell us when we cut west. We'll go that way for a mile or so and then head straight out into the Gulf."

★

Chapter 17 - Sailing

Mort passed us in the channel and led the way out into the Gulf. Davi was on Mort's boat, and both of us were charged with watching the shore for the enemy. Mike and one of Mort's crew were charged with watching for aircraft. I saw several Humvees approaching on the main road by the docks and radioed Davi. The sun was just below the horizon, and the dark was yielding a soft hazy light.

I said, "Enemy vehicles by our dock. They have mounted machine guns. The dumbasses have all of their lights on."

Mort checked the depth and said, "Cut right now! Follow us."

The enemy had not spotted us yet, and we would soon be around the mouth of the channel and out of sight. We were almost out of their line of vision when I saw the vehicles flying towards the closest point of land in our direction. I yelled, "Everyone, take cover!" as I radioed the warning to Davi.

The vehicles stopped and started firing at us, missing short and wide, but were getting closer. "I yelled, "Start firing! I'll watch through the binoculars and guide you into the target."

The team fired all eight SAWs at the vehicles hitting water most of the time until I talked them closer and closer to the enemy. Then we unleashed the .50 cal. BMGs on the bastards. The tracer's glow enabled us to walk the bullets onto the targets. The .50s had the range to devastate the Humvees, and soon both were on fire and the crews dead. The remaining troops popped up and fired a few times, but only two rounds hit Mort's boat, with none hitting ours. The .50 cal. BMGs wiped them out.

We moved past their line of sight and started angling out to sea as we stayed out of their line of fire. Mort radioed to Aaron, "Keep a close watch on the sky. They could have helicopters."

The sky was clear, and yet there were no helicopters, so we sailed due south. Mort waited for six hours before calling us to make sure we were out of the line of sight radio range, and no one could easily track us. Our small handheld radios only had a range of ten miles over water.

We sailed at seven knots, and as expected, it would take another day to get out of the range of aircraft.

There hadn't been time to cover our long-range plan. Aaron said, "I'll give you the short version tonight. We'll stop for an hour, lash the boats together and give you the full briefing."

I said, "Sounds good. Where are we heading."

Aaron said, "Many of our compounds around the world have recently come under attack by an unknown enemy. This, coupled with the invasion of the USA by multiple countries, makes it necessary to head to one of our compounds in South America.

Initially, we are sailing to Belize and then on to Aruba or perhaps French Guiana if necessary. Before we arrive in Belize, we'll stop at the easternmost point of the Yucatan Peninsula to fish and search for game. While there, we'll try to smoke and sundry the fish and meat.

This is not a long trip, but we will pace ourselves as though it were. We will catch rainwater and fish at every opportunity. We need and intend to conserve all supplies for the proverbial rainy day. Get used to eating a lot of fish until we find, and grow our own food."

I replied, "Mort, we understand, and everyone here will do their best to make sure we are conserving our supplies. I'm not sure what fish we can catch in the open Gulf moving at seven knots, but we'll give it a try. "

Nodding his head, Aaron said, "No, you're right, well, unless you're fond of flying fish. The deep waters of the Gulf are akin to a desert. We'll wait until we are off the coast of the Yucatan to do any serious fishing."

We made two large rain catchers out of spare sails and placed one on each ship. We rigged them to quickly put them in place during the day and left them in place at night. They were roughly ten feet by twelve with a low end that funneled water into four plastic two hundred-gallon international bulk carriers. It often rains in the Gulf, and we intended to catch as much water as possible.

Trolling artificial lures was moderately productive, but we would go for hours before we caught anything. Still, we ate fish every day and soon had our fill. Even Mort asked the galley staff to cook some beef stew on the third day.

On the morning of the fourth day, Sam was on lookout on the yacht. He saw something and yelled, "Land ho! I see land."

I asked, "Where?"

He replied, "South, dead ahead," he yelled, pointing in the direction of his sighting.

I had just taken over the watch from Ben and trained my binoculars ahead. I saw a green mass about ten miles ahead.

The yacht cut power, and I saw Mort waving to drop the sails, which we quickly accomplished, well, not as soon as a more competent crew does. Still, we dropped sail in, for us, record time.

We brought the boats together, and Mort gave us his plan. "Radar doesn't show anything but the land ahead. Everyone has to keep an eye out for pirates or government troops. Either would be bad for us. We need to divide into hunting and fishing teams. We don't need any water thanks to our rain catchers, but I want a couple hundred pounds of both meat and fish, in addition to what we eat while we stay here."

Mike, Ben, Davi, Paul, and I took one of the Zodiacs to shore to hunt while the others stayed back to fish or pull guard duty. We each took a compound bow with plenty of arrows along with our usual weapons.

Mort said, "This area was sparsely settled before TSHTF, but why take chances shooting when we are all proficient with the bows."

We landed the Zodiac about five miles east of a village called Holbocks, which was on a peninsula that formed the north end of a large bay. We landed, hid the boat, and walked inland to start hunting. There were hundreds of monkeys, birds, and small lemur-type animals, but nothing we wanted to eat.

Davi scolded us with, "If you go hungry for a week, you will eat monkey. It's not bad roasted over an open fire."

I huffed, "I'll take your word for it. Let's find a pig, cow, deer, or two hundred rabbits."

We hunted for two hours and only had a small pig to show for our effort. The pig field dressed down to about 25 pounds. I placed it in a plastic bag and threw it over my shoulder.

I said, "We'll starve at this rate."

Davi shushed me and pointed to the ground. "She whispered, "Those tracks are from a big cat. These are from a small woman or a child. The cat is stalking the human. Let's hurry."

"Davi, should we risk being seen to save someone we don't know," blurted Ben.

I replied, "What if it was your wife?"

We walked for ten minutes when we heard a terrifying roar up ahead. Davi motioned for us to follow her. We only covered about fifty feet when we saw a large black cat trying to shake a young woman from a tree. The cat looked like a Panther and was twice the size of a big German Shepherd. The young girl was about 15 feet up in the tree, clinging for dear life while beating on the cat with a club.

I notched an arrow, drew my bow back, and shot an arrow deep into the side of the cat. It turned, looked at me, and charged.

I reached for another arrow, brought it to the bow, notched it on the string when I heard a shot as the Panther crashed down on top of me. I pushed and shoved to get the big cat off me and, finally, with Davi's help, managed to roll the beast off me.

I walked away with only a few deep scratched from its front claws and knew I was lucky to be alive. "Davi, thanks for your timely and accurate shot."

Davi snickered, "I'm always saving your sorry ass. Come on, we need to check on the girl."

Mike and Paul coaxed her down from the tree and tried to make sense of her Spanish.

Davi and I walked up, and I heard the girl say, "We must go. They're searching for me."

I couldn't catch every word, but my high school Spanish class was finally coming in handy. I replied, "Who's searching for you, and why are they searching for you," in my broken Spanish.

Her reply scared me more than the Panther. My translation of what she said was, "The Cartel, and I'm one of their slaves. My friends and I escaped this morning. The Panther killed her and would have killed me if you had not arrived. Hurry, we must go. They'll kill all of us."

I translated for the team and said, "Let's get back to the boat now and get out of here."

We ran back to the boat, only stopping once for a minute to rest. Mike fired up the Zodiac, and we headed full speed back to the sailboat.

Davi said, "Don't use the radios. They might overhear us and pinpoint the signal."

It only took a few minutes to motor back to our sailboat. We immediately told everyone about our new friend and that we had to haul ass out of here. The team quickly stowed the fishing gear, hauled in the anchors, and prepared to head back out to sea.

I said, "Mort told us to head on to Cancun and try to trade or purchase food there."

The young girl took me off to the side and said, "No, Cancun. Cartel own Cancun."

I yelled to my friends and said, "Does anyone speak Spanish?"

Callie replied, "Dad, you know I took five years of Spanish. I'll talk to her."

A few minutes later, Callie filled us in on why the girl was adamant about not going to Cancun. "Dad, this drug Cartel has taken over this end of Mexico down to the north end of Panama. Cancun is their headquarters. We must head out to sea, and we must not even think about landing anywhere until we are south of Panama.

Oh, and her name is Susan Imelda Herrera Garcia."

I signaled for Mort to head due west out to sea, and we remained on that heading for ten hours before I radioed Mort. We agreed to head southeast for another ten hours as fast as the sailboat would go before deciding where to go.

We tied the boats together for thirty minutes to have a meeting, and as usual, Mort led the discussion. I rather enjoyed the role of X.O. Besides, Mort was more qualified to serve as the leader of our band of gypsies than I was.

Mort said, "My friends, I think we take the girl at her word and skip landing until we clear Panama. I suspect that some War Lord will also control Venezuela.

This means that we have to live off our supplies longer than planned. On the other hand, and it's a big hand, we can try the Cayman Islands or Jamaica for food. While I don't know much about the Caymans, I'm sure Jamaica will be, again, run by pirates. I think we should definitely give it a wide berth."

We voted to try the Caymans for food and water if needed. The Grand Cayman Island was just over three hundred eighty miles, or two to three days sailing time from our current location.

The Cayman Islands didn't pan out. We were met at sea by friendly but firm natives who offered water but no food.

We heard, "You Gringos are flooding down south to escape the Mexicans, Russians, and Cubans. We don't want you. No one wants you. Go home."

They gave us water and told us to move on. We did.

Aaron, are you sure that any of the Israeli compounds survived. We are going to starve if we don't find a home soon."

He replied, "I can't guarantee anything. I pray every night. I see no option other than to move on and find a place. We need to decide on heading down the east side of South America or up the west side to the Pacific. Our little flotilla would struggle during any trip around the Horn. It's a pity that the Panama Canal is owned by the Chinese."

I said, "Aaron, everyone is getting worn out from not knowing if we will find a place to call home."

***

We decided to stay on the east side of South America. The days were getting longer, hotter, and more humid as we headed southeast. It seems really odd to us that hot and cold no longer seem to matter as much now as they had before the lights went out...humanity adapts, and the Earth abides.

We are tougher and never sweat the small stuff anymore. We laugh more, dance, and have time for our friends. We tell more jokes and never take offense when kidded. The people around us are our family, our clan. We didn't know what lay ahead. Pirates, War Lords, or paradise, but we knew the USA had gone down the toilet, and we vowed never to become slaves to any man or government. We had resolved to live free or die trying.

"Dad, Susan has an idea of where we can find a home."

I looked at Callie and started to tell her to tell Susan to mind her own business when I remembered my manners and said, "Please, ask Susan to join us."

Susan walked up to the table, sat down between Mike and me, and said, "I told Callie that my last name is Herrera Garcia. That's not true. My real name is Aimee Bassot. I'm from the island of Martenvous, which is not far from here."

I had to stop, look at her, and say, "You're speaking in perfect English."

"Yes, I speak seven languages. I was on vacation from school in Cancun when I was kidnapped by those asshole drug lords."

I frowned, "Go on."

She said, "My father, Henri Bassot, is the highest-ranking military officer on Martenvous. He's the Capitaine de Vaisseau, the French Naval and Air Forces commander stationed at Fort Saint Charles. He'll reward you if you take me home."

I shook my head, "I thought you were Spanish."

She looked me in the eyes. "I didn't know you or trust you at first. Martenvous is a French Island. I know you can find a home there."

Martenvous was two hundred miles southeast from us, with Grenada and Trinidad due south. We decided to try Martenvous first and hope Aimee/Susan wasn't playing us. My French is much better than my Spanish.

☆

Chapter 18 - Martenvous

Aimee told us about her home. "The island of Martenvous is only forty miles long by fifteen miles wide, and the native population is around four hundred thousand before the lights went out up north. The capital and largest city is Fort de Ville. My dad lives on the base at Fort Saint Charles."

I asked, "Have you heard anything about life on the island since the lights went out?"

She said, "No, but we had power in Cancun, so I would hope things are pretty much normal."

Mort, Aaron, and I spent some time quizzing Aimee about the island and what we might face upon our arrival.

We were cautious and stopped 15 miles due west of the island and continued listening to our shortwave and walkie-talkie radios. We didn't want to be surprised by drug lords or pirates again. The shortwave radio had the usual banter from survivors around this half of the world. Depending on atmospheric conditions, we heard people from a thousand miles away or fifteen. Most were asking for help, and some were warning people not to approach their part of the world.

The one common theme was that most were barely getting by and were living off the land. It greatly concerned us that even countries not affected by the EMP blasts were struggling to survive.

"I'm concerned that we might not be as welcome as Aimee thinks. This was a resort island that got away from farming when the tourist industry skyrocketed. The island won't support 400 thousand people," said Aaron

I replied, "I was thinking the same thing and am worried that many others like us have left the USA and other countries and flooded the islands."

Aaron said, "Let's lay low and listen to our radios before we sail into a trap or get run off at gunpoint."

We all agreed and held to an area ten miles away from the coast. We continued to listen and heard some communications that excited us and other communications that concerned us.

Davi urged, "Aaron, Zack, come here quick!"

Aaron said, "Just a minute. "What have you heard."

"Listen. I'll translate," said Davi.

The person was speaking in French.

"...we have the rebels surrounded. They're ready to surrender."

Another French voice replied, "No, do not take any prisoners. They're traitors. Shoot them all."

The first voice said, "Sir, there are over a hundred men and women."

"I said, shoot them all."

"Oui, mon Capitaine, right away."

Before what we heard sank into our minds, Aimee ran up, saying, "That was my father. What did he say?"

Aaron replied, "Did Martenvous have any civil unrest before the lights went out?"

Aimee said, "No more than any country. Why do you ask?"

Aaron said, "Your father just gave the orders to shoot a hundred men and women trying to surrender. There was an attack on a food storage warehouse. The military fought the attackers off and chased them into the mountains, where they boxed them into a canyon. Your father gave orders to shoot them all."

Aimee cried out, "No, there must be a mistake. My father is a kind and gentle man. He wouldn't kill his own people. They must be an army from another island."

I spoke up, "She has a point. There are dozens of islands in the area. It's easy to see that one might try to steal from the other. We need to keep an open mind but remain cautious."

The following day we heard the next transmission that was in English, "Charles, we are heading back to Barbados. Get your people back to the boats. We were given an hour to get out of Martenvous, or they would sink our boats."

A voice replied, "The bastards won't help us."

"No, the ship's captain said they don't need more mouths to feed and will sink us with their canons if we don't leave."

The voice said, "I think he meant more black mouths to feed."

"We are loading now. Will meet you 15 miles south to decide where to go."

The voice said, "Roger out."

The transmission ended.

We also heard regular radio stations giving weather reports, local news, and music. The two stations sounded as though there hadn't been over a year of mayhem in the world. The announcers were very upbeat and joked a lot.

***

After a hard day's work, Captain Henri Bassot relaxed by the pool, with his mistress by his side. "Mon Cher, order Champagne cocktails and a shrimp platter to hold us over until dinner. Please tell my chef to prepare lobster and filets for dinner. Oh, tell him I want a chocolate cake for dessert. Let him know to

570

expect eighteen guests from the French consulate. We will also have the English and Russians to dinner tonight."

The tall, leggy blonde walked over to the bar, picked up the phone, called the Captain's assistant, and passed the instructions on to her.

He waved at a black woman who served as his maid and said, "Rub some sunblock on my back and legs."

"Oui, my Captain."

She looked over at him with disgust carefully hidden behind wide, bright brown eyes and a big smile as she saw his naked body. She picked up the sunblock, poured some on her hands, and began rubbing it on his back, legs, and buttocks. He rolled over, and she applied the sunblock to his chest, the front of his legs, and then to his private parts.

She was a beautiful thirty-year-old woman who had been told to serve the Captain or leave the island. She shared his bed when the blonde wasn't available. She looked up, saw the blonde walking towards them, and moved away from him back to her station.

The blonde walked up to Henri, grabbed him, and said, "I know you're sleeping with your maid, but don't have her rubbing your dick in public."

He said, "I'll do as I please, and you'll shut up unless you want to become a plantation worker."

An hour later, his senior Chief of Staff came to him to say, "Our radar has spotted two boats about ten miles east of our coast. I told our ships to intercept the boats and hold them until they receive your instructions."

"Mai Oui, Andre."

***

Mort spotted several boats on the radar between the island and us, hoping none were military vessels. "Zack, we are being hailed by someone claiming to be with the French Navy."

571

Aaron had already grabbed the mic and asked in French, "To whom am I speaking?"

"I'm Lieutenant Devereau. Who are you, your home port, and where's your destination?"

Aaron said, "We are Americans from the USA seeking a new home."

The lieutenant replied. "Stop your engines and prepare to be boarded."

I said, "Aaron, can we outrun them?"

"No."

Aaron then answered, "We are cutting our engines, but it's too deep to anchor. One of our boats is a sailboat, so it can't totally stop."

"Je comprends. Have it put out its sea anchor."

"We will."

"Je comprends? What the hell does that mean?" asked a nervous Mike.

Aaron replied, "It means I understand."

"Oh, okay, then."

It was an hour until the ship came into sight. It was a frigate with a 5-inch deck gun and several twin mounted fifty. Cal BMGs. The vessel stopped about half a mile away with the five incher aimed at us and launched two Zodiacs armed with French-made squad machineguns.

Each boat had six men who quickly boarded and searched our vessels. We tried to speak to them, but they shoved us out of the way and poked their rifles into our sides.

The leader finally walked up to Aaron and said in English, "Sorry for the rough treatment, but we have had several ships try to land with bad intentions. Some of your homegrown terrorists tried to take over our home a few months ago. I believe you have heard of the Black Panthers and Black Separatist Movement."

Aaron said, "Yes, they were causing trouble back home before the lights went out."

"Well, thousands of them left the USA and are trying to take over their own Caribbean Island to forge a new homeland."

Aaron said, "Sorry that you had to go through that. We are looking for a new home and just want to contribute and work hard."

The lieutenant asked, "Why do you have so many machine guns on your boats?"

"As you probably know, there are pirates on the oceans and many bad people out there. Drug gangs are trying to take over the world."

The lieutenant said, "I'll call our Captain, and he'll tell me what to do with you."

I said, "Could you tell Captain Bassot that we have brought his daughter, Aimee, back to him safely?"

Aimee went over and introduced herself to the astonished Lieutenant. He keyed his mic and said in French, "Tell Captain Bassot that we have rescued his daughter, Aimee."

In a few minutes, Aimee was talking with her father and was in tears. She was transferred to the frigate and rushed at full speed to Fort Saint Charles.

The boarding crews stayed with us and guided us into the harbor, where our boats were chained to the docks. The boarding crew confiscated our machine guns and all other weapons except for our sidearms.

Aaron watched the boarding team leave the boat only to stand guard on the dock. "Aren't we glad we hid most of our weapons and ammo? I don't trust these people."

About an hour later, the Lieutenant came down to us and said, "I would like to pass on Captain Bassot's compliments, along with an invitation to your leaders to attend a homecoming party for his daughter. The party starts at 7:00 tomorrow evening. We can provide formal clothes if required. I have to inform you that we do not allow firearms on our streets, so please, leave your sidearms on the boats."

We gave them the correct sizes for Davi, Ally, Aaron, Mort, and me. The clothes and some hygiene products were delivered at noon the next day.

We woke up to find breakfast awaiting us in a tent on the dock. There were croissants, cheeses, jams, ham, and fruit. Lunch was served in the same tent. The meals were delicious.

At breakfast, Ally nudged me and said, "Am I wrong, or are Joan and Forrest always together these days?"

I looked over at the following table, and Joan laughed at something Forrest said and had her hand on his shoulder. "Yep, I see the same and have also seen them slip off to the side quite a bit. They swim alone, too."

Ally said, "I'm glad she found someone, and those children will have a great Mama."

I laughed, "And she won't be chasing your husband."

She replied, "Well, of course, there's that, but hey, she's not your type anyway.

I agreed but thought, apparently out loud, that I was married to Joan for 16 years, and how could she not be my type.

Ally pinched my inner thigh under the table and whispered, "Your type is me."

The time passed as we continued to listen to radio traffic while watching the Fort and the town from our boats. We saw two more frigates and numerous smaller gunboats come and go past the dock.

Much of the chatter on the walkie-talkies was confusing. There appeared to be a revolt against the Captain, and the French leaders, another rebellion against white rule, and the farmers were fighting everyone. It sounded like a hot mess. We even heard some of the Black Separatist propaganda.

I said, "Aaron, I think we have walked into a mess. There appear to be several groups fighting for control of Martenvous."

574

Aaron said, "And the Captain has most of the firepower. Let's try to not piss him off."

I thought for a minute and said, "We need to hide some weapons."

I shouldn't have been surprised at how devious Davi could be. She found the perfect place to hide a substantial cache of weapons.

***

Aimee told her father about her perils. "Father, it was terrible. I flew to Cancun from New Orleans a few days before the USA was attacked. Jennifer, Connie, and I were on the beach having some drinks and sunning ourselves when it came on the news. The Americans and Canadians panicked the first day, and all of them tried to go back home. All flights to the USA and Canada were canceled. I tried to get a flight for us, but they canceled all flights the next day. That's when I got scared."

Her father asked, "How did you join the Americans?"

She replied, "It's a long story, but we were kidnapped by a drug cartel and made to do despicable things to survive."

Her father cringed, "My poor daughter."

"We escaped from the cartel's compound on the north end of Yucatan, where Connie and Jennifer were killed by the lions the cartel sent to kill us. The Americans were hunting food and killed the lion just before it ate me. They saved me and took me with them."

He hugged her and said, "Oh my God, what a terrible experience. We owe the Americans for saving your life."

She smiled, "Yes, Father. They're good people, and they're just looking for a home. Please help them."

He replied, "We need more good people to help us with this invasion."

"Father, what invasion?"

He frowned, "Revolutionaries from Cuba and the USA have infiltrated the black community and convinced some of them that they're slaves and that they must kill all whites."

She said, "But blacks have most of the leadership positions and have a great life here."

"The revolutionaries have convinced a sizable part of our less fortunate population that the blacks on our side are also slaveholders. We have won most battles, but the constant war has hurt our farming, and we are running short of food, which makes the problem worse."

Aimee asked, "Can I go see the Americans?"

"They're coming to our house for your homecoming party. You will see them tonight."

She smiled, "Oh, tres joie. I want to rest, and then I'll tell you about my entire misadventure."

"Aimee, did you catch the name of the cartel or any of its leaders?"

"Yes, it's the Cortez Cartel."

Captain Bassot gave orders. "Lieutenant, plan a mission to destroy the Cortez Cartel. I believe they're based in Yucatan."

"Sir, they're 3,000 Kilometers away. We don't have any planes or ships with that range. We don't have enough fuel to send frigates, either. The same cartel controls the fuel shipped out of Venezuela, and we haven't had a shipment in months. I'll put a plan together, but it would be a one-way mission."

Bassot replied, "I'm sorry. You're correct. My love for my daughter is clouding my judgment."

"Sir, there's something we can do."

"And what's that."

The lieutenant said, "They get most of their drugs from South America. We can sink their ships with the drugs. It's only about 1,500 Kilometers to the coast of Columbia."

Bassot said, "That's still beyond our range. Keep thinking, and let me know when you come up with a plan. I must say, however, that I do like the idea of sinking their drugs. Yes, I like it very much."

The lieutenant said, "Sir, one last thought. The leader of the Cortez cartel is actually from Grenada and lives there most of the time. He has killed all of the Grenadian leadership and rules the country as a dictator."

A wicked grin flooded across Bassot'sface. "And Grenada is only 290 Kilometers away."

"Yes, sir, we could mount an attack and eliminate the leader of the men who captured your daughter. Though most certainly, one of his lieutenants will assume his place, we will, at least, let them know that punishment from our forces will be swift and terrible."

Bassot said, "Develop a plan to stop the drug trade in our area and kill the entire cartel contingent on Grenada. I also want fuel from Venezuela. We must also have fuel for our power generation plant, or we will all soon be in the dark."

"Oui, mon Capitaine.

***

Governor's Palace

The Island of Martenvous,

A former French Protectorate

Aimee looked lovely and gushing. "Hello. I'm so glad to see you. This is my Father, Captain Henri Bassot. Where are Callie and her husband? I wanted to see them again."

Bassot said, "Aimee, that's my fault. I just invited their leaders to the dinner. We can have your other friends over tomorrow."

Aaron replied, "We are pleased to be here with you and to be in your beautiful country."

Bassot shook our hands. "I must thank you for saving my daughter and bringing her back to me. She tells me that you have had a dangerous trip and are looking for a home. We shall discuss that tomorrow, but I'll tell you now that we welcome you with open arms."

The Captain introduced us to the island leadership and dignitaries before we were served drinks and dinner. I noticed that the leadership was an equal mix of blacks and whites, but all servants were black. I felt that they didn't have a race problem as much as a rich vs. poor problem.

Bassot looked at me. "Zack, I must admire you and the others for covering over 3,000 Kilometers in two small motor yachts. That was quite a trip."

I smiled and stared back at him. "It was one motor yacht and a 62 foot Beneteau sailboat. The sailboat was one of the best built and can easily handle long ocean voyages."

He said, "I'm familiar with Beneteau. It's a French company. So, many of you were soldiers?"

I frowned and said, "Only a few. The rest of us had to learn on the fly."

Bassot pointed to his lieutenant. "My Lieutenant told me that you were also heavily armed."

I nodded, "We had several FN249 SAWs and two .50 cal. BMGs on each boat."

I stopped there when I realized I was giving way too much information. He was asking too many questions for my liking. I wondered where he was going in his mind.

We had dined on seafood, steak, and numerous vegetables before a flaming dessert was served. I hadn't eaten so well in several years. I got a feeling that we ate enough food to feed a small village of the local people. There was music and dancing after the meal, and I have to say that Ally and I thoroughly enjoyed the party. It was a brief respite from the post-apocalyptic world that had engulfed our lives for over a year. Still, on this occasion, we were carefree and didn't have a care in the world for over four hours that night.

***

Bassot saw the lieutenant walk into the room. "Lieutenant, you do know that our visitors have a sailboat that can travel around the world without fuel. The crew needs only food and water."

"Sir, that's brilliant. I'll put a plan together that combines our Special Forces and their sailboat. Perhaps we can find another large sailboat. We can attack the drug routes all of the way back to the Yucatan and everything between here and Columbia. We just need to increase the boat's firepower."

"Not exactly my thoughts, but we are on the same page. Learn more about the boat and report back to me."

***

Aaron, Mort, and I were summoned to meet with Captain Bassot the next day for lunch. The note stated that he wanted to discuss our future as residents of Martenvous. We arrived at noon sharp and found another meal fit for a king laid out by the pool.

An aide to the Captain asked us to be seated and begin our lunch since the Captain was detained and would join us in a few moments. I pointed out to Aaron that I saw the staff hide food in their pockets several times.

"Zack, I saw the same thing last night at the homecoming party. I get a feeling that it's great to be rich on this island, but being poor could be not so good."

Captain Bassot arrived before we could finish the conversation. He came with the Lieutenant and his Chief of Staff. They joined us for lunch and general chit-chat for an hour before getting down to business. "Gentlemen, I want to formally welcome you to Martenvous, the most beautiful island in the Caribbean. We hope you will want to make this your home but will understand if

579

you decide to continue your quest to find a suitable home. While we weren't hit by the EMP blasts, our island has had several setbacks due to the attacks on Europe and the USA."

Aaron interrupted and asked, "Pardon me, sir. Can you give us an update on the state of the world? We are aware of the attacks on the USA and Israel but know almost nothing about Europe and the rest of the world."

Bassot said, "Certainly. The initial attacks were on the USA, the EU countries, and Canada. French intelligence told us it was a joint attack by the North Koreans and Iran. When Israel realized it was to be eliminated, they launched all of their nuclear weapons at their enemies. Iran, Syria, Iraq, and other Muslim countries were devastated by atomic blasts.

They also bombed China, Moscow, and several other countries with EMP blasts. Israel is a nuclear wasteland, as is most of the Middle East. Now, what's left of the Russian, Cubans, and Chinese are rushing into Canada and the USA to get their share of the pie. The USA has bombed Mexico and Cuba, which stopped their attacks, but they're trading nukes with Russian and Chinese forces. No one can win that game, and we could all die from nuclear fallout."

Aaron said, "Thank you, that fills in the gaps in what we had heard. How has Martenvous fared?"

"France was devastated and told us we are on our own. We relied on trade with France and the USA for most of our food. Unfortunately, we had starvation and riots as the food ran out. Thousands died during the riots, and over a hundred thousand fled to other islands.

We quickly increased our farming and fishing industries but are just catching up to the demand for our own people. Sadly we have to turn away ships full of people every day who think we can feed them."

I asked, "Why would you take us into your society?"

"You saved my daughter, and I believe you have skills that could prove very valuable to our country. Surviving in the USA and then a long voyage to get here makes you survival experts."

I said, "Thanks. We appreciate your comments and are glad to have helped Aimee."

Bassot said, "Oui, you're, of course, welcome. Now down to our situation. You're free to leave us or stay and become members of our community, but there are rules. The basic rules that affect you're:

- You can't have guns on our island.

- You can't vote for two years.

- You have to find a job within 60 days.

- We are increasing the size of our military, and everyone between 16 and 50 has to serve in our National Guard.

- You must become French citizens and learn French, which is our national language.

- If you decide to leave, we will fill your water tanks but won't give you any food for your voyage."

- If you decide to stay, you will receive free housing, food for 60 days, free medical care, and all the rights of a French Citizen."

I replied, "That's a lot to digest. It sounds very attractive, but can we go back to our group and discuss the offer? Oh, one question."

"Oui?"

I asked, "Do the National Guard troops keep their guns at home as the Swiss do?"

Bassot answered, "No. We keep the arms at Fort Saint Charles and several Police Stations."

I shook his hand, "Thanks. We will give you our answer before the deadline."

He said, "Certainly, and take these leaflets that cover the rules and benefits that I just mentioned."

I said, "Thanks for the great lunch and covering the ground rules."

Bassot said, "I'd like to hear back with your answer in three days."

"Of course, and that sounds reasonable."

Bassot looked at Aaron and then me. "We will want every adult to tell us their answer in private. We don't want anyone coerced. I hope that's not a problem."

I said, "Not at all. We don't force anyone to do anything, and they're free to leave the group at any time."

Bassot stopped us. "Sorry, I forgot to ask, but how did you get the SAWs and heavy machine guns?"

I looked him in the eye and said, "Great question. The USA is in chaos. There are many abandoned US Armories across the country. We found an abandoned one and took what we needed."

***

Ally huffed, "Zack, you have to be kidding. They want to take our guns. I like what I see so far, but who's to say that pirates won't attack and run right over these French military types. Everyone else has beaten them in war."

I said, "I have the same concerns, but playing Devil's advocate, two years ago, would you worry about not having a gun?"

Ally was pissed. "That's not fair. It was a different time, and even then, my bastard husband had guns in the house."

"I just want us to make a good decision and not one based on our recent trials and tribulations."

Ally was still mad and gritted her teeth. "Darling, ... we will make a decision based on facts."

"Bull shit, I'm not giving up my guns to any tinpot dictator," replied Davi. "I can live with the rest of the conditions."

I said, "I think we all agree on the guns. Let's lay out the rest of the facts," said Aaron.

"We know or suspect the following:

1. No guns.

2. Military service.

3. They're fighting one or two opposing groups.

4. The poor inhabitants are fed up with the French Aristocracy.

5. The military appears to govern the island.

6. The island had 380 thousand people and now has about 150 thousand. What happened to the others?

7. Food is scarce, but the rich are throwing banquets.

The list makes for the start of a revolution, and I don't want to be trapped in someone else's war."

We laid out our list of issues and the rules and benefits the Captain gave us to our entire team. We discussed each item one at a time, and then we allowed everyone to have a say in our town hall meeting.

Most were for leaving, but 18 of our forty-one people wanted to stay and call the island home. The ones wanting to stay were Sam, Jacob, and half of Mort's people from Bayou La Batre. The rest of us were adamant about leaving.

***

The Captain watched as his men wanded us with metal detectors before we could enter the meeting room. This was a surprise even though we knew the citizens weren't allowed to have guns.

We were all seated in chairs facing Captain Bassot and his Chief of Staff. The Captain welcomed us and turned the meeting over to his Chief of Staff, who promptly covered the rules and benefits.

He took a few questions and then said, "You will now go through the black door to announce your decision to our official. Parents, take your children with you, but parents must be momentarily separated when you declare your decision. That reminds me, if a mother and father make different decisions, children under 16 must stay or go with the father. There are no exceptions. Now, go through the door when requested."

We all filed through the door and told a clerk our decision, and then she told us to leave through one of two doors.

I was the next to last to declare my decision and found myself being herded onto a bus by armed guards. I noticed there were two buses and that the bus I was on had my friends who wanted to leave Martenvous.

I sat down next to Aaron and asked, "What the fuck is going on?"

Aaron said, "One of the guards told us that we were being taken to temporary housing until we were prepared to leave the island, and the others were being taken to their houses."

I asked, "Why can't we stay on the boats?"

Aaron said, "I asked, and the guard replied that he just follows orders."

The bus trip took only twenty minutes and ended at a beautiful resort. The guard told us to use the beach houses during our stay. Dinner would be served in the dining room at 7:00 sharp.

Before we could head to the beach houses, the Lieutenant drove up and said, "Sorry for our poor communications. You will stay here for the next week or two while we prepare your sailboat for your trip.

It will receive a small cannon, several recoilless rifles, two more .50 cal. BMGs, anti-aircraft capability, and enough food and water for a ninety-day ocean voyage.

We want to make sure you can survive long enough to find the paradise you seek. Captain Bassot felt that saving his daughter was worth giving you the food. Our Captain and his staff will meet with you several times before you depart. They'll be better able to answer your questions."

We started asking questions, and the Lieutenant answered with, "That's all I have to say. Enjoy the beach and resort. Do not try to leave."

Mort gathered us around as soon as the Lieutenant left to say, "I know this was a surprise, but remember we are unknown visitors in another country. Our governments would do the same thing. Isolate the visitors, keep them happy, vet them, and if they're harmless to send them on their way."

This made sense and calmed us down. He avoided a revolt that day. I just hoped he was correct about the Captain's intentions. I still wondered why they were now giving us food.

***

Aimee visited the next day and spent half-day swimming and enjoying the company of Callie and Paul. She made a point of talking with me that day. "Zack, I want to thank you again for saving my life, and my father wants to repay you by making sure you have a safe voyage to your new home. I twisted his arm a bit to help you with the food.

I also told him that any pirates that you killed wouldn't attack us later. I'm sorry that you don't want to stay here, but understand that Americans don't necessarily like our customs and rules. You should go where you will be happy, but remember that most Latin American and South American countries have the same anti-gun policies and different views of your Bill of Rights."

I said, "You're welcome. It was the right thing to do, and we would do it again. It's a shame that the drug lords of the world are gaining power during these trying times. We do appreciate your countries assistance and these beautiful beaches. We have been struggling to survive so long, and it's great to see our people laughing and enjoying this resort."

Amiee frowned, "My father will have his staff meet with you starting tomorrow to get your input into the modifications to the sailboat. He wants to make sure that you're safe while you're on your mission."

I said, "We love it here, but we can't wait to find a place of our own."

Aimee looked down at her feet. "You will have maps and limited access to the internet tomorrow. Perhaps you can find an island in the Caribbean to make your home. Terrible people govern a few of those islands. Perhaps with your military skills, you can make one your new home. My dad will give you the locations of two islands that could make a wonderful home."

The young woman was either incredibly savvy or had been prepped by her father. What she said made a lot of sense. After she had left, I met with Aaron, Mort, Mike, and Davi. I told them what Aimee had passed on, and we had a lively discussion.

Mort said, "I think the Captain wants us to eliminate a threat by killing off one of his enemies on a nearby island."

I said, "I don't know. Much of what she said makes sense. If we don't settle at one of the Israeli compounds, all of this part of the world is much like Martenvous,"

Aaron added, "We should be able to contact one of our compounds through the internet or their phone system. It appears the EMP blasts did not harm their electronics this far south. We also need to ask more questions now that she opened the door to alternatives."

I said, "In any case, the 'Patriots' still have some bad guys to fight and many days of uncertainty ahead."

***

We continued to eat well, swim in the ocean, and enjoy the best vacation anyone ever had while thinking about where life would take us and where our new home would be. I could go for living on this island even if Aaron and Davi were nervous about Captain Bassot's intentions.

"Come on, Ally, let's go for a swim."

"Hon, do you have a plan?"

I replied, "I always have a plan."

586

The End

Of Frozen Apocalypse but thanks to my fan's request I've added a more to the story to answer some dangling questions. Enjoy "The Final Ending."

*

The Day America Died!

The Final Ending

Post-Apocalyptic Survival Fiction

by

AJ Newman

*

Acknowledgments

This book is dedicated to Patsy, my beautiful wife of thirty-six years. She assists with everything from Beta reading to censor duties. She enables me to write, golf, and enjoy my life with her and our mob of Shih Tzus.

Thanks to Patsy, Cheryl, Richard S, and David, who are Beta readers for this novel. They gave many suggestions that helped improve the cover and readability of my book.

Thanks to Dee Cooper @ https://angryeaglepublishing.com/ for proofreading and editing this novel.

Thanks to WMHCheryl at http://wmhcheryl.com/services-for-authors/ for the great final proofreading and suggestions on improving the accuracy and helping me to tell a better story.

Thanks to Dee Cooper at Dauntless Cover Design for the fantastic cover.
AJ Newman

Copyright © 2021 Anthony J Newman. All rights reserved.

This book is a work of fiction. All events, names, characters, and places are the author's imagination or are used as fictitious events. That means I thought up this whole book from my imagination, and nothing in it is true.

All rights reserved. None of this publication may be copied or reproduced without prior written permission from the publisher.

As they say on TV, don't try anything you read in this novel. It's all fiction and stuff I made up to entertain you. Buy some survival books if you want to learn how to survive in the apocalypse.

Published by Newalk LLC.
Henderson, Kentucky

Key Character List

Zack Johnson – Divorced, electrical engineer, prepper, and car mechanic. He has a 16-year-old daughter and ex-wife. Had a farm close to Owensville, Ky. He is the hero in this series. Married Ally Stone.

Callie Johnson - Zack's daughter, who lived in Anderson, KY, with her mom. Married Paul Stone.

Ally Stone –A woman rescued by Mike when the SHTF. She has two kids, Paul and Susie. Becomes Zack's wife.

Joan Johnson – Zack's ex-wife. A bossy woman who lived in Anderson, Kentucky, where she's a restaurant manager.

Mike Norman – Joan's brother and Zack's best friend. Like Zack, he is a prepper. He is an auto mechanic and outdoorsman.

Sally Green – She was headed home when Zack saved her. A Strong-willed woman who does what it takes to survive.

Davi Gold – Aaron's daughter. She is an ex-Israeli Mossad agent. She falls for Zack but has to move on to complete her mission in the USA.

Aaron Gold – Davi's father, 55, and an ex- Israeli military pilot. Retired and had a large farm in southern Illinois. He became Zack's mentor.

Sharon Gold – Davi's mother and a Professor of Chemistry at the University of Illinois.

Paul Stone – Ally's son and becomes very helpful on the farm. Becomes Callie's boyfriend and then her husband at the end of book II.

Mort - Aaron's friend and another ex-patriot Jew from Israel.

Aimee Bassot - A young woman Zack saved from a drug cartel and the daughter of Captain Bassot.

Captain Henry Bassot - Military commander of Martenvous and a dictator.

Lieutenant Harry Devereau - Bassot's right arm man. A young man who has eyes for Davi.

*

The island of Martenvous was only forty miles long by fifteen miles wide. The native population was around four hundred thousand before the lights went out in the north. The capital and largest city was Fort de Ville.

Chapter 1- Safety for Liberty

Fort de Ville, Martenvous – Spring 2039

Hi! I'm Zack Johnson. I finally made time to tell the rest of my survival story. It starts just like it ended. The sun was warm, Ally felt good in my arms. I could almost forget the apocalypse and the dozens of people I'd killed to get to the safety of this tropical island. Todd, Prescott, and the countries attacking the USA were only distant thoughts these days. For the last two months, we'd given up fighting every day to find food and kill those trying to kill us.

Over the past year, I'd changed from being a divorced, depressed guy to the leader of this intrepid group. I'd been a prepper with survival skills, but now, all adults and most kids were accomplished in the art of self-defense and killing the enemy. Hand-to-hand, knife fighting, and long-range sniping were among the group's skill sets. Davi and Aaron had honed our military skills and developed us into a credible fighting force.

We lay on the secluded beach and soaked in the sunshine. Ally nipped my ear and brought me back to reality. "A penny for your thoughts."

"I was thinking about how beautiful my wife is and how much I love her?"

Ally chuffed. "Zack Johnson, I am beautiful. That is true, but you are full of BS. What were you really thinking? Damn, it's that thing we can't talk about."

I kissed her and tried to untie her Bikini. She bit harder. "Ouch, that hurt."

"Zack, you're lying on a secluded beach with a half-naked, and I might say a beautiful as well as willing woman, and you're off in la-la land. How am I going to start producing a baby without a little bit of help?"

I kissed her and held her bronzed body in my arms. "We're only practicing making babies. Remember no babies until that thing we can't talk about is over."

My mind was on more pressing things. For my mind to wander away from my gorgeous wife was something I'd rarely experienced since Ally and I were married. She'd blossomed from a plain housewife who'd almost given up on life to become a vibrant lady warrior. Did I fail to mention she was the sexiest woman I'd ever known, and the time in the sun had made her more beautiful? So anyway, suffice it to say it took a lot to get me to stop ... well, you know. This story is about the apocalypse and not my love life.

***

We'd all been given easy jobs and enjoyed the good life on Martenvous, as did all of the wealthy people. If you were poor, your life sucked. There was no middle class on the island. Bassot had confiscated their wealth and made them trudge each day to the fields and mines. The beach, the food, and hot steamy nights with Ally were all on my mind. Well, that's what I wanted everyone, including Captain Bassot, our benevolent dictator, to think.

Captain Bassot's rules for our crew were:

- You can't have guns on our island.
- You can't vote for two years.
- You have to find a job within 60 days.
- We are increasing the size of our military, and everyone between 16 and 50 has to serve in our National Guard.
- You must become French citizens and learn French, which is our national language.
- If you decide to leave, we will fill your water tanks but won't give you any food for your voyage.
- If you decide to stay, you will receive free housing, food for 60 days, free medical care, and all the rights of a French Citizen.

Two months ago, half of our group voted to stay on the island and make it their home. The half my group was in voted to leave. The leader of the island, Captain Bassot, had told us he would refit and supply our boat so we could leave. We could see work being performed on our sailboat, but very little work was done on the motor yacht. I couldn't figure out why the delay or what Bassot's plan was for us. We played along and waited for a chance to leave.

My friends and family wanted to stage a revolt, kill Bassot, and liberate the island. I put my foot down in public and ensured everyone complied while a select group schemed to free us from this dictator.

Benjamin Franklin said, *"Those who would give up essential Liberty, to purchase a little temporary Safety, deserve neither Liberty nor Safety."* Yes, we had food and safety but zero freedom. Bassot had taken our guns when he took our freedom. Old Ben was right. Without freedom, a person has nothing. We didn't like nothing. These thoughts were constantly on my mind. That's what I'd been thinking about when Ally jumped my ass on the beach.

My little secret team was made up of my most trusted people. Davi, the Israeli Mossad superwoman, and Aaron, her father and ex-Israeli military were now trusted friends. Mike, my best friend and confidant, Mort, another ex-patriot Israeli, and Ally, my wife, and an overall wise person, made up our revolt team. I trusted the others but wanted to keep a tight rein on our plans and bring people in when necessary. I also wanted them to appear to be enjoying the good life and have the usual complaints. Secrecy was the key to success.

We held our meetings every third day in one of the group's apartments. Fearing that Bassot had bugged the apartments, we passed notes and then destroyed them during the session. I kept a small fire going in a metal wastebasket to burn the evidence if we were raided.

Davi scratched furiously across the pad, "Our boats are being fitted with two Ma Deuces, four twin SAWs, and a dozen cases full of Rocket Propelled Grenades were loaded on board this week."

Mort shook his head while penning his response, "Bassot is going to force us to fight his enemy, or he is stealing our sailboat for his navy."

I didn't like where this was going. I wrote, "Davi, could we fetch our weapons and hide them? We might need them in an emergency."

I passed the note around to everyone. Mike read it and then scribbled his reply, "The bastards perform a search of our rooms every few days!"

Davi wrote, "No, they would be found. We need to get them just before we leave or have to have them."

I think it's easy to see that these meetings were tedious, to say the least. Most of the work being done to develop an action plan for our escape was spying on Bassot's military and civilian leaders. Our best guess was that Bassot had over three hundred sailors and five hundred soldiers at his command. They were well-armed and trained. These men weren't gangbangers.

***

Paul and Callie joined us on the beach. I could hear Paul's voice booming through the foliage long before we saw them through the palm trees. Then we heard Callie. "Put your clothes on and stop the hanky-panky!"

Ally gave her the finger. "Child, we adults always behave when out in public. You should try it sometime."

Callie stuck her tongue out at Ally. "Ally, you do know that you just mentioned my dad and adult at the same time. Besides, he's been like a coon dog chasing a bitch in heat ever since you two got together."

Paul laid their blanket on the ground and made the time-out sign while stifling a snicker. "Whoa! Callie! You just called your dad a dog and stepmom a bitch."

I groaned. "I resemble that. What man wouldn't chase a hot babe like Ally? Hey! You didn't mention Forrest sniffing around your Mom."

Paul whispered, "The coast is clear. We can talk."

Callie said, "I didn't mean that like it sounded."

Ally gave her the finger again. "I know, dear. Bless your heart."

I persisted. "Callie, how are Forrest and your mom doing? I've noticed he's living in her cottage."

My daughter chuckled. "Forrest and his kids are darlings. He waits on mom like a princess. He's kind and considerate. Nothing like that asshole pervert Todd she almost married."

I couldn't help myself. "Is your mom still mad at Mike for taking a dump in Todd's Corvette?"

She laughed. "I'd forgotten about that. Uncle Mike is the man!"

I tired of the give and take. "Okay, ladies. Let's call a catfight truce. We need to talk. Paul has some concerns about our stay in paradise. Paul?"

They drew near to each other while still lying on their blankets. Paul said, "Zack, you know I trust your opinion and leadership ...."

I interrupted, "I feel a *but* coming."

Paul cleared his throat. "But, we've stayed here too long. Our folks are getting too comfortable. If we don't leave soon, we'll never leave. Callie and I want to develop a plan to retake our boats and get away as soon as possible."

Callie grimaced and avoided looking me in the eye. She said, "Dad, we trust you, but this crap has gone on too long. You only appear to want to make love on the beach and play canasta with a small group of our friends. I don't know what's going on in your mind, but it's not like you to settle for slavery."

I drew them in closer. Our heads almost touched. "What's wrong with making love on the beach?"

Callie huffed and gritted her teeth before I made the timeout sign. "Ally, I think it's time to bring the kiddos in on the game plan."

***

Ally and I stayed on the beach alone after my daughter and her husband left. I needed Ally's opinion on handling Callie since she'd changed quickly before my eyes from my petite teenager to a

596

grown married woman. We were deep in discussion when I heard a noise in the woods not far from us. I glanced above Ally to see a large man running toward us swinging a big assed machete. His face was contorted, and he screamed gibberish as he ran toward us. My pulse raced as I tried to push Ally under and behind me. I reached for my pistol a bit too late and had to meet him empty-handed. I jumped over Ally and hit the man while I blocked his arm holding the huge knife.

My left shoulder hit the man at the same time my right hand closed on his wrist, bringing the machete down. I'd successfully blocked the knife, but the man slammed my stomach with a blow delivered by his right fist. The bastard had unbelievable strength. I fell but didn't lose my grip on his wrist. Tripping over Ally's legs, I dragged the man with me. He was one strong SOB, and I was losing the fight when I heard him scream. Ally was using his balls for a punching bag while she bit his calf. I used the distraction to bite his forearm and wrench the knife from his hand. I struck him on the shoulder with the flat side of the blade.

The man swung and punched me on my cheek. I saw stars but kept the knife in hand and hit him on the butt with the business end on the machete. He yelped, and I hit him again above his ankle, severing his Achilles tendon. He fell to the ground with Ally clamped to his leg, still punching him in the groin. I swung the machete again and split his skull open. The fight ended.

Ally spat several times and washed her mouth out with a swig of wine. "That was a big son of a bitch."

I sat beside her as I huffed and took a long pull from the wine bottle. "I don't think he likes me."

Ally took the bottle and took a long drink. "He's Muslim, Black, and has those damned anarchist tattoos that were all in the news before the doo-doo hit the fan. Why would he attack us?"

"I don't know, but I think the sumbitch was acting crazy. He was probably on PCP or Meth. Let's not tell the Captain. I'll bury him in the jungle and cover the spot with leaves."

Ally stopped me. "We make a great team. I punch 'em, and you stab 'em."

I shivered when I thought this could have ended differently. "We have to be more careful. This island paradise has a few snakes."

After arriving back at our beach cabin, I told my team about the attack. I also told everyone to make sure they never traveled alone. My description of the episode held their attention. They were sitting in the front of their seats, leaning toward me. Then I told them how Ally joined in the fight by biting the asshat's leg and punching his balls. Mike had just taken a swig of beer, blew it out his nose, and sprayed all of us. The others laughed but stopped when the beer hit them.

Joan wiped beer from her nose. "Mike, you are an asshole."

Mike drug a hand across his mouth. "But I'm your asshole, and you love me."

"Only because you're my retarded brother."

***

The traitor first came to me about two weeks after we landed on Martenvous. She filled me in on what the island was like before the apocalypse. Captain Bassot had started out a good man, but the power went to his head. Overnight he'd become the absolute ruler of the island. Absolute power corrupts absolutely.

She took my hand and begged. "I need your help."

I looked at her and wondered what the heck I could do to help this woman. Old Zack would have had a quick but flirting answer. "What can I do for you?"

She reached out and shook my hand. "The Captain has let this new power go to his head. He's starving our people and treating most everyone like peasants. He has two women vying for his bed every day, and that alone has caused distractions for him. He's screwing most of the beautiful women on his staff while our once wonderful Island is destroyed."

I looked deep into her eyes and saw genuine concern and fear. "But what can I do, and why should I do it?"

598

She implored, "You can do a great deal, and the reason is you won't find a better place than this to make a good home. Every island in the Caribbean has these tin-pot dictators and drug lords. You and your people can make a difference here with my help. The Captain must go!"

I caught a glimpse of someone watching us from the shadows. I continued to look at the produce and speak without looking at her. I still wasn't convinced. "How can I trust you since the Captain trusts you?"

She turned to walk away when a person approached. She looked over her shoulder. "By my deeds," she said as she walked away."

The person skulking around was Davi. She asked, "What did she want?"

I smiled and then frowned. "I don't know. She just said how great Martenvous was and asked if we were enjoying our stay."

"Bull shit!" Davi walked away and then looked over her shoulder and smiled.

I thought the woman could read my mind.

*

Chapter 2 – The game so far

The beach by our beach houses.

Paul raised his voice, and his nose wrinkled. "What plans?"

Ally grinned. "So you think all we've been doing is fornicating on the beach and becoming complacent?" She turned to me. "The plan is working."

Callie scratched her jaw. "What plan?"

I looked around and scanned the beach. We were about fifty feet from the tree line, and I couldn't see anyone. "The plan to get our complacent asses off this island. Your two roles have been to be dissatisfied and whine about getting off the island. Ya done good. I heard you tell Aimee about how you loved Martenvous but were eager to get away and find a permanent home."

Callie said, "We didn't say anything that would harm our group!"

I reached across Paul and patted her on the back. "Callie, you two had critical roles in convincing Aimee that we were not planning anything, and you weren't happy about it. We need Captain Bassot fat, dumb, and content for our plan to work. I'll add both of you into the loop on the goals and begin to get your input.

The short story is we have hidden weapons and are gathering intelligence on Bassot's military and his enemies. We also have made a connection with one of the farmers who hate Bassot."

Callie looked down and frowned. "I feel guilty plotting against my friend's father."

Ally beat me to speak. "Don't feel guilty because Aimee isn't your friend and feeds everything she hears back to her father. We've tested her several times with bogus information concerning the locals."

Callie's eyes opened wide. "Dad, you don't trust me but trust me to spill my guts to Aimee."

Tears rolled down my daughter's eyes. "Callie, I do trust you, but this was need to know, and you had no need to know until recently. I also needed you to do exactly what you did. I know you'd never mention anything about our team that would harm us. I did count on you to mention to Aimee about the waiter who stole Aaron's watch. You also passed on the bogus info about one of the servants who was supposed to have been spying on Bassot. That guy was actually a spy from Cuba working to kill all of us."

Callie dried her tears. "What can Paul and I do to help?"

I looked around the area. "Davi will get with you. She'll give you a list of common household items she needs to help with our escape. I'll also give you a list of people to watch and report their movements back to me."

Paul fidgeted. "Zack, I'm sorry I doubted you."

601

Ally saw Callie pulling on her hair. "You were right about how we appeared to be just making love on the beach without a care. That was our part in fooling Bassot. Of course, your dad and I probably enjoyed our roles more than you two enjoyed yours."

Callie blushed and grinned at Ally, "You do know that several people saw you two naked on the beach doing it."

Ally's face quickly matched Callie's. "I know. That was the hard part for me. I'm really a private person, especially with showing my private parts."

Paul got back to business. "When?"

I was still guarded about timelines and plans. "Sooner than later."

Callie was still curious. "What assignments do our other people have?"

I clenched my jaw and then exhaled. "Girl, I trust you, but that is a need to know thing, and you don't need to know."

Callie laughed and said, "I was just wondering if Davi or Joan was put up to seducing any of Bassot's men."

Ally's eyes snapped toward me. I snickered. "Callie, are you jealous of some lady getting the job to seduce a sailor? Do you want to seduce one of Bassot's men?"

Paul stuttered, "Hey ... wait ... a dar ... darn minute. Hell no!"

Ally and I forced a laugh. I said, "We wouldn't ask anyone to do that. That is unless someone like Callie volunteers."

Paul's face bloomed with crimson blush, and he took Callie in his arms and said, "I'm the only sailor she is going to seduce."

Callie's fists were balled tightly, and her eyes squinted. "Dad ... that hurt. Joking is okay, but that went too far."

She stormed away with Paul in tow.

Oh shit! I had treated my daughter as an equal and pulled her leg a bit too far. Apologies were needed.

***

Mike snorted, "Oh crap! I'll bet Callie blew a cork! What possessed you to talk with her like that? Hell, that's something I'd do."

I slunk down in my seat and took a drink of my beer. "I don't know, except maybe she's been acting and living like an adult for over a year. She's Davi's mini me as it is. I hate to say it, but she'll be equally at home rocking babies or slitting throats. I think she'll have it easier than Davi since she had a soft side early in life."

Mike cringed, "Yes, I agree. When I first met Davi and found you only had eyes for Geena, I attempted to use the famous Norman charm to melt her down. She looked me in the eyes and said, 'Stop trying that shit on me and try it on one of these bimbos.' No one says, bimbos."

Mike Norman and I'd been best friends ever since I could remember. We went to grade school, high school, and some college together. Mike had always been a ladies man while I was a bit awkward around women. I jumped out of that mode when Joan divorced me.

I said, "Mike let's change the subject. I have a spy in Bassot's inner circle. We have spies in the farmers. I need you to develop spies in the anarchists. I know that will be tough since they are African Americans, Hattians, and Black islanders from Martenvous. Just let me know what you'll need."

603

Mike's eyes opened wide, and he sat back in his chair with his fingers locked behind his head. "That will be a piece of cake. I'll get that done right after I find the Holy Grail."

I gave him a pat on the back. "Davi is an expert in infiltration and developing spy rings."

Mike laughed, "She can get spies but not a boyfriend."

I sneered, "Maybe she's looking for qualities that you don't possess."

***

Later that day, I saw Lieutenant Devereau sneaking a peek at a woman on the beach. The white thong Bikini accentuated her rather shapely and gorgeous tanned body. Even I, the perfect husband, stared at the woman for a few seconds until she rolled over and it was Davi. I instantly felt guilty. Then, I grinned from ear to ear.

I had seen a mutual attraction, and at first thought, it was a shame he was the enemy. Now, the idea of Davi using her charm on the lieutenant to gain information grew on me. I'd thought back to how I'd met Davi and suddenly remembered that Davi had never paired up with any of the men. I had wondered about that but never had the nerve to ask her. Of course, I'd been attracted to her, but the damned truth was she scared me. Any woman who could cut your head off and piss down your throat, frankly, scared the shit out of me. Maybe the first time in my life, my big head actually won a battle concerning women.

I walked up behind Devereau, humming an old tune, so I didn't appear to be sneaking up on him. I cleared my throat. "Lieutenant, she is beautiful, isn't she?"

He stammered for a few seconds. "Sir! I don't want to leave the impression that I was spying or stalking the young lady."

I raised my hand. "No need to apologize for watching a gorgeous young lady on a public beach. I had to stop and enjoy the view myself. Davi is one of my best friends, and I think she'd like you to approach her. She doesn't have a boyfriend, and I know she'd like to get to know you better."

Lieutenant Devereau said, "Are you sure? She seems so cold and impersonal around our leadership."

I chuckled, "What do you expect from an ex-Mossad agent. She could break both of us in half if we were a threat. I know her, and she can be gentle and thoughtful. The girl also has a funny streak that will keep you laughing. That is once you get to know her. I'll put in a good word for you if you want."

He said, "I thought your group was anxious to leave Martenvous."

I mentally crossed my fingers. "The extra month of living in paradise has mellowed my team a bit. We kinda vacillate on leaving on a good day. To be truthful, the rebels worry us. The ones that arrived from the USA tried to ruin our country and are trying to ruin yours. If we could eliminate them, this would be a great place to stay. I hope the Captain is working on a plan to stop them before they spread their evil."

***

The black clad figure crept through the jungle and arrived at the top of Mount St. Peter. I thought I knew who the person was, but the darkness hid their features. This was the second time I'd followed the stealthy bastard. Four days ago, I'd spotted someone sneaking through the trees quite by accident. The dark figure wore only black and blacked out its face. The dark clad figure was almost invisible in the dark below the tree canopy.

The first time, a truck was hidden in the brush, and the asshat got in and drove off, leaving me behind. The following day, news spread across the island that one anarchist leader and two drug cartel members had been assassinated during a meeting.

The anarchists controlled the northern tip of the island, including the mountain. The top of the mountain was actually a dormant volcano and where their headquarters were located. I watched for the dark clad person every night to no avail until the fourth night. I guessed he was heading to the truck and ran as fast as I could. I snuck into the back of the truck and stayed hidden for over an hour as the truck lurched along dirt roads. He parked the truck halfway up a mountain.

I walked behind the shadowy figure the last three miles up the mountain without being seen. I was getting good at this clandestine ninja crap, even if I do say so myself. He stopped short of a small group of heavily guarded shacks located in a clearing, nearly at the top of the old volcano. I watched as he searched through his rucksack and pulled out several objects. Then he low crawled to the back of two buildings and came back only holding his pistol.

The guy hauled ass down the mountain through the brush, not caring about the noise he made. This was good because he would have heard me about fifty feet behind him. He'd only covered a hundred yards when the still of the night was shattered by two powerful explosions. Men yelled, and women screamed. Gunfire erupted behind us, and searchlights lit up the night. The ninja warrior froze for several minutes.

I watched carefully around me and saw something out of the corner of my eyes. He had raised his rifle to shoot at something moving in front of him. It was then I rose and fired my AR. Two men had gotten between us and were stalking the ninja guy. I shot both of them, not twenty feet from the man. I was flat on the ground when he turned and saw the dying men. The dark figure bolted through the brush, but I was still pinned down.

It took me the rest of the night to get home since I'd missed my ride in the back of his truck. The arduous trip home gave me time to figure out who the ninja warrior was. I decided to keep the secret a while longer.

Ally stood in the doorway, stamping her feet. "Where have you been? I know you told me you were trying to catch someone sneaking around, but the other times you were only gone for a few hours. It's 9:30, and you missed breakfast."

I kissed her and started to speak. She pushed back. "Oh! Hell, no! Tell me what happened."

I smiled and stretched. "I followed the man in black to an old pickup. I hid in the bed and ended up on top of Mount St. Peter. Can you believe that bastard blew up some anarchist's camp? I shot two men trying to kill this ninja guy and missed my ride back home. I walked twenty miles back home through the jungle. That about sums it up."

Ally's lips thinned. She looked up to the sky and then back at me. "Why did you save this man?"

Thinking quickly, I took her by the hand to the kitchen. "He is either a friend of ours and an enemy of our enemy or an enemy of ours and an enemy of our enemy."

Ally huffed. "So an enemy of my enemy is a friend? That crap could get your ass hung out to dry. Besides, I think you screwed that quote up."

"You know what I mean."

Chapter 3 – Hanky Panky

The Beach

The white thong Bikini accentuated Davi's gorgeous tanned body. She stretched and posed to make maximum use of her assets. She knew Lieutenant Devereau had been watching her ever since they'd landed on the island and was watching her now. The truth was that Davi was also interested in the Lieutenant, so she didn't balk at seducing the young lieutenant when I floated it by her.

The lieutenant left, so I took the opportunity to talk with Davi on the beach. "I'm sure you saw the lieutenant gawking at you."

Davi giggled. Yes, giggled. I'd never heard her giggle before today. "He's cute and likes to watch me when I'm on the beach. He's a bit timid. Hey, did Ally let you off the leash?"

I choked, "No ... I ... err ...I'm not on a leash."

She snickered, "You were looking just as much as he was today."

I had been busted. "I'm happily married, but any man would stop and look at a beautiful woman lying half-naked on the beach."

She toyed with me. "I can take the rest off if you'd like."

"Davi, you never showed any interest in men before. I thought you might be gay or something," I blurted out.

"You bastard. I gave you every chance to show interest, and you didn't."

I recovered quickly. "Davi, you are one of the most beautiful and sexy women I've ever met. However, you are also the scariest woman I've ever met. Every time I tried to flirt with you, you scared me off. Several times I had to stop and check to see if I still had my balls."

She chuckled, "I can be a bit intense. So strong women scare you?"

I fired back at her. "No! I like strong women. Ally is a strong woman but has a soft side. I'm scared of women who could slit my throat in bed if I pissed them off."

Davi nodded, "You have a point there. Do you think Harry would be scared of me?

"Who the hell is Harry?"

She blushed. "The handsome lieutenant."

I raised an eyebrow teasing her, "You just blushed. Have you ever blushed in your life? Harry wants to get in your knickers and has a case of puppy love. If you ever want to find true love and not just one night stands, you'd better wall off scary Davi and show the sexy, caring, and thoughtful side of you. You can always pull the other Davi out when you need to slit a throat."

Tears formed in her eyes, but she quickly wiped them away. "I don't know how to do that. I try and fail every time."

I had a brainstorm or a brain fart, depending on how Davi took my following statement. "Davi, I care for you and want you to be happy. Could you hold back your ego and show your soft side just enough to allow Ally to help you find that inner softness."

Davi glared at me then smiled. "My first reaction was to kick you in the nuts for that, but I realize I need help. Do you really think Ally would be able to stop gloating and help me?"

I never lied to people I loved. "Davi, Ally will gloat a bit, but you will never see or feel it. She will be damned happy that you aren't after me."

Davi reached up and kissed me on the cheek. "Please talk with her."

I nodded and then stuck a finger into her shoulder. "I told you to not be by yourself. There could be another attack."

Davi only smiled, "If someone attacks, I'll bring his ear to you? Remember you said I was scary."

***

Davi only had been alone a few minutes when she saw the movement in the trees out of the corner of her eye. She pretended to add some sunscreen when she hefted her dagger. The two women came running in Davi's direction from a hundred feet away. Davi squinted and smiled when she saw the lead woman was much faster and would arrive a few seconds sooner. Davi waited until the woman was twenty feet away and sprang upward like a leopard. She eviscerated the woman with one slash and stood ready for the next attack as the first woman died with her bowels spilled at Davi's feet.

The second machete wielding assassin was a petite lady who had an evil smirk on her face. She screamed incoherent words just as Davi sidestepped and pushed her from behind. The woman fell forward, and she writhed in agony with the machete sticking out of her back. She'd suffered several sliced organs and blood vessels. Davi stood over the bodies, shaking her head. "Amateurs."

Davi dragged the bodies into the jungle and used one of the machetes to bury them. She calmly took the big knives down to the beach and washed the blood from them and her dagger. Davi then washed her hands and checked her makeup before going to her cottage.

Davi knocked on my door, and I let her enter. She brought her right hand from behind her. "I have some trophies for you."

I saw the ears and choked. "They sent two huge men with little ears to kill you?!"

Davi smiled, "No! They were women. One big one and a small one. They are buried in the sand where I was sunbathing this morning."

"Davi, please tell the others and do not go anywhere alone again. Please get rid of those ears before I puke."

Davi looked at the ears, yawned, and held them up to her ears. "You know, I might make earrings from these."

***

The following day, I told the group why Paul and Callie were joining the secret team, and only Aaron's eyebrows raised. I wrote, "How is everyone doing with their assignments?"

Aaron scowled and looked at me. He wrote, "I've been able to add two more spies from the farmers. Their leader wants to meet with us."

I drummed my fingers on the table. I wrote, "Good, set it up for this week."

Aaron still frowned. He wrote, "Their leader wants to know who our leader is."

I chuckled. "People in hell want ice water." Then I wrote, "We'll both meet with their leader and tell him our leader wants to remain anonymous for now. To clarify – I am our leader. Aaron is the general in charge of our military. Aaron reports to me."

Mike wrote, "We know that. One of the house staff let it slip that the Captain has become a bit ... let's say, perverted in taking his pleasures with the women staff members. He whipped one with a buggy whip a couple of days ago."

Several wrote, "Damn!"

Davi wrote, "I received an anonymous note that led me to a cache of weapons and ammunition. There were a dozen older ARs, six 9 mm pistols, about five pounds of C4, and plenty of ammunition. The note also said, "My first deed.""

I didn't react and then wrote, "So, we have some secret help. Did you hide the weapons?"

Davi looked at me a bit too long. She wrote, "No. I left them where they were. It was a good hiding spot in a hollow tree not far from my cabin."

Mike wrote, "Davi and I have a plan to develop a spy in the anarchists. She's a maid on Bassot's staff."

I wrote, "Great on the spy plan. Everyone check with all your sources to find out who's trying to kill us."

***

I watched Ally brush her teeth from the bed in our tiny cabin. "Darling, I have to ask you to do something for our team that might stick in your craw."

Ally rinsed her mouth and pointed her toothbrush at me. "That sounds ominous. You'd never ask me to do something against my will, so shoot."

I gulped. "I need you to help Davi develop her soft side."

Ally's eyes opened wide. "Tell me more."

I jumped in and told her about our conversation. "She's interested in the lieutenant."

"Harry?"

I shook my head. "How did you know his name?"

She smiled, "I asked. He came up to me and asked about Davi earlier in the week. He wanted to know if she had a husband or was dating."

My interest was piqued. "Well?"

Ally pointed the toothbrush at me again. "I told him that I hadn't seen her with a man since I'd known her. I then said Davi focused on our survival and took her responsibility seriously. I wanted to say the bitch needs to get laid and find a steady fellow. I did say she is more relaxed now and would welcome his interest."

"Thank you. That was handled perfectly to fit into our plans. I need Davi to get in good with Harry and get him to spill the beans on Bassot's military."

Ally poked me on the shoulder. "Seduce is the correct word."

I looked her in the eyes. "I hope she does get laid. She's wound up tighter than an eight-day clock. It might mellow her out."

Ally frowned. "Exactly what do I have to do to help Da ... vi get laid?"

I swallowed and rubbed my jaw. "You need to help her tone the warrior side down and help her act like a normal woman when she's not killing people."

Ally broke out in laughter, stumbled into me, and flopped down on the bed. "She scares you shitless, and that's why she didn't hook up with you before I arrived. This is too funny! Our fearless leader and my hubs is afraid of a woman and didn't jump in bed with her to keep his balls intact."

My face was hot, and my fists clenched, then I snickered. "How long have you known?"

She chuckled, "Babe, the Zack I got to know was a horn dog before the apocalypse and would jump at a chance to get a good-looking woman in bed. Saving Callie and Geena's death made a major impact on you. I think I also helped you muddle through some issues. Of course, I'll help Davi get Harry in bed so she'll stop making eyes at my hubby. Now make love to me like you mean it and forget about that Israeli hussy."

Chapter 4 – Scheming

Fort de Ville, Martenvous

My new friend met with me at the farmer's market. She had a fruit basket and was beautiful in her sundress with brilliant flowers on a white background. She had the island tan that was framed nicely by her white sundress. I walked up beside her and checked out some bananas. "Your first deed was great, but what does it prove beside you have connections. I don't have anything against the Captain."

She picked up some grapes and stuck one in her mouth. "You will have once Bassot sends you to invade Grenada while he holds your wife and daughter hostage."

I started to raise my voice but only squeaked. "How do you know this?"

She grinned, "The Captain's male staff members like em young. They talk in bed."

I looked at her and felt sad. "You love your country so much you'd sleep with those assholes?"

She sighed and said, "I've done a lot of things that leave a bad taste in my mouth since I learned of the Captain's perversion and atrocities."

Before I could speak, she grinned and said, "That didn't come out right. I will do anything to rid the island of the Captain and his henchmen."

I believed her. "I need to know how to gain the Captain's trust while I work to stop the anarchists from Cuba and the USA. I think they must be stopped before dealing with the Captain or the other evil factions."

She nodded and chewed on another grape. "I think you're right about the anarchists, but the Captain has your boats ready to sail to Grenada. I know you're meeting with the leader of the farmer group. Meet me at the end of Paris Boulevard on the beach tomorrow at noon."

"What if someone sees us?"

She plucked another grape. "No one will. If they do, we'll kill them if they aren't friends."

I began to think I'd met another Davi and could be playing with fire. I walked away, and Davi was hiding in the tree line. Shit! I walked into a crowd and walked around a corner. I ran to the end of the building and waited in a dark alley. I saw Davi in the light and walked up behind her as quietly as possible. Davi whirled around with a roundhouse kick. I caught her foot and dumped her on the sand. "Davi, it's me, Zack. Put that knife away."

I stuck my hand out and pulled her to her feet. "Why were you surveilling me?"

Davi kept a tight grip on my hand. "I've always watched over you even after you married Ally. You are important to me."

I squeezed her hand. "Davi, you are important to me also. Go ahead and ask me what's on your mind."

Davi's pursed lips and blush confused me. Then she asked, "Are you sleeping with that bitch?"

"No! Believe it or not, she is trying to convince me to keep our people on the island. She thinks we can help make her country free and prosperous."

Davi's head shook, and her eyebrows rose before she let my hand drop. "You told the truth and then lied to me. I can read you like a book."

I came clean with her. "She is going to help us defeat the evil rebels, help the farmers, and overthrow Bassot."

"Are you shitting me?"

I raised my hands. "Lower your voice. No. I'm not kidding you. She contacted me and delivered the weapons. I trust her. I do not want anyone else to know about her, even Ally."

Davi sighed. "Zack, don't get mad, but did you have to seduce her to get her on our side?"

I took her hand and placed the other on her shoulder. "No, I couldn't do that to Ally. I know we have to do things that don't feel right, but I won't do that."

Davi's frown turned into a grin. "But you want me to sleep with Harry to pump him for info and help."

She was a very intelligent person, so I didn't try to BS her. Besides, she could tell if I was lying. "I do want you to obtain information from Harry. How you do that is up to you. But, don't shit me! You are interested in him and wouldn't mind at all sharing your bed with him."

She chuckled. "You can also read my mind. I wasted too much time on you and now need some male companionship. Even I have a biological clock and would like to have a husband and rug rats one day."

***

Aaron and I were to meet with George Gagnon the following day at the place she'd told me to go. The location on the desolate beach was five miles from our cabin. We rode bicycles all but the last quarter mile and then walked through the jungle to the beach. We were four hours early so I could watch to see if it could be an ambush. We hid in the bushes and sat on the sand, eating some fruit for breakfast. I washed it down with a swig of wine and then scanned the beach.

Aaron looked across the water to the opposite side. "You've developed a habit that will help keep you alive. Too many leaders have been ambushed before a meeting."

I looked past Aaron and scanned up the beach to the ocean. "Davi taught me well."

The beach was in a sheltered cove that was an eighth-mile deep and as wide at the opening to the sea. A large creek flowed into the bay a hundred feet from us, and the water looked inviting. Only the lower class people came to this beach because it had brown sand thanks to the creek's mud that washed into the bay. The lower class folks worked during the week, so it was deserted that day.

Three hours later, two men broke through the trees only a few yards from us. We heard them walking through the thick undergrowth and hid when they got close to us. They scanned the beach with field glasses and then walked deeper into the trees and walked toward the ocean.

Aaron watched the men. "They think they're being stealthy but sound like an elephant busting through the jungle."

We waited for another thirty minutes until three men and a woman walked out of the trees on the same beach we were on but a couple hundred yards closer to the ocean. Aaron studied them through the binoculars. "I recognize one man and the woman. They are our spies. Let's go to them."

We walked out of the tree line and waved at the farmer group. They saw us and waved back. They were as wary of meeting anyone on the island as we were. I had Davi and Ally hiding in the brush with two of the rifles that my new friend had given us. They were my security. I wondered if the farmers had any hidden snipers.

We shook hands, and George Gagnon introduced himself as their leader. He was a short, stout man with dirty clothes and calloused hands. He spoke like a peasant using colloquial language for a few minutes. I was surprised when he started talking with much more sophistication. He saw my surprised look. "I was educated at Harvard and had a doctorate in sociology. I became a farmer when Bassot closed the universities and told us to find a real job. My family owned a small farm on the other side of the island, so I knew farming. I didn't know how power would create a monster from a once good man."

I looked around at his group. "Let's get down to business. First, I want to offer our services to train your people on military tactics, hand-to-hand fighting, and a few other basic military tactics that will make them much more effective and help them live longer."

Gagnon looked at Aaron. "Is he your leader, or are you?"

Aaron pointed at me. "Zack is our leader. I am the leader of our small fighting force. I report to him. You need to listen to him."

Gagnon huffed, "We've done well so far without your help."

I motioned to my snipers. Ally then Davi stepped out of the tree line and waved at us. "We don't want to insult you, but you need training in most fighting and security tactics. Always get to a meeting place several hours before the meeting to make sure there isn't an ambush already set up."

Gagnon balked and said, "Two of my men scoped out the area two hours ago."

I shook my head. "We know. My snipers, Aaron, and I watched them look around for a few minutes and melt back into the bush."

Gagnon tensed and cracked his knuckles. "I'm just a lowly professor. What do I know about fighting? Please provide the necessary training."

Aaron spoke. "I will send two of our best to help improve your fighting skills. This will take two weeks. They will only train your trainers who will pass on their knowledge to the rest of your group. They will also train your team how to make explosives, set up ambushes, and run a guerilla war."

Gagnon thanked us profusely, "Our people will use the training wisely."

I glanced at Aaron. "Are you aware of any attacks on anyone besides Bassot's men by the anarchists?"

Gagnon rubbed his jaw. "Yes, there have been several attempted attacks on the old white ruling class. They all have personal body guards, so none of the attacks were successful, so far."

***

My new friend was curious the next day about how the meeting with Gagnon went. "Gagnon is a strange bird. What was your opinion of him?"

I stood in front of the household goods in the small store inspecting a butcher knife. "That he is. He's like most revolutionaries. Long on get up and go but not much ability to get the job done. He can stir up the people but isn't an effective leader, or more importantly, he's not a fighter."

She only said one word. "Bingo!"

I looked into her eyes and blushed. "How do you know what it takes to fight in a revolt?"

She bowed and then whispered, "I don't. I can't open a jar of pickles, but I keep a big strong man around to provide the muscle. I know enough to know that the farmers would only last a couple of days in an all-out fight. They haven't been crushed yet because the Captain sees the drug cartel as more threatening. The farmers are third in line on his hit list."

Frown lines spread across my face. "Who's number two?"

She selected a steak knife. "The anarchists"

"So, what's next on your list to bother me with?"

My new friend stepped around me and motioned for the shopkeeper. "You are going to wipe out the drug cartel on Grenada and then the anarchists."

"What the f ...?" The shopkeeper walked up and interrupted me. She asked about the steel and would the knife keep its edge. He assured her it would.

621

I started over. "That sounds like the Captain's plan. Why help him solidify his grip on the island?"

Her face looked angelic then a devious grin appeared. "If you defeat the Captain, you have to fight the drug lords and anarchists by yourself. Why not use the Captain to defeat them and then defeat the Captain when he trusts you the most?"

*

Chapter 5 – My plan

Fort de Ville, Martenvous

The Lieutenant sought my advice on how to approach Davi. He'd joined the military in France at seventeen and had only dated the girls in his backward village. Harry's social skills were limited. He knew how to be a gentleman and eat with the right fork but was clueless when it came to courting a woman.

Harry met with me at a small café at the entrance to the palace. It was one of the few still open and catered to the island's elite and military officers. He was clearly uncomfortable but blurted out. "I need your help. Davi is so well, strong. I've only dated the girls in my village back when I was a teen. How do I start with such a sophisticated lady?"

I wanted to take this as seriously as possible but still gave him my proven Zack Johnson horn dog method. "Bump into her at the market or other safe place. Introduce yourself. Tell her she's pretty. Tell her you'd like to take her on a tour of the island or walk on the beach. Be yourself. Above all, listen to her. Most men don't listen because they are fixated on the prize at the end of the romantic talk. Now, for Davi, stay away from military talk and don't ask her how many people she's killed. Seriously, you don't want to know."

Harry nodded and had a cherry glow on his cheeks. "That's simple. Does it work?"

I crossed my fingers. "Of course it does. That's how I got Ally."

He fidgeted and then cleared his throat. "Do you think Davi will stay on the island?"

I'd thrown the bait out, and now it was time to set the hook. "As a matter of fact, Davi and I had this discussion the other day. She agrees that if the Captain got rid of the anarchists, the island would be a great place to live. The farmer's revolt could easily be undermined by infiltrating it and eliminating the leaders. The others would disband. The secret to keeping the farmers happy is to allow them to keep more of the food they produce and back off the heavy-handed approach."

Harry was a bit surprised. "It's that easy?"

"Yes, ridding the island of the anarchists is the tough part. I'd set up a small surveillance team to find their leaders and then send hunter-killer teams out to kill the leaders first and then capture the rest of the scum. I hate to say it, but they must all be eliminated, or they'll just come back on you later."

Harry asked, "Why don't you tell Captain Bassot your thoughts?"

The hook was firmly set. "Captain Bassot is one to approach carefully. If he feels that I think I know how to lead better than he does, he might just get pissed. No, he'll have to ask for my advice. You won't get into Davi's panties talking with me. Go!"

Harry stuttered. "I'm a gentleman and wouldn't ...."

I smiled, "Bullshit."

***

Yes, I ran straight to Davi and told her the clumsy lieutenant would be trying to bump into her. "Harry came to me this morning and asked for advice on how to get in your pants?"

Davi choked and spewed wine on me. "Liar! He's a nice guy and would take a week or two before he even tried anything."

Wiping my face and wondering if the stain would come out of my white shorts, I said, "He didn't exactly say that, but he's very, very, very interested in *seeing* you."

"Don't you think one *very* would have been enough, and the way you said *seeing* sounded dirty."

I snickered, "Hey, you know me. I'm just a teenaged boy with girls on my mind. Seriously, the lieutenant is a gentleman, and you will have to make the first move. He's well trained in manners and how to behave around the elite, but he's socially awkward around women. Just be patient with him."

Davi shook her head. "It's weird having a man I couldn't conquer giving advice to my new boyfriend."

I exhaled loudly. "If I'd met you and didn't know what a badass you are, I'd have been all over you. You are everything a man wants, well, except for the emasculation part. Make damned sure the bad assed Davi stays hidden, and you'll do okay. How are you and Ally getting along?"

Davi frowned, and I gulped. "Zack, we talked and buried the hatchet. I ..."

625

"In her head?"

Davi punched me on the shoulder. "No, we're friends now. She sounds a lot like you with her advice. Be yourself but not the lady warrior. Instead, be kind and gentle. Shake my ass and wear low-cut blouses. Wear my thong Bikini and get him on a blanket on the beach. She says the same stuff that you do, but it's not crude and dirty like you talk to me. Damn, I just figured out that you talk with me like you would with Mike because you see me as your buddy and not a hot woman."

Her tears flowed. I was at a loss for words, but that didn't keep me from opening my mouth. "Davi, you are a hot sexy young woman. You acted tougher than Mike or I could ever hope to be, so I switched from trying to date you to make you one of my best friends. Don't do that with Harry, and you'll be that hot young chick that I missed out on when we first met."

Davi sniffled. "Zack, you'll always be my best friend. You care for me enough to tell me what I need to hear, not what I want to hear. Ally does that also. Did you know that she's not afraid of me? She was only afraid that I'd take you away from her. I assured her that would never happen."

I kissed her on the forehead. "Now go forth, my child and seduce young Harry and turn him to the good side."

Davi giggled, "I plan to do a lot more than that with him. I haven't been with a man in almost a year."

"TMI! TMI!"

Davi chortled, "I thought buddies talked like that."

"Men buddies do. It's kind of weird hearing a woman talk like that even if they're your best friend. Don't even come back and try to give me details like Mike used to do."

She huffed, "A lady never tells."

We spent the rest of the meeting discussing what I needed Harry to hear so he could pass it on to the Captain. It took quite a bit of arm twisting, but Davi finally agreed to move the Drug Cartel ahead of the anarchists.

Davi didn't exactly give up on the anarchists. "Zack, I'll support going after the thugs on Grenada first, but I'm also going to tickle the anarchists a little while we wipe out the bastards on Grenada."

I replied, "Works for me. Besides, I'm not stupid. I guessed a while back that you are the ninja asshole who's been bombing and assassinating the anarchists. Who did you think shot those two asshats that were about to kill you two weeks ago."

Her eyes were wide open as she turned to me. "I thought I was being careful to not get caught. Give me your word not to tell anyone. "

"Davi, I know you better than anyone but maybe your father. You hated how the anarchists were torturing innocent people and intimidating everyone. They would purge the good islanders and invite more thugs from the USA and Cuba. I won't tell anyone."

Davi pulled me to her and hugged me. "You saved my life. I owe you."

"No! I owe you for always having my back. I'll always back your play." I patted her on the back.

I filled Ally in on my conversation with Davi, well, most of it anyway. I kept the ninja warrior stuff to myself. We agreed that she'd be a better girlfriend if she listened, but meek Harry might not be tough enough for her.

627

***

Mike had been busy during the following week. He and Davi met with the lady who worked as a maid for Captain Bassot. Davi had told Mike that the maid was a beauty and slept with Bassot. The palace sources informed Davi that the Captain's mistress and daughter were furious that he was sleeping with a lowly islander.

Mike saw the woman walk out of the bushes. "Damn, she's gorgeous. I see what the Captain sees in her."

Davi huffed, "Is that all you men think about?"

Mike turned to Davi. "Yes, but we married men mainly think about our wives."

Davi shook her head. "You and your twin brother are so full of bull. Let's go see the lady."

The lady saw us and smiled. "You are the Israeli woman."

"Yes, I'm Davi Gold. I hear we have some of the same goals."

The gorgeous black woman extended her hand. "I'm Jade Allard."

Mike said, "I'm Mike, and that's not your real name."

Jade replied, "Do you really care what my name is when I can help you cut the Captain's nuts off and render his military useless."

628

Davi scratched her neck and yawned. "Talk is cheap. What can you deliver?"

Jade smirked, "More than you can imagine. My people have been treated well but always as second-class citizens. We'd gained political power in the past five years, but Bassot dissolved the government and installed puppets that do his bidding. He was once a good man before he let this evil power take over. We were lovers for nine years before the apocalypse. His wife knew but was happy as long as her lifestyle suited her, and Bassot kept me hidden from others."

Mike wanted to crack a joke but uncharacteristically kept a harsh tone. "What made you turn against him?"

Mike saw a frown and then tears. She gulped. "He killed my aunt and uncle. He also brought another woman into the palace. He takes her everywhere but is ashamed of me because I'm not one of the elites."

Davi covered the kind of information Aaron and I needed and then ended the meeting. Mike watched the lady blend into the trees. "Why doesn't she just kill him in his sleep?"

Davi thought for a minute. "Because one of his officers would take over and could be worse for the island."

Mike clenched his fists. "So we're in for a fight."

***

Lieutenant Harry Devereau strolled to Davi's favorite beach on Saturday with a boogie board and a picnic basket. His fingers were crossed until he saw her in the pink Bikini. Now he worried about losing his courage. He walked toward the bathing beauty who lay on her stomach with her top off, soaking up the sun.

Davi pretended to read a book as she caught Harry's motion in her peripheral vision. She saw him mumbling to himself. "Come on over here and sit down by me."

Harry was only a few yards away when his feet tangled, and he stumbled and almost fell on Davi. His arm flew over her and wrapped over her bare back. She tilted her sunglasses up to her forehead. "Darn, I thought you were super timid, and here you go trying to feel me up on a public beach."

Harry stuck his finger under her chin. "You are the most beautiful woman I've ever seen. My knees go week every time I see you."

Davi smiled. "Now, take your hand off my back and tie my Bikini top. Then we can talk, and you can tell me why it took you so long to get the nerve to approach me."

Harry tied the strings and plopped down beside her, fidgeting. "I joined the military right out of high school. I lived in a small village and spent most of my time on the family farm in Southern France. I didn't learn much about girls before I joined the service."

Davi rolled over and laid her head on Harry's lap. She looked up into his brown eyes. "Of course, all soldiers frequent the ladies in the red light district. You didn't catch any STDs, did you?" Davi bit her tongue. "I'm sorry about that. When I get nervous, I joke around."

His face burning, Harry bent down and kissed her. Davi reached up and pulled him down to her. They finally came up for breath. Harry's face was inches away. "Why would a beautiful woman be nervous?"

She kissed him again. "For the same reason, you were nervous. I was a military brat, and my dad trained me to be a warrior. I joined the military at fifteen and didn't have time for boys. I'm as socially backward as you are. I like that. We can learn together."

The following two hours were spent learning all about their lives before the shit hit the fan. Harry opened up to her about his dislike for military life but never said a bad word about Bassot. However, after wine and sandwiches plus two hours of making out on the blanket, Harry opened up. He disliked the way the military was forced to treat the farmers and islanders. He was no fan of Bassot.

Davi carefully told him that she wanted to stay on the island, but her group was anxious about the anarchists taking over the island. Davi liked Harry and didn't have to act as they explored each other's bodies after moving the blanket into the nearby stand of trees. She felt a bit guilty using him but overcame that and enjoyed the rest of the day.

From time to time, she'd caught a reflection from the woods across the way and thought Mike or Zack was watching them. She gave them a show they'd never forget, nor would Harry.

Later, she told me about her taunting us. It wasn't me or Mike watching her. I told her that I'd never watch her like that.

Davi blushed and looked down to her feet. "Who the hell was watching?"

*

Chapter 6 The Captain's plan

Fort de Ville, Martenvous – The Palace

Aaron and I met Captain Bassot for breakfast every other Friday since we had landed on the island. He'd told us the meeting was to stay in touch with the people who'd saved his daughter and to convince us to stay on the island. Bassot was always late for the meeting. Aaron and I had learned we were expected to eat on time and then watch him eat while we talked. I always thought it was one way to show us he was more powerful than we were.

Bassot walked in, and I about choked on my last bit of sunny-side-up eggs. The woman kissed him and then left the room. She was the woman who'd been with the farmers at the meeting. Damn, there was more than one spy in Bassot's circle of friends. By the way, this one dressed, she was definitely friendly.

Bassot turned to us and smiled. "One of my adoring subjects. She just stopped by this morning to show her appreciation for my strong leadership."

I clapped my hands. "I guess it's the same all over the world. The movie stars and leaders get all the hot chicks."

Bassot took it as a compliment and laughed. "I have figured out that even though Aaron is the strongest militarily speaking, that you are the leader of your merry band. I also noted that you have a hot chick for a wife."

I didn't want to push him too far. "Yes, I'm the leader of this band of survivors. Aaron has years of military experience and is the leader of our small fighting force. We haven't talked about what our group has done to survive. We've had to fight the same tin-pot dictators and anarchists as you have on the island. We were always out manned and out gunned. We won many battles, but when we heard the Cubans, Russians, and Chinese were heading our way, we knew we couldn't win."

This captured Bassot's interest. "How did you win battles with a, pardon me for saying so, rag-tag group of people?"

Aaron replied, "We won the hearts and minds of most of the locals and used guerilla tactics to shred their capacity to fight. We ambushed their leaders, ambushed their men, and got the locals on our side by helping them with food and weapons."

I sat there hoping Aaron had his fingers crossed. "Aaron and his wife even smuggled food by decorating a semi with Biohazard signs and wearing level four protective gear."

Bassot laughed then said, "One of my officers has formed an attachment to that Israeli beauty in your group. He's young and might be a bit awkward for such a sophisticated woman."

I chuckled, "Davi is anything but sophisticated. She can whip any man or woman on both our teams, but she has devoted her life to her country. She's just right for Harry."

Aaron smiled, "My daughter is quite fond of the Lieutenant. They'll make a good couple if we stay here."

Bassot took a breath and exhaled, "The lieutenant told me you were very worried about the anarchists taking over the island. I've contained them but haven't been successful in wiping them out. What would you do differently?"

I spoke from the heart. "Aaron will cover the military part. I'll cover the big picture. You're tilting away at three windmills but need to focus on one. You need to lighten up on the general population and start programs to make their lives better. Make the farmers your friends instead of treating them like necessary evils. Without the produce and meat they supply, this island will die off in less than a year. Start programs to help them be more efficient and keep more of what they produce. Then you can concentrate on the anarchists while not worrying about a general revolt of your people."

Bassot's smile disappeared. "You are correct. I've had to have a stern hand during the apocalypse. The anarchists are the major problem. Your small group can be a force for good or a threat. I need your help. I have a threat that is just right for your group to solve for me. Frankly, I don't want you to leave us because I see your group as vital to our island's survival. My people don't know how to survive. My military and leadership would starve on their own, and our farmers and the general population would kill themselves fighting useless wars. I want to go back to a democratically elected leader when we can get the enemies defeated, but I need your help."

I looked at Aaron. "Aaron and our team would be glad to assist you. We love this place, but as I said to you a couple of months ago, we love our freedom. Aaron will take a day or two and get back to you on his strategy to defeat the anarchists. I will do the same for the civil unrest. All we ask is if this works to be allowed to live in peace and prosper as the island gets back on its feet."

Bassot stuck his hand out. "Those sound like reasonable requests. Let's rebuild our island."

We didn't speak of the meeting until we were on the beach with Davi and Mike. I filled them in on the discussion. Davi shrugged her shoulders. "I don't know what to think. He sounds genuine but so did Adolf Hitler back in the 1930s."

I said, "I don't trust the Captain any more than he trusts us. The day we get rid of the anarchists is the day the Captain has to go, or he'll kill or imprison us."

Aaron nodded, "This will take precise planning."

Mike frowned at me and then smiled. "I know you've come to expect a joke from me, but I think we need to take the time to diagram all of the factions, spies, and motives. We have spies in every group now, and I, for one, think we need to figure out how to solve this problem without getting shot or blown up, again."

***

Captain Henri Bassot called his officers and island dignitaries together the next day and held a surprise meeting. The waiters served champagne and hors d'oeuvres to the sizable crowd. Trumpets blared as Bassot entered the grand ballroom of the palace. He smiled and waved at his subjects.

He clapped his hands, and the trumpets ceased. Bassot stepped up to the podium. "I am glad to announce that our beautiful island has turned the corner and is on its way to normalcy again after the horrible apocalypse. In honor of this great accomplishment, my superiors have promoted me to General of the Army, Navy, and Air Force.

I am loosening our emergency rules regarding the eighty percent tax on farmers and rancher's crops and livestock to celebrate this feat. The tax is now only fifty percent and will be further reduced to only thirty percent at the end of the year. Further reductions will occur as our island completes its recovery. I'm also reducing the tax on food by half and increasing the amount of food going to the disabled, elderly, and sick. Our island is doing much better under my guidance, and we must share the improvements with everyone."

The room erupted in applause, but many of the island's elites were left shaking their heads. The taxes had been split between them and Bassot. They were eager to find out what their cut would be after the reduction.

Bassot called for his trusted Lieutenant. "Harry, you are much too valuable to only be a lowly lieutenant. You have been promoted to Major Harry Devereau. You will receive a fifty percent pay increase and lodging suitable for a major's status. Now, down to business. This might be a bit touchy, but I need you to pump your new love for any information that might help us. We need to determine what her leaders' plans are for my island. I also need you to convince her that the drug cartels are our largest threats."

Harry's eyes shifted from the Captain to the window and back. "Of course, sir, I can have fun with her and still be of service to my mentor. Is there anything in particular that you want to know?"

Bassot was proud of the young man he'd mentored for the past six years. "Just keep your ears open. How soon will their boats be ready to tackle the Grenada gangsters?"

Harry replied, "They have been fitted with the best weapons we can spare. My men will load the food when you give me a couple of days warning that they are to sail."

Bassot shook his protégés hand. "Great, it will be in a week or so. Keep working on Davi."

***

Harry drove his staff car to Davi's cabin and knocked on her door. Davi looked out the window with her pistol in hand and saw the 2038 Cadillac gleaming in the sun. She opened the door and let Harry into the living room. Harry took her into his arms and whispered, "Let's go on a ride."

She tucked her pistol behind her back in a paddle holster when Harry turned to leave. "Harry, you sound so mysterious."

Harry drove them to an old fort that overlooked the south end of the island. The ancient cannons were long gone, many years ago. The government kept the grounds clean and weeds free for the tourists. He took a picnic basket and blanket from the back seat and led Davi up a flight of steps to one of the gun batteries. He spread the blanket on the stone floor and beckoned Davi to join him.

The wine flowed, and soon they embraced. Davi slid down and lay with her head on his lap while chatting about the good old days before the bombs fell. Harry ran his fingers through her hair and caressed her cheek, and kissed her. Davi lifted his shirt and kissed his taught stomach. He was surprised. "Why did you do that?"

Davi rose up. "It was the only part of your body I could reach to kiss. If you don't like it, I'll never do it again."

Harry shivered and said, "No! Please do it. I just didn't want to go too fast with you."

Davi kissed him. "I think we passed go fast the other day on the blanket in the trees."

637

Davi pulled his shirt over his head and planted kisses all over his chest. She was afraid she'd scared him off when his hands began to roam. She grinned and looked him in the face. "Harry, you are a virgin! You won't be when we leave this damned rock."

Chapter 7 - Davi's Struggle

My beach cottage

Ally opened the door and ushered Davi into our modest beach house. I was in the shower getting ready for dinner after a long day planning our strategy to defeat the Grenada drug runners. I tried not to listen, but hey, I'm just as curious as the next guy.

Ally saw the ear-to-ear smile Davi sported. "You got the lieutenant in bed, didn't you?"

Davi frowned, "I wish it had been a bed. My ass will have bruises for a month. He took me to an old stone fort for a picnic. He was moving a bit too slow, so I began kissing his tummy."

I could hear Ally chuckle. "I'll bet that got his motor running."

Davi gasped, "Oh! Boy! Did it! We had our clothes off, and ... well, ... you know a few minutes later ... anyway the boy has stamina is all I'll say. I was exhausted."

Ally laughed aloud, "And had a bruised ass. So the boy isn't as backward as we thought."

Davi took a deep breath and closed her eyes. "No! He was still backward. Three hours later, I'd taught him everything I know. He's coming to my cottage next time. It was heaven except for the torture from the stone."

I walked into the room and said, "I couldn't help but hear you deflowered Harry."

Davi exclaimed, "Don't you dare ask Harry for details."

I snickered, "I'd only do that if Mike was involved."

Ally pinched my chest. "You'd better not be asking for details from anyone about any lady."

"Yes, dear. Now, stop!"

Ally gave me a pinch. "Now go and tell Mike everything you know and leave us adults alone."

I made the time-out sign. "Davi, did you cover the items I wanted to be discussed?"

Davi's face scrunched up, and her middle finger appeared. "I'm doing that tomorrow. He was too busy to talk."

I quickly left and went to Mike's house. I would never tell him about Davi's bedroom exploits. She meant too much to me to dishonor her. Mike and I talked about life in general until Sally served us cold sandwiches and a bowl of soup. Oh! Yeah! Mike tried to get me to tell him everything Davi had told me. I didn't, and Mike was disappointed that I didn't trust him.

I looked my best friend in the eye. "Mike, you are my best friend. Not counting Ally, Davi is my second best friend in life. If you told me a secret, I'd keep it forever. Davi deserves the same."

Mike grumbled. "Damn, ya got me there. If she was a man, you'd tell me everything."

I grinned, "I would because us guys see sexual tales as fair game for discussion. Women see it as a betrayal."

Mike suddenly looked up. "Is it okay if I ask her to tell me the details?"

I sometimes wonder about the boy. "Mike, old buddy, yes, but make sure you wear a steel cup over your gonads. Davi can be a bit testy."

Davi caught me the next day and seemed to be bubbling over but didn't say anything. She walked up humming a show tune and snapping her fingers. She saw me and got serious. We talked about the anarchists and Bassot but nothing more. Then after I didn't speak for a few minutes, she broke the ice. "You haven't asked me anything about my ... uh ... adventure with Harry."

I placed my hands on her shoulders. "Davi, that adventure was a very private thing between only Harry and you. It's none of my business. You seem sad. I thought you were over the moon last evening."

Davi looked at her feet. "I'd never done it before."

"What the f ... uh heck? You talked a good story. Well, it doesn't matter. Both of you are now experienced."

Davi had tears flowing. I'm not good with women's tears. She moaned, "Will he think I'm a slut?"

"Where the hell did you get that idea?"

She sniffled and wiped her nose on her shirt. "I enjoyed it so much. I was afraid he'd stop, so I took over and did everything to him that I'd ever heard of or seen on my laptop."

I inhaled deeply and then lifted her chin to look her in the eyes. "I think he is the luckiest man on the face of the planet. Well, except for me, thanks to Ally. You just made him the happiest man in the world."

She grinned. "Do you think so?"

I nodded. "Yes. Now to business. Give me the details about what Harry said about the island, Bassot, and life in general."

She'd given me the highlights, so I didn't learn much more. "Do you think the lieutenant is dissatisfied enough to join our team?"

She drummed her fingers on the wall. "I'm not sure. Harry is sending the right signals, but before I ask him to join us, I want to make sure he's not playing us while we're trying to play him."

She looked down at her feet. I stuck a finger under her chin and drew her gaze to mine. "Do you feel guilty?"

She exhaled. "Yes."

I asked, "Do you care for him and would have done what you did if he was just a nice guy you'd met on the street?"

Her eyes watered. "I think I'm falling in love with him."

She sniffled, and I wiped the tears away. "You are saving him from the Captain. You wouldn't want a man in your life that could abuse the island's people or kill innocent folks. I think he's a good guy in a bad situation. Using your assets to get his mind straight is nothing to be ashamed of, girl."

She blew her nose. "Thanks, Zack. I needed a pep talk."

As I walked back to my cottage, I thought that I'd gotten mixed up in a bunch of teenagers with raging hormones in a situation comedy. The pep talk made Davi feel better, but I felt like crap. Asking my good friend to prostitute herself to infiltrate the enemy weighed heavy on my mind.

***

Mike and Sally were lounging on the beach with Paul and Callie when I arrived. "Hey, I see beach bums!"

Sally gave me the usual bird. "And tell me again why we need to leave paradise."

Paul looked up at me. I didn't speak. Paul caught Sally's eye. "The cat set a trap with wonderful cheese. Now Bassot is playing nice with us. When he gets what he wants, he won't need us anymore. Then he eats us."

Mike rubbed some oil on his wife's back. "I think I've said that same thing many times. She still loves the island."

I nodded to Sally. "Sally is right."

Sally sat upright. "Could someone record this for posterity?"

I said, "Smartass! Mike, you need to beat her more often. Seriously, this island is perfect except for the Captain, the anarchists, and the drug lords wanting to take it all away from us. That's why I'm here."

Mike rubbed Sally's shoulders. "Sally didn't kill you for that beating remark, so I guess we'll listen to your plan."

Callie stood up with her hands on her hips. "I'm not doing anything that harms Aimee."

A frown covered my face, and my muscles tensed. "Callie, you can't always lead with your heart. Aimee is a big girl. If she

643

stands with the Captain, she's probably going to get hurt. We won't look to hurt her. I'm here to fill you in and prepare you for dinner and a meeting at my place. Aaron and the leaders in his group and our leaders will discuss who to take to eliminate the Grenada cartel. Davi and I have decided that has to be the first major move. Then we attack the anarchists and the Captain at the same time."

Paul's head bobbed, and his mouth twitched as he digested the information. "So, we need to build a team to attack the cartel. Later, we attack the anarchists with the Captain's help but turn on the Captain as soon as the anarchists appear to be defeated. Great plan!"

I was proud of the young man. "Yep, that sums it up. Now, we know about half of our folks want to stay here and half want to leave. How many can we count on to fight to make this island suit our needs?"

***

Davi had met Harry for some afternoon delight at her cabin. I ran into her as she walked out the door to go find me. "Well, hello there, Miss blushing and whisker burned lady. No time for all that *heing and sheing* stuff today. We need to work on our plan to handle Grenada. We need a list of names we can count on when the doo doo hits the fan."

Davi stopped, turned around, and walked to the deck behind her beach bungalow. "Hello, Zack, nice day. How are you doing? You suck at chitchat. I'm in a great mood. Do not spoil it!"

She meant business. So I said, "Good afternoon Davi. How are you doing today, and can we work on our plans now?"

She dropped several turds into the punchbowl and left me gasping.

Chapter 8 – More Planning

I closed my mouth and didn't talk for a minute while I digested what Davi had dropped on me. "Please repeat all of that slowly so I can digest it this time."

Davi took a deep breath and repeated what she'd said before. "Harry is madly in love with me."

I interrupted, "In lust, maybe. Love takes a while. Get on to the important stuff."

She pursed her lips and shook a balled fist at me. "Shut your pie hole and listen! Harry loves me and wants us to get married after we get back from Grenada."

Interrupting was what I do. "We, as in Harry, is going with us?"

"Listen and stop interrupting. Asshole! Harry and ten to twenty of his loyal men are going with us to whip up on the cartel. The Captain wants to make sure we're successful."

My eyes were wide open, and my pulse raced. My fists clenched. "Why the hell do we need them ....?"

"Shut up and listen!" Davi snorted. "Harry loves me ... shut up ... he is only bringing men loyal to him. They aren't loyal to the Captain. Harry is on our side. He's the one supplying arms and leadership to the farmers. He also is working with your new friend that I'm not free to talk about."

Davi stopped talking, and I didn't say a word. She fidgeted. "Well, Zack, what do you have to say?"

"You told me to shut up."

Davi hit me on the chest with a balled fist. It hurt. I smiled. "Do you trust him?"

She shrugged and didn't look me in the eyes. "I want to trust Harry, but every fiber in my body ... well, most fibers say this is too easy. I've been asking myself if he's playing me better than I'm playing him."

She was right. This was too easy, but we needed to go with the flow and take care of the cartel. "I think your judgment is correct. We work closely with him and let him earn our trust."

Davi giggled, "I like working closely with him."

"I'll bet you do. Maybe I can talk with him and get a feel."

Davi snapped her fingers. "I forgot something he asked me. He asked if I could trust you and Aaron. I told him, I trust my Dad, and I trust you with my life. He told me that he was jealous of you at first, but that changed when you told him how to get into my pants."

I choked and then gulped. "That was private men talk."

She laughed, "I know, and I was honest about our relationship. I told him that you were afraid of me and only had eyes for Ally. I also told him I wasted almost a year pining after you."

I didn't know what to say because I'd caught a longing look in her eyes. "This makes it more important to choose the right people for our little trip to Grenada. Hey, I just thought, does he know about your ninja routine?"

Davi stood up and went to a kitchen cabinet. She held up several blocks of C4. "Yes, and he's supplying me with ammunition, explosives, and logistics. Oh, and no one will be searching our cabins."

We finished the meeting by making a list of our best fighters who we knew would be loyal team members. We then gathered our leadership team and went to Aaron's cabin.

***

Aaron and Davi's mom, Sharon, knew that Davi had been dating Harry. Aaron disapproved at first because of the Captain and his iron-fisted rule of the island. Aaron seated everyone around the living room while Sharon served drinks to them. I looked around the room. Aaron's friend and ex-Israeli soldier, Mort, Davi, Ally, Mike, Paul, Callie, Aaron, and Sharon were seated.

I broke the ice. "We will start with me giving a brief update, Davi covering Bassot's military, and Mike and Aaron updating us on our spy ring. Then we make plans to invade Grenada. I'll begin."

I gave them updates on my new friend's help, our need to take out the cartel, and a brief description of our long-term plan. I ended by asking a question. "Do you think most of the ones that wanted to leave would change their minds if we got rid of the Captain, cartel, and anarchists?"

Everyone replied that the entire crew loved the island and would stay if the rules matched those of the United States.

Davi took over and surprised all by telling them about her exploits as the ninja warrior killing and blowing up anarchist's buildings. Aaron smiled in approval. Sharon, not so much. She said, "Davi, I know you are trained, but that was extremely dangerous for you to do by yourself."

Davi winked at me. "Mom, I was cautious and didn't take any chances." Davi then told us what she could about Harry and his relationship with Bassot. "Harry is falling in love with me, and I care deeply for him. We will see where that goes. Harry is a bit disillusioned with Bassot's leadership. He is among a large group in the island's military who want him to lighten up on the heavy-handed approach to managing people. They also hate that he caters to the rich and pisses on the regular islanders. I'm working on him a bit without being too obvious."

Mike snickered, "I'll bet you are...."

He stopped abruptly when Davi's mom cut her eyes at him. Mike quickly regrouped. "I'll bet he's madly in love and wrapped around your little finger."

Davi shook her head. "Mike, Harry is his own man, and seducing him would be too obvious. I will treat him as a friend or enemy, depending on how this turns out. I must add that Harry will be commanding a group of ten to twenty of Bassot's men on our trip to Grenada."

That was a shocker to most of the room. Aaron raised his hands. "If I were Bassot, I'd do the same. Davi thinks Harry is competent, and his group will be welcome. We just have to worry about Bassot and his men turning on us after we kill off the anarchists."

Mike and Aaron then covered the spy group's inroads into Bassot's team and the anarchists. Jade had told them that the attacks had demoralized the anarchists' followers since dozens of them had died during the attacks but only one of the leaders. Jade then told Aaron that Bassot couldn't be trusted and planned to deal with us after his enemies were defeated.

I led the discussion concerning who should go on the mission and who should stay behind. "Mort, how many of your team is willing to fight to free the island?"

Mort scowled. "Not if we win all of the battles and have another of Bassot's men take over where he left off. We want a democratic government."

I stood up and said, "If we go to attack Grenada. I plan to take over the island and set up a Constitutional Republic based on the US Constitution. However, I plan to make additions that install term limits and limit federal power over citizens. Voting integrity and assuring everyone can fairly vote will be stressed."

Mort didn't smile much but cracked a grin. "Thanks, we thought that was the plan. The Captain has hundreds of men, several heavily armed ships, and the elites' support. Can we defeat him?"

I looked around the room and knew exactly what to say. "One of my favorite quotes is, "Cut off a rattle snake's head, and it won't rattle longer." Bassot will be dealt with during the assault on the anarchists, right after we eliminate the drug cartel."

Davi added, "Harry shared the intelligence they've gathered on the cartel. They have light machine guns, RPGs, and plenty of AKs and handguns. No mortars or artillery."

I caught their attention. "Davi and I will sneak ashore and perform a quick recon mission to verify that information before we attack. I'm afraid they might use Grenadians as human shields. I don't want to make new enemies, so Aaron placed two spies on the island weeks ago. They reported there is a resistance movement and are eager to work with us. Davi and I will take weapons, ammunition, and explosives to the group. They will perform attacks on outposts on the side of the island furthest from the cartel's headquarters to draw the cartel's force away from their leaders. We slip in and wipe them out. Then it's just a matter of mopping up and turning the island over to the resistance."

I ended the meeting. "That's all, folks. I need Aaron and Davi for a few minutes to discuss our meeting tomorrow with the Captain."

Davi asked, "Should I be in the meeting since Harry will certainly be there."

I handled that concern. "You are one of my most trusted *lieutenants* and are necessary for helping plan the mission. Harry can stay home before I go in without you. Harry and you will behave professionally, and I don't expect any issues. Now, the question is how much we tell Bassot. Does he need to know about our spies and the resistance?"

Aaron's head shook before I finished speaking. "No! We only tell him what Harry and we are going to do. Even Harry doesn't need to know that we have extra help. We can say, "We're so happy they had a resistance and joined us in the fight.""

Davi and I agreed.

I walked with Ally and Davi back toward our cottages. "Davi, can you feel Harry out on what happens to Grenada after we eliminate the cartel?"

Davi poked Ally in the side. "He asked me to feel out Harry and didn't make it sound dirty. Is your boy growing up?"

Ally chuckled. "God knows I've tried to raise him right. I did a great job with Paul, but I fear I adopted Zack too late. I'm used to his boyish pranks and filthy mind. I kinda find them charming, now."

I squeezed her hand. "I resemble that."

Davi finally answered my question. "I was going to ask you if I could do that. I have a feeling Harry is close to being fed up with Bassot."

***

Later that night, Davi lounged on her couch with Harry's head on her lap. They'd just finished making love and were enjoying a glass of wine. Davi took a chance. "Harry, I've tried to keep our professional and private lives apart. I love you, and I don't want you to compromise yourself or your beliefs. We'll soon be attacking the cartel. What does Bassot plan to do with Grenada? Are we going to leave and let the inhabitants take the island back over and rule it in peace?"

Harry nuzzled against her. "Bassot compromises my beliefs every day. I love you and trust you. Bassot wants to take over Grenada and make their people into slaves to grow food and supply raw materials to make Martenvous a better place to live. Don't pass out, but I'd like to stay on Grenada with my most trusted men and make it a great place to live in freedom."

Davi bent over and kissed Harry passionately. Harry caught his breath. "I think you like my plan."

651

She kissed him again. "I like your plan and want to discuss it with you and Zack tomorrow. Now, we're going back to my bedroom."

*

Chapter 9 – Bassot's Dream

Ally made pancakes the following day along with Canadian bacon and orange juice. I pigged out and stuffed my face as Paul and Callie watched in awe. "Dad, save some for us. Paul and I are skinny people and need nutrition too."

Ally placed several pancakes on each of their plates. "Dig in, boys and girls. I like to see my family eat."

I'd just taken a bite of bacon when there was a knock on the back door, and a second later, Davi's head popped through. "Zack, I need ... are those blueberry pancakes?"

Ally said, "Pull up a chair but watch them. They bite if you get near their food."

Ally set a plate in front of Davi and gave her some pancakes before serving herself. "Zack, pass the syrup. You have to share. The butter too, please!"

Davi's mouth was full, but she managed to speak. "Harry and I need to talk with you before the meeting at ten with Bassot. Oh! Shit!" She ran to the door. "Come on in, Harry. This is my adopted family. I believe you know everyone."

Ally jumped up and made more pancakes while I set a plate and eating utensils in front of our new guest. I dropped back into my chair. "Harry, Davi says you need to speak to me."

Harry had just taken a bite. "Uh, I uh! We probably need to talk in private."

I waved my hand around the table. "I trust everyone in this room with my life, and you can trust them with what you were going to say to me."

Harry fiddled with his fork and pancake. "I could be killed if what I say leaks out. Davi, is this okay?"

"Darling, you can trust them," Davi said and took his hand.

Harry fidgeted with his fork and started to put a forkful into his mouth. "I'd planned the liberation of Grenada before we knew who you all were. My plan was to convince Captain Bassot that the drug cartel was much more powerful than it really was. Then I'd take a large force made up of mainly soldiers and sailors that were like-minded and loyal to me. We'd take the island, kill the drug assholes, and start a free government. Of course, I'd have scuttled the ships that remained behind. Then we could take in refugees from Martenvous and help set up a more powerful resistance over here."

I listened carefully. I mulled over what he'd said. "Harry, welcome to the family. Your plans and ours dovetail in together quite well. I have a few good surprises for you. Let's eat and then cover our mutual plans before we meet Bassot in three hours. I want us to be together on what we tell him but have a few small disagreements."

Harry took a breath and placed his arm around Davi. "I agree and might have a few good surprises for you. One thing I must say is that when the Captain figures out we double crossed him, there can't be any of your people on the island, or he'll kill them."

***

Aaron, Davi, Mike, and I walked into the palace promptly at nine forty-five. I had our plans in a folder and thought we were ready for about anything Bassot could throw at us. As I expected, Bassot made us wait an hour before we were ushered into his dining room. The asshat liked to meet while enjoying a meal. I walked into the room first and saw Jade sitting on his lap. She saw me and winked before any one of my crew could see her. She stood up, kissed Bassot, and left the room. That gave me an idea.

Bassot turned his attention to a blonde woman and didn't seem to care if we saw him fondle her as she was leaving. The man was corrupted absolutely with his fleeting absolute power. "Captain Bassot, we are here and ready to discuss our plans to eliminate the cartel on Grenada."

Bassot stood up and shook my hand. He pointed to the stars on his shoulder. "General Bassot is the correct salutation. I was recently promoted."

I faked a smile. "Congratulations, General. I'm glad your superiors saw your talent and rewarded you appropriately."

Bassot leaned forward. "Did Harry tell you that I promoted him to Major? He's my protégé, and I trust him implicitly. He will be in charge of this operation. Oh! I hear that one of your right arm ladies and Harry have been, I guess, working very well together. Davi, you are radiant today even in your camouflage shirt and pants."

Davi bowed slightly. "Thanks, and yes, Harry and I have similar interests in military strategies and tactics."

I almost choked. "I have our plans ready to discuss."

Harry looked at me and frowned. This threw me a curve. Bassot snapped his fingers, and two men rolled in a whiteboard and a large flip chart. "I've taken the liberty of making a few changes to my original plans. Flip the page, please."

One of the men turned the page to show a map of Martenvous and the islands around the area. The map covered the Lesser Antilles from Puerto Rico to Grenada, including Barbados. Nine larger islands and a handful of small ones were highlighted. Martenvous was almost in the center of the island chain.

Bassot pulled a laser pointer from his jacket pocket. "I plan to add all of the islands to the French Protectorate. Of course, I will be the governor of this new French-ruled empire. Eliminating the drug cartel will shore up the south end of my new empire. The islands between Martenvous and Grenada are poorly defended. St. Lucia has a small but well-armed police force. It won't cause too much trouble for Major Devereau and your force. The rest will fall like dominoes. Then we take Dominica north of us. Guadeloupe will be a tough nut to crack but not impossible. I think Harry might stand offshore with the two frigates and shell the shit out of them before your two forces storm the island."

Harry looked as nervous as a dog crapping razor blades. I stood up and clapped. Aaron and the rest of my team followed my lead. "Bravo! General, this is brilliant. Of course, you'll need some loyal subjects to manage each island for you. A select few who can get the most out of the islanders to benefit you and Martenvous to bring it back to glory and end suffering."

Harry stood up and walked to the General. "Sir, my hat is off to you. I'd only had small plans to talk you into adding Grenada. This is why I admire you so much. I have a lot to learn."

The Captain ... err ... General glowed with pride for his plan. "I'm pleased that you all see what my plan can do for me, Martenvous, and you. I have plenty of people without the ability to lead that suck up to me every day. Only a few of the old money elites on this island have a clue what it takes to start a business or manage people. Zack, you have built a strong team. We can do great things together."

I walked up to the flip chart. "General, we can start on the global plans the day after we run the anarchists off the island. How much do you want to be involved?"

The General motioned to the second man who'd been silent so far. "Harry, introduce Captain Monet."

Harry asked Monet to join him. "Charles is my XO and will be in charge of all planning and organization. Zack and my team will work with him to deliver the results our leader desires. This team will be unstoppable."

I read between the lines and figured out that Monet was a trusted ally of the Generals. "I like the organization and can't wait to begin the planning for the larger picture."

Harry tapped on the whiteboard and flipped the next chart. "This is our proposed timeline for conquering Grenada and then the other islands in order."

Aaron gazed at the timeline. "This only gives a few days per island. Each one could take weeks."

Captain Monet huffed and walked in front of the flipchart. "My plan takes into account all foreseeable delays. What are your concerns?"

Aaron wrapped his arms around his chest and walked to the chart. "Unless you plan to use some type of chemical or biological weapon, we'll have to take the island through hand-to-hand combat. Of course, we'll use the cannons and mortars from the ships, but they'll only be effective on buildings and large gatherings of people."

The General slammed his fist on the table. "Captain Monet is a graduate of the French Military Academy and is an expert. We go with his schedule."

I paused, stood up, and pointed to Monet. "How many battles have you fought in or led people into?"

Monet choked. "None, but I have studied war tactics and successful battles at the war college."

I pointed to Aaron and Davi. "Aaron led the Israeli forces in the famous Battle of the Negev and several other major victories against the terrorist states. Davi has led Special Forces teams into hostile countries, sabotaged their infrastructure, and assassinated military leaders. I'd listen to them."

The General's face flushed, and he visibly shook. To my surprise, he calmly said, "I agree. Captain, work with Aaron to address his concerns. The timetable only reflects my dreams of uniting the Lesser Antilles into our own sovereign country. There is no hard timeline. Monet, Aaron, and Harry, please go to the meeting room next door and hammer out your issues."

Aaron took Davi with him. I stood there with Mike waiting on an ass chewing from the General. He smiled and pointed at Mike. "Mike hasn't said anything during the meeting. Why did you bring him? Does he have military skills?"

I squinted and turned to my goofy friend. "A good leader surrounds himself with the best, most experienced people he can find. He also has to have a few people who will call bullshit when he hears a stupid or questionable idea. Those people don't have to be the best in the field. They have to be loyal but not afraid to stop up the works and question the experts. Mike is one of the best survivalists I know. He has my back, and I have his. He isn't always right but always makes me think things through when others press their ideas. He's saved my life more times than I can count."

Bassot slumped in his chair and scratched his jaw. "Do you see my *Mike* anywhere around me?"

My heart raced, and I felt my heart pound in my ears. "Harry could become your Mike. However, you have to trust him and listen to him. The worst thing a leader can do is be like the king with no clothes. Monet wants to please you too much. He will get people killed. You need to develop a couple of people you trust to help you steer your efforts to make your dreams come true. I hate to say it, but if we conquered all of the islands tomorrow, you don't have enough loyal and competent men and women to help govern them."

Bassot stretched and stiffened his back. "I see two men like that in front of me now. There are two more in the meeting next door. I need your team to help me fulfill my dream. I think I have plenty of the young pups like Harry, but the older ones have lived like elites and allowed their underlings to manage the island. The truth is Martenvous had become an elite cesspool. In my attempt to keep the island from disintegrating, I fell into the trap of settling for the same bad leadership. I also liked the women and power. I became Caligula!"

I jumped in and maybe over my head. "You have identified the problem. Now you need to reflect on what went wrong and how to do it better going forward. I think you can only succeed if you get most of your subjects to support your policies. My team has fallen in love with Martenvous and would gladly stay and contribute if we defeat the anarchist and cartel. We also have to make the farmers our friends. That can be done."

Bassot stood up, followed by Mike and me. "You've given me a lot to think about. While I may have appeared that I didn't like what I heard, I want to assure you that I did need to hear it and make changes. Could you give me your thoughts about how to get the farmers on my side?"

I took a deep breath and scratched my jaw. "I'll be glad to help with the farmers or anything else. I will ask you to write two lists. The first is your complaints about them. The second is a list of what they want. Then give an honest effort to see if you can meet them in the middle."

Mike and I left the General and joined the others in the planning room. We worked until noon. I told Monet that the General gave me a task with my comrades, and we would leave for lunch and be back in two hours.

We lunched at one of the cafes close to the palace. Mike plopped into his seat. "Man, that took some balls to tell the Gen ... er ...al that he was full of crap!"

Davi's head snapped around. Her mouth opened, and nothing came out. I raised my hand. "I said it diplomatically. The man is over his head and knows it. He's pissed off everyone on the island and surrounded himself with incompetent yes men."

Aaron lowered his head and rubbed his hand on his bald scalp. "Does he have a clue about how to get out of this mess?"

Mike wiggled in his seat like a puppy about to piss on your carpet. "He thinks we can become his right-hand men and women. He sees each of us managing an island."

Davi blew wine across the table. "Shut up! Are you shitting me?"

I chuckled and then nodded. "He all but gave us our choice of islands. He needs us to help groom Harry and others for those jobs down the road. He sees Harry as his only truly loyal man."

Aaron filled Mike and me in on the discussions in the planning session. "We learned our ships have been ready for several weeks. They have been made into gunships. We also learned that Monet is an educated fool. I believe the General put Monet's plan in front of us to see if we are yes men."

What's that phrase they say in mysteries? I believe it's, *and the plot thickens.*

*

Chapter 10 – Sailing! Again!

The Caribbean Ocean – off the west side of St. Lucia.

Our sailboat led the small flotilla south to Grenada. We were traveling at five knots with a favorable wind. We wanted to pass St. Lucia about two to three miles from the coast. We planned to bypass all of the islands at about that distance. The Beneteau yacht was slower than usual due to the addition of dozens of machine guns, mortars, and a five-inch recoilless rifle.

Davi suggested we sail close to the islands to draw out any pirates of rogue military units. The sailboat looked harmless but bristled with heavy and light machine guns. Harry and most of his men were on one of Bassot's two frigates assigned to my task force. We kept one frigate traveling a mile further out to sea from the island so our sailboat would hide it from prying eyes. The other followed a couple of miles behind. Anyone daring to come out to sea to attack us would get a hell of a surprise.

I heard Joan yell out, "I see St. Lucia!"

Everyone scrambled to their combat stations. Mort's men manned the .50 caliber heavy machine guns while my folks manned the old M60 7.62 caliber machine guns and the four SAWS. Davi and I manned the recoilless rifle, and Paul and Callie manned one of the mortars. Ten of Harry's men filled in where needed.

Two older motor yachts came into view. There were armed men on the deck, but we didn't see any heavy weapons, just AKs and ARs. Davi wanted to blow them out of the water, but I said they could just be concerned about us being the bad guys. I let them approach and addressed them. "We are friendly. What do you want?"

A man yelled through a megaphone. "Your boats and women."

The tarp flew off the recoilless rifle, and a few seconds later, the gun barked, and the boat exploded. Pieces rained down while Mort's men pounded the second boat with .50 caliber incendiary bullets. The boat caught on fire, and the gas tank exploded.

Men jumped off the last boat and floated helplessly. Davi sneered, took aim, and raked the floundering men. The SAW ripped the men to shreds. Sharks began feeding on them, and the water churned as they fed. When the machine guns stopped firing. I called out, "Well, do you feel better?"

Davi high-fived me. "That will teach the filthy perverts to mistreat women."

Harry's voice boomed over the radio. "There's a larger vessel heading your way. Steer away from shore, and we'll greet him."

We heard the cannon fire and could see smoke with our binoculars but couldn't see the pirate vessel sink. We heard several loud explosions, and then Harry spoke over the radio. "We wanted to capture the vessel, but it put up a short flight. Only a few small arms fire hit the side of our frigate. The pirate ship rests with Davey Jones. I always wanted to say that as a kid!"

The rest of the short voyage to Grenada was peaceful.

***

Grenada

The crescent moon was hidden by the clouds at midnight on our first day off the southeast coast of Grenada. The air was calm, and the RIB boats cut through the water to the desolate beach. My stomach fluttered as it always did before I went on a mission. Paul and Ben looked at me and gave thumbs-up signs. I must have looked pretty bad. I took a deep breath and gazed at Ally, Joan, Callie, Ben, Paul, Mike, and Sally. The rest of the team sat behind them. "You know your jobs. Harry's Marines will load the weapons and explosives in the trucks that had better be waiting on the beach. Davi will take her team to Brizan, and I'll take mine plus ten Marines to St. George. We duck and cover while the frigates pound the asshats. Then we mop up the survivors. Any questions?"

There weren't any.

Harry had stationed one frigate off the coast at St. George and the other at Brizan, which were the two cartel strongholds. They would begin shelling the designated targets just before the sun rose at five. This gave us enough time to drive to the two cities, which were less than ten miles as the crow flies from our landing zone. Luck was with us. Both cartel bases were both situated in industrial warehouses.

Davi had flashed the expected two short, three long, and two short light flashes. We were rewarded with a long, short, and two long flashes. Davi slapped me on the back. "The resistance will meet us on the beach just east of Chochu. We're five minutes from landing. Check your weapons in case the landing zone is hot."

The resistance team met us on the beach. They hugged us and thanked us for coming to their aid. Their leader hugged me and then said, "We've been very busy with the explosives you delivered yesterday during your scouting mission. Our teams will begin eliminating as many of the cartel's outposts an hour before the shelling begins. Zack, your idea to find their homes and take them out before they can react is brilliant! We have resistance members waiting to kill the bastards."

I was cautiously optimistic, but the tide appeared to be turning in our favor. We quickly loaded the trucks with the second batch of weapons and explosions this week. This would resupply the resistance fighters after the fight had been won.

The road was narrow and deserted. Gas was in short supply, so most of the running cars were sparingly used. We arrived a half-mile from the cartel's headquarters an hour and a half later. Our night vision goggles (NVG) gave us a significant advantage over the drug gang. I sent my two-man teams to their assigned locations and told them to wait until four am before taking out any of the gang.

Time passed slowly. I counted down and saw the minute hand hit four o'clock. I placed the crosshairs of my suppressed .308 sniper rifle on my target. Taking a deep breath and then holding it, I squeezed the trigger. The gun bucked, and the man fell. The next target fell a few seconds later. I could only hear a few pops in the distance as my teams took out the guards.

Twenty minutes later, the shelling began. The shells exploded upon impact and lit up the night. Harry and his crew were very proficient, and every shell hit the industrial complex. A shell must have hit an ammo dump because a tremendous explosion rocked the earth, knocking Ally and me to the ground. Large chunks of steel and masonry flew through the air and rained down on us. As soon as I knew what had happened, I shoved Ally down the embankment. We slid on the dew-covered grass to the bottom, where I helped her into the culvert nearby and joined her. I saw several pairs of eyes in the dark, and all but a small pair of eyes scurried out the other end. I knew the eyes belonged to a rat, so I calmly walked us, and soccer kicked the little bastard out the other end of the pipe. The culvert was only four feet high on the inside, but it had eight feet of soil and a concrete road above it.

Ally gasped. "Was that a rat?"

I held her close. "A dead rat, now."

Before I could brag about kicking a field goal, we were knocked to the floor. The secondary explosions weren't over. I rolled on top of Ally, and several chunks of the shattered culvert fell on top of me. Something huge had hit the road above us, rattling us against the concrete walls. More concrete chips and dirt fell on us. A large chunk grazed my right arm, but I took the brunt of the falling debris. Only a few smaller pieces hit my wife. Ally grunted when the silt stopped falling. "Either make love to me or get off."

I swam through the debris around us and helped her to her knees. "Come on. We need to scramble to our targets. The shelling has stopped."

Ally sighed and took a deep breath. "My mind is willing, but my body says, *"screw this.""*

I helped her shove the dirt and concrete pieces out of our way. We crawled out of the culvert and moved up the embankment. We shuddered when our eyes saw the scene in front of us. All of the dozen or so buildings were gone. Smoke rolled from several fires, and huge chunks of the building lay scattered around us for as far as I could see. Raw, twisted girders stood by themselves above the devastation. The smell of cordite and burning rubber filled the air.

There were no living bodies, just chunks, and pieces of bodies. Ally saw a shattered head with an eyeball hanging out. She stumbled backward and emptied her stomach. I held her hair back and gave her a drink. She took my arm and wiped her mouth on my shirt.

I heard a noise behind me. "I'm Jose. I'm the leader of the resistance. You're Zack?"

I nodded.

He stuck out his hand. "The fight is over. You saw how this one ended. The other group in Brizan fared better, but the survivors were picked off as they tried to regroup after the shelling. Go, find your people and meet us for a celebration breakfast at the city's courthouse."

We found Mike and Sally first. Sally had a nasty cut on her head but was okay. Mike saw us and pulled Sally behind him. "That was one hell of an explosion. We could have used that ammunition."

Ally snorted. "Shut up, Mike. We need to find our team."

Ally tended to the cut on Sally's head while Mike and I looked for the rest of our team. We walked past a collapsed overpass when I heard a voice coming from the rubble. My heart pounded as I ran to the source of the sound. Mike and I frantically dug through the ruins and found my daughter. The overpass had broken in the middle creating a void beneath both ends. Callie and Paul were unharmed because they were further away from the explosion. The massive concrete structure had saved their lives.

I held Callie and wiped away her tears, but she kept crying. Paul held her hand. "Zack, she saw a huge object fall on the truck that Ben and his wife jumped under. They must be dead."

I gave Callie to Paul and went to find Ben. We found Ben and his wife's remains under a large truck. They'd scrambled under the truck for shelter from the falling debris, and, well, it wasn't pretty. We buried their remains the best we could and went on to search for the rest of our team. I still cringe years later at the gruesome scene. That's all I have to say about that.

Mike and I walked west around the crater's perimeter and heard laughing coming from the other side of several trucks. We snuck up on the people and were relieved to see Davi and the rest of our team drinking wine and celebrating. I walked up to Davi, and she threw her arms around me and gave me a kiss on the lips. I held her at arm's length. "Davi, the resistance leader told us the fight for the island is over."

Davi shoved a bottle of wine into Mike's hands. "Yes, we won! The resistance took out over a hundred of the cartel's men before we started sniping. Harry's shelling took out the entire leadership. There are a few rats left alive, but the resistance is hunting them down. They will be killed on sight."

I exhaled and looked around at my friends. "Ben and his wife were killed by falling debris. Mike and I buried them. Let's say a prayer for them."

I gave an impromptu eulogy for the couple and then said the Lord's Prayer. "We were lucky to only lose two of us in this fight. We have to get better at this."

Jose, the resistance leader, walked into the group with Ally, Paul, and Callie. "The fighting is done. It's time to celebrate."

I yelled, "Stop! Yes, we won this battle, but the war isn't over. Others will come and try to take this island from you. We need to get all of the islands to join into a mutual defense pact."

*

Chapter 11 – Wow!

Sailing

Davi stayed on Harry's frigate during the trip home. They were married by the frigate's captain in a small ceremony with Harry's officers and us. Harry left a frigate offshore with the intent of making the island its home base. He didn't care what Bassot would do. He knew we had to strengthen and protect our expanding nation. I was shocked he wasn't worried about Bassot's reaction to making that decision without input from his boss and mentor.

After the wedding, I caught Harry. "I didn't see Captain Monet, your executive officer, at the wedding."

Harry smiled and pointed to Davi. She grinned. "That damned ninja fellow tossed their bodies to the sharks. Only men and women loyal to Harry are left on all our boats and ships."

We left Mort and several of his people on Grenada to help improve the island's organization. Most of their leaders and all of their politicians had been murdered by the cartel. They knew they needed help, and we knew we needed their food and raw materials. The cartel had treated the farmers and ranchers very well, so they actually increased production during the apocalypse. Forrest and Joan loved the island, so I appointed Forrest to be our contact and liaison for Grenada. Jose agreed with the concept of a mutual defense pact and began selling the idea to his people. We were off to a great start on nation-building.

We stayed for four days before hauling in our anchors and going back to Martenvous. Jose wanted all of us to stay and help lead their rebuilding efforts. I told him we would help and be there for his home island, but we had a mess to clean up of our own.

I wanted to know Bassot's reaction to the taking of Grenada and the elimination of the cartel. Still, we didn't break radio silence since we didn't want to attract any attention from the pirates known to be sailing these waters. I ordered everyone to rest because I feared we might have a fight on our hands when we met with Bassot. I gathered my inner circle and started plotting Bassot's demise. When I learned that Davi was traveling on Harry's ship, I had prepared her to lobby Harry about planning to get rid of Bassot ASAP. She liked the idea but wasn't sure that Harry was on board with killing Bassot. Harry preferred jail for his mentor.

Aaron looked at me. "I like your idea for developing two plans. We kill or jail Bassot, and with Harry's help, we take over the island and install a Constitutional Republic form of government."

Mike snickered, "I say we slit his throat while he's getting laid by the maid. Hey, it rhymes. I made a poem."

I shook my head. "Mike, this is a serious topic. Maybe we pay the maid to kill the bastard."

Ally said, "Remember, the maid is one of our spies in the Anarchist's camp. She'd love to kill Bassot, but that would compromise her ability to keep spying for us."

Paul raised his hand. "We know Bassot has to go, but who else has to go? Harry will take care of any military supporters loyal to Bassot, but there are several of the elites on the island who help prop up Bassot's reign of terror."

I knew exactly who would understand what was needed. "We're close enough to use a short-range walkie-talkie. I'm calling my contact to set that part in motion."

I keyed the mic. "French wine sucks."

A minute later, we heard, "American men are wussies."

I laughed at her reply, but Callie gulped. "I know that ...."

I stopped her. "Keep it to yourself for now?"

"Hello, my friend. We need to discuss who are Zebra's major supporters."

She laughed and replied, "I'm way ahead of you. Let's meet at the usual place."

I answered, "Will do."

Ally pinched me and then whispered in my ear. "Who's the woman?"

I whispered back to her. "I'll fill you in later."

Mike chuckled. "Jealousy is a bad thing. That sounded like a young French gir .... . Oh! Shit!"

***

Martenvous

We entered the harbor with Harry's frigate leading the way. The early evening breeze was cool as the sun set behind us as we gazed at the island. Suddenly, fireworks exploded above the harbor! I grabbed my binoculars and saw hundreds of people celebrating on the docks. Fireworks shot into the air, people were dancing, and a band played in a pavilion just off the docks.

I changed the channel on my walkie-talkie. "French wine sucks!"

I received an immediate answer. "The king is dead! Long *die* the king!"

My thinking ground to a halt, sputtered, and caught fire. "Isn't Bassot *your* father?"

Aimee Bassot laughed. "My father is Gagnon. I'll explain later. Come on in and celebrate our freedom."

I yelled, "Anchor here until I get a straight answer."

Harry's voice broke into what I thought was a secure and secret channel. "Bassot died around lunchtime. One of his lovers didn't love him as much as he thought they did. Go ahead and dock so Aimee and I can fill you in on our little secret."

My friends heard the exchange. Questions flooded into me. "I can only say that Aimee has been helping us get rid of her father. Well, Bassot apparently isn't her father, but anyway, Bassot is dead, and you know as much as I do now."

Harry and Aimee were treated like royalty. The islanders knew we helped but focused their praise on the two homegrown founding fathers and mothers of their revolution. We couldn't pry them away from their adoring fans. I was a bit jealous. My team had planned and executed the revolt against Bassot. Aimee and

Harry had just shot cannons at thugs and killed Bassot. Oh! Well! Our reward would be a peaceful life.

The party never ended that night. Ally and I went to sleep at dawn. Mike, Sally, Paul, and Cassie left the party with us and retired for the night. The sound of beating on our door woke us up. Ally lifted her head off my chest. "If that's your dumb assed buddy, go tell him to go home."

She tucked her head under a pillow as I left the room to answer the door. The knocking continued. I yanked the door open, yelling," Stop knocki ...."

Davi pushed me aside, her and Harry entered the living room. "Davi, what in the sam hell do you want this early in the morning?"

Harry chuckled. "It's early evening, and Davi and I haven't been to bed. Well, not to sleep, anyway. Here take a drink. We are a bit drunk but have sobered up a couple of times since we last saw you and Ally. Ally! Wake up!"

Davi caught Ally when Ally stormed around the corner. "Ally, I want to thank you for all your help. Now take a sip and listen."

Ally took a large swig of the wine and glared at Davi.

Davi cleared her throat, took a drink, and filled in the gaps on what had transpired during the past two days. "Bassot was caught cheating on Aimee's mother. Aimee's mother had an affair with Gagnon to get even. Bassot found out about the affair, killed Aimee's grandparents, and kept her mom locked in their house for years. He never found out Aimee wasn't his daughter. Aimee found out everything when Bassot killed her mom while she was away at school. Gagnon and her aunt told her everything. That covers Aimee's motivation."

"Harry, tell them why you hated Bassot."

Harry stuttered and then took a deep breath. "Several years ago, I fell in love with the daughter of one of Bassot's maids. She fell for me, and we were meeting secretly. Bassot had never seen her before, but one day she came to find her mom, and Bassot attacked her and raped her."

Harry took another deep breath. "Her mom and I vowed to kill the SOB two years ago, but I talked her into waiting for the right time. When I found your group, I knew the time had arrived."

The hamster wheel in my brain was turning at a furious pace. "Jade is the mother of your friend."

Harry choked but then looked at Davi. "Yes, and Jade cut the SOB's throat."

The hamster kept the wheel busy. "What about the anarchists?"

"Jade, Gagnon, and Aimee took out their leaders, and Gagnon's men are hunting the survivors as we speak. I provided modern weapons to the farmers, and they are busy cleaning house."

Information overload set in quickly. "You mean we won the war, and none of us had to fight Bassot or the anarchists?"

Davi laughed. "Zack, we helped more than anyone. You jump-started their resistance movement. We infiltrated their groups and learned who their leaders were. The most significant thing we did was to give them confidence and support. They were fed up but didn't have the courage to act."

Ally asked, "Where is Aimee? Callie will want to hear from her."

Harry said, "Aimee is off to St. Lucia to start their revolution and grow our new alliance and possible new nation."

I frowned and gazed out the window. "Why didn't she stay here long enough to enjoy our victory?"

Harry smiled at his new wife. "For the same reason, Davi, Paul, and my Special forces are going to Dominica. There's a bad group that's taken over the island and making life miserable for the locals."

Ally jumped up. "Does Callie know Paul is going?"

Davi nodded. "Yes, and she tried to go with Paul, but I told her to stay home and prepare her nest."

Ally's face scrunched, and then her eyes flew open. "Is she pregnant?"

Davi hugged Ally. "Yes, but let her tell you."

*

Chapter 12 – Back to Better than Normal

Fort de Ville

Ally and I swam in the clear ocean water. She was more playful than usual, and we behaved like newlyweds. The ocean wasn't cool but much cooler than the hot assed air on the island. The sun hung low on the horizon, and the sky was red. I tried to remember that old saying about 'Red sky in morning, sailor take warning, red at night, sailors delight,' or something like that. Anyway, we had just had a delightful swim and were ready to grill some steaks.

Time had quickly passed since the coup that freed Martenvous. Three months was a short time for a country to go from a dictator to a free society. Aimee and Harry had no sympathy for the elites who'd backed Bassot. They disappeared by the dozens, and their land and wealth were shared by the islanders.

For the first time since the apocalypse, we were back to almost normal. Hell, it was better than normal. Ally, Susie, and I now lived in a lovely home close to the new governor, Aaron. Aaron and Sharon lived in a beautiful house, and he turned the governor's mansion into a museum. Harry was now the Commander of our military, with Davi and Mort as his closest advisors.

Trade between Grenada and Martenvous had brought much-needed medical supplies and several doctors. Aaron opened up the food warehouses and allowed the farmers to keep their crops and trade or sell the products on the open market. The government only kept five percent to help feed the disabled and poor. The island's people felt free but hoped this wasn't a ploy to gain their confidence and be betrayed again.

The anarchists were decimated, and the farmers were happier. I say happier because they liked the progress but still had doubts Aaron and Harry would follow through with the promises to install a Constitutional Republic form of government with Senators and House of Representatives elected by the people. Aaron appointed Mr. Gagnon, the farmers' leader, to the first senator position of the seven needed. Gagnon was allowed to appoint another senator and three House of Representatives of the thirty-three positions to be filled.

I had been pressed into being the Mayor of Fort de Ville and replaced the corrupt politician who never listened to his people. I now knew how difficult it was to please a large group of people. The first thing I did was dissolve the town's council and hold an election to start fresh. The people loved this move, and we were on a roll fixing issues and ensuring fairness. I always hated favoritism and rooted it out anytime I found it.

Forrest and Joan were living in Grenada. He'd taken the position of liaison between the Governor of Grenada and Aaron. Forrest and Joan were married right after Bassot had been dealt with. Forrest is a part-time teacher at the high school, and Joan stays home taking care of Forrest's children. She finally got her dream of being married to an important man and not having to work. Not having to kill thugs was a bonus. They will return to Martenvous after a year or two. I hoped for them a much more extended stay. Callie loved having her mother two days travel away from her and Paul. Joan was the busy body mother-in-law.

Paul had survived his work with Davi to free Dominica. Dominica had also decided to join our mutual defense alliance. He and Cassie had taken up farming on land close to her uncle Mike. Paul had made friends with Mr. Gagnon's son and received help learning how to tend his new land. Paul had learned how to garden and raise bees at his mom's hand, but the thing that made him a big hit with the Gagnons was Paul's beer-making skills. Ally had taught him well. Ally and Paul started a brewpub in Fort de Ville and shared her favorite ales with the islanders. I was happy because I would get free beer.

Grenada was doing much better than expected. Once the cartel had been wiped out, their previous leaders took charge and quickly took care of their people's needs. They were a big help in restoring stability to Martenvous. They sent supplies, food, and doctors to assist in our rebuilding. They were pleased to become a part of the larger group and began lobbying the islands around them to join the new Commonwealth of the Lesser Antilles.

***

Callie couldn't catch her breath as she dialed the old rotary phone. "Dad, there's water pouring out on the floor from the hot water heater, and Paul is out in the field!"

I laid the wallpaper down and said, "Hold on! Ally, I have to help Callie! Callie, find the cold water line at the top of the heater. There should be a valve. Turn the water off."

Callie put the phone down and returned a few minutes later. "Got it, but water is still flowing out of the bottom."

"Callie, it's a thirty-gallon tank. It will flow until it's empty."

Ally gave me a dirty look. "You are a good dad, but this paper won't hang itself."

Ally was busy decorating the baby's room. Oh! I failed to mention we were pregnant. Ally was apprehensive about motherhood at her age, but we wanted a baby in our lives. Little Mike or little Sally would grow up with their niece or nephew. We'd finally felt safe enough to have children.

Ally yelled! "Get your butt in here. Hanging wallpaper is a two-person job."

Yes, she was a bit irritable with all the hormones and stuff. "Yes, dear! I had to take a call from Aaron. The farmers want Mike and me too ...."

Ally huffed, "Do I look like I give a crap what anyone wants. Hold this while I align it."

"Yes, dear."

Hey! Happy wife, happy life. Ally was actually stressed out due to her brewpub startup while also redecorating our new home. I couldn't slack off at work, so I decided to hire an assistant for the brewpub and a helper for the house. It was terrific to deal with common husband-wife issues and not kill people, snakes, and wolves to survive. I didn't sweat the small stuff anymore. I just smiled and said, "Yes, dear. Yes, Callie, or screw you, Mike. I could get used to this part of the apocalypse.

We'd lived through the worst times the Earth had seen in over two thousand years and were now thriving. I prayed every night that the other larger countries would leave us alone. Of course, the signs posted all around the islands in our mutual defense group warning about our smallpox and ebola infections have scared everyone away so far.

The End

OF

The Final Ending

and end of The Day America Died! series.

Check out my other series:

Old Man's War - Book 1 of 3 my Old Man's Apocalypse series.
At 58, Jeff Mann had spent the first two years of the apocalypse hiding from the rest of the world to survive. He only ventured out from time to time to find food or to run off any criminals and scumbags that stopped on the Gulf Coast island on the way to the mainland to spread their depravity. He'd survived the riots, looting, and starvation but wouldn't tolerate the chaos and corruption coming to his island. Jeff begins a crusade against the chaos after saving two women from the degenerate criminal's grasp. Can one man and two women make a difference in a world gone mad? Should they try to fight the depravity or hide?

War Dogs: Heading Home - Book 1 of 3 of my War Dogs series
Post-Apocalyptic Sci-Fi survival Fiction
Severely wounded Staff Sergeant Jason Walker and his Military Working
Dog, MMax, are being shipped home. An EMP blast causes their plane to
crash. Having survived two disasters, they face the Apocalypse and the
struggle to get home. Will there be anything left to return to?
Ebook, Paperback, and audio.- Narrated by Roger Wayne

**Prepper's Apocalypse – Book 1 of 3 of my Prepper's Apocalypse
series.**
Post-Apocalyptic Sci-Fi survival Fiction

Tom's and his family's vacation ended with a devastating EMP attack on
the USA during his family's return flight from Hawaii to San Francisco.
Surviving the plane crash only caused them to confront the chaos of the
apocalypse head-on. Their fellow survivors were helpless and lacked the
skills to survive. Tom, his sister, and their grandma endure the perilous
trip from San Francisco to their ranch in Southern Oregon, using their
prepper skills to keep them alive during the anarchy and chaos around
them.

**The Day America Died: New Beginnings - Book 1 of my
Prepper's Apocalypse series.**
Post-Apocalyptic Sci-Fi survival Fiction
Rogue nations using primitive nuclear weapons create shattering EMP
blasts. The country is transported back 150 years. Zack is 2,000 miles
from Home. He knows he only has a limited amount of time to get to his
daughter and take her to the safety of his Kentucky farm. But can he
reach Callie before she comes to harm or is placed in a relocation camp?
With the odds stacked against him, Zack will do anything it takes.
Zack Johnson is no hero, but he does have some
valuable skills to help him survive. The country had
degenerated into violence and dog-eat-dog scenarios.
People are killing their fellow citizens for a scrap of
decaying bread or a sip of water.

Thanks for reading my novels.
Please leave a great review on Amazon. Thanks
Remember to read my other books on Amazon.
AJ Newman

682

To contact or follow the author, please like my page and leave comments at
https://www.facebook.com/aj.newmanauthor.5?ref=bookmarks
For you MeWe folks: https://mewe.com/i/anthonynewman5

To view other books by AJ Newman, go to Amazon to my author's page:
http://www.amazon.com/-/e/B00HT84V6U

A list of my other books follows at the end.

Thanks, AJ Newman

Books by AJ Newman

Solar Flare:
Prelude to an Apocalypse
Solar Chaos (to be published in spring 2023)

Old Man's Apocalypse:
Old Man's War
Old Man's Journey
Old Man's Destiny

Prepper's Apocalypse
Prepper's Apocalypse
Prepper's Collapse
Prepper's Betrayal – (mid-spring 2021)

John Logan Mysteries" The Human Syndrome

Extinction Level Event
Extinction
Immune: The Hunted

War Dogs
Heading Home
No One Left Behind
Amazon Warriors
War Dogs   Trilogy

EMP:
Perfect Storm
Chaos in the Storm

Cole's Saga series:
Cole's Saga
FEMA WARS

American Apocalypse:
American Survivor
Descent into Darkness
Reign of Darkness
Rising from the Apocalypse

After the Solar Flare:
Alone in the Apocalypse
Adventures in the Apocalypse

Alien Apocalypse:
The Virus
Surviving

A Family's Apocalypse Series:
Cities on Fire

Family Survival

The Day America Died:
New Beginnings
Old Enemies
Frozen Apocalypse
The Day America Died!   Trilogy

The Adventures of Jon Harris:
Surviving
Hell in the Homeland
Tyranny in the Homeland
Revenge in the Homeland
Apocalypse in the Homeland
Jon Returns

AJ Newman and Mack Norman
Rogue's Apocalypse:
Rogues Origin
Rogues Rising
Rogues Journey

A Samantha Jones Murder Mystery:
Where the Girls Are Buried
Who Killed the Girls?

These books are available on Amazon: https://www.amazon.com/AJ-Newman/e/B00HT84V6U/ref=dp_byline_cont_ebooks_1

To contact the Author, please leave comments @
https://www.facebook.com/aj.newmanauthor.5?ref=bookmarks

About the Author

AJ Newman is the author of 41 science fiction and mystery novels, plus 17 audiobooks published on Amazon and Audible. He was born and raised in a small town in western Kentucky. His Dad taught him how to handle guns early in life, and he and his best friend Mike spent summers shooting .22 rifles and fishing.

Reading is his passion, and he fell in love with science fiction. He graduated from USI with a degree in Chemistry but made a career working in manufacturing and logistics, but he always fancied himself as an author.

AJ served six years in the Army National Guard in an armored unit and spent six years performing every function on M48 and M60 army tanks. This gave him great respect for our veterans who lay their lives on the line to protect our country and freedoms.

AJ resides in Henderson, Kentucky, with his wife Patsy and their four tiny Shih Tzus, Sammy, Cotton, Callie and Benny. All except Benny are rescue dogs.

Made in the USA
Middletown, DE
27 September 2023

39490407R00411